PENGUIN CLASSICS

PAMELA

SAMUEL RICHARDSON was born in Derbyshire in 1689, the son of a London joiner. He received little formal education and in 1707 was apprenticed to a printer in the capital. Thirteen years later he set up for himself as a stationer and printer and became one of the leading figures in the London trade. As a printer his output included political writing, such as the Tory periodical *The True Briton*, the newspapers *Daily Journal* (1736–7) and *Daily Gazeteer* (1738), together with twenty-six volumes of the *Journals* of the House of Commons and general law printing. He was twice married and had twelve children.

His literary career began when two booksellers proposed that he should compile a volume of model letters for unskilled letter writers. While preparing this Richardson became fascinated by the project and a small sequence of letters from a daughter in service, asking her father's advice when threatened by her master's advances, formed the germ of *Pamela; or, Virtue Rewarded* (1740–41). *Pamela* was a huge success and became something of a cult novel. By May 1741 it reached a fourth edition and was dramatized in Italy by Goldoni, as well as in England. His masterpiece, *Clarissa or, the History of a Young Lady*, one of the greatest European novels, was published in 1747–8. Richardson's last novel, *The History of Sir Charles Grandison*, appeared in 1753–4. His writings brought him great personal acclaim and a coterie of devoted admirers who liked to discuss with him the moral aspects of the action in the novels. Samuel Richardson died in 1761 and is buried in St Bride's Church, London.

PETER SABOR is Professor of English at Université Laval, Quebec. His publications include *Horace Walpole: A Reference Guide*, *Horace Walpole: The Critical Heritage*, *Samuel Richardson: Tercentenary Essays* (co-edited with Margaret Anne Doody), a collected edition of Frances Burney's plays and editions of works by Sarah Fielding, John Cleland, Frances Burney and Thomas Carlyle.

MARGARET ANNE DOODY is Andrew W. Mellon Professor in the Humanities and Professor of English at Vanderbilt University, where she is presently Director of the Comparative Literature Program. Her publications include *A Natural Passion: A Study of the Novels of Samuel Richardson*, *The Daring Muse: Augustan Poetry Reconsidered* and *Frances Burney: The Life in the Works*, as well as two novels, *Aristotle Detective* and *The Alchemists*. She has also edited *Evelina* for Penguin Classics.

SAMUEL RICHARDSON

PAMELA;
OR, VIRTUE REWARDED

Edited by Peter Sabor
with an introduction by
Margaret A. Doody

PENGUIN BOOKS

PENGUIN BOOKS

Published by the Penguin Group
Penguin Books Ltd, 27 Wrights Lane, London W8 5TZ, England
Penguin Putnam Inc., 375 Hudson Street, New York, New York 10014, USA
Penguin Books Australia Ltd, Ringwood, Victoria, Australia
Penguin Books Canada Ltd, 10 Alcorn Avenue, Toronto, Ontario, Canada M4V 3B2
Penguin Books (NZ) Ltd, Private Bag 102902, NSMC, Auckland, New Zealand

Penguin Books Ltd, Registered Offices: Harmondsworth, Middlesex, England

First published 1740
Published in the Penguin English Library 1980
Published in Penguin Classics in 1985
22

This edition and Notes copyright © Peter Sabor, 1980
Introduction copyright © Margaret A. Doody, 1980
All rights reserved

Printed in England by Clays Ltd, St Ives plc
Set in Monotype Fournier

CONTENTS

Introduction by Margaret A. Doody   7

Note on the Text   21

Selected Further Reading   23

PAMELA   26

Notes   517

INTRODUCTION

WHEN *Pamela, or Virtue Rewarded* appeared in two volumes in November 1740 it was soon what we should call a 'best seller', the first example of that phenomenon in the history of English fiction. Everybody read it; there was a 'Pamela' rage, and Pamela motifs appeared on teacups and fans. Many praised the novel enthusiastically both for its liveliness and its morality, but some condemned the work as undignified and low, seeing in the servant girl's story a pernicious 'levelling' tendency. *Pamela* has never ceased being a controversial work. It is certainly a revolutionary book. It changed the life of the novel as a literary genre, pointing out new directions in subject, style and form.

By the standards of polite society, the author, Samuel Richardson, was scarcely less 'low' than his narrating heroine. Richardson (1689–1761), son of a respectable working-class man, had had a little schooling (we still do not know quite how much) and always loved reading, but by the standards of his contemporaries he was not an educated man, as he had no knowledge of Latin and Greek, and he was certainly not a gentleman. In his early teens he was apprenticed to a printer, and until middle age his life was spent in building up his own business. Before he became a novelist he had done a little writing connected with his trade, such as composing prefaces, and he had produced a handbook for apprentices and a version of Aesop's *Fables*. Then in 1739 Rivington and Osborn, booksellers, asked him to produce a little book of sample letters, the sort of book which provides models of business and personal letters to assist the semi-literate. The 'letter-writer' had been a minor genre of popular literature for over a century, and it was customary for authors to indulge in a certain amount of character-drawing and humour, especially in capturing the phrases and cadences of country bumpkins. Richardson became unexpectedly fascinated by his new project, and a small sequence of letters from a daughter in service, asking her father's advice when she is threatened by her master's advances, became the germ of *Pamela*. *Familiar Letters on Important Occasions* was put aside until the novel was finished.

The inspiration of creating Pamela's narrative in letters and of letting her speak for herself in her own manner (which might be termed the country style) Richardson owed to the letter-writer. But he owed another and larger debt to English popular fiction of his lifetime. Until recently, literary historians have been largely content to deal only with the early masters of the novel, Defoe and Richardson, but in fact, as MacBurney and Richetti have shown, there were a great number of novels appearing between 1700 and 1740, though few of these had a very long life or attracted widespread attention. A large proportion of these little novels were by women, and dealt with the experiences of women in the trials of love. Some are stories of love and courtship, others of love and seduction (or even rape). The authors show their heroines, however constrained by law and convention to endure restriction and passivity, as women who think, feel, analyse, react. Woman takes the centre of the stage as a consciousness. In the novels or novellas of writers like Elizabeth Rowe, Mary Davys, Jane Barker or Eliza Heywood, the heroine, however disadvantaged, can implicitly defy the world of masculine authority around her by becoming the centre of the narrative, with masculine characters only figures in her story.

Richardson adapted this popular feminine and domestic fiction, seeing in it the possibilities the earlier authors only hint at; he raises this 'low' fiction to another level. It becomes part of the tradition of the novel, in the mainstream not only of English but also of European fiction. It is remarkable that Fielding, who writes consciously within the classical and continental tradition, had a great influence on English literature, but little immediate effect on other European works, whereas the novels of Richardson, homegrown as they are, were to have considerable importance in the development of European literature. *Pamela*, which we with hindsight can see presages the era of the French Revolution and of Romanticism, was to influence Rousseau, Diderot, Goethe and Pushkin.

The novel is revolutionary in its depths, not just on the surface, though there are overt statements which have far-reaching significance. When Pamela says 'my *soul* is of equal importance with the soul of a princess', she is, as Roger Sharrock points out, making an obvious Christian statement, and the statement has social implications. Pamela is threatened by Mr B., who uses and abuses his power as a man, as an employer, and as a member of the governing class. He is the local J.P., so Pamela cannot turn to the law because her oppressor *is* the law. He subjects her to a form of imprisonment, and threatens rape. The novel is constructed out of Pamela's power of defiance.

'And pray,' said I, (as we walked on) 'how came I to be his property? What right has he in me, but such as a thief may plead to stolen goods?' 'Was ever the like heard!' says she. 'This is downright rebellion, I protest!'

The virtue that is rewarded is in large measure the virtue of rebellion.

It is not just the occasional phrase which gives the reader this contact with revolt, with the questioning of hierarchy. The novel itself lacks (ostensibly) the controlling, authoritative and soothing presence of the monarchical author. The real author refuses to appear, calling himself an editor (this device was not in itself new). The heroine tells her own story, but in that telling she has no final authority. Heroines like Roxana or Jane Eyre tell their stories after everything is finished and the pattern of a life can be seen – they know what the end is, what the point is. Pamela as she tells her story is always in the middle of her own experience. Her narration is fresh, even to herself; she hasn't the advantage over us of having thought it through, of having arranged her experience over the years. There is only one point at which Richardson lets go of this method of narration, the linking passage explaining the abduction; in *Clarissa* he was to achieve complete disappearance.

The novel in letters had existed before Richardson, but not in any work of the same scope. Since the success of *Lettres portugaises* (1669), which was thought of as a collection of real-life letters by a Portuguese nun to the French cavalier who had abandoned her, the epistolary mode had been recognized as presenting the voice of love – and of course there was the classical and poetic precedent of Ovid's *Heroides*. The authors of English popular feminine fiction had used the epistolary mode occasionally, but customarily only for heightened passion; the more intensely feelings are expressed, the less we see of individual character or local circumstance. Richardson, coming to the novel from the direction of the 'letter-writer', creates a disconcertingly individual character and very definite social circumstances. The kind of novel which Richardson discovered in *Pamela* and developed in *Clarissa* exploits the idea of 'the moment'. The heroine writes 'to the moment'; all her actions and thoughts take place in a moving halo of time. Pamela is confusedly aware of the significance of particular moments, but she cannot create a novelistic plot out of these moments, any more than we can in our own lives as we move from Tuesday into Wednesday. Her attempts to see pattern or something like novelistic plot are, like our own, fragmentary, soon superseded by something else. When she tries to get up a 'plot' with the feeble Williams (and she is quite delighted at her own cleverness) it crumbles very rapidly, and nothing much has happened.

It has often been said – and rightly – that *Pamela* begins a literary tradition which leads to the novels of Proust, Joyce and Virginia Woolf. But letters do not provide a Woolfian 'stream-of-consciousness'. Writing a letter supposes some degree of articulate wakefulness, a sense of order and a desire to communicate. Thoughts are no longer in the muddle of the psyche, but are moving outward into the world; in Dryden's phrase the writer is 'moving the sleeping images of things towards the light'. Richardson's imagination is deeply fascinated by the point where unconscious personal (and archetypal) feelings and perceptions come from the deeps to the surface – where the planes of the outer world and the inner meet. All Richardson's major characters are, in effect, authors, as if the authorial occupation were in itself a great primary image of the work of consciousness in the human being. Pamela wishes to correspond, in all senses of the word; it is part of her frustration that at times her letters cannot get through to anybody, and a more important and constant frustration that her letters as they emerge into the outer world do not quite correspond with the mind of anyone else in that world (save, of course, the minds of the readers of Richardson). She is alone; her perceptions, her integrity, her passions do not seem to fit in with the world, or other people's ideas. Her parents are good-hearted but inadequate readers of Pamela (they wish her to marry Williams); Simon Darnford and Parson Peters reject and rebuff her; Mr B. is infuriated and mocks her. Ultimately, Mr B. becomes her reader, almost the ideal reader, allowing her freedom of choice and then initiating a real, not dictatorial, correspondence with her. They correspond.

The effect of the novel depends upon Pamela. Richardson has given his character an enormous job to do, for it is her voice alone which is to carry the narrative. She must have a language of her own. All novelists have to wrestle with at least two languages – their own, and that of at least one character. We might find a phrase and call these 'fictional dialects'. Actually, an author has several dialects, and so does each major character. Pamela's language is the central problem for the novelist, as Richardson showed in his continual revisions; responding to criticism of novel and heroine as vulgar, he refined the language to some extent, as we can see in the differences between this, his last version of the novel, and the first edition. Generally, the refinement consists in giving Pamela fewer words and more connected sentences rather than in sweeping away striking phrases or vulgar usages. Indeed, the author's constant interest in vulgarisms, varieties of common speech – in dialects – can be seen in the rewritten and amplified scene at the farm, where the farmer is now given direct (instead of reported) speech, in country language: '*he will not come* NERST *her*', 'a quite *otherguess* light'. The author also provides new psychological motivation for the farmer, a despiser of women who wants to use Pamela as an object lesson to his own daughter. A little family tyrant is well created in the new scene with its physical objects and gestures: 'pulling out his spectacles', 'then slap went his hand upon the board'. Richardson was always fascinated by the power politics of small groups, especially families, and the gestures which manifest power struggles and emotional tensions. Even when personages were originally conceived merely to serve the narrative, Richardson was not satisfied with leaving them as blank counters, but went back and worked them up into full-blooded characters.

His revisions were by no means all in the cause of refinement. Mrs Jewkes's crude sexy joke about Pamela's not wanting to marry a clergyman is an addition, and there are other extra touches of description: her neigh of laughter, her 'ugly horse-lip'. Mrs Jewkes was evidently in some sense one of Richardson's favourite characters. Her rewritten appearances in the second volume give her heightened comic importance; at Pamela's wedding-party, Mrs Jewkes 'waddled to us with two bottles of Rhenish, (what she herself dearly loves)'.

All these comic characters are communicated to us through

Pamela; it is, after all, her language which gives us the description of Mrs Jewkes's horse-lip, of her waddling and neighing. Pamela has to convey the other characters' essence so it is felt in what they say or do. Pamela's own language fits in with theirs and is in contrast to it. When she is talking to or of Mr B. her language is sometimes much more elevated than his, but it is often strikingly colloquial ('Hay, you know, *closet* for that, Mrs Jervis!'), blunt in contrast with his uneasy pretensions. She always has a greater range of 'fictional dialects' than any other character in the novel. Richardson never wished to relinquish any of Pamela's various dialects, though he toned down some in places so as not to overshadow others too much. He wants to maintain the common style, the self-dramatization, the bounce, and the vigorous if limited sense of humour which are all aspects of his character. We cannot get away from her fascinating and irritating lowness:

I have read of a good bishop, that was to be burnt for his religion; and he tried how he could bear it, by putting his fingers into the lighted candle: so I t'other day tried, when Rachel's back was turned, if I could not scour a pewter plate she had begun. I see I could do it by degrees; it only blistered my hand in two places.

All the matter is, if I could get plain-work enough, I need not spoil my fingers. But if I can't, I will make my hands as red as a blood-pudding, and as hard as a beechen trencher, but I will accommodate them to my condition.

Several fictional dialects are blended together here: one is derived from Protestant martyrology, another from the practical language of the kitchen. The latter is then touched with the language of beauty-care, and this in turn is overthrown by the vigorous image of 'blood-pudding', in a sentence that begins with the language of the cot, rather than of the kitchen of the Great House, and ends with two high, abstract words that are still in keeping with the general tone.

Someone who can scour pewter may be a servant; someone who can speak of making her hands as red as a blood-pudding and as hard as a beechen trencher is certainly of the servant class. This is no fine lady masquerading as a country maid. Pamela's voice is insistent, unignorable, like a physical presence. The letters embody her and she them – that this is more than a metaphor can be felt in the scene where Mr B. reaches into her bodice to grab her manuscripts. The letters are physical objects within the story. This is a very physical book. We can believe it is really about sex and sexuality, not because we are told so but because we can feel this is in the narrative, with its forceful earthiness. The imagery throughout is of plain physical objects, appealing to the senses: 'earth', 'wool', 'beans', 'sunflower', 'shoes', 'cow', 'wine', 'cake', 'grass', 'brick', 'pond'. These things all belong to Pamela's world, her frame of reference. Pamela is, I believe, the first important heroine in English fiction who works for a living, and could earn a living by the work of her hands. She thinks like a servant, because she is one. We see this in the very first letter, where real regrets for the loss of the dead lady are mixed with worries about the security of her job and a lively interest in the four guineas paid as honest wages and sent home, carefully if cynically wrapped up. No other heroine has burst upon the world with such an inelegant concern over a few coins.

Pamela is not daintily free of her social position – it has conditioned the way she thinks, speaks and acts. Pamela is an individual in particular social and historical circumstances of which she is less conscious than the (absent) author. The novel as a genre has always accommodated this vision of unimportant people in history; in reading novels we hear the news about people who are not kings and queens and great chiefs, who have never been heard of before. Lazarillo and Don Quixote and Gil Blas and Pamela and Tom Jones are not legendary, and not leaders; they do not control their society but are trying to make their way in it. But, as Ronald Paulson has pointed out, the early novel, embarrassed by classical tradition, could deal with unimportant characters from the low to middle classes only by treating them satirically. Richardson's *Pamela* gives us an unsatiric view of a lower-class person. Defoe's characters offer the only precedent in English fiction, but Moll and Roxana have a raffishness, a sort of gallows-foot dash, in their outlaw position as thieves and whores. Richardson's character is an honest and well-meaning person from a fairly stable background and she wants, like most of us, to live an honest life within her own social world. When this seems impossible she is heroic enough to choose an unsuccessful position as the alternative to doing wrong and losing her own identity. She is as heroic as Maggie Tulliver in her moral choices (though better treated in the end) but the heroism is indivisible from her whole personality, and she *is* a teenaged servant girl.

It is sometimes difficult for the twentieth-century reader to understand what Richardson's contemporaries would have grasped immediately – the full meaning of Pamela's social position, which might well be compared to that of a black servant girl in the American South in the earlier part of our own century. Her use of language indicates her background, origin and status – and these make her, in Mr B.'s world, an inferior, commonly thought of almost as another species of being. Readers who have pointed out that Pamela is in love with Mr B. from the outset have always been partly right – but she does have real reason to fear him, and genuinely rebels when he tries to make an unChristian and perverse use of their feelings for each other. Mr B. himself is not individually guilty, for he has been conditioned by the assumptions of his own class. Sir Simon Darnford says

'Why, what is all this, my dear, but that our neighbour has a mind to his mother's waiting-maid! . . . I don't see any great injury will be done her. He hurts no *family* by this.'

Mr B. is both promulgator and victim of a code which deliberately sets up not just a double but a triple standard. Men of all classes are expected to take casual sexual pleasure – though it's better for poor men not to roam too much. Middle- and upper-class young ladies have chastity most explicitly demanded of them (for worldly reasons of family and descent) but lower-class girls are not supposed to set any such value on themselves – they are there for sexual convenience. So thoroughly has gentle society accepted this notion that a lower-class girl who makes any fuss about yielding her virginity must be guilty of hypocrisy – after all, one knows what they are all like, really. Richardson was horrified at being taken for a leveller, but this pernicious code he attacks unsparingly, and the extirpation of it demands new assumptions about class, property, authority and identity.

Pamela rebels against this code, but she has no illusions about her social condition as one of the 'poor people'. She knows that marriage cannot be expected as the logical outcome or possible result of her resistance. It is the reader who sees that marriage is the only right end to the story, the only sexual relationship which allows of equality and integrity, acknowledges Pamela's value as a person, not a thing.

The story is of course a highly charged love story with a happy ending. But Mr B. is not a dashing hero like Mr Rochester (though the resemblance between their two novels has been seen since one of the first reviews of *Jane Eyre*). The narrative permits us to see Mr B. through Pamela's eyes, so in the context of the novel he is subordinate to her, and the authority of masculinity and class is overthrown here too. We know more about him than she does; we don't see the awe-ful person she sees. He is the ruler of her small world, but the reader realizes that this fox-hunting young country squire would be considered something of a bumpkin himself at St James's; going to court is a big occasion for him, and he wants to show Pamela his get-up – no lord or earl would behave in this naïve small-beer manner. We see that Mr B. is rebelling against his mother's influence over him, and trying to fit in with the conventions of his peer-group in becoming a swaggering seducer, an abductor. He tries on a great many roles before us and Pamela; he is alternatively aristocratic, friendly, magisterial, blustering. We can see the weaknesses in this unromantic hero–villain as he sulks and shows off. But Pamela too has a (feminine) power of analysis, and she writes down what she thinks, learning more about him as she goes on. She captures Mr B. in words, even more thoroughly than he captures her in his Lincolnshire house – this is a shock to him, as if a specimen of rock should turn and analyse the geologist. Mr B. is not the master as long as Pamela can think and write, and yet it is to that thinking self that he is attracted. In trying on his little rape-scenarios he makes an absurd error, sinning against his own feelings as much as hers; he wants love, but finds that difficult to acknowledge. He feels threatened by a woman unless he can control her and make the sexual relationship undangerous to himself (and hence, unreal).

Both characters are youthful, in a state of flux and experiment. Neither is yet fully formed. Traditionally the novel delights in adolescents, in portraying the processes in which the formless becomes formed. A novelist may desire to promote a standard of maturity which replaces youthful flounderings, but the novel itself, as a genre, is always trying to subvert this by suggesting irreplaceable values in adolescent perceptions and confusions.

There is a continual sense that the younger generation can change, redeem, or find freedom from the limitations and errors of the past. The novel is the genre of historical hope. Richardson, in portraying his young characters, daringly embraces the undefined and chaotic. His novels as works of art have their own form, but he wants it to seem that the work grows into its own natural shape without artificial control. He loves the formless, the radiant zigzag becoming. The reader of *Pamela* is immersed in the destructive element – thoughts, wishes, sudden perceptions, vanishings – all a flow without apparent direction. Everything is changeable. The world Richardson makes us see is a world being made, and being made by perceivers. It is not an accident but a necessary coincidence of history that Richardson arose out of the culture which produced Locke, Berkeley and Hume. The action of *Pamela* is always internal: everything that happens is mediated through the narrator's consciousness.

That consciousness is not itself a literary consciousness. Pamela is a kind of reverse of Don Quixote. Don Quixote makes all his experience a reflection of the literature he has read. Pamela finds what she has read totally inadequate to what she is experiencing. Some of her fictional dialects develop from works she has read, but they are too far away from her situation and too limited to be truly satisfactory. We have seen her picking on an incident in the life of a martyr as a model, and we smile at the distance between the two and the unconscious arrogance of the borrowing. Again, she lights on the fable of the ant and grasshopper as an exemplar. But she is not a martyred bishop, or a grasshopper, and her own intense and unique life keeps spilling over and out of any ready-made literary frame. She has to create a language of her own that will make sense of her life. A motif of suspense underneath the story, like a base line below the melody, is Pamela's search for and creation of a language. In the first letter, she and her parents are evidently almost on a level, almost at one (though the reader sees more than the Andrews who play Watson to our Holmes throughout). We soon realize that Pamela is growing beyond her parents, as she experiences feelings and perceptions which they could not imagine, and with these acquires a language which becomes her own major dialect, which has room for subtlety and paradox, for complexity, and for perplexities that cannot be answered by any simple facts or maxims: 'Is it not strange that love borders so much upon hatred?'

Pamela's achievement is related to her creative labour of memory. All that stands between random discrete 'moments' and chaos is the capacity of the mind to remember, sometimes even against the will, and in the process individual consciousness gains its unique form. Pamela writing her letters, and even perforce collecting them about her person like a walking anthology of herself, achieves a portable creation of memory, an imitation of the universal work which finds identity in memory. The novel as a genre has always been deeply concerned with the activity and proclivities of remembering. The memory does not readily cast aside what is trivial or embarrassing or distracting – it is not hierarchical; it holds the commonplace *madeleine* in deeper reverence than Venice. What Pamela has to remember inevitably grows, becomes larger and more complex, like the book itself as we read it. The pages we have turned are the memory, and like the heroine we can turn back and refer to particular moments which might not have been fully understood when the experience was happening. When Mr B. wants to censor and suppress Pamela's papers, he is trying, like the dictator of a conquered land, to render her a region without a history, without a memory, and hence without an identity save that which he chooses to give her.

The emphasis on memory suits the story's pattern – which, after all the talk about absconding authors, we must acknowledge Richardson did give it – a pattern of repetition and variation. Mr B.'s attempt on Pamela when she is with the cooperative Mrs Jewkes is a variation on his earlier attempt when Pamela was with the decent Mrs Jervis. Pamela is imprisoned – escapes – is imprisoned again. There is a heartbeat rhythm of constriction–release–constriction.

Within the story there are countering elements – support for the status quo, jokes against the heroine – which seek to subvert that story: 'Don't stand dilly-dallying, sir. She cannot exclaim worse than she has done ...'. All the criticisms ever made of the heroine have been made first within the novel itself. Mrs Jewkes stands in for the baser side of the reader, the aspect of ourselves which wants a quick consummation and can feel some contempt for the egotism of an unimportant servant girl: 'so much pining and whining for nothing at all'. When Mrs Jewkes voices such feelings for us we see what they imply.

The novel is large enough to permit a variety of counter-responses within itself. It parodies the Romance, and also allows us to see that the Romance proper offers a critique of this tale of prosaic people in the flat eastern counties of England. The story is both a universal human action, dealing with matters as serious as the perversion of sex into power, and the human need for freedom – *and* equally and at the same time the story of two countrified young people, bumptious, ignorant, egotistical. Pamela is not the heroine of Romance, all beautiful and good; she has very human limitations and natural, unglamorous qualities. Richardson goes out of his way to achieve mixed effects, puzzling readers who would like literature to be clear, who can accept a chaste Marina but not a chaste servant maid who is capable of some self-pity, self-dramatization and self-love. The scene in which Pamela, dressed in her new country garb, looks at herself in the glass has been seized upon as exhibiting the character's vanity, and hence her determination to ensnare Mr B. with her beauty. The scene is more subtle than that. Of course, looking in the mirror is not exactly a sin in a sixteen-year-old girl. But Pamela is not gazing for idle pleasure, but in order to confirm a decision. In choosing to go away, to lose job and prospects and income and to tumble down a narrow social ladder, she requires the reassurance of seeing that she is still herself. Richardson knows perfectly well that the circumstance includes some degree of self-dramatization and 'vanity'; really, he is making us ask, perhaps uncomfortably, whether these qualities can always be simply classified as 'bad'. Pamela's comparison of herself with the bishop (see p. 109) is self-dramatizing and conceited though there is real heroism in her disproportionate reaction. Pamela responds to the best of her ability to a difficult situation, but her responses, from moment to moment, are off-balance, absurd, comic – though not entirely comic – to the observer. Within the novel Pamela is called 'a comical girl', and so she is. The novel suggests that all of us, even in our most serious trials and decisions, have an element of absurdity. Richardson refuses to allow us to put good and bad qualities in separate piles. Here also there is a questioning of hierarchies and established orders of things. We might all want to agree that whereas rebellion against unjust power, perseverance, honesty, integrity are good, qualities like self-pity, self-dramatization and vanity are bad – but does any human being attain the first category of qualities without some mixture of the second? Richardson is in effect asking whether we haven't found it far too easy to lump a great many necessary psychological energies under easy pejorative labels.

Pamela is good, but she is funny. She is funny and brave in her imprisonment – not in the tower of Romance, but in a stolid old-fashioned manor house among farms. Her jailor is not the black-a-vised ruffian or monstrous harem-guard of more exotic fiction, but fat talkative Mrs Jewkes who prides herself on her notable store of home remedies. Pamela spills out her angry feelings about Mrs Jewkes in a highly comic descriptive passage. The description of the 'broad, squat, pursy *fat thing*' is, as Pamela admits, 'poor and helpless spite'. But impotent and undignified expressions of wrath – like the childhood gesture of sticking one's tongue out behind a teacher's back – are not psychologically useless. It is important to Pamela to be able to let herself know she isn't giving in, so what is foolish has a real value.

There is a more subtle kind of comedy, involving mixed effects, in the scene by the pond where the antagonistic lovers begin to become truly reconciled. We should look at the changes rung throughout the scene on words like 'sincere', 'frank', 'honest'. In a proper love story, this scene would be tender and straightforward; instead, it is full of odd little comic curlicues of play-acting and illogicality. Mr B. promises to be 'sincere' for the present – with the right to change tomorrow; he thinks sincerity can be taken up provisionally, and he is trying to use the power of 'sincerity' to sound Pamela's feelings. Mr B. promises to be sincere, believes he is so, and at once becomes histrionic, egotistical and demanding. The characters' conversation in this scene goes round in circles; logically, it gets nowhere. The hero explains why he can't marry the heroine, and the heroine asks to go back to her family. Apparently, nothing has changed, yet in fact a great deal does happen in the dialogue of feelings rather than of logic. Sincerity does bring them together, even with all the falsehood, posturing and evasion involved in their attempts. When human beings start being 'sincere' with each other, a lot of sludge inevitably comes up from the sacred fount – but in human affairs, Richardson suggests, nothing is unmixed, nothing is statically 'pure'.

This is a novel deliberately created out of mixed languages, impure effects, awkward gestures, failures and inelegant self-revelation. It is also for these reasons a humane and generous book, kind to human imperfections and hopeful for human growth. The silliness, delusion and egotism which cling to human thought and actions like flesh to bone are redeemable, may even have in themselves the seed and motive of virtue. Everything is growing and changing and developing – like the seeds of the beans Pamela planted, or the seed of the child which is growing in Mr B.'s wife at the end of the novel. No process ever comes to an end, as long as life lasts, because consciousness doesn't come to an end, nor the natural world whose impulses it shares. The novel has a sense of the inexhaustible in life. There is no reason for an end to the story.

Richardson defies the conventions of 'an ending' by running right past it. The wedding of Mr B. and Pamela is not an end, but a beginning, and also a continuation of their lives before. Mr B.'s marriage was at first a secret affair, but he has to come to terms with it as an aspect of his whole self, which includes his social being. He has to bring it to the light. What is private has to become public before it is fully itself, just as imagination has to become articulate. Mr B. has to connect his present with his past, and Pamela is now drawn into sharing his past, his memories and affections – a process which involves her in an encounter with his violent sister, horrified at the misalliance, and produces other shocks as well. She and Mr B. never finish learning about each other or themselves.

Marriage does not put an end to the eternal process of living and being surprised. There are forces in Nature itself always pushing us forward, and in this novel (as not in *Clarissa*) Nature is in sympathy with the higher spiritual force within the psyche which makes us desire development, a larger and nobler identity, even if that nobler identity is never finally realized. The novel is telling us that human beings are sacred, even with their shortcomings. Sacredness and absurdity are consubstantial, as they are in Pamela's letters, those sacred imperfections.

M.D.

NOTE ON THE TEXT

THE publication history of *Pamela*, like that of Richardson's two subsequent novels, is complex. It was first published anonymously in two volumes in November 1740; a revised edition with a lengthy introduction was published in February 1741, and three further revised editions were published in that year. In December 1741 a two-volume sequel was published, written in response to numerous criticisms, parodies and spurious continuations of the original work. In 1742 a deluxe, illustrated octavo edition of all four volumes was published, in which the text was again revised and the much criticized introduction replaced with a voluminous table of contents summarizing each letter and journal entry. Two further revised editions of the first part of *Pamela* were published in 1746 and 1754, and shortly after Richardson's death in 1761 another four-volume edition was published, containing what was subsequently assumed to be the final text of the novel.

During the 1750s, however, Richardson had undertaken an extensive revision of *Pamela*, making numerous stylistic alterations while adding and deleting phrases, sentences, paragraphs and even lengthy passages of several pages. These changes were made in an interleaved copy of the octavo edition. Richardson did not print the resulting text during his lifetime, but it was preserved by his daughters after his death, and finally used as the copy text for an edition of *Pamela* published in 1801. The provenance of this edition was first demonstrated in an article by Richardson's biographers, Eaves and Kimpel, of 1967; the interleaved copy text, however, is not known to have survived.

There are, then, three principal versions of *Pamela*: the original, two-volume novel of 1740; the intermediate revised editions of 1741–61; and the last revised text of 1801.

The present edition of the first part of *Pamela*, based on a facsimile reprint of the 1801 text (Garland Publishing Company, 1974), and incorporating corrections made to that text in an edition of 1810, makes Richardson's final version generally available for the first time. Some emendations have been made for the convenience of the modern reader, according to the following principles:

1. Richardson's spelling has been retained, except that elliptical spellings (past participles ending in '*d*, *tho*', *thro*', etc) have been expanded, and the long s (f) has been replaced by the modern s.

2. Punctuation, similarly, is left intact, except that (a) quotation marks have been supplied where necessary, and the running quotation marks used by Richardson deleted; (b) large numbers of dashes, often used by Richardson to indicate a change of speaker, have been deleted, and others, used to introduce dialogue, have been replaced with commas. Dashes indicating interruption or agitation, however, have been retained.

3. The setting-out of parallel passages has been rationalized.

4. Obvious misprints have been corrected.

5. Capitalization and italicization have not been altered.

I would like to acknowledge my gratitude to T. C. Duncan Eaves and Ben D. Kimpel, who kindly made available their unpublished collation of the 1801 and 1810 editions; and to Christine Rees, Peter Dixon, Linda Cooke and Margaret Doody for their assistance and advice.

SELECTED FURTHER READING

BIOGRAPHY

Margaret Anne Doody, 'Samuel Richardson', *Dictionary of Literary Biography*, vol. 39, *British Novelists, 1660–1800*, Martin C. Battestin (ed.), Gale Research Company, 1985

T. C. Duncan Eaves and Ben D. Kimpel, *Samuel Richardson: A Biography*, Oxford University Press, 1971

A. D. McKillop, *Samuel Richardson: Printer and Novelist*, University of North Carolina Press, 1936; Shoestring Press, 1960

GENERAL WORKS ON RICHARDSON

Donald L. Ball, *Samuel Richardson's Theory of Fiction*, Mouton, 1971

R. F. Brissenden, *Samuel Richardson*, Longmans, Green & Co. for the British Council, 1958

Elizabeth B. Brophy, *Samuel Richardson: The Triumph of Craft*, University of Tennessee Press, 1974

John Carroll (ed.), *Samuel Richardson: A Collection of Critical Essays*, in the series *Twentieth Century Views*, Prentice-Hall, 1969
—(ed.), *Selected Letters of Samuel Richardson*, Oxford University Press, 1964

Margaret Anne Doody, *A Natural Passion: A Study of the Novels of Samuel Richardson*, Oxford University Press, 1974

Margaret Anne Doody, 'Saying "No", Saying "Yes": The Novels of Samuel Richardson', *The First English Novelists: Essays in Understanding*, J. M. Armistead (ed.), University of Tennessee Press, 1985

Brian Downs, *Richardson*, Routledge & Kegan Paul, 1928

Rita Goldberg, *Sex and Enlightenment: Women in Richardson and Diderot*, Cambridge University Press, 1984

Morris Golden, *Richardson's Characters*, University of Michigan Press, 1963

Anthony M. Kearney, *Samuel Richardson*, Routledge & Kegan Paul, 1968

Mark Kinkead-Weekes, *Samuel Richardson: Dramatic Novelist*, Routledge & Kegan Paul, 1973

Ira Konigsberg, *Samuel Richardson and the Dramatic Novel*, University of Kentucky Press, 1968

Gerald Levin, *Richardson the Novelist, the Psychological Patterns*, Humanities Press, 1978

A. D. McKillop, *The Early Masters of English Fiction*, University of Kansas Press, 1956; Constable, 1962.

Valerie Grosvenor Myer (ed.), *Samuel Richardson: Passion and Prudence*, Vision Press, 1986

Marijke Rudnik-Smalbraak, *Samuel Richardson: Minute Particulars within the Large Design*, Leiden University Press, 1983

William M. Sale, Jr, *Samuel Richardson: Master Printer*, Cornell University Press, 1950

Ian Watt, *The Rise of the Novel*, Chatto & Windus, 1957; Penguin, 1963

Cynthia Griffin Wolff, *Samuel Richardson and the Eighteenth-Century Puritan Character*, Archon Books, 1972

ON PAMELA

Jennifer Brady, 'Readers in Richardson's *Pamela*', *English Studies in Canada*, 9 (1983), 164–76

Terry J. Castle, 'P/B: *Pamela* as Sexual Fiction', *Studies in English Literature*, 22 (1982), 469–89

Rosemary Cowler (ed.), *Twentieth Century Interpretations of Pamela: A Collection of Critical Essays*, Prentice-Hall, 1969

Robert A. Donovan, *The Shaping Vision*, Cornell University Press, 1966

John Dussinger, *The Discourse of the Mind in Eighteenth-Century Fiction*, Mouton, 1974

T. C. Duncan Eaves and Ben D. Kimpel, 'Richardson's Revisions of *Pamela*', *Studies in Bibliography*, 20 (1967), 61–88

—(ed.), *Pamela*, Houghton Mifflin, 1971

Robert A. Erickson, 'Mother Jewkes, Pamela and the Midwives', *English Literary History*, 43 (1976), 500–516

Robert Folkenflik, 'A Room of Pamela's Own', *English Literary History*, 39 (1972), 585–96

James Louis Fortuna, Jr, '*The Unsearchable Wisdom of God*': A Study of Providence in Richardson's *Pamela*, University of Florida Press, 1980

Philip Gaskell, *From Writer to Reader: Studies in Editorial Method*, Clarendon Press, 1978

Bernard Kreissman, *Pamela-Shamela*, University of Nebraska Press, 1960

Gwendolyn Needham, 'Richardson's Characterization of Mr B. and Double Purpose in *Pamela*', *Eighteenth Century Studies*, 3 (1970), 433–74

Roy Roussel, *The Conversation of the Sexes: Seduction and Equality in Selected Seventeenth- and Eighteenth-Century Texts*, Oxford University Press, 1986

Peter Sabor, 'The Cooke-Everyman Edition of *Pamela*', *The Library*, 32 (1977), 360–66

Roger Sharrock, 'Richardson's *Pamela*: The Gospel and the Novel', *Durham University Journal*, n.s. 27 (1966), 67–74

Janet Todd, '*Pamela*: or the Bliss of Servitude', *British Journal for Eighteenth-Century Studies*, 6 (1983), 135–48

BIBLIOGRAPHY

Richard Gordon Hannaford, *Samuel Richardson: An Annotated Bibliography of Critical Studies*, Garland, 1980

William Merritt Sale, Jr, *Samuel Richardson: A Bibliographical Record of his Literary Career with Historical Notes*, Yale University Press, 1936

Sarah W. R. Smith, *Samuel Richardson: A Reference Guide*, G. K. Hall, 1984

PAMELA;

OR,

VIRTUE REWARDED.

IN A

SERIES OF LETTERS

FROM A BEAUTIFUL

YOUNG DAMSEL TO HER PARENTS:

AND AFTERWARDS

IN HER EXALTED CONDITION,

BETWEEN

HER, AND PERSONS OF FIGURE AND QUALITY,

UPON THE

MOST IMPORTANT AND ENTERTAINING SUBJECTS, IN GENTEEL LIFE.

IN FOUR VOLUMES.

VOL. I.

PUBLISHED IN ORDER TO CULTIVATE THE PRINCIPLES
OF VIRTUE AND RELIGION IN THE MINDS OF THE
YOUTH OF BOTH SEXES.

A NEW EDITION, BEING THE FOURTEENTH,
WITH NUMEROUS CORRECTIONS AND ALTERATIONS.

London:

Printed for J. Johnson, G. G. and J. Robinson, R. Baldwin,
W. J. and J. Richardson, F. and C. Rivington, Ogilvy and
Son, Otridge and Son, P. Macqueen, J. Nunn, W. Lane,
G. Wilkie, Vernor and Hood, Lackington, Allen, and Co.
Cadell and Davies, C. Law, Longman and Rees, T. Hurst,
and J. Wallis.

1801.

ADVERTISEMENT

TO THE FOURTEENTH EDITION

THE Booksellers think it necessary to acquaint the Public, that the numerous alterations in this Edition were made by the Author, and were left by him for publication.

It cannot be material to state here the reasons why the Work has not sooner appeared in this altered and improved form.

But it may be proper, for the satisfaction of the Public, to mention, that they have been favoured with the copy, from which this Edition is printed, by his only surviving daughter, Mrs Anne Richardson.[2]

March 30, 1801

PREFACE

IF to *divert* and *entertain*, and at the same time to *instruct* and *improve* the minds of the YOUTH of *both sexes:*

If to inculcate *religion* and *morality* in so easy and agreeable a manner, as shall render them equally *delightful* and *profitable:*

If to set forth in the most exemplary lights, the *parental*, the *filial*, and the *social* duties:

If to paint VICE in its proper colours, to make it *deservedly odious*; and to set VIRTUE in its own amiable light, to make it look *lovely:*

If to draw characters with justness, and to support them distinctly:

If to raise a distress from *natural* causes, and excite a compassion from *just* ones:

If to teach the man of *fortune* how to *use* it; the man of *passion* how to *subdue* it; and the man of *intrigue*, how, gracefully, and with honour to himself, to *reclaim:*

If to give *practical* examples, worthy to be followed in the most *critical* and *affecting* cases, by the *virgin*, the *bride*, and the *wife:*

If to effect all these good ends, in so probable, so natural, so *lively* a manner, as shall engage the passions of every sensible reader, and attach their regard to the story:

And all without raising a *single idea* throughout the whole, that shall shock the exactest purity, even in the warmest of those instances where Purity would be most apprehensive:

If these be laudable or worthy recommendations, the *Editor* of the following Letters, which have their foundation both in *Truth* and *Nature*, ventures to assert, that all these ends are obtained here, together.

Confident therefore of the favourable reception which he ventures to bespeak for this little Work, he thinks any *apology* for it unnecessary: and the rather for two reasons: 1st, Because he can appeal from his *own* passions, (which have been uncommonly *moved* in perusing it) to the passions of *every one* who shall read with attention: and, in the next place, because an *Editor* can judge with an impartiality which is rarely to be found in an *Author*.

CONTENTS[4]

I. *To her Parents*. Recounting her lady's death. – Her master's kindness to her. Sends them money.

II. *From her Parents*. Are much concerned for her lady's death: cautions her against having *too* grateful a sense of her master's favour to her. Further cautions and instructions.

III. *To her Father*. She resolves to prefer her Virtue to life itself. Apprehends no danger at present from her master's favour.

IV. *To her Mother*. Lady Davers praises her beauty, and gives her advice to keep the men at a distance. Intends to take her to wait upon her own person.

V. *To her Parents*. Mrs Jervis's the housekeeper's worthy conduct in the family, and friendship to her. She is quite fearless of danger; and why.

VI. *To the same*. Farther instances of her master's goodness to her. Her joyful gratitude upon it. He praises her person to Mrs Jervis.

VII. *To her Father*. Reciting other particulars of her master's bounty to her. A little apprehensive; but hopes without reason.

VIII. *From her Father*. Inforcing his former cautions and instructions. Is easier, since he knows she has Mrs Jervis to advise with.

IX. *To her Parents*. Her master refuses to let her go to Lady Davers. His pretended reason for it. Lady Davers seemingly apprehensive for her. Still hopes the best, and will give them notice of all that happens.

X. *To her Mother*. Acquaints her, that now her master's designs against her are apparent. That she had written down the particulars of all; but that somebody had stolen her letter. Will write at the first opportunity another, revealing all: but is watched and blamed by her master, for spending so much time in writing.

XI. *To her Mother*. Cannot find her letter; so recites her master's free behaviour to her in the summer-house. Her virtuous resentment. Refuses his offers of money. He injoins her to secrecy, pretending he only designed to try her.

XII. *To her Mother*. Desires Mrs Jervis to permit her to lie with *her*: and tells her all that had passed. Mrs Jervis's good advice. Her master's angry behaviour to her. She wishes she had never been taken from her low condition.

XIII. *From her Parents*. Their concern and apprehensions for her. They think it best for her to return to them; but are the easier, as she lies with Mrs Jervis.

XIV. *To her Father*. Relating a conversation between her master and Mrs Jervis about her. He will have it, that she is an artful and designing girl. Orders Mrs Jervis to caution her how she writes out of the house the affairs of his family.

XV. *To her Mother*. Her master upbraids her with revealing to Mrs Jervis what he had ordered her to keep secret: and tries to intimidate her. Her moving Expostulation. He offers freedoms to her. She escapes from him into another room, and falls into a fit. Mrs Jervis interpose in her behalf. He appoints the next day for her and Mrs Jervis to attend him.

XVI. *To her Parents*. His imperious manner intimidates Mrs Jervis. Pamela's courage. He threatens that she shall return to her former low condition. Her affecting behaviour on this occasion.

XVII. *From her Parents.* They tell her, how welcome her return will be to them, as she will come innocent and honest.

XVIII. *To her Parents.* Mrs Jervis gives her opinion, that he will never attempt her again; and that she may stay, if she will ask it as a favour.

XIX. *To the same.* Mrs Jervis again advises her to ask to stay. Her reasons to the contrary. How the love of her fellow servants affects her. Mr Longman the steward's kindness to her.

XX. *To the same.* Provides a neat, home-spun suit of cloaths, that when she returns to her parents, she may not appear above her condition.

XXI. *To the same.* Mrs Jervis tells her of how much consequence she is to her master, and his expressions in her favour. Is uneasy at Mrs Jervis's wishing her to stay.

XXII. *To the same.* A rough expression of her master to her, overheard by the butler. The servants concerned, that she is to go away. Mr Jonathan the butler's kindness, and concern at what he had heard her master say to her. Instance of Mr Longman's favour to her.

XXIII. *To the same.* Description and characters of several neighbouring ladies, who rally her master on her account. She hopes to set out in a few days.

XXIV. *To the same.* Puts on her home-spun dress. What passes on that occasion between Mrs Jervis, her master, and herself. A Note from Mr Jonathan, warning her of her danger.

XXV. *To the same.* Her master hides himself in their closet, and overhears a discourse against himself between Mrs Jervis and her, as she is undressing for bed. Finding himself discovered, he rushes out. Her terror. She falls into fits.

XXVI. *To the same.* Mrs Jervis gives her master warning. He agrees that they shall go away both together.

XXVII. *To the same.* She is to stay a week longer for Mrs Jervis's going with her. Her master asks her opinion of a new birth-day suit of cloaths. He owns to Mrs Jervis, that he had an eye upon Pamela in his mother's life-time. Her surprize at his wickedness, and at that of several gentlemen in the neighbourhood.

XXVIII. *To the same.* Mrs Jervis is permitted to stay. Mr Longman intercedes for Pamela, and desires her to humble herself. Her affecting behaviour hereupon.

XXIX. *To the same.* Mrs Jervis's kind offer of money to her; which she declines accepting of; and why. Yet laments that, as things have fallen out, she had been brought up wrong by her lady: but hopes to make her mind bend to her condition. She divides her cloaths into three bundles, and desires Mrs Jervis to inspect them. Her moving conduct and reasonings on this occasion. She discovers, to her great surprize, that her master had heard all she had said: upbraids Mrs Jervis upon it, and repeats her wishes to be safe with her parents.

XXX. *To the same.* Her master treats her kindly. Bespeaks her confidence in him. Avows his love to her. Intimates, that he will make all her family happy. Protests he has no view to her dishonour: and tells her, that if she will stay but a fortnight longer, she shall find her account in it. The different agitations of her mind on this occasion.

XXXI. *To the same.* She declares to him her determination to go. He offers her a sum of money for her father, and intimates, that he will find her a husband, who shall make her a gentlewoman. She, by writing, signifies to him her resolution to go to her parents. Finding her determined, he gives leave for his travelling chariot and Lincolnshire coachman to carry her, and sends her five guineas. Her verses on her departure.

Here the Editor gives an account of Pamela's being carried to her master's seat in Lincolnshire, instead of to her father's. Of John's treacherous baseness, in relation to her letters. The copy of a letter from Mr B. to her father, containing his pretended reasons for not permitting her to go to them. Of her parents' grief. Of her father's visit to Mr B.; and of what passed between Mrs Jervis, Mr B., and the old man, on that occasion. Copy of a letter from Pamela to Mrs Jervis, written by a prescribed form.

XXXII. *From Pamela to her Parents.* She bewails her wretched condition, and exclaims against the vile trick put upon her. Gives an account of her being carried to a farmer's house, on the way to Lincolnshire; and of her conversation with the farmer, his wife, and daughter. A letter from her master to her. Copy of another to the farmer. She endeavours to engage the farmer in her favour; but to no purpose. Resolves, if possible, to make a party on the road, or at the inn where the coachman next puts up; but there is met by Mrs Jewkes. She reproaches the coachman. Tampers, but to no purpose, with Mrs Jewkes.

Her JOURNAL

Begun for her amusement, and in hopes to find some opportunity to send it to them. Has hopes of moving Mr Williams, her master's chaplain, to assist her escape.

SUNDAY. Mrs Jewkes's insolence to Mr Williams; and still greater to her. Describes the person of the bad woman. John arrives with a letter from her master to her, requiring her to copy a prescribed form of a letter to her parents, to make them easy. She complies for their sakes; and writes a moving one to her master.

MONDAY. John's excessive concern on reflecting upon his own baseness, makes Mrs Jewkes suspect he loves Pamela, and narrowly watch him: however, he privately drops a letter, which Pamela takes up, in which he confesses his treachery to her. Her surprize upon it.

TUESDAY, WEDNESDAY. Her contrivance to correspond with Mr Williams. Contents of her first letter to him, reciting her dangers, and begging him to assist her to escape.

THURSDAY. Further instances of Mrs Jewkes's insolence to her. Mr Williams's answer to her letter, declaring his readiness to assist her, and proposing the means. Her reply; desires that a key may be made by his to the garden backdoor. She is permitted to angle; and hooks a carp, which, moved by a reflection upon her own case, she throws in again.

FRIDAY, SATURDAY. Mrs Jewkes tricks her out of her little stock of money. She receives a letter from her master, offering if she will invite him down, to put Mrs Jewkes into her power, and to permit Mrs Jervis to attend her. Mr

Williams acquaints her, that he has been repulsed by every one to whom he has applied in her favour; but shall soon procure the key she desires, and means to escape. She writes to tell him that she fears her master's coming may be sudden; and that therefore no time is to be lost. Her moving letter to her master, in answer to his; in which she absolutely denies her consent to his coming down.

SUNDAY. Is concerned she has not the key. Turns the cxxxviith psalm to her own case.

MONDAY, TUESDAY, WEDNESDAY. Is pleased, that Mr Williams has got a large parcel of her papers, to send away to her parents. Mrs Jewkes suspects, by his looks, that he is in love with Pamela, and pretends to wish it to be a match between them. His third letter, intimating, that she has but one way honourably to avoid the danger she is in; and that is, by marrying. Modestly tenders himself. Her answer.

THURSDAY, FRIDAY, SATURDAY. Mr Williams promises to assist her to his power, though she has not so readily come into his proposal as he wished.

SUNDAY. She tells her parents that Mr Williams has received a letter from her master, and Mrs Jewkes another, confirming the contents of it, letting him know that he has now a living fallen that will make him happy, and intimating that he designs him Pamela for his wife. Commanding Mrs Jewkes, in that to her only, to let him know that they approve of each other. Pamela suspects the intent of these letters. Cautions Mr Williams upon his honest joy; but yet hopes to be soon permitted to go to her father and mother. Mrs Jewkes presses her to encourage Mr Williams's address. Mr Williams intends to write a letter on his own account to her parents. She begs they will not encourage his address.

MONDAY Morning. Mr Williams is attacked by supposed robbers, on his return to the village. His letter to Mrs Jewkes, giving an account of the disaster. Pamela's mistrusts increase. Refuses to accompany Mrs Jewkes to make him a visit. In her absence, has great temptations to make her escape: but is unable to resolve upon it.

MONDAY Afternoon. Mrs Jewkes returns from visiting Mr Williams. Rallies Pamela, and makes a jest of his fright. Declares she had got out of him all that was plotting between him and her. Advises her to send a letter of thanks to her master, for his favour to her, in relation to Mr Williams: On her refusal, declares her to be quite unfathomable. Pamela still more and more apprehensive.

TUESDAY, WEDNESDAY. Mrs Jewkes's change of temper to Mr Williams. He is surprized at it. Pamela writes to him, blaming his openness. Desires to know what he had said to Mrs Jewkes; and proposes to resume the project of escaping.

THURSDAY. His answer. Thinks Mr B. neither can nor dare deceive him in so black a manner. Contents of the advices he has received in relation to Mr B.'s motions. Tells her what he had, and what he had not, owned to Mrs Jewkes. Her reply; in which she expresses great uneasiness and doubts; and impatiently wishes for the horse he had undertaken to procure for her.

FRIDAY. Mr Williams thinks her too apprehensive. Doubts not, that things *must* be better than she apprehends. He sends her a letter from her father, in which he approves of Mr Williams's address.

SATURDAY, SUNDAY. Mrs Jewkes quarrels with Mr Williams. Pamela is more and more convinced there is mischief brewing.

MONDAY, TUESDAY. All now out! Two letters brought from Mr B.; one to herself, filled with upbraidings and menaces; the other to Mrs Jewkes; wrongly, as by mistake, delivered to each. In that to Mrs Jewkes he declares his utmost resentment against Pamela, for her supposed encouragement of Mr Williams's address. Resolves to have Mr Williams arrested. Her affliction and despair. Her apprehensions of Colbrand the Swiss.

WEDNESDAY. Mr Williams actually arrested. She forms a new stratagem for her escape. Overhears Mrs Jewkes, in her cups, acknowledge to Colbrand, that the robbery of Mr Williams was a contrivance of hers, to come at his letters.

THURSDAY, FRIDAY, SATURDAY, SUNDAY. All her contrivances ruined. Is tempted to drown herself. Her soliloquy by the pond side. Refuges herself, half-dead with her bruises and distress, behind a pile of fire-wood. Mrs Jewkes's fright on missing her: and cruelty on finding her in the wood-house, though unable to stand up, or help herself.

SUNDAY *Afternoon*. She dreads the coming of her master. Her generous concern for him on hearing of a danger which he had escaped. She wonders at herself, for this concern of hers. She hears that John Arnold is turned away; and that Mr Longman, Mr Jonathan, and Mrs Jervis, are in danger of losing their places, for offering to intercede in her favour.

MONDAY, TUESDAY, WEDNESDAY. Mrs Jewkes more and more insolent to her.

THURSDAY. Apprehends from some particular dispositions, that her master will soon come. Her contemplations on his pretended love to her.

FRIDAY. Mrs Jewkes apprehending that she designs another escape, locks her up, and takes away her shoes; but of a sudden returns them, and orders her to dress herself handsomely, in order to receive a visit from Lady Darnford's two daughters. She refuses to obey her, and will not be made a shew of.

Five o'Clock. She thinks she hears the young ladies' coach. Resolves not to go down to them. Steps to the window; and, to her utmost surprize and terror, beholds her master just arrived.

Seven o'Clock is come, and she has not yet seen him. Doubts not that something is resolving against her. Is full of confusion and grief.

SATURDAY *Morning*. Her master's harsh treatment of her. Mrs Jewkes's vile instigations. Pamela's appeal to him against her. He sides with the wicked woman; and orders her to withdraw, and he will send her a few lines, her answer to which shall decide her doom.

SATURDAY *Noon*. Sends Proposals to her in writing, to live with him as his mistress. Her noble and resolute answer. Mrs Jewkes's vile instigations.

SATURDAY *Night*. He sends Mrs Jewkes for her. She refuses attending him in his chamber.

SUNDAY. Her master, in a letter to Mrs Jewkes, pretends that he shall not be at home till the next evening; and orders her not to trust Pamela without another's lying with her as well as herself. She sees this letter, through Mrs Jewkes's pretended carelessness, and rejoices at this further reprieve.

TUESDAY *Night*. She gives the particulars of the worst attempt he had yet made, and of Mrs Jewkes's wicked assistance. Her narrow escape. She falls into fits; which so affect her master, that he desists from his wicked purpose; and when she is recovered, comforts her.

WEDNESDAY *Morning*. He sends for her to walk with him in the garden. She likes not him, nor his ways. He resents an expression which his free usage provoked from her. She expostulates with him on his proceedings.

WEDNESDAY *Night*. Her master's great kindness and favour to her before Mrs Jewkes. Mrs Jewkes's respectful behaviour to her upon it. He admires her prudence. She has hopes that he will act honourably by her. But, on a sudden, he damps all again, and leaves her in a state of uncertainty.

THURSDAY *Morning*. Mr B. being to go to Stamford, tells her, that he will take it kindly, if she will confine herself pretty much to her chamber till he returns. His reasons for it. She promises not to stir any where without Mrs Jewkes.

FRIDAY *Night*. A gipsey finds means to drop a letter for her, intimating a sham marriage designed. Her passionate reflections on this occasion.

SATURDAY *Noon*. Her master returns. Mrs Jewkes seizes a parcel of her papers, and carries them to him.

SATURDAY, *Six o'clock*. She intreats him to return her papers unread. He refuses. Her sharp expressions hereupon make him angry with her. She endeavours to pacify him. Having read the papers, he sends for her, and insnaringly discovers that she has papers of a later date than these, and insists upon seeing them. She refuses; but he frightens her into a compliance.

SUNDAY *Morning*. On reading her last papers, which contain her temptations at the pond, he is greatly moved. His kind behaviour to her; yet, apprehending that this kindness is but consistent with the sham marriage she dreads, she still insists upon going to her parents. He falls into a rage hereupon, and bids her begone from his presence.

SUNDAY *Three o'Clock*. Her reflections upon the haughtiness of people in a high condition. Is surprized by a message from Mrs Jewkes, that she must instantly leave the house. Prepares to go, but cannot help being grieved. The travelling chariot is drawn out. Colbrand is getting on horseback. Wonders where all this will end.

The JOURNAL *continued* [Volume II]

SUNDAY *Night, near Nine o'Clock*. Mrs Jewkes insults her on her departure. Her wicked hints to her master in her hearing. He rebukes the vile woman for them. Pamela blesses him on her knees for it. Wonders she could be so loth to leave the house. The chariot drives away with her. She can hardly think but she is in a dream all the time.

Ten o'Clock. A copy of her master's letter to her, delivered at a certain distance, declaring his honourable intentions, had she not unseasonably preferred going to her parents. She laments that she gave credit to the gipsey-story. Accuses her heart of treachery to her.

MONDAY *Morning, Eleven.* Thomas the groom overtakes her with a second letter from her master, declaring, that he finds he cannot live without her. That if she will return, it will lay him under the highest obligation. Her reasonings with herself, whether to go back, or to proceed. At last, resolves to oblige him.

TUESDAY *Morning.* Her master's gratitude on her return. Description of Mrs Jewkes's constrained complaisance and officiousness to her. Her master orders that she be left entirely at her own liberty to go and come as she pleases, and the chariot to be at her service. Acquaints her, that he had set Mr Williams at liberty, and taken his bond. He gives her a letter to peruse from Lady Davers, who threatens, that if he should marry Pamela she will renounce all relation to him; but proposes that he will give her a sum of money, and marry her to some fellow of her own degree. Pamela's serious reflections upon the pride of people of birth and condition.

WEDNESDAY *Morning.* Her master takes an airing with her in the chariot. An interesting conversation between them. Her delightful prospects. He clears up, to her satisfaction, the gipsey's information. Tells her that the neighbouring ladies intend to make him a visit, on purpose to see and admire her. She resolves, throughout her future life, to rely on Providence, who has brought such real good to her out of such evil appearances.

THURSDAY. He declares his intentions of marriage. His kindness to her in a particular instance, when she dreaded he would have been disobliged. She has hopes that her master will be reconciled to Mr Williams.

FRIDAY. She gives the particulars of what passed in the visit of the neighbouring gentry, who admire her. Miss Polly Darnford particularly fond of her.

FRIDAY *Afternoon.* Her father's unexpected arrival, while all the guests are together. Is kindly received by her master, and all his fears for his daughter's virtue dissipated. The company greatly affected at the first interview between her father and her.

SATURDAY. Her master offers to dismiss Mrs Jewkes. He is pleased with her forgiving temper. Takes an airing with her father and her, and designedly falls in with Mr Williams. His kindness to that gentleman. Gives him up his bond, and requests him to officiate next day in his newly fitted up chapel.

SUNDAY. Mr Williams accordingly officiates. Her father performs the clerk's part with applause. Mr B.'s pleasant remarks on her paraphrase on the cxxxviith psalm. Mr Andrews joyfully takes leave, to carry the good tidings of all these things to his wife.

MONDAY. Mr B. brings her a licence, and presses for the day. The Thursday following fixed upon.

TUESDAY. Her serious reflections on the near prospect of her important change of condition. Is diffident of her own worthiness. Prays for humility, that her new condition may not be a snare to her.

WEDNESDAY, THURSDAY. Her alternate fears and exultation, as the day draws nigh. His generous and polite tenderness to her. Her modest, humble and thankful returns.

THURSDAY *Afternoon.* Her nuptials celebrated. Her joyful exultations to her parents upon it. Mrs Jewkes's dutiful and submissive behaviour to her. The different aspect everything bears to her, now that her prison is become her palace.

FRIDAY *Evening*. Instances of his politeness and generosity to her. He kindly complies with her intercession in favour of Mr Longman, Mrs Jervis, Jonathan, and John Arnold, whom he had dismissed.

SATURDAY *Morning*. Copy of Mr B.'s letter to Mr Longman, and of hers to Mrs Jervis, in the kindest manner desiring them to take possession, with Jonathan, of their former offices. Rejoices in her happiness, and prays that her will to do good may be enlarged with her opportunities.

SATURDAY *Evening*. Mr B.'s kind intentions towards her parents. His annual allowance to her for private charities.

SUNDAY. His rules to her, in relation to dress, and to different parts of family management; and to her own deportment, on particular occasions. With other interesting particulars.

MONDAY. In Mr B.'s occasional absence, Lady Davers, with her nephew, arrive. Particulars of the harsh treatment she met with from that lady.

TUESDAY. Lady Davers's outrageous behaviour to her brother on his return. At last a happy reconciliation takes place. Pamela gives the particulars of a conversation between Mr B. and herself, when alone, in which he tells her what he expects from her future conduct. She is a little tinctured with jealousy upon a charge made by Lady Davers, in her passion, of an intrigue between him and Miss Sally Godfrey.

WEDNESDAY. She relates briefly to Lady Davers her past trials and distresses, who is greatly delighted with her story; and desires to see all her papers.

WEDNESDAY *Night*. The neighbouring gentry take leave of Mr and Mrs B. on their setting out for Bedfordshire. Mrs Jewkes, with tears, begs her to forgive her past wickedness to her. Miss Darnford and Mrs B. agree upon a correspondence by letters. Her value and esteem for that young lady.

SATURDAY. Lady Davers sets out for her own seat; and Mr and Mrs B. for Bedfordshire. Her emotions on her arrival as mistress of the house she was lately turned out of. Her kind reception of Mrs Jervis, and affable behaviour to the servants. Mr B.'s generosity to her.

SUNDAY *Night*. Has the pleasure to think, she is not puffed up with this great change of condition.

MONDAY. Her justice and generosity with respect to her father's creditors, &c.

WEDNESDAY *Evening*. Mr B. brings home to dinner with him four of the neighbouring gentry. What passed on that occasion. She tells her parents, how much Mr B. is pleased with their undertaking to manage the Kentish estate, as he had directed her to propose to them.

THURSDAY. Mr B. carries her to breakfast ten miles off, to a neat dairy-house; and by surprize introduces to her Miss Goodwin, the daughter he had by Miss Sally Godfrey. Her generous and affecting behaviour on this occasion. As they return, he gives the moving particulars of that amour, and of the lady's remarkable penitence and prudence.

MONDAY *Morning*. She gives an account of their public appearance the preceding day, at church; and of what passed in the morning and afternoon on that occasion.

TUESDAY. An affecting instance of Mr B.'s goodness to her, in settling his affairs in such a manner, that, in case of his death without children by her, neither she nor her parents should lie at the mercy of his heirs. Other tender particulars on this affecting occasion. Her verses on humility.

FRIDAY. The most considerable of the neighbouring gentry visit them, to congratulate their nuptials, and all join to admire her. She resolves to have no other pride but in making deserving objects happy. Relates, that Lady Davers has sent for her papers, and promises that her lord and she will soon be *her* guests. Hopes, as Miss Goodwin grows older, she shall have her committed to her care. Has just received the news, that her parents are on the point of setting out to be with her. Prays for a happy meeting. Impatiently longs for it.

VOLUME I

My dear Father and Mother,

I have great trouble, and some comfort, to acquaint you with. The trouble is, that my good lady died of the illness I mentioned to you, and left us all much grieved for the loss of her; for she was a dear good lady, and kind to all us her servants. Much I feared, that as I was taken by her ladyship to wait upon her person, I should be quite destitute again, and forced to return to you and my poor mother, who have enough to do to maintain yourselves; and, as my lady's goodness had put me to write and cast accompts,⁵ and made me a little expert at my needle, and otherwise qualified above my degree, it was not every family that could have found a place that your poor Pamela was fit for: But God, whose graciousness to us we have so often experienced, put it into my good lady's heart, on her death-bed, just an hour before she expired, to recommend to my young master all her servants, one by one; and when it came to my turn to be recommended (for I was sobbing and crying at her pillow) she could only say, 'My dear son!' and so broke off a little; and then recovering, 'Remember my poor Pamela!' And those were some of her last words! O how my eyes overflow! Don't wonder to see the paper so blotted!

Well, but God's will must be done! and so comes the comfort, that I shall not be obliged to return back to be a burden to my dear parents! For my master said, 'I will take care of you all, my good maidens; and for you, Pamela,' (and took me by the hand; yes, he took my hand before them all), 'for my dear mother's sake, I will be a friend to you, and you shall take care of my linen.' God bless him! and pray with me, my dear father and mother, for a blessing upon him: For he has given mourning⁶ and a year's wages to all my lady's servants; and I having no wages as yet, my lady having said she would do for me as I deserved, ordered the housekeeper to give me mourning with the rest, and gave me with his own hand four guineas, and some silver, which were in my lady's pocket when she died; and said, if I was a good girl, and faithful and diligent, he would be a friend to me, for his mother's sake. And so I send you these four guineas for your comfort. I formerly sent you such little matters as arose from my lady's bounty, loth as you was always to take any thing from me: But Providence will not let me want; and I have made, in case of sudden occasions, a little reserve (besides the silver now given me) that I may not be obliged to borrow, and look little in the eyes of my fellow-servants: And so you may pay some old debt with part; and keep the other part to comfort you both. If I get more, I am sure it is my duty, and it shall be my care, to love and cherish you both; for you have loved and cherished me, when I could do nothing for myself. I send them by John our footman, who goes your way; but he does not know what he carries; because I seal them up in one of the little pill-boxes,[7] which my lady had, wrapped close in paper, that they may not chink; and be sure don't open it before him.

I know, my dear father and mother, I must give you both grief and pleasure; and so I will only say, pray for your Pamela; who will ever be

Your dutiful Daughter.

I have been scared out of my senses; for just now, as I was folding up this letter, in my late lady's dressing-room, in comes my young master! Good sirs! how I was frightened! I went to hide the letter in my bosom, and he, seeing me tremble, said smiling, 'To whom have you been writing, Pamela?' I said, in my confusion, 'Pray your honour, forgive me! Only to my father and mother.' 'Well, then, let me see what a hand you write.' He took it, without saying more, and read it quite through, and then gave it me again; and I said, 'Pray your honour, forgive me!' Yet I know not for what: For he was not undutiful to *his* parents; and why should he be angry that I was dutiful to *mine*! And indeed he was not angry; for he took me by the hand, and said, 'You are a good girl, to be kind to your aged father and mother. I am not angry with you for writing such innocent matters as these; *though you ought to be wary what tales you send out of a family.* Be faithful and diligent; and do as you should do, and I like you the better for this.' And then he said, 'Why, Pamela, you write a pretty hand, and *spell* very well too. You may look into any of my mother's books to improve yourself, so you take care of them.'

To be sure I did nothing but curt'sy and cry, and was all in confusion, at his goodness. Indeed, he was once thought to be wildish; but he is now the best of gentlemen, I think!

But I am making another long letter: So will only add to it, that I shall ever be

Your dutiful Daughter,
PAMELA ANDREWS.

LETTER II

HER FATHER IN ANSWER

My dear Child,

Your letter was indeed a great trouble, and some comfort, to me, and to your poor mother. We are troubled, to be sure, for your good lady's death, who took such care of you, and gave you learning, and for three or four years past has always been giving you clothes and linen, and every thing that a gentlewoman need not be ashamed to appear in. But our chief trouble is, and indeed a very great one, for fear you should be brought to any thing dishonest or wicked, *by being set so above yourself*. Every body talks how you are come on, and what a genteel girl you are; and some say, you are very pretty; and, indeed, when I saw you last, which is about six months ago, I should have thought so myself, if you was not our child. But what avails all this, if you are to be ruined and undone! Indeed, my dear Pamela, we begin to be in great fear for you; for what signify all the riches in the world, with a bad conscience, and to be dishonest? We are, it is true, very poor, and find it hard enough to live; *though once*, as you know, *it was better with us*. But we would sooner live upon the water, and, if possible, the clay of the ditches I contentedly dig, than live better at the price of our dear child's ruin.

I hope the good 'squire has no design; but, as he was once, as you own, a little wildish, and as he has given you so much money, and speaks so kindly to you, and praises your coming on; and, Oh! that frightful word, that he would be kind to you, if you would do as *you should do*; these things make us very fearful for your virtue.

I have spoken to good old widow Mumford about it, who, you know, has formerly lived in good families; and she gives us some comfort; for she says, it is not unusual, when a lady dies, to give what she has about her person to her waiting-maid, and to such as sit up with her in her illness. But then, *why should he smile so kindly upon you?* Why should he take such a poor girl as you by the hand, as your letter says he has done twice? Why should he deign to read your letter written to us, and commend your writing and spelling? Indeed, indeed, my dearest child, our hearts ake for you; and then you seem so full of *joy* at his goodness, so *taken* with his kind expressions (which, truly, are very great favours, if he means well) that we *fear* – Yes, my dear child, we *fear* – you should be *too* grateful, and reward him with that jewel, your virtue, which no riches, nor favour, nor any thing in this life, can make up to you.

I, too, have written a long letter; but will say one thing more; and that is, that in the midst of our poverty and misfortunes, we have trusted in God's goodness, and been honest, and doubt not to be happy hereafter, if we continue to be good, though our lot is hard here: But the loss of our dear child's virtue would be a grief that we could not bear, and would very soon bring our grey hairs to the grave.

If, then, you love *us*, if you wish for *God*'s blessing, and *your own* future happiness, we charge you to stand upon your guard; and, if you find the least thing that looks like a design upon your virtue, be sure you leave every thing behind you, and come away to us; for we had rather see you all covered with rags, and even follow you to the church-yard, than have it said, a child of our's preferred any worldly conveniencies to her virtue.

We accept kindly of your dutiful present; but till we are out of our pain, cannot make use of it, for fear we should partake of the price of our poor daughter's shame: So have laid it up in a rag among the thatch, over the window, for a while, lest we should be robbed.

With our blessings, and our hearty prayers for you, we remain,
Your careful, but loving Father and Mother,
JOHN AND ELIZ. ANDREWS.

LETTER III

I must needs say, my dear father, that your letter has filled me with trouble: for it has made my heart, which was overflowing with gratitude for my master's goodness, suspicious and fearful; and yet,

I hope I shall never find him to act unworthy of his character; for what could he get by ruining such a poor young creature as me? But that which gives me most trouble is, that you seem to mistrust the honesty of your child. No, my dear father and mother, be assured, that, by God's grace, I never will do any thing that shall bring your grey hairs with sorrow to the grave. I will die a thousand deaths, rather than be dishonest any way. Of that be assured, and set your hearts at rest; for although I have lived above myself for some time past, yet I can be content with rags and poverty, and bread and water, and will embrace them, rather than forfeit my good name, let who will be the tempter. And of this, pray rest satisfied, and think better of

Your dutiful Daughter.

My master continues to be very affable to me. As yet I see no cause to fear any thing. Mrs Jervis the house-keeper too is very civil to me, and I have the love of every body. Sure they can't *all* have designs against me because they are civil! I hope I shall always behave so as to be respected by every one; and that nobody would do me more hurt, than I am sure I would do them.

Our John so often goes your way, that I will always get him to call, that you may hear from me, either by writing (for it keeps my hand in) or by word of mouth.

LETTER IV

My dear Mother,

As my last was to my father, in answer to his letter, I will now write to you; though I have nothing to say but what will make me look more like a vain hussy, than any thing else: however, I hope I shan't be so proud as to forget myself. Yet there is a secret pleasure one has to hear one's self praised. You must know, then, that my Lady Davers, who, I need not tell you, is my master's sister, has been a month at our house, and has taken great notice of me, and given me good advice to keep myself to myself. She told me I was a very pretty wench, and that every body gave me a very good character, and loved me; and bid me take care to keep the fellows at a distance; and said, *that* I might do, and be more valued for it, even by themselves.

But what pleased me much, was what I am going to tell you; for at table, as our butler Jonathan told Mrs Jervis, and she me, my master and her ladyship talking of me, she told him she thought me the prettiest wench she ever saw in her life; and that I was too pretty to live in a batchelor's house; since no lady he might marry, would care to continue me with her. He said, I was vastly improved, and had a good share of prudence, and sense above my years; and it would be pity, that what was my merit should be my misfortune. 'No,' said my lady, 'Pamela shall come and live with me, I think.' With all his heart, he replied; he should be glad to have me so well provided for. 'Well,' said she, 'I'll consult my lord about it.' She asked, how old I was; and Mrs Jervis said, I was fifteen last February. 'O!' said she, 'if the wench' (for so she calls us maiden-servants) 'takes care of herself, she'll improve yet more and more, as well in her person as mind.'

Now, my dear mother, though this may look too vain to be repeated by me, yet are you not rejoiced, as well as I, to see my master *so willing to part with me?* This shews that he has nothing bad in his heart. But John is just going away, and so I have only to say, that I am, and will always be,

Your honest, as well as dutiful Daughter.

Pray make use of the money. You may now do it safely.

LETTER V

My dear Father and Mother,

John being to go your way, I am willing to write, because he is so willing to carry any thing for me. He says it does him good at his heart to see you both, and to hear you talk: you are both so sensible, and so honest, that he always learns something from you to the purpose. It is a thousand pities, he says, that such worthy hearts should not have better luck in the world! and wonders, that you, my father, who are so well able to teach, and write so good a hand, succeeded no better *in the school you attempted to set up*; but was forced to go to such hard labour. But it is more pride to me that I am come of such honest parents, than if I had been born a lady.

I hear nothing yet of going to Lady Davers; and I am very easy at present here: for Mrs Jervis uses me as if I were her own daughter, and is a very good woman, and makes my master's interest her own. She is always giving me good counsel, and I love her, next to you two, I think, best of any body. She keeps such good rule and order, as makes her mightily respected by us all; and takes delight to hear me read to her. And all she loves to hear read is good books, which we read very often when we are alone; so that I am ready, with such good employment, to think that I am at home with you. She heard one of our men, Harry, who is no better than he should be, speak freely to me; I think he called me his pretty Pamela; and took hold of me, as if he would have kissed me (for which, you may be sure, I was very angry) and she took him to task, and was as angry at him as I could be; and told me she was very well pleased to see my prudence and modesty, and that I kept all the fellows at a distance. And, indeed, though I am sure I am not proud, but carry it civilly to every body, I cannot bear to be looked upon by these men-servants as they are apt to look upon me; and as I generally break-fast, dine, and sup, with Mrs Jervis, (so good is she to me) I am very easy that I have so little to say to them. Not but they are very civil to me in the main, for Mrs Jervis's sake, who they see loves me; and they stand in awe of her, knowing her to be a gentle-woman born, though she has had misfortunes.

I am going on again with a long letter; for I love writing, and shall tire you. But when I began, I only intended to say, that I am quite fearless of any danger now: and indeed cannot but wonder at myself, (though your caution to me was owing to your watchful love) that I should be so foolish as to be so uneasy as I have been: for I am sure my master would not demean himself so, as to think upon such a poor girl as I, for my harm. For such a thing would ruin his credit as well as mine, you know: who, to be sure, may expect one of the best ladies in the land. So no more at present; but that I am

Your ever dutiful Daughter.

LETTER VI

My master has been very kind since my last; for he has given me a suit of my late lady's clothes, and half a dozen of her shifts, and six fine handkerchiefs,[8] and three of her cambric aprons, and four

Holland ones.[9] The clothes are fine silk, and too rich and too good for me, to be sure. I wish it was no affront to him to make money of them, and send it to you: that would do me more good.

You will be full of fears, I warrant now, of some design upon me, till I tell you, that he was with Mrs Jervis when he gave them me; and he gave her a great many good things at the same time, and bid her wear them in remembrance of her good friend, his mother. And when he gave me these fine things, he said, 'These, Pamela, are for you. Have them made fit for you, when your mourning is laid by, and wear them for your good mistress's sake. Mrs Jervis commends your conduct; and I would have you continue to behave as prudently as you have done hitherto, and every body will be your friend.'

I was so affected with his goodness, that I could not tell what to say. I curt'sied to him, and to Mrs Jervis for her good word; and said, I wished I might be deserving of his favour, and her kindness: and nothing should be wanting in me, to the best of my knowledge.

O how amiable a thing is doing good! it is all I envy great folks for!

I always thought my young master a fine gentleman, as every body, indeed, says he is: but he gave these good things to us both with such a graciousness, that I thought he looked like an angel.

Mrs Jervis says, he asked her, if I kept the men at a distance; for, he said, I was very pretty; and to be drawn in to have any of them, might be my ruin, and make me poor and miserable betimes. She never is wanting to give me a good word, and took occasion to launch out in my praise, she says. But I hope she said no more than I shall try to deserve, though I may not deserve it at present. I am sure I will always love her next to you and my dear mother. So I rest

Your ever-dutiful Daughter.

LETTER VII

My dear Father,

Since my last, my master gave me more fine things. He called me up to my late lady's closet,[10] and pulling out her drawers, he gave me two suits of fine Flanders laced head-clothes,[11] three pair of fine silk shoes,[12] two hardly the worse, and just fit for me (for my lady had a very little foot), and the other with wrought silver buckles in them; and several ribands and top-knots[13] of all colours; four pair of fine white cotton stockings, and three pair of fine silk ones; and two pair of rich stays.[14] 'Your poor lady, Pamela,' said he, 'was finely shaped, though in years, and very slender.' I was quite astonished, and unable to speak for a while; but yet I was inwardly ashamed to take the stockings; for Mrs Jervis was not there: if she had, it would have been nothing. I believe I received them very aukwardly; for he smiled at my aukwardness, and said, 'Don't blush, Pamela: dost think I don't know pretty maids wear shoes and stockings?'

I was so confounded at these words, you might have beat me down with a feather. For, you must think, there was no answer to be made to this. And besides, it was a little odd, I thought, and so I thought before, that he himself should turn over my lady's apparel, and give me these things with his own hands, rather than to let Mrs Jervis give them to me. So, like a fool, I was ready to cry; and went away curt'sying and blushing, I am sure, up to the ears; for, though there was no harm in what he said, yet I did not know how to take it. But I went and told all to Mrs Jervis, who said, God put it into his heart to be good to me, and I must double my diligence. It looked to her, she said, as if he would fit me in dress for a waiting-maid's place on Lady Davers's own person.

But still your fatherly cautions came into my head, and made all these gifts nothing near to me what they would have been. But yet, I hope, there is no reason. So I will make myself easy; and, indeed, I should never have been otherwise, if you had not put it into my head; for my good, I know very well. But, may be, without these uneasinesses to mingle with these benefits, I might be too much puffed up: so I will conclude, all that happens is for our good; and God bless you, my dear father and mother; and I know you constantly pray for a blessing upon me. Who am, and shall always be,

Your dutiful Daughter.

LETTER VIII

Dear Pamela,

I cannot but renew my cautions on your master's kindness, and his free expression to you about the stockings: yet there may *not* be, and I hope there *is not*, any thing in it. But when I reflect, that there *possibly* may, and that if there *should*, no less depends upon it than my child's happiness in this world and the next; it is enough to make one fearful for you. Arm yourself, my dear child, for the worst; and resolve to lose your life rather than your virtue. What though the doubts I filled you with lessen the pleasure you would have had in your master's kindness; yet what signify the delights that arise from a few fine clothes, in comparison with a good conscience ?

These are indeed very great favours that he heaps upon you, but so much the more to be suspected. As you say, it would have been more proper for Mrs Jervis to have been the dispenser of them to you, if he had so thought fit. I can't say I much like of it, that it was not so.[15] I trust that you will be always on your guard: yet, when you say, *he looked so amiably, and like an angel*, how afraid I am, that they should make too great an impression upon you! For, though you are blessed with sense and prudence above your years, yet I tremble to think, what a sad hazard a poor maiden, of little more than fifteen years of age, stands against the temptations of this world, and a designing young gentleman, if he should prove so, who has so much *power* to oblige, and has a kind of *authority* to command as your master. Methinks I could wish, so could your mother, that you might be taken by good Lady Davers. That would be an high honour; and what is of more account, a great ease to our hearts concerning your virtue.

But if this be, or be not to be, I repeat my charge to you, my dear child, on both our blessings, to be on your guard; there can be no harm in that: and since Mrs Jervis is so good a gentlewoman, and so kind to you, I am the easier a great deal, and so is your mother; and we hope you will hide nothing from her, and take her counsel in every thing. So, with our blessings, and assured prayers for you, more than for ourselves, we remain

Your loving Father and Mother.

Besure don't let people's telling you, you are pretty, puff you up: for you did not make yourself, and so no praise can be due to you for it.

It is virtue and goodness only, that make the true beauty. Remember that, Pamela.

LETTER IX

I am sorry, my dear father and mother, to write you word, that the hopes I had of going to wait on Lady Davers, are quite over. My lady would have had me; but my master, as I heard by-the-bye, would not consent to it. He said, her nephew might be taken with me, and I might draw him in, or be drawn in by him; and he thought, as his mother loved me, and committed me to his care, he ought to continue me with him; and Mrs Jervis would be a mother to me.

Mrs Jervis tells me, my lady shook her head, and said, '*Ah! Brother!*' and that was all. And as you have made me fearful, by your cautions, my heart at times misgives me. But I say nothing yet of your cautions, or of my own uneasiness, to Mrs Jervis; not that I mistrust her, but for fear she should think me presumptuous, and vain, and conceited, to have any fears about the matter, from the great distance between such a gentleman, and so poor a girl. But yet Mrs Jervis seemed to build something upon Lady Davers' shaking her head, and saying, '*Ah! Brother!*' and no more.

God, I hope, will give me his grace; and so I will not, if I can help it, make myself too uneasy; for I hope there is no occasion. But every little matter that happens, I will acquaint you with, that you may continue to me your good advice, and pray for

Your thoughtful PAMELA.

LETTER X

My dear Mother,

You and my good father may wonder you have not had a letter from me in so many weeks: but a sad, sad scene has been the occasion of it. For, to be sure, now it is too plain, that all your cautions were well-grounded. O my dear mother, I am miserable! truly miserable! But yet, don't be frighted, I am honest! And I hope God, of his goodness, will keep me so!

O this angel of a master! this fine gentleman! this gracious benefactor to your poor Pamela! who was to take care of me at the prayer of his good dying mother! who was so apprehensive for me, lest I should be drawn in by Lord Davers's nephew, that he would not let me go to Lady Davers's: This very gentleman (yes, I *must* call him gentleman, though he has fallen from the merit of that title) has degraded himself to offer freedoms to his poor servant: he has now shewed himself in his true colours, and, to me, nothing appears so black and so frightful.

I have not been idle; but had writ from time to time, how he, by sly mean degrees, exposed his wicked views: but somebody stole my letter, and I know not what is become of it. It was a very long one. I fear, he that was mean enough to attempt bad things in one respect, did not stick at *this*. But be it as it will, all the use he can make of it will be, that he may be ashamed of *his* part; I not of *mine*: for he will see I was resolved to be virtuous, and gloried in the honesty of my poor parents.

I will tell you all, the next opportunity; for I am watched very narrowly; and he says to Mrs Jervis, 'This girl is always scribbling; I think she may be better employed.' And yet I work very hard with my needle, upon his linen, and the fine linen of the family; and am, besides, about flowering him a waistcoat.[16] But, Oh! my heart's almost broken; for what am I likely to have for my reward, but shame and disgrace, or else ill words, and hard treatment! I'll tell you all soon, and hope I shall find my long letter.

Your most afflicted Daughter.

Perhaps I *he* and *him* him too much: but it is his own fault if I do. For why did he lose all his dignity with me?

LETTER XI

Well, my dear mother, I can't find my letter, and so I'll try to recollect it all.

All went well enough, in the main, for some time after my last letter but one. At last, I saw some reason to be suspicious; for he would look upon me, whenever he saw me, in such a manner, as shewed not well: And one day he came to me, as I was in the summer-house in the little garden, at work with my needle, and Mrs Jervis was just gone from me; and I would have gone out; but he said, 'Don't go, Pamela; I have something to say to you; and you always fly me, when I come near you, as if you were afraid of me.'

I was much out of countenance you may well think; and began

to tremble, and the more when he took me by the hand; for no soul was near us.

'Lady Davers,' said he, (and seemed, I thought, to be as much at a loss for words as I) 'would have had you live with *her*; but she would not do for you what I am resolved to do, if you continue faithful and obliging. What say you, my girl?' said he, with some eagerness; 'had you not rather stay with me than go to Lady Davers?' He looked so, as filled me with fear; I don't know how; wildly, I thought.

I said, when I could speak, 'Your Honour will forgive me; but as you have no lady for me to wait upon, and my good lady has been now dead this twelvemonth, I had rather, if it would not displease you, wait upon Lady Davers, *because*—'

I was proceeding, and he said a little hastily, '— *Because* you are a little fool, and know not what's good for yourself. I tell you, I will make a gentlewoman of you, if you are obliging, and don't stand in your own light.' And so saying, he put his arm about me, and kissed me.

Now, you will say, all his wickedness appeared plainly. I struggled, and trembled, and was so benumbed with terror, that I sunk down, not in a fit, and yet not myself; and I found myself in his arms, quite void of strength; and he kissed me two or three times, with frightful eagerness. At last I burst from him, and was getting out of the summer-house; but he held me back, and shut the door.

I would have given my life for a farthing. And he said, 'I'll do you no harm, Pamela; don't be afraid of me.'

I said, 'I won't stay.'

'You *won't*, hussy! Do you know whom you speak to?'

I lost all fear, and all respect, and said, 'Yes, I do, sir, too well! Well may I forget that I am your servant, when you forget what belongs to a master.'

I sobbed and cried most sadly. 'What a foolish hussy you are!' said he: 'Have I done you any harm?' 'Yes, sir,' said I, 'the greatest harm in the world: You have taught me to forget myself, and what belongs to me; and have lessened the distance that fortune has made between us, by demeaning yourself, to be so free to a poor servant. Yet, sir, I will be bold to say, I am honest, though poor: And if you were a prince, I would not be otherwise than honest.'

He was angry, and said, 'Who, little fool, would have you other-wise? Cease your blubbering. I own I have undervalued myself; but it was only to try you. If you can keep this matter secret, you'll give me the better opinion of your prudence: And here's something,' added he, putting some gold in my hand, 'to make you amends for the fright I put you in. Go, take a walk in the garden, and don't go in till your blubbering is over: And I charge you say nothing of what has past, and all shall be well, and I'll forgive you.'

'I won't take the money indeed, sir,' said I: 'I won't take it.' And so I put it upon the bench. And as he seemed vexed and confounded at what he had done, I took the opportunity to open the door, and hurried out of the summer-house.

He called to me, and said, 'Be secret, I charge you, Pamela; and don't go in yet.'

O how poor and mean must those actions be, and how little must they make the best of gentlemen look, when they offer such things as are unworthy of themselves, and put it into the power of their inferiors to be greater than they!

I took a turn or two in the garden, but in sight of the house, for fear of the worst; and breathed upon my hand to dry my eyes, because I would not be too disobedient.

My next shall tell you more.

Pray for me, my dear father and mother; and don't be angry, that I have not yet run away from this house, so late my comfort and delight, but now my terror and anguish.

I am forced to break off hastily.

Your dutiful and honest Daughter.

LETTER XII

Well, my dear mother, and now I will proceed with my sad story.

After I had dried my eyes, I went in, and began to ruminate with myself what I had best to do. Sometimes I thought I would leave the house, and go to the next town, and wait an opportunity to get to you; but then I was at a loss to resolve whether to take away the things he had given me or no, and *how* to take them away: Some-times I thought to leave them behind me, and only go with the clothes I had on: But then I had two miles and a half, and a bye-way to the town; and being pretty well dressed, I might come to some harm, almost as bad as what I would run away from; and then, maybe, thought I, it will be reported, I have stolen something, and so was forced to run away: And to carry a bad name back with me to my dear parents, would be a sad thing indeed! O how I wished for my grey russet[17] again, and my poor honest dress, with which you fitted me out for going to this place, when I was not twelve years old, in my good lady's days! Sometimes I thought of telling Mrs Jervis, and taking her advice; but then I thought of his command to be secret; and who knows, thought I, but he may be ashamed of his actions, and never attempt the like again? And as poor Mrs Jervis depended upon him, through misfortunes that had attended her, I thought it would be a sad thing to bring his displeasure upon her for my sake.

In this perplexity; now considering, now crying, and not knowing what to do, I passed the time in my chamber till evening; when desiring to be excused going to supper, Mrs Jervis came up to me, and said, 'Why must I sup without you, Pamela! Come, I see you are troubled at something; tell me what is the matter?'

I begged I might be permitted to lie with her on nights; for I was afraid of spirits, and they would not hurt such a good person as she. 'That was a silly excuse,' she said; 'for why was you not afraid of spirits before?' [Indeed I did not think of that]. 'But you shall be my bed-fellow with all my heart,' added she, 'let your reason be what it will; only come down to supper.' I begged to be excused; for, said I, 'I have been crying so, that it will be taken notice of by my fellow-servants as they come in and out; and I will hide nothing from you, Mrs Jervis, when we are alone.'

She was so good as to indulge me; but made haste to come up to bed; and told the female servants, that I should lie with her, because she could not rest well, and she would get me to read her to sleep; for she knew I loved reading, she said.

When we were alone, I told her all that had passed; for, ruminating on every thing, I thought, though he had bid me not, yet if he should come to know I had told, it would be no worse; for to keep a secret of such a nature, would be, as I apprehended, to deprive myself of the good advice which I never wanted more; and might encourage him to think I did not resent it as I ought, and would keep *worse secrets*, and so make him do *worse by me*. Was I right, my dear mother?

Mrs Jervis could not help mingling tears with my tears; for I cried all the time I was telling her the story, and begged her to advise me what to do; and I shewed her my dear father's two letters, and she praised the honesty and inditing of them, and said pleasing things to me of you both.

But she begged I would not think of leaving my service; 'for,' said she, 'in all likelihood, as you behaved so virtuously, he will be ashamed of what he has done, and never offer the like to you again: Though, my dear Pamela, I fear more for your prettiness than for any thing else; because the best man in the land might love you.' So she was pleased to say. She wished it was in her power to live independent; then she would take a little private house, and I should live with her like her daughter.

And so, (as you ordered me to take her advice), I resolved to stay to see how things went, except he was to turn me away. So, my dear father and mother, it is not disobedience, I hope, that I stay; for I could not expect a blessing, or the good fruits of your prayers for me, if I was disobedient.

All the next day I was very sad, and began my long letter. He saw me writing, and said (as I mentioned) to Mrs Jervis, 'That girl is always scribbling; methinks she might find something else to do'; or to that purpose. And when I had finished my letter, I put it under the toilet,[18] in my late lady's dressing-room, whither nobody comes but myself and Mrs Jervis, besides my master; but when I came up again to seal it, to my great concern, it was gone; and Mrs Jervis knew nothing of it; and nobody knew of my master's having been near the place in the time: So I have been sadly troubled about it: But Mrs Jervis, as well as I, thinks he has it, some how or other; and he appears cross and angry, and seems to shun me, as much as he said I did him. It had better be so than worse!

But he has ordered Mrs Jervis to bid me not pass so much time in writing; which is a poor matter for such a gentleman as he to take notice of, as I am not idle other-ways, if he was not apprehensive of the subject I wrote upon. And this has no very good look.

But I am a good deal easier since I sleep with Mrs Jervis; though after all, the fears I live in on one side, and his displeasure at what I do on the other, make me more miserable than enough.

O that I had never left my little bed in your loft![19] To be thus exposed to temptations on one hand, or disgusts on the other! How happy was I a while ago! How contrary now! Pity and pray for

Your afflicted PAMELA.

LETTER XIII

My dearest Child,

Our hearts bleed for your distress, and the temptations you are exposed to. You have our hourly prayers; and we would have you flee this evil great house and man, if you find him in the least inclined to renew his freedoms. You ought to have done it at first, had you not had Mrs Jervis to advise with.

We have, indeed, great comfort, when we reflect upon your past conduct, and that you have been bred to be more ashamed of dishonesty than poverty: But as we can't see but your life must be a burden to you, through the great apprehensions always upon you; and as we consider that it may be presumptuous to trust too much to your own strength; and that you are but very young; and that the devil may put it into his head to use some stratagem, of which great men are full, to decoy you; I think you had better come home to share our poverty with safety, than live with so much discontent in a plenty, that itself may be dangerous.

God direct you for the best! While you have Mrs Jervis for an adviser, and bed-fellow, (and O my dear child, that was prudently done of you!) we are easier than we should otherwise have been. And so committing you to the Divine Protection, remain,

Your truly loving,
and careful, Father and Mother.

LETTER XIV

Mrs Jervis and I, my dear father and mother, have lived very comfortably together for this fortnight past; for my master was all that time at his Lincolnshire estate, and at Lady Davers's. But he came home yesterday. He had some talk with Mrs Jervis soon after, and mostly about me. He said to her, it seems, 'Well, Mrs Jervis, I know Pamela has your good word; but do you think her of any use in the family?' She told me, she was surprised at the question; but said, that I was one of the most virtuous and industrious creatures she ever knew. 'Why that word *virtuous*?' said he. 'Was there any reason to *suppose* her otherwise? Or has any body taken it into their heads to try her?' 'Who, sir,' said she, 'dare to offer any thing to her in such an orderly and well-governed house as yours, and under a master of so good a character?' 'Your servant, Mrs Jervis; but pray, if any body *did*, do you think Pamela would let *you* know it?' 'She is,' replied she, 'an innocent young creature, and I believe has so much confidence in me, that she would take my advice as soon as she would her mother's.' '*Innocent!* again; and *virtuous*, I suppose! Well, Mrs Jervis, you abound with your epithets! But I will give you my opinion of her: I don't think this same favourite of yours so very artless a girl, as you imagine.' 'I am not to dispute with your honour,' replied Mrs Jervis; 'but I dare say, if the men will let her alone, she'll never trouble herself about them.' 'Why, Mrs Jervis,' said he, 'are there any men that will *not* let her alone, that you know of?' 'No, indeed, sir; she keeps herself so much to herself, and yet behaves so prudently, that they all esteem her, and shew her as great respect, as if she was a gentlewoman born.'

'Ay,' says he, 'that's her art, that I was speaking of: But let me tell you, the girl has vanity and conceit, and pride too, or I am mistaken; and, perhaps, I could give you an instance of it.' 'Sir,' said she, 'you can see further than such a poor silly [20] woman as I can; but I never saw any thing but innocence in her.' 'And *virtue* too, I'll warrant,' said he. 'But suppose I could give you an instance, where she has talked a little too freely of the kindnesses that have been shewed her from a *certain quarter*; and has had the vanity to impute a few kind words, uttered in mere compassion to her youth and circumstances, into a design upon her, and even dared to make free with names that she ought never to mention but with reverence and gratitude; what would you say to that?' 'Say, sir!' replied she, 'I cannot tell what I should say. But I hope Pamela is incapable of such ingratitude.'

'Well, no more of this silly girl,' said he; 'you may only advise her, as you are her friend, not to give herself too much licence upon the favours she meets with; and if she stays here, that she will not write the affairs of my family purely for an exercise to her pen and her invention. I tell you, she is a subtle, artful little gypsey, [21] and time will shew you that she is.'

Was ever the like heard, my dear father and mother? It is plain he did not expect to meet with such a repulse, and mistrusts that I have told Mrs Jervis, and has my long letter too, that I intended for you; and so is vexed to the heart. But I can't help it. I had better be *thought* artful and subtle, than *be* so, in *his* sense; and as light as he makes of the words *virtue* and *innocence* in me, he would have made a less angry construction, had I *less deserved* that he should do so; for then, may be, my *crime* would have been my *virtue* with him; wicked gentleman as he is!

I will soon write again; but must now end with saying, That I am, and will always be,

Your honest Daughter.

LETTER XV

My dear Mother,

I broke off abruptly my last letter; for I feared he was coming; and so it happened. I put the letter into my bosom, and took up my work, which lay by me; but I had so little of the *artful*, as he called it, that I looked as confused, as if I had been doing some great harm.

'Sit still, Pamela,' said he, 'and go on with your work, for all me. You don't tell me I am welcome home after my journey to Lincolnshire.' 'It would be hard, sir,' said I, 'if you were not always welcome to your honour's own house.'

I would have gone; but he said, 'Don't run away, I tell you. I have a word or two to say to you.' O how my heart fluttered! 'When I was a *little kind* to you,' said he, 'in the summer-house, and you behaved so *foolishly* upon it, as if I had intended to do you great harm, did I not tell you, you should take no notice of what passed to any creature? And yet you have made a common talk of the matter, not considering either my reputation, or your own.' 'I made a common talk of it, sir!' said I: 'I have nobody to talk to, hardly –'

He interrupted me, '*Hardly!* you little equivocator! what do you mean by *hardly*? Let me ask you, Have you not told Mrs Jervis for one?' 'Pray your honour,' said I, all in agitation, 'let me go down; for it is not for *me* to hold an argument with your honour.' 'Equivocator, again!' and took my hand, 'why do you talk of an *argument*? Is it holding an argument with me, to answer a plain question?

Answer me to what I asked.' 'O good sir,' said I, 'let me beg you will not urge me further, for fear I forget myself again, and be *saucy*.'

'Answer me then, I bid you, Have you not told Mrs Jervis? It will be *saucy* in you, if you don't directly answer my question.' 'Sir,' said I (and fain would have pulled my hand from him), 'perhaps I should be for answering you by another question, and that would not become me.' 'What is it you would say?' replied he; 'speak out.'

'Then, sir,' said I, 'why should your honour be so angry I should tell Mrs Jervis, or any body else, what passed, if you intended no harm?'

'Well said, pretty *innocent* and *artless*! as Mrs Jervis calls you,' said he; 'and is it thus, insolent as you are! you taunt and retort upon me! But still I will be answered directly to my question.' 'Why then, sir,' said I, 'I will not tell a lye for the world: I *did* tell Mrs Jervis; for my heart was almost broken; but I opened not my mouth to any other.' 'Very well, bold-face,' said he, 'and equivocator again! You did not open your *mouth* to any other; but did you not *write* to some other?' 'Why now, and please your honour,' said I, (for I was quite courageous just then) 'you could not have asked me this question, if you had not taken from me my letter to my father and mother, in which (I own it) I had broke my mind freely to them, and asked their advice, and poured forth my griefs!'

'And so I am to be exposed, am I,' said he, '*in* my own house, and *out* of my house, to the whole world, by such a saucebox?' 'No, good sir,' said I, 'and I pray your honour not to be angry with me; it is not *I* that expose you, if I say nothing but the truth.' He was then very angry, and called me assurance; and bid me remember to whom I was talking.

'Pray, sir,' said I, 'of whom can a poor girl take advice, if it must not be of her father and mother, and such a good woman as Mrs Jervis, who, for her sex-sake, should give it me when asked?' 'Insolence!' he then called me, and stamped with his foot. I fell down on my knees, and said, 'For heaven's sake, your honour, pity a poor creature, that knows nothing, but how to cherish her virtue and good name: I have nothing else to trust to; and though poor and friendless here, yet I have always been taught to value honesty above my life.' 'Honesty, foolish girl!' said he. 'But is it not one part of honesty to be dutiful and grateful to your master?' 'Indeed, sir,' said I, 'it is impossible I should be ungrateful to your honour, or disobedient, or deserve the names of boldface and insolent, which you are pleased to call me, but when your commands are contrary to that first duty, which shall ever be the principle of my life!'

He seemed to be moved, and rose up, and walked into the great chamber two or three turns, leaving me on my knees; and I threw my apron over my face, and laid my head on a chair, and cried as if my heart would break, but had no power to go from the place.

At last he came in again, but with mischief in his heart! and raising me up, he said, 'Rise, Pamela, rise; you are your own enemy. Your perverse folly will be your ruin: I am very much displeased with the freedoms you have taken with my name to my house-keeper, as also to your father and mother; and you may as well have *real* cause to take these freedoms with me, as to make my name suffer for *imaginary* ones.' And saying so, he lifted me up, and offered to set me on his knee.

O how I was terrified! I said, like as I had read in a book a night or two before, 'Angels and saints, and all the host of heaven, defend me![22] And may I never survive one moment, that fatal one in which I shall forfeit my innocence!' 'Pretty fool!' said he, 'how will you forfeit your innocence, if you are obliged to yield to a force you cannot withstand? Be easy, for let the worst happen that can, *you'll* have the merit, and *I* the blame; and it will be a good subject for letters to your father and mother, and a pretty tale moreover for Mrs Jervis.'

He then, though I struggled against him, kissed me, and said, 'Who ever blamed Lucretia?[23] The shame lay on the ravisher only: and I am content to take all the blame upon myself; as I have already borne too great a share for what I have deserved.' 'May I,' said I, 'Lucretia like, justify myself by my death, if I am used barbarously?' 'O my good girl!' replied he, tauntingly, 'you are well read, I see; and we shall make out between us, before we have done, a pretty story for a romance.'

He then offered to kiss my neck. Indignation gave me double strength, and I got from him by a sudden spring, and ran out of the room; and the door of the next chamber being open, I rushed into it, and threw-to the door, and it locked after me; but he followed me so close, he got hold of my gown, and tore a piece off, which hung without the door; for the key was on the inside.

I just remember I got into the room. I knew nothing further till afterwards, having fallen down in a fit; and there I lay, till he, as I suppose, looking through the key-hole, 'spied me upon the floor,[24] and then he called Mrs Jervis, who, by his assistance, bursting open the door, he went away, seeing me coming to myself; and bid her say nothing of the matter, if she were wise.

Poor Mrs Jervis thought it was worse, and cried over me as if she was my mother; and I was two hours before I came to myself; and just as I got on my feet, he coming in, I fainted away again; and so he withdrew: But he staid in the next room to hinder any body from coming near us, that his vile proceedings might not be known.

Mrs Jervis gave me her smelling-bottle,[25] and had cut my laces,[26] and sat me in a great chair, and he called her to him: 'How is the girl?' said he: 'I never saw such a fool in my life. I did nothing at all to her.'

Mrs Jervis could not speak for crying. So he said, 'She has told you, it seems, that I was kind to her in the summer-house, although I assure you, I was quite innocent then as well as now, and I desire you to keep this matter to yourself, and let not my name be freely used.'

'O, sir,' said she, 'for your honour's sake, and for Christ's sake –' But he would not hear her, and said, 'For *your own* sake, I tell you, Mrs Jervis, say not a word more. I have done her no harm. And I will not have her stay in my house; prating, perverse fool, as she is! But since she is so apt to fall into fits, or at least to pretend to do so, prepare her to see me to-morrow after dinner, in my mother's closet, and do you be with her as a witness to what shall pass between us.'

And so he went out in a passion, and ordered his chariot[27] to be got ready, and went a visiting somewhere.

Mrs Jervis then came to me. I told her all that had happened, and said I was resolved not to stay in the house: And she replying, He seemed to threaten that I should not; 'I am glad of that,' said I; 'then I shall be easy.' So she told me all he had said to her, as above.

Mrs Jervis is very loth I should go; and yet, poor woman! she begins to be afraid for herself; but would not have me ruined for the world. She says, To be sure he means no good; but may-be, now he sees me so resolute, he will give over all attempts: And that I shall better know what to do after to-morrow, when I am to appear before a very bad judge, I doubt.

How I dread this to-morrow's appearance! Would to heaven, I could tell how to get away before the time came! But be as assured, my dear parents, of the honesty of your poor child, as I am of your prayers for

Your dutiful daughter.

O this frightful to-morrow! how I dread it!

LETTER XVI

I know, my dear parents, that you longed to hear from me soon; and I sent to you as soon as I could.

Well! you may believe how uneasily I passed the time, till his appointed hour came. Every minute, as it grew nearer, my terrors increased; and sometimes I had great courage, and sometimes none at all; and I thought I should faint, when it came to the time my master had dined. I could neither eat nor drink; and, do what I could, my eyes were swelled with crying.

At last he went up to the closet, which was my good lady's dressing-room; a room I once loved, but then dreaded.

Don't your heart ake for me? I am sure mine fluttered about like a new-caught bird in a cage. O Pamela, said I to myself, why art thou so fearful! Thou hast done no harm! What, if thou fearest an unjust judge, when thou art innocent, wouldst thou do before a just one, if thou wert guilty? Have courage, Pamela, thou knowest the worst! And how much happier a choice is poverty with honesty, than plenty with wickedness!

So I cheared myself; but yet my poor heart sunk, and my spirits were quite broken. Every thing that stirred, I thought was to call me to my account. I dreaded it, and yet I wished it to come.

Well, at last he rung the bell; O, thought I, that it was my passing-bell!

Mrs Jervis went up, with a full heart enough, poor good woman! He said, 'Where's Pamela? Let her come up, and do you come with her.'

She came to me; I was ready to go with my feet, but my heart was with my dear father and mother, wishing to share your poverty and content. I went up, however.

O how can wicked men seem so steady and untouched, with such black hearts, while poor innocents stand like malefactors before them!

He looked so stern, that my heart failed me, and I wished myself any where but there, though I had before been summoning up all my courage. Good heaven, said I to myself, give me courage to stand before this naughty master! O soften him, or harden me!

'Come in, fool,' said he, angrily, as soon as he saw me (and snatched my hand with a pull); 'you may well be ashamed to see me, after your noise and nonsense, and exposing me as you have done.'

I ashamed to see *you*! thought I: Very pretty indeed! But I said nothing.

'Mrs Jervis,' said he, 'here you are both together: Do you sit down; but let her stand, if she will' (Ay, thought I, if I *can*; for my knees beat one against the other). 'Did you not think, when you saw the girl in the way you found her in, that I had given her the greatest occasion for complaint, that could possibly be given to a woman; and that I had actually ruined her, as she calls it? Tell me, *could* you think any thing less?' 'Indeed,' said she, 'I feared so at first.' 'Has she told you what I did to her, and *all* I did to her, to occasion the folly, by which my reputation might have suffered in your opinion, and in that of all the family? Inform me, what has she told you?'

She was a little too much frighted, as she owned afterwards, at his sternness; and said, 'Indeed she told me you *only* pulled her on your knee, and kissed her.'

Then I plucked up my spirit a little. '*Only!* Mrs Jervis,' said I; 'and was not that enough to shew me what I had to fear? When a master of his honour's degree demeans himself to be so free as *that* to such a poor servant as me, what is not to be apprehended? But your honour went further; and talked of Lucretia, and her hard fate. Your honour knows you went too far for a master to a servant, or even to his equal; and,' bursting into tears, 'I cannot bear it.'

Mrs Jervis began to excuse me, and to beg he would pity a poor maiden, who had such a value for her reputation. He said, 'I speak it to her face, I think her pretty, and I thought her humble, and one that would not grow upon my favours, or the notice I took of her; but I abhor the thought of compelling her to any thing. I know better what belongs to myself; but I was bewitched by her, I think, to be freer than became me; though I had no intention to carry the jest farther.'

What poor stuff was all this, my dear mother, from a man of his sense! But see how a bad cause, and bad actions, confound the greatest wits! It gave me a little more courage then; for innocence, I find, in a low fortune, and not strong mind, has many advantages over guilt, with all its riches and wisdom.

'Your honour,' said I, 'may call this jest or sport, or what you please; but indeed, sir, it is not a jest that becomes the distance between a master and a servant.' 'Do you hear, Mrs Jervis?' said he, 'do you hear the pertness of the creature? I had a good deal of this sort before in the summer-house, and yesterday too, which made me rougher with her than perhaps I had otherwise been.'

'Pamela, don't be pert to his honour,' said Mrs Jervis; 'you should know your distance; you see his honour was only in jest.' 'O dear Mrs Jervis,' said I, 'don't *you* blame me too. It is very difficult for a servant to keep her distance to her master, when her master departs from his dignity to her.'

'See again!' said he; 'could you believe this of the young baggage, if you had not heard it?' 'Good, your honour,' said the well-meaning gentlewoman, 'pity and forgive the poor girl: She is but a girl, and her virtue is very dear to her; and I will pawn my life for her, she will never be pert to your honour, if you'll be so good as not to molest her any more, nor frighten her again. You saw, sir, by her fits, the terror she was in: She could not help it; and though your honour intended her no harm, yet the apprehension was almost death to her; and I had much ado to bring her to herself.'

'O the little hypocrite!' said he; 'she has all the arts of her sex; they were *born* with her. I told you a while ago, you did not know her. But this was not the reason principally of my calling you before me together: I find I am likely to suffer in my reputation by the perverseness and folly of this girl. She has told you all, and perhaps more than all; nay, I make no doubt of it; and she has written letters (for I find she is a mighty letter writer!) to her father and mother, and to *others*, as far as I know; in which, representing herself as an angel of light, she makes her kind master and benefactor, a devil incarnate.' (O how people will sometimes, thought I, call themselves by their right names!) 'And all this,' added he, 'I won't bear; and so I am resolved she shall return to the condition she was taken from; and let her be careful how she uses my name with freedom when she is gone from me.'

I brightened up at once at these welcome words: I threw myself upon my knees at his feet, with a most sincere, glad heart; and said, 'May your honour be for ever blessed for your resolution! Now I shall be happy. And permit me, on my knees, to thank you for all the benefits and favours you have heaped upon me; for the opportunities I have had of improvement and learning, through my good lady's means, and yours. I will now forget all your honour has offered to me: And I promise you, that I will never let your name pass my lips, but with reverence and gratitude: And so God Almighty for ever bless your honour!'

Then rising, I went away with a much lighter heart than I came into his presence with: And fell to writing this letter.

And thus all is happily over.

And now, my dearest father and mother, expect soon to see your poor daughter, with an humble and dutiful mind, returned to you: And don't fear, but I know how to be as happy with you as ever: For I will lie in the loft, as I used to do; and pray let my little bed be got ready; and I have a small matter of money, which will buy me a suit of clothes, fitter for my condition than what I have; and I will get Mrs Mumford to help me to some needle-work; and fear not, my being a burden to you, if my health continues. I know I shall be blessed, if not for my own sake, for both *your* sakes, who have, in all your trials and misfortunes, preserved so much integrity, as makes every body speak well of you. But I hope he will let good Mrs Jervis give me a character, for fear it should be thought I was turned away for dishonesty.

And so, my dear parents, may you be blest for me, and I for you! And I will always pray for my master and Mrs Jervis. So good night; for it is late, and I shall be soon called to-bed.

I hope Mrs Jervis is not angry with me. She has not called me to supper; though I could have eat nothing, if she had. But I make no doubt I shall sleep purely to-night, and dream that I am with you, in my dear, dear, happy loft once more.

So good night again, my dear father and mother, says

Your honest, though poor Daughter.

Perhaps I shan't come this week, because I must get up the linen, and leave in order every thing belonging to my place. So send me a line, if you can, to let me know if I shall be welcome, by John, who will call for it as he returns. But say nothing of my coming away to him, as yet; for it will be said, I blab every thing.

LETTER XVII

My dearest Daughter,

Welcome, welcome, ten times welcome, shall you be to us; for you come to us innocent, and happy, and honest; and you are the staff of our old age, and our comfort. And though we cannot do for you as we would, yet fear not we shall live happily together; and what with my diligent labour, and your poor mother's spinning, and your needle-work, I make no doubt we shall do better and better. Only your poor mother's eyes begin to fail her; though I bless God, I am as strong, and able, and willing to labour as ever; and O my dear child, your virtue has made me, I think, stronger and better than I was before. What blessed things are trials and temptations, when we have the strength to resist and subdue them!

But I am uneasy about those same four guineas. I think you should give them back again to your master; and yet I have broken them. Alas! I have only three left; but I will borrow the fourth, if I can, part upon my wages, and part of Mrs Mumford, and send the whole sum back to you, that you may return it against John comes next, if he comes again before you.

I want to know how you come. I fancy honest John will be glad to bear you company part of the way, if your master is not so cross as to forbid him. And if I know time enough, your mother will go one five miles, and I will go ten on the way, or till I meet you, as far as one holiday will go; for that I can get leave to make on such an occasion: And we shall receive you with more pleasure than we had at your birth, or than we ever had in our lives.

And so God bless you, till the happy time comes! say both your mother and I; which is all at present, from

Your truly loving Parents.

LETTER XVIII

My dear Father,

I thank you and my mother a thousand times for your goodness to me, expressed in your last letter. I now long to get my business done, and to be with you. I have been quite another thing since my master has turned me away; and as I shall come to you an honest girl, what pleasure it is to what I should have had, if I could not have seen you but as a guilty one! Well, my writing time will soon be over, and so I will make use of it now, and tell you all that has happened since my last letter.

I wondered Mrs Jervis did not call me to sup with her, and feared she was angry; and when I had finished my letter, I longed for her coming up. At last she came; but seemed shy and reserved; and I said, 'My dear Mrs Jervis, I am glad to see you: You are not angry with me, I hope.' She said, she was sorry things had gone so far; and that she had a great deal of talk with my master, after I was gone; and that he seemed moved at what I said, and at my falling on my knees to him, and my prayer for him, at my going away. He said, I was a strange girl; he knew not what to make of me: 'And is she gone?' said he: 'I intended to say something else to her, but she behaved so oddly, that I had not power to stop her.' She asked, if she should call me again? He said, 'Yes'; and then, 'No, let her go; it is best for her and for me too; and she *shall* go. Where she had it, I can't tell; but I never met with the fellow of her in my life, at any age.' She said, he had ordered her not to tell me all: But she believed he never would offer any thing to me again, and I might stay, she fancied, if I would beg it as a favour; though she was not *sure* neither.

'I stay! dear Mrs Jervis,' said I; 'why 'tis the best news that could have come to me, that he will let me go. I long to return to my former condition, as he threatened I should. My father and mother are poor and low in the world, it is true. I have often grudged myself the affluence I have lived in, through my dear lady's goodness to me, while they have lived so hardly. I am no bad needlewoman, you know; and never was an idle girl: And who knows, if I can get work, but I may be able to contribute to their comforts, instead of being a charge upon them? A rich thought, that, Mrs Jervis! Let me enjoy it.'

Mrs Jervis, dear good soul! wept over me, and said, 'Well, well, Pamela, I did not think I had shewed so little love to you, as that you should express so much joy upon leaving me. I am sure I never had a child half so dear to me as you are.'

I wept to hear her so good to me, as indeed she has always been; and said, 'What would you have me to do, dear Mrs Jervis? I love you next to my own father and mother, and to leave you is the chief concern I have at quitting this place; but must it not be to my certain ruin if I stay? After such offers and such threatenings, and his comparing himself to a wicked ravisher, in the very time of his last offer; and turning it into a jest, that we should make a pretty story in romance; can I stay, and be safe? Has he not under-valued himself twice? And does it not behove me to beware of the third time, for fear he should lay his snares surer; for, perhaps, he did not expect that a poor servant would resist her master? And must it not be looked upon as a sort of warrant for such actions, if I stay after this? It would be an encouragement, in short, to renew his attempts, as it would make him believe himself forgiven, for what ought not to be forgiven.'

She hugged me to her, and said, 'Where gottest thou all thy knowledge, and thy good notions, at these years? I shall always love thee. But, Pamela, do you *resolve* to leave us?'

'Yes, my dear Mrs Jervis,' said I; 'for, as matters stand, how can I do otherwise? But I will finish the duties of my place first, if I may; and hope you will give me a character, as to my honesty; that it may not be thought I was turned away for any faults committed.' 'A character! ay, that I will,' said she; 'I will give thee such a character as never girl at thy years deserved.' 'And I am sure,' said I, 'I will always love and honour you, as my third best friend, wherever I go, or whatever becomes of me.'

And so we went to bed, and I never waked till it was time to rise; which I did, as blithe as a bird, and went about my business with pleasure.

But I believe my master is exceedingly angry with me; for he passed by me two or three times, and would not speak to me; and towards evening he met me in the passage leading to the garden, and said such a word to me as I never heard in my life from him, to man, woman, or child; for he first said, 'This creature's always in my way, I think.' I said, standing up as close as I could, (and the entry was wide enough for a coach[28] too) 'I hope I shan't be long in your honour's way.' 'D—n you!' said he, (that was the hard word) 'for a little witch; I have no patience with you.'

I trembled to hear him say so; but I *saw* he was vexed; and as I am going away, I minded it the less. It is not to be wondered at, my dear parents, when a person will do wicked things, that he will speak wicked words. May God keep out of the way of wicked things and wicked words,

Your dutiful Daughter.

LETTER XIX

Our John having no opportunity to go your way, I write again, and send both letters at once. I can't say, yet, when I shall get away, nor how I shall come; because Mrs Jervis shewed my master the waistcoat I am flowering for him, and he said, 'It looks well enough: I think the creature had best stay till she has finished it.'

There is some private talk carried on betwixt him and Mrs Jervis, that she don't tell me of; but yet she is very kind to me, and I don't mistrust her at all. I should be very base if I did. But, to be sure, she must oblige him, and keep all his lawful commands; and other, I dare say, she will not keep: She is too good, and loves *me* too well; but *she* must stay when *I* am gone, and so must get no ill-will.

She has been at me again to humble myself, and ask to stay. 'But what have I done, Mrs Jervis?' said I: 'If I have been a sauce-box and a bold-face, and pert, and a creature, as he calls me, have I not had reason? Tell me from your own heart, dear Mrs Jervis, what would *you* think, or how would *you* act in *my* case?'

'My dear Pamela,' said she, and kissed me, 'I don't know how I should act, or what I should think. I hope I should act as *you* do: But I know nobody else that would. My master is a fine gentleman; he has a great deal of wit and sense, and is admired, as I know, by half a dozen ladies, who would think themselves happy in his addresses. He has a noble estate; and yet I believe he loves my good maiden, though his servant, better than all the ladies in the land; and he has tried to overcome his love, because you are so much his inferior; and 'tis my opinion he finds he can't; and that vexes his proud heart, and makes him resolve you shan't stay; and so he speaks so cross to you, when he sees you by accident.'

'Well, but, Mrs Jervis,' said I, 'let me ask you, If he can stoop to like such a poor girl as me, what can it be *for*? He may, perhaps, think I may be good enough for his harlot; and those things don't disgrace men, that ruin poor women. And so he may make me great offers, and may, perhaps, intend to deck me out in finery, the better to gratify his own pride;[29] but I should be a wicked creature indeed, if, for the sake of riches or favour, I should forfeit my good name; yea, and worse than any other young body of my sex; because I can so contentedly return to my poverty again, and think it less disgrace to be obliged to live upon rye-bread and water, as I used to do, than to be a harlot to the greatest man in the world.'

Mrs Jervis had her eyes full of tears. 'God bless you, my dear love!' said she; 'you are my admiration and delight. How shall I do to part with you!'

'Well, good Mrs Jervis,' said I, 'let me ask you now: You and he have had some talk, and you may not be suffered to tell me all. But do you think, if I were to ask to stay, that he is sorry for what he has done? ay, and *ashamed* of it too? for I am sure he ought, considering his *high*, and my *low* degree, and how I have nothing in the world to trust to but my honesty: Do you think, in *your own* conscience now (pray answer me truly) that he would never offer any thing to me again, and that I could be safe?'

'Don't, my dear child,' said she, 'put thy questions to me, with that pretty becoming earnestness in thy look. I know this, that he is vexed at what he has done; he was vexed the *first* time, more vexed the *second* time.'

'Yes,' said I, 'and so he will be vexed, I suppose, the *third* and the *fourth* time too, till he has quite ruined your poor maiden; and who will have cause to be vexed then?'

She clasped me to her bosom, and called me dear pretty creature, and said it was no wonder that my master could not help loving me. And that, if I stayed, she hoped the best; since many a man had been ashamed of his wicked attempts upon a repulse, who never would have been ashamed had he succeeded.

'Ill trusting, my dear Mrs Jervis,' said I, 'to the honour of a man who has no virtue; and who has shewn himself as he has shewn himself. I *think*,' said I, (and I hope I should have grace to *act accordingly*) 'that I should not give way to his temptations on *any* account; but it would be very presumptuous in me to rely upon my own strength, against a man of his qualifications and estate, and who is my *master*; and thinks himself intitled to call me bold-face, and what not? only for resisting his vile attempts: and that, too, where the good of my soul and body is concerned. How then, Mrs Jervis,' said I, 'can I *ask*, or *wish* to stay?'

'Well, well,' says she, 'as he seems in earnest that you shall *not*, I hope it is from a good motive; for fear he should be tempted to disgrace *himself* as well as *you*.' 'I have thought of that too, Mrs Jervis,' said I, 'for I would be glad to think of him with that duty that becomes me: But if he had meant me well, he would have let me go to Lady Davers, and not have hindered my preferment. And he would not have said, I should return to my low condition, when by his mother's goodness I had been taken out of it; but that he intended to fright me, and *punish* me, as he thought, for not complying with his wickedness: and this shews me well enough what I have to expect from his future goodness, except I will deserve it at his own dear, dear price.'

She was silent, and I added, 'Well, there's no more to be said; I must go, that's certain: My chief concern will be how to part with *you*; and indeed with *every body*; for all my fellow-servants have loved me, and you and they will cost me a sigh and a tear too, now-and-then, I am sure.'

And so I fell a crying: I could not help it. For it is a pleasant thing to be in a house among a great many fellow-servants, and to be beloved by them all.

Nay, I should have told you before now, how kind and civil Mr Longman, our steward, is. Vastly courteous, indeed, on all occasions! And he said once to Mrs Jervis, he wished he was a young man for my sake; I should be his wife, and he would settle all he had upon me, on marriage; and, you must know, he is reckoned worth a power of money.

I take no pride in this; but bless God, and you, my dear parents, for your good lessons, that I have been enabled so to carry myself, as to have every body's good word: Not but that our cook one day, who is a little snappish and cross some times, said once to me, 'Why this Pamela of *ours* goes as fine as a lady. See what it is to have a fine face! I wonder what the girl will come to at last.'

She was warm with her work; and I stole away; for I seldom go down into the kitchen; and I heard the butler say, 'Why, Jane, nobody has your good word: what has Mrs Pamela [30] done to you? I am sure *she* offends nobody.' 'And what,' said the foolish wench, 'have I said to her, *foolatum*; [31] but that she was pretty?'

They quarrelled afterwards, I heard: I was sorry for it, but troubled myself no more about it. Forgive this silly prattle, from

Your dutiful Daughter.

Mrs Jervis is very desirous that I should stay to finish the waistcoat. She believes my master will make me an *honest* present, as I may say, when it is done. Good gentlewoman! she is loth to part with me. She says, she will be my watchful guardian till it is done; though she hopes there will be no occasion for her care. [32] I never, I must say, did a prettier piece of work; and I am up early and late to get it done; for I long to come to you.

LETTER XX

I did not, my dear father and mother, send my last letters so soon as I hoped, because John (whether my master mistrusts or no, I can't say) had been sent to Lady Davers's, instead of Isaac, who used to go thither; and I could not be so free with, nor so well trust Isaac; though he is very civil to me too. So I was forced to stay till John returned.

As I may not have opportunity to send again soon, and yet as I know you keep my letters, and read them over and over, (so John told me) when you have done work, (so much does your kindness make you love all that comes from your poor daughter) and as it may be some little pleasure to me, perhaps, to read them myself, when I am come to you, to remind me what I have gone through, and how great God's goodness has been to me (which, I hope, will further strengthen my good resolutions, that I may not hereafter, from my bad conduct, have reason to condemn myself from my own hand, as it were): For all these reasons, I say, I will write as I have time, and as matters happen, and send the scribble to you as I have opportunity; and if I do not every time in form, subscribe as I ought, I am sure you will always believe, that it is not for want of duty. So I will begin where I left off, about the talk between Mrs Jervis and me, on her wishing me to ask to stay.

Unknown to Mrs Jervis, I put a project, as I may call it, in practice. I thought with myself some days ago – Here I shall go home to my poor father and mother, and have nothing on my back that will be fit for my condition; for how should your poor daughter look with a silk night-gown, silken petticoats,[33] cambrick head clothes, fine Holland linen, laced[34] shoes, that were my lady's! And how in a little while must these have looked, like old cast offs indeed, and I looked upon as such for wearing them! And people would have said, (for poor folks are envious as well as rich) 'See there Goody Andrews's daughter turned home from her fine place! What a tawdry figure she makes! And how well that garb becomes her poor parents circumstances!' And how should I look, thought I, even if I could purchase home-spun clothes, to dwindle into them one by one, as I got them? May-be, an old silk gown, and a linsey-woolsey[35] petticoat, and the like. So, thought I, I had better get myself at once equipped in the dress that will become my condition; and though it may look poor to what I have been used to wear of late days, yet it will serve me, when I am with you, for a good holiday and Sunday suit, and what, by a blessing on my industry, I may, perhaps, make shift to keep up to.

So, as I was saying, unknown to any body, I bought of Farmer Nichols's wife and daughters, a good sad-coloured[36] stuff, of their own spinning, enough to make me a gown and two petticoats; and I made robings and faceings[37] of a pretty bit of printed callico I had by me.

I had a pretty good camblet quilted coat,[38] that I thought might do tolerably well; and I bought two flannel under-coats; not so good as my swan-skin[39] and fine linen ones, but what will keep me warm, if any neighbour should get me to go out to help 'em to milk, now-and-then, as sometimes I used to do formerly; for I am resolved to do all your neighbours what kindness I can; and I hope to make myself as much beloved about you, as I am here.

I got some pretty good Scots cloth,[40] and made me, at mornings and nights, when nobody saw me, two shifts; and I have enough left for two shirts, and two shifts, for you, my dear father and mother. When I come home, I'll make 'em up, and desire your acceptance of them.

Then I bought of a pedlar, two pretty-enough round-eared caps,[41] a little straw hat, and a pair of knit mittens, turned up with white callico; and two pair of ordinary blue worsted hose, that make a smartish appearance, with white clocks,[42] I'll assure you! and two yards of black riband for my shift-sleeves, and to serve as a necklace; and when I had 'em all come home, I went and looked upon them once in two hours, for two days together: for you must know, though I lie with Mrs Jervis, I keep my own little apartment still for my clothes; and nobody goes thither but myself. You'll say, I was no bad housewife to have saved so much money; but my dear good lady was always giving me something.

I believed myself the more obliged to do this, because, as I was turned away for what my *good master* thought want of duty; and as he expected *other* returns for his presents, than I intended to make him, so I thought it was but just to leave his presents behind me, when I went away.

Don't trouble yourself about the four guineas, nor borrow to make them up; for they were given me, with some silver, as I told you, as a perquisite,[43] being what my lady had about her when she died; and, as I hope for no wages, I am so vain as to think I have deserved all that money in the fourteen months since my lady's death: for she, good soul! overpaid me before, in learning and other kindnesses. Had *she* lived, none of these things might have happened! But I ought to be thankful 'tis no worse. Every thing will turn out for the best; that's my confidence.

So, as I was saying, I have provided a new and more suitable dress, and I long to appear in it, more than ever I did in any new clothes in my life; for then I shall be soon after with you, and at ease in my mind. But I am forced to break off. – Here comes Mrs Jervis.[44]

LETTER XXI

Now I will tell you what passed between Mrs Jervis and me. She hoped, she said, seeing me in a little hurry, on her coming in, that she was not unwelcome. She could not endure that I should be so much by myself.

'I always,' said I, 'rejoice to see my dear Mrs Jervis.'

'I have had,' said she, 'a world of talk with my master about you.'
'I am sorry,' said I, 'that I am made of so much consequence as to
be talked of by him.' 'O,' replied she, 'I must not tell you all; but
you are of more consequence to him than you *think* for–'

'Or *wish* for,' said I; 'for the fruits of being of consequence to
him, might be to make me of none to myself, or any body else.

'But I suppose,' proceeded I, 'that I am of so much consequence
to him as to vex him, if it be but to think, he can't make a fool of
such a one as I; and that is a rebuke to the pride of his high condition, which he did not expect, and knows not how to put up
with.'

'There may be something in that,' said she; 'but indeed, Pamela,
he is very angry with you *too*; and calls you perverse; wonders at
his own folly for having taken so much notice of you. He was
willing to shew you the more favour, he says, because of his
mother's love for you, and recommendation; and he had thoughts
of continuing it to you for your own sake, could you have known
how to comport yourself as you ought to do. But he saw that too
much notice–'

'*Too much notice*, indeed, Mrs Jervis,' said I. 'Do you think I
should ever have forgot my duty as a servant, if he had not forgot
his as a master?'

'He says you *shall* go,' replied she; 'for he thinks it won't be for
his reputation to keep you: but he wished (don't speak of it for the
world, Pamela) that he knew a lady of birth, just such another as
yourself, and he would marry her to-morrow.'

I coloured as red as the very scarlet, I believe; but said, 'Yet if I
were the lady of birth, and he would offer to be rude first, as he has
twice done to me, I don't know whether I would have *him*: for *she*
that can bear an insult of that kind, I should think not worthy to be
a gentleman's wife; any more than I should look upon him as a
gentleman, that could offer it. But, dear Mrs Jervis,' added I, very
seriously, 'let me say, that I am now more full of fears than ever.
Never, for the future, I beseech you, think of putting me upon
asking to stay. To tell me that my master likes me, when I know
what end he aims at, is abomination to my ears; and I shan't think
myself safe, till I am at my poor father's and mother's.'

She was a little angry with me, 'till I assured her, that I had not
the least uneasiness on her account, but thought myself safe in her

protection and friendship. And so we dropped the discourse for that time.

I hope to have finished this waistcoat in two days; after which, I have only some fine linen to get up, and shall then let you know how I contrive as to my passage; for the heavy rains will make it sad travelling on foot: but, perhaps, I shall be able for a small matter to procure a place in Farmer Nichols's one-horse-chaise, [45] which goes to — market twice a week with his wife or daughter: [46] and that, you know, is upwards of ten miles on the way. But I hope to let you know more.

P. A.

LETTER XXII

All my fellow-servants have now some notion, that I am to go away; but can't imagine for what. Mrs Jervis tells them, that my father and mother, growing in years, cannot live without me; and so I go home to them, to help to comfort their old age; but they seem not to believe that to be the reason: because the butler heard my master ask me very roughly, as I passed by him in the entry leading to the hall, how long I was to stay here; and tell me, calling me *idle girl*, that I minded my pen more than my needle. Little things for such a gentleman as he is to say, and to ask, had there not been a reason.

He seemed startled, when he saw the butler, as he entered the hall, where Mr Jonathan stood. 'What do *you* here?' said he. The butler was confounded; and so was I; for, never having been taxed so roughly, I could not help crying; and got out of both their ways to Mrs Jervis, and made my complaint. 'This love,' said she, 'is the deuce! in how many strange shapes does it make people shew themselves! And in some the farthest from their hearts.'

So one, and then another, has been since whispering, 'Pray, Mrs Jervis, are we to lose Mrs Pamela?' as they always call me. 'What has she done?' And then she tells them as above, about going home to you.

My master came in, just now, to speak to Mrs Jervis about household matters, having some company to dine with him to-morrow; and I stood up, and having been crying, at his roughness in the entry, I turned away my face.

'You may well,' said he, 'turn away your cursed face. Mrs Jervis, how long is she to be about this waistcoat?' *Cursed face!* What words were these!

'Sir,' said I, 'if your honour had pleased, I would have taken the waistcoat with me; and though it may be now finished in a few hours, I will do so still, and remove out of your house and sight for ever so hated a creature.'

'Mrs Jervis,' said he, (not speaking to me) 'I believe this little villain of a girl has the power of witchcraft; for she bewitches all that come near her. She makes even *you*, who should know better what the world is, think her an angel of light.'

I offered to go away; for I believed he wanted me to ask to stay in my place, for all this his great wrath and hard words; and he said, 'Stay here! stay here when I bid you!' and snatched my hand. I trembled, and said, 'I will, I will!' for he hurt my fingers.

He seemed to have a mind to say something to me; but broke off abruptly, and said, 'Begone!' And away I hurried; and he and Mrs Jervis had a deal of talk, as she told me; and in it he expressed himself vexed to have spoken in Mr Jonathan's hearing.

Now you must know, that Mr Jonathan, our butler, is a very grave good sort of old man, with his hair as white as silver; and an honest worthy man he is. Hurrying down stairs from my master and Mrs Jervis, as I told you, into the parlour, there was he. He took my hand, but in a gentler manner than my master did, with both his; and he said, 'Ah, sweet, sweet Mrs Pamela! what is it I heard but just now! I am sorry at my heart; but I am sure I will sooner believe *any body* in fault than *you*.' 'Thank you, Mr Jonathan,' said I; 'but as you value your place, don't be seen speaking to such an one as me.' I cried too; and slipt away as fast as I could from him, for his own sake, lest he should be seen to pity me.

And now I will give you an instance how much I am also in the favour of Mr Longman, our steward.

I had lost my pen some-how; and my paper being written out, I stepped to Mr Longman's office, and begged him to give me a pen or two, and two or three sheets of paper. 'Ay, that I will, my sweet maiden!' said he; and gave me three pens, some wafers,[47] a stick of wax, and twelve sheets of paper; and coming from his desk, where he was writing, he said, 'Let me have a word or two with you, my sweet little mistress' (for so these two good old men often call me; for I believe they love me dearly): 'I hear bad news: that we are going to lose you: I hope it is not true?'

'Yes, it is, sir,' said I; 'but I was in hopes it would not be known till I went away.'

'What a dickens,'[48] said he, 'ails our master of late! I never saw such an alteration in any man in my life. He is pleased with nobody, as I see; and by what Jonathan tells me just now, he was quite out of the way[49] with *you*. What could *you* have done to him, trow?[50] Only Mrs Jervis is a very good woman, or I should have feared *she* had been your enemy.'

'Mrs Jervis,' said I, 'is a just good woman, and, next to my father and mother, the best friend I have in the world.' 'Well then,' said he, 'it must be worse. Shall I guess? You are too *pretty*, my sweet mistress, and it may be, too *virtuous*. Ah! have I not hit it?'

'No, good Mr Longman,' said I, 'don't think any thing amiss of my master; he is cross and angry with me, that's true; but possibly I may have given occasion for it; and because I chuse to go to my father and mother rather than stay here, he may perhaps think me ungrateful. But you know, sir, that a father and mother's comfort is the dearest thing of all others to a good child.' 'Sweet excellence!' said he, 'this becomes *you*; but I know the world and mankind too well; though I must hear, and see, and say nothing! And so a blessing attend my little sweeting, wherever you go!' And away went I, with a court'sy and thanks.

Now it pleases one, my dear father and mother, you must think, to be so beloved. How much better, by good fame and integrity, it is to get every one's good word but *one*, than by pleasing *that one*, to make *every one else* one's enemy, and be a wicked creature besides! I am, &c.

LETTER XXIII

We had a great many neighbouring gentlemen, and their ladies, this day at dinner; and my master made a fine entertainment for them. And Isaac and Mr Jonathan, and Benjamin waited at table. And Isaac tells Mrs Jervis, that the ladies will by and by come to see the house, and have the curiosity to see me; for, it seems, they said to

my master, when the jokes flew about, 'Well, Mr B—, we understand, you have a servant-maid, who is the greatest beauty in the
county; and we promise ourselves to see her before we go.'

'You will do her too much honour, ladies,' said he. 'The wench
is well enough; but no such beauty as you talk of. She was my
mother's waiting-maid, as you know; and her friends being low in
the world, my mother on her death-bed recommended her to my
compassion. She is *young*, and every thing is *pretty* that is *young*.'

'Ay, ay,' said one of the ladies, 'that's true; but if your mother
had *not* recommended her so kindly, there is so much merit in
beauty, that I make no doubt, but such a fine gentleman as somebody is thought to be, would have wanted no inducement to be
generous to it.'

They all laughed at my master: and he, it seems, laughed for
company; but said, 'I don't know how it is, but I see with different
eyes from other people; for I have heard much more talk of her
prettiness, than I think it deserves: She is well enough, as I said; but
her greatest excellence is, that she is humble, courteous, and faithful,
and makes all her fellow-servants love her: My house-keeper, in
particular, doats upon her; and you know, ladies, that Mrs Jervis is
a woman of discernment: And as for Jonathan here, and my good
old steward Longman, if they were younger men, I am told, they
would fight for her. Is it not true, Jonathan?' 'By my troth, sir,'
answered Jonathan, 'I never knew her peer; and all your honour's
family are of the same mind as to her.' 'Do you hear, ladies?' said
my master. 'Well,' said the ladies, 'we will make a visit to Mrs
Jervis by and by, and hope to see this paragon.'

I believe they are coming; and will tell you the rest by and by. I
wish they had come, and were gone. Why should they make me the
subject of their diversion?

Well, these fine ladies however made their visit to Mrs Jervis in
her office, that was the pretence. I would have been absent, if I
could; and did step into the closet; so they saw me not when they
came in.

There were four of them, Mrs Arthur at the great white house on
the hill, Mrs Brooks, Miss Towers,[51] (Miss she is called, being a
single lady, and yet cannot be less than thirty years of age) and the
other, it seems, a countess, of some hard name, I forget what.

Now, if I shall not tire you, I will give you some little account of the characters and persons of these four ladies; for when I was hardly twelve years old, you used not to dislike my descriptions.

You must know, then, that Mrs Arthur is a comely person, inclinable to be fat; but very easy with it, and has pretty good features, though a little too masculine, in my opinion. She has the air of a person of birth, and seems by it to shew, that she expects to be treated as such; and has a freedom and presence of mind in all she *says* or *does*, that sets her above being in the least conscious of imperfection in *either*. It is said, she is pretty passionate in her family on small occasions, and reminds her husband, now and then, that he is not of birth equal to her own; though he is of a good gentleman's family too: and yet her ancestor was ennobled, it seems, but two reigns ago.[52] On the whole, however, she bears no bad character, when her passion is over; and will be sometimes very familiar with her inferiors: yet, Mrs Jervis says, Lady Davers is more passionate[53] a great deal; but has better qualities, and is more bountiful. Mr Arthur has the character of a worthy gentleman, as gentlemen go; for he drinks hard, it seems; so indeed all the gentlemen around us do, except my master, who has not *that* vice to answer for. I am sure, I have a double reason to wish – for *his* sake as well as my *own* – he had no worse! But let that pass, at present.

Mrs Brooks is well descended, though not of quality.[54] And has as much pride as if she *was*, if I can guess by her scornful looks: For being a tall thin lady, and of a forbidding kind of aspect, she looks *down* upon one, as it were, with *so* much disdain! Yet she has no bad character in her family; she does not talk much, but affects to be thought a lady of great discernment. Her spouse bears a pretty good character; but he gives himself great airs of jesting and rallying upon serious things; and particularly on matrimony, which is his standing jest, whenever his lady is not by. And some people impute this to him as wit: but I remember a saying of my good lady's, 'That any body might have a character for wit, who could give themselves the liberty to *say* what would shock others to *think*.'

The countess is not only noble by marriage, but by birth: But don't you wonder to find *me* scribble so much about *family* and *birth*? When, had I reason to boast of it, I should, if I know my own mind, very little value myself upon it; but, contrarily, think with the poet I have heard quoted, That VIRTUE *is the only nobility*.[55]

But, indeed, even we inferiors, when we get into genteel families, are infected with this vanity; and though we cannot brag of our *own*, we will sometimes pride ourselves in that of our *principals*. But, for my part, I cannot forbear smiling at the absurdity of persons even of the first quality, who value themselves upon their *ancestors* merits, rather than *their own*. For is it not as much as to say, they are conscious they have *no other*?

But how strangely I run on! Let me proceed with the countess's character, and don't think me too bold, to take these freedoms with my betters. Her ladyship is not handsome, yet has such an affable look, that one cannot chuse but respect her. But then, with this affable aspect, she has an air that shews, as if she could not easily be daunted. And I don't know how it is, but one of the chief beauties of the sex seems banished from the faces of ladies, in these days: for they not only don't know how to blush themselves, but they laugh at any innocent young creature that does, as rustic and half-bred; and (as I have more than once heard them) toss their jests about, and their *double meanings*, as they own them, as freely as the gentlemen. But whatever reputation these freedoms may give to their *wit*, I think they do but little credit to their *hearts* – For, does not the observation hold severely against such, *That out of the abundance of the heart the mouth speaketh?* [56] The husband of the countess (what makes me forget his title?) it seems, is a bad man, and a bad husband, and her ladyship lives very unhappily with him; and this all the world knows; for he is a *lord*, and *above* the world's opinion. And indeed I never heard of any couple so happy as *you*, my dear parents, though you labour so hard for a poor livelihood. But Providence gives one thing to one, and another to another. No one has *every thing*. But to you, my dear father and mother, is given *content*; and that is better than all the riches in the world, without it.

But Miss Towers outdoes all the ladies in the neighbourhood for wit and repartee; and her conversation is mightily coveted by every body, gentlemen as well as ladies: for no one, they say, can be sad in her company. She has something smart and humourous to say to every body, and on every occasion: so that, though she were to speak a silly thing, (and that I have the boldness to think she has many a one, on visits to my lady) yet every body has such an opinion of her, that they are prepared to laugh and applaud, before she opens her lips. Then she is of family, as indeed they all are; and some call her lady:[57] but, indeed, you know we simple bodies are used to give that title to all fine folks, who live upon their means. Miss Towers is well-shaped, is of an easy deportment, and has no one ill feature, taken separately: yet I know not how it is; but they seem as if they were not well put together, if I may so say. It was talked, that the rakish 'Squire Martin of the Grove, and this lady, were to make a match; but she refused him, because of his free life: for though she takes great liberties of speech, and can't help it, being a *wit*, as they call it, yet she is a lady of virtue, and *morals*, at least. But what a length have I run! It is time to return to their visit to Mrs Jervis.

They entered the room with great flutter, laughing heartily at something Miss Towers had said, as she came along. Mrs Jervis stood up at their appearance: 'So, Mrs Jervis,' says one of the ladies, 'how do you do? We are all come to inquire after your health.' 'I am much obliged to you, ladies,' said Mrs Jervis. 'But,' said the countess, 'we are not *only* come to ask after Mrs Jervis's health neither: We are come to see a rarity besides.' 'Ay,' says Mrs Arthur, 'I have not seen your lady's Pamela these two years, and they tell me she is grown wondrous pretty.'

Then I wished I had not been in the closet; for when I came out, they must needs know I heard them: but I have often found, that bashful people owe themselves a spite, and frequently confound themselves more, by endeavouring to avoid confusion.

'Why, yes,' said Mrs Jervis, 'Pamela is very pretty indeed; she is but in the closet there: Pamela, pray step hither.'

I came out, covered with blushes; and they smiled at one another.

The countess took my hand. 'Why, indeed,' she was pleased to say, 'report has not been too lavish, I'll assure you. Don't be ashamed, child' (and stared full in my face); 'I wish I had just such a face to be ashamed of.'

Mrs Arthur said, 'Ay, my good Pamela, I say as her ladyship says: don't be so much ashamed; though indeed your blushes become you. I think your good lady departed made a sweet choice of such a pretty attendant. She would have been mighty proud of you, as she always was praising you, had she lived till now.'

'Ah! madam,' said Mrs Brooks, 'do you believe, that so *dutiful* a son as our neighbour, who always *admired* what his mother *loved*, does not pride himself, for all what he said at table, in such a pretty maiden?'

She looked with such a malicious sneering countenance, I cannot abide her.

Miss Towers, with her usual free air, said, 'Well, Mrs Pamela, I can't say I like you so well as these ladies do; for I should never care, if I had a husband, and you were *my* servant, to have *you* and your *master* in the same house together.'

Then they all set up a great laugh.

They are ladies, my dear father, and ladies may say any thing.

Says Miss Towers, 'Can the pretty image *speak*, Mrs Jervis? I vow she has *speaking* eyes! O you little rogue,' said she, and tapped me on the cheek, 'you seem born to undo, or to be undone!'

'God forbid, madam,' said I, 'it should be *either*! I beg leave to withdraw; for the sense I have of my unworthiness, renders me unfit for such a presence.'

I then went away, with one of my best court'sies to each lady; and Miss Towers said, as I went out, 'Prettily said, I vow!' And Mrs Brooks said, 'See that shape! I never saw such a face and shape in my life; why she must be better descended than you have told me.'

They went to my master, it seems, so full of *me*, that he had much ado to stand it; but as their praises were very little to my reputation, I am sure I take no pride in them; and I fear they will make no better for me. This gives me another cause for wishing myself out of this house.

This is Thursday morning, and next Thursday I hope to set out; for I have finished my task, and my master is very cross! I am vexed that his crossness affects me so. If ever he had any kindness towards me, for his mother's sake, I believe he now hates me heartily.

Is it not strange that love borders so much upon hatred? But this wicked love is not like the true virtuous love, to be sure. And how must this hatred have been increased, if he had met with a base compliance?

How happy am I, to be turned out of doors, with that sweet companion, my *innocence*! 'O may that be always my companion! And while I presume not upon my own strength, and am willing to avoid the tempter, I hope the divine grace will assist me.'

Forgive me, that I repeat in my letter part of my hourly prayer. I owe every thing, next to God's goodness, to your piety and good lessons, my dear parents; my dear *poor* parents! I say that word with pleasure; for your *poverty* is my *pride*, as your integrity shall be my imitation.

As soon as I have dined, I will put on my new clothes. I long to have them on. I know I shall surprise Mrs Jervis with them; for she shan't see me till I am full-dressed. John is come back, and I'll soon send you some of what I have written. I find he is going early in the morning; and so I'll close here, that I am

Your most dutiful Daughter.

Don't lose your time in meeting me; because I am so uncertain. It is hard, if some how or other I can't get a conveyance. But it may be that my master won't refuse to let John bring me. John is very careful, and very honest; and you know John as well as I; for he loves you both.

LETTER XXIV

I shall write on, as long as I stay, though I should have nothing but sillinesses to write; for I know you divert yourselves on nights with what I write, because it is mine. John tells me how much you long for my coming; but he says, he told you, he hoped something would happen to hinder it.

I am glad you did not tell him the occasion of my going away; for if my fellow-servants were to guess the reason, it were better so than to have it from you or me; besides, I really am concerned that my master should cast away a thought upon such a poor creature as me; for besides the disgrace, his temper is quite changed; and I begin to believe what Mrs Jervis told me, that he likes me, and can't help it; and is vexed he cannot.

Don't think me presumptuous and conceited; for it is more my concern than my pride, to see such a gentleman so much under-value himself in the eyes of his servants, on my account. But I am to tell you of my new dress to-day.

And so, when I had dined, up stairs I went, and locked myself into my little room. There I tricked myself up [58] as well as I could in my new garb, and put on my round-eared ordinary cap; but with a green knot,[59] however, and my home-spun gown and petticoat, and plain leather shoes; but yet they are what they call Spanish leather. A plain muslin tucker [60] I put on, and my black silk necklace, instead of the French necklace my lady gave me; and put the ear-rings out of my ears, and when I was quite equipped, I took my straw hat in my hand, with its two green strings, and looked about me in the glass, as proud as any thing. To say truth, I never liked myself so well in my life.

O the pleasure of descending with ease, innocence, and resigna-tion! Indeed there is nothing like it! An humble mind, I plainly see, cannot meet with any very shocking disappointment, let fortune's wheel turn round as it will.

So I went down to look for Mrs Jervis, to see how she liked me.

I met, as I was upon the stairs, our Rachel, who is the house-maid; and she made me a low curt'sy, and I found did not know me. I smiled, and went to the housekeeper's parlour: and there sat good Mrs Jervis at work. And, would you believe it, *she* did not know me at first; but rose up, and pulled off her spectacles; and said, 'Do you want *me*, young woman?' I could not help laughing, and said, 'Hey-day! Mrs Jervis, what! don't you know me?' She stood all in amaze, and looked at me from head to foot. 'Why, you surprise me,' said she; 'what, Pamela, thus metamorphosed! How came this about?'

As it happened, in stepped my master; and my back being to him, he thought it was a stranger speaking to Mrs Jervis, and withdrew again; and did not hear her ask, if his honour had any commands for her? She turned me about and about and I shewed her all my dress, to my under-petticoat; and she said, sitting down, 'Why, I am all in amaze: I must sit down. What can all this mean?'

I told her, I had no clothes suitable to my condition, when I returned to my father's; and so it was better to begin here, as I was soon to go away, that all my fellow-servants might see I knew how to suit myself to the state I was returning to.

'Well,' said she, 'I never knew the like of thee. But this sad preparation for going away, (for now I see you are quite in earnest) is what I know not how to get over. O my dear Pamela, how can I part with you!'

My master rung in the back-parlour, and so I withdrew, and Mrs Jervis went to attend him. It seems he said to her, 'I was coming in to let you know that I shall go to Lincolnshire, and perhaps to my

Lord Davers's, and be absent some weeks. But pray, what pretty neat damsel was that with you?'

She says, she smiled, and asked, if his honour did not know who it was.

'No,' said he, 'I never saw her before. Farmer Nichols, or Farmer Brady, have neither of them such a tight⁶¹ smart lass for a daughter, have they? Though I did not see her face neither.'

'If your honour won't be angry,' said she, 'I will introduce her into your presence; for I think she outdoes our Pamela.'

'That can't be,' he was pleased to say: 'but if you can find an excuse for it, let the girl come in.'

Now I did not thank her for this, as I told her afterwards; for it brought a great deal of trouble upon me, as well as crossness, as you shall hear.

She then stepped to me, and told me, I must go in with her to my master. 'But,' said she, 'for goodness sake, let him find you out; for he don't know you.' 'O fie, Mrs Jervis,' said I, 'how could you serve me so? Besides, it looks too free both *in me*, and *to him*.'

'I tell you,' said she, 'you *shall* come in; and pray don't reveal yourself till he finds you out.'

So I went in, foolish creature that I was! yet I must have been seen by him another time, if I had not then. And she would make me take my straw hat in my hand.

I dropped a low curt'sy, but said never a word. I dare say he knew me as soon as he saw my face; but was as cunning as Lucifer. He came up to meet me, and took me by the hand, and said, 'Whose pretty maiden are you? I dare say you are Pamela's sister, you are so like her; so neat, so clean, so pretty! Why, child, you far surpass your sister Pamela!'

I was all confusion, and would have spoken; but he took me about the neck. 'Why,' said he, 'you are very pretty, child: I would not be so free with your *sister*, you may believe; but I must kiss *you*.'

'O sir,' said I, as much surprized as vexed, 'I am Pamela. Indeed I am Pamela, *her own self*!'

'Impossible!' said he, and kissed me, for all I could do. 'You are a lovelier girl by half than Pamela'; and again would kiss me.

This was a sad trick upon me, and what I did not expect; and Mrs Jervis looked like a fool, as much as I, for her officiousness. At last I disengaged myself, and ran out of the parlour, very much vexed, you may well think.

He talked a good deal to Mrs Jervis, and at last ordered me to attend him again; and insisting on my obedience, I went, but very unwillingly. As soon as he saw me, 'Come in,' said he, 'you *little villain*!' (I thought men only could be called villains); 'who is it you put your tricks upon? I was resolved never again to honour you with my notice; and so you must disguise yourself, to attract me, and yet pretend, like an hypocrite as you are—'

'I beseech you, sir,' said I, 'do not impute disguise and hypocrisy to me. I have put on no disguise.' 'What a plague,' said he, for that was his word, 'do you mean then by this dress?'

'I mean, may it please your honour,' said I, 'one of the honestest things in the world. I have been in disguise, indeed, ever since my good lady your mother took me from my poor parents. I came to my lady so low in garb, that these clothes I have on are a princely suit, to those I had then. And her goodness heaped upon me rich clothes, and other bounties: and as I am now returning to my parents, I cannot wear those good things without being laughed at; and so have bought what will be more suitable to my degree.'

He then took me in his arms, and presently pushed me from him. 'Mrs Jervis,' said he, 'take the little witch from me; I can neither *bear*, nor *forbear* her.' (Strange words these!) 'But stay; you shan't go!—Yet begone!—No, come back again.'

I thought he was mad, for my share; for he knew not what he would have. I was going, however; but he stepped after me, and took hold of my arm, and brought me in again: I am sure he made my arm black and blue; for the marks are upon it still. 'Sir, sir,' said I, 'pray have mercy; I will, I will come in.'

He sat down, and looked at me, and, as I thought afterwards, as silly as such a poor girl as I. At last he said, 'Well, Mrs Jervis, as I was telling you, you may permit her to stay a little longer, till I see if Lady Davers will have her; provided she humble herself, and ask this as a favour, and is sorry for her pertness, and the liberty she has taken with my character, as well out of the house, as in it.'

'Your honour indeed told me so,' said Mrs Jervis.

I was silent and motionless too. 'What a thankless creature!' said he. 'Do you hear, statue, you may stay a fortnight longer, till I see Lady Davers. Can you neither speak, nor be thankful?'

'Your honour frights me so,' said I, 'that I can hardly speak: but I have only to beg, as a favour, that I may go to my father and mother.'

'Why, fool,' said he, 'won't you like to go to wait on Lady Davers?'

'Sir,' replied I, 'I was once fond of that honour; but you were pleased to say, I might be in danger from her ladyship's nephew, or he from me.'

'Impertinence!' said he. 'Do you hear, Mrs Jervis, do you hear how she retorts upon me?' And he looked very angry, and coloured.

I then fell a weeping; for Mrs Jervis said, 'Fie, Pamela, fie!' And I said, 'My lot is very hard, indeed! I am sure I would hurt nobody: and I have been, it seems, guilty of indiscretions, which have cost me my place, and my master's favour. And when the time is come, that I should return to my poor parents – Good, your honour, what have I done, that I must be used worse than if I had robbed you!'

'Robbed me!' said he; 'why so you have, girl; you *have* robbed me.'

'Who! I, sir?' said I: 'have I robbed you? Why then you are a Justice of Peace, and may send me to gaol, if you please, and bring me to a trial for my life! If you can prove that I have robbed you, I am sure I ought to die.'

Now I was quite ignorant of his meaning; though I did not like it when it was afterwards explained, neither. Well, thought I, at the instant, what will this come to at last, if the poor Pamela shall be thought to be a thief! And how shall I shew my face to my honest parents, if I am but suspected?

'But, sir,' said I, 'let me ask one question, and not displease you; for I don't mean disrespectfully: Why, if I have done amiss, am I not left to be discharged by your house-keeper, as other maid-servants usually are? Why should you so demean yourself to take notice of me? For indeed I am not of consequence enough for my master to concern himself, and be angry, about such a creature as I am.'

'Do you hear, Mrs Jervis, how pertly I am interrogated? Why, sauce-box,' says he, 'did not my good mother desire me to be kind to you? And have you not been always distinguished by me, more than a common servant has reason to expect? And does your ingratitude upbraid me for this?'

I said something mutteringly, and he vowed he would hear it. I begged excuse; but he insisted upon it. 'Why then,' replied I, 'if your honour must know, I said, That my good lady did not desire your kindness to extend to the *summer-house* and her *dressing-room*.'

Well, this was a little saucy, you'll say! And he flew into *such* a passion, that I was forced to run for it; and Mrs Jervis said, It was happy I got out of his way.

Why, what makes him then provoke one so? I'm almost sorry for it; but I would be glad to get away at any rate: for I begin to be more afraid of him than ever.

Just now Mr Jonathan sent me these lines. Bless me! what shall I do?

'Dear Mrs Pamela, Take care of yourself; for Rachel heard my master say to Mrs Jervis, who, she believes, was pleading for you, "Say no more, Mrs Jervis; for by G— I will have her." Burn this instantly.'

O pray for your poor daughter! I am called to go to bed by Mrs Jervis; for it is past eleven; and I am sure she shall hear of it; for all this is owing to her, though she did not mean any harm. But I have been, and am, in a strange fluster; and I suppose too, she'll say, I have been full pert.

O my dear father and mother, power and riches never want advocates: but, poor gentlewoman! she cannot live without him: and he has been very good to her.

Perhaps I shall send this in the morning; but may-be not; so won't conclude: though I can't say too often, that I am (yet with great apprehensions)

Your most dutiful Daughter.

LETTER XXV

O let me, my dear parents, take up my complaint, and say, Never was poor creature so barbarously used, as your Pamela! Indeed, my dear father and mother, my heart is just broken! I can neither write as I should do, nor let it alone; for to whom but to you can I vent my griefs, and keep my heart from bursting! Wicked, wicked man! I have no patience when I think of him! But yet, don't be frighted – for – I hope – I am honest! But if my head and my heart will let me, you shall hear all.

John went your way in the morning; but I have been too much distracted to send by him; and have seen nobody but Mrs Jervis, and Rachel, and one I hate to see, or be seen by: and indeed I hate now to see any body. Strange things I have to tell you, that happened since last night, that good Mr Jonathan's letter, and my master's harshness, put me into such a fluster. But I will keep you no longer in suspence.

I went to Mrs Jervis's chamber; and there my wicked master had hid himself (base gentleman as he is), in her closet, where she has a few books, chest of drawers, and such-like. Ever since the summer-house affair, till this sad night, (when I neglected my caution), I always used to look into that closet, and another in the room, and under the bed; and, indeed, being displeased with Mrs Jervis for what had happened in the day, I thought of nothing else but being angry with her.

I sat myself down on one side of the bed, and she on the other, and we began to undress ourselves; but she on that side next the closet, that held the worst heart in the world. 'So,' said Mrs Jervis, 'you won't speak to me, Pamela! I find you are angry with me.' 'Why, Mrs Jervis,' said I, 'so I am, a little; it would be wrong to deny it. You see what I have suffered by your forcing me in to my master: and a gentlewoman of your years and experience must needs know, that it was not fit for me to pretend to be any body else for my own sake, nor with regard to my master.'

'But,' said she, 'who would have thought it would have turned out so?' 'Aye,' said I, little thinking who heard me, 'Lucifer always is ready to promote his own work and workmen. You presently saw what use he made of it, pretending not to know me, on purpose to be free with me: and when he took upon himself to know me, to quarrel with me, and use me hardly: and you too,' said I, 'to cry "Fie, fie, Pamela!" cut me to the heart: for that encouraged him.'

'Do you think, my dear,' said she, 'that I would encourage him? I never said so to you before; but since you force it from me, I must tell you, that ever since you consulted me, I have used my utmost endeavours to divert him from his wicked purposes: and he has promised fair; but to say all in a word, he doats upon you; and I see it is not in his power to help it.'

Luckily I said nothing of the note from Mr Jonathan; for I began to suspect all the world almost: but I said, to try Mrs Jervis, 'Well then, what would you have me do? You see he is for having me wait on Lady Davers now.'

'Why, I'll tell you freely, my dear Pamela,' said she, 'and I trust to your discretion to conceal what I say: My master has been often desiring me to put you upon asking him to let you stay.'

'Let me interrupt you, Mrs Jervis,' said I, 'to tell you that it was not the pride of my *heart*, but the pride of my *honesty*, that made me resolve against asking to stay: for, what must have been the case? Here my master has been very rude to me, once and twice. He has given me warning to leave my place, and uses me very harshly; perhaps, to frighten me to his purposes, as he supposes I would be fond of staying (as indeed I should, if I could be safe; for I love you and every one in the house, and value him, if he would act as my master). Well then, as I know his designs, what would have been my asking to stay, but an indirect allowance of all that he has done, and an encouragement of his further wicked devices?'

'You say well, my dear child,' says she; 'and for all these considerations, and for what I have heard this day, after you ran away (and I am glad you went as you did), I cannot persuade you to stay; and shall be glad, which is what I never thought I could have said, that you were well at your father's; for if Lady Davers will entertain you, she may as well have you from thence as from hence.'

'There's my good Mrs Jervis!' said I; 'God will bless you for your good counsel to a poor maiden, that is hard beset. But pray what did he say when I was gone?'

'Why,' says she, 'he was very angry at your hints of the *summer-house*, and *dressing-room*.'

'He would hear them,' said I. 'I think I was very bold; but it was in a good cause. Besides, Mrs Jervis, consider, it was the truth; if he does not love to hear of the *summer-house* and the *dressing-room*, why should he not be ashamed to continue in the same bad mind?'

'But,' said she, 'when you had muttered this to yourself, you might have told him any thing else.'

'Well,' replied I, 'I cannot tell a wilful lie, and so there's an end of it. Lord bless me! I wish I was well out of the house, though it was at the bottom of a wet ditch, on the wildest common in England; for I find that *you* now give him up, and think there is danger in staying.'

'It signifies nothing,' said she, 'to tell you all he said; but it was enough to make me fear you would not be so safe as I could wish; and, upon my word, Pamela, I don't wonder he loves you; for, without flattery, you are a charming girl! and I never saw you look more lovely in my life, than in that same new dress of yours. And then it was such a surprize upon us all! I believe truly, you owe some of your danger to the lovely *appearance* you made.'

'Hush!' said I, 'Mrs Jervis, did you not hear something stir in the closet?' 'No, silly girl!' said she; 'your fears are always awake.' 'But indeed,' said I, 'I think I heard something rustle.' 'May be,' says she, 'the cat may be got there: but I hear nothing.'

I was hush! but she said, 'Pr'ythee, my good girl, make haste to-bed. See if the door be fast.' I did, and was thinking to look in the closet; but hearing no more noise, thought it needless, and so went again and sat myself down on the bed-side, and proceeded to undress myself. And Mrs Jervis, being by this time undressed, went into bed, and bid me hasten, for she was sleepy.

I don't know why, but my heart sadly misgave me: indeed, Mr Jonathan's note was enough to make it do so, with what Mrs Jervis had said. I pulled off all my clothes to an under petticoat; and then hearing a rustling again in the closet, I said, 'Heaven protect us! but I must look into this closet, before I come to bed.' And so was going to it slip-shoed,[62] when, O dreadful! out rushed my master, in a rich silk morning gown.[63]

I screamed, and ran to the bed; and Mrs Jervis screamed too; and he said, 'I'll do you no harm, if you forbear this noise; but otherwise take the consequence.'

Instantly he came to the bed-side (for I had crept into it, to Mrs Jervis, with my coat[64] on, and my shoes); and, taking me in his arms, said, 'Mrs Jervis, rise, and just step up stairs, to keep the maids from coming down at this noise: I'll do no harm to this rebel.'

'O, for heaven's sake! for pity's sake! Mrs Jervis,' said I, 'if I am not betrayed, don't leave me; and, I beseech you, raise all the house!'

'No,' said Mrs Jervis, 'I will not stir, my dear lamb; I will not leave you. I wonder at you, sir!' and kindly threw herself upon my coat, clasping me round the waist. 'You shan't hurt this innocent; for I will lose my life in her defence. Are there not,' added she, 'enough wicked ones in the world for your base purpose, but you must attempt such a lamb as this!'

He was in a rage, and threatened to throw her out of the window; and to turn her out of the house the next morning. 'You need not, sir,' said she; 'for I will not stay in it. God defend my poor Pamela till to-morrow, and we will both go together.' 'Let me, Pamela,' said he, 'expostulate with you but one moment.' 'Pray, my dear,' said Mrs Jervis, 'don't hear a word, except he leaves the bed, and goes to the other end of the room.'

Mrs Jervis was about my feet, and upon my coat. The wicked wretch still had me in his arms. I sighed, and screamed, and then fainted away.

'Pamela! Pamela!' said Mrs Jervis, as she tells me since, 'O—h!' and gave another shriek, 'my poor Pamela is dead for certain!'

And so, to be sure, I was for a time; for I knew nothing more (one fit following another) till about three hours after, as it proved to be, I found myself in bed, and Mrs Jervis sitting up on one side, with her wrapper[65] about her, and Rachel on the other; and no master, for the wicked wretch was gone. But I was so overjoyed, that I hardly could believe myself; and I said, (which were my first words), 'Mrs Jervis, can I be *sure* it is you? Rachel, can I be *sure* it is you? Tell me! can I? Where have I been?'

'Hush, my dear,' said Mrs Jervis; 'you have been in fit after fit. I never in my life was so frightened.'

By this I judged Rachel knew nothing of the matter; and it seems my wicked master had, upon Mrs Jervis's second noise on my fainting away, slipped out; and, as if he had come from his own chamber, disturbed by the screaming, went up to the maids' room (who hearing the noise, lay trembling, and afraid to stir) and bid them go down and see what was the matter with me and Mrs Jervis. And he charged Mrs Jervis to say not a word of what had passed; and on that condition he would forgive her for what she had said and done. So the maids came down; for the men lie in the out-houses; and all went up again, when I came to myself a little, except Rachel, who sat up with me, and to bear Mrs Jervis company. I believe they guess the matter to be bad enough; though they dare not say any thing.

When I think of my danger, and the freedoms he actually took, though I believe Mrs Jervis saved me from worse, and she says she did, I am almost beside myself.

At first I was afraid of Mrs Jervis; but I am fully satisfied she is very good, and I should have been lost but for her; and she takes on grievously about it. Had she gone out of the room, to still the maids, as he bid her, he would certainly have shut her out, and then what would have become of your poor Pamela! I must leave off a little; for my eyes and my head are greatly disordered.

LETTER XXVI

I did not rise till ten o'clock, and I had all the concerns and wishes of the family, and multitudes of inquiries about me. My wicked master went out early to hunt; but left word, he would be in to breakfast. And so he was.

He came up to our chamber about eleven. He seemed to have neither sorrow nor shame. He was above both; for he was our *master*, and put on sharp anger at first.

I had great emotions at his entering the room, and threw my apron over my head, and wept as if my heart would break.

'Mrs Jervis,' said he, 'since I know *you*, and *you* know *me*, so well, it will be difficult for us to live together for the future.'

'Sir,' said she, 'I will take the liberty to say, that, if I did not express my resentment for the usage this poor girl has met with, and in my chamber too, I ought to be looked upon by the dear lamb as the worst of women. I know my obligations, sir, to you and your family; and shall ever acknowledge them. But on this occasion it behoves me to say, whatever be the consequence to myself, that I desire not to stay. Be pleased, therefore, to let poor Pamela and me go away together.'

'With all my heart,' said he; 'and the sooner, the better.' She wept. 'I find,' says he, 'this girl has made a party of the whole house in her favour.'

'Her innocence deserves the love of us all,' said she, very kindly: 'and, pardon me, sir, but I never could have thought, that the son of my dear, good lady departed, could have so forfeited his honour, as to endeavour to destroy a virtue he ought to protect.'

'No more of this, Mrs Jervis,' said he; 'I will not bear it. As for

Pamela, she has a lucky knack of falling into fits when she pleases. But the cursed yellings of you both made me not myself. I intended no harm to her, as I told you, if you'd have forborne your squallings; and I *did* no harm neither, but to myself; for I raised a hornet's nest about my ears, that, as far as I know, may have stung to death my reputation.'

'You will be pleased, sir,' said Mrs Jervis, 'to order Mr Longman to take my accounts: they shall all be ready by to-morrow. As for Pamela, she is at liberty, I hope, to go away with me.'

I sat still; for I could not speak, nor look up, so extremely did his presence discompose me; but I was sorry to hear myself the unhappy occasion of Mrs Jervis's losing her place. I hope, for both their sakes, that matters may be still made up between them.

'Well,' said he, 'let Longman make up your accounts, as soon as you will; and Mrs Jewkes, my Lincolnshire house-keeper, shall come hither in your place, and won't be less obliging, I dare say, than *you* have been.' 'I never, sir,' said she, 'disobliged you till now; and, permit me to say, that the regard I have for your honour –'

'No more, no more,' said he, 'of such antiquated topics. I have been no bad friend to you; and I shall always esteem you, though you have not been so faithful to my secrets as I could have wished, and have laid me open to this girl, which has made her more apprehensive of me than she had occasion to be.'

'Well, sir,' said she, 'after what passed yesterday, and last night –'

'Still, Mrs Jervis, still reflecting upon me, and all for imaginary faults! for what harm have I done the girl? I won't bear your impertinence. But yet, in respect to my mother, I am willing to part with you upon good terms: though you ought both of you to reflect on your last night's freedom of conversation, in relation to me; which I should have resented more than I do, but that I am conscious I acted beneath myself in stepping into your closet; where I might have expected to hear a multitude of impertinence between you.'

'You have no objection, I hope, sir,' said she, 'to Pamela's going away on Thursday next, as she intended.' 'You are mighty solicitous,' returned he, 'about Pamela: but, no, not I; let her go as soon as she will: she is a foolish girl, and has brought all this upon herself; and upon me more trouble than she can have had from me:

I will never more concern myself about her. I have a proposal made me, since I have been out this morning, that I shall perhaps embrace; and so wish only, that a discreet use may be made of what is past; and there's an end of every thing with me, as to Pamela, I assure you.'

I clasped my hands together through my apron, overjoyed at this, though I was soon to go away: for, wicked as he has been to me, I wish his prosperity with all my heart, for my good old lady's sake.

'Well, Pamela,' said he, 'you need not now be afraid to speak to me; tell me what you lifted up your hands at?' I said not a word. Said he, 'If you like what I have said, hold out your hand.' I held it out through my apron; for I could not speak to him; and he took hold of it, and pressed it, though less hard than he did my arm the day before. 'What does the little fool cover her face for?' said he. 'Pull your apron away; and let me see how you look after your freedom of speech of me last night. No wonder you are ashamed to see me. You know you were very free with my character.'

I could not stand this insult, as I took it to be, considering his behaviour to me; and I then spoke and said, 'O the difference between the minds of thy creatures,[66] good God! how shall some be cast down in their innocence, while others can triumph in their guilt!'

And so saying, I went up stairs to my chamber, and wrote all this; for though he vexed me by his taunting, yet I was pleased to hear he was likely to be married, and that his wicked intentions were laid aside as to me.

I hope I have passed the worst; or else it is very hard. And yet I shall not think myself quite safe till I am with you: for, methinks, after all, his repentance and amendment are mighty suddenly resolved upon. *But the Divine Grace is not confined to space,*[67] and remorse may have smitten him to the heart, and I hope has, for his treatment of me!

Having opportunity, I send this to you now, which I know will grieve you to the heart. But I hope I shall bring my next scribble myself: and so conclude, though half-broken hearted,

Your ever-dutiful Daughter.

LETTER XXVII

I am glad, my dear father, that I desired you not to meet me. John says you won't, on his telling you, that he is sure I shall get a conveyance by Farmer Nichols's means: but as for the chariot he talked to you of, I can't expect that favour: and besides, I should not care for it, because it would look so much above me. But Farmer Brady, they say, has a chaise with one horse, as well as Farmer Nichols, and one or other we can either borrow or hire, though money runs a little low, after what I have laid out; but I don't care to say so here, though I warrant I might have what I would of Mrs Jervis, or Mr Jonathan, or Mr Longman; but then how shall I pay it, you'll say? And besides, I don't love to be too much obliged.

But the chief reason I'm glad you don't set out to meet me, is the uncertainty; for it seems I must stay another week still, and hope certainly to go Thursday after. For poor Mrs Jervis will go at the same time, she says, and can't be ready before.

Oh! that I was once well with you! Though he is very civil too at present, and not so cross as he was; and yet he is as teazing another way, as you shall hear. For yesterday he had a rich suit of clothes brought home, which they call a birth-day suit;[68] for he intends to go to Court next birth-day; and our folks will have it, he is to be made a lord. I wish they would make him an honest man, as he was always thought to be; but, alas for me! I have not found him such.

And so, as I was saying, he had these clothes brought home, and he tried them on. And before he pulled them off, he sent for me, when nobody else was in the parlour with him. 'Pamela,' said he, 'you are so neat and so nice in your own dress, that you must be a judge of ours. How are these clothes made? Do they fit me?' What a poor vanity was this! But I suppose he could not think of a better pretence to send for me in to him. 'I am no judge, sir,' said I; and curtesying, would have withdrawn. But he bid me stay.

His waistcoat stood on end with lace,[69] and he looked very grand. But what he offered so lately has made me very serious, and his familiar talk to me very apprehensive.

He asked me, why I did not wear my usual clothes? (for, you must know, I still continue in my new dress). 'Though I think,' says he, 'that every thing looks well upon you.' 'I have no clothes, sir,' said I, 'that I ought to call my own, but these: and it is no matter what such an one as I wear.' 'You look very serious, Pamela,' said he: 'I see you can bear malice.' 'Yes, so I can, sir,' replied I, 'according to the occasion!' 'Your eyes always look red, I think. Are you not a fool, to take an innocent freedom so much to heart? I am sure, you, and that other fool, Mrs Jervis, frightened me by your hideous squalling, as much as I could terrify you.'

'Give me leave to say, sir, that if your honour could be so much afraid of your own servants knowing of your attempts upon a poor creature, that is under your protection while she is in this house, surely you ought to be more afraid of God Almighty, in whose presence we all stand, and to whom the greatest, as well as the least, must be accountable, let them think what they please.'

He took my hand, in a kind of good-humoured mockery, and said, 'Well urged, my pretty teacher! When my Lincolnshire chaplain dies, I'll put thee on a gown and cassock, and thou'lt make a good figure in his place!'

'I wish,' said I – and there I stopt. He would hear what I was going to say. 'If you will, sir, it was this – I wish your honour's conscience would be your preacher, and then you would need no other chaplain.'

'Well, well, Pamela,' said he, 'no more of this unfashionable jargon. I did not send for you so much for your opinion of my new suit, as to tell you, you are welcome to stay (since Mrs Jervis desires it) till she goes.'

'*Welcome to stay*, sir!' repeated I. 'I hope you will forgive me saying, that I shall rejoice when I am out of this house!'

'Well,' said he, 'you are an ungrateful girl; but I am thinking it would be pity, with these soft hands, and that lovely skin,' (still holding my hand, and fooling with it) 'that you should return again to hard work, as you must, if you go to your father's; I would, therefore, advise Mrs Jervis to take a house in London, and let lodgings to us members of parliament, when we come to town; and such a pretty daughter, as you may pass for, will always fill her house, and she'll get a great deal of money.'

This was a barbarous joke, you will own, my dear parents. An insult from his pride and plenty upon our meanness and want; and so was the more cruel.

Being ready to cry before, the tears gushed out; and I would fain have withdrawn my hand from his, but could not; and then I said, 'Your treatment of me, sir, has been just of a piece with these words. But do you do well to put yourself upon a foot, as I may say, with such a poor maiden as me? And let me ask you, sir, whether this becomes your fine clothes, and a master's station?'

'Charmingly put,' said he. 'But why so serious, my pretty Pamela? Why so grave?' And would kiss me. But my heart was full; and I said, 'Let me alone! I *will* tell you, if you were a king, and insulted me as you have done, that you have forgotten to act like a gentleman: and I won't stay to be used thus! I will go to the next farmer's, and there wait for Mrs Jervis, if she must go: and I'd have you know, sir, that I can stoop to the meanest work, even that of your scullions, rather than bear such ungentlemanly imputations.'

'I sent for you in,' said he, 'in high good humour; but 'tis impossible to hold it with such an impertinent. However, I'll keep my temper. But while I see you here, pray don't put on those dismal grave looks! Why, girl, you should forbear 'em, if it were but for your pride-sake; for the family will think you are grieving to leave the house.' Was not this poor for such a gentleman? 'Then, sir,' said I, 'I will try to convince them, as well as your honour, of the contrary; for I will endeavour to be more chearful while I stay, for that very reason.'

'I will set this down by itself,' replied he, 'as the first time that ever what I advised had any weight with you.' 'And I will add,' returned I, 'as the first advice you have given me of late, that was fit to be followed!'

He laughed, and I snatched my hand from him, and hurried away as fast as I could. Ah! thought I, married! I'm sure 'tis time you were married, or at this rate no honest maiden ought to live with you.

How easy it is to go from bad to worse, when once people give way to vice! But do you think, my dear father, that my master shewed any great matter of wit in this conversation with his poor servant? But I am now convinced that *wickedness* is *folly* with a witness.[70] Since, if I may presume to judge, I think he has shewn a great deal of foolishness, as well in his sentiments and speeches, as in his actions to me; and yet passes not for a silly man, on other occasions, but the very contrary. Perhaps, however, he despises me too much to behave otherwise than he does to such a poor girl.[71]

How would my poor lady, had she lived, have grieved to see him sunk so low! But perhaps, in that case, he would have been better. Though he told Mrs Jervis he had an eye upon me, in his mother's life-time; and that he intended to let me know as much by-the-bye! Here's shamelessness! Sure the world must be near at an end; for all the gentlemen about are almost as bad as he! And see the fruits of such examples! There is 'Squire Martin in the Grove has had three lyings-in in his house, in three months past; one by himself, and one by his coachman, and one by his woodman; and yet he has turned neither of them away. Indeed, how can he, when they but follow his own vile example?

But what sort of creatures must the women be, do you think, to give way to such wickedness? This it is that makes every one be thought of alike. What a world do we live in! for it is grown more a wonder, that the men are *resisted*, than that the women *comply*. This, I suppose, makes me such a sauce-box, and bold-face, and a creature; and all because I won't be indeed what he calls me.

But I pity these poor creatures: one knows not what arts and stratagems men may devise to gain their vile ends. For do I not see, by my narrow escapes, what hardships poor maidens go through, whose lot it is to go out to service; especially to houses where there is not the fear of God, and good rule kept by the heads of the family.

But it is time to put an end to this letter, which I do, by sub-scribing myself, what I shall ever be,

Your dutiful Daughter.

LETTER XXVIII

John, my dear father and mother, says that you wept when you read the last letter, that I sent by him. I am sorry you let him see that you did; for they all mistrust already how matters are; and as it is no credit, that I have been *attempted*, though it is, that I have *resisted*; yet I am sorry they have cause to think so evil of my master from any of us.

Mrs Jervis has made up her accounts with Mr Longman, but nevertheless will stay in her place. I am glad of it, for her own sake, and for my master's; for she has a good master of him; so indeed all have but poor me! and he has a good housekeeper in her.

Mr Longman, it seems, took upon him to talk to my master, how faithful and careful of his interests she was, and how exact in her accounts; and he told him, there was no comparison between her accounts and Mrs Jewkes's, at the Lincolnshire estate.

He said so many fine things, it seems, of Mrs Jervis, that my master sent for her in Mr Longman's presence, and said, Pamela might come along with her: I suppose to mortify me, that I must go, while she was to stay: but as, when I go away, I was not to go *with her*, nor *she with me*, I did not matter it much: only it would have been creditable to such a poor girl, had the housekeeper been to bear me company, when I went.

'Well, Mrs Jervis,' said my master to her, 'Mr Longman says you have made up your accounts with him, with your usual fidelity and exactness. I had a good mind to make you an offer of continuing with me, if you can be a little sorry for your hasty words, which were far from being so respectful as I have deserved from you.'

She seemed at a loss what to say, because Mr Longman was there; and she could not speak of the occasion of those words, which was *me*.

'Indeed, Mrs Jervis,' said Mr Longman, 'I must needs say before your face, that since I have known my master's family, I have never found such good management in it, nor so much love and harmony neither. I wish the Lincolnshire estate were as well served!' 'No more of that,' said my master; 'but Mrs Jervis may stay if she will; and here, Mrs Jervis, pray accept of these guineas, which, at the close of every year's accounts, I will present you with, besides your salary, as long as I find your care so useful and agreeable.' And he gave her five guineas.

She made a low court'sy, and thanking him, looked towards me, as if she would have spoken for me.

He took her meaning, I believe; for he said, 'Indeed I love to encourage merit and obligingness, Mr Longman; but I can never be equally kind to those who don't deserve it at my hands, as to those who do'; and then he looked full at me. 'Mr Longman,' continued he, 'I said that girl might come in with Mrs Jervis, because they love to be always together: for Mrs Jervis is very good to her, and loves her as well as if she were her daughter. But else –'

Mr Longman, interrupting him, said, '*Good* to Mrs Pamela! Ay, sir, and so she is, to be sure! But every body must be good to her; for –'

He was going on. But my master said, 'No more, no more, Mr Longman! I see old men are taken with pretty young girls, as well as other folks; and fair looks hide many a fault, where a person has the art to behave obligingly.' 'Why, and please your honour,' said Mr Longman, 'every body –' and was going on, I believe, to say something more in my praise; but he interrupted him, and said, 'Not a word more of this Pamela. I can't let her stay, I assure you; not only because of her pertness, but because of her writing out of my family all the secrets in it.'

'Ay!' said the good old man; 'I'm sorry for that too! But, sir! –' 'No more, I say,' said my master; 'for my reputation is so well established,' (mighty fine, thought I!) 'that I care not what any body writes or says of *me*: but to tell you the truth, (not that it need go further) I think of changing my condition soon; and, you know, young ladies of birth and fortune will chuse their own servants, and that's my chief reason why Pamela can't stay. As for the rest,' said he, 'the girl is a good sort of girl, take her all together; though I must needs say, a little pert, since my mother's death, in her answers, and gives me two words for one, which I can't bear; nor is there reason I should, you know, Mr Longman.'

'No, to be sure, sir; but 'tis strange, methinks, she should be so mild and meek to every one of us in the house, and forget herself where she should shew most respect!'

'Very true, Mr Longman, but so it is, I assure you: and it was from her pertness, that Mrs Jervis and I had the misunderstanding: and I should mind it the less, but that the girl (there she stands, I say it to her face) has sense above her years, and knows better.'

I was in great pain to say something, but yet I knew not what, before Mr Longman; and Mrs Jervis looked at me, and walked to the window to hide her concern for me. At last, I said, 'It is for *you*, sir, to say what you please; and for *me* only to say, God bless your honour!'

Poor Mr Longman faltered in his speech, and was ready to cry. Said my insulting master to me, 'Why pr'ythee, Pamela, now shew thyself as thou art, before Mr Longman. Can'st thou not give *him* a specimen of that pertness which thou hast exercised where it least becomes thee?'

Was he wise for this, my dear father and mother? Did he not deserve all the truth to be told? Indeed I did say, 'Your honour may play upon a poor girl, that you know *can* answer, but *dare* not.'

'Insinuating girl,' replied he, 'say the worst you *can* before Mr Longman, and before Mrs Jervis. And as you are going away, and have the love of every body, I would be a little justified to my family, that you have no reason to complain of hardships from me, as I have of pert saucy answers from you, besides exposing me in your letters.'

'Surely, sir,' said I, 'I am of no consequence equal to this, in your honour's family, that such a great gentleman as you should need to justify yourself about me. I am glad Mrs Jervis stays with your honour, and I know I have *not deserved* to stay; and more than that, I don't *desire* to stay.'

'Ads-bobbers!' [72] said Mr Longman, and ran to me; 'don't say so, don't say so, dear Mrs Pamela! We all love you dearly; and pray down of your knees, and ask his honour's pardon, and we will all become pleaders in a body; and I and Mrs Jervis at the head of it, to beg his honour's pardon, and to continue you, at least till his honour marries.'

'No, Mr Longman,' said I, 'I cannot ask to stay; nor would I stay, if I might. All I desire, is, to return to my poor father and mother; and though I love you all, I *won't* stay.'

'O well-a-day, [73] well-a-day!' said the good old man, 'I did not expect this! When I had got matters thus far, and had made all up for Mrs Jervis, I was in hopes to have got a double holiday of joy for all the family, in procuring *your* pardon too.'

'Well,' said my master, 'this is a little specimen of what I told you, Mr Longman. You see there's a spirit you did not expect.'

Mrs Jervis went out. She told me after, that she could stay no longer, to hear me so hardly used; and must have spoken, had she stayed, what would have never been forgiven her.

I looked after her, to go too; but my master said, 'Come, Pamela, give another specimen, I desire you, to Mr Longman: I am sure you must, if you will but *speak*.'

Was it not cruel, my dear father, to make such sport of a poor girl? 'Well, sir,' said I, 'since it seems your greatness wants to be justified by my lowness, and I have no desire you should suffer in the sight of your family, I will say, on my bended knees,' (and I kneeled down) 'that I have been a very faulty, and a very ungrateful creature to the *best* of masters: I have been very perverse and saucy; and have deserved nothing at your hands, but to be turned out of your family with shame and disgrace. I therefore have nothing to say for myself, but that I am not *worthy* to stay, and so cannot *wish* to stay, and *will* not stay: and so God Almighty bless you, and you, Mr Longman, and good Mrs Jervis, and every living soul of the family! and I will pray for you as long as I live.' And so I rose up, and was forced to lean upon my master's elbow-chair,[74] or I should have sunk down.

The good old man wept more than I, and said, 'Ads-bobbers, was ever the like heard! 'Tis too much, too much! I can't bear it. As I hope to live, I am quite melted. Dear sir, forgive her: the poor thing prays for you; she prays for us all! She owns her fault, yet *won't* be forgiven! I profess I know not what to make of it.'

My master himself, hardened wretch as he was, seemed a little moved, and took his handkerchief out of his pocket, and walked to the window: 'What sort of a day is it?' said he. And then getting a little more hard-heartedness, he added, 'Well, you may be gone from my presence! Thou art a strange medley of inconsistence! but you shan't stay after your time in the house.'

'Nay, pray, sir, pray, sir,' said the good old man, 'relent a little. Ads-heartlikins![75] you young gentlemen are made of iron and steel, I think: I'm sure,' said he, 'my heart's melted, and is running away at my eyes. I never felt the like before.' Said my cruel master, with an imperious tone, 'Get out of my presence, girl! I can't bear you in my sight.'

Indeed I wanted to be out of his sight, as much as he did to have me gone: but I trembled so, that I was forced to go holding by the wainscot[76] all the way with both my hands, and thought I should hardly have got to the door: but when I did, as I hoped this would be my last interview with this terrible hard-hearted master, I recovered presence of mind enough to turn about, and with a low court'sy, and my hands clasped, to say, 'God bless you, sir! God bless *you*, Mr Longman!' And I went into the lobby leading to the great hall, and dropped into the first chair; being unable to get further.

I leave all these things to your reflection, my dear parents; but I can write no more. My heart is almost broken! indeed it is! O when shall I get away? Send me, good God, in safety, once more to my poor father's peaceful cot![77] – and there the worst that can happen will be joy in perfection to what is now borne by

Your distressed Daughter.

LETTER XXIX

I must write on, though I shall come so soon; for now I have hardly any thing else to do. I have finished all that lay upon me, and only wait the good time of setting out. Mrs Jervis said, 'You must be low in pocket, Pamela, for what you have laid out'; and so would have presented me with two guineas of her five; but I could not take them of her, because, poor gentlewoman! she pays old debts for her children that were extravagant, and wants them herself. This, however, was very good of her.

I am sorry I shall have but little to bring with me; but I know *you* will not. And I will work the harder, when I come home, if I can get a little plain-work,[78] or any thing to do. But all your neighbourhood is so poor, that I fear I shall want work; except, perhaps, Dame Mumford can help me to something, from any of the good families she is acquainted with.

Here, what a sad thing it is! I have been brought up wrong, as matters stand. For you know that my good lady, now in heaven, loved singing and dancing; and, as she would have it I had a voice, she made me learn both; and often and often has she made me sing her an innocent song, and a good psalm too, and dance before her: And I must learn to flower and draw too, and to work fine work with my needle; why, all this too I have got pretty tolerably at my fingers end, as they say; and she used to praise me, and was a good judge of such matters.

Well now, what is all this to the purpose, as things have turned about?

Why, no more nor less, than that I am like the grasshopper in the fable,[79] which I have read of in my lady's books, as follows:

'As the ants were airing their provisions one winter, a hungry grass-hopper, (*as suppose it was poor me*) begged a charity of them. They told him, that he should have wrought in summer, if he would not have wanted in winter. "Well," says the grasshopper, "but I was not idle neither; for I sung out the whole season." "Nay, then," said they, "you'll e'en do well to make a merry year of it, and dance in winter to the tune you sung in summer." '

So I shall make a fine figure with my singing and dancing, when I come home to you! To be sure, I had better, as things stand, have learned to wash and scour, and brew and bake, and such like. But I hope, if I can't get work, and can meet with a place, to learn these soon, if any body will have the goodness to bear with me till then: for, notwithstanding what my master says, I am strangely mistaken in myself, if I have not an humble and a teachable mind; and next to God's grace, *that* is all my comfort: for I shall think nothing too mean that is honest. It may be a little hard at first; but woe to my proud heart, if I find it so, on trial; for I will make it bend to its condition, or break it.

I have read of a good bishop[80] that was to be burnt for his religion; and he tried how he could bear it, by putting his fingers into the lighted candle: so I t'other day tried, when Rachel's back was turned, if I could not scour a pewter plate she had begun. I see I could do it by degrees; it only blistered my hand in two places.

All the matter is, if I could get plain-work enough, I need not spoil my fingers. But if I can't, I will make my hands as red as a blood-pudding,[81] and as hard as a beechen trencher,[82] but I will accommodate them to my condition. I must break off; here's somebody coming.

'Tis only our Hannah with a message from Mrs Jervis. But here is somebody else. Well, it is only Rachel.

I am as much frighted as were the city mouse and the country mouse,[83] in the same book of Fables, at every thing that stirs. Oh! I have a power of these things to entertain you with in winter evenings, when I come home. If I can but get work, with a little time for reading, I hope we shall be very happy, over our peat fires.

What made me hint to you, that I should bring but little with me, is this:

You must know, I did intend to do, as I have done this afternoon: and that is, I took all my clothes, and all my linen, and I divided them into three parcels, as I had before told Mrs Jervis I intended to do; and I said, 'It is now Monday, Mrs Jervis, and I am to go away on Thursday morning betimes;[84] so though I know you don't doubt my honesty, I beg you will look over my poor matters, and let every one have what belongs to them; for,' said I, 'you know

I am resolved to take with me only what I can properly call my own.'

'Let your things,' said she, 'be brought down into the green-room, and I will do any thing you would have me do.'

I did not know her drift then; to be sure she meant well; but I did not thank her for it, when I did know it.

I fetched them down, and laid them in three parcels, as before; and when I had done, I went to call her to look at them.

Now in this green-room is a closet, with a sash-door[85] and a curtain before it; for there she puts her sweet-meats and such things; and into this closet my master had got unknown to me; I suppose while I went to call Mrs Jervis: and she has since owned, it was at his desire, when she told him something of what I intended, or else she would not have done it: though I have reason, I'm sure, to remember the last closet-work.

So I said, when she came up, 'Here, Mrs Jervis, is the first parcel. I will spread it all before you. These are the things my good lady gave me. In the first place,' said I – and so I went on describing the clothes and linen, mingling blessings, as I proceeded, on my lady's memory for her goodness to me: and when I had turned over that parcel, I said, 'Well, so much for the first parcel, Mrs Jervis, containing my lady's gifts.'

'Now I come to the presents of my dear virtuous master: Hay, you know, *closet* for that, Mrs Jervis!'

She laughed, and said, 'I never saw such a comical girl in my life! But go on.' 'I will, Mrs Jervis,' said I, 'as soon as I have opened the bundle'; for I was as brisk and as pert as could be, little thinking who heard me.

'Now here, Mrs Jervis,' said I, 'are my ever-worthy master's presents'; and then I particularized all those in the second bundle.

After which, I turned to my own, and said:

'Now comes poor Pamela's bundle, and a little one it is, to the others. First, here is a callico night-gown, that I used to wear o' mornings. It will be rather too good for me when I get home; but I must have something. Then there is a quilted calimanco[86] coat, and my straw hat with green strings; and a piece of Scots cloth, which will make two shirts and two shifts, the same I have on, for my poor father and mother. And here are four other shifts; and here are two pair of shoes; I have taken the lace off, which I will burn,[87] and this, with an old silver buckle or two, will fetch me some little matter at a pinch.

'What do you laugh for, Mrs Jervis?' said I. 'Why you are like an April day; you cry and laugh in a breath.

'Here are two cotton handkerchiefs and two pair of stockings, which I bought of the pedlar'; (I write the very words I said) 'and here too are my new-bought knit mittens: and this is my new flannel coat, the fellow to that I have on. And in this parcel pinned together are several pieces of printed callico, remnants of silks, and such-like, that, if good luck should happen, and I should get work, would serve for robings and facings, and such-like uses. And here too are a pair of pockets, and two pair of gloves. Bless me!' said I, 'I did not think I had so many good things!

'Well, Mrs Jervis,' said I, 'you have seen all my store, and I will now sit down, and tell you a piece of my mind.'

'Be brief, then,' said she, 'my good girl'; for she was afraid, she said afterwards, that I should say too much.

'Why then the case is this: I am to enter upon a point of equity and conscience, Mrs Jervis, and I must beg, if you love me, you will let me have my own way. Those things there of my lady's I can have no claim to, so as to take them away; for she gave them me, supposing I was to wear them in her service, and to do credit to her bountiful heart. But since I am to be turned away, you know, I cannot wear them at my poor father's; for I should bring all the little village upon my back: and so I resolve not to have *them*.

'Then, Mrs Jervis, I have far less right to these of my worthy master's: for you see what was his intention in giving them to me. So they were to be the price of my shame, and if I *could* make use of them, I should think I should never prosper with them. So in conscience, in honour, in every thing, I have nothing to say to thee, thou *second, wicked* bundle!

'But,' said I, 'come to my arms, my dear *third* parcel, the companion of my poverty, and the witness of my honesty; and may I never have, as I shall never deserve, the least rag that is contained in thee, when I forfeit a title to that innocence which I hope will ever be the pride of my life! and then I am sure it will be my highest comfort at my death, when all the riches and pomp in the world will be more contemptible than the vilest rags that can be worn by beggars!' And so I hugged my *third* bundle.

'But,' said I, 'Mrs Jervis,' (and she wept to hear me) 'one thing more I have to trouble you with, and that's all.

'There are four guineas, you know, that came out of my good lady's pocket, when she died, that, with some silver, my master ordered me: now these same four guineas I sent to my poor father and mother, and they have broken them; but would make them up, if I would: and if you think it should be so, it shall. But pray tell me honestly your mind: as to the three years before my lady's death, do you think, as I had no wages, I may be supposed to be quits? By quits, I cannot mean that my poor services should be equal to my lady's goodness; for that is impossible. But as all her learning, and education of me, as matters have turned, will be of little service to me now; for to be sure it had been better for me to have been brought up to hard labour, since that I must turn to at last, if I can't get a place: so I say, by quits I only mean, as I return all the good things she gave me, whether I may not set my little services against my keeping; and I am sure my dear good lady would have thought so, had she lived: but that is now out of the question. Well then, I would ask, whether, in above this year that I have lived with my master, as I am resolved to leave all his gifts behind me, I may not have earned, besides my keeping, these four guineas, and these poor clothes here upon my back, and in my third bundle? Now tell me your mind, freely, without favour or affection.'

'Alas! my dear maiden,' said she, 'you make me unable to speak to you at all: to be sure it will be the highest affront that can be offered, for you to leave any of these things behind you. And it is impossible but my master must know that you do.'

'Well, well, Mrs Jervis,' said I, 'I don't care; I shall mean no affront: but I have been too much used to be snubbed and hardly treated by my master, of late. I have done him no harm; and I shall always pray for him, and wish him happy. But I don't deserve these things, I know I don't. Then I cannot wear them if I should take them: so they can be of no use to me: And I trust I shall not want the poor pittance, that is all I desire to keep life and soul together. Bread and water I can live upon, Mrs Jervis, with content. Water I shall get any where; there is nourishment in water, Mrs Jervis: and if I can't get me bread, I will live like a bird in winter upon hips and haws, and at other times upon pig-nuts,[88] and potatoes, or turneps, or any thing. So what occasion have I for these things? But all I ask is about these four guineas, and if you think I need return them?'

'To be sure, my dear, you need not,' said she; 'you well earned them by that waistcoat only.'

'No, I think not *so*, in *that* only; but in the linen, and other things that have passed under my hands, do you think I have?'

'Yes, yes,' said she, 'and more.'

'And my keeping allowed for, I mean,' said I, 'and these poor clothes that I have on, besides? Remember *that*, Mrs Jervis.'

'Yes, my dear odd one, no doubt but you have!'

'Well then,' said I, 'I am as happy as a princess! I am quite as rich as I wish to be! And, once more, my dear third bundle, I will hug thee to my bosom. And I beg you will say nothing of all this till I am gone, that my master may not be so angry, since he has so far undervalued himself, as to take notice of such a poor girl as I, but that I may go in peace; for my heart, without other matters, will be ready to break to part with you all.' And then I was forced to wipe my eyes; and good Mrs Jervis wept till she sobbed again.

'Now, Mrs Jervis,' proceeded I, 'as to one matter more: and that is, my master's last usage of me, before Mr Longman.'

'Pr'ythee, dear Pamela,' said she, 'step to my parlour, and fetch me a paper I left on my table. I have something to shew you in it.'

'I will,' said I, and stepped down; but that, it seems, was only a fetch[89] to take the orders of my master. She afterwards told me, that he said he thought two or three times to have burst out upon me; but he supposed he should hardly have had patience with the prattler, as he called me; and bid her not let me know he was there. And so went away. But I tripped up again so nimbly (for there was no paper) that I just saw his back, as if coming out of that green-room, and going into the next that was open. I whipped in, and shut the door, and bolted it. 'O Mrs Jervis,' said I, 'what have you done by me? I see I can't confide in any body. I am beset on all hands! Wretched Pamela! where shalt thou expect a friend, if Mrs Jervis joins to betray me?' She was surprized, but made so many protestations of her good intentions, that I forgave her. She told me all, and that he owned I had made him wipe his eyes two or three times. She hoped good effects from this incident; and reminded me, that I had said nothing but what would rather move compassion than resentment. But O that I was safe from this house! for never poor creature sure was so terrified as I have been for months together! I am called down from this most tedious scribble. I wonder what will next befal

Your dutiful Daughter.

Mrs Jervis says, she is sure I shall have the chariot to carry me home to you. Though this will look too great for me, yet it will shew as if I was not turned away quite in disgrace. The travelling chariot is come from Lincolnshire, and I fancy I shall go in that; for the other is quite grand.

LETTER XXX

I write again, though I shall probably bring to you what I write in my pocket; for I shall have no writing, nor, I hope, writing time, when I come to you. This is Wednesday morning, and I am to set out to you to-morrow morning: but I have had more trials, and more vexation; but of another nature, though all from the same quarter.

Yesterday my master, after he came from hunting, sent for me. I went with great terror; for I expected he would be in a fine passion with me for my freedom of speech in the green-room: so I was resolved to begin first, with submission, to disarm his anger; and I fell upon my knees as soon as I saw him; and said, 'Good sir, let me beseech you, as you hope to be forgiven yourself, and for the sake of my dear good lady your mother, who recommended me to you in her last words, to forgive me all my faults: and only grant me this favour, the last I shall ask you, that you will let me depart your house with peace and quietness of mind, that I may take such a leave of my fellow-servants as befits me; and that my heart be not quite broken.'

He raised me up, with a kinder aspect than ever I had known; and said, 'Shut the door, Pamela, and come to me in my closet: I want to have a little serious talk with you.'

'How can I, sir,' said I, 'how can I?' and wrung my hands. 'O, pray, sir, let me go out of your presence, I beseech you.'

'By the G—d that made me,' said he, 'I'll do you no harm. Shut the parlour-door, and come to me in my library.'

He then went into his closet, which is his library, and full of rich pictures besides; a noble apartment, though called a closet, and next the private garden, into which it has a door that opens. I shut the parlour door as he bid me; but stood at it irresolute. 'Place some confidence in me,' said he: 'surely you may, when I have spoken thus solemnly.' So I crept towards him with trembling feet, and my heart throbbing through my handkerchief.

'Come in,' said he, 'when I bid you.' I did so. 'Pray, sir,' said I, 'pity and spare me.' 'I will,' said he, 'as I hope to be saved.' He sat down upon a rich settee, and took hold of my hand, and said, 'Don't doubt me, Pamela. From this moment I will no more consider you as my servant; and I desire you'll not use me with ingratitude for the kindness I am going to express towards you.'

This both alarmed and emboldened me; and he said, holding both my hands between his, 'You have too much good sénse not to discover, that I, in spite of my heart, and all the pride of it, cannot but love you. Yes, look up to me, my sweet-faced girl! I *must* say I love you; and have put on a behaviour to you, that was much against my heart, with intent to make you say or do something that should provoke me.'

I was unable to speak; and he, seeing me too much confounded to go on in that strain, said, 'Well, Pamela, let me know in what situation of life your father is: I know he is a poor man; but is he as low and as honest as he was when my mother took you?'

Then I could speak a little; and with a down look, (and I felt my face glow like fire), I said, 'Yes, sir, as *poor* and as *honest* too, and that is my pride.' 'I will do something for him,' said he, 'if it be not your fault, and make all your family happy.' 'Ah! sir,' said I, 'he is happier already than ever he can be, if his daughter's virtue is to be the price of your favour. And I beg you will not speak to me on the *only* side that can wound me.' 'I have no design of that sort,' said he. 'O sir,' said I, 'tell me not so, tell me not so!' ''Tis easy,' said he, 'to be the making of your father, without injuring *you*.' 'If this, sir, can be done, let me know how; and all I can do with innocence shall be the study of my life to do. But Oh! what can such a poor creature as I do, and do my duty?' 'I would have you,' said he, 'stay a week or a fortnight longer, and behave your-self obligingly to me; and all shall turn out beyond your expectation. I see,' said he, 'you are going to answer otherwise than I would have you; and I begin to be vexed that I should thus meanly ask you to stay: but yet I will tell you, that your behaviour before Longman, when I treated you a little harshly, and you could so well have vindicated yourself, has quite charmed me. And though I am not pleased with all you said yesterday while I was in the closet, yet you have moved me more to admire you than before; and I am awakened to see more worthiness in you, than ever I saw in any woman in the world. All the servants, from the highest to the lowest, doat upon you, instead of envying you; and look upon you in so superior a light, as speaks what you ought to be. I have seen more of your letters than you imagine,' (this surprised me) 'and am quite charmed with your manner of writing, and with many of your sentiments so much above your years; and for all these reasons I love you to extravagance. Now, Pamela, when I have stooped to acknowledge all this, you must oblige me by staying another week or fortnight, which will give me time to bring about some certain affairs; and you shall see how much you may find your account in your compliance.'

I trembled to feel my poor heart giving way. 'O good sir,' said I, 'spare a poor maiden, that cannot look up to you, and speak. My heart is full: and why should you wish to ruin me?' 'Only oblige me,' said he, 'in staying a fortnight longer, and John shall carry word to your father, that I will see him in the mean time, either here, or at the Swan in his village.' 'O sir,' said I, 'my heart will burst; but on my bended knees I beg you to let me go to-morrow, as I designed: and don't offer to tempt a poor creature, whose whole will would be to do yours, if innocence would permit.' 'It shall permit,' said he; 'for I intend no injury to you, God is my witness!' 'Impossible!' said I; 'I cannot, sir, believe you, after what has passed: how many ways are there to ruin poor creatures! Good God, protect me this *one* time, and send me but to my dear father's cot in safety!' 'Strange, damned fate,' says he, 'that when I speak so solemnly, I can't be believed!' 'What *should* I believe, sir?' returned I; 'what *can* I believe? What have you said, but that I am to stay a fortnight longer? and what then is to become of me?' 'My pride of birth and fortune (damn them both!' said he, 'since they cannot obtain credit with you, but must add to your suspicions) will not let me descend, all at once; and I ask you but a fortnight's stay, that, after this declaration, I may pacify those proud demands upon me.'

O how my heart throbbed! and I began (for I did not know what I did) to say the Lord's prayer. 'None of your beads to me, Pamela,' said he; 'thou art a perfect nun, I think.'

But I said aloud, with my eyes lifted up to heaven, '*Lead me not into temptation; but deliver me from evil*, O my good God!'

He pressed me in his arms, and said, 'Well, my dear girl, then you stay this fortnight, and you shall see what I will do for you. I'll leave you a moment, and walk into the next room, to give you time to think of it, and to shew you I have no design upon you.'

This, I thought, did not look amiss.

He went out, and I was tortured with twenty different doubts in a minute: sometimes I thought, that to stay a week or fortnight longer in this house to obey him, while Mrs Jervis was with me, could not be attended with bad consequences. But then, thought I, how do I know what I may be *able* to do? I have withstood his *anger*; but may I not relent at his *kindness*? How shall I stand *that*! Well, I hope, thought I, by the same protecting grace, in which I will always confide! But then what has he promised? Why he will make my poor father and mother's life comfortable. O! said I to myself, that is a rich thought; but let me not dwell upon it, for fear I should indulge it to my ruin. What can he do for *me*, poor girl as I am! What can his greatness stoop to! He talks, thought I, of his pride of heart, and pride of condition! O these are in his *head* and in his *heart* too, or he would not confess them to me at *such* an instant. Well then, thought I, this can be only to seduce me! And when I reflected, that after this open declaration of what he called his love, he would probably talk with me on that subject *more plainly* than ever, and that I should be possibly *less* armed to withstand him; and further, that if he meant nothing but honour, he would have spoken before Mrs Jervis; and when the odious frightful first closet came again into my head, and my narrow escape upon it; and farther reflected, how easy it might be for him to send Mrs Jervis and the maids out of the way; and so that all the mischief he designed might be brought about in less than that time; when I reflected on all these things, I resolved to go away, and trust all to Providence, and nothing to myself. And you shall hear how thankful I ought to be for being enabled to take this resolution.

But just as I have written to this place, John sends me word that he is going this minute your way; and so I will send you thus far, and hope, by to-morrow night, to ask your blessings, at your own happy abode, and tell you the rest by word of mouth; and so I remain till then, and for ever,

Your dutiful Daughter.

LETTER XXXI

I told you my resolution, my happy resolution, as I have reason to think it: and just as I had taken it he came in again, with great kindness in his looks; and said, 'I make no doubt, Pamela, you will stay this fortnight to oblige me.' I knew not how to frame my words so as to deny, and yet not make him storm: but thus I answered, 'Forgive, sir, your poor distressed maiden: I know I cannot possibly deserve any favour at your hands, that can conflict with innocence; and I beg you will let me go to my father.' 'Thou art the greatest fool,' said he, 'I ever knew. I tell you I will *see* your father; I'll send for him hither to-morrow, in my travelling chariot, if you will; and I'll let him know what I intend to do for *him* and for *you*.'

'What, sir, may I ask you, can that be? Your honour's noble estate will easily enable you to make *him* happy, and not unuseful perhaps to *you* in some respect or other. But what price am I to pay for all this?' 'You shall be happy as you can wish,' said he, 'I do assure you: and here I will now give you this purse, in which are fifty guineas, which I will allow your father yearly, and find an employment for him suitable to his liking, that shall make him deserve *that* and *more*. I would give you still more for him; but that perhaps you would suspect I have a design upon you.'

'O sir, take back your guineas; I will not touch one, nor will my father, I am sure, till he knows what is to be done *for* them; and particularly what is to become of *me*.'

'Why then, Pamela,' said he, 'suppose I find a man of probity, and genteel calling, for a husband for you, that shall make you a gentlewoman as long as you live?'

'I want no husband, sir,' said I; for now I began to see him in all his black colours: yet being so much in his power, I thought I would a little dissemble.

'But,' said he, 'you are so pretty, that, go where you will, you can never be free from the designs of some or other of our sex; and I shall think I don't answer the care of my dying mother for you, who committed you to me, if I don't provide you a husband to protect your virtue and your innocence: and a worthy one I have thought of for you.'

O black, perfidious creature! thought I, what an implement art thou in the hands of Lucifer, to ruin the innocent heart! Yet still I dissembled; for I feared much both him and the place I was in. 'But whom, pray, sir, have you thought of?' 'Why,' said he, 'young Williams, my chaplain, in Lincolnshire, who will make you happy.'

'Does he know, sir,' said I, 'anything of your honour's intentions?' 'No, my girl,' answered he, and kissed me (much against my will; for his very breath was now poison to me); 'but his dependence upon my favour, and your beauty and merit, will make him rejoice at my kindness to him.' 'Well, sir,' said I, 'then it is time enough to consider of this matter; and it cannot hinder me from going to my father's: for what will staying here a fortnight longer signify to this? Your honour's care and goodness may extend to me *there*, as well as *here*; and Mr Williams, and all the world, shall know that I am not ashamed of my father's poverty.'

He would kiss me again; and I said, 'If I am to think of Mr Williams, or of anybody, I beg, sir, that *you* will not be so free with me.' 'Well,' said he, 'but you stay this next fortnight, and in that time I will have both Williams and your father here; and when they two have agreed upon the matter, you and Williams shall settle it as you will. Mean time, take and send only these fifty pieces to your father, as an earnest of my favour; and I'll make you all happy.' 'Sir,' said I, 'I beg at least two hours to consider of this.' 'I shall,' said he, 'be gone out in one hour; and I would have you write to your father what I propose, and John shall carry your letter, and take the purse with him for the good old man.' 'Sir,' said I, 'I will let you know, in one hour, my resolution.' 'Do so,' replied he, and gave me another kiss, and let me go.

How I rejoiced that I had got out of his clutches! So I write you this, that you may see how matters stand; for I am resolved to come away, if possible.

So here was a trap laid for your poor Pamela. I tremble to think of it! What a scene of wickedness was here contrived for all my wretched life! Black-hearted wretch, how I hate him! For at first, as you will see by what I have written, he would have made me believe other things; and this of Mr Williams, I suppose, came into his head after he walked out from his closet, to give himself time to think how to delude me better: but the covering was now too thin, and easy to be seen through.

I went to my chamber, and the first thing I did was to write to him; for I thought it was best not to see him again, if I could help it; and I put it under his parlour-door, after I had copied it, as follows:

'*Honoured Sir*,
'Your last proposal convinces me, that I ought to go to my father, if it were but to ask his advice about Mr Williams. I am so set upon it, that I am not to be persuaded. So, honoured sir, with a thousand thanks for all favours, I will set out to-morrow early; and the honour you designed me, as Mrs Jervis tells me, of your chariot, there will be no occasion for; because I can hire, I believe, Farmer Brady's chaise. So, begging you will not take it amiss, I shall ever be

Your dutiful Servant.

As to the purse, sir, my poor father, to be sure, won't forgive me, if I take it, till he can know how to deserve it: which is impossible.'

So he has just now sent Mrs Jervis, to tell me, That since I am resolved to go, go I may, and that the travelling chariot shall be ready; but that he will never trouble himself about me as long as he lives. Well, so I get out of the house, I care not; only I should have been glad I could with innocence have made you, my dear parents, happy.

I cannot imagine the reason of it, but John, who I thought, was gone with my last, is but now going; and he sends to know if I have anything else to carry. So I break off to send you this with the former.

I am now preparing for my journey, and about taking leave of my fellow-servants. And if I have not time to write, I must tell you the rest, when I am so happy as to be with you.

One word more: I slip in a paper of verses, on my going; sad poor stuff! but as they come from me, you'll not dislike them, perhaps. I shewed them to Mrs Jervis, and she took a copy of them; and made me sing them to her; and in the green-room too; but I looked into the closet first. I will only add, That I am

Your dutiful Daughter.

Let me just say, That he has this moment sent me five guineas by Mrs Jervis, as a present for my pocket: so I shall be very rich; for as *she* brought them, I thought I might take them. He says he won't see me; and I may go when I will in the morning; and *Lincolnshire Robin* shall drive me: but he is so angry, he orders that nobody shall go out at the door with me, not so much as into the court-yard. Well! I can't help it! but does this not expose him more than *me*?

But John waits, and I would have brought this and the other myself; but he says, he has put up the former among other things, and so can take both as well as one.

John is very good, and very honest; I am under great obligations to him. I would give him a guinea, now I'm so rich, if I thought he'd take it. I hear nothing of the clothes my lady and my master gave me; for I told Mrs Jervis I would not take them; but I fancy, by a word or two that dropped, they will be sent after me. What a rich Pamela you'll have, if they should! But as I can't wear them, if they do, I don't desire them; and, if I have them, will turn them into money, as I can have opportunity.

Well, no more – I'm in a violent hurry!

VERSES *on my going away*[90]

I

Attend, my fellow-servants dear,
A grateful song demands your ear;
The dictates of a heart sincere,
   Presented you by Pamela.

II

I long have had a blissful fate;
Exalted by the good and great,
Yet to her former humble state
   Content returns your Pamela.

III

Whate'er kind heav'n has designed,
Still may I keep an equal mind,
To the Eternal Will resigned,
            And happy must be Pamela.

IV

For what indeed is happiness
But conscious innocence and peace?
And that's a treasure I possess;
            Thank heav'n, that gave it Pamela.

V

My future lot I cannot know:
But this, I'm sure, where-e'er I go,
Whate'er I am, whate'er I do,
            I'll be the grateful Pamela.

VI

Yet something more remains to say:
God's holy will be sure obey;
And for our bounteous master pray,
            As ever shall poor Pamela.

VII

For, O we *pity* should the great,
Nor *envy* their superior state;
Temptations always round them wait,
            Exempt from which are such as we.

VIII

Their riches, gay deceitful snares!
Inlarge their fears, increase their cares;
Their servants' joy surpasses theirs;
            At least, so judges Pamela.

IX

Glad to my parents I return;
Nor for their low condition mourn;
Since grace and truth their souls adorn,
            They're high and great to Pamela.

x

On GOD all future good depends:
Serve him. And so my sonnet ends.
O may he make you rich amends,
         For all your loves to Pamela.

Here it is necessary the reader should know, that when Mr B. found Pamela's virtue was not to be subdued, and he had in vain tried to conquer his passion for her, he had ordered his Lincolnshire coachman to bring his travelling chariot from thence, in order to prosecute his base designs upon the innocent virgin; for he cared not to trust his Bedfordshire coachman, who, with the rest of the servants, so greatly loved and honoured the fair damsel. And having given instructions accordingly, and prohibited his other servants, on pretence of resenting Pamela's behaviour, from accompanying her any part of the way to her father's, that coachman drove her five miles on her way; and then turning off, crossed the country, and carried her onward towards Mr B.'s Lincolnshire estate.

It is also to be observed, that the messenger of her letters to her father, who so often pretended business that way, was an implement in his master's hands, and employed by him for that purpose; and always gave her letters first to him, and his master used to open and read them, and then send them on; by which means, as he hints to her (as she observes in one of her letters, p. 116), he was no stranger to what she wrote. Thus every way was the poor virgin beset.[91] The intriguing gentleman thought fit to keep back from her father her three last letters; in which she mentions his concealing himself to hear her partitioning out her clothes, his last effort to induce her to stay a fortnight, his pretended proposal of the chaplain, and her hopes of speedily seeing them, as also her verses; and to send himself a letter to her father, which is as follows:

Honest Goodman Andrews,
You will wonder to receive a letter from me, but I have two motives for writing. *The one*, to acquaint you, that I have discovered the strange correspondence which has for some time past been carried on between you and your daughter, by means of my servant, John Arnold: whose part in it I shall resent as becomes me.

Strange correspondence, I call it, as the concerns of my family are exposed in it, and as great and indecent liberties are taken with my character.

The other, that it has also come to my knowledge, that the girl has a love affair with a young clergyman, for whom I intend to provide; but who at present has no other dependence, than my favour.

As to the *first*, I must tell you, that you ought not to have countenanced such culpable freedoms in the girl. Nor would you, I presume (for I am told that you are a prudent man), if you had known, as is the truth, that ever since the death of her kind lady, she has given herself up to the reading of novels and romances, and such idle stuff, and now takes it into her head, because her glass tells her she is pretty, that every body who looks upon her is in love with her. Hence, silly girl! her misrepresentations of those innocent familiarities of mine to her, on certain benevolent occasions (for I am a young man, and pride is not one of my failings) about which she so much alarms you; and which I was the less scrupulous about, as they were really innocent; as the girl was a favourite of my mother; and as I had no mean opinion, young as she is, of her discretion, as well as of her modesty. But there is a time of life, Goodman Andrews, which may be looked upon as a test of prudence in girls, and in which misconduct blasts many a shining hope.

I say not this, however, to excite your apprehensions. With all her new-shewn faults, I think her a modest and a virtuous girl. If I did not, she would not engage the least of my cares for her, though so earnestly recommended to me by my mother in her last moments.

She has already acquainted you, that she is dismissed from my service; and you expect her soon with you. But you must not be surprized, that you see her not quite so soon as both you and she might hope. For I have thought it worthy of my promises made to her late dear lady, to send her for a little while out of the parson's way, to a family of great repute; where she will have extraordinary opportunities of improvement, and be treated with great kindness. I will tell you my motives for taking this step; and the rather, as I took it without waiting for your concurrence.

In the first place, you yourself as you must needs acknowledge, have not acted so *prudently* as might have been expected from a man of your years, on the occasion I have mentioned: and she, perhaps, has been as free to others, as to you (young girls know no bounds to their vanity!) for she is become a mighty letter-writer.

In the next place, there was so much subtlety used, that (as I was resolved to serve and save them both) time was not allowed for consulting you.

For, you must know, that when challenged on proofs incontestibly clear, she would *not own* her regard for the young parson. Nor that either you or her mother knew anything of the matter. Nor would the young fellow acknowledge, that there was anything between them. I am very angry with him: a man of his cloth to deny facts so plainly proved, as must shew, that if he had not a view to marriage, he had worse.

Then my mother's love for the girl, and her recommendation of her to me, gave her a sort of title to my care, and the rather, as you, her honest father, cannot do anything for them, should they marry. I have no doubt, but the foolish fellow would have followed her, had she gone to you: and you might have had difficulty enough to keep asunder two headstrong young people, who, by coming together before they had means to live, might have been the ruin of each other, were his views ever so honourable.

When the living falls, to which I have thoughts of preferring him, and he is thereby in a way to maintain a wife, let them (if *you* have no objection) come together in God's name. All my generous and condescending cares for them both, will then be answered.

I have written a long letter to you, Goodman Andrews: and I have no doubt, if you have a grateful heart, but you will think me entitled to your thanks. But I desire not to be answered but by your good opinion, and by the confidence which you may repose in my honour. Being

Your hearty Friend to serve you.

It is easy to guess at the poor old man's concern upon reading this letter, from so considerable a man. He knew not what course to take, and had no manner of doubt of his daughter's innocence, and that foul play was designed her. Yet he sometimes hoped the best, and was ready to believe the surmised correspondence between the clergyman and her, having not received the letters she wrote, which would have cleared up that matter.

But after all, he resolved, as well to quiet his own as her mother's uneasiness, to undertake a journey to Mr B.'s, and leaving his poor wife to excuse him to the farmer who employed him, he set out that very evening, late as it was; and travelling all night, found himself soon after daylight at Mr B.'s gate, before the family was up: and there he sat down to rest himself, till he should see somebody stirring.

The grooms were the first he saw, coming out to water their horses; and he asked in so distressful a manner, what was become of Pamela, that they thought him crazy; and said, 'Why, what have you to do with Pamela, old fellow? Get out of the horses' way.' 'Where is your master?' said the poor man; 'pray, gentlemen, don't be angry: my heart is almost broken.' 'He never gives anything at the door, I assure you,' says one of the grooms; 'so you'll lose your labour.' 'I am not a beggar *yet*,' said the poor old man; 'I want nothing of him, but my Pamela! O my child! my child!'

'I'll be hanged,' said one of them, 'if this is not Mrs Pamela's father.' 'Indeed, indeed,' said he, wringing his hands, 'I am'; and weeping, 'Where is my child, where is my Pamela?' 'We beg your pardon, father,' said one of them; 'but she is gone home to you: how long have you been come from home?' 'O! but last night,' said he; 'I have travelled all night: is the 'squire at home, or is he not?' 'Yes, but he is not stirring,' said the groom, 'as yet.' 'Thank God for that!' said he; 'thank God for that! Then I hope I may be permitted to speak to him.' They asked him to go in, and he stepped into the stable, and sat down on the stairs there, wiping his eyes, and sighing so bitterly, that it grieved the servants to hear him.

The family was soon raised, with the report of Pamela's father coming to enquire after his daughter; and the maids would fain have had him go into the kitchen. But Mrs Jervis, having been told of his coming, arose, and hastened down to her parlour, and took him in with her, and there heard all his sad story, and read the letter. She wept bitterly; but yet endeavoured before him to hide her concern; and said, 'Well, Goodman Andrews, I cannot help weeping to see you weep; let nobody see my master's letter, whatever you do. I dare say your daughter's safe.'

'But I see,' said he, 'that *you*, madam, know nothing about her: if all was right, so good a gentlewoman as you are, would have been let into the secret. To be sure you thought she was with me!'

'My master,' replied she, 'does not always inform his servants of his proceedings; but you need not doubt his honour: you have his hand for it. And you may see he can have no design upon her, because he is not from hence, and does not talk of going hence.' 'That is all I have to hope for!' said he; 'that is all, indeed! But –' and was going on, when the report of his coming having reached Mr B. he came down, in his gown and slippers, into the parlour where he and Mrs Jervis were talking.

'What's the matter, Goodman Andrews? what's the matter?' 'O my child!' said the good old man; 'give me my child! I beseech you, sir.' 'Why, I thought,' says Mr B., 'that I had satisfied you about her: sure you have not the long letter I sent you, written with my own hand.' 'Yes, yes, but I have, sir, and that brought me hither; and I have walked all night.' 'Poor man!' returned he, with great seeming compassion, 'I am sorry for it, truly! Why your daughter has made strange confusion in my family; and if I thought it would have disturbed you so much, I would e'en have let her have gone home; but what I did was to serve *her* and *you* too. She is very safe, I do assure you, Goodman Andrews; and you may take my honour for it, I would not injure her for the world. Do you think I *would*, Mrs Jervis?' 'No, I hope not, sir!' said she. '*Hope not!*' said the poor man, 'so do I! but, pray, sir, give me my child; that is all I desire; and I'll take care no clergyman shall come near her.'

'Why, London is a great way off,' said Mr B. 'and I can't send for her back presently.' 'What, then, sir,' said he, 'have you sent my poor Pamela to London?' 'I would not have it said so,' replied Mr B., 'but I assure you, upon my honour, she is quite safe and satisfied, and will quickly inform you by letter, that she is. She is in a reputable family, no less than a bishop's; and is to wait on his lady, till I get the matter over that I mentioned to you.'

'O how shall I know this?' replied he. 'What!' said Mr B. pretending anger, 'am I to be doubted? Do you believe I can have any design upon your daughter? And if I had, do you think I would take such methods as *these* to effect it? Why, surely, man, thou forgettest whom thou talkest to!' 'O, sir,' said he, 'I beg your pardon; but consider my dear child is in the case: let me know what bishop, and where; and I'll travel to London on foot to see my daughter, and then shall be satisfied.'

'Why, Goodman Andrews, I believe thou hast read romances

as well as thy daughter, and thy head's turned with them. May I not have my word taken? Do you think, once more, I would offer anything dishonourable to your daughter? Pr'ythee, man, recollect a little who I am. But if I am not to be believed, what signifies talking?' 'Pray forgive me, sir,' said the poor man; 'but there is no harm to say, What bishop's, and where he lives?' 'What, and so you'd go troubling his lordship with your impertinent fears and stories! Will you be satisfied, if you have a letter from her within a week (it may be less if she be not negligent), to assure you all is well with her?' 'Why that,' said the poor man, 'will be some comfort.' 'I can't answer for her negligence,' said Mr B. 'if she don't write. But if she should send a letter to you, Mrs Jervis (for I desire not to see it; I have had trouble enough about her already) be sure you send it by a man and horse the moment you receive it, to her honest father.' 'To be sure I will,' answered she. 'Thank your honour,' said the good man. 'But must I wait a whole week for news of my child? It will be a year to me.'

'I tell you,' said Mr B. 'it must be her own fault, if she don't write: it is what I insisted upon for my own reputation; and I shall not stir from this house, I assure you, till she is heard from, and that to satisfaction.' 'God bless your honour,' said the poor man, 'as you say and mean the truth.' '*Amen, Amen,* Goodman Andrews,' returned Mr B., 'you see I am not afraid to say *Amen.* So, Mrs Jervis, make the good man welcome, and let me have no uproar about the matter.'

He then, whispering her, bid her give him a couple of guineas to bear his charges home; telling him, he should be welcome to stay there till the letter came, and he would then be convinced of his honour, and particularly that he should not leave his own house for some time to come.

The poor man staid and dined with Mrs Jervis, and in hopes to hear from his beloved daughter in a few days, accepted the present, and set out for his own house.

Mean time Mrs Jervis, and all the family, were in the utmost grief for the trick put upon the poor Pamela, and she and the steward represented it to their master in as moving terms as they durst: but were forced to rest satisfied with his general assurances of intending her no dishonour; which, however, Mrs Jervis little believed, from the pretence he had made in his letter, of the correspondence between Pamela and the young clergyman; which she knew to be all mere invention; though she durst not say so.

But the week after they were made a little more easy, by the following letter brought by an unknown hand, and left for Mrs Jervis. How procured, will be shewn in the sequel.

Dear Mrs Jervis,

I must acquaint you, that instead of being carried by Robin to my father's I have been most *vilely tricked*,[92] and am driven to a place which I am not at liberty to mention. I am not, however, used unkindly, *in the main*; and I write to beg of you to let my dear father and mother (whose hearts must be well-nigh broke) know that I am well, and that I am, and *by the Grace of God*, ever will be, their honest, as well as dutiful daughter. I am, dear Mrs Jervis,

> *Your obliged Friend,*
> PAMELA ANDREWS.

I must neither send date nor place: but have most solemn assurances of honourable usage. *This is the only time my low estate has been a trouble to me, since it has subjected me to the terrors I have undergone. Love to your good self, and all my dear fellow-servants. Adieu! Adieu! But pray for your poor* PAMELA.

This, though it was far from quieting Mrs Jervis's apprehensions, was shewn to the whole family, and to Mr B. himself, who pretended not to know how it came; and Mrs Jervis sent it away to the good old couple. They at first suspected it was forged, and not their daughter's hand; but finding the contrary, they were a little easier; and having enquired of all their acquaintance, what could be done, and no one being able to put them in a way how to proceed, with effect, on so extraordinary an occasion, against so rich and so resolute a man; and being afraid to make matters worse (though they saw plainly enough that she was in no bishop's family, and so mistrusted all the rest of his story), they applied themselves to prayers for their poor daughter, and for a happy issue to an affair that almost distracted them.

We shall now leave the honest old pair, praying for their dear Pamela; and return to the account she herself gives of all this;

having written it journal-wise, to amuse and employ her time, in hopes some opportunity might offer to send it to her friends, (and, as was her constant view) that she might afterwards look back upon her dangers; and either approve or repent of her conduct in them.

LETTER XXXII

O my dearest Father and Mother,

Let me write, and bewail my miserable fate, though I have no hope that what I write can be conveyed to your hands! I have now nothing to do but write, and weep, and fear, and pray! But yet what can I hope for, when I seem to be devoted as a victim to the will of a wicked violator of all the laws of God and man! But, gracious Father of all Mercies, forgive me my impatience. Thou best knowest what is fit for thine handmaid! And as Thou sufferest not thy poor creatures to be tempted above what they can bear, I will resign myself to thy will. And still, I hope, desperate as my condition seems, that as these trials are not the effects either of my presumption or vanity, I shall be enabled to overcome them, and in thine own good time be delivered from them.

Thus do I hourly pray! And! O join with me, my dear parents! But, alas! how can you know, how can I reveal to you, the dreadful situation of your poor daughter! The unhappy Pamela may be undone, before you can know her hard lot!

O the unparalelled wickedness of such men as these, who call themselves gentlemen! who pervert the bounty of Providence to them, to their own everlasting perdition, and to the ruin of oppressed innocence!

But now I will tell you what has befallen me. And yet how shall you receive what I write? Here is no honest John to carry my letters to you! And, besides, I am watched in all my steps; and no doubt shall be, till my hard fate ripen his wicked projects for my ruin. I will every day, however, write my sad state; and some way, perhaps, may be opened to send the melancholy scribble to you. But when you *know* it, what will it do but aggravate your troubles? For what, alas! can the abject poor do against the mighty rich, when they are determined to oppress?

I will begin with my account from the last letter I wrote you, in which I inclosed my poor verses; and continue it at times, as I have opportunity; though, as I said, I know not how it can reach you.

The often wished-for Thursday morning came, when I was to set out. I had taken my leave of my fellow-servants over-night and a mournful leave it was to us all: for men, as well as women-servants, wept to part with me; and, for *my* part, I was over-whelmed with tears on the affecting instances of their love. They all would have made me little presents; but I would not take any-thing from the lower servants. But Mr Longman would make me accept of several yards of Holland, and a silver snuff-box, and a gold ring, which he desired me to keep for his sake; and he wept over me; but said, 'I am sure, so good a maiden God will bless; and though you return to your poor father again, and his low estate, yet Providence will find you out: remember I tell you so; and *one* day, though I may not live to see it, you *will* be rewarded.' 'O dear Mr Longman,' said I, 'you make me too rich; and yet I must be further indebted to you: for I shall be often scribbling' (I little thought it would so soon be my only employment), 'and I will beg you, sir, to favour me with some paper; and as soon as I get home, I will write you a letter, to thank you for all your kindness to me; and a letter also to good Mrs Jervis.'

This was lucky; for I should have had none else, but at pleasure of my surly governess, as I may call her; but now I can write to ease my mind, though I can't send it to you; and write what I please, since she knows not how well I am provided: for good Mr Longman gave me above forty sheets of paper, and a dozen pens, and a little phial of ink; which last I wrapped in paper, and put in my pocket, and some wax and wafers.

'O dear sir,' said I, 'you have set me up. How shall I requite you?' He said, 'By a kiss, my fair mistress'; and I refused it not; for he is a good old man.

Rachel and Hannah wept when I took my leave; and Jane, who sometimes used to be a little cross to me, and Cicely too, cried very much, and said they would pray for me: but Jane, I doubt, will forget that; for, poor soul! she seldom prays for herself!

Then Arthur the gardener, our Robin the coachman, and Lincolnshire Robin too, who was to carry me, were very civil; and both had tears in their eyes; which I thought then very good-natured in Lincolnshire Robin, because he knew but little of me.

But it now appears too plainly, that he might well be concerned; for he had then his instructions, it seems, and knew he was to be an implement to entrap me.

Then our other three footmen, Harry, Isaac, and Benjamin, and grooms, and helpers, were very much affected likewise; and the poor little scullion-boy, Tommy, was overwhelmed with grief.

They had got all together over-night, expecting to be differently employed in the morning; and they all begged to shake hands with me, and I kissed the maidens, and prayed to God to bless them all; and thanked them for all their love and kindness to me: and indeed I was forced to leave them sooner than I wished, because I could not stand it. Harry (I could not have thought it; for he is a little wildish, they say) wept till he sobbed again. John, poor honest John, was not then come back from you. But as for the butler, Mr Jonathan, he could not stay in company.

I thought to have told you a great deal about this; but I have worse things to employ my pen.

Mrs Jervis, good Mrs Jervis, wept all night long. I comforted her all I could: and she made me promise, that if my master went to London to attend parliament, or to Lincolnshire, I would come and stay a week with her. And she would have given me money; but I would not take it.

Next morning came, and I wondered I saw nothing of poor honest John; for I waited to take leave of him, and thank him for all his civilities to me and to you: but I suppose he was sent further by my master, and so could not return; and I desired to be remembered to him.

And when Mrs Jervis told me, with a sad heart, the chariot was ready, with four horses to it, I was just as if I was sinking into the ground, though I wanted to be with you.

My master was above stairs, and never asked to see me. I was glad of it in the main; but, false heart! he knew that I was not to be out of his reach. O preserve me, heaven, from his power, and from his wickedness!

They were none of them suffered to go with me one step, as I writ to you before; for he stood at the window to see me go. And in the passage to the gate (out of his sight) there they stood, all of them, in two rows; and we could say nothing on each side, but, 'God bless you!' and 'God bless you!' But Harry carried my own bundle, my third bundle, as I was used to call it, to the coach, and some plum-cakes, and diet-bread,[93] made for me over night, and some sweet-meats, and six bottles of Canary wine,[94] which Mrs Jervis would make me take in a basket, to chear our hearts now-and-then, when we got together, as she said. And I kissed all the maids again, and shook hands with the men again; but Mr Jonathan and Mr Longman were not there; and then I went down steps to the chariot, leaving Mrs Jervis weeping as if she would break her heart.

I looked up when I got to the chariot, and I saw my master at the window, in his gown; and I curt'sied three times to him very low, and prayed for him with my hands lifted up; for I could not speak; indeed I was not able. And he bowed his head to me, which made me then very glad he would take such notice of me; and in I stepped, and my heart was ready to burst with grief; and could only, till Robin began to drive, wave my white handkerchief to them, wet with my tears. And at last away he drove, Jehu-like,[95] as they say, out of the court-yard: and I too soon found I had cause for greater and deeper grief.

Well, said I to myself, at this rate of driving I shall soon be with my father and mother; and till I had got, as I supposed, half way, I thought of the good friends I had left. And when, on stopping for a little bait[96] to the horses, Robin told me I was near half way, I thought it was high-time to dry my eyes, and remember to whom I was going; as then, alas for me! I thought. So I began with the thoughts of our happy meeting, and how glad you would both be, to see me come to you safe and innocent; and I tried to banish the other gloomy side from my mind: but yet I sighed now and then, in remembrance of those I had so lately left. It would have been ungrateful, you know, not to love those who shewed so much love for me.

It was about eight in the morning when I set out; and I wondered, and wondered, as I sat, and more when I saw it was about two, by a church-dial in a little village we passed through, that I was still more and more out of my knowledge. Hey-day, thought I, to drive at this strange rate, and to be so long going little more than twenty miles, it is very odd! But, to be sure, thought I, Robin knows the way.

At last he stopped, and looked about him, as if he was at a loss for the road; and I said, 'Mr Robert, sure you are out of the way!' 'I'm afraid I am,' answered he: 'but it can't be much; I'll ask the first person I see.' 'Pray do,' said I; and he gave his horses a little hay; and I gave him some cake, and two glasses of Canary wine; and he stopped about half an hour in all. Then he drove on very fast again.

I had so much to think of, of the dangers I now doubted not I had escaped, of the good friends I had left, and my best friends I was going to, and the many things I had to relate to you; that I the less thought of the way, till I was startled out of my meditations by the sun beginning to set, and still the man driving on, and his horses in a foam; and then I began to be alarmed all at once, and called to him; and he said, he had wretched ill luck, for he had come several miles out of the way, but was now right, and should get in still before it was quite dark. My heart began then to misgive me, and I was much fatigued; for I had had very little sleep for several nights before; and at last I called out to him, and said, 'Lord protect me, Mr Robert; how can this be! In so few miles to be so much out! How can this be?' He answered fretfully, as if he was angry with himself; and said, he was bewitched, he thought. 'There is a town before us,' said I. 'What do you call it? If we are so much out of the way, we had better put up there; for the night comes on apace.' 'I am just there,' said he. ''Tis but a mile on one side of the town before us.' 'Nay,' replied I, 'I may be mistaken; for it is a good while since I was this way; but I am sure the face of the country here is nothing like what I remember it.'

He still pretended to be much out of humour with himself; and at last stopped at a farm house, about two miles beyond the village I had seen; and it was then almost dark, and he alighted, and said, 'We must put up here. I know the people are very worthy people; and I am quite out.'

Lord, thought I, be good to the poor Pamela! And I prayed most fervently for the Divine Protection.

The farmer's wife, and maid, and daughter, came out; and the wife said, 'What brings you this way at this time of night, Mr Robert? And with a gentlewoman too?' Laying then all circumstances together, the blackest apprehensions filled my mind, and I fell a crying, and said, 'God give me patience! I am undone for certain! Pray, mistress, do you know 'Squire B. of Bedfordshire?'

The wicked coachman would have prevented her from answering me; but the daughter said, 'Know his worship! yes, surely! why he is my father's landlord!' 'Then,' said I, 'I am undone, undone for ever! O wicked wretch! what have I done to *you*,' said I to the coachman, 'to induce you to serve me thus? Vile tool of a wicked master!' 'Faith,' said the fellow, 'I'm sorry this task was put upon me: but I could not help it. But make the best of it now. These are very civil reputable folks; and you'll be safe here, I assure you.' 'Let me get out,' said I, 'and I'll walk back to the town we came through, late as it is. For I will not enter this house.'

'You will be very well used here, I assure you, young gentle-woman,' said the farmer's wife, 'and have better conveniences than any where in the village.' 'I matter not conveniences,' said I: 'I am betrayed and undone! As you have a daughter of your *own*, pity me, and let me know, if your landlord be here!' 'No, I assure you, he is not,' said she.

And then came the farmer, a good sort of man, grave, and well-behaved; and he spoke to me in such honest-seeming terms, as a little pacified me; and seeing no help for it, I went in; and the wife immediately conducted me up stairs to the best apartment, and told me, that was mine as long as I stayed; and nobody should come near me but when I called. I threw myself on the bed in the room, tired and frightened to death almost, and gave way to my grief.

The daughter came up, and said, Mr Robert had given her a letter to give me; and *there* it was. I raised myself, and saw it was the hand and seal of the wicked wretch my master, directed To Mrs Pamela Andrews. This was a little better than to have *him* here; though, if he had, he must have been brought through the air; for I thought *I* was.

The good woman (for I began to see things about a little reputable, and no guile appearing in them, but rather a face of concern for my grief) offered me a glass of some cordial[97] water, which I accepted, for I was ready to faint; and then I sat up in a chair. And they lighted a brush-wood fire; and said, if I called, I should be waited upon instantly; and so left me to ruminate on my sad condition, and to read my letter, which I was not able to do presently. After I was a little come to myself, I found it to contain the following words:

'*Dear* PAMELA,

'The regard[98] I have for you, and your obstinacy, have constrained me to act by you in a manner that I know will give you equal surprize and apprehension. But, by all that is good and holy, I intend nothing dishonourable by you! Suffer not your fears therefore to incite a behaviour in you, that will be disreputable to yourself, as well as to me, in the eyes of the people of the house where you will be when you receive this. They are my tenants, and very honest civil people.

'You will by this time be far on your way to the place I have allotted for your abode for a few weeks, till I have managed some particular affairs; after which I shall appear to you in a very different light, from that in which you may at present, from your needless apprehensions, behold me.

'To convince you, mean time, that I intend to act by you with the utmost honour, I do assure you, that the house to which you are going, shall be so much at your command, that I will not myself approach it without your leave. Make yourself easy therefore; be discreet and prudent; and a happy event shall reward your patience.

'I pity you for the fatigue you will have, if this comes to your hand in the place where I have directed it to be given you.

'I will write to your father, to satisfy him that nothing but what is strictly honourable is intended you by

Your true Friend.'

I but too well apprehended, that this letter was written only to pacify me for the present; but as my danger was not so immediate as I had had reason to dread, and as he had promised to forbear coming to me, and that he would write to you, my dear father, to quiet your concern, and that you might contrive some way to help me, I was a little more easy than before: and made shift to taste of a boiled chicken they had got for me. But the table was hardly taken away, when the coachman came (with a look of a hangman, as I thought) and calling me *madam* at every word, begged that I would get ready to pursue my journey by five in the morning, or else he should be late in. I was quite grieved at this; for I began not to dislike my company, considering how things stood, and was in hopes to get a party among them, by whose connivance I might throw myself into some worthy protection in the neighbourhood, and not be obliged to go forward.

However, I returned a slight answer to the wicked Robert; and, since my time was intended to be short, I resolved to make the best use of it; and therefore, as soon as he was withdrawn, I began to tamper with the farmer and his wife,[99] and was going to represent my case to them, when the farmer interrupted me, and said, They were well informed of the matter; and hinted, that young women in this age were too apt to throw themselves away, to their own disparagement, and to the grief of their friends.

I told them, that this was far from being my case; that I was a young creature who had been taken into Mr B.'s family to wait upon his mother, who was the best of ladies: and that since her much lamented death, finding I could not live in it with reputation and safety, I was resolved to quit it, and return to my parents, who were the worthiest people in the world, but of low fortunes and degree: but that, when I was in expectation of being carried to them, I had been betrayed, and brought hither, in the way to a worse place, no doubt. That as they had a daughter of their own (who sat by us, and seemed moved by my story, and the earnest manner in which I told it; for I could not help mingling my words with my tears) I besought them to take pity of a helpless young maiden, who valued her honour above her life; and to whose ruin they would be accessary, if they did not contribute to save her when it was in their power so to do. And of that I was sure such good worthy people as they seemed to be, would not for the world be guilty.

'That, for certain,' replied the farmer, 'we would not: but hark you me, young gentlewoman, let me tell you we have very good authority to question the truth of your relation; and have reason to think, that all will be well with you, if you act up to the discretion that seems to be in you, and if you will be governed by your best friends.'

'The authority you speak of,' returned I, 'must be from some vile story told you by this wicked coachman, and I beg you will call him in: and when he comes, you shall find he will not be able to gainsay me. Dear, good, worthy people, let him be called in.'

'No need of *that*, young gentlewoman,' replied the farmer. 'We have better authority than Mr Robert's. Our worthy landlord himself has informed us, under his own hand, how matters stand with you: and really I must say, it never was a good world since young women would follow their own headstrong wills, and resolve to dispose of themselves without the knowledge and consent of those who were born before them.' And here he slapt his clenched fist upon the table, and looked with a peevish earnestness upon his daughter, and then upon his wife.

You may believe that this intelligence very much affected and surprized me; since it discovered the deep arts of my wicked master, and how resolved he seems to be on my ruin, by the pains he takes to deprive me of all hopes of freeing myself from his power. I begged, however, that they would be so kind as to let me see what my master had written. The good woman said she knew not if that would be proper. 'Not proper!' said I. 'Can there be anything in a letter that has convinced such good people as you seem to be, of the justice of the writer's intentions, that is not proper to be shewn to one who is most interested in the contents of the letter? Let me see it, I beseech you, that I may either take shame to myself, or defend my character, which is all I have in the world to trust to.'

'Well, I think you may see it,' said the farmer, 'I *think* you may. There it is,' pulling it out of his pocket-almanack-book.

I read its contents, and afterwards procured leave to take a copy of it; which follows:

'*Farmer* MONKTON,[100]

'I send to your house, for *one night* only, a young gentlewoman, *much against her will*, who has deeply embarked in a love affair, which, if carried on to effect, must be *her* ruin, as well as the ruin of the person to whom she wants to betroth herself; and for whom I have *as much regard as I have for her*.

'As I know the step I have taken will oblige her father, [*See, my dear father!*] when he knows my motives, I have directed her to be carried to one of my houses (where she will be well used), in order to try, if, by absence and by expostulation, they can both, or either of them, be brought to know their own interest.

'I am sure you will use her kindly; for, excepting this matter, *which she will not own*, [*A wicked wretch, I am sure!*] she wants not either sense or prudence.

'I have written a letter to her, which Robert will give her at your house. The girl *is lively*, and will be out of humour, possibly, on the supposed disappointment of her love scheme. I have therefore written nothing in it but what may tend to soothe her, and have not hinted to her [*O the artful wretch!*] the true reason for the step I have taken. [*What reason have I for apprehensions from such a false-hearted contriver!*] Young people of that sex, you know, Farmer Monkton, think hardly of everything that thwarts their headstrong inclinations. Nor had I given myself all this trouble to thwart her, had not my dear mother recommended her to my care in her last hours; and were the young fellow in a way to maintain her. It is an ungrateful thing to endeavour to save people against their will. [*God forgive me, my dear father! But how do I hate this vile hypocritical master!*]

'I will acknowledge any trouble you shall be at on this occasion the first opportunity, though I shall not be that way, while the young creature is at the house to which I shall send her, that I may not give reason for suspicions. We live, you know, farmer, in a censorious world.'

And do not such actions, and such contrivances as those of this wicked man, justify the world's censoriousness? Indeed they do!

He then concludes with his regards to the good woman; and this was looked upon, by both the farmer and his wife, as mighty condescending: and to be sure he designed it should.

I was greatly shocked, you may well think, at the wicked arts of this abominable gentleman. Gentleman shall I call him? He says, you see, too cunningly for me, that *I would not own* this pretended love affair; so that he has prepossessed them with a doubt of the truth of all I could say in my own behalf. And as they are his tenants, and as all his tenants love him, (for he has some amiable qualities, and so he had need) I found all my hopes in a manner frustrated. And the thought of this, at first reading the letter, so affected me, that I wept bitterly; and could not forbear saying, that the wicked writer was as much too hard for me in his contrivances, as he was too powerful for me in his riches. And not entering directly upon my defence, the farmer the less doubted the truth of what the letter contained, and began to praise my master's care and concern for me; and to caution me against receiving the addresses of anyone, without the advice and consent of my friends; and so made me the subject of a lesson for his daughter's improvement: at the same time intimating, that I should be guilty of great unworthiness, if I presumed to suggest anything to the discredit of a gentleman, who, in this proceeding, could have no view but to my good; and to that of the young man whom I was supposed to love. Laying great weight upon his landlord's resolution not to come this way, while I was at the house he proposed to send me to; and this purposely that he might not give room *for foul suspicions*.

This raised me from my wailing fit. I told them, that all that was suggested in the letter was false, abominably false: that I was not in love with any man breathing; and that my master's vile contrivances had made it necessary I should acquaint them with the whole truth.

This I did; and afterwards read to them his letter to me; and gave it such comments as I thought it would well bear.

The old couple at first seemed much at a loss what to think, or what to say. They looked upon one another; and the honest woman shook her head, and seemed to pity me, while the daughter shed tears at my relation, and still in more abundance, at my earnest appeal to her father and mother for their protection.

This gave me a momentary hope; and I was proceeding with my appeal to move them in my behalf, when the old farmer, pulling out his spectacles, desired that he might be suffered himself to read his *honour's* letter to me; as he called one of the wickedest of men.

I gave him the letter; but found by the event, that he only seemed to wish to read it in order to acquit his landlord.

'My dear,' said he to his wife (looking upon the letter with his spectacles on, and now and then upon her, and now and then upon me, and sometimes upon his daughter), 'I know not what to say to this business. To be sure there is something very odd in the story, as this young gentlewoman tells it: but does not his honour say, that this step of his *will oblige her father*?'

I would then have spoken; but he desired to be heard with patience.

'Does he not tell us, Dorothy, in the letter he was so good as to write to us, that *she will not own her love*? And *will* she own it?' said the silly old man. 'Well then; so far so good. And does he not say, that he has written to her *to soothe her*? Very good of so great a man, I think: and that *he has not told her the motive of his doings?* And does not this also come out to be true? And does he not say, *that he will not come* NERST[101] *her, that he may not give occasions for foul suspicions?* And does he not tell us what is the nature of *headstrong girls?* Too well we know what that is, Dorothy.' And then he frowningly looked upon his daughter, who cast her eyes down, and blushed. 'And does he not say, that this young gentlewoman here will be *out of humour at her disappointment?* And do not the free things she *have* said of his honour shew this also to be true?'

Again I would have spoken; but he angrily desired to be heard out. I am sure the man is a tyrant over his wife and daughter; not such a one as you, my dear father.

'Well,' proceeded he, 'and does not his honour promise, *by all that's good and holy* (solemn and serious words, I do assure you!) that he intends nothing dishonourable by her? Bless my heart, young mistress! what would you have more? And who ever knew the 'squire worse than his word, though but in common matters, and where he sweareth not to it? And does he not say, that his care of her is owing to his dutiful remembrance of his mother, the best of ladies, God rest her soul! And can he break his promise to a dying mother? He cannot; no man can be so wicked as that comes to. Furthermore, does he not say, that if the young man was in the way to maintain a wife, he would not give himself all this trouble? *An ungrateful thing, indeed*, (True, says his honour. His honour is a wise man, look ye, do you see?) *to endeavour to save people against their will.*' And then he looked fiercely at his poor meek daughter.

'And here again,' proceeded the tedious old man, (and now I was glad that he had almost gone through the vile letter), 'does not his honour say, that when he has managed some particular affairs (put the young man in a way, no doubt) he shall appear in a quite *otherguess*[102] light than he now does? And that an happy event shall reward her patience? And that the house she is going to, shall be at her command? A great thing, I assure you! And does he not promise to write to her father, to make him quiet and easy? Come, come, young mistress, I see not that the least dishonour is intended you. Be prudent and discreet, therefore, as his honour advises. It is a fearful thing to reflect upon the mischiefs that it is in the power of women to do to the reputation of us men. I once had some slurs;

but who has escaped them, sooner or later, that has had concerns with the sex? So be patient and contented, and all will be well, as far as I can see. And there is an end of the matter.'

And then he swelled strangely, half over the table, as I thought, proud of his fine speech and wisdom.

I in vain attempted, when he had made an end, to convince him and his wife of the truth of my relation, and of the reality of my danger, and the more from the wicked glosses my master took so much pains to put upon his proceedings with so poor and so inconsiderable a girl as I am, and as he ought to think me. A fine gentleman's notions of the word *honour*, I moreover said, and those of us common people, might be very different. He might also be a generous and kind landlord, and yet not a virtuous man; and the treatment I had received from him at his house, and his present violent proceedings, to carry me to one of his houses, when I was to have gone to my father and mother, were strong and unquestionable evidences, that he meant me not honourably. In vain, I say, did I endeavour to convince them of the justice of these and other observations. The farmer declared, that he could never question his landlord's honour so solemnly given: adding, that although great and learned men had different ways of thinking and acting from others, as in this case, yet he was confident that all would turn out right at last. And one very vile hint he gave (to be sure, my dear father and mother, the man, though a man in years, cannot be a right good man!), passing an angry eye, as of contempt, from me to his daughter, and then to his wife, 'A strange to-do these girls make,' said he, 'and all for what? Why truly they can hardly be kept from running away with one man, yet make a mighty pother with their virtue and their fears from another. I say, 'tis humour and folly, and nothing else, and not goodness.'

And then slap went his hand upon the board. I thought I never saw a man put on so ugly a look in my life. His daughter does not seem to be a forward girl. But, as I said before, he must be a tyrant, and no good man at the bottom.

I could have given him an answer he would not have liked; but was willing to carry it fair, though half spiritless at the repulse I had met with; for, thought I, if I can but get a little more time to stay here, who knows but I may contrive some way to escape? I therefore told the farmer and his wife, how much I was fatigued, and begged they would give me entertainment with them a little longer than that night. I was sure, I said, that their landlord himself would not be against it, if he knew how much I was disordered with the journey and my apprehensions.

They said, they were loth to deny me anything in their power, as I had seen the 'squire had wished them to treat me kindly. If therefore Mr Robert could dispense with his orders, they should not refuse me.

Robert was sent for up. He came. I told him that I found myself so much fatigued, that I could not think of setting out so soon the next morning as he expected. But he told me that he must follow his orders; and that setting out so early would break the neck of my journey, as he phrased it; God forgive me! But I was ready to wish that the necks – I think I must not say what I wished both to the master and the man.

Nevertheless, I told the farmer and his wife, before Robert's face, that if they would give me leave to stay one day more, this surly coachman, who must needs think all was not fair that he was employed about, and who had no right to controul me, should not compel me to go with him. But they said, that as I had owned myself to be the servant of the squire, they were of opinion that they ought not to intermeddle between a man of his rank and his servant. They were under great obligations to their landlord, they added, and they expected repairs, and other favours from him; and as they doubted not that I might depend upon his honour so solemnly given, and under his hand and seal too, they did not chuse to disoblige him. So I was forced to give up all hope from them.

I had very little rest that night; and next morning early was obliged to set out. They were so civil, however, as to suffer their servant-maid to accompany me five miles onward, as it was so early; and then she was set down, and walked back.

Notwithstanding this disappointment, I was not quite hopeless, that I might yet find means to escape the plots of this wicked designer. And as I was on the way in the chariot, after the maid had left me, I thought of an expedient which gave me no small comfort.

This it was. I resolved that when we came into some town to bait, as Robert, I doubted not, must do for the horses sake, (for he drove at a great rate) I would apply myself to the mistress of the house, and tell her my case, and refuse to go further.

Having nobody but this wicked coachman to contend with, I was very full of this project; and depended so much on its success, that I forbore to call out for help, and for rescue, as I may say, to different persons whom we passed; and who, perhaps, would have heard my story, and taken me out of the hands of a coachman: yet two of these were young gentlemen; and how did I know but I might have fallen into difficulties as great as those I wanted to free myself from.

After very hard driving, we reached the town at which this too faithful servant to a wicked master proposed to put up. And he drove into an inn of good appearance. But you may believe, my dear father and mother, that I was excessively alarmed, when, at my being shewn a room, I was told that I was *expected* there, and that a little entertainment was provided for me. Yet was neither met nor received at my alighting by any body who had so provided for me.

Nevertheless, I was determined to try what could be done with relation to my project with the mistress of the inn; and for fear of the worst, to lose no time about it. I sent for her in, therefore, and making her sit down by me, I said, 'I hope, madam, you will excuse me; but I must tell you my case, and that before anybody comes in, who may prevent me. I am a poor unhappy young creature, to whom it will be a great charity to lend your advice and assistance, as I shall appear to deserve your pity. And you seem to be a good sort of gentlewoman, and one who would assist an oppressed innocent person.'

'Yes, madam,' said she, 'I hope you guess right, and I have the happiness to know something of the matter before you speak. Pray, call my sister Jewkes.' Jewkes! Jewkes! thought I, I have heard of that name; for I was too much confounded to have a clear notion of anything at the moment.

Then the wicked creature appeared, whom I had never seen but once before, and I was frighted out of my wits. Now, thought I, am I in a much worse situation than I was at the farmer's.

The naughty woman came up to me with an air of confidence, and kissed me, 'See, sister,' said she, 'here's a charming creature!' and looked in such a manner as I never saw a woman look in my life.

I was quite silent and confounded. But yet, when I came a little to myself, I was resolved to steal away from them, if I could; and once being a little faintish, I made that a pretence to take a turn into the garden for air: but the wretch would not trust me out of her sight; and the people I saw being only those of the house, who, I found, were all under the horrid Jewkes's direction, and pre-possessed[103] by her, no doubt, I was forced, though with great reluctance, to set out with her in the chariot; for she came thither on horseback with a man-servant, who rode by us the rest of the way, leading her horse. And now I gave over all thoughts of redemption.

Here are strange pains, thought I, taken to ruin a poor innocent, helpless, and even *worthless* young creature. This plot is laid too deep, and has been too long hatching, to be baffled,[104] I fear. But then, I put up my prayers to God, who I knew was able to save me, when all human means should fail: and in him I was resolved to confide.

You may see (yet, O! that kills me; for I know not whether ever you can see what I now write, or not) what sort of woman this Mrs Jewkes is, compared to good Mrs Jervis, by this.

Every now and then she would be staring in my face, in the chariot, and squeezing my hand, and saying, 'Why, you are very pretty, my silent dear!' And once she offered to kiss me. But I said, 'I don't like this sort of carriage, Mrs Jewkes; it is not like two persons of one sex to each other.' She fell a laughing very confidently, and said, 'That's prettily said, I vow! Then thou hadst rather be kissed by the other sex? 'Ifackins,[105] I commend thee for that!'

I was sadly teazed with her impertinence, and bold way; but no wonder; she was housekeeper at an inn, before she came to my master. And indeed she made nothing to talk boldly on twenty occasions in the chariot, and said two or three times, when she saw the tears trickle down my cheeks, I was sorely hurt, truly, to have the handsomest and finest young gentleman in five counties in love with me!

So I find I am got into the hands of a wicked procuress, and if I had reason to be apprehensive with good Mrs Jervis, and where everybody loved me, what a dreadful prospect have I now before me, in the hands of such a woman as this!

O Lord bless me, what shall I do! What shall I do!

About eight at night we entered the court-yard of this handsome, large, old, lonely mansion, that looked to me then, with all its brown nodding horrors of lofty elms and pines about it, as if built for solitude and mischief. And here, said I to myself, I fear, is to be the scene of my ruin, unless God protect me, who is all sufficient.

I was very ill at entering it, partly from fatigue, and partly from dejection of spirits: and Mrs Jewkes got some mulled wine, and seemed mighty officious to welcome me thither. And while she was absent (ordering the wine) the wicked Robin came in to me, and said, 'I beg a thousand pardons for my part in this affair, since I see your grief, and your distress; and I do assure you, that I am sorry it fell to my task.'

'Mighty well, Mr Robert!' said I; 'I have heard that the hangman at an execution usually asks the poor creature's pardon, and then pleads his duty, and calmly does his office. But I am *no* criminal, as you *all* know; and if I could have thought it my duty to comply with a wicked master, I had saved you in particular the merit of this vile service.'

'I am sorry,' said he, 'you take it so. But everybody don't think alike.'

'Well,' said I, 'whatever your thoughts may be, *you* have done *your* part, Mr Robert, towards my ruin, very faithfully; and will have cause to be sorry, perhaps, at the long run, when you shall see the mischief that comes of it. You knew I had reason to think that I was to be carried to my father's; and I can only, once more, thank you for *your* part in this vile proceeding. God forgive you!'

Mrs Jewkes came in as he went out. 'What have you said to Robin?' said she; 'the foolish fellow is ready to cry,' and she laughed as she spoke, as if she despised him for his remorse. 'I need not be afraid of *your* following his example, Mrs Jewkes,' said I: 'I have been telling him, that he has done *his* part to my ruin: and he now can't help it! So his repentance does *me* no good; I wish it may *him*.'

She calls me *madam* at every word; paying that undesired respect to me, as you shall hear, in the view of its being one day in my power to serve or dis-serve her, if ever I should be so vile as to *be* a *madam* to the wickedest designer that ever lived. Poor creatures *indeed* are such as will court the favour of wretches who obtain undue power, by the forfeiture of their honesty! And such a poor creature is this woman, who can madam up an inferior fellow-servant, in such views; and who yet, at times, is insolent enough; for it is her true nature to be insolent.[106]

'I do assure you, madam,' said she, 'I should be as ready to cry as Robin, if I should be the instrument of doing you harm.'

'It is not in *his* power to help it now,' said I; 'but *your* part is come, and *you* may chuse whether you will contribute to my ruin or not.' 'Why, look ye, look ye, madam,' said she, 'I have a great notion of doing my duty to my master; and therefore you may depend upon it, if I can do *that*, and serve *you*, I will: but you must think, if *your* desire, and *his* will, come to clash once, I shall do as he bids me, let it be what it will.'

'Pray, Mrs Jewkes,' said I, 'don't *madam* me so: I am but a silly poor girl, set up by the gambol of fortune, for a may-game;[107] and now I am to be something, and now nothing, just as that thinks fit to sport with me. Let us, therefore, talk upon a foot together; and that will be a favour done me; for I was at best but a servant girl; and now am no more than a discarded poor desolate creature; and no better than a prisoner. God be my deliverer and comforter!'

'Ay, ay,' says she, 'I understand something of the matter. You have so great power over my master, that you will be soon mistress of us all; and so, I will oblige you, if I can. And I must and will call you madam; for I am instructed to shew you all respect, I assure you.' See, my dear father, see what a creature this is!

'Who instructed you to do so?' said I. 'Who! my master, to be sure,' answered she. 'Why,' said I, 'how can that be? You have not seen him lately.' 'No, that's true; but I have been expecting you here sometime,' [O the deep laid wickedness! thought I] 'and besides, I have a letter of instructions by Robin; but, perhaps, I should not have said so much.' 'If you would shew me those instructions,' said I, 'I should be able to judge how far I could, or could not, expect favour from you, consistent with your duty.' 'I beg your excuse, fair mistress, for *that*,' returned she; 'I am sufficiently instructed, and you may depend upon it, I will observe my orders; and so far as they will let me, so far will I oblige you; and that is saying all in one word.'

'You will not, I hope,' replied I, 'do an unlawful or wicked thing, for any master in the world.' 'Look-ye,' said she, 'he is my master; and if he bids me do a thing that I *can* do, I think I *ought* to do it; and let him, who has power to command me, look to the *lawfulness* of it.' 'Suppose,' said I, 'he should bid you cut my throat, would you do it?' 'There's no danger of that,' replied she; 'but to be sure I would not; for then I should be hanged; since that would be murder.' 'And suppose,' said I, 'he should resolve to ensnare a poor young creature, and ruin her, would you assist him in such wickedness? And do you not think, that to rob a person of her virtue, is worse than cutting her throat?'

'Why now,' said she, 'how strangely you talk! Are not the two sexes made for each other? And is it not natural for a man to love a pretty woman? And suppose he can obtain his desires, is that so bad as cutting her throat?' And then the wretch fell a laughing, and talked most impertinently, and shewed me, that I had nothing to expect either from her virtue or compassion. And this gave me the greater mortification; as I was once in hopes of working upon her by degrees.

We ended our argument, as I may call it, here; and I desired her to shew me to the apartment allotted for me. 'Why,' said she, 'lie where you list, madam; I can tell you, I must sleep with you for the present.' '*For the present!*' said I, and torture then wrung my heart! 'But is it in your *instructions*, that you must be my bed-fellow?' 'Yes, indeed,' replied she. 'I am sorry for it,' said I. 'Why,' said she, 'I am wholesome, and cleanly too, I'll assure you.' 'I don't doubt that,' said I; 'but I love to lie by myself.' 'How so?' returned she; 'was not Mrs Jervis your bed-fellow at the other house?'

'Well,' said I, quite sick of her and my condition, 'you must do as you are instructed. I can't help myself; and am a most miserable creature.'

She repeated her insufferable nonsense, 'Mighty miserable indeed, to be so well beloved by one of the finest gentlemen in England!'

I am now come down in my writing to this present SATURDAY, *and a deal I have written*

My wicked bed-fellow has very punctual orders, it seems; for she locks me and herself in, and ties the two keys (for there is a double door to the room with different locks) about her wrist, when she goes to-bed. She talks of the house having been attempted to be broke open two or three times; whether to fright me, I can't tell; but it makes me fearful; though not so much as I should be, if I had not other and greater fears.

I slept but little last night, and arose, and pretended to sit by the window which looks into the spacious gardens; but I was writing all the time, from break of day, to her getting up, and after, when she was absent.

At breakfast she presented the two maids to me, the cook and house-maid: poor souls they seem to be, and equally devoted to her and ignorance.

There are (besides the coachman Robert) a groom, a helper, a footman; all strange creatures, that promise nothing; and all likewise devoted to this woman. The gardener looks like a good honest man; but he is kept at distance, and seems reserved. Yet who knows, but I may find a way to escape before my wicked master comes?

I wondered I saw not Mr Williams the clergyman, but would not ask after him, apprehending it might give some jealousy to Mrs Jewkes; but when I had seen the rest, he was the only one I had hopes of; for I thought his cloth would set him above assisting in my ruin. But in the afternoon he came; for it seems he has a little Latin school in the next village, about three miles distant, on the small profit of which he lives content, in hopes that something better will soon fall out through my master's favour.

He is a sensible, and seems to be a serious young gentleman; and when I saw him, I confirmed myself in my hopes of him; for he seemed to take great notice of my distress and grief (which I could not hide if I would) though he was visibly afraid of Mrs Jewkes, who watched all our motions and words.

He has an apartment in the house; but only comes hither on Saturday afternoons and Sundays: and he preaches sometimes for the minister of the village.

I hope to go to church with him to-morrow: sure it is not in her instructions to deny me! My master cannot have thought of *every* thing; and something may strike out for me there.

I have asked her, for a feint, to help me to pens and ink, though I have been using my own so freely, when her absence would permit; for I desired to be left to myself as much as possible. She says she will oblige me; but then I must promise not to send any thing I write out of the house, without her seeing it. I said, I wanted only to divert my melancholy; for I loved writing, as well as reading; but I had nobody to send to, she knew well enough.

'No, not at *present*, may be,' said she; 'but I am told you are a great writer, and it is in my instructions to see all you write; so look you here,' added she, 'I will let you have a pen and ink and two sheets of paper; for this employment will divert you: but, as I told you, I must always see your writing, be the subject what it will.' 'That's very hard,' said I; 'but may I not have to myself the closet in the room where we lie, with the key to lock up my things?' 'I believe I may consent to that,' answered she; 'and I will set it in order for you, and leave the key in the door. And there is an harpsichord too,' said she. 'Mr Williams says it is in tune, and you may play upon it to divert you; for I know my old lady taught you music: and you may, moreover, take what books you will out of my master's library. You love books too well to damage them.'

This was agreeable enough. These books and my pen will be all my amusement; for I have no work given me to do; and though the harpsichord be in tune, I am sure I shall not find my mind in tune to play upon it. I went directly, and picked out some books from the library, with which I filled a shelf in the closet she gave me possession of; and from these I hope to receive improvement, as well as amusement. But no sooner was her back turned, than I set about hiding a pen of my own here, and another there, for fear I should come to be denied, and a little of my ink in a broken china-cup, and a little in a small phial I found in the closet; and a sheet of the paper here-and-there among my linen, with a bit of the wax, and a few of the wafers, given me by good Mr Longman, in several places, lest I should be searched; and something I hope may happen to open a way for my deliverance, by these or some other means. How happy shall I think myself, if I can by any means get away before my wicked master arrives! If I cannot, what will become of your poor Pamela? Since he will have no occasion, I am sure, to send this vile woman out of the way, as he would have done Mrs Jervis once!

I was going to beg your prayers, as I used to do; but, alas! you cannot know my distress; yet I am sure I have your hourly prayers. I will write on, as things happen, that if a way should open, my scribble may be ready to be sent to you. If I can escape with my innocence, with what pleasure shall I afterwards read these my letters, as I may call them!

O how I want such an obliging honest-hearted man as John Arnold!

SUNDAY

Alas! Alas! I am denied by this barbarous woman to go to church! And she has behaved very rudely to poor Mr Williams, for pleading for me. I find he is to be forbid the house, if she pleases. Poor gentleman! all his dependence is upon my master, who intends to give him a very good living when the incumbent dies; and he has kept his bed these four months of old age and dropsy.

Mr Williams pays me great respect, and I see pities me; and would perhaps assist me in an escape from these dangers, if I knew how to communicate my thoughts to him. I should be very much grieved to ruin a poor young gentleman, by engaging him to favour me: yet one would do any thing that one honestly might, to preserve one's innocence; and Providence would, perhaps, make it up to Mr Williams!

Something, I hope, will offer. Mr Williams whisperingly hinted just now, that he wanted an opportunity to speak to me.

The wretch (I think I will always call her the *wretch* henceforth) insults me more and more. I was but talking to one of the maids just now, indeed a little to sound her; and she popped upon us, and said, 'Nay, madam, don't offer to tempt poor innocent country wenches to betray their trust: you wanted her, I heard you say, to take a walk with you. But I charge you, Nan, never stir with her, nor obey her, without letting me know it; no, not in the smallest trifles. I say, walk with you!' repeated she, with disdain, 'and where would you go, I tro'?' 'Why, barbarous Mrs Jewkes,' said I, 'only to look a little up the elm walk, since you would not let me go to church.'

'Nan,' said she, to shew me how much they were all in her power, and to carry her insolence to the utmost height, 'pull off madam's shoes, and bring them to me. I have taken care of her others.' 'Indeed she shan't,' said I. 'Nay,' said Nan, 'but I must, if my mistress bids me; so pray, madam, don't hinder me.' And so, indeed, (would you believe it?) she took my shoes off; I was too much surprized to make resistance. I have not yet power to relieve my mind by my tears. I am quite stupified!

Now I will give you a picture of this wretch! She is a broad, squat, pursy,[108] *fat thing*, quite ugly, if any thing human can be so called; about forty years old. She has a huge hand, and an arm as thick – I never saw such a thick arm in my life. Her nose is flat and crooked, and her brows grow down over her eyes; a dead, spiteful, grey, goggling eye: and her face is flat and broad; and as to colour, looks as if it had been pickled a month in saltpetre. I dare say she drinks. She has a hoarse man-like voice, and is as thick as she's long; and yet looks so deadly strong, that I am afraid she would dash me at her foot in an instant, if I were to vex her. So that with a heart more ugly than her face, she is at times (especially when she is angry) perfectly frightful: and I shall be ruined, to be sure, if heaven protects me not; for she is very, very wicked.

What poor and helpless spite is this! But the picture is too near the truth notwithstanding. She sent me a message just now, that I shall have my shoes again, if I will let her walk with me (let her *waddle* with me rather, she should have said) in the garden.

Since I am so much in the power of this hated wretch, I will go with her. O for my worthy, dear Mrs Jervis! Or, rather, to be safe with my dear father and mother!

I have just now some joy to communicate to you. This moment I am told John, honest John, is come on horseback! A blessing on his faithful heart! What pleasure does this news give me! But I'll tell you more by-and-by. I must not let her know I am so glad to see this worthy John. But, poor man! he looks sad, as I see him out of the window! What can be the matter! I hope you, my dear parents, are well, and Mrs Jervis, and Mr Longman, and every body, my master not excepted – for I wish him to live, and repent of all his wickedness.

O my dear father! what a world do we live in!

Here is John arrived, as I told you. He came to me, with Mrs Jewkes, who whispered, that I would say nothing about the shoes, for my *own* sake, as she said.

John saw my distress, by my red eyes, and my haggard looks, I suppose; and his own eyes ran over, though he would have hid his tears, if he could, from Mrs Jewkes. 'O Mrs Pamela!' said he; 'O Mrs Pamela!' 'Well, honest fellow-servant,' said I, 'I cannot help it at present: I am obliged to *your* honesty and kindness, however.' And then he wept more.

My heart was ready to break to see his grief; for it is a touching thing to see a man cry. 'Tell me the worst,' said I, 'honest, worthy John, tell me the worst. Is my master coming?' 'No, no,' said he, and sobbed. 'Well,' said I, 'is there any news of my poor father and mother? How do they do?' 'I hope, well,' said he; 'I know nothing to the contrary.' 'There is no mishap, I hope, to Mrs Jervis, or Mr Longman, or to any of my fellow-servants!' 'No,' with a long N—o, as if his heart would burst. 'Well, thank God then!' said I.

'The man's a fool,' said Mrs Jewkes, 'I think; what ado is here! why, sure thou'rt in love, John. Dost thou not see young madam is well? What ails thee, man?' 'Nothing at all,' said he; 'but I am such a fool, as to cry for joy to see good Mrs Pamela. But,' turning to me, 'I have a letter for you.'

I took it, and saw it was from my master; so I put it in my pocket.

'And here is one for you, Mrs Jewkes,' continued he; 'but yours, Mrs Pamela, requires an answer, which I must carry back early in the morning; or *to-night*, if you please to write time enough for me to set out.'

'You have no more notes or letters, John,' said Mrs Jewkes, 'for Mrs Pamela, have you?' 'No,' answered he, 'I have only, besides the letter, every body's kind love and service.' 'Aye, to us *both*, to be sure,' said Mrs Jewkes.

I retired to read the letter, blessing John as I went, and calling him a good man.

This is a copy of it.

'*Dear* PAMELA,

'I send purposely to you on an affair that concerns you very much, and me somewhat, but chiefly for your sake. I am sensible that I have proceeded by you in such a manner as may justly alarm you, and give concern to your honest friends. All my pleasure is, that I *can* and *will* make you amends for the uneasiness I have given you. I sent to your father the day after your departure, and assured him of my honour to you; and made excuses, such as ought to have satisfied him, for your not going to him. But he came to me next morning, and expressed so much uneasiness, on account of your health and welfare, that, in pity to him, and to your mother (whose apprehensions, he said, would be greater than his own, since he himself was willing to rely upon my solemn assurances of acting honourably by you), I promised that he should see a letter written from you to Mrs Jervis, to satisfy him that you are well, and not unhappy.

'As compassion to your aged parents, for whom you have so laudable an affection, is solely my motive, I have no doubt but you will oblige me with transcribing, in the form of a letter, directed to Mrs Jervis, to be sent to them, the few inclosed lines. And the *less* doubt have I, as in writing them, I have put myself as near as possible in your situation, and expressed your sense with a warmth, that I fear will have too much possessed you. I must desire that you will not alter one tittle of the prescribed form. If you do, it will be impossible for me to send it, or that it should answer the considerate end which I propose by it.

'I have already promised you, that I will not approach you without your consent. If I find you easy, and satisfied in your present abode, I will keep my word. Nor shall your restraint last long: only till I have managed an affair with Lady Davers;[109] which once determined, I will lose no time to convince you of the honour of my intentions in your favour. Mean time, I am,

Your true Friend, &c.'

The letter he prescribed for me was this:

'*Dear Mrs* JERVIS,

'I must acquaint you, that instead of being carried by Robin to my father's, I have been driven to a place which I am not at liberty to mention. I am not, however, used unkindly; and I write to beg of you to let my dear father and mother, whose hearts must be well-nigh broke, know that I am well; and that I am, and ever will be, their honest as well as dutiful daughter. I am, dear Mrs Jervis,

Your obliged friend, PAMELA ANDREWS.

'I must neither send date nor place; but have most solemn assurance of honourable usage.'

I knew not what to do on this most strange request. But my heart bled so much for you, my dear father, who had taken the pains to go yourself, and enquire after your poor daughter, as well as for my mother, that I resolved to write, and pretty much in the above* form, that it might be sent to pacify you, till I could let you, some-how or other, know the true state of the matter. I shall inclose a copy, and what I write to my wicked master himself:

'What, sir, have I done, that I should be singled out to be the *only* object of your cruelty? And how can I have the least dependence upon your solemn assurances, after what has passed, and being not permitted to write to my friends, or to let them know where I am?

'Nothing but your promise of not seeing me here in my deplorable bondage, can give me the least ray of hope.

'Do not, I beseech you, drive your distressed servant upon a rock, that may be the ruin both of her soul and body! You don't know, sir, how dreadfully I *dare*, weak as I am of heart and intellect, were I to find my virtue in danger. Why, O why, should a poor unworthy creature, who ought to be below the notice of such a gentleman as you, be made the sport of a high condition? Can there be any other reason assigned for your proceedings by her, but this one, that she is not able to defend herself, nor has a friend that can right her?

'I have, sir, in part to shew my obedience, but, indeed, I own, more to give ease to the minds of my poor distressed parents, followed pretty much the form you have prescribed for me, in a letter to Mrs Jervis; and the alterations I have made (for I could not help a few), are of such a nature, as, though they shew my just discontent, yet must answer the end you are pleased to say you propose by this letter.

'For God's sake, sir, give me reason, and speedy reason, by setting at liberty a poor creature, who has done nothing to deserve confinement, to join with all the rest of your servants to bless that goodness which you have been accustomed to extend to every one, and till of late used to shew to the now deeply afflicted

PAMELA.'

I thought, when I had written this letter, and that which he had prescribed, it would look like placing a confidence in Mrs Jewkes,

*See p. 129. Her alterations and additions are there in a different character.

to shew them to her; and I shewed her, at the same time, my master's letter to me; for, I believed, the value he expressed for me, would give me credit with one who professed in every thing to serve him, right or wrong; though I have so little reason, I fear, to pride myself in that credit: and I was not mistaken; for she is at present mighty obliging, and runs over in my praises.

I am now come to MONDAY, *the 5th day of my bondage*

I was in hope to have an opportunity to have a little private talk with John, before he went away; but it could not be. The poor man's excessive sorrow made Mrs Jewkes take it into her head, that he loves me; and so when he was to set out on his return this morning, and I desired to see him, she would needs accompany him to my closet, as I call it. The poor wretch (you shall by-and-by know why I call John a poor wretch) was as full of concern at taking leave, as he was at his first seeing me. I gave him the two letters in one cover: but Mrs Jewkes, as I should have told you, would make me shew them to her before I sealed them up, (and put a private mark on the cover) lest I should inclose any thing else, as indeed I had intended to do.

At the man's going away, he dropt a bit of paper, close rolled up, in my sight, just as she turned her back to go down stairs. I took it up unobserved; and was excessively surprized, when, on returning to my closet, I opened it, and read as follows.

'*Good Mrs* PAMELA,
'I am grieved to tell you how much you have been deceived, and betrayed, and that by such a vile dog as I. Little did I think it would come to this. But I must say, if ever there was a rogue in the world, it is me. I have all along shewed your letters to my master: he employed me for that purpose; and he saw every one before I carried them to your father and mother; and then sealed them up, and sent me with them. I had some business that carried me that way, but not half so often as I pretended: and as soon as I heard how it was, I was ready to hang myself. You may well think I could not stand in your presence. O vile, vile wretch, to bring you to this! If you are ruined, I am the rogue that caused it. All the justice I can do you, is to tell you, you are in vile hands; and I am afraid

will be undone, in spite of all your sweet innocence; and I believe I shall never live, after I know it. If you can forgive me, you are exceeding good; but I shall never forgive myself, that's certain. Howsomever, it will do you no good to make this known; and mayhap I may live to do you service. If I can, I will. I am sure I ought. Master kept your last two or three letters, and did not send them at all. I am the most abandoned wretch of wretches.

J. ARNOLD.

'You see your undoing has been long hatching. Pray take care of your sweet self. Mrs Jewkes is a devil: but in my master's other house you have not one false heart, but myself. Out upon me for a villain!'

My dear father and mother, when you come to this place, I make no doubt your hair will stand an end, as mine does! O the deceitfulness of the heart of man! This John, whom I took to be the honestest of men; whom you also took to be so; who was always praising you to me, and me to you, and for nothing so much as for our *honest* hearts; this *very* fellow was all the while a vile hypocrite, and a perfidious wretch, and helping to carry on my ruin.

But he says so much of himself, that I will only sit down with this sad reflection – That power and riches never want tools to promote their vilest ends, and that there is nothing so hard to be known as the heart of man. I can but pity the poor wretch, since he seems to have great remorse, and I believe it best to keep his wickedness secret.

One thing I should mention in this place: John brought down, in a portmanteau, all the clothes and things which my lady and my master had given me, and moreover, two velvet hoods, and a velvet scarf,[110] that used to be worn by my lady; but I have no pleasure in them, nor in any thing else.

Mrs Jewkes had the portmanteau brought into my closet, and she shewed me what was in it; but then locked it up, and said, she would let me have what I would out of it, when I asked; but if I had the key, it might make me want to go abroad: and so the confident woman put it in her pocket.

I gave myself over to sad reflections upon this strange and surprising discovery of John's deceitfulness, and wept much for him, and for myself too; for now I see, as he says, that my ruin has been long contriving, and that I can make no doubt what my master's *honourable* professions will end in. What a heap of hard names does the poor fellow call himself! But if John deserves those names, what must that wicked master deserve, who set him to work? And who, not content to be corrupt himself, endeavours to corrupt others, who would have been innocent if left to themselves! and all to carry on a base plot against a poor creature, who never did him harm, nor withheld him any; and who can still pray for his happiness, and his repentance.

I cannot but wonder what these *gentlemen*, as they are called, can think of themselves for these vile doings? John had *some* inducement; for he hoped to please his master, who rewarded him, and was bountiful to him; and the same may be said, bad as she is, for this same odious Mrs Jewkes. But what inducement has my master for taking so much pains to do the devil's work for him? If he loves me, as 'tis falsely called, must he therefore lay traps for me, to ruin me, and to make me as bad as himself? I cannot imagine what good the undoing of such a poor creature as I can procure him! To be sure, I am a very worthless body. People indeed say I am handsome; but if I am, should not a gentleman prefer an honest servant to a guilty harlot? And must he be *more* earnest to seduce me, because I dread of all things to be seduced, and would rather lose my life than my honesty?

These are strange things to me; I cannot account for them; but surely nobody will say, that these fine gentlemen have any tempter but their own base wills! This wicked master could run away, when he apprehended his servants might discover his vile attempts upon me in that sad closet affair; but is it not strange, that he should not be afraid of the All-seeing Eye, from which even that base, plotting heart of his, in its most secret motions, cannot be hidden?

TUESDAY *and* WEDNESDAY

Mrs Jewkes took me with her a little turn for an airing in the chariot, and I have walked several times in the garden; but she was always with me. And having no opportunity to write yesterday, I will now put both days together.

Mr Williams came to see us, and took a walk with us one of the times; and while her back was turned (encouraged by the hint he had before given me) I said, 'Sir, I see two tiles upon that parsley-bed: might not one cover them with mould, with a note between them, on occasion?' 'A good hint!' said he: 'let that sun-flower by the back-door of the garden be the place; I have a key to that door; for it is my nearest way to the village.'

What inventions will necessity push one upon! I hugged myself at the thought; and she coming to us, he said, as if he was continuing a discourse we were in, 'No, not very pleasant.' 'What's that? what's that?' said Mrs Jewkes. 'Only,' said he, 'the village, I am saying, is not very pleasant.' 'Indeed,' said she, ''tis not.' 'Are there any gentry near it?' said I. And so we chatted on about the town, to deceive her. But I intended no hurt to anybody by my deceit.

We then talked of the garden, how large and pleasant, and the like; and sat down on the turfted[111] slope of the fish-pond, to see the fishes play upon the surface of the water; and she said, I should angle, if I would.

'I wish,' said I, 'you'd be so kind to fetch me a rod and baits.' 'Pretty mistress!' said she, 'I know better than that, I assure you, at this time.' 'Indeed, I mean no harm,' said I. 'Perhaps not,' replied she; 'but we will angle a little to-morrow.' Mr Williams, who is much afraid of her, changed the discourse. I sauntered in, and left them to talk by themselves; but he went away to the village; and she was soon after me.

I had got to my pen and ink; but, on her coming, I put what I was writing in my bosom, and asked her for more paper. She questioned me as to that she had given me before, 'You know,' said I, 'that I have written two letters, and sent them by John.' (O how the very mentioning of his name, poor guilty fellow, grieves me!) 'Well,' said she, 'you have some left: one sheet did for those two letters.' 'Yes,' said I, 'but I used half another for a cover, you know; and see how I have scribbled the other half,' and so I shewed her a parcel of broken scraps of verses, which I had tried to recollect, and had written purposely that she might think me usually employed in such an idle way. 'Ay,' said she, 'so you have; well, I'll give you two sheets more; but I must see how you dispose of them.' Well, thought I, I hope still, Argus,[112] to be too hard for thee. Now Argus, the poets say, had an hundred eyes, and was set to watch with them all, as she does, with her goggling ones.

She brought me the paper, and said, 'Now, Mrs Pamela, let me see you write something.' 'I will,' said I; and took the pen and wrote, 'I wish Mrs Jewkes would be so good to *me*, as I would be to *her*, if I had it in my power.' 'That's pretty, now,' said she: 'well, I hope I am; but what then?' 'Why then' (*wrote I*) 'she would do me the favour to let me know, what I have done to be made her prisoner; and what she thinks is to become of me.' 'Well, and what then?' said she. 'Why then, of consequence' (*scribbled I*) 'she would let me see her instructions, that I may know how far to blame, how far to acquit her; and what to hope from her.'

Thus I fooled on, to shew her my fondness for scribbling (for I had no expectation of any good from her) that so she might suppose I employed myself, as I said, to no better purpose at other times: for she will have it that I am upon some plot, I am so silent, and love so much to be by myself.

She would have me write on a little further. 'No,' said I, 'you have not answered me.' 'Why,' said she, 'what can you doubt, when my master himself assures you of his honour?' 'Ay,' said I; 'but lay your hand to your heart, Mrs Jewkes, and tell me, if you yourself believe him.' 'Yes,' said she, 'to be sure I do.' 'But,' said I, 'what do *you* call honour?' 'Why,' said she, 'what does *he* call honour, think you?' 'Ruin! shame! disgrace!' said I, 'I fear.' 'Pho, pho!' said she; 'if you have any doubt about it, he can best explain his own meaning: I'll send him word to come and satisfy you, if you will.' 'Horrid creature!' said I, in a fright. 'Can you not stab me to the heart! I'd rather you would, than say such another word! But I hope there is no thought of his coming.'

She had the wickedness to say, 'No, no; he don't intend to come, as I know of: but, if I was he, I would not be long away.' 'What means the woman?' said I. 'Mean!' said she (turning it off); 'why, I mean, I would come, if I was he, and put an end to all your fears – by making you as happy as you wish.' ''Tis out of his power,' said I, 'to make *me* happy, great and rich as he is! but by leaving me innocent, and giving me liberty to go to my father and mother.'

She went away soon after, and I ended my letter, in hopes to have an opportunity to lay it in the appointed place. I then went to her, and said, 'I suppose, as it is not dark, I may take another turn in the garden.' ''Tis too late,' said she; 'but if you will go, don't stay; and, Nan, see and attend madam,' as she called me.

I went towards the pond, the maid following me, and dropped purposely my *hussey*:[113] and when I came near the tiles, I said, 'Mrs Ann, I have dropped my *hussey*; be so kind as to look for it: I had it by the pond-side.' She went back to look, and I flipped the note between the tiles, and covered them as quick as I could with the light mould, quite unperceived; and the maid finding the *hussey*, I took it, and sauntered in again, and met Mrs Jewkes coming to seek after me. What I wrote was this:

'*Reverend Sir*,
'The want of opportunity to speak my mind to you, I am sure, will excuse this boldness in a poor creature that is betrayed hither, I have reason to think, for the worst of purposes. You know something, to be sure, of my story, my native poverty, which I am not ashamed of, my late lady's goodness, and my master's designs upon me. 'Tis true, he promises honour; but the honour of the wicked is disgrace and shame to the virtuous. And he may think he keeps his promises, according to the notions he may allow himself to hold; and yet, according to mine, and every good person's, basely ruin me.

'I am so ill treated by this Mrs Jewkes, and she is so ill-principled a woman, that as I may soon want the opportunity which the happy hint of this day affords to my hopes, I throw myself at once upon your goodness without the least reserve: for goodness I see, sir, in your looks, I hope it from your cloth, and I doubt it not from your inclination, in a case circumstanced as my unhappy one is. For, sir, in helping me out of my present distress, you perform all the acts of religion in one; and the highest mercy and charity, both to body and soul, of a poor wretch, that, believe me, sir, has at present, not so much as in thought, swerved from innocence.

'Is there not some way to be found out for my escape, without danger to yourself? Is there no gentleman or lady of virtue in this neighbourhood, to whom I may fly, only till I can find a way to get to my father and mother? Cannot Lady Davers be made acquainted with my sad story, by your conveying a letter to her? My parents are low in the world: they can do nothing, but break their hearts for me; and that, I fear, will be the deplorable case.

'My master promises, if I will be easy, as he calls it, in my present lot, that he will not come down without my consent. Alas! sir, this is nothing: for what is the promise of a person, who thinks himself intitled to act as he has done by me? If he comes, it must be for no good; and come, to be sure, he will, when he thinks he has silenced the clamours of my friends, and lulled me, as no doubt he hopes, into a fatal security.

'Now, therefore, sir, is all the time I have to work and struggle for the preservation of my honesty. If I stay till he comes, I am undone. You have a key to the garden back-door; I have great hopes from that. Study, good sir, and contrive for me. I will faithfully keep your secret.

'I say no more, but commit this to the happy tiles, in the bosom of that earth, where I hope my deliverance will take root, and bring forth such fruit as may turn to my inexpressible joy, and your reward, both here and hereafter: as shall ever pray

Your oppressed humble Servant.'

THURSDAY

This completes a terrible week since my setting out, in hopes to see you, my dear father and mother. O how different were my hopes then, from what they are now! Yet who knows what these happy tiles may produce!

But I must now tell you, how I have been beaten by Mrs Jewkes! It is very true! And thus it came about.

I was very impatient to walk in the garden, to see if any thing had offered answerable to my hopes. But this wicked Mrs Jewkes said I should not go without *her*; and she was not at leisure to go with me. We had a great many words about it; for I told her, It was very hard to be denied to walk by myself in the garden for a little air; but must be dogged and watched, as if I were a thief.

She pleaded her instructions, and said, she was not to trust me out of her sight. 'You had better,' said she, 'be easy and contented, I assure you; for I have stricter orders than you have yet found put in force. Don't I remember,' added she, 'your asking Mr Williams if there were any gentry in the neighbourhood? This makes me suspect, that you want to get away to some of them, and din their ears[114] with your dismal story, as you call it.'

My heart aked at this hint; for I was afraid by it, that she had found my letter under the tiles. But at last, seeing me vexed and surprized, she said, 'Well, since you are set upon it, you may take a turn, and I will be with you in a minute.'

When I was out of sight of her window, I speeded towards the hopeful place; but was soon forced to slacken my pace, by her odious voice. 'Hey-day! why so nimble, and whither so fast?' said she. 'What! are you upon a wager?' I stopped for her till she had waddled up to me; and she held by my arm, half out of breath: so I was forced to pass by the hopeful spot, without daring to cast an eye towards it.

The gardener was at work a little further, and I stopt to look upon what he was about, and began to talk to him in the way of his art; but she said softly, 'My instructions are, not to let you be familiar with the servants.' 'Are you afraid,' said I, 'that I should confederate with them to commit a robbery on my master?' 'Perhaps I am,' said the odious wretch; 'for to rob him of yourself, would be the worst robbery, in his opinion, that you could commit.'

'And pray,' said I, (as we walked on) 'how came I to be his property? What right has he in me, but such as a thief may plead to stolen goods?' 'Was ever the like heard!' says she. 'This is downright rebellion, I protest! Well, well, lambkin,' (which the foolish creature often calls me) 'if I was in his place, he should not have his property in you long questionable. I would not stand shill-I, shall-I,[115] as he does; but put you and himself both out of your pain.' 'Jezebel,'[116] said I, (I could not help it) and was about to say more; but she gave me a severe blow upon my shoulder. 'Take that,' said she; 'who is it you call Jezebel?'

I was excessively surprised; for you, my dear father and mother, never beat me in your lives; and looked round, as if I wanted somebody to help me; but saw nobody; and said, at last, putting my hand to my shoulder, 'Is this also in your instructions? Am I to be *beaten* too?' And fell a crying, and threw myself on the grass-walk we were upon. 'Jezebel!' repeated she, in a great pet, 'Jezebel! Marry come up![117] I see you have a spirit; you must and shall be kept under. I'll manage such a little provoking thing as you, I warrant ye! Come, rise; we'll go in a-doors, and I'll lock you up, and you shall have no shoes, nor any kindness from me, I assure you.'

I did not know what to do. And I blamed myself for my free speech; for now I had given her some pretence; and oh! thought I, here have I unseasonably, by my mal-pertness,[118] ruined the only project I had left.

The gardener saw what passed; but she called to him, 'What do you stare at, Jacob? Pray, mind what you are upon.' And away he walked to another quarter, out of sight.

Well, thought I, I must put on the dissembler a little, I see. She took my hand roughly, 'Come, get up,' said she, 'and come in a-doors. I'll Jezebel you!' 'Why, dear Mrs Jewkes!' said I. 'None of your dears, and your coaxing!' said she; 'why not Jezebel again?' She was in a violent passion, I saw. And again I blamed myself for provoking her. 'If you don't rise, and go in,' said she, 'of your own accord, I can take such a slender creature as you under my arm, and carry you in. You don't know my strength.' 'Indeed I do,' said I, 'too well; and will you not use me worse, when I am within?' I arose. She muttered to herself all the way, 'I to be a Jezebel with you, that have used you so well!' and such-like.

When I came near the house, I said, sitting down upon a settle-bench,[119] 'Well, I will *not* go in, till you say, you forgive me, Mrs Jewkes. If you will forgive my calling you that name, I will forgive your beating me.' She sat down by me; and, after some angry words, 'Well, I think I will forgive you this time,' said she; and kissed me, as a mark of reconciliation. I told her, I wished she would let me know what her instructions were, and the liberty she could allow me, in which case she should find that I would, if possible, confine myself within the prescribed bounds, and not expect more from her than she could grant me.

'This,' said she, 'is something like: I wish I could give you all the liberty you desire; for you must think it is no pleasure to me to tie you to my petticoat: but people that will do their duty, must have some trouble; and what I do is to serve as good a master, to be sure, as lives.' 'Yes,' said I, 'to every body but me!' 'He loves you too well,' returned she, 'and thence arise your grievances; so you ought to bear them.' '*Love!*' repeated I. 'Such love is a thousand times worse than his hate would be.' 'Come,' said she, 'don't let the wench see you have been crying, nor tell *her* any tales; for you won't tell them fairly, I am sure; and I'll send her to attend you; and you shall take another walk in the garden, if you will: perhaps it will get you a stomach to your dinner; for you don't eat enough to keep life and soul together. You are beauty to the bone,' added the strange wretch, 'or you could not look so well as you do, with so little stomach, so little rest, and so much pining and whining for nothing at all.' Say what you will, wicked woman as you are, thought I, so I can be rid of your bad tongue and bad company. She left me, and sent the maid to walk with me. I hoped now to find some opportunity to come at my sun-flower. But I walked the other way, to take that spot in my return, to avoid suspicion.

I forced my discourse to the maid; but it was all upon general matters; for I find she is asked after everything I say and do. When I came near the place, I said, 'Pray, step to the gardener, and ask him to gather me a sallad.' She called out, 'Jacob!' I told her, he could not hear her so far off. And when she had stepped about a bow-shot from me, I stooped down, and took a letter, without direction, from between the tiles, and thrust it in my bosom. She was with me before I could well secure it; and I trembled like a fool, that I feared I should discover myself. 'You seem frighted, madam,' said she. 'I *am* frighted,' answered I; and a lucky thought just then entered my head: 'I stooped to smell at the sun-flower, and a great nasty worm running into the ground, startled me; for I can't abide worms.' 'Sun-flowers,' said she, 'don't smell.' 'So I find,' replied I. We then walked in; and Mrs Jewkes said, 'You have not staid long; you shall go another time.'

I went up to my closet, locked myself in, and opening my letter, found the contents to be these that follow:

'I am infinitely concerned for your distress. I most heartily wish it may be in my power to serve and save so much innocence, beauty, and merit. My whole dependence is upon Mr B. and I have a near view of being provided for, by his favour to me. But yet I would sooner forfeit all my hopes in him, (trusting in God for the rest) than not assist you, if possible. I never looked upon Mr B. in the light he now appears in to me, in your case. To be sure, he is no professed debauchee. But I am entirely of opinion you should, if possible, get out of his hands, and especially as you are in very bad ones in Mrs Jewkes's.

'We have in this neighbourhood the widow Jones, mistress of a good fortune, and a woman of virtue. We have also old Sir Simon

Darnford. His lady is a good woman; and they have two daughters, virtuous young ladies. All the rest are but middling people, and traders, at best. I will represent your case, if you please, either to Mrs Jones or Lady Darnford, in hopes they will afford you protection. I see no probability of keeping myself concealed in this matter; but will, as I said, risque all things to serve you; for I never saw a sweetness and innocence like yours; and your hard case has attached me entirely to you; for I know, as you so happily express yourself, if I can serve you in this affair, I shall thereby perform all the acts of religion in one.

'As to Lady Davers, I will convey a letter, if you please, to her; but it must not be from our post-house.[120] And let this be a caution to you in other respects; for the man owes all his bread to Mr B. and his place too; and I believe, by something that dropped from him over a can[121] of ale, has his instructions. You don't know how you are surrounded: all which confirms me in your opinion, that no honour is meant you, let what will be professed; and I am glad you want no caution on that head.

'Give me leave to say, that I had heard much in your praise, but, I think, greatly short of what you deserve, both in person and mind: my eyes convince me of the one, your letter of the other. I will not enlarge any further than to assure you, that I am, and will be, to the best of my power,

Your faithful Friend and Servant,
ARTHUR WILLIAMS.

'I will go once every morning, and once every evening, after school-time, to look for your letters. I will go in, and return without entering the house, if I see the coast clear: otherwise, to avoid suspicion, I will go in.'

In answer to this agreeable letter, I wrote instantly as follows:

'*Reverend Sir,*
'How suitable to your function, and your character, is your kind letter! God bless you for it! I now think I am beginning to be happy. I should be sorry to have you suffer on my account; but if you should, I hope it will be made up to you an hundred-fold by that God whom you so faithfully serve. I should be too happy,

could I ever have it in my power to contribute in the least to it. But alas! to serve me, must be for God's sake only; for I am low in fortune; though in mind, I hope, too high to do a mean or unworthy deed, were it even to gain a kingdom. But I lose time.

'Any way you think best, I shall be pleased with; for I know not the persons, nor in what manner it is proper to apply to them. I am glad of the hint you so kindly give me of the man at the post-house. I was thinking of opening a way to serve myself by letter, when I could have opportunity; but I see more and more, that I am indeed strangely surrounded with dangers; and that there is no dependence to be made on my master's professions.

'I should think, sir, if either of those ladies would give leave, I might some way get out by means of your key; and as it is impossible, watched as I am, to know when it can be, suppose, sir, you could get one made by it, and put it, the next opportunity, under the sun-flower! I am sure no time is to be lost; because it is my wonder, that Mrs Jewkes is not jealous about this key; for she forgets not the minutest thing. But, sir, if I had a key, and, if these ladies would *not* shelter me, I could get away from hence. And if once out of the house, they could have no pretence to force me in again; for I have done no harm, and hope to make my story good to any compassionate person; and by this means *you* need not be known. Torture should not wring from me anything to your detriment, I assure you.

'One thing more, good sir. Have you no correspondence with my master's Bedfordshire family? I inclose a letter of a deceitful wretch (for I can trust you with anything) poor John Arnold. Its contents will tell you, why I inclose it. Perhaps, by John's means, I might be informed of my master's motions, and particularly as to his intentions of coming hither, and the time; for come he will, I have no doubt; and that is my dread. You will see, sir, that John seems desirous to atone for his treachery to me. I leave this hint for you to improve upon, and am, Reverend Sir,

Your ever obliged and thankful Servant.

'I hope, sir, by your favour, I could send a little packet, now-and-then, some how, to my father and mother. I have a little stock of money, about five or six guineas: shall I put half into your hands, to defray the charge of a man and horse, or any other incidents?'

I had but just time to transcribe this letter, before I was called to dinner; and I put that for Mr Williams, with a wafer in it, into my bosom, to get an opportunity to deposit it.

Of all the flowers in the garden, the sun-flower surely is the loveliest! It is a propitious one to me! How nobly my plot succeeds! But I begin to be afraid my writings may be discovered; for they grow bulky: I stitch them hitherto in my under-coat, next my linen. But if this brute should search me! I must try to please her, and then she will not.

I am but just come from a walk in the garden; and have deposited my letter by a simple wile. I got some horse-beans;[122] and we took a turn in the garden, to angle. She baited the hook, and I held it, and soon hooked a noble carp. 'Play it, play it,' said she. I did, and brought it to the bank. A sad thought just then came into my head; and I took it gently off the hook, and threw it in again; and O the pleasure it seemed to have, on flouncing in, when at liberty! 'Why this?' says she. 'O Mrs Jewkes! I was thinking this poor carp was the unhappy Pamela. I was comparing myself to my naughty master. As *we* deceived and hooked the poor carp, so was I betrayed by false baits; and when you said, *play it, play it,* it went to my heart, to think I should sport with the destruction of the fish I had betrayed: I could not but fling it in again; and did you not see the joy with which it flounced from us? O that some good merciful person would procure me my liberty in like manner; for I cannot but think my danger equal!'

'Lord bless thee!' said she, 'what a thought is that!' 'Well, I can angle no more,' said I. 'I'll try *my* fortune,' said she, and took the rod. 'Do,' answered I, 'and I will plant life, if I can, while you are destroying it. I have some horse-beans here, and will go and stick them into one of the borders, to see how long they will be coming up; and I will call the bed I put them in, my garden.'

By this simple contrivance, I hope, my dear father and mother, I shall have an opportunity to convey to you my letters, if I cannot get away myself. Let the wicked woman smile at my simplicity if she will; I have now a pretence to bend my steps to that spot; and if the mould should look a little fresh, it won't be so much suspected.

She mistrusted nothing of this; and I went and stuck in here and there my beans, for about the length of five ells,[123] on each side of the sun-flower; and easily deposited my letter. And not a little proud am I of this contrivance. Sure something will do at last!

FRIDAY, SATURDAY

I have just now told you a trick of mine: I will now tell you a trick of this wicked woman's. She came to me, 'I have a bill,' said she, 'which I cannot change till to-morrow; and a tradesman instantly wants his money; and I don't love to turn poor trades-folks away without their money: have you any about you?' 'I have a little,' replied I: 'how much will do?' 'Oh!' said she, 'I want ten pounds.' 'Alas!' said I, 'I have but six guineas, and a very trifle of silver.' 'Lend me what you have,' said she, 'till to-morrow. I will return it you then without fail.' O my folly! I gave her the six guineas, and she went down stairs: and when she came up again, she laughed, and said, 'Well, I have paid the tradesman.' 'I hope,' said I, 'you'll repay me to-morrow.' The wretch, laughing loud, replied, 'Why, what occasion have you for money? To tell you the truth, lambkin, I did not want it. I only feared you might make a bad use of it; and now I can trust Nan with you a little oftener, especially as I have got the key of your portmanteau; so that you can neither corrupt her with money nor fine things.'

Never did any body look more silly than I! How I fretted to be so foolishly taken in! And the more, as I had hinted to Mr Williams, that I would put part of it into his hands to defray the charges of my sending to you. I cried for vexation! And now, my dear father, I have not five shillings left to support me, were I to get away! Was ever such a fool! I *must* be priding myself in my contrivances, truly! 'Was this vile trick in your instructions, *wolfkin*?' said I, as she called me *lambkin*. 'Jezebel, you mean, child!' said she. 'Well, I now forgive you heartily; let's kiss and be friends!' 'Out upon you!' said I; 'I cannot bear you.' But I durst not call her names again, being afraid of the weight of her huge paw, which I have once felt.

The more I think of this thing, the more I am grieved, and the more do I blame myself.

This night the man from the post-house brought a letter for Mrs Jewkes, in which was one inclosed to me: she brought it up to me. 'Well, my good master don't forget us,' said she. 'He has sent you a letter; and see what he writes to *me*.' So she read, That he hoped her fair charge was well, happy, and contented. That he did not doubt her care and kindness to me; and that she could not use me too well.

'There's a master for you!' said she: 'sure you will love and pray for him.' I desired her to read the rest. 'No, no,' said she, 'but I won't.' 'Are there,' said I, 'any orders for taking away my shoes, and for beating me?' 'No,' said she; 'nor does he call *me* Jezebel: but I thought we had forgiven one another.'

This is a copy of his letter to me:

'*My dear* PAMELA,

'I begin to repent already, that I have bound myself by promise, not to see you till you give me leave. Can you place so much confidence in me, as to *invite* me down? Assure yourself, that you shall not have cause to repent of your obligingness. Consider *who* it is that urges you to give him leave to go to his own house, as a favour. I the more earnestly press for your consent, as Mrs Jewkes acquaints me, that you take your restraint very heavily; and that you neither eat nor rest well; and yet I cannot take off this restraint, till I have had some discourse with you, that must tend to make you one of the happiest of women. It is your *interest*, therefore, my dear girl, to give me a dispensation from my promise, in order to shorten the time of this restraint. John, on his return from you, acquainted me with your uneasiness, in such terms, as, I must own, somewhat alarmed me. But surely your resentment will not throw you upon a rashness that might encourage a daring hope. This fellow hinted to me (in his superabundant concern for you) that Mrs Jewkes used you with unkindness. If, on my arrival at the *Hall*, I find this to be so, I will put that woman entirely in your power; you shall, if you please, dismiss her for ever from my service; and Mrs Jervis, or whom else you please, shall attend you in her place.

'Till I have settled two or three points of consequence with Lady Davers, I do not think myself at liberty to explain further my intentions in your favour. But of this you may assure yourself, that I mean to act by you with the utmost honour; for your merit and innocence have very tenderly impressed me. But you must place some confidence in me. I cannot bear to be mistrusted by those to whom I intend kindness.

'I look upon the letter you wrote at my request, to be shewn to your father and mother (who are entirely easy upon it) as one instance of the confidence I wish for. And you shall not, I repeat, have reason to repent it.

'Mrs Jewkes will convey to me your answer. Let it be such as I wish for. And you will inexpressibly oblige

Your true Friend.'

True friend! Wicked man! O my dear parents! what a *true friend* is he, who seeks to gain the confidence of a young creature, his servant, in order to ruin her! I have no doubt of his intent. He may think it doing me honour, and no doubt but he does, by setting me above want, to make me a kept and vile creature! There are those who, perhaps, would think such offers from such a man no dishonour, the more's the pity: but you, my dear parents, have too well instructed me, to permit me to be of that mind. What can there be to settle between Lady Davers and him, that can concern such a poor girl as I am? If there were any thing, could he not trust me with a secret that was to make for my good, if he believed I should think it for my real good? O the artful deluder! My *innocence*, he says, *has very tenderly impressed him*! Yet, to seek to destroy what has engaged him; and so to make me an abandoned wretch! Have I not heard you both talk enough of these subjects, and what false hearts these men have?

I was so much convinced of his baseness by this very letter, that, comparing its contents with the trick he had played me, and with the situation I am in with this bad woman set over me, I became the more impatient in my hopes to find a letter from Mr Williams, that might open a prospect for me to escape the alarming danger.[124]

I took an evening turn, as I called it, in Mrs Jewkes's company; and coming to the place, I stopt, and said, 'Do you think, Mrs Jewkes, any of my beans can have struck[125] since yesterday?' She laughed, and said, 'You are a poor gardener; but I love to see you divert yourself.'

She passing on, I found my good friend had deposited, and slipping it into my bosom (for her back was towards me), 'Here,' said I, drawing her back by the sleeve, having a bean in my hand, 'is one of them; but it has not stirred.' 'No, to be sure,' said she, and turned upon me a most wicked jest,[126] unbecoming a woman's mouth. When I came in, I hurried to my closet, and read as follows:

'I am sorry to tell you, that I have had a repulse from Mrs Jones. She is concerned at your case, she says; but don't care to make herself enemies. I applied to Lady Darnford, and told her, in the most pathetic terms I could think of, your sad story, and shewed her your more pathetic letter. I found her well-disposed; but she would advise with Sir Simon, she said, who, by-the-by, is not a man of a character famous for virtue. She did, in my presence; and he said, "Why, what is all this, my dear, but that our neighbour has a mind to his mother's waiting-maid! And if he takes care she wants for nothing, I don't see any great injury will be done her. He hurts no *family* by this."'

So, my dear father and mother, it seems, that *poor* peoples virtue is to go for nothing.

'"And I think, Mr Williams, you, of all men, should not engage in this affair, against your friend and patron."

'He spoke this in so determined a manner, that it silenced the lady; and I had only to beg no notice should be taken of the matter, as proceeding from *me*.

'I have hinted your case to Mr Peters, the minister of this parish; but I am concerned to say (for he bears an irreproachable character)[127] that he imputed selfish views to me, as if I would make an interest in your affections, by my zeal. And when I represented the duties of our function, and the like, and protested my disinterestedness, he coldly said, I was very good; but was a young man, and knew little of the world. And though it was a thing to be lamented, yet when he and I should set about to reform mankind in this respect, we should have enough upon our hands; since, such attempts, he said, were too common and too fashionable to be decried with success by private clergymen. And then he uttered some reflections upon the conduct of the present fathers of the church, in regard to the first personages of the realm, as a justification of his coldness on this score.

'I represented the different circumstances of your case: that other women lived in a state of guilt *by their own consent*; but to serve you, was to save an innocence that had but few examples. And then I shewed him your letter.

'He said, it was prettily written; and he was sorry for you; and that your good intentions ought to be encouraged. "But what," said he, "would you have *me* to do, Mr Williams?" "Why, suppose, sir." said I, "that, if she can make her escape, you should give her shelter in your house, with your spouse and niece, till she can get to her friends!" "What, and embroil myself with a man of Mr B.'s power and fortune! Not I, I assure you! And I would have you consider what you are about: for Mr B. is a man of strong passions; and by what you have told me, and the letter you have shewed me, seems determined to carry his point. I am sorry," added he, "for the young woman; but see not that our embroiling ourselves for her, with such a man as he is, will do her any service. The case, the more's the pity! is too common. And if she is so pretty, as you say, she might have fallen into worse hands; for he is not an ungenerous man, nor profligately wicked, except in this case: and it is what all young gentlemen will do."

'This is what Mr Peters was pleased to say; and I am greatly concerned for him, I assure you. However, I am not discouraged by this ill success, let what will follow as to myself, if I can serve you.

'I besought Mr Peters to take no notice of my application to him. He promised that he would not: and I am sure I may rely upon his word. He would be glad you were safe, I dare say: but, poor gentleman! he is like too many of us. He wants courage, when a man of power is in the case.[128]

'I do not hear, as yet, that Mr B. is coming. I am glad of your hint relating to that unhappy fellow, John Arnold. Something, perhaps, will strike out from that, which may be useful.

'As to your pacquets, if you seal them up, and lay them in the usual place, (if you find it not suspected) I will watch an opportunity to convey them; but if they are large, you had best be very cautious. This evil woman, I find, mistrusts me.

'I just hear, that the gentleman is dying, whose living Mr B. has promised me. I have almost a scruple to take it, as I am acting so contrary to his desires; but I hope he will one day thank me for it.

'As to money, don't think of it at present. Command all in my power to do for you, without reserve.

'I believe, when we hear he is coming, it will be best to make use of the key, which I shall soon procure you; and I can borrow a horse for you, I believe, to wait within half a mile of the back-door, that opens to the pasture; and will contrive by myself, or by somebody else, to have you conducted to some place of present safety. So don't be discomforted, I beseech you. I am, excellent Mrs Pamela,

Your faithful Friend, &c.'

I made a thousand sad reflections upon the former part of this honest gentleman's kind letter; and, but for the hope he gave me at last, should have given up my case as quite desperate. I then wrote to him, to thank him most gratefully for his kind endeavours. In my letter, I lamented the little concern the gentry he applied to, had shewn for a case so circumstanced; the wickedness of the world, first to give way to such iniquitous fashions, and then plead the frequency of them, in order to excuse themselves from attempting to amend them; and how unaffected people were with the distresses of others. I waved my former hint of writing to Lady Davers; since *that*, I feared, would only serve to harden her brother, and make him come down the sooner, and to be more determined on my ruin; besides, that it might make Mr Williams suspected to be the person by whose means such a letter was conveyed. My lady, I told him, both loved and feared her brother; and it was a doubt whether, if her ladyship *would* interest herself in my behalf, it would have any effect upon him: that, therefore, I would entirely rely upon his assistance in the key and the horse, which he had offered to procure for me. I acquainted him with my master's desire to be permitted, as he called it, to come down: a condescension vastly too great, did he not build upon that my requested permission (could he obtain it) a kind of indirect consent to his vile views. I was fearful, I said, that his coming might be sudden, and therefore thought no time was to be lost: and acquainted him with the abominable trick of this base woman, in borrowing my little money, and refusing to restore it; on the contrary, glorying in her artful wickedness in getting it from me.

I was so closely watched, that I had not opportunity to take a copy of the letter I wrote. But when I had it ready in my bosom, I was easy.

I was guilty of art in my turn; for I told her, that I wanted to have her advice upon the letter of my master to me. She was highly pleased. 'Ay,' said she, 'this is something like, and now we will take a turn in the garden, or where you please.' I pretended it was indifferent to me; but at the same time led into the garden, and began to talk to her of my master's letter; though I did not acquaint her with *all* the contents; mentioning to her only that he wanted my consent to come down, and hoped she used me kindly, and the like. And I said, 'Now, Mrs Jewkes, let me have your advice as to this.' 'Why, then,' said she, 'I will give it you freely: e'en send to him to come down: it will highly oblige him, and I dare say you'll fare the better for it.' 'How the *better*?' said I. 'I dare say, you think yourself, that he intends my ruin.' 'I hate,' said she, 'that foolish word *ruin*! Why ne'er a lady in the land lives happier than you may do, if you will, or be more honourably used.'

'Well, Mrs Jewkes,' said I, 'I shall not at this time dispute with you about the words *ruin* or *honourable*; for I find we have quite different notions of both: but now I will speak plainer than ever I did. Do you think he intends to make proposals to me, as to a kept mistress, or kept slave rather, or do you not?' 'Why, lambkin,' said she, 'what dost thou think, thyself?' 'I fear,' said I, 'he does.' 'Well,' said she, 'but if he does (for I know nothing of the matter, I assure you), you may have your own terms. I see that you may do anything with him.'

I could not bear this to be spoken, though it was what I had long feared; and began to exclaim in passionate terms. 'Nay,' said she, 'he may marry you, as far as I know.' 'No, no,' said I, 'that cannot be. I neither desire nor expect it. His high condition in the world does not permit me to have such a thought. And the whole of his conduct by me shews but too plainly what his base views are; yet you would have me invite him to come down, would you? What, Mrs Jewkes, invite my ruin?'

'Ruin!' said she, and put up her ugly horse-lip:[129] 'It is what *I* would do, in your place; and if it was to be as you *think*, I should rather be out of my pain, than live in continual apprehensions, as you do.' 'An *hour* of innocence,' replied I, 'is worth an *age* of guilt: and were my life to be made ever so miserable by it, I should never forgive myself, if I were not to lengthen out to the longest minute the time of my innocency. Who knows what Providence may do for me?'

'Who knows,' said she, 'as he loves you so well, but you may move him in your favour by your prayers and tears? Prayers and tears you are a good one at, lambkin.' [Was she not an odious wretch? A woman! surely she cannot have the nature of a woman!] 'And for that reason,' continued she, 'I should think you had better let him come down.'

'A *good one at prayers and tears*, Mrs Jewkes! You are a wicked woman' ('Jezebel,' said she) 'thus to make a jest of the calamity of a poor young creature, designed, as perhaps you know, for a sacrifice!'

She only laughed – Ugly creature! She only laughed – You cannot imagine how ugly she is when she laughs. How must she look when she cries?[130]

'I will write to him,' continued I, 'because he expects an answer; else, perhaps, he will make my silence a pretence to come down. How can a letter go?'

'I will take care of that,' said she; 'it is in my instructions.' Ay, thought I, so I suppose, by the hint Mr Williams gave me about the post-house.

The gardener coming by, I said, 'Mr Jacob, I have planted a few beans, and I call the border where I have planted them my garden. It is just by the door, out yonder, I'll shew it you; pray, don't dig them up.' I went on with him; and when we had turned the alley, out of her sight, and were near the place, 'Pray,' said I, 'fetch me a few more beans, or a few pease.' He smiled, I suppose, at my foolishness, but went on, nodding his compliance; and I popped my letter to Mr Williams under the mould, and stepped back, as if waiting for his return. She was not far off. He presently came back with some beans. She followed him; and whispering me, 'I am afraid of some fetch!' said she. 'You don't use to send on such simple errands.' I was frighted. 'My master writes,' proceeded she, 'that I must have all my eyes about me; for though you are as innocent as a dove, yet you are as cunning as a serpent.[131] But I'll forgive you, if you cheat *me*.'

I then thought of my money, and could have called her names, had I dared: and I said, 'Pray, Mrs Jewkes, now you talk of forgiving me if I cheat *you*, be so kind as to pay me my money; for though I have no occasion for it, yet I know you was but in jest, and intended to give it me again.' 'You shall have it in a proper time,' said she; 'but indeed, I was in earnest to get it out of your hands, for fear you should make an ill use of it.'

We cavilled upon this subject as we walked in, and I went up to write my letter to my master; and, as I intended to shew it her, I wrote accordingly as to her part of it; for I made little account of his offer of Mrs Jervis to me, instead of this wicked woman (however agreeable that would have been) nor indeed of anything he said: for were his designs honourable, in the just sense of the word, he needed not to have caused me to be run away with, and confined as I am. Here follows a copy of my letter:

'*Honoured Sir*,
'When I consider how easily you might make me happy, since all I desire is to be permitted to go to my father and mother: when I reflect upon your former proposal to me, in relation to a certain person, not one word of which is now mentioned; and upon my being in so strange a manner run away with, and still kept here a miserable prisoner; do you think, sir, (pardon your poor servant's freedom; my fears make me bold) that your general assurances of honour, can have the effect upon me, that, were it not for these things, all your words ought to have? O sir! I too much apprehend, that *your* notions of honour and *mine* are very different. And I have no other hope but in your continued absence. If you have any proposals to make me, that are consistent with your *honourable* professions, in *my* humble sense of the word, a few lines will communicate them to me, and I will return such an answer as befits me.

'Why, sir, must I be close watched, a wretched prisoner! hindered from stirring out, from speaking to any body, from going so much as to church to pray for you, who have been till of late so generous a benefactor to me; why, sir, I humbly ask, why all this, if you mean honourably? Pardon me, I hope you will; but as ·to *seeing you*, I cannot bear the dreadful apprehension. Whatever you have to propose, whatever you intend by me, let my assent be that of a free person, mean as I am, and not of a slave, who is to be threatened and frightened into a compliance with measures which you yourself, if I may judge by your conduct towards me, think I would naturally abhor. My restraint is indeed hard upon me. I am very uneasy under it. Shorten it, I beseech you, if you would wish me to avoid a rashness worse than that you seem to be apprehensive of. For, let me say, that if I am made desperate, you know not what the wretched Pamela *dare do*, rather than submit to dishonour. I am, sir,

> *Your greatly oppressed*
> *and very unhappy Servant.*'

After I had taken a copy of this, I folded it up; and Mrs Jewkes coming, just as I had done, sat down by me, and said, when she saw me direct it, 'I wish you would tell me if you have taken my advice, and consented to my master's coming down.' 'If it will oblige you,' said I, 'I will read the whole letter to you.' 'That's good,' said she; 'then I'll love you dearly.'

I read it to her, and she praised me much for my wording it; but said, she thought I pushed the matter very close; and it would better bear *talking* of, than *writing* about. She wanted an explanation of what I wrote about the proposal in relation to a *certain person*; but I said, she must take it as she heard it. 'Well, well,' said she, 'I make no doubt you understand each other, and will do so more and more.'

I sealed up the letter, and she undertook to send it away.

SUNDAY

As I now knew it would be in vain to expect leave to go to church, I did not ask for it; and was the less felicitous on this head, because, if I *might* have permission to go, the sight of the neighbouring gentry, who had rejected Mr Williams's proposal in my favour, would have given me great regret and sorrow; and it was impossible I should have edified under any doctrine preached by Mr Peters: so I applied myself to my private devotions.

Mr Williams came yesterday, and this day, as usual, and took my letter; but having no good opportunity, we avoided speaking to each other: but I was concerned I had not the key; for I would not have lost a moment to procure one, had I been *him*, and he *me*. Mrs Jewkes came up, and wanted me sadly to sing her a psalm, as she had often on common days importuned me for a song upon the harpsichord, which I always declined, because of my sad situation; as now I did, on account of my spirits being so low that I could hardly speak, nor cared to be spoken to; but when she was gone, I remembering the cxxxviith psalm to be affecting, turned to it, and took the liberty to alter it somewhat nearer to my case, as follows:

I

When sad I sat in Brandon-hall,[132]
   All guarded round about,
And thought of ev'ry absent friend,
   The tears for grief burst out.

II

My joys and hopes all overthrown,
   My heart-strings almost broke,
Unfit my mind for melody,
   Much more to bear a joke;

III

Then she to whom I pris'ner was,
   Said to me tauntingly,
'Now chear your heart, and sing a song,
   And tune your mind to joy.'

IV

'Alas!' said I, 'how can I frame
   My heavy heart to sing,
Or tune my mind, while thus enthralled
   By such a wicked thing!'

V

But yet, if from my innocence
   I, e'en in thought should slide,
Then let my fingers quite forget
   The harpsichord to guide.

VI

And let my tongue within my mouth
   Be locked for ever fast,
If I rejoice, before I see
   My full deliv'rance past.

VII

And thou, Almighty, recompence
    The evils I endure,
From those who seek my sad disgrace,
    So causeless, to procure.

VIII

Remember, Lord, this Mrs Jewkes,
    When with a mighty sound,
She cries, 'Down with her chastity,
    Down to the very ground!'

IX

E'en so shalt thou, O wicked one,
    At length to shame be brought;
And happy shall all those be called,
    That my deliv'rance wrought.

X

Yea, blessed shall the man be called
    That shames thee of thy evil;
And saves me from thy vile attempts,
    And thee, too, from the d—l.

MONDAY, TUESDAY, *and* WEDNESDAY

I write now with a little more liking, because Mr Williams has got a large parcel of my papers safe, in his hands, to send them to you, as he has opportunity; so I am not quite *uselessly* employed; and I am delivered, besides, from the fear of their being found, if I should be searched. I have been permitted to take an airing five or six miles, with Mrs Jewkes: but, though I know not the reason, she watches me more closely than ever; so that Mr Williams and I have, by consent, discontinued, for these three days, the sun-flower correspondence.

The poor cook-maid has had a sad mischance; for she has been hurt by a vicious bull in the pasture, by the side of the garden, not far from the back-door. Now this pasture I am to cross, which is about half a mile, and then is a common, and near that a private horse-road, where I hope to find an opportunity for escaping, as soon as Mr Williams can get me a horse, and has made all ready for me: for he has got me the key, which he put under the mould, just by the door, as he found an opportunity to hint to me.

He just now has signified, that the gentleman is dead, whose living he has had hope of; and he came pretendedly to tell Mrs Jewkes of it; and so could speak this to her, before me.

She wished him joy. See what the world is? one man's death is another man's joy: thus we thrust out one another! My hard case makes me serious.

He found means to slide a letter into my hands, and is gone away: he looked at me with such respect and solemnness at parting, that Mrs Jewkes said, 'Why, madam, I believe our young parson is half in love with you.' 'In love with me, Mrs Jewkes!' said I; 'Mr Williams knows better.' 'Why,' said she, (I believe to sound me) 'I can't see you can either of you do better; and I have lately been so touched for you, seeing how heavily you apprehend dishonour from my master, that I think it is pity you should not have Mr Williams.'

I knew this must be a fetch of her's, because, instead of being troubled for me, as she pretended, she watched me closer, and him too: I therefore said, 'There is not a man living that I desire to marry. To keep myself honest, and to be a comfort and assistance to my poor parents, is the very top of my ambition.' 'Well, but,' said she, 'I have been thinking very seriously, that Mr Williams would make you a good husband; and as he will owe all his fortune to my master, he will be very glad, to be sure, to be obliged to him for a wife of his chusing: especially such a pretty one, and one so ingenious,[133] and genteelly educated.'

This gave me a doubt, whether she knew of my master's intimation of that sort formerly: I asked her, if she had reason to surmise, that *that* was in view? 'No,' she said; it was only her own thought; but it was very likely, that my master had either that in view, or something better for me. But, if I approved of it, she would propose such a thing to our master directly.

She then gave a detestable hint, that I might take resolutions upon it, of bringing such an affair to effect. I told her, I abhorred her vile insinuation; and as to Mr Williams, I thought him a good civil sort of man; but as, on one side, he was above me; so on the other, I said, of all professions, I should not like a clergyman for my husband. She wondered at that, she said, as I had such a religious turn. 'Why, Mrs Jewkes,' said I, 'my dislike of a clergyman proceeds not from disrespect to the function. Far otherwise.' 'Why, indeed, as you say,' answered she [I did *not* say so], 'there are a great many fooleries among lovers, that would not so well become a starched band and cassock. E'fackins, thou hast well considered of the matter.' And then she *neighed*, as I may say, if neighing be the laugh of a horse. I think I do hate her. Must not, my dear mother, this woman be a bad woman to the very core? She turns every thing into wickedness. She saw I was very angry, by my colouring at her, I suppose; but I said nothing;[134] and finding she could make nothing of me, she changed the discourse.

I will open his letter by-and-by, and give you the contents of it; for she is up and down so much, that I am afraid of her surprising me.

Well, I see that I shall be under no necessity to make advances to Mr Williams, if I were disposed to think of him, as I am sure I am not. This is his letter:

'I am at a loss to express myself, lest I should appear to you to have a selfish view in the service I wish to do you. But I really know but one effectual and honourable way for you to extricate yourself from the dangerous situation you are in. It is that of marriage with some person whom you could make happy in your approbation. As for my own part, an engagement of that kind would be, as things stand, my *apparent* worldly ruin. But yet, so great is my veneration for you, and so entire my reliance on Providence upon so just an occasion, that I should think myself but too happy, if I might be accepted. I would, in this case, forego all my expectations, and be your conductor to some safe distance. But why do I say, *in this case?* That I will do, whether you think fit to reward me so eminently or not. And I will, the moment I hear of Mr B.'s setting out, (and I think now I have settled a very good method of intelligence of all his motions) get a horse ready, and myself to conduct you. I refer myself wholly to your goodness and direction, and am, with the highest respect,

Your most faithful humble Servant.

'Don't think this a sudden resolution. I always admired your character; and the moment I saw you, wished to serve so much excellence.'

What shall I say, my dear father and mother, to this unexpected declaration? I want now, more than ever, your advice. But, after all, I have no mind to marry: I had rather live with you. But yet, I would marry a man who begs from door to door, and has no home nor being, rather than endanger my honesty. Yet I cannot, me-thinks, young as I am, bear the thoughts of being a wife. After a thousand different thoughts, I wrote as follows:

'*Reverend Sir,*

'I am greatly confounded at the contents of your last. You are much too generous, and I cannot bear you should risque all your future prospects for me. Yet I cannot think of your offer without equal concern and gratitude; since nothing but to avoid a ruin, that would be otherwise unavoidable, could induce me, young as I am, to think of a change of condition; and so, sir, you ought not to accept of such an involuntary compliance, as mine would be, were I, upon the *last* necessity, to yield to your very generous proposal. I will rely wholly upon your goodness, in assisting my escape; but shall not, on *your* account principally, *think* of the honour you propose for me, at present; and never, but at the pleasure of my parents, who, low as they are in circumstances, in such a weighty point, are as much intitled to my duty, as if they were ever so rich. I beg you, therefore, sir, not to think of any thing from me, but everlasting gratitude, which will always bind me to be

Your most obliged Servant.'

THURSDAY, FRIDAY, SATURDAY. *the 14th, 15th, and 16th of my Bondage*

Mrs Jewkes has received a letter, and is much civiller to me, and Mr Williams too, than she used to be. I wonder I have not one in answer to mine to my master. I suppose he is angry. I am not the more pleased for her civility; for she is very cunning, and as watch-ful as ever. I laid a trap to get at her instructions, which she carries in the bosom of her stays; but it has not succeeded.

My last letter went safe to Mr Williams, by the old conveyance, so that he is not suspected. He has intimated, that though I have not come so readily as he hoped I would into his scheme, yet his diligence shall not be slackened, and he will leave it to Providence and myself, to dispose of him as he shall be found to deserve. He has signified to me, that he shall soon send a special messenger with the pacquet to you, and I have added to it what has occurred since.

SUNDAY

I am just now quite astonished! I hope all is right! But I have a strange turn to acquaint you with.

Mr Williams and Mrs Jewkes came to me both together; he in ecstasies, she with a strange fluttering sort of air. 'Well,' said she, 'Mrs Pamela, I give you joy! I give you joy! Let nobody speak but me!' Then she sat down, as out of breath, puffing and blowing. 'Every thing,' proceeded she, 'turns as I said it would! Why, there is to be a match between you and Mr Williams! Well, I always thought it. Never was so good a master! Go to, go to, naughty mistrustful Mrs Pamela – Nay, Mrs Williams,' said the forward creature, 'I may as good as call you; you ought on your knees to beg my master's pardon a thousand times for mistrusting him.'

She was going on; and he, poor man! wanted, I saw, to edge in a joyful word; but I said, 'Don't torture me thus, I beseech you, Mrs Jewkes. Let me know all! Ah! Mr Williams,' said I, 'take care, take care!' 'Mistrustful again!' said she; 'why, Mr Williams, shew her your letter; and I will shew her *mine*: they were brought by the same hand.'

I trembled at the thoughts of what this might mean; and said, 'You have so surprised me, that I cannot stand, nor hear, nor read! Why did you come up in such a manner to attack such weak spirits?' 'Shall we, Mrs Jewkes,' said Mr Williams, 'leave our letters with Mrs Pamela, to give her time to recover from her surprize?' 'Ay,' said she, 'with all my heart; here is nothing but flaming honour and good-will!' And so saying, they left me their letters, and withdrew.

My heart was quite sick with the surprize; so that I could not presently read them, notwithstanding my impatience; but after a-while, recovering, I found the contents thus strange and un-expected:

'*Mr* WILLIAMS,

'The death of Mr Fownes has now given me the opportunity I have long wanted, to make you happy, and that in a double respect: for I shall soon put you in possession of his living, and (if you have the art of making yourself well received) of one of the loveliest wives in England. She has not been used (as she has reason to think) according to her merit; but when she finds herself under the protection of a man of virtue and probity, with a competency to maintain her in the handsome manner to which she has been of late years accustomed, I am persuaded she will forgive those seeming hardships which have paved the way to so happy a lot, as I hope it will be to you both. I have only to account for my conduct, and good intentions with regard to her, which I shall do, when I see you: but as I shall soon set out for London, I believe it will be a month first. Mean while, if you can prevail with Pamela, you need not suspend for *that* your mutual happiness; only let me have notice of it first, and that she approves of your addresses; since, in so material an article, she ought entirely to be her own mistress; as I assure you, on the other hand, I would have you be absolutely your own master, that nothing may be wanting to complete your mutual felicity. I am, my old school-fellow,

> *Your Friend.*'

Was ever the like heard! Lie still, my throbbing heart! This is the letter Mrs Jewkes left with me:

'*Mrs* JEWKES,
'You have been very careful and diligent in the task, which, for reasons I shall hereafter explain, I had imposed upon you. Your trouble is now almost at an end; for I have written my intentions to Mr Williams so particularly, that I need say the less here, because he will not scruple, I believe, to let you know the contents of my letter. I have only one thing to mention; it is, that if you find what I have hinted to him will be in the least disagreeable to either, you assure them both, that they are at entire liberty to pursue their own inclinations. I hope you continue your civilities to the mistrustful, uneasy Pamela, who now will begin to think justly of my honour in the discharge of the promise I made to my mother in the girl's favour.

'When I have a few lines from her in acknowledgment of her injurious mistrusts of my honour, and to express her gratitude on this occasion, I shall not scruple to write a letter to her, to assure her, and Mr Williams, of my further intentions for their mutual benefit.

Your Friend, &c.'

I had hardly time to transcribe these letters, though writing so much, I write pretty fast, before they came up again, in high spirits; and Mr Williams said, 'I am glad at my heart, dear Mrs Pamela, that I was *before-hand* in[135] my declarations to you: this generous letter has made me the happiest man on earth; and, Mrs Jewkes, you may be sure, that if I can procure this fair-one's consent, I shall think myself –'

I interrupted the good man (for considering my master's treatment of me before at his other house, my being carried off as I was, and kept a prisoner here, I could not but be upon my guard; this woman too, so very artful and wicked) and said, 'Ah, Mr Williams! take care, take care; don't let –' There I stopped, and Mrs Jewkes said, 'Still mistrustful! I never saw the like in my life! But I see,' said she, 'I was not wrong, whilst my old orders lasted, to be wary of you both. I should have had a hard task to prevent you, I find; for, as the saying is, *Nought can restrain consent of twain.*'[136]

I wondered not at her taking hold of his joyful indiscretion. I took her letter, and said, 'Here, Mrs Jewkes, is your letter. I thank you for letting me see it; but I have been so long in a maze, that I can say nothing of this for the present. Time will bring all to light. Here, sir, is yours: may every thing turn to your happiness! I give you joy of my master's goodness in the living.' 'It will not be a *living*,' replied he, 'without you.' 'Forbear, sir,' said I: 'while I have a father and mother, I am not my own mistress: and I will see myself quite at liberty, before I shall think myself fit to make a choice.'

Mrs Jewkes held up her eyes and hands, and said, 'Such art, such caution, such cunning, for thy years! Well!' 'Why,' said I, (that he might be more on his guard) 'though I hope there cannot be deceit in this, I have been so used to be made a fool of by fortune, that I can hardly tell how to govern myself; and am almost an infidel as to mankind. But, I hope, I may be wrong; henceforth, Mrs Jewkes, I will consult you in every thing,' (*that I think proper*, said I to myself) for to be sure, though I may forgive her, I can never love her.

She left Mr Williams and me, a few minutes, together; and I said, 'Consider, sir, consider what you have done.' ' 'Tis impossible,' said he, 'there can be deceit.' 'I hope so,' replied I; 'but what necessity was there for you to talk of your *former* declaration? Let *this* be as it will, *that* could do no good, especially before this woman. Forgive me, sir; they talk of womens promptness of speech; but, indeed, I see an honest heart is not to be trusted with itself in bad company.'

He was going to reply; but, though her task is said to be ALMOST (I took notice of that word) at an end, she came up to us again; and said, 'Well, I had a good mind to shew you the way to church to-morrow.'

I was glad of this, because, though in my present doubtful situation I should not have chosen it, yet I would have encouraged her proposal, to be able to judge, by her being in earnest or otherwise, whether one might depend upon the rest. But Mr Williams again indiscreetly helped her to an excuse, by saying, that it was now best to defer it *one* Sunday, and till matters were riper; and she readily took hold of it, and confirmed his opinion.

After all, I hope the best; but if this should turn out to be a plot, nothing I fear but a miracle can save me. But sure the heart of man is not capable of such black deceit. Besides, Mr Williams has it under my master's own hand, and he dare not but be in earnest; and then again, his education, and parents example, have neither of them taught him such very black contrivances. So I will hope for the best!

Mr Williams, Mrs Jewkes, and I, have been all three walking together in the garden; and she pulled out her key to the back-door, and opening it, we walked a little way in the pasture. Mr Williams pointed at the sun-flower, as we passed it, but I was forced to be very reserved to him; for the good man has no guard, no caution at all. In the pasture, at a distance, we looked at the bull that hurt the cook-maid, who is got pretty well again. An ugly, surly, grim creature. Mrs Jewkes said, that was not the first mischief he had done. You know, my dear mother, that I was always from childhood afraid of a bull; and you used to tell me, that as cows for their meekness and usefulness were to be likened to good women; so bulls, when fierce and untameable, were to be compared to wicked men: and thence you gave me such cautions and instructions, to avoid such libertine men, as have had a place in my memory ever since.[137]

Mr Williams, Mrs Jewkes, and I, have just supped together; and I cannot yet think but all must be right. Only I am resolved not to marry, nor to give any encouragement to Mr Williams, beyond the civility due to so good a man: at least till I am with you, and have the approbation of you both. So young a girl! I think I should be very forward were I to shew any inclination to be so soon a wife. My reverence for the character is too great to make me hope, that I could, for one while, acquit myself tolerably in the station of a good clergyman's wife; and if I were ever to be so preferred, I hope, by God's grace, not to disgrace the character.[138]

Mr Williams said, *before* Mrs Jewkes, he would send a messenger with a letter to my father and mother. How indiscreet! But I desire you will give no answer, till I have the happiness of seeing you; which now I hope for soon.

He will, in my pacquet, send you a most tedious parcel of stuff, of my *oppressions*, my *distresses*, my *fears*. I will send this with it (for Mrs Jewkes gives me leave to write to my father, which looks well); and I am glad I can conclude, after all my sufferings, with my *hopes*, to be soon with you, which I know will give you comfort. And so, begging the continuance of your prayers and blessings, I subscribe myself

Your ever dutiful Daughter.

I have so much time upon my hands, that I must write on to employ myself. The Sunday evening, where I left off, Mrs Jewkes asked me, if I chose to lie by myself? I said, Yes, with all my heart, if she pleased. 'Well,' said she, 'after to-night you shall.'

I asked her for more paper; and she gave me a little phial of ink, eight sheets of paper, which she said was all her store, (for now she would get me to write for her to our master, if she had occasion) and six pens, with a piece of sealing-wax. This also looks mighty well!

She pressed me very much, when she came to-bed, to give encouragement to Mr Williams, and said many things in his behalf; and blamed my shyness to him. I told her, I was resolved to give no encouragement, till I had talked to my father and mother. She said, she fancied I thought of somebody else, or I could never be so insensible. I assured her, as I could do very safely, that there was not a man on earth I wished to have; and as to Mr Williams, he might do better by far; and I had proposed so much happiness in living with my poor father and mother, that I could not think of any scheme of life with pleasure, till I had tried that.

I asked her just now for my money; and she said it was above, in her strong box, but that I shall have it to-morrow. All these things continue to look well.

Mr Williams would go home this night, though late, because he would dispatch a messenger to you with a letter he had proposed from himself, and with my pacquet. But again I say, pray don't encourage him; for he is much too heady and precipitate as to this matter, in my way of thinking; though to be sure, he is a very good man, and I am much obliged to him.

MONDAY *Morning*

Alas! Alas! we have bad news from poor Mr Williams. He has had a sad mischance; fallen among rogues in his way home last night; but by good chance has saved my papers. This is the account he gives of it.

'*Good Mrs Jewkes*,

'I have had a sore misfortune in going from you. When I had got as near the town as the dam, and was going to cross the wooden bridge, two fellows got hold of me, and swore bitterly they would kill me, if I did not give them what I had. They rummaged my pockets, and took from me my snuff-box, my seal-ring,[139] my corkscrew, and half a guinea, and some silver, and halfpence; also my handkerchief, and two or three letters I had in my pocket. By good fortune the letter Mrs Pamela gave me was in my bosom, and so that escaped; but they bruised my head and face, and cursing me for having no more money, tipped me into the dam, crying, "Lie there, parson, till to-morrow!" My shins and knees were bruised much in the fall against one of the stumps; and I had like to have been suffocated in water and mud. To be sure, I shall not be able to stir out this day or two: for I am a fearful spectacle! My hat and wig I was forced to leave behind me, and go home a mile and a half without; but they were found next morning, and brought me with my snuff-box, which the rogues must have dropped. My cassock is sadly torn, as is my band. You need not question, but that I was much frightened; for a robbery in these parts has not been known of many years. Diligent search is making after the rogues. My kindest respects to good Mrs Pamela. If *she* pities my misfortunes, I shall be the sooner well, and fit to wait on her and you. This did not hinder me writing a letter, though with great pain, as I do this; [*To be sure, this good man can keep no secret!*] and sending it away by a man and horse, this morning. I am, good Mrs Jewkes,

Your most obliged humble Servant.

'Heaven be praised, it is no worse! I find I have got no cold, though miserably wet from head to foot. My fright, I believe, prevented me from catching cold; for I was not rightly myself for some hours, and know not how I got home. I will write a letter of thanks this night, if I am able, to my kind patron, for his inestimable goodness to me. I wish I was enabled to say all I hope, with regard to the *better part* of his bounty to me, incomparable Mrs Pamela.'

The brute laughed, when she had read this letter, till her fat sides shook. 'I can but think,' said she, 'how the poor parson looked, after parting with his pretty mistress in such high spirits, when he found himself at the bottom of the dam! And what a figure he must cut in his tattered band and cassock, and without hat and wig! I warrant,' added she, 'he was in a sweet pickle[140] when he got home.' I said, I thought it was very barbarous to laugh at such a misfortune. But she replied, As he was safe, she laughed; otherwise she should have been sorry: and she was glad to see me so much concerned for him. It looked *promising*, she said.

I heeded not her reflection; but as I have been used to causes for mistrusts, I cannot help saying, that I don't like this thing: and their taking his letters most alarms me. How happy it was, they missed my pacquet! I know not what to think of it! But why should I let every accident break my peace? Yet it *will* do so, while I stay here.

Mrs Jewkes is very earnest with me, to go with her in the chariot, to visit Mr Williams. She is so officious to bring on the affair between us, that being a cunning, artful woman, I know not what to make of it. I have refused her absolutely, urging, that except I intended to encourage his suit, I ought not to do it. And she is gone without me.

I have strange temptations to get away in her absence, notwith-standing all these fine appearances. 'Tis sad to have nobody to advise with! I know not what to do. But, alas for me! I have no money, if I should get away, to buy any body's civilities, or to pay for necessaries or lodging. But I will go into the garden, and resolve afterwards.

I have been in the garden, and to the back-door: and there I stood, my heart up at my mouth.[141] I could not see I was watched: so this looks well. But now, if any thing should happen amiss; if my master should come down, and use me ill, I should never forgive myself for losing such an opportunity as this. Well, I will go down again, and see if all is clear, and how it looks out at the back-door in the pasture.

I have been down again, and ventured to open the door, and went out about a bow-shot into the pasture; but there stood that horrid bull, staring me full in the face, with fiery saucer eyes,[142] as my antipathy to the creature made me think; and especially as the poor cook-maid's misfortune came strongly into my mind. So I got in again for fear he should come at me. And here again I am at my pen. Nobody saw me, however.

Do you think there are such things as witches and spirits? If there be, I believe in my heart, Mrs Jewkes has got this bull on her side. But yet, what could I do without money or a friend? O this wicked woman, to trick me so! Then I know not one step of the way, nor how far to any house or cottage; or whether I could obtain protection if I got to a house: and now the robbers are abroad too, I may run into dangers as great as those I want to escape from; nay, much greater, if the present not unpromising appearances hold: and sure my master cannot be so black a creature, as that they should not! What can I do? I have a good mind to try for it once more; but then I may be pursued and taken; and it will be worse for me; and this wicked woman perhaps will again beat me, take my shoes away, and lock me up.

But after all, if my master should mean *well*, he cannot be angry at my fears, were I to get away; and nobody can blame me; and I can more easily be induced, when I am with you, and when all my apprehensions are over, to consider his proposal of Mr Williams for me, than I could do here; and he pretends, as you have read in his letter, he will leave me to my choice: why then should I be afraid? I will go down again, I think! Direct me, O Thou who art the preserver of the innocent! direct me what to do!

I went down resolved to get away, if possible; but the gardener was at work in sight of the door. I loitered about, in hopes he would leave that quarter: but he continued digging there. So I came up again. Fool that I was! could I not have thought of some errand to send him out of the way? As I continue writing here, when I ought to act, that will shew you my strange irresolution, and how I am distressed between my hopes and my fears![143] But I will go down again, and contrive to send this busy gardener with a message, that will keep Mrs Jewkes still longer with Mr Williams, in hopes of my fetching her home, with the maid Nan to bear me company. What a contriver is your Pamela become! *Necessity is truly said to be the mother of invention.*

Well, here I am, come back again! frighted, like a fool, out of all my purposes! The gardener was in another part of the garden, far enough from the back-door; and I had unlocked it, and actually got a good way over the pasture; when I looked, and saw the horrid bull, as I thought, making to get between me and the door, and another bull coming towards me the other way. Well, thought I, here seems to be the spirit of my master in one bull, and Mrs Jewkes's in the other; and now I am gone for certain! 'O help!' cried I, like a fool, nobody near me! and ran back to the door as swift as if I flew. When I had got the door in my hand, I ventured to look back, to see if these supposed bulls were coming; and I saw they were only two poor cows, grazing in distant places, that my fears had made so terrible to me.

But as every thing is so frightful to me, and as things have not so black an appearance as they had at first, I will not think of escaping: and, indeed, if I were to attempt it, and were to have got at distance from this house, I should too probably be as much terrified at the first strange man that I met with. I have heard it said, *That there can be no prudence without apprehension*:[144] but I am persuaded, that fear brings one into more dangers, than the caution, that goes along with it, delivers one from.

I then locked the door, and put the key in my pocket; and was but just come from the door, when the maid Nan appeared in sight, and made my escape impossible, if I would have attempted it.

Do I not appear to you, my dear parents, to be weaker even than a child, to be thus terrified by the bull and the robbers? But had I had my money, I should have had more courage, as that would have probably made me a protecting friend, till I had got to you. But this, however, I think, that had I supposed my case as desperate as I lately thought it, I dare say that I should have reasoned myself into courage enough to venture not only the bull, but the robbers.

MONDAY *Afternoon*

Mrs Jewkes is returned from her visit. 'I would have you set your heart at rest,' said she to me; 'for Mr Williams will do very well again. He is not half so bad as he fancied. O these scholars! they have not the hearts of mice! He has only a few scratches on his face; which I suppose he got by grabbling[145] among the gravel, at the bottom of the dam, to try to find a hole in the ground, to hide himself from the robbers. His shin and his knee are hardly to be seen to ail any thing. He says in his letter, he was a frightful spectacle: he might be so when he first came in-a-doors; but, only for a few groans when he thinks of his danger, or tells his story, I see nothing is the matter with him. So, Mrs Pamela, I would have you be very easy about it.'

'I am glad of it,' said I, 'for all your jokes, Mrs Jewkes.'

'Well,' continued she, 'he talks of nothing but you; and when I told him, I would fain have persuaded you to come with me, the man was out of his wits with his gratitude to me: and so has laid open all his heart to me, and told me all that has passed, and all that was contrived between you two.'

This alarmed me prodigiously; and the more, as I had seen, in two or three instances, that his honest heart could keep nothing, believing every one as undesigning as himself.

'Ah! Mrs Jewkes, Mrs Jewkes,' said I, 'this might have done, had he had any thing that he could have told you of. But you know well enough, that had we been disposed to hold the most innocent conversation with each other, we had no opportunity for it.'

'No,' said she, 'that's very true, Mrs Pamela; not so much *as for that declaration*, that he owned before me he had found opportunity to make you. Come, come, no more of these shams with me! Perhaps I am as cunning as you. However,' added she, 'all is well now; because my *watchments* are now over, by my master's direction. How have you employed yourself in my absence?'

I could not conceal my apprehensions of what might have passed between Mr Williams and her; and she said, 'Well, Mrs Pamela, since all matters are likely to be so soon and so happily ended, let me advise you to be a little less concerned at his discoveries: and make *me* your confident, as *he* has done, and I shall think you have some favour for me, and reliance upon me, and perhaps you will not repent it.'

She was so earnest, that I mistrusted that her kindness to Mr Williams in her visit to him was only to get out of him what she could. 'Why, Mrs Jewkes,' said I, 'is all this fishing about for something, where there is nothing, if there be an end of your *watchments,*[146] as you call them?'

'Nothing,' said she, 'but womanish curiosity, I assure you; for one is naturally led to find out matters, where there is such privacy affected.'

'Let me know, Mrs Jewkes, what he has told you; and then I'll give an answer to your curiosity.'

'I don't care,' said she, 'whether you do or not; for I have as much as I wanted from him; and I despair of getting out of you, my little dear, any thing you have not a mind I should know.'

'Well,' said I, 'let him have said what he will, I care not: for I am sure he can say no harm of me; and so let us change the talk.'

I was the easier, indeed, because she gave me no hint of the key and the door, which she would have done, had he told her every thing. And so she gave up me, and I her, as despairing to gain our ends of each other.

But I am sure he must have said more than he should. And I am the more apprehensive, because she has now been actually, these two hours, writing; though she pretended she had given me up all her stores of paper, and that I should write for her.

I begin to wish I had ventured every thing, and gone off when I might. To what evils does a cowardly heart expose one! O when will this state of doubt and uneasiness end!

She has just been with me, and says she shall send a messenger to Bedfordshire; and he shall carry a letter of thanks for me, if I will write it, for my master's favour to me. 'I have no thanks to give,' said I, 'till I am with my father and mother: and, besides, I sent a letter, as you know, but have had no answer to it.' She said, she thought her master's letter to Mr Williams was sufficient; and the least I could do, was to thank him, if but in two lines. 'No need of that,' replied I; 'for I don't intend to have Mr Williams: what then is that letter to me?' 'Well,' said she, 'I see thou art quite unfathomable!'

I don't like all this. O my foolish fears of bulls and robbers! for now all my uneasiness begins to double upon me. What can this uncautious man have said! What she has got out of him, is, no doubt, the subject of her long letter.

She is now mighty silent and reserved, to what she was, and says nothing but No, or Yes, to what I ask. Something must be hatching, I doubt! the rather, as she does not keep her word about my lying by myself, and restoring my money; to both which points she returned suspicious answers, saying, as to the one, 'Why, you are mighty earnest for your money! I shan't run away with it': and to the other, 'Goodlack! you need not be so willing to part with me for a bed-fellow, till you are sure of one you *like better*.' This cut me to the heart, and at the same time stopped my mouth.

TUESDAY, WEDNESDAY

Mr Williams has been here; but we have had no opportunity to talk together: he seemed confounded at Mrs Jewkes's change of temper and reservedness, after her kind visit; and much more at what I am going to tell you.

He asked, if I would take a turn in the garden with Mrs Jewkes and him. 'No,' said she, 'I can't go.' 'May not Mrs Pamela,' said he, 'take a walk?' 'No,' replied she, 'I desire she won't.' 'Why, Mrs Jewkes?' said he; 'I am afraid I have somehow disobliged you.' 'Not at all,' answered she; 'but I suppose you will soon be at liberty to walk together as much as you will: and I have sent a messenger for my last instructions, about *this* and *more* weighty matters; and when they come, I shall leave you to do as you think fit; but till then, it is no matter how little you are together.'

This alarmed us both; and he put on, as I thought, a self-accusing countenance. So I went behind her back, and held my two hands together, flat, with a bit of paper I had, between them, and looked at him. He seemed to take me, as I intended, intimating the renewing of the correspondence by the tiles.

I left them together, and retired to my closet, to write a letter for the tiles; but having no time for a copy, I will give you the substance only.

I expostulated with him in it on his too great openness and easiness to fall into Mrs Jewkes's snares; told him my apprehensions; and gave briefly the reasons for my fears; I desired to know what he had told her; and intimated, that I thought there was the highest reason to resume our project of escaping by the back-door.

I put this in the usual place, in the evening, and now wait with impatience for an answer.

THURSDAY

I have the following answer:

'*Dear Mrs Pamela*,
'I am utterly confounded, and must plead guilty to all your just reproaches. I wish I were master of but half your discretion. I hope, after all, this is only a touch of this ill-woman's temper, to shew her power and importance: for I think Mr B. neither can nor dare deceive me in so black a manner. I would expose him all the world over, if he did. But it *is not*, *cannot* be in him. I have received a letter from John Arnold, in which he tells me, that his master is preparing for his London journey; and believes, he will come into these parts afterwards: but he says, Lady Davers is at their house, and is to accompany her brother to London, or meet him there, he knows not which. John professes great zeal to serve you: and I find he refers to a letter he sent me before, but which is not come to my hand. I *think* there can be no treachery; for it is a particular friend at Gainsborough[147] to whom I have ordered him to direct; and this letter of John's is come safe to my hands by this conveyance; for well I know, I durst trust nothing to Brett, at the post-house here. I own I am in a little pain, at present; for I was, indeed, too open with Mrs Jewkes; led to it by her dissimulation, and by her warm wishes to make me happy with you. I hinted, that I would not have scrupled to have procured your deliverance by any means: and that I had proposed to you, as the only honourable one, marriage with

me. But I assured her, though she would hardly believe me, that you discouraged my application. Which is too true! But not a word did I mention to her of the back-door, or key.

'But don't be too much concerned. I hope all will end well: we shall soon hear, whether it will be necessary to resume our former scheme. If it be, I will lose no time to provide a horse for you, and another for myself; for I can never do either God or myself better service, though I were to forego all my expectations for it in this world. I am

Your most faithful humble Servant.'

Mrs Jewkes continues still sullen and ill-natured, and I am almost afraid to speak to her. She watches me as close as ever, and pretends to wonder why I shun her company as I do.

I have just put under the tiles this earnest letter:

'*Reverend Sir,*
'Every thing gives me additional disturbance. The miscarried letter of John Arnold makes me suspect a trick. Yet am I loth to think myself of so much importance, as to suppose every one in a plot against me. Are you sure, however, that the London journey is not to be a Lincolnshire one? May not John, who has been once a traitor, be so again? Why *need* I be thus in doubt? If I could have the hoped for horse, I would, rather than live thus in terror, throw the reins on his neck, and trust to Providence as my only safeguard. I am loth to think of embroiling you; now just upon the edge of your preferment. Yet, sir, I fear your fatal openness will make you suspected as an accessary to my escape, were I to be able to effect it, even without you.

'Were my *life* in question, instead of my *virtue*, I would not wish to involve any body in the least difficulty for so worthless a poor creature. But, O sir! my *soul* is of equal importance with the soul of a princess, though in quality I am but upon a foot with the meanest slave.

'Save thou, my innocence, good Heaven! and happy shall I be, although an early death were to be my lot; since that would put an end to all my troubles.

'Forgive my impatience: but my presaging mind bodes horrid mischiefs! Every thing looks dark around me; and this woman's impenetrable sullenness and silence, (without any apparent reason for either) from a behaviour of a sudden so very *contrary*, bid me fear the worst. Blame me, sir, if you think me wrong; and let me have your advice what can be done by

Your most afflicted Servant.'

FRIDAY

I have received this half-angry answer from Mr Williams; but what is dearer to me than all other letters in the world could be, was yours, my dear father, inclosed in his.*

* The following is a copy of her father's letter:

' *My dearest Daughter*,
'Our prayers are at length heard, and we are overwhelmed with joy. O what sufferings, what trials have you gone through! Blessed be the Divine Goodness, which has enabled you to withstand so many temptations! We have not yet had leisure to read through in course[148] your long accounts of all your hardships. I say *long*, because I wonder how you could find time and opportunity for them; but otherwise, they are the delight of our spare hours; and we shall read them over and over, as long as we live, with thankfulness to God, who has given us so virtuous and so discreet a daughter. How happy is our lot, in the midst of our poverty! O let none ever think children a burden to them; when the poorest circumstances can produce so much riches in a *Pamela*! Persist, my dear daughter, in the same excellent course; and we shall not envy the highest estate, but defy the great world to produce such a daughter as ours.

'I said, we had not read through all yours in course. We were too impatient, and so turned to the end; where we find your virtue within view of its reward, and your master's heart turned to see the folly of his ways, and the injury he had intended to our dear child. For, to be sure, my dear, he *would* have ruined you, if he could. But seeing your virtue, his heart is touched, and he has, no doubt, been awakened by the Divine Goodness, rewarding your prudence.

'We don't see, that you can do any way so well, as to come into the present proposal, and make Mr Williams, the worthy Mr Williams! (God bless him) happy. And though we are poor, and can add no merit, no fortune to our dear child, but rather must be a disgrace to her, as the world will think; yet I hope I do not sin in my pride, to say, that there is no good man, of a common degree, (especially as your late lady's kindness gave you such good opportunities, which you have had the grace to improve) but may think himself happy in you. But, since you say you had rather *not* marry at present, far be it from us to advise you to act against your inclinations! So much prudence as you have shewn in all your conduct, would make it very wrong in us to mistrust it in this, or to offer to direct you in your choice. But, alas! my child, what can *we* do for you: To involve you in our difficulties, and make you a partaker in

'*Madam*,

'I think you are too apprehensive by much. I am sorry for your uneasiness. You may depend upon me, and all I can do. But I make no doubt of the journey being really intended to London, nor of John's contrition and fidelity. I have just received, from my *Gainsborough* friend, this letter, as I suppose, from your father, in a cover, directed for me, as I had desired. I hope it contains nothing to add to your uneasiness. Pray, dearest Mrs Pamela, lay aside your fears, and wait a few days for the issue of Mrs Jewkes's letter, and mine of thanks to Mr B. Things, I hope, *must* be better than what you expect. Providence will not desert such piety and innocence; and be this your comfort and reliance: which is the best advice that can at present be given by

Your most faithful humble Servant.'

The above is Mr Williams's sharp letter. But, O my dear father, what inexpressible comfort has your letter given me! You ask, *What* can you do for me? What is it you *cannot do* for your child! You can give her the advice she *has so much* wanted, and *still* wants. and will *always* want: you can confirm her in the paths of virtue, into which you first conducted her; and you can pray for her, with hearts more pure, than are to be met with in palaces! Oh! how I long to throw myself at the feet of you both, and receive from your lips, the blessings of such good parents! But, alas! how are my prospects again overclouded to what they were when I closed my last parcel! More trials, more dangers, I fear, must your poor Pamela have to struggle with: but through the Divine Goodness, and your prayers, I hope, at last, to get well out of all my difficulties, and the rather, as they proceed not from my own vanity and presumption!

---

our poverty, after you have lived in such plenty, would but *add* to our afflictions. But it will be time enough to talk of these things, when we have the pleasure you now put us in hope of, of seeing you with us; which God grant. *Amen, Amen,* say

Your most indulgent Parents, Amen.

'Our humblest service and thanks to the worthy Mr Williams. Again, we say, God bless him for ever!

'O what a deal we have to say to you! God give us a happy meeting! We understand the 'squire is setting out for London. He is a fine gentleman. I wish he was as good. But I hope he will now reform.'

But I will proceed with my hopeless story.

I saw Mr Williams was a little nettled at my impatience; and so I wrote to assure him I would be as easy as I could, and wholly directed by him; especially as my father, whose respects to him I mentioned, had assured me, my master was setting out for London, which he must have some-how from his own family, or he would not have written me word of it.

SATURDAY, SUNDAY

Mr Williams has been here both these days, as usual; but is still very indifferently treated by Mrs Jewkes. To avoid suspicion, I left them together, and went up to my closet, and staid there most of the time he was here. He and she, I found by her, had a quarrel. At going away, he told her, he would very little trouble the house, till he had an answer to his letter, from Mr B. 'The less, the better,' she answered. I thought it best to be silent, when she told me this.

I am satisfied there is mischief brewing, and shall begin to hide my papers, and be more and more circumspect.

MONDAY, TUESDAY, *the 25th and 26th Days of my heavy Restraint*

I have still stranger things to write than I had before. A messenger is returned, and now (O wretched; wretched Pamela! what at last will become of me!) all is out! The messenger brought two letters, one to Mrs Jewkes, and one to me: but, as the greatest wits may be sometimes mistaken, they being folded and sealed alike, that for *me*, was directed to Mrs Jewkes; and that for *her*, was directed to me. But the contents of both are equally dreadful and abominable.

She brought me up that directed for me, and said, 'Here's a letter for you. I will ask the messenger a few questions, and then I will read that which is brought me with it.'

She went down, and I broke open in my closet that she gave me, and found it directed, *To Mrs* PAMELA ANDREWS. But when I opened it, it began, Mrs Jewkes. I was quite confounded; but, thought I, this may be a lucky mistake; I may discover something. And so I read on these horrid contents:

'*Mrs* JEWKES,

'What you write has given me no small disturbance. For a girl, distinguished by me, to be so ready to run away with a fellow, and that upon so short an acquaintance, in order to avoid me; and at a time when I had given her the strongest assurances of my honour, is what I cannot bear to think of. Ungrateful creature! But I reserve the *fool's plaything*[149] for my future vengeance; and I charge you to double your diligence, that she may not escape it.

'I send this by an honest Swiss, who attended me in my travels; a man I can trust; and let him be your assistant: for the *artful creature*, by her seeming innocence and simplicity, may have got a party, perhaps, among my few servants with you, as she has here. Even John Arnold, whom I confided in, and favoured more than any other of my fellows, has proved an execrable villain; and shall meet his due reward for it.

'As to that *college novice*, Williams, I need not bid you take care he see not this *forward creature*; for I have ordered Mr Shorter, my attorney, to throw him instantly into gaol,[150] for money he has had of me, which I had intended never to carry to account against him.

'Holy hypocrite! How knew he that I designed dishonour to the *painted gewgaw*?[151] Had he been governed by no worse motives than those of compassion for a young creature whom he had thought innocent and in danger, ought he not, as his function and my favour for him would have warranted, to have expostulated with me? But he was not content to enter into an intrigue with the *saucy designer*, to supplant me his patron and best friend: he has exposed me by an application in her behalf, to the whole family of Sir Simon Darnford, to receive and protect against me, this *plotting little villain of a girl*, when he had got her away from my house. Of this Sir Simon has informed me. Disgraceful application! Officious and base intermeddler! It is easy to guess at his vile motives: more impure, more sensual than those of him, whom he wanted to rob of the *fair idiot*. Yet, ungrateful wretch! to expect preferment from me! Well does he deserve that ruin, that utter ruin, which awaits so black, so odious a treachery!

'Colbrand, my trusty Swiss, will obey you without reserve, if you cannot confide in my other servants with you.

'As for the girl's denying, that she encouraged his declaration, I believe it not. 'Tis certain the *speaking picture*,[152] with all that pretended innocence and bashfulness, would have run away with him. I now hate her perfectly; and though I will do nothing to her *myself*, yet I can bear, for the sake of my revenge, and my *injured honour*, and *slighted offers*, to see any thing, even what *she most fears*, be *done to her*; and then she may be turned loose to her evil destiny, and echo to the woods and groves her piteous lamentations for the loss of her fantastic innocence, which the romantic idiot pretends to value herself upon.

'I shall go to London with my sister Davers; and the moment I can disengage myself, which may be in three weeks from this time, I will be with you, and decide *her fate*. Mean time, be doubly careful; for this innocent, as I have warned you, is full of contrivances. I am, &c.'

I had but just read this dreadful letter through, when Mrs Jewkes came up, in a great fright, guessing at the mistake, and that I had her letter; and she found me with it open in my hand, just ready to faint.

'What business,' said she, 'had you to read my letter?' and snatched it from me. 'You see,' said she, looking upon it, 'it begins Mrs Jewkes at top: you ought, in manners, to have read no further.' 'Add not,' said I, 'to my afflictions! I shall soon be out of all your ways! This is too much! too much! I never can support this.' And threw myself upon the couch in my closet, and wept bitterly.

She went out, and when she had read the letter, came in again: 'Why this,' said she, 'is a sad letter indeed. I am sorry for it: but I feared you would carry your niceties too far.' 'Leave me, leave me, Mrs Jewkes,' said I, 'for a-while: I cannot talk!' 'Poor heart!' said she; 'well, I'll come up again presently, and hope to find you better. But here, take your own letter: I wish you well; but this is a sad mistake!' And so she put down by me that which was intended for me. But I had no spirit to read it at that time. O man! man! hard-hearted cruel man! what mischiefs art thou not capable of!

I sat ruminating, when I had a little come to myself, upon the contents of this wicked letter; and had no inclination to look into my own. The bad names, *fool's plaything, artful and forward creature, painted gewgaw, villain of a girl, speaking picture, romantic idiot,* are hard words for your poor Pamela! and I began to think, whether I was not indeed a very naughty body, and had not done vile things:

but when I thought of his having discovered poor John, and of Sir Simon's mean officiousness, in telling him of Mr Williams, together with what he had resolved against him, in revenge for his goodness to me, I was quite dispirited; and yet still more, about that horrible Colbrand, and what he could *see done to me*; for then I was ready to gasp for breath, and my heart quite failed me. Then how dreadful are the words, that he will *decide my fate* in three weeks! Gracious heaven, said I, strike me dead, before that time, with a thunderbolt, or provide some way for my escaping these threatened mischiefs!

At last, I took up the letter directed for Mrs Jewkes, but designed for me; and I found *that* little better than the other. These are the hard words it contains:

'Well have you done, perverse, forward, artful, yet foolish Pamela, to convince me, before it was too late, of my weakness in believing you to be a mirror of bashful modesty, and unspotted innocence. Specious hypocrite! Mean-spirited girl! It was *degree*, not *man*, that gave you apprehension. You could not repose the least confidence in one whom you had known for years, and who, under my good mother's misplaced favour for you, in a manner had grown up with you; but you could enter into an intrigue, and even lay plots to run away with a man you never knew, till within these few days past. Mean-spirited, ungrateful, forward, and low girl, as I *think* you, I must repeatedly *call* you!

'What though I had excited your fears, in sending you one way, when you hoped to go another; yet, had I not engaged, in order to convince you of my resolution to do honourably by you, not to come near you without your own consent? Yet how have you requited me? The very first fellow that came in your way, you have practised upon, corrupted too, and thrown your *forward* self upon him; after having by your insinuating arts, and bewitching face, induced him to break through all the ties of honour and gratitude to me; and that at a time when the happiness of his future life depended upon my favour.

'As, therefore, you would place no confidence in me, my honour owes you nothing; and in a little time you shall find how much you have erred in treating, as you have done, a man, who was once

Your affectionate and kind Friend.'

What cruel reproaches! *Mean-spirited*, and *low*, and *forward*: if I am *low*, I am not *mean-spirited*. I wish I could not say, It is he that, *high* as he thinks himself, is *mean-spirited*. It is *degree*, not *man*, he says, that gives me apprehension. What can he mean by it? A *mirror of bashful modesty and unspotted innocence, he thought me!* What business has he to think of me at all? And so, because he thought me modest and innocent, he must seek to make me impudent and guilty.

His dear mother, my good lady, did not, and would not to this day, have thought her favours *misplaced*, I dare say: but I know what she would have thought of him, for such vile doings to her poor servant-girl.

In a manner grown up with me! What an abasement does wickedness make pride submit to! *Brought up with him!* How can he say so! Was he not abroad for some time? And when, of late, at home, how has he eyed me with scorn sometimes! How has the *mean* girl been ready to tremble under his disdainful eye! How have I fought for excuses to get from my lady, when he came to visit her in her apartment, though bid to stay, perhaps! *Brought up with him!* I say – *Brought up with him!* He may as well say, The poor frighted pigeon brought up with the hawk! He has an eye like a hawk's, I am sure! and a heart, I verily think, as cruel! *Mean-spirited!* he says not true when he calls me *mean-spirited*. *Forward* he shall not find me. *Ungrateful!* I should abhor myself if I were capable of *ingratitude. Low!* what a poor reproach is that from a gentleman! But if I am *low*, I am *honest*; so am in this better than those who are high and dishonest. *What though he had excited my fears!* What business had he to excite my fears? What business had he to *send me one way*, to his wicked house, and vile woman, *when I hoped to go another*, to *you*, my dear, worthy parents! *The very first fellow!* I scorn his reflection! He is mistaken in your Pamela. You know what I writ about Mr Williams; and if you, and my mother, and my own heart acquit me, what care I? – I had almost said. But these are after reflections. At the reading of his letter, I was quite broken-hearted.[153]

Alas for me! said I to myself, what a fate is mine, to be thus thought artful, and forward, and ungrateful! when all I intended was to preserve my innocence; and when all the poor little shifts, which his superior wicked wit and cunning have rendered ineffectual, were forced upon me in my own necessary defence!

When Mrs Jewkes came up to me again, she found me bathed in tears. She seemed, as I thought, to be moved to some compassion; and finding myself now entirely in her power, and that it is not for me to provoke her, I said, 'It is now, I see, in vain for me to contend against my evil destiny, and the superior arts of my barbarous master. I will resign myself to Providence; that, I hope, will still protect me. But you see how this poor Mr Williams is drawn in and undone; I am sorry I am made the cause of *his* ruin: poor, poor man! to be thus involved, and for my sake too! But, if you'll believe me,' said I, 'I gave no encouragement to what he proposed, as to marriage; nor would he have proposed it, I believe, but as the only honourable way he thought left to save me: and his principal motive to it all, was virtue and compassion to one in distress. What other view could he have? You know I am poor and friendless. All I beg of you is, to let the worthy gentleman have notice of my master's resentment; and let him fly the country, and not be thrown into gaol: this will answer my master's end as well; for it will as effectually hinder him from assisting me, as if he were in a prison.'

'Ask me,' said she, 'to do any thing that is in my power, consistent with my duty and trust, and I will do it; for I am sorry for you both. But, to be sure, I shall keep no correspondence with him, nor allow you to do it.'

I offered to talk of a duty superior to that she mentioned, which would oblige her to help distressed innocence, and not permit her to go the lengths enjoined by lawless tyranny; but she plainly bid me be silent on that head; for it was in vain to attempt to persuade her to betray her trust. 'All I have to advise you,' said she, 'is to be easy; lay aside all your contrivances and arts to get away, and make me your friend, by giving me no reason to suspect you; for I glory in my fidelity to my master: and you have both practised some strange sly arts, to make such a progress as he has owned there was between you, so seldom as, I thought, you saw one another; and I must be more circumspect than I have been.'

This doubled my concern; for I now apprehended I should be much closer watched than before.

'Well,' said I, 'since I have, by this strange accident, made such a discovery, let me read over again that horrid letter of yours, that I may get it by heart, and with it feed my distress, and make calamity familiar to me.' 'Then,' said she, 'let me read yours again.' I gave her mine, and she lent me hers; and so I took a copy of it, with her leave; because, as I said, I would by it prepare myself for the worst. And when I had done, I pinned it on the head of the couch. 'This,' said I, 'is the use I shall make of this wretched copy of your letter; and here you shall always find it wet with my tears.'

She said, She would go down to order supper, and insisted upon my company, when it was ready: I would have excused myself; but she putting on a commanding air, I was forced to submit. The moment I went down, she took my hand, and presented me to the most hideous monster I ever saw in my life. 'Here, Monsieur Colbrand,' said she, 'here is *your* pretty ward, and *mine*; let us try to make her time with us easy.' He bowed, and put on his foreign grimaces, and seemed to bless himself! and, in broken English, told me, I was happy in de affections of de vinest gentleman in de varld! I was quite terrified. I will describe him to you, my dear father and mother, if now you will ever see this; and you shall judge if I had not reason, especially as I knew not that he was to be at supper.

He is a giant of a man, for stature; taller, by a good deal, than Harry Mawlidge, in your neighbourhood, and large-boned, and scraggy; and has a hand – I never saw such a one in my life. He has great staring eyes, like the bull's that frightened me so; vast jaw-bones sticking out; eye-brows hanging over his eyes; two great scars upon his forehead, and one on his left cheek; huge whiskers and a monstrous wide mouth; blubber[154] lips, long yellow teeth, which his lips hardly cover, even when he is silent; so that he has always a hideous grin about his mouth. He wears his own frightful long hair, tied up in a great black bag;[155] a black crape neckcloth, about a long ugly neck; and he has something on his throat, that sticks out, as I may say, like a wen.[156] As to the rest, he was dressed well enough, and had a sword on, with a dirty red knot[157] to it; leather garters, buckled below his knees; and a foot – near as long as my arm, I verily think.

'I fright de young lady,' said he; and offered to withdraw; but she forbid him.

I sat not long with them; but went up to my closet. My heart ached all the time I was at table, being unable to look upon him without horror; and this brute of a woman, though she knew how great my distress was, *before* this addition to it, no doubt did it on purpose to strike more terror into me. And indeed it had its effect;

for when I went to-bed, I could think of nothing but his hideous person, and my master's more hideous actions. These thoughts so affected me, that I dreamed they were both coming to my bed-side with the worst designs; and jumped out of bed, waking in terror. Mrs Jewkes was alarmed. I told her my dream: the wicked creature only laughed, and said, All I feared was no more than a dream; and when it was over, and I was well awake, I should laugh at it as such. Was there ever such an abominable wretch?

And now I am come to the close of WEDNESDAY, *the 27th day of my imprisonment*

Poor Mr Williams is actually arrested, and carried away to Stamford.[158] Unhappy man! his over-security and openness of heart have ruined us both! I was but too well convinced, that we ought not to have lost a moment's time. But he was half angry, and thought me impatient: and then his fatal confessions, and the detestable artifice of my master! What will become of us both!

But one stratagem I have just thought of, though attended with this discouraging circumstance, that I have neither friends nor money, nor know one step of the way, were I actually out of the house. But let bulls, and bears, and lions, and tygers, and, what is worse, false, treacherous, deceitful man, stand in my way, I cannot be in more danger than I now think myself in: for I rely not upon his three weeks; since, now he is in such a rage, and has already begun his vengeance on poor Mr Williams, it is but too probable, that he may come down to Lincolnshire before he goes to London.

My device is this: I will endeavour to get Mrs Jewkes to go to bed before me; as she often does, while I sit locked up in my closet. Her first sleep is generally very sound, and the moment she drops into it, she never fails by snoring to give one notice of it. And if, on her doing so, I can but get out between the two bars of the window, (for you know I am very slender, and I have tried, and find I can get my head through) then I can drop upon the leads underneath, which are little more than my height. These leads are over a little summer parlour, which juts out towards the garden; and as I am light, I can easily drop from them; for they are not high from the ground: then I shall be in the garden; and shall not fail to make use of the key of the back-door, which I have, and so let myself out.

But I have another piece of management still in store; good Heaven succeed to me my well-meant devices!

I have read of a great captain,[159] who, being in danger, leaped overboard, into the sea; and his enemies, as he swam, shooting at him with bows and arrows, he unloosed his upper garment, and took another course, while they stuck that full of their darts and arrows; and he escaped, and lived to triumph over them all. So I will slip off my upper petticoat, and throw it into the pond, with my handkerchief; for it is likely, when they miss me, and cannot find me elsewhere, they will go to the pond, supposing that I may have drowned myself; and, when they see some of my clothes floating there, they will be all employed in dragging the pond, which is a very large one. I shall not, perhaps, be missed till the morning, and this will give me opportunity to get a great way off: and I am sure I will run for it when I am out. And so I trust that Providence will direct my steps to some place of safety.

O my dear parents! don't be frighted when you come to read this! But all will be over before you can see it; and so God direct me for the best. My writings, for fear I should not escape, I will bury in the garden; for, to be sure, I shall be searched, and used dreadfully, if I can't get off. And so I will close here, for the present, to prepare for my plot. Prosper thou, O Gracious Protector of oppressed innocence! this last effort of thy poor handmaid; that I may escape the crafty devices and snares that have begun to entangle me; and from which, but by this one trial, I see no way of escaping! And, Oh! whatever becomes of me, bless my dear parents, and protect poor Mr Williams from ruin! for he was happy before he knew me.

Just now, just now! I heard Mrs Jewkes, who is in her cups, own to the horrid Colbrand, that the robbing of poor Mr Williams was a contrivance of her's, and executed by the groom and a helper, in order to seize my letters upon him, which they missed. They are now both laughing at the dismal story, which they little think I overheard. O how my heart akes! for what are not such wretches capable of?

Past Eleven o' Clock

Mrs Jewkes is come up, and gone to bed; and bids me not stay long after her. O for a dead sleep for the treacherous brute! I never saw her so much in liquor, and that gives me hopes. I have tried again, and find I can get my head through the iron bars. I am now all prepared. I hope soon to hear her fast; [160] and now I'll seal up these and my other papers, my last work, and to Providence commit the rest! Once more, God bless you both! and send us a happy meeting! if not here, in his heavenly kingdom! *Amen.*

THURSDAY, FRIDAY, SATURDAY, SUNDAY, *the 28th, 29th, 30th, and 31st days of my distress*

And distress indeed! For here I am still! And every thing has been worse and worse! O the unhappy Pamela! Without any hope left, and ruined in all my contrivances! But do you, my dear parents, rejoice with me, even in this low plunge of my distress; for your poor child has escaped from an enemy worse than any she ever met with; an enemy she never thought of before, and was hardly able to stand against: I mean the weakness and presumption, both in one, of her own mind! which, had not the Divine Grace interposed, would have sunk her into everlasting perdition!

I will proceed, as I have opportunity, with my sad relation: for my pen and ink (in my now doubly-secured closet) is all I have to employ myself with: and indeed I have been so weak, that till yesterday evening, I have not been able to hold a pen.

I took with me but one shift, besides what I had on, and two handkerchiefs, and two caps, which my pocket held, (for it was not for me to encumber myself) and all my stock of money, which was but five or six shillings, to set out for I knew not whither; and got out of the window, not without some difficulty, sticking a little at my shoulders and hips; but I was resolved to get out, if possible. The distance from the window to the leads was greater than I had imagined, and I was afraid I had sprained my ancle; and the distance from the leads to the ground, was still greater; but I got no hurt considerable enough to hinder me from pursuing my intentions. So, being now in the garden, I hid my papers under a rose-bush, and covered them over with mould, and there I hope they still lie.

Then I hied[161] away to the pond: the clock struck twelve, just as I got out; and it was a dark misty night, and very cold; but I was not then sensible of it.

When I came to the pond-side I flung in my upper coat, as I had designed, and my handkerchief, and a round-eared cap, with a knot pinned upon it; and then ran to the door, and took the key out of my pocket, my poor heart beating all the time, as if it would have forced its way through my stays. But how miserably was I disappointed, when I found that my key would not open the lock! The wretch, as it proved, had taken off the old lock, and another was put on! I tried and tried before I was convinced it was so; but feeling about found a padlock on another part of the door; then how my heart sunk! I dropped down with grief and confusion, unable to stir for a while. But my terror soon awakened my resolution; for I knew that my attempt, if I escaped not, would be sufficient to give a pretence for the most outrageous insults from the woman; and for the cruelest treatment from my master; and to bring him down the sooner to put his horrid purposes in execution; I therefore was resolved, if possible, to get over the wall; but that being high, had no other hope to do it, than by help of the ledges of the door, which are very strong and thick. I clambered up, therefore, upon them, and upon the lock, which was a great wooden one; and reached the top of the door with my hands; which shut not close to the wall; and then, little thinking I could climb so well, I made shift to lay hold on the top of the wall with my hands: but, alas for me! nothing but ill luck! no escape for poor Pamela! The wall being old, the bricks I held by, gave way, just as I was taking a spring to get up; and down came I, and received such a blow upon my head, with one of the bricks, that it quite stunned me; and I broke[162] my shins and my ancle besides, and beat off the heel of one of my shoes.

In this dreadful way, flat upon the ground, I lay, for I believe five or six minutes; and then trying to get up, I sunk down again two or three times. My left hip and shoulder were sadly bruised, and pained me much; and besides my head bled quite down into my neck, as I could feel, and aked grievously with the blow I had with the brick. Yet these hurts I valued not; but crept a good way upon my knees and hands, in search of a ladder I just recollected to have seen against the wall two days before, on which the gardener was nailing a nectarine branch, that was loosened from the wall: but no ladder could I find. What, now, thought I, must become of the miserable Pamela! Then I began to wish myself again in my closet, and to repent of my attempt, which I now censured as rash; but that was because it did not succeed.

God forgive me! but a sad thought came just then into my head![163] I tremble to think of it! Indeed my apprehensions of the usage I should meet with, had like to have made me miserable for ever! O my dear, dear parents, forgive your poor child! But being then quite desperate, I crept along, till I could raise myself on my staggering feet; and away limped I! What to do, but to throw myself into the pond, and so put a period to all my terrors in this world! But, oh! to find them infinitely aggravated in a miserable *eternity*! had I not by the *Divine Grace* been with-held.

As I have escaped this temptation, I will tell you my conflicts on this dreadful occasion, that the Divine mercies may be magnified in my deliverance; and in that I am yet on this side the dreadful gulph, from which there could have been no return.

It was well for me, as I have since thought, that I was so bruised as I was; for this made me the longer before I got to the water; and gave time for a little reflection, for a ray of grace to dart in upon my benighted mind; and so, when I came to the pond-side, I sat myself down on the sloping bank, and began to ponder my wretched condition; and thus I reasoned with myself:

Pause here a little, Pamela, on what thou art about, before thou takest the dreadful leap; and consider whether there be no way yet left, no hope, if not to escape from this wicked house, yet from the mischiefs threatened thee in it!

I then considered, and after I had cast about in my mind, every thing that could make me hope, and saw no probability; a wicked woman, devoid of all compassion! a horrid abetter just arrived in this dreadful Colbrand! an angry and resenting master, who now hated me, and threatened me with the most dreadful evils! and that I should, in all probability, be soon deprived even of the opportunity I now had before me, to free myself from all their persecutions! What hast thou to do, distressed creature, *said I to myself*, but to throw thyself upon a merciful God, (who knows how innocently thou sufferest) to avoid the merciless wickedness of those who are determined on thy ruin?

And then, thought I (and O that thought was surely of the devil's instigation; for it was very soothing and powerful with me) these wicked wretches, who now have no remorse, no pity on me, will then be moved to lament their misdoings; and when they see the dead corpse of the miserable Pamela dragged out to these dewy banks, and lying breathless at their feet, they will find that remorse to soften their obdurate hearts, which, now, has no place in them! And my master, my angry master, will then forget his resentments, and say, 'Alas!' and it may be, wring his hands. 'This is the unhappy Pamela! whom I have so causelessly persecuted and destroyed! Now do I see she preferred her honesty to her life. She, poor girl! was no hypocrite, no deceiver; but really was the innocent creature she pretended to be!'

Then, thought I, will he, perhaps, shed a few tears over the corpse of his persecuted servant; and, though he may give out, it was disappointment, and (in order to hide his own guilt) love for poor Mr Williams; yet will he be inwardly grieved, and order me a decent funeral, and save me, or rather *this part* of me, from the dreadful stake, and the highway interment:[164] and the young men and maidens in my father's neighbourhood will pity poor Pamela! But yet I hope I shall not be the subject of their ballads and their elegies, but that my memory, for the sake of my dear father and mother, may quickly slide into oblivion!

I was once rising, so indulgent was I to this sad way of thinking, to throw myself in: but again my bruises made me slow; and I thought, What art thou about to do, wretched Pamela? How knowest thou, though the prospect be all dark to thy short-sighted eye, what God may do for thee, even when all human means fail? God Almighty would not lay me under these sore afflictions, if he had not given me strength to grapple with them, if I will exert it as I ought: and who knows, but that the very presence I so much dread, of my angry and designing master, (for he has had me in his power before, and yet I have escaped) may be better for me, than these persecuting emissaries of his, who, for his money, are true to their wicked trust, and are hardened by that, and a long habit of wickedness, against compunction of heart? God *can* touch his heart in an instant: and if this should *not* be done, I can *then* but put an end to my life by some other means, if I am so resolved.

But how do I know, thought I, on the other hand, that even *these bruises* and *maims* that I have got, while I pursued only the laudable escape I had meditated, may not have been the means of furnishing me with the kind opportunity I now have of surrendering up my life, spotless and unguilty, to that merciful Being who gave it!

But then recollecting, Who gave thee, said I to myself, presumptuous as thou art, a power over thy life? Who authorized thee to put an end to it? Is it not the weakness of thy mind that suggests to thee that there is no way to preserve it with honour? How knowest thou what purposes God may have to serve, by the trials with which thou art now exercised? Art *thou* to put a bound to the Divine Will, and to say, '*Thus much will I bear, and no more?*' And wilt thou *dare* to say, That if the trial be augmented and continued, thou wilt sooner die than bear it? Was not Joseph's exaltation owing to his unjust imprisonment?[165]

If, despairing of deliverance, I destroy myself, do I not in effect, question the power of the Almighty to deliver me? And shall I not, in that case, be guilty of a sin, which, as it admits not of repentance, cannot be hoped to be forgiven? And wilt thou, to shorten thy *transitory* griefs, *heavy* as they are, plunge both body and soul into *everlasting* misery! Hitherto, Pamela, thought I, thou art the innocent, the suffering Pamela; and wilt thou, to avoid thy sufferings, be the guilty aggressor? How do I know but that the Almighty may have permitted these sufferings as trials of my fortitude, and to make me, who perhaps have too much prided myself in a vain dependence on my own foolish contrivances, rely wholly on his grace and assistance?

Then again, thought I, wilt thou suffer in *one* moment, all the good lessons of thy poor honest parents, and the benefit of their example, (who have persisted in doing *their* duty with resignation to the Divine Will, amidst the extreme degrees of disappointment, poverty, and distress, and the persecutions of merciless creditors) to be thrown away upon thee; and bring down, as in all probability this thy rashness will, their grey hairs with sorrow to the grave, when they shall understand, that their beloved daughter, slighting the tenders of Divine Grace, despairing of the mercies of a protecting God, has blemished, in this *last act*, a *whole* life, which those dear parents had hitherto approved and delighted in?

What then, presumptuous Pamela, dost thou *here?* thought I: quit with speed these perilous banks, and fly from these dashing waters, that seem in their meaning murmurs, this still night, to reproach thy rashness! Tempt not God's goodness on the mossy banks, which have been witnesses of thy guilty purpose; and while thou hast power left thee, avoid the temptation, lest thy grand enemy, now, by Divine Grace, repulsed, return to the assault with a force that thy weakness may not be able to resist! And lest thou in one rash moment destroy all the convictions, which now have awed thy rebellious mind into duty and resignation to the Divine Will!

And so saying, I arose; but was so stiff with my hurts, so cold with the dew of the night, and the wet grass on which I had sat, as also with the damps arising from so large a piece of water, that with great pain I got from this pond, which now I think of with terror; and bending my limping steps towards the house, took refuge in the corner of an out-house, where wood and coals are laid up for family use: there, behind a pile of fire-wood, I crept, and lay down, as you may imagine, with a heart just broken; expecting to be soon found out by cruel keepers, and to be worse treated than ever I yet had been.

This, my dear father and mother, is the issue of your poor Pamela's fruitless enterprize; and who knows, if I had got out at the back-door, whether I had been at all in a better case, moneyless, friendless, as I am, and in a strange place! But blame not your poor daughter too much: nay, if ever you see this miserable scribble, all bathed and blotted with my tears, let your pity get the better of your reprehension! But I know it will.

I must leave off for the present; for my strength and my will are at this time far unequal to each other. But yet I will add, that though I should have praised God for my deliverance, had I been freed from my wicked keepers, and my designing master; yet I have more abundant reason to praise him, that I have been delivered from a worse enemy—*Myself!*

I will continue my sad relation.

It seems Mrs Jewkes awaked not till day-break; and not finding me in bed, she called out for me; and no answer being returned, arose and ran to my closet. Finding me not there, she searched under the bed, and in another closet; having before examined the chamber-door, and found it as she had left it, quite fast, and the key, as usual, about her wrist. For if I could have stole that from her, in her dead sleep, and got out at the chamber-door, there were two or three passages, and doors to them all, double-locked and barred, to go through, into the great garden; so that there was no way to escape, but out of the window; and of that window I dropped from, because of the summer parlour under it; the other windows being a great way from the ground.

She says, she was excessively alarmed. She instantly raised the two maids, who lay not far off, and then the Swiss; and finding every door fast, she said, I must be carried away, as St Peter was, out of prison, by some angel.[166] It is a wonder she had not a worse thought.

She says, she wept, wrung her hands, and ran about like a mad woman, little thinking I could have got out of the closet-window, between the iron bars; and indeed I don't know whether I could do so again. But at last, finding that casement open, they concluded it must be so; and ran out into the garden, and found my footsteps in the mould of the bed which I dropped down upon from the leads: and so speeded away all of them, that is to say, Mrs Jewkes, Colbrand, Nan, and the gardener, who by that time had joined them, towards the back door, to see if that was fast, while the cook was sent to the out-offices to raise the men-servants, and make them get horses ready, to take each a several way to pursue me.

But it seems, finding that door double-locked and padlocked, and the heel of my shoe, and the broken bricks, they verily concluded I was got away by some means over the wall; and then, they say, Mrs Jewkes seemed like a distracted woman: till at last Nan had the thought to go towards the pond, and there seeing my coat, and cap and handkerchief, in the water, cast almost to the banks by the motion of the waves, she thought it was me, and screaming out, ran to Mrs Jewkes, and said, 'O madam, madam! here's a piteous thing! Mrs Pamela lies drowned in the pond!'

Thither they all ran; and finding my clothes, doubted not but I was at the bottom; and then they all, Swiss among the rest, beat their breasts, and made most dismal lamentations; and Mrs Jewkes sent Nan to the men, to bid them get the drag-net ready, and leave the horses, and come to try to find the poor innocent, as she, it seems, *then* called me, beating her breast, and lamenting my hard hap;[167] but most what would become of them, and what account they should give to my master.

While every one was thus differently employed, some weeping and wailing, some running here and there, Nan came into the wood-house; and there lay poor I, so weak, so low, and so dejected, and withal so stiff with my bruises, that I could not stir nor help myself to get upon my feet. And I said, with a low voice, (for I could hardly speak) 'Mrs Ann, Mrs Ann!' The creature was sadly frighted, but was taking up a billet[168] to knock me on the head, believing I was some thief, as she said; but I cried out, 'O Mrs Ann, Mrs Ann! help me, for pity's sake, to Mrs Jewkes! for I cannot get up.' 'Bless me!' said she, 'what! you, madam! Why our hearts are almost broken, and we were going to drag the pond for you, believing you had drowned yourself. Now,' said she, 'shall we be all alive again!'

Without staying to help me, she ran away to the pond, and brought all the crew to the wood-house. The wicked woman, as she entered, said, 'Where is she? Plague of her spells, and her witch-crafts! She shall dearly repent of this trick, if my name be Jewkes'; and coming to me, took hold of my arm so roughly, and gave me such a pull, as made me scream out, (my shoulder being bruised on that side) and drew me on my face. 'O cruel creature!' said I, 'if you knew what I have suffered, it would move you to pity me!'

Even Colbrand seemed to be concerned, and said, 'Fie, madam, fie! you see she is almost dead! You must not be so rough with her.' The coachman Robin seemed to be sorry for me too, and said, with sobs, 'What a scene is here! Don't you see she is all bloody in her head, and cannot stir?' 'Curse of her contrivances!' said the horrid creature; 'she has frightened *me* out of my wits, I'm sure. How the d—l came you here?' 'O,' said I, 'ask me now no questions, but let the maids carry me up to my prison; and there let me die decently, and in peace!' Indeed I thought I could not live two hours.

'I suppose,' said the tygress, 'you want Mr Williams to pray by you, don't you? Well, I'll send for my master this minute! Let him come and watch you himself, for me; for there's no such thing as a woman's holding you, I'm sure.'

The maids took me up between them, and carried me to my chamber; and when the wretch saw how bad I was, she began a little to relent.

I was so weak, that I fainted away, as soon as they got me up stairs; and they undressed me, and got me to-bed, and Mrs Jewkes ordered Nan to bathe my shoulder, and arm, and ancle, with some old rum warmed; and they cut from the back part of my head, a little of the hair, for it was clotted with blood; and put a family plaster[169] to the gash, which was pretty long, but not deep. If this woman has any good quality, it is, it seems, in a readiness and skill to manage in cases where sudden accidents happen in a family.

After this, I fell into a pretty sound and refreshing sleep, and lay till near twelve o'clock, tolerably easy, yet was feverish, and anguishly inclined. The wretch took a great deal of care of me: but for what end? Why, to fit me to undergo more troubles; for that is the sad case.

She would have made me rise about twelve; but I was so weak, I could only sit up till the bed was made, and then was helped into it again; and was, as they said, delirious some part of the afternoon. But having a tolerable night on Thursday, I was a good deal better on Friday, and on Saturday my feverishness seeming to be gone, arose. I was so amended by evening, that I begged her to allow me to sit in my closet by myself. I assured her, that all my contrivances to escape were at an end. She had caused it to be double barred the day before; and consented; but first she made me tell her the whole story of my enterprize; which I did very faithfully. She expressed her wonder at my resolution, but told me frankly, that I should have found it a hard matter to get out of my master's power, let me have escaped to whom I would; for that she was provided with a warrant from my master (who is a justice of peace in this county, as well as in the other) to get me apprehended, on suspicion of wronging him.

O my dear parents, how deep-laid are the mischiefs designed to fall on my devoted head! Surely, I cannot be worthy of all this contrivance! This shews me that there was too much in what was hinted to me formerly at the other house, that my master swore he would *have* me! Preserve me, Heaven! from being *his*, in his own wicked sense of the word!

I must add, that now this woman sees me recover so fast, she uses me worse, and has abridged me of paper all but one sheet, which I am to produce, written or unwritten, on demand. She has also reduced me to one pen. Yet my hidden stores stand me instead. But she is more and more spiteful and cross; and tauntingly calls me Mrs Williams, and says every thing that she thinks will vex me.

SUNDAY *Afternoon*

Mrs Jewkes has thought fit to give me an airing for three or four hours this afternoon. I am a good deal better; but health is a blessing hardly to be coveted in my circumstances, since that but exposes me to the danger I am in continual apprehensions of; whereas a weak and sickly state might possibly move compassion for me. O how I dread the coming of this angry and incensed master! Yet why is he angry? Why incensed? I am sure I have done him no harm!

Just now we heard, that he had like to have been drowned in crossing a stream, a few days ago, in pursuing his game. What is the matter, that, with all his ill usage of me, I cannot hate him? To be sure, in this, I am not like other people! He has certainly done enough to make me hate him; but yet when I heard his danger, which was very great, I could not in my heart forbear rejoicing for his safety; though his death would have set me free. Ungenerous master! If you knew this, you surely would not be so much my persecutor! But for my late good lady's sake, I must wish him well; and O what an angel would he be in my eyes yet, if he would give over his attempts, and reform!

Well, I hear by Mrs Jewkes, that John Arnold is turned away, being detected in writing to Mr Williams; and that Mr Longman, and Mr Jonathan the butler, have incurred his displeasure, for offering to speak in my behalf. Mrs Jervis too is in danger; for all these three, it seems, went together to beg in my favour; for now it is known where I am.

Mrs Jewkes has received a letter; but she says the contents are too bad for me to know. They must be bad indeed, if they be worse than what I have already seen.

Just now the horrid creature tells me, as a secret, that she has reason to think my master has found a way to satisfy my scruples: it is, by marrying me to this dreadful Colbrand, and buying me of him on the wedding-day, for a sum of money! Was ever the like heard? She says it will be my duty to obey my husband; and that Mr Williams, as a punishment, will be forced to marry me to that dreadful wretch: and that when my master has paid for me, and I am surrendered up, the Swiss is to go home again, with the money, to his former wife and children; for, she says, it is the custom of those people to have a wife in every nation.[170]

But this, to be sure, is horrid romancing! Yet, improbable as it is, it may possibly serve to introduce some plot now hatching. With what strange perplexities is my mind agitated! Perchance, some sham-marriage may be designed on purpose to ruin me: but can a husband sell his wife against her own consent? And will such a bargain stand good in law? But what is law, what is any thing with the lawless? And if I am bought and sold, and taken away by the vile purchaser, what will a legal punishment for wickedness committed, avail the irretrievable injured!

MONDAY, TUESDAY, WEDNESDAY, *the 32nd, 33rd, and 34th Days of my Imprisonment*

Nothing has offered in these days but squabblings between Mrs Jewkes and me. She is worse and worse to me. I vexed her yesterday, because she talked filthily; and told her she talked more like a vile London prostitute, as I had heard them spoke of at the Bedfordshire-house, than a gentleman's housekeeper; and she thinks she cannot use me bad enough for it. Bless me! she curses and storms at me like a trooper, and can hardly keep her hands off me. You may believe she must talk very wickedly to make me say such words: indeed what she said cannot be repeated; and she is a disgrace to her sex. And then she ridicules me, and laughs at my notions of virtue; and tells me, impudent creature as she is! what a fine bed-fellow I shall make for my master, with such whimsical notions about me! Do you think this is to be borne? And yet she talks worse than this, if possible! Quite abominably. What vile hands am I put into!

THURSDAY

I have now the greatest reason, to apprehend my master will be here soon; for the servants are busy in setting the house to rights; and a stable and coach-house are cleaning out, that have not been used some time. I ask Mrs Jewkes, but she tells me nothing, nor will hardly answer me when I ask her a question. Sometimes I think she puts on these airs, purposely to make me wish for, what I most of all things dread, my master's coming down. But if he *does* come, where is his promise of not seeing me without I consent to it? But, it seems, *his honour owes me nothing*! So he tells me in his letter. And why? Because I am willing to keep mine. Indeed, he says, *he hates me perfectly*; and it is plain he does, or I should not be left to the mercy of this woman.

FRIDAY, *the 36th Day of my Imprisonment*

I took the liberty yesterday afternoon, finding the gates open, to walk out before the house; and ere I was aware, had got to the bottom of the long row of elms; and there I sat myself down upon the steps of a sort of broad stile, which leads into the road that goes towards the town. Seeing myself got thus far from the house, why cannot I now, thought I, get quite off? But I was discouraged on seeing the country on this side quite open as far as the eye could reach. The warrant Mrs Jewkes told me of, also helped to intimidate me. But before I could resolve, or if I had resolved, could get out of sight of pursuers,[171] I saw a whole posse of men and women from the house, running towards me, as in a fright. At first I wondered what was the matter, till they came nearer; and I found they were all alarmed, thinking I had attempted to get off. There was first the horrible Colbrand, running with his long legs, well-nigh two yards at a stride; then there was one of the grooms, poor Mr Williams's robber, a sad fellow! Then I spied Nan, half out of breath; and the cook-maid after her; and, lastly, came, waddling, as fast as she could, Mrs Jewkes, exclaiming most bitterly, as I found, against me. Colbrand said, 'O how you have frighted us all!' And went behind me, lest I should run away, as I suppose.

I sat still, that they might suppose I had no view to get away. When Mrs Jewkes came within hearing, I found she was in a rage, charging me with my contrivances; and when she came up to me, the barbarous creature struck at me with her horrid fist, and, I believe, would have felled me, had not Colbrand interposed and said, He saw me sitting still, looking about me, and not seeming to have the least inclination to get away. But this would not serve: she ordered the two maids to take me each by an arm, and lead me back into the house, and up stairs; and there I have been locked up ever since, without shoes; and last night I was forced to lie between her and Nan. And I find she is resolved to make a handle[172] of this against me, and in her own behalf. Indeed, what with *her* usage, and my own apprehensions of *still worse*, I am quite weary of my life.

Just now she has been with me, and given me my shoes, and has laid her insolent commands upon me, to dress myself in a suit of clothes out of the portmanteau, which I have not seen lately, against three or four o'clock; for, she says, she is to have a visit from Lady Darnford's two daughters, who come purposely to see me. And so she gave me the key of the portmanteau. But I will not obey her; and I told her I would not be made a shew of, nor see the ladies. She left me, saying, It should be worse for me, if I did not. But how can that be?

Five o'Clock is come

And no young ladies! So that I fancy – But, hold! I hear their coach, I believe. I'll step to the window. I won't go down to them, I am resolved.

Mercy on me! What will become of me! Here is my master come in his fine chariot! What shall I do? Where shall I hide myself? What shall I do? Pray for me! But, oh! you will not see this!

Seven o'Clock

Though I dread to see him, yet do I wonder I have not. To be sure something is resolving against me, and he stays to hear all her stories. I can hardly write; yet, as I can do nothing else, I know not how to lay down my pen. How crooked and trembling the lines! Why should the guiltless tremble so, when the guilty can possess their minds in peace?

SATURDAY Morning

Now let me give you an account of what passed last night; for I had no power to write, nor yet opportunity, till now.

This vile woman held my master in talk till half an hour after seven; and he came hither about five in the afternoon. And then I heard his voice on the stairs, as he was coming up to me. What he said was about his supper. He ordered a boiled chicken, with parsley and butter. And up he came!

He put on a stern and haughty air. 'Well, perverse Pamela,

ungrateful creature!' said he (for my first salutation) 'you do well, don't you, to give me all this trouble and vexation?'

I could not speak; but throwing myself on the floor, hid my face, and was ready to die with grief and apprehension. 'Well may you hide your face!' said he, 'well may you be shamed to see me, vile forward creature, as you are!' I sobbed, and wept, but could not speak. And he let me lie, and went to the door, and called Mrs Jewkes. 'There,' said he, 'take up that fallen angel! Once I thought her as innocent as an angel of light; but now I have no patience with her. The little hypocrite prostrates herself thus, in hopes to move my compassion, and expects, perhaps, that I will raise her from the floor myself. But I shall not touch her: no,' said the cruel man, 'let such fellows as Williams be taken in by her artful wiles! I know her now, and plainly see, that she is for any fool's turn, that will be caught by her.'

I sighed, as if my heart would break! And Mrs Jewkes lifted me upon my knees; for I trembled so, I could not stand. 'Come,' said she, 'Mrs Pamela, learn to know your best friend! confess your behaviour, and beg his honour's forgiveness of all your faults.'

I was ready to faint; and he said, 'She is mistress of arts, I assure you; and will mimick a fit, ten to one, in a minute.'

I was struck to the heart at this; but could not speak presently. I only lifted up my eyes to heaven! And at last made shift to say, 'God forgive you, sir!'

He seemed in a great passion, and walked up and down the room, casting sometimes an eye upon me, and seeming as if he would have spoken, but checked himself. And at last he said, 'When she has *acted* this her *first part* over, perhaps I will see her again, and she shall *soon* know what she has to trust to.'

And so he went out of the room: and I was sick at my very heart! 'Surely,' said I, 'I am the wickedest creature that ever breathed!' 'Well,' said the impertinent, 'not so wicked as *that* neither; but I am glad you begin to see your faults. There is nothing like humility! Come, I'll stand your friend, and plead for you, if you'll promise to be more dutiful for the future. Come, come,' added the wretch, 'this may be all made up by to-morrow morning, if you are not a fool.' 'Begone, hideous woman!' said I; 'and let not my afflictions be added to by thy inexorable cruelty, and unwomanly wickedness.'

She gave me a push, and left me in a violent passion, and as I found, made a story of this; and told my master that I had such a spirit, there was no bearing it.

I laid me down on the floor, and had no power to stir, till the clock struck nine, when the wicked woman came up again. 'You must come down-stairs,' said she, 'to my master; that is, if you please, spirit.' 'I believe,' said I, 'I cannot stand.' 'Then,' said she, 'I'll send up Mons. Colbrand to carry you down.'

I called her cruel creature. She lifted me up by my arm and insisted on my going down. I could not resist, she pulling me along to the stairs-head. I trembled all the way down-stairs; and when I came to the bottom, she stept into the parlour before me; and a new servant, who waited on him instead of John, withdrew as soon as I came in. By-the-way, he has a new coachman too, which looks as if he has also turned away Bedfordshire Robin.

'I thought,' said he, when I came down, 'you should have sat at table with me, while I was in these parts, and when I had not company: but as I find you unworthy of that honour, and that you prefer my menials to me, I call you down to wait on me, while I sup, that I may have some talk with you, and throw away as little time as possible upon you.'

'Sir,' said I, 'I think it an honour to be allowed to wait upon you.' But I was forced to stand behind his chair, that I might hold by it. 'Fill me,' said he, 'a glass of that Burgundy.' I went to do it; but my hand shook so, that I could not hold the salver with the glass on it, and spilt some of the wine. So Mrs Jewkes poured it for me, and gave it me to carry on the salver. I carried it as well as I could; and made a low curt'sy in offering it. He took it, and said, 'Stand behind me, out of my sight.'

'You tell me, Mrs Jewkes,' said he, 'that she remains very sullen still, and eats nothing.' 'No,' said she, 'not so much as to keep life and soul together.' 'And is always crying, you say too?' 'Yes, sir,' answered she, 'I think she is, for one thing or other.' 'Ay,' said he, 'your young wenches will feed upon their tears; and their obstinacy will serve them for meat and drink. I think I never saw her look better in my life! But I suppose she lives upon love. This sweet Mr Williams, and her little villainous plots together, have kept her alive and well; for mischief, love, and contradiction, are the natural food of women.'

My heart was too full to allow me to speak.

'And so you say that she had *another* project, but yesterday, to get away?' 'She denies it herself,' said she; 'but it had all the appearance of one. I'm sure she put me into a fearful pucker[173] about it. I am glad, with all my heart, your honour is come; and hope, whatever be your honour's intention concerning her, you will quickly let her know her fate; for you will find her as slippery as an eel, I assure you!'

'Sir,' said I, falling on my knees at his feet, and, not knowing what I did, clasping his knees, 'Have mercy upon me, and hear me, concerning that wicked woman's usage of me–'

He cruelly interrupted me, and said, 'I am satisfied she has done her duty: it signifies nothing what you say against Mrs Jewkes. That you are here, little hypocrite as you are, pleading your cause before me, is owing to her care of you; else you had been with the parson. Wicked girl,' added he, 'to tempt a man to undo himself, at a time when I was on the point of making him happy for his life!'

I arose, but said, with a deep sigh, 'I have done! I have done! I have a strange tribunal to plead before. The poor sheep, in the fable, had such a one; when it was tried before the vulture, on the accusation of the wolf!'[174]

'So, Mrs Jewkes,' said he, 'you are the wolf, I the vulture, and this the poor harmless lamb, on her trial before us. You don't know how well read this innocent is in reflection. Her memory always serves her, when she has a mind to display her own romantic innocence, at the price of other people's characters.'

'Well,' said the aggravating creature, 'this is nothing to what she has called me. I have been a Jezebel, a London prostitute, and what not. But I am contented with her ill names, now I see it is her fashion, and she can call your honour a vulture.'

'I had no thought,' said I, 'of comparing my master–' and was going on: but he said, 'Don't prate, girl!' 'No,' said she, 'it don't become you, I'm sure.'

'Well,' said I, 'since I must not speak, I will hold my peace: but there is a righteous Judge, who knows the secrets of all hearts! and to him I appeal.'

'See there!' said he: 'now this meek, good creature is praying for fire from heaven upon us! She can curse most heartily, in the spirit of Christian meekness, I assure you! Come, saucy-face, give me another glass.'

I poured out the wine, and offered it to him, as well as I could; but wept so, that he said, 'I suppose I shall have some of your tears in my wine!'

When he had supped, he stood up, and said, looking at me, I don't know how, yet with a jeering look too, 'How happy for you it is, that you can, at will, make your speaking eyes overflow in this manner, without losing any of their brilliancy! You have been told, I suppose, that you are *most* beautiful in your tears! Did you ever,' said he to *her*, (who all this while was standing in one corner of the parlour) 'see a more charming creature than this? Is it to be wondered, that I undervalue myself thus to take notice of her? See,' and took the glass with one hand, and turned me round with the other, 'what a shape! what a neck! what a hand! and what a bloom in that bewitching face! But who can describe the tricks and artifices, that lie lurking in her little, plotting, guileful heart! 'Tis no wonder the poor parson was infatuated with her! I blame *him* less than I do *her*; for who could expect such artifice in so young a sorceress?'

I went to the further part of the room, and leaned my face against the wainscot; and, in spite of all I could do to refrain, sobbed, as if my heart would break. 'I am surprised, Mrs Jewkes,' said he, with a very careless air, 'at the mistake of the letters you tell me of! But I am not afraid any body should read what I write. I don't carry on private correspondences, and reveal every secret that comes to my knowledge, and then corrupt people to carry my letters, against their duty, and all good conscience.

'Come hither, hussy,' added he; 'you and I have a long reckoning to make up. Why don't you come, when I bid you?' 'Fie upon it! Mrs Pamela,' said she: 'what! not stir, when his honour commands you to go to him! Who knows but his goodness will forgive you?'

He came to me (for I had no power to stir) and put his arms about my neck, and would kiss me; I struggled. 'Don't be a fool, Pamela,' said he. And then loosing his arms with an air, 'Well, Mrs Jewkes, were it not for the thought of this cursed parson, I believe in my heart, I could *yet* forgive this intriguing girl; and, so great is my weakness, take her to my bosom.'

'O,' said the sycophant, 'you are very good, sir! very forgiving indeed! But,' added the profligate wretch, 'I hope your honour *will* be so good as to forgive her still, and take her to yourself. If you do, you will certainly bring her to a better sense of her duty, by to-morrow morning.'

Could any thing, in womanhood, be so vile? I had no patience: but yet grief and indignation choaked up the passage of my words; and I could only stammer out a passionate exclamation to Heaven, to protect my innocence: but the word *innocence* was the subject of their ridicule.

'Forgive her,' said he, and paused, as if he was considering whether he could forgive me or not, 'No, I cannot yet forgive her neither. She has given me great disturbance; she has brought great discredit upon me, both abroad and at home; she has corrupted all my servants at the other house; she has despised me for my condescension, and sought to run away with this ungrateful parson. And surely I ought not to forgive her.'

Yet, with all this wretched grimace, he put his arm about my neck, and so rudely kissed me, that I struggling said, 'I will *die*, sir, before I will submit to this treatment!' 'Consider, Pamela,' said he, in a threatening tone, 'consider where you are; and don't play the fool: if you do, a more dreadful fate awaits you than you can imagine. But take her up-stairs, Mrs Jewkes, and I'll send a few lines to her to consider of; and let me, Pamela, have your answer in the morning. Till then you have to resolve: and after that, if you stand in your own light,[175] your doom will be irrevocable.' Thus dismissed, I hurried up-stairs, and gave myself up to grief, in expectation of what he would send: but yet I was glad of this night's reprieve!

He sent me nothing, however. And about twelve o'clock Mrs Jewkes and Nan came up, as the night before, to be my bedfellows; and I would go to bed with some of my clothes on; at which they muttered sadly, Mrs Jewkes particularly. Indeed I would have sat up all night, if she would have let me: and I might as well; for I had but very little rest that night, apprehending this woman would let my master in. She did nothing but praise him, and blame me; but I answered her as little as I could.

He has that officious Sir Simon Darnford to dine with him to-day, whose family sent to welcome him into the country; and, it seems, the old baronet wants to see me. So I suppose I shall be sent for, as Samson[176] was, to make sport for him. Here I am, and must bear it all!

Twelve o' Clock, SATURDAY Noon

Just now he has sent me up, by Mrs Jewkes, his proposals. They are, my dear parents, to make me a vile kept mistress. So here are the *honourable intentions* all at once laid open! But you will see how they are accommodated to what I should have most desired, with regard to your welfare, could I have honestly promoted it. I have answered, as I'm sure you will approve. I fear there will be nothing omitted to ruin me, and though my poor strength may not be sufficient to defend me, yet I will be innocent of crime in the sight of God; and to him leave the avenging of all my wrongs.

I shall write to you my answer against his articles; and hope the best, though I dread the worst. But if I should come home to you ruined and undone, let me hope that you will pity your poor Pamela, and encourage her to look up to your worthy faces, for the short remainder of her life. Long, I am sure, I shall not survive my disgrace. Yet I ask neither your pity nor your forgiveness, if my ruin be not more owing to my misfortune than to my fault.

HIS PROPOSALS

The following ARTICLES are proposed to your serious consideration. Let me have an answer, in writing, to them. Only remember, that I will not be trifled with; and that what you give for answer, will absolutely decide your fate, without expostulation or further trouble:

I. If you can convince me, that the hated Williams has had no encouragement from you in his addresses; and that you have no inclination

MY ANSWER

Forgive, sir, the spirit your poor servant is about to shew in her answer to your ARTICLES. Not to be warm, and in earnest, on such an occasion, would shew a degree of guilt, that my soul abhors. I will not trifle with you, sir, nor act like one who is doubtful of her own mind, in a point that wants not one moment's consideration. And I therefore return the ANSWER following, let what will be the consequence:

I. As to the first article, sir, it may behove me (that I may not deserve, in your opinion, the opprobrious terms of *forward*, and *artful*, and such-like) to declare solemnly, that Mr Williams for him, in preference to me: then I will offer the following proposals to you, which I will punctually make good.

never had the least encouragement from me; and I believe his principal motive was the apprehended duty of his function, to assist, so contrary to his apparent interest, an innocent person, in distress. You may, sir, the rather believe me, when I declare, that I know not the man breathing I would wish to marry.

II. I will directly make you a present of five hundred guineas, which you may dispose of as you please: and will give it into the hands of any person you shall appoint to receive it; and expect no favour from you till you are satisfied in the irrevocable possession of it.

II. As to your second proposal, I reject it with all my soul. Money, sir, is not my chief good: may God Almighty desert me, whenever I make it so; and whenever, for the sake of that, I can give up my title to that blessed hope which will stand me instead, at a time when millions of gold will not purchase one happy reflection on a past mis-spent life!

III. I will likewise directly make over to you a purchase I lately made in Kent, which brings in 250l. per annum, clear of all deductions. This shall be made over to you in full property to you and your descendants for ever. Your father shall be immediately put into possession of it in trust for you and yours. And I will make up deficiencies, if such should happen, to the amount of that clear yearly sum, and allow your father, besides, fifty pounds a-year, for his life, and for that of your mother, for his care and management of this your estate.

III. Your third article, sir, I reject for the same reason; and am sorry you could think my poor honest parents would enter into their part of it, and be concerned for the management of an estate, which would be owing to the prostitution of their daughter. Forgive, sir, my warmth on this occasion; but you know not the poor man, and the poor woman, my ever dear father and mother, if you think, that they would not much rather chuse to starve in a ditch, or rot in a noisome[177] dungeon, than accept of the fortune of a monarch, upon such wicked terms. I dare not say all that my full mind suggests to me on this grievous occasion. But indeed, sir, you know them not; nor shall the terrors of death, in its most frightful forms, ever make me act unworthy of such poor honest parents!

IV. I will, moreover, extend my favour to any other of your relations, that you may think worthy of it.

IV. Your fourth article I take upon me, sir, to answer as the second and third. If I have any friends that want the favour of the great, may they *ever* want it, if they are capable of desiring it on unworthy terms.

V. I will order patterns to be sent you for chusing four complete suits of rich clothes, that you may appear with reputation, as if you were my wife. And I will give you the two diamond rings, and ear-rings, the solitaire[178] and diamond necklace, and buckles that were bought to present to Miss Tomlins, if the treaty of marriage that was so near taking place between her and me had been brought to effect: and will confer upon you still *other* favours, as I shall find myself obliged, by your affection and good behaviour.

V. I do assure you, sir, that I have greater pride in my honest poverty and meanness, than I can have in dress and finery purchased with guilt. Believe me, sir, I think such things less become the low born Pamela, than the rags your good mother raised me from. Your rings, sir, your solitaire, your necklace, your ear-rings, and your buckles, will better befit some lady of degree, to whom you may give a lawful claim to them than me. To lose the best jewel, my virtue, would be poorly recompensed by the jewels you propose to give me. What should I think, when I looked upon my finger, or saw, in the glass, those diamonds on my neck, and in my ears, but that they were the price of my honesty; and that I *wore* those jewels outwardly, because I had none inwardly? When I come to be proud and vain of gaudy apparel, and outside finery, then (which I hope will never be) may I rest my principal good in such trifles, and despise for them the more solid ornaments of a good fame and a chastity inviolate.[179]

VI. Now, Pamela, will you see what a value I set upon the free-will of a person *already* in my power; and who, if these proposals are not accepted, shall find, that I have not taken all these pains, and risqued my reputation, as I have done, with-

VI. I know, sir, by woeful experience, that I am in your power: I know all the resistance I can make will be poor and weak, and perhaps stand me in little stead: I dread your *will* to ruin me is as great as your *power*: yet, sir, will I dare to tell you, that I will make no free-will offering of my virtue. All I *can* do, poor as that *may* be, I *will* do, to preout resolving to gratify my passion for you at all adventures.[180] And it will behove you to consider, whether it is not better for you to comply upon terms so advantageous to you, and so beneficial to your father and mother, and other friends, than to be mine without condition or equivalent.

VII. You shall be mistress of my person and fortune, as much as if the foolish ceremony had passed. All my servants shall be yours; and you shall chuse any one of them for your particular attendant: and if your conduct be such, as I have reason to be satisfied with it, I know not (though I will not engage for this) but I may, after a twelvemonth's cohabitation, marry you; for if my love increases for you, as it has done for many months past, it will be impossible for me to deny you any thing.

And now, Pamela, consider well of the premises. Consider, that it is in your power to make yourself, and all your friends, happy: but this will be over this very day, irrevocably over; and you shall find, if obstinate, all you would be thought to fear, without the least benefit to yourself. But if you sig-

serve my honour: and then, if I cannot escape the violence of man, I can safely appeal to the great God my only refuge, with this consolation, that my will bore no part in the violation.

VII. Give me leave to say, sir, that to the ceremony you call *foolish*, you yourself owe your being, and the mother, my dear and ever honoured lady and mistress, who bore you. Would she, sir, think you, have stooped to be the mistress of the *person* and fortunes of a king on such terms?[181] For her sake, as well as for God's sake, let me beseech you, sir, it is all I beg, to be allowed to return to my native poverty unviolated. I heard you once say, that a certain great commander, who could live upon lentils, might well refuse the bribes of the greatest monarch:[182] and, I hope, as I can contentedly live in the meanest manner, that I am above making an exchange of my honesty for all the riches of the Indies.

Give me leave to say, in answer to what you hint, that you may, in a twelvemonth's time, marry me, if you shall be satisfied with my good behaviour; that *this* weighs less with me, if possible, than any thing else you have said. For, in the first place, there is an end of all merit, and all good behaviour, on my side (if I have *now* any) the moment I consent to your proposals. And I shall be so far from nify to me your compliance, and this you need only to do by desiring to see me, I will instantly set about securing to you the full effect of these proposals. One word only more: if, my dear girl, you value yourself, your friends, or my favour, let me experience a grateful return on this occasion: and I will forgive you all that's past!

expecting such an honour, that I will pronounce, that I should be most *unworthy* of it. What, sir, would the world say, were you to marry your harlot? That a man of your rank, should stoop, not only to marry the low-born Pamela, but to marry a low-born prostitute?

Yet, after all, dreadful is the thought, that I, a poor, weak, friendless, unhappy creature, am too fully in your power! But permit me, sir, to pray, as I now write, on my knees, That before you resolve upon my ruin, you yourself will weigh well the matter. Hitherto, sir, though you have taken large strides towards this heinous sin, yet are you on *this* side the commission of it. When once it is done, nothing can recal it! And where will be your triumph? What glory will the spoils of such a weak enemy yield you? Let me but enjoy my poverty with honesty, is all my prayer; and I will *bless* you, and *pray for* you, every moment of my life! Think, O think, before it is yet too late, what remorse will attend your dying hour, when you come to reflect, that you have ruined, perhaps soul and body, a wretched creature, whose only pride was her virtue! And how pleased you will be, on the contrary, if in that tremendous moment you shall be able to acquit yourself of a crime so foul, and to plead in your own behalf, that you suffered the earnest supplications of an unhappy wretch to prevail with you to be innocent yourself, and let her remain so!

May God Almighty, whose mercy so lately saved you from the peril of perishing in deep waters, (on which I hope you will give me *cause* to congratulate you) touch your heart in my favour, and save *you* from this *sin*, and *me* from this *ruin*! To Him do I commit my cause; and to Him will I give the glory, and night and day pray for you, if I may be permitted to escape this great evil!

Finally, sir, have pity, I beseech you have pity on

Your poor oppressed
broken-spirited Servant.

I took a copy of this for your perusal, my dear parents, if I shall ever be so happy to see you again; and at night, when Sir Simon was gone, my master sent Mrs Jewkes to *remind me*, was the word, that I had not let him know, *I desired to see him*: my answer was, I had written as he commanded; giving the paper to her for him.

She carried it down to him; but returned presently with it, saying, I must go down with it myself.

I went trembling; and yet I heartened myself up, so as that, in such a cause, I might shew as little fear as possible.

'Well,' said he, as soon as I came into his presence, 'Have you considered my proposals?' 'I have, sir,' said I; 'and there is my answer: but pray let me not stay to see you read it.'

'Is it owing to your bashfulness,' said he, 'or to your obstinacy that you would not have me read it before you?'

I offered to go away; and he said, 'Don't run from me; I won't read it till you are gone.' But taking hold of my struggling hand, 'Tell me, Pamela, whether you comply with my proposals, or not?'

'Sir,' said I, 'you will see presently; pray don't hold me.' 'Did you well consider,' said he, 'before you wrote?' 'I did, sir,' replied I. 'If it be not what you think will please me,' returned he, 'take it back again, dear girl, and reconsider it; for if I have this as your absolute answer, and don't like it, you are undone. Let me tell you, I will not meanly sue where I can command. I fear,' added he, looking sternly in my face, 'by your manner, it is not what I like. And let me tell you, that I cannot bear denial. If the terms I have offered are not sufficient, I will augment them to two thirds of my estate; for,' said he, and swore a dreadful oath, 'I cannot live without you and since the thing is gone so far, I *will not*!' He then clasped me in his arms, in such a manner as quite frighted me; and kissed me two or three times.

I got from him, and ran up stairs, and shut myself in the closet, extremely terrified and uneasy.

In an hour's time he called Mrs Jewkes down to him; and I heard him very high in passion: and I heard her say, It was his own fault: there would be an end of all my perverseness, if he was once resolved; and such-like impudent aggravations.

I am resolved not to go to bed this night, if I can help it. Lie still, lie still, my poor fluttering heart! What will become of me!

Almost Twelve o'Clock SATURDAY *Night*

He sent Mrs Jewkes, about ten o'clock, to bid me come to him. I asked her, 'Whither?' She said she would shew me.

I followed her three or four steps, and saw her making to his chamber, the door of which was open: 'I cannot go thither!' said I, and stopt. 'Don't be foolish,' said she; 'but come; no harm will be done to you!' 'Well,' said I, 'if I die, I cannot go thither.'

I heard him say, 'Let her come in, or it shall be worse for her.' 'Well,' said I, 'I cannot go thither, indeed I cannot'; and so I went back again into my closet; yet was afraid of being fetched by force.

But she came up soon after. 'You have done your business with my master, I can tell you,' said she. 'He hates you now, as much as he once loved you. A fine piece of work! But he'll do nothing to you himself. Come, make haste to bed. My master is gone to his.' 'I will not go to bed this night, that's certain!' said I. 'Then,' said she, 'you shall be *made* to come to bed; and Nan and I will undress you.'

I knew neither prayers nor tears would move this wicked woman: but I said, 'If I do go to bed, I am sure you will let my master in, and I shall be undone!' 'Mighty piece of *undone*!' said the wretch. 'But he is too much exasperated against you, to be so familiar with you, I will assure you! No, no,' continued she, 'you'll be disposed of another way soon, I can tell you, for your comfort: And I hope your *husband* will have your obedience, though nobody else can.' 'No husband in the world,' said I, 'shall make me do an unjust or base thing.' 'That will soon be tried,' replied she; and Nan coming in, 'What,' said I, 'am I to have *two* bed-fellows again, these warm nights?' 'Yes, slippery one,' answered she, 'you are; and that till you can have *one good one* instead of us.' 'This is like you, Mrs Jewkes,' said I. '*Out of the abundance of the heart.* But it will do you no harm to let me sit all night in the great chair.' 'Nan,' said she, 'undress my young lady. If she won't let you, I'll help you: and if neither of us can do it quietly, we'll call my master to do it for us; though I think it an office more worthy of Monsieur Colbrand!' 'You are very wicked,' said I. 'I know it,' replied she: 'I am a Jezebel, and a London prostitute, you know.'

'You did great feats,' said I, 'to tell my master all this poor stuff! But you did not tell him how you beat me.' 'No, *lambkin*,' (a word

I had not heard a good while) 'that I left for you to tell; and you was going to do it, if the *vulture* had not taken the *wolf*'s part, and bid the poor *lamb* be silent!' 'No matter for your fleers,[183] Mrs Jewkes,' said I; 'though I cannot be heard in my defence here, yet a time will come, when I *shall* be heard, and when your own guilt will strike you dumb.' 'Ay, spirit!' said she, 'and the *vulture* too! Must we *both* be dumb? Why that, lambkin, will be pretty! When that time comes,' proceeded the wicked creature, 'you'll have all the talk to yourself! And how will the tongue of the pretty lambkin then bleat out *innocence* and *virtue*, and *honesty*, till the whole trial be at an end!' 'You are a wicked woman, Mrs Jewkes,' said I; 'and if you thought any thing of another world, could not talk thus. But no wonder! It shews what hands I am got into!' 'Ay, so it does,' returned she; 'but I beg you'll undress, and come to bed, or I believe your innocence won't keep you from *still worse* hands.' 'I will come to bed,' said I, 'if you will let me have the keys in my own hand; not else, if I can help it.' She came to me, and took me in her huge arms, as if I were a feather; said she, 'I do this to shew you, what a poor resistance you can make against me, if I pleased to exert myself; and so lambkin,' setting me down, 'don't say to your *wolf*, I *won't* come to bed! But undress, undress I tell you. And, Nan, pray pull off my young lady's shoes.' 'No, pray don't,' said I, 'I will come to bed presently, since I can't help it.'

And so I went to the closet, and scribbled a little. And she being importunate, I was forced to go to bed; but with some of my clothes on, as the former night; and she let me hold the two keys; for there are two locks, there being a double door; and I got a little sleep that night, having had none for two or three nights before.

I can't imagine what she means; but Nan offered to talk a little once or twice; and she snubbed her, and said, 'I charge you, wench, don't open your lips before me! And if you are asked any questions by Mrs Pamela, don't answer her one word, while I am here!' But she is a lordly woman to the maid-servants, and that has always been her character. O how unlike good Mrs Jervis in every thing.

SUNDAY *Morning*

Knowing that my master was dressing, in order to go to church, and seeing through my window the chariot getting ready, How happy, thought I, should I be, if I could go to that holy place, where I have not been for so long a time! How can such a wicked wretch as my master, with such bad designs in his heart, have the courage to shew his face there! I would pray for him as well as for myself, thought I, if I might be permitted to go: and should even be glad to interest the whole congregation in my prayers. In this thought I took up my pen. And what, said I to myself, should be the form of such an address to the congregation? Perhaps this – and I wrote down this for myself:

The prayers of this congregation are earnestly desired by a poor distressed creature, for the preservation of her virtue and innocence.

And this for my master and myself:

The prayers of this congregation are earnestly desired for a gentleman of great worth and honour, who labours under a temptation to exert his great power to ruin a poor, distressed, worthless maiden.

Mrs Jewkes came up: 'Always writing!' said she; and would see it. And strait, against my earnest entreaties, carried it down to my master. He looked upon it, and said, 'Tell her, she shall soon see how her prayers are answered. She is very bold: but as she has rejected all my favours, her reckoning for all is not far off.'

I looked after him out of the window, and he was charmingly dressed: to be sure, he is a handsome, fine gentleman: what pity his heart is not so good as his appearance! Why can't I hate him? But don't be uneasy, if you should see this; for it is impossible I should love him; for his vices all *ugly him over*, as I may say.

My master sends word, that he shall not come home to dinner: I suppose he dines with this Sir Simon Darnford.

I am much concerned for poor Mr Williams. Mrs Jewkes says, he is confined still, and takes on much. All his trouble is brought upon him for my sake: my master, it seems, will have his money from him. This is very hard, for it is three fifty pounds, which he gave him, as he thought, as a salary for three years that he has been with him. But there was no agreement between them; and he absolutely depended on my master's favour. How generous was he to run these risques for the sake of oppressed innocence! I hope he will meet with his reward in due time.

SUNDAY *Evening*

Mrs Jewkes has received a line from my master. I wonder what it is; for his chariot is come home without him. But she will tell me nothing; so it is in vain to ask her. I am so fearful of plots and tricks, I know not what to do. For, now my disgrace is avowed, what can I think? To be sure the worst will be attempted! But if I must suffer, let me not, good Heaven! be long a mournful survivor! Only let me not sinfully shorten my time!

This woman left upon the table, in the chamber, the following letter of my master's to her; and on seeing it there, I bolted myself in till I had transcribed it: you'll see how tremblingly, by the crooked lines. I wish poor Mr Williams's release at any rate; but this letter makes my heart ach. Yet I have another day's reprieve, thank Heaven!

'*Mrs* JEWKES,
'I have been so pressed on Williams's affair, that I shall set out this afternoon, in Sir Simon's chariot-and-six,[184] and with Mr Peters, who is his intercessor, for Stamford; and shall not be back till to-morrow evening, if then. As to your ward, I am thoroughly incensed against her. She has withstood her time; and now, would she sign and seal to my articles, it is too late. I shall discover something, perhaps, by him; and will, on my return, let her know, that all her ensnaring speciousness shall not save her from the fate that awaits her. But let her know nothing of this, lest it put her upon plots and artifices. Besure trust her not without another with you at night, lest she venture the window in her foolish rashness: for I shall require her at your hands.

Yours, &c.'

I had but just finished taking a copy of this, and laid the letter where I had it, and unbolted the door, when she came up in a great fright, for fear I should have seen it; but I being in my closet, and that lying as she left it, she did not mistrust. 'O,' said she, 'I was afraid you had seen my master's letter here, which I carelessly left on the table. Well,' continued she, 'I wish poor Mr Williams well off; I understand my master is gone to make up matters with him; which is very good of him. To be sure he is a very forgiving gentleman.' 'Why,' said I, as if I had known nothing of the matter, 'how can he make up matters with him? Is not Mr Williams at Stamford?' 'Yes,' said she, 'I believe so; but Parson Peters pleads for him, and he is gone with him to Stamford, and will not be back to-night: we have, therefore, nothing to do, but to eat our suppers betimes,[185] and go to-bed.'

So I have one more good honest night before me: who can tell what the next may be? But I know that I have your prayers at all times joined with my own.

TUESDAY *Night*

For the future, I will always mistrust most, when appearances look fairest. O your poor daughter, what has she not suffered since Sunday night, the time of her worst trial, and fearfullest danger!

O how I shudder to write you an account of this wicked interval of time! For, my dear parents, will you not be too much frightened and affected with my distress, when I tell you, that his journey to Stamford was all abominable pretence? For he came home privately, and had well-nigh effected all his vile purposes in the ruin of your poor daughter; and that by such a plot as I was not in the least apprehensive of: and you'll hear what a vile unwomanly part that wicked wretch, Mrs Jewkes, acted in it.

Take the dreadful story as well as I can relate it.

The maid Nan is fond of liquor, if she can get at it; and Mrs Jewkes happened, or designed, as is too probable, to leave a bottle of cherry-brandy in her way, and the wench drank more of it than she should; and when she came to lay the cloth, Mrs Jewkes perceived it, and rated at [186] her most sadly. The wretch has too many faults of her own, to suffer any of the like sort in any body else, if she can help it; and she bade her get out of her sight, when we had supped, and go to bed, to sleep off her liquor, before we came to bed. And so the poor maid went muttering up stairs.

About two hours after, which was near eleven o'clock, Mrs Jewkes and I went up to go to-bed; I pleasing myself with what a charming night I should have. We locked both doors, and saw poor Nan, as I thought, sitting fast asleep, in an elbow-chair, in a dark corner of the room, with her apron thrown over her head and neck. But oh! it was my abominable master, as you shall hear by and by.

And Mrs Jewkes said, 'There is that beast of a wench fast alseep! I knew she had taken a fine dose.' 'I will wake her,' said I. 'Let her sleep on,' answered she, 'we shall lie better without her.' 'So we shall,' said I; 'but won't she get cold?'

'I hope,' said the vile woman, 'you have no writing to-night.' 'No,' replied I, 'I will go to-bed when you go, Mrs Jewkes.' 'That's right,' answered she; 'indeed I wonder what you can find to write about so continually. I am sure you have better conveniences of that kind, and more paper, than I am aware of. Indeed I had intended to rummage you, if my master had not come down; for I spied a broken tea-cup with ink, which gave me a suspicion: but as he is come, let him look after you, if he will. If you deceive him, it will be his own fault.'

All this time we were undressing; and I fetching a deep sigh, 'What do you sigh for?' said she. 'I am thinking, Mrs Jewkes,' answered I, 'what a sad life I live, and how hard is my lot. I am sure the thief that has robbed is much better off than I, bating [187] the guilt; and I should, I think, take it for a mercy to be hanged out of the way, rather than live in these cruel apprehensions.'

So, being not sleepy, and in a prattling vein, I began to give a little history of myself, in this manner.

'My poor honest parents,' said I, 'in the first place, took care to instil good principles into my mind, till I was almost twelve years of age; and taught me to prefer goodness and poverty, if they could not be separated, to the highest condition; and they confirmed their lessons by their own practice; for they were of late years remarkably poor, and always as remarkably honest, even to a proverb; for, *As honest as Goodman* ANDREWS, was a bye-word.

'Well, then comes my late dear good lady, and takes a fancy to me, and said she would be the making of me, if I was a good girl: and she put me to sing, to dance, to play on the harpsichord, in order to divert her melancholy hours; and also taught me all manner of fine needle-works; but still this was her lesson, "*My good Pamela, be virtuous, and keep the men at a distance.*" Well, so I did; and yet, though I say it, they all respected me; and would do any thing for me, as if I were a gentlewoman.

'But then, what comes next? Why, it pleased God to take my good lady; and then comes my master: and what says he? Why, in effect, it is "*Be not virtuous*, Pamela."

'So here have I lived above sixteen years in virtue and reputation; and, all at once, when I come to know what is good, and what is evil, I must renounce all the good, all the whole sixteen years innocence, which, next to God's grace, I owed chiefly to my parents and to my lady's good lessons and examples, and chuse the evil; and so, in a moment's time, become the vilest of creatures! And all this, for what, I pray? Why, truly, for a pair of diamond ear-rings, a solitaire, a necklace, and a diamond ring for my finger; which would not become me: for a few paltry fine clothes; which, when I wore them, would make but my former poverty more ridiculous to every body that saw me; especially when they knew the base terms I wore them upon. But, indeed, I was to have a great parcel of guineas beside; I forget how many; for had there been ten times more, they would not have been so much to me, as the honest six guineas you tricked me out of, Mrs Jewkes.

'Well, but then I was to have I know not how many pounds a year for my life; and my poor father (fine encouragement indeed!) was to be the manager for the abandoned prostitute, his daughter: and then (there was the jest of it!) my kind, forgiving, virtuous master would pardon me all my misdeeds.

'And what, pray, are all these violent misdeeds? Why, they are, for daring to adhere to the good lessons that were taught me; for not being contented, when I was run away with, in order to be ruined; but contriving, if my poor wits had been able, to get out of danger, and preserve myself honest.

'Then was he once jealous of poor John, though he knew John was his own creature, and helped to deceive me.

'Then was he outrageous against poor Mr Williams; and him has this good, merciful master thrown into gaol! and for what? Why, truly, for that being a divine, and a good man, he was willing to forego all his expectations of interest, and assist a poor creature, whom he believed innocent!

'But, to be sure, I must be *forward, bold, saucy*, and what not, to dare to attempt an escape from certain ruin, and an unjust confine-ment. Poor Mr Williams! how was he drawn in to make marriage proposals to me! O Mrs Jewkes! what a trick was that! The honest gentleman would have had but a poor catch of me, had I consented to be his wife; but he, and *you* too, know I did not want to marry *any body*. I only wanted to go to my poor parents, and not to be laid under an unlawful restraint, and which would not have been attempted, but only that I am a poor destitute young creature, and have no friend that is able to right me.

'So here, Mrs Jewkes,' said I, 'have I given my history in brief. I am very unhappy: and whence my unhappiness? Why, because my master sees something in my person that takes his present fancy; and because I would not be ruined; why, therefore, to chuse, I must, and I shall be ruined! And this is all the reason that can be given!'

She heard me run on all this time, while I was undressing, without any interruption; and I said, 'Well, I must go to the two closets, ever since an affair of the closet at the other house, though he is so far off. And I have a good mind to wake this poor maid.' 'No, don't,' said she, 'I charge you. I am very angry with her, and she'll get no harm there; and if she wakes, she will find her way to-bed well enough, as there is a candle in the chimney.'

So I looked into the closets; and kneeled down in my own, as I used to do, to say my prayers, and this with my under clothes in my hand;[188] and passed by the supposed sleeping wench, in my return. But little did I think, it was my wicked, wicked master in a gown and petticoat of her's, and her apron over his face and shoulders. To what meannesses will not Lucifer make his votaries stoop, to gain their abominable ends!

Mrs Jewkes by this time was got to-bed, on the further side, as she used to do; and I lay close to her, to make room for the maid, when she should awake. 'Where are the keys?' said I, 'and yet I am not so much afraid to-night.' 'Here,' said the wicked woman, 'put your arm under mine, and you shall find them about my wrist, as they used to be.' I did so, and the abominable designer held my hand with her right hand, as my right arm was under her left.

In less than a quarter of an hour, hearing the supposed maid in motion, 'Poor Nan is awake,' said I; 'I hear her stir.' 'Let us go to sleep,' replied she, 'and not mind her: she'll come to bed, when she's quite awake.' 'Poor soul!' said I, 'I'll warrant she will have the head-ach finely to-morrow for this.' 'Be silent,' answered she, 'and go to sleep; you keep me awake. I never found you in so talkative a humour in my life.' 'Don't chide me,' said I; 'I will say but one thing more: do you think Nan could hear me talk of my master's offers?' 'No, no,' replied she, 'she was dead asleep.' 'I am glad of that,' said I; 'because I would not expose my master to his common servants; and I knew you were no stranger to his *fine* articles.' 'I think they *were* fine articles,' replied she, 'and you were bewitched you did not close with them: but let us go to sleep.'

So I was silent: and the pretended Nan (O wicked, base, villainous designer! what a plot, what an unexpected plot was this!) seemed to be awaking; and Mrs Jewkes, abhorred creature! said, 'Come, Nan! What, are you awake at last? Pr'ythee come to-bed, for Mrs Pamela is in a talking fit, and won't go to sleep one while.'

At that, the pretended she came to the bed-side; and sitting down in a chair concealed by the curtain, began to undress. 'Poor Mrs Ann,' said I, 'I warrant your head aches most sadly! How do you do?' No answer was returned. 'You know I have ordered her not to answer you,' said the abominably wicked woman: this plot, to be sure, was laid when she gave her these orders the night before.

The pretended Nan (how shocking to relate!) then came into bed, trembling like an aspen-leaf; and I (poor fool that I was!) pitied her much. But well might the barbarous deceiver tremble at his vile-dissimulation, and base designs.

What words shall I find, my dear mother, (for my father should not see this shocking part) to describe the rest, and my confusion, when the guilty wretch took my left arm, and laid it under his neck as the vile procuress held my right; and then he clasped me round the waist!

'Is the wench mad?' said I. 'Why, how now, confidence?' thinking still it had been Nan. But he kissed me with frightful vehemence; and then his voice broke upon me like a clap of thunder: 'Now, Pamela,' said he, 'is the time of reckoning come, that I have threatened!' I screamed out for help; but there was nobody to help me: and both my hands were secured, as I said. Sure never poor soul was in such agonies as I: 'Wicked man!' said I; 'wicked, abominable woman! Good Heaven, this *one* time! this *one* time, good Heaven, deliver me, or strike me dead this moment!' And then I screamed again and again.

'One word with you, Pamela!' said he. 'Hear me but one word! Hitherto you find I offer nothing to you.' 'Is this *nothing*,' said I, 'to be in bed here? To hold my hands between you?'

'Hear me, Pamela.' 'I will hear, if you will this moment leave the bed, and take this vile woman from me!'

Said she, (O disgrace of womankind!) 'Don't stand dilly-dallying, sir. She cannot exclaim worse than she has done; and will be quieter when she knows the worst.'

'Silence!' said he to her. 'I must say one word to you, Pamela: it is this; you now see, that you are in my power! You cannot get from me, nor help yourself: yet have I not offered any thing amiss to you. But if you resolve not to comply with my proposals, I will not lose this opportunity. If you do, I will yet leave you. I abhor violence.[189] Your compliance, my dear girl, shall intitle you to all I offered you in my proposals.'

'O sir,' exclaimed I, 'leave me, do but leave me, and I will do any thing I ought to do.' 'Swear then to me,' said he, 'that you will accept my proposals!' And then (for this was all detestable grimace)[190] he put his hand in my bosom.[191]

With struggling, fright, terror, I quite fainted away, and did not come to myself soon; so that they both, from the cold sweats I was in, thought me dying. And I remember no more, than that, when, with great difficulty, they brought me to myself, she was sitting on one side of the bed, with her clothes on; and he on the other, in his gown and slippers.

When I saw them there, I sat up in my bed, nothing about my neck, without any regard to what appearance I must make: and he soothing me with an aspect of pity and concern, I put my hand to his mouth, and said, 'O tell me, yet tell me not, what I have suffered in this distress!' And I talked quite wild, and knew not what; for I was on the point of distraction.

He most solemnly, and with a bitter imprecation, vowed, that he had not offered the least indecency; that he was frightened at the terrible manner I was taken with the fit: that he would desist from his attempt; and begged but to see me easy and quiet, and he would leave me directly, and go to his own bed. 'O then,' said I, 'take with you this most wicked woman, this vile Mrs Jewkes, as an earnest that I may believe you!'

'And will you, sir,' said the wicked wretch, 'for a fit or two, give up such an opportunity as this? I thought you had known the sex better. She is now, you see, quite well again!'

This I heard; more she might say; but I fainted away once more, at these words, and at his clasping his arms about me again. And when I came a little to myself, I saw him sit there, and the maid Nan, holding a smelling-bottle to my nose, and no Mrs Jewkes.

He said, taking my hand, 'Now will I vow to you, my dear Pamela, that I will leave you the moment I see you better, and pacified. Here's Nan knows, and will tell you, my concern for you. I vow to Heaven, that I have not offered any indecency to you. And since I found Mrs Jewkes so offensive to you, I have sent her to the maid's bed. The maid only shall stay with you to-night; and but promise me, that you will compose yourself, and I will leave you.' 'But,' said I, 'will not Nan also hold my hand? And will not she let you come in again?' He swore that he would not return that night. 'Nan,' said he, 'do you go to-bed to the dear creature, and say all you can to comfort her: and now, Pamela, give me but your hand, and say you forgive me, and I will leave you to your repose.'

I held out my trembling hand, which he vouchsafed to kiss; and again demanding my forgiveness, 'God forgive you, sir,' said I, 'as you will be just to what you promise!' And he withdrew, with a countenance of remorse, as I hoped; and Nan shut the doors, and, at my request, brought the keys to-bed.

This, O my dear parents! was a most dreadful trial. I tremble still to think of it. I hope, as he assures me, he was not guilty of indecency; but have reason to be thankful that I was disabled in my intellects. Since it is but too probable, that all my resistance, and all my strength, otherwise would not have availed me.

I was so weak all day on Monday, that I could not get out of bed. My master shewed great tenderness for me; and I hope he is really sorry, and that this will be his last attempt; but he does not say so neither.

He came in the morning, as soon as he heard the door open: and I began to be fearful. He stopped short of the bed, and said, 'Rather than give you apprehensions, I will come no further.' 'Your honour, sir,' said I, 'and your mercy, is all I have to beg.'

He sat down on the side of the bed, and asked kindly, How I did? He bid me be composed; and said, I still looked a little wildly. 'Pray, sir,' said I, 'let me not see this infamous Mrs Jewkes: I cannot bear her in my sight.' 'She shan't come near you all this day, if you will promise to compose yourself.' 'Then, sir, I will try.' He pressed my hand very tenderly, and went out.

What a change does this shew! May it be lasting! But, alas! he seems only to have altered his method of proceeding; and retains, I doubt, his wicked purpose!

On Tuesday about ten o'clock, when he heard I was up, he sent for me down into the parlour. As soon as he saw me, he said, 'Come nearer to me, Pamela.' I did, and he took my hand, and said, 'You begin to look well again: I am glad of it. You little rogue,' was his free word, 'how did you frighten me on Sunday night!' 'Sir,' said I, 'pray name not that night'; my eyes overflowing at the remembrance: and I turned my head aside.

'Place some little confidence in me,' said he. 'I know what those charming eyes mean, and you shall not need to explain yourself. I do assure you, that the moment you fainted away, I quitted the bed, and Mrs Jewkes did so too. I put on my gown, and she fetched her smelling-bottle, and we both did all we could to restore you; and my passion for you was all swallowed up in the concern I had for your recovery; for I thought I never saw a fit so strong and violent in my life; and feared we should not bring you to yourself again. My apprehensions for you, might possibly be owing to my folly, and my unacquaintedness with what your sex *can* shew when they are in earnest. But this I repeat to you, that your mind may be entirely comforted: all that I offered to you was before you fainted away. You yourself are sensible, that that was rather what might excite your fears, than deserve your censure. You have nothing, therefore, to make yourself uneasy at, or to reproach me with on the occasion you take so much at heart.'

'What you refer to, sir,' said I, 'was very bad: and it was too plain, you had the worst designs.' 'When I tell you the truth in one instance,' replied he, 'you may believe me in the other. I know not, I declare, beyond that lovely bosom, that you are a woman; but that I *did* intend what you call *the worst*, is most certain: and though I would not too much alarm you now, I could curse my weakness and my folly, which makes me own, that I cannot live without you. But, if I am master of myself, and my own resolution, I will not attempt to compel you to any thing.' 'Sir,' said I, 'you may easily keep your resolution, if you will send me out of your way, to my parents; and that is all I beg.'

' 'Tis a folly to talk of it,' said he. 'You must not, shall not go. And if I could be assured you would not attempt it, your stay here should be made agreeable to you.' 'But to what end, sir, am I to stay?' said I: 'you yourself seem not sure you can keep your own present good resolutions; and what would you think of me, were I to stay to my danger, if I *could* get away in safety? And what will the world –'

'The world, pretty simpleton!' interrupted he: 'what has the world to do between you and me? But I now sent for you for two reasons; the first is, to engage you to promise me for a fortnight to come, that you will not offer to go away without my consent; and this I expect for *your own* sake, that I may give you more liberty. The second, that you will see Mrs Jewkes, and forgive her. She is much concerned, and thinks, that, as all her fault was her obedience to me, it would be very cruel to sacrifice her, as she calls it, to your resentment.'

'As to the first, sir,' said I, 'it is a hard injunction: and as to the second, considering Mrs Jewkes's vile unwomanly wickedness, and her endeavours to instigate you to ruin me, when you, from your returning goodness, seemed to have some compassion for me, it is still harder. But to shew my compliance in all I *can* comply with' [for you know, my dear parents, I might as well make a merit of complying, when my refusal would stand me in no stead] 'I will consent to both.'

'That's my good girl!' said he, and kissed me. 'This is quite prudent, and shews me, that you don't take insolent advantage of my passion for you; and will, perhaps, stand you in more stead than you are aware of.'

He then rung the bell, and said, 'Call down Mrs Jewkes.' She came down, and he took my hand, and put it into hers; and said, 'Mrs Jewkes, I am obliged to you for your diligence and fidelity; but Pamela must be allowed to think *she* is not; because the service I employed you in was not so agreeable to her, as I could have wished she would have thought it; and you were not to favour her, but obey me. But yet I assure you, at the very first word, she has *once* obliged me, by consenting to be reconciled to you; and if she gives me no great cause, I shall not, perhaps, put you on such disagreeable service again. Now, therefore, be you once more bedfellows and board-fellows, as I may say, for some days longer; and see that Pamela sends no letters nor messages out of the house, nor keeps a correspondence unknown to me, especially with that

Williams; and, as for the rest, shew the dear girl all the respect that is due to one I must love, and who yet, I hope, will deserve my love; and let her be under no unnecessary restraints. But your watchful care is not, however, to cease: and remember, that you are not to disoblige *me*, to oblige *her*; and that I will not, cannot, yet part with her.'

Mrs Jewkes looked very sullen, and as if she would be glad still to do me a good turn, if it lay in her power.

I took courage then to drop a word or two for poor Mr Williams; but he was angry, and said, he could not endure to hear his name, in *my* mouth.

I begged for leave to send a letter to you, my dear father. So I should, he said, if he might read it first. But this did not answer my design; and yet I would have sent you such a letter as he might have seen, if I had been sure my danger was over. But that I cannot; for he now seems to be taking another method: a method which I am still more apprehensive of, than I was of his more open and haughty behaviour; because he may now perhaps resolve to watch an opportunity, and join force with it, when I least think of my danger: for now he seems all kindness. He talks of love without reserve; and makes nothing of allowing himself the liberty of kissing me, which he calls innocent; but which I do not like; since for a master to take such freedoms with a servant, has meaning too much in it, not to alarm.

Just this moment I have a confirmation of what I thought of his designs in his change of behaviour to me; for I over heard him say to the wicked woman, who very likely (for I heard not what she said) had been instigating him again, 'I have begun wrong. Terror does but add to her frost. But she is a charming girl; and may be thawed by kindness. I should have sought to melt her by love.'

What an abominable man is this! Yet his mother so good a woman! He says I must stay a fortnight. What a dangerous fortnight may this be to your poor girl! But I trust that God will enable me (as is my constant prayer) to be proof against his vileness.

WEDNESDAY *Morning*

This wicked man – He cannot deserve to be called a gentleman. I believe I shall lose all my reverence for him. He seems to be putting in practice his vile arts. He sent for me down. I went. There was no helping that, you know. 'We will take a walk in the garden,' said he, taking my hand, and led me into it. What signified denying to go? Should he have base designs, thought I, I am as much in danger in the house, with such a vile woman, as in the garden. But what I had heard, you may suppose, was in my head, and I could not but be apprehensive: though I dared not to own I had over heard what he said, lest he should think me a listener: but if I was, in such a situation, I am excusable.

He presently began by squeezing my hand; and then, truly, all the way we walked, he would put his arm about my waist. I would have removed his arm: but he called me little fool! and bid me not mistrust his honour. Had he not told me, he said, that I might rely upon it? And it would be better for me if I did.

He then said abundance of kind and praiseful things, enough to make me proud, had not his designs been so apparent.

After walking about, he led me into a little alcove in the further part of the garden, which having a passage through it, I the less resisted; and still the less, as he had led me through once without stopping;[192] but then stopping in it, he began to be very teazing. He made me sit on his knee; and still on my struggling against such a freedom, he bid me rely on his honour, solemnly assuring me that I might. But then kissing me very often, though I resisted every time, I told him, at last, and would have got from him, that I would not stay with him in this place. I would not be so freely used. And I wondered he could so demean himself. I told him, moreover, that he would level all distance between us, and I should lose all reverence for him; though he was the son of my ever-honoured lady.

He held me fast notwithstanding, professing honour all the time with his mouth, though his actions did not correspond. I begged and prayed he would let me go: and had I not appeared quite regardless of all he said, and resolved not to stay, if I could help it, I know not how far he would have proceeded: for I was forced at last to fall down upon my knees.

He then walked out with me, still bragging of his honour, and his love. 'Yes, yes, sir,' said I, 'your honour is to destroy mine, and your love is to ruin me, I see it too plainly. But, indeed, I will not walk out with you, sir, any more.'

'Do you know,' said he, 'whom you talk to, and where you are?'

You may believe I had reason to think him not so decent as he should be; for I said, 'As to *where I am*, sir, I know it too well, and that I have no creature to befriend me: and, as to *whom I talk to*, sir, let me ask you, what you would have me answer?'

He put his arm round me, and his other hand on my neck; which made me more angry and bold; and he said, 'Who then am I?' 'Why,' said I, (struggling from him, and in a great passion) 'to be sure, you are Lucifer himself in the *shape* of my master, or you could not use me thus.' 'These are too great liberties,' said he, in anger; 'and I desire, that you will not repeat them, for your own sake: for if you have no decency towards *me*, I'll have none towards *you*.'

I was running from him; and had got at a little distance, when he in a haughty tone, called out, 'Come back! Pamela, come back when I bid you!' Too well I knew, as I told you before, that every place was alike dangerous to me; and that I had nobody to run to for safety: and I stopped at his call; for he stopped too, as if to see if I would obey him, and perhaps to have a pretence against me if I did not; or in disdain to run after such a girl as me. 'How can I, sir,' said I, throwing abroad my supplicating arms, 'how can I go back, to a gentleman who has so demeaned himself to his poor servant girl?' 'Come back,' repeated he, in a still more haughty tone, throwing out in a threatening manner one arm, and looking taller than usual, as I thought, and he is a tall, and very majestic man. 'Come back, when I bid you'; still not moving a pace towards me.

What could I do? With unwilling feet, and slow, I went back; and seeing him look angry, I held my hands together, and wept, and said, 'Pray, sir, forgive me.' 'No,' said he, 'rather say, pray, Lucifer, forgive me. You have given me a character, Pamela, and blame me not if I act up to it.'

'Sir,' said I, 'let me beg you to forgive me. I am really sorry for my boldness; but indeed, you don't use me like a gentleman; and how can I express my resentments, if I mince the matter, while you are indecent?'

'Precise fool!' said he, 'what indecencies have I offered you? I was bewitched I had not gone through my purpose last Sunday night; and then your licentious tongue had not given the worst interpretation to little puny freedoms, that shew my love and my folly at the same time. But begone,' said he, taking my hand, and tossing it from him, 'and learn more wit. I will lay aside my foolish regard for you, and assert myself. Be gone,' said he, again, with a haughty air.

'If, sir,' said I, 'I am not to go for good, I cannot quit your presence till you pardon me. On my knees I beg you will': and I kneeled to him. 'I am truly sorry for my boldness. But I see how you go on: now you soothe me, and now threaten me: and have you not as good as avowed my ruin? What then is left me but words? And can these words be other than such strong ones as shall shew the detestation, which, from the bottom of my heart, I have for every attempt upon my virtue? Judge for me, sir, I hope you are not the most hard-hearted of men! judge for me, and pardon me.'

'Pardon you,' said he, 'what! when you have the boldness to justify yourself in your fault? Why don't you say, you never will again offend me?' 'I will endeavour, sir,' said I, 'always to preserve that decency towards you, that veneration for you, which is due from me to the son of that ever-honoured lady, who taught me to prefer my honesty to my life. Command from me, sir, that life, and I will lay it down with pleasure, to shew my obedience to you. But I cannot be patient, I cannot be passive, when my virtue is in danger. For God's sake, sir, seek not to destroy the fabric which your good mother took so much pleasure in building up.'

He seemed affected, yet angrily said, he never saw such a fool in his life! And walking by the side of me some yards without saying a word, he at last went in, bidding me attend him in the garden after dinner.

WEDNESDAY *Night*

I have now, my dear parents, such a scene to open to you, that I know will alarm both your hopes and your fears, as it does mine. And this it is:

After my master had dined, he took a turn into the stables, to look at his stud of horses; and afterwards, when he came in, he opened the house-keeper's parlour-door, where Mrs Jewkes and I sat at dinner. At his entrance, we both rose up; but he said, 'Sit still, sit still: proceed with your dinner. Mrs Jewkes has told me, that you have but a poor appetite.' 'A poor one, indeed,' said Mrs Jewkes. 'A pretty good one, sir,' said I, '*considering*.' 'None of your

considerings!' said he, 'pretty-face'; and tapped me on the cheek. I
blushed, but was glad he was so good-humoured; though I could
not tell how to sit before him, nor how to behave myself. 'I know,
Pamela,' said he, 'you are a carver: my mother used to say so.' 'My
lady, sir,' said I, 'was very good to me, in every thing; and would
always make me do the honours of her table, when she was with her
few select friends that she loved.' He bid me carve that chicken. I
did so. 'Now,' said he, taking a fork, and putting a wing upon my
plate, 'let me see you eat that.' I obeyed; but was much abashed at
his freedom and condescension. And you can't imagine how Mrs
Jewkes looked, and how respectful she seemed to me, and called me
good madam, I assure you, urging me to take a little bit of tart.

My master took two or three turns about the room, musing and
more thoughtful than ever before I had seen him; and at last he went
out, saying, 'I am going into the garden: you know, Pamela, what I
said to you before dinner.' I stood up, and court'sied, saying, I
would attend his honour. 'Do, good girl,' said he.

'Well,' said Mrs Jewkes, 'I see how things will go. O *madam*,' as
she called me again, 'I am sure you are to be our mistress; and then
I know what will become of me.' 'Ah! Mrs Jewkes,' said I, 'if I can
but keep myself virtuous, 'tis the most of my ambition; and I hope
no temptation shall make me otherwise.'

Notwithstanding I had no reason to be pleased with his treatment of me before dinner, yet I made haste to attend him.

I found him walking by the side of that very pond, which,
through a sinful despondence, had like to have been so fatal to me.
And it was by the side of this pond, and not far from the place where
I had that dreadful conflict, that my present hopes, if I am not to be
betrayed by them, began to dawn. And sometimes I have the presumption to hope fo r an happy omen from hence; as if the Almighty would shew your poor daughter, how well she did, to put
her affiance [193] in his goodness, and not to throw away herself,
because her ruin, in her short-sighted apprehension, seemed at the
time to be inevitable.

'Well, Pamela,' he was pleased to say, 'I am glad you wanted not
intreaty, or a new command, to come to me. I love to be obliged.
Give me your hand.' I did so; and he looked at me very steadily,
and pressing my hand all the time, at last said, 'I will now talk to
you in a serious manner.

'You have a good deal of prudence, and a penetration beyond your *years*, and, as I thought, beyond your *opportunities*. You seem to me to have an open, frank, and generous mind; and in person you are so lovely, that in my eyes, you excel all your sex. All these accomplishments have engaged my affections so deeply, that, as I have often said, I cannot live without you; and I would divide, with all my soul, my estate with you, to make you mine upon my own terms.' Here he paused. 'Ah, sir,' said I, offering gently to withdraw my hand; but he held it the faster. 'Hear me out,' said he. 'These terms you have absolutely rejected; yet in such a manner as makes me admire you more. Your pretty chit-chat to Mrs Jewkes the last Sunday night, so full of beautiful simplicity, half disarmed my resolution, before I approached your bed. And I see you on all occasions so watchful for your virtue, that though I hoped to find it otherwise, I cannot but confess, my passion for you is increased by it. But now what shall I say further, Pamela? I will make you my adviser in this matter; though not, perhaps, my definitive judge.

'You cannot believe,' proceeded he, 'that I am a *very* abandoned man. I have hitherto been guilty of no *very* enormous actions. The causing you to be carried off to this house, and confining you here, may, perhaps, be one of the most violent actions of my life. Had I been utterly given up to my passions, I should before now have gratified them, and not have shewn that remorse and compassion for you, which have reprieved you more than once when absolutely in my power.

'But, what can I do? Consider the pride of my condition. I cannot endure the thought of marriage, even with a person of equal or superior degree to myself; and have declined several proposals of that kind: how, then, with the distance between us, in the world's judgment, can I think of making *you* my wife? Yet I must have you; I cannot bear the thoughts of any other man's supplanting me in your affections. And the very apprehension of that has made me hate the name of Williams, and use him in a manner unworthy of my nature.

'Now, Pamela, judge for me; and, since I have told you thus candidly my mind, and I see yours is big with some important meaning, by your eyes, your blushes, and that sweet confusion which I behold struggling in your bosom, tell me with like openness and candour, what you think I ought to do, and what you would have me do.'

It is impossible for me to express the agitations of my mind on this unexpected declaration, and made in so condescending a manner; for, alas for me! I found I had need of all my poor discretion, to ward off the blow which this treatment gave to my most guarded thoughts. I threw myself at his feet; for I trembled, and could hardly stand. 'O sir,' said I, 'spare your poor servant's confusion! O spare the poor Pamela!' 'Speak out,' said he, 'and tell me, what you think I ought to do?' 'I cannot say what you *ought* to do,' answered I: 'but I only beg you will not seek to ruin me; and if you think me virtuous, if you think me sincerely honest, let me go to my poor parents. I will vow to you, that I will never suffer myself to be engaged without your approbation.'

Still he insisted upon a more explicit answer to his question, of what I thought he *ought* to do. And I said, 'As to *my* poor thoughts, of what you ought to do, I must needs say, that, indeed, I think you ought to regard the world's opinion, and avoid doing any thing disgraceful to your birth and fortune; and therefore, if you really honour the poor Pamela with your favour, a little time, absence, and the conversation of worthier persons of my sex, will effectually enable you to overcome a regard so unworthy of your condition: and this, sir, is the best advice I can offer.'

'Charming creature! lovely Pamela!' said he, (with an ardour that was never before so agreeable to me) 'this generous manner is of a piece with all the rest of your conduct. But tell me still more explicitly, what you would advise me to in the case.'

'O sir,' said I, 'take not advantage of my credulity, and of my free and open heart: but were I the first lady in the land, instead of the poor abject Pamela Andrews, I would, I *could* tell you. But I can say no more.' And I held down my face, all covered over with confusion.

O my dear father and mother! now I know you will indeed be concerned for me, since now I am concerned for myself: for now I begin to be afraid, I know too well the reason why all his hard trials of me, and my black apprehensions, would not let me hate him.

But be assured still, by the Divine Aid, that I shall do nothing unworthy of your Pamela; and if I find that this appearance of true love is only assumed to delude me, I shall think nothing in this world so vile and so odious; and nothing, if he be not the worst of his kind, (as he says, and I hope, he is not) so desperately guileful as the heart of man.

He generously said, 'I will spare your confusion, Pamela, but I hope, I may promise myself, that you can love me preferably to any other man; and that no one in the world has had any share in your affections; for I am very jealous in my love, and if I thought you had a secret whispering in your soul, though it had not yet come up to a wish, for any other man breathing, I should not forgive *myself* for persisting in my affection for you; nor *you*, if you did not frankly acquaint me with it.'

As I still continued on my knees, on the grass border by the pond-side, he sat himself down on the grass by me, and putting his arm round me, 'Why hesitates my Pamela?' said he. 'Can you not answer me with truth, as I wish? If you cannot, speak, and I will forgive you.'

'O sir,' said I, 'it is not that I cannot most readily answer your question; indeed it is not: but what you once said to Mrs Jewkes, when you thought I was not in hearing, comes across my mind; and makes me dread, that I am in more danger than ever I was in my life.'

'I will not answer, too fearful and foolish Pamela,' said he, 'how long I may hold in my present mind; for my pride struggles hard within me; and if you doubt me, I have no obligation to your confidence or opinion. But at present I am sincere in what I say: and I expect you will be so too; and answer directly my question.'

'I find, sir,' said I, 'I know not myself; and your question is of such a nature, that I only want to tell you what I heard, and to have your kind answer to it; or else, what I can truly say to your question, may pave the way to my ruin.'

'Well,' said he, 'you may say what you have over-heard; for, in not answering me directly, you put my soul upon the rack; and half the trouble I have had with *you*, would have brought to my arms some one of the finest ladies in England.'

'O sir,' said I, 'my virtue is as dear to me, as if I was of the highest quality; you know, that I have had but too much reason for apprehensions. But I will tell you what I heard.

'You talked to Mrs Jewkes of having begun wrong with me, in

trying to subdue me with terror; and of frost, and such-like; and that you would, for the future, change your conduct, and try to *melt* me, that was your word, by kindness. I fear not, sir, the grace of God supporting me, that any acts of kindness will make me forget what I owe to my virtue; but, sir, I may, I find, be made more miserable by such acts, than by terror; because my nature is frank, and I cannot be ungrateful, and if I should be taught a lesson I never yet learnt, with what regret should I descend to the grave, to think, that I could not hate my worst enemy! And that, at the last great day, I must stand up as an accuser of the unhappy soul, that I could wish it in my power to save!'

'Exalted girl!' said he, 'what a thought is that! Why, now, Pamela, you excel yourself. You have given me a hint that will hold me long. But, sweet creature, tell me what is this lesson, which you never yet learnt, and which you are so afraid of being taught?'

'If, sir, you will again generously spare my confusion, I need not speak it: but this I will say, in answer to the question you seem most solicitous about, that I never yet saw the man to whom I wished to be married. I hoped for nothing but to return to my poor parents; and to employ myself in serving God, and comforting them; and you know not, sir, how you disappointed me in my proposed honest pleasures, when you sent me hither.'

'Well then,' said he, 'I may promise myself, that neither regard for the parson, nor for any other man, is any the least secret motive of your stedfast refusal of my offers?' 'Indeed, sir, you may; and, as you was pleased to ask, I answer, that I have not the least shadow of a wish or thought in favour of any man living.'

'But,' said he, '(for I am foolishly jealous, and yet my jealousy shews my fondness for you) have you not encouraged Williams to think you will be his?' 'Indeed, sir, I have not; but the very contrary.' 'And would you not have had him,' said he, 'if you had got away by his means?' 'I had resolved, sir,' said I, 'in my mind, otherwise; and he knew it, and the poor man –' 'I charge you,' said he, 'say not a word in his favour! You will excite a whirlwind in my soul, if you name him with kindness; and then you will be borne away with the tempest.'

'I have done, sir.' 'Nay, but do not have done; let me know the whole. If you have any regard for him, speak out; for it would end dreadfully for *you*, for *me*, and for *him*, if I found, that you disguised any secret of your soul from me, in this nice particular.'

'If ever, sir, I have given you cause to think me sincere –' 'Say then,' said he, interrupting me with great vehemence, and taking both my hands between his, 'declare, as if you were in the presence of God, that you have not any the least shadow of regard for Williams, or any other man.'

'As I wish God to bless me, sir, and to preserve my innocence, I have not.' 'I will believe you, Pamela,' said he. 'In time, perhaps, I may better bear that man's name. If I am convinced that you are not prepossessed, my vanity makes me assured, that I need not to fear a place in your regard, in preference to any other man. But yet it piques my pride, to think that you were so easily, and at such a short acquaintance, brought to run away with that college novice!'

'May I, sir, be heard one word? Let me not incur your indignation and I will tell you, perhaps, the unnecessary and imprudent, but yet, the whole truth.

'My honesty (I am poor and lowly, and am not intitled to call it *honour*) was in danger. I saw no means of securing myself from your avowed attempts. You had shewed you would not stick at little matters; and what, sir, could any body have thought of my sincerity, when I declared that I preferred my virtue to all other considerations, if I had not escaped from these dangers, if I could have found any way to do it? I am not going to say any thing for him; but indeed, sir, it was I that put him upon assisting my escape. I got him to enquire, if there were any gentry in the neighbourhood, who would protect me; and prevailed upon him – Don't frown at me, good sir, for I must tell you the whole truth! – to apply to a lady named Jones; and to Lady Darnford; and he was so good as to apply to Mr Peters the minister: but they all refused me; and then it was he let me know, that there was no honourable way to avoid the dangers I apprehended but marriage. I declined his expedient; and he agreed to assist me for God's sake.'

'Now,' said he, 'you are going –' Interrupting him, 'Pray, sir,' said I, 'don't be angry; I have just done. I would only say, that rather than have staid to be ruined, I would have thrown myself upon the poorest beggar that ever the world saw, if I had thought him honest. And I hope, when you duly weigh all matters, you will forgive me, and not think me so bold and so forward a creature as you have been pleased to call me.'

'Well,' said he, 'even in this your last speech, which, let me tell you, shews more your integrity of heart, than your prudence, you have not over-much pleased me. But I *must* love you; and it vexes me not a little that I must. But tell me, Pamela; for now the former question recurs; since you so much prize your virtue; since all attempts against that, are so odious to you; and since I have avowedly made several of these attempts, do you think it is possible for you to love me *preferably* to any other man?'

'Ah! sir,' said I, 'and here my doubt recurs, that you may thus graciously treat me, to take advantage of my credulity.'

'Still perverse and doubting! Cannot you take me as I am at present? I have told you that I am now sincere and undesigning, whatever I may be hereafter.'

'Ah! sir, what can I say? I have already said too much, if – But do not bid me say how well.' And then, my face glowing as the fire, I, all abashed, leaned upon his shoulder, to hide my confusion.

He clasped me to him with ardour, and said, 'Hide your dear face in my bosom, my beloved Pamela; your innocent freedoms charm me! But then say – How well – what?'

'If you will be good,' said I, 'to your poor servant, and spare her, she cannot say too much! But if not, she is doubly undone! Undone indeed!'

'I hope my present temper will hold,' replied he; 'for I tell you frankly, that I have known, in this agreeable hour, more sincere pleasure than I ever experienced in the guilty tumults, that my desiring soul drove me into, in the hopes of possessing you on my own terms. And, Pamela, you must pray for the continuance of this temper; and I hope your prayers will get the better of my temptations.'

His goodness overpowered all my reserves. I threw myself at his feet, and embraced his knees. 'What pleasure, sir, you give me, at these gracious words, is not lent your poor servant to express! I shall be too much rewarded for all my sufferings, if this goodness hold! God grant it may, for your own soul's sake, as well as for mine! And oh! how happy should I be, if–'

He stopped me, and said, 'But, my dear girl, what must we do about the world, and the world's censure? Indeed, I cannot marry!'

Now was I again struck all of a heap. However, soon recollecting myself, 'Sir,' said I, 'I have not the presumption to hope for such an honour. If I may be permitted to return in peace and safety to my poor parents, to pray for you there; it is all I at present request. This, sir, after all my apprehensions and dangers, will be a great pleasure to me. And, if I know my own heart, I shall wish you happy in a lady of suitable degree; and rejoice most sincerely in every circumstance that shall make for the happiness of my late good lady's beloved son.'

'Well,' said he, 'this conversation, Pamela, is gone farther than I intended it. You need not be afraid, at this rate, of trusting yourself with *me*: But it is I, that ought to be doubtful of myself, when I am with *you*. But before I say any thing further on this subject, I will take my proud heart to task; and, till then, let every thing be as if this conversation had never passed. Only, let me tell you, that the more confidence you place in me, the more you will oblige me; and that your doubts will only beget *cause* of doubts.' And with this ambiguous saying, he saluted [194] me in a more formal manner, if I may so say, than before, and lent me his hand; and we walked towards the house, side-by-side, he seeming very thoughtful and pensive, as if he had already repented him of his goodness.

What shall I do, what steps take, if all this be designing! To be sure, if he be false, as I may call it, I have gone too far, much too far! I am ready, on the apprehension of this, to bite my forward tongue, for what I said, or rather to beat my more forward heart, that dictated to that poor tongue. But sure, at least, he must be sincere at the *time*! He could not be such a practised dissembler. If he could, O how desperately wicked is the heart of man! And where could he learn all these barbarous arts? If so, it must be native surely to the sex! But, silent be my rash censurings! Be hushed, ye stormy tumults of my disturbed mind! For have I not a father who is a man! A man who knows no guile, who would do no wrong; who would not deceive or oppress, to gain a kingdom: how then can I think it is native to the sex? And I must also hope my good lady's son cannot be the *worst* of men! If he be, hard was the lot of the excellent woman that bore him! But much harder the hap of your poor Pamela, who has fallen into the power of such a man. But yet I will trust in God, and hope the best; and lay down my tired pen for this time.

Thursday *Morning*

Somebody rapped at our chamber-door this morning as soon as it was light: Mrs Jewkes asked who it was? My master said, 'Open the door, Mrs Jewkes!' 'O,' said I, 'for Heaven's sake, Mrs Jewkes, don't!' 'Indeed,' said she, 'but I must.' 'Then,' said I, and clung about her, 'let me slip on my clothes first.' But he rapped again, and she broke from me; and I, in terror, folded myself in the bed-clothes. He entered, full dressed, and very richly,[195] and said, 'So fearful, Pamela, after what passed yesterday between us!' 'O sir, sir!' said I, 'I fear my prayers have wanted their wished effect. I beseech you, sir –' He interrupted me, 'No need of your foolish fears. I shall say but a word or two, and go away.'

'After you went up-stairs,' said he, (sitting down by the bed-side) 'I had an invitation to a ball, which is to be this night at Stamford, on occasion of a wedding; and I am going to call on Sir Simon, and his lady and daughters; for the bride is a relation of theirs: so I shall not be at home till Saturday. I come therefore to caution *you*, Mrs Jewkes, before Pamela, (that she may not wonder at being more closely confined, than for these three or four days past) that nobody sees her, or delivers any letter to her in that space; for a person has been observed lurking about, and inquiring after her; and I have been well informed, that either Mrs Jervis, or Mr Longman, has written a letter, with a design of having it conveyed to her: and,' said he, 'you must know, Pamela, that I have ordered Mr Longman to make up his accounts, and have dismissed Jonathan, and Mrs Jervis, since I have been here; for their behaviour has been intolerable, and they have made such a breach between my sister Davers and me, as we shall never, perhaps, make up. Now, Pamela, I shall take it kindly, if you will confine yourself to your chamber pretty much for the time I am absent, and not give Mrs Jewkes cause of trouble or uneasiness; and the rather, as you know she acts by my orders.'

'Alas! sir,' said I, 'I fear all these good people have suffered on my account!' 'They have,' said he, 'for their impertinence in your favour. Never was there a girl of your station and degree, who set a large family in such a ferment, as you have done mine, by their cares for you. But let that pass. You know both of you my pleasure; and, in part, the reason of it. I shall only say, that I have had such a letter from my sister, as I could not have expected; and Pamela,' said he, 'neither you nor I have reason to thank her, as you shall know, perhaps, at my return. Let all the gates be fastened; nor let any body go to the gate, without you, Mrs Jewkes.' 'I'll be sure,' said she, 'to obey your honour.' 'I will give Mrs Jewkes no trouble, sir,' said I, 'and will keep pretty much in my chamber, and not stir so much as into the garden without her; to shew you I will obey in every thing I *can*. But I begin to fear –' 'Ay,' said he, 'more plots and contrivances, don't you? But I'll assure you, you never had less reason; and I tell you the truth; for I am really going to Stamford *this time*; and upon the occasion I tell you. And so, Pamela, give me your hand, and one kiss, and then I am gone.'

I durst not refuse.

He and Mrs Jewkes had a little talk without the door; and I heard her say, 'You may depend, sir, upon my care and vigilance.'

He went in his coach, very richly dressed, as I mentioned, which looks as if what he said was true: but I have been used to so many tricks, and plots, and surprizes, that I know not what to think. But I mourn for poor Mrs Jervis.

So here is Mr Williams; here is poor wicked John; here is good Mrs Jervis, and Mr Longman, and Mr Jonathan, turned away for me! Mr Longman is rich indeed, and so need the less matter it; but I know it will grieve him: and for poor Mr Jonathan, I am sure it will cut that good old servant to the heart. Alas for me! What mischiefs am I the occasion of? Or, rather, my master, whose actions towards me, have made so many of my kind friends forfeit his favour!

I am very sad about these things: if he really loved me, methinks he should not be so angry that his servants loved me too. I know not what to think.

FRIDAY *Night*

I have removed my papers from under the rose-bush; for I saw the gardener begin to dig near that spot; and I was afraid he would find them.

Mrs Jewkes and I were this morning looking through the iron gate that fronts the elms, and a gypsey-like woman made up to us, and said, 'If, madam, you will give me some broken victuals, I will tell you both your fortunes.' I said, 'Let us hear our fortunes, Mrs Jewkes.' 'I don't like these sort of people,' said she; 'but we will hear what she will say to us, however. I shan't fetch you any victuals, woman; but I will give you some pence.' But Nan coming out, she said, 'Fetch some bread, and some of the cold meat, and you shall have your fortune told, Nan.'

This, you'll think, like some of my other matters, a very trifling thing to write about. But, mark the discovery of a dreadful plot, which I have made by it. What can I think of this wicked, this very wicked man! Now will I hate him most heartily. Thus it was:

Mrs Jewkes had no suspicion of the woman, the iron gate being locked, and she on the outside, and we on the inside; and so put her hand through, to be told her fortune. The woman, muttering over a parcel of cramp [196] words, said, 'Why, madam, you will marry soon, I can tell you.' Mrs Jewkes seemed pleased, and said, 'I am glad to hear that'; and shook her fat sides with laughing. The woman looked most earnestly at *me* all the time, as if she had meaning. Then it came into my head, from my master's caution, that possibly this woman might be employed to try to get a letter into my hands; and I was resolved to watch all her motions. 'What sort of a man shall I have, pray?' said Mrs Jewkes. 'A man younger than yourself,' answered the woman, 'and a very good husband he'll prove.' 'I am glad of that,' said she, and laughed again. 'Come, Mrs Pamela, let us hear *your* fortune.'

The woman came to me, and took my hand. 'O!' said she, 'I can't tell your fortune: your hand is so white and fine, I cannot see the lines: but,' said she, and, stooping, pulled up a little tuft of grass, 'I have a way for that'; and so rubbed my hand with the mould part of the tuft. 'Now,' said she, 'I can see the lines.'

Mrs Jewkes was very watchful of all her ways, and took the tuft, and looked upon it, lest any thing should be in that. And then the woman said, 'Here is the line of Jupiter crossing the line of life; and Mars – Odd, my pretty mistress,' said she, 'you had best take care of yourself; for you are hard beset, I'll assure you. You will never be married, I can see; and will die of your first child.' 'Out upon thee, woman!' said I; 'better thou hadst never come hither!'

'I don't like this,' said Mrs Jewkes, whispering. 'It looks like a cheat: pray, Mrs Pamela, go in this moment.' 'So I will,' said I; 'for I have enough of fortune-telling.'

The woman was very desirous to tell me more; which added to Mrs Jewkes's suspicions. She threatened her: and away went the woman, having told Nan her fortune, that she would be drowned.

This thing ran strongly in all our heads; and we went, an hour after, to see if the woman was lurking about, and took Monsieur Colbrand for our guard. Looking through the iron gate, he 'spied a man sauntering about the middle of the walk; which filled Mrs Jewkes with still stronger suspicions: and she said, 'Mr Colbrand, you and I will walk towards this fellow, and enquire what he saunters there for; and, Nan, do you and Mrs Pamela stay at the gate.'

Then opening the iron gate, they walked down towards the man; and I, guessing that the woman, if employed, must mean something by the tuft of grass, cast my eyes towards the spot whence she pulled it, and saw more grass pulled up, and in a little heap: then I doubted not something was there for me; so I walked to it, and standing between that and Nan, 'The wild flower,' said I, 'that grows yonder near that elm, the fifth from us on the left, is a very pretty one; pray pluck it for me.' 'It is a common weed,' answered she. 'No matter,' replied I; 'pray fetch it for me: there are beautiful colours in some weeds.'

She went from me to fetch it, and the moment she turned her back, I stooped, and pulled up a good handful of the grass, and in it a bit of paper, which I put instantly into my bosom, dropping the grass, my heart fluttering at the odd adventure! I then would have gone in; but the maid desired me to stay till Mrs Jewkes returned.

I was all impatience to read this paper. And when Colbrand and she came back, 'Certainly,' said she, 'there is some reason for my master's caution: I can make nothing of this sauntering fellow; but, to be sure, there was some roguery in the gypsey.' 'Well,' said I, 'if there was, she lost her aim, you see!' 'Ay, very true,' said she; 'but that was owing to my watchfulness; and you was very good to go away when I spoke to you.'

When we came in, I hasted up stairs to my closet, and found the billet to contain, in a hand that seemed disguised, and the spelling bad, the following words:

'Twenty contrivances have been thought of to let you know your danger; but all have proved in vain. Your friends hope it is not yet too late to give you this caution, if this paper reaches your hands. Mr B. is absolutely determined upon your ruin: and because he despairs of effecting it any other way, he will pretend great love and kindness to you, and that he will marry you. You may expect a parson for this purpose in a few days, or rather a man in a parson's habit; but who is indeed a sly, artful fellow, a broken[197] attorney, whom he has hired to personate a minister. The man has a broad face, pitted much with the small-pox. So take care of yourself. Doubt not this advice. Perhaps you'll have had but too much reason already to confirm you in the truth of it. From your zealous well-wisher,

SOMEBODY.'

Now, my dear father and mother, what shall we say of this truly diabolical master! How shall I find words to express my griefs! And here too, I have as good as confessed that I love him! But I will break this forward heart of mine, if it will not be taught to hate him! What a plot is here laid to ruin me, and by my own consent too! No wonder he did not improve his wicked opportunities, when he had such a project as *this* in reserve! How dreadful must have been my condition, when I had found myself a guilty harlot, instead of a lawful wife! This is indeed too much, too much for your poor Pamela! And as I hoped all the worst was over, and that I had the pleasure of beholding a reclaimed gentleman, and not an abandoned libertine. What *now* must your poor daughter do! O the wretched, wretched Pamela!

SATURDAY *Noon, One o' Clock*

My master is come home, and to be sure, has been where he said. So *once* he has told truth; and this matter seems to be gone off without a plot: no doubt he depends upon this sham-marriage! He has brought a gentleman with him to dinner; and so I have not seen him yet.

Two o' Clock

I am very sorrowful, and have a new reason to be so; for just now, as I was in my closet, busied in opening the parcel I had hid under the rose-bush, to see if it was damaged by lying so long, who but Mrs Jewkes should come upon me by surprize! She immediately laid her hands upon it: for she had been looking through the key-hole, it seems.

I know not what I shall do! For now he will see all my private thoughts of him, and all the secrets of my heart. What a careless creature am I!

You know I had the good luck, by Mr Williams's means, to send you all my papers down to Sunday night, the 17th day of my imprisonment. But now these papers contain all my matters, from that time, to Wednesday the 27th day of my distress: as you may now, perhaps, never see them, I will briefly mention their contents.

In these papers, then, are included, An account of Mrs Jewkes's arts, to draw me in to approve of Mr Williams's proposal for marriage; and of my refusing to do so; and desiring you not to encourage his suit to me. Of Mr Williams's being wickedly robbed, and a visit of the bad woman's to him; whereby she discovered all his secrets. Of my inclining to get off, while she was gone; and being ridiculously prevented by my foolish fears. An acknowledgment of my having the key of the back-door. An account of Mrs Jewkes's writing to my master all the secrets she had discovered of Mr Williams; and of her behaviour to me and him upon it. Of the continuance of my correspondence with Mr Williams by the tiles; begun in the parcel you had. Of my reproaches of Mr Williams for revealing the secrets of his heart to Mrs Jewkes. His letter to me in answer, threatening to expose my master, if he deceived him; and in which he mentions John Arnold's correspondence with him, and a letter which John sent, and was intercepted, as it seems. An account of the correspondence being carried on by a friend of Mr Williams's at Gainsborough; and of his design of providing a horse for me, and one for himself, in order to get me off; and of what Mr Williams had owned to Mrs Jewkes; and of my discouraging his proposals. Then it contained a pressing letter of mine to Mr Williams, urging him to oblige me with the means of escaping, before my master came; with his half-angry answer to me. There was also in this parcel your good letter to me, my dear father, sent to me by Mr Williams's conveyance; in which you tell me, you would have me encourage Mr Williams, but leave it to me to pursue my own inclinations; but in which, however, fortunately enough, you take notice of my being disinclined to marry. Also the substance of my answer to Mr Williams's chiding letter, in which I promise more patience, &c. Likewise a dreadful letter of my master to Mrs Jewkes, which, by mistake, was directed to me; and one to me, directed, by like mistake, to her; and very free reflections of mine upon both. I had also expressed on that occasion great concern for Mr Williams's being deceived and ruined; and gave an account of Mrs Jewkes's glorying in her wicked fidelity; together with a sad description of Monsieur Colbrand, a person he sent down to assist Mrs Jewkes in watching me. My concern was also farther expressed in them for poor Mr Williams's being arrested and thrown into gaol; nor did I in them spare my master on this occasion. Then they contain ample particulars of a contrivance of mine, to make my escape by the back-door; having, to amuse them, first thrown my petticoat and handkerchief into the pond: an attempt that had like to have ended very dreadfully for me! And then again I lament the ruin of Mr Williams as owing to his endeavours to serve me: and lastly, I relate that I overheard Mrs Jewkes brag of her contrivance to rob Mr Williams, in order to get at my papers; which, however, he preserved, and sent safe to you.

These, down to the issue of my unfortunate plot to escape, are, to the best of my remembrance, the contents of the papers, which this merciless woman seized: for, how badly I came off, and what followed, I still have safe (as I hope) sewed in my under-coat, about my hips.

In vain were all the prayers and tears that I could use to this vile woman, to prevail upon her not to shew them to my master. She had now, she said, found out the reason why I chose to be so much alone; and why I was always employed in writing. Often and often, she told me, she had searched every place she could think of, for writings, to no purpose till now. And she hoped there was nothing in them but what *any body* might see. 'For,' said she, 'you know, you are *all innocence*!' 'Insolent creature,' said I, 'I am sure you are *all guilt*! And so you must do your worst; for now I can't help myself; and I see there is no mercy to be expected from you.'

Just now, as my master was upon the stairs, (coming up to me, as I believe) she met him, and gave him my papers. 'There, sir,' said she; 'you always said Mrs Pamela was a great writer; but I never could get any thing of hers before.'

He took them, and went down to the parlour again. And what with the gypsey affair, and what with this, I could not think of going down to dinner; and she told him that too; and so I suppose I shall have him up-stairs, as soon as his company is gone.

SATURDAY, *Six o'Clock*

My master came up, and in a pleasanter manner than I expected, said, 'So, Pamela, we have seized, it seems, your treasonable papers?' 'Treasonable! sir,' said I, very sullenly. 'Ay,' said he, 'I suppose so; for you are a great plotter; but I have not read them yet.'

'Then, sir,' said I, 'it will be truly generous in you *not* to read them; but to give them to me again unread: they are written to my father and mother only.' 'What,' replied he, 'can you write to them that I may not see? I must read them before I return them.' 'Give me leave to say, sir,' said I, 'that you served me not well in the letters I used to write formerly. Was it worthy of the character of such a gentleman to contrive to get into your hands, by that false John Arnold, what your poor servant wrote to her father and mother?' 'Yes,' said he, 'by all means, every line that such a servant as *my* Pamela writes, be it to whom it will.'

Your Pamela! thought I. Then the sham-marriage came into my head; and indeed it has not been out of it since the gypsey affair. 'But,' said he, 'have you any thing in these papers you would not have me see?' 'To be sure, sir,' replied I, 'there is; for what one writes to one's father and mother is not for every body to see.' 'Nor,' answered he, 'am I every body.'

'It was not to your disadvantage,' added he, 'that I did see the letters you hint at; for they gave me a very high opinion of you: and if I had not loved you, do you think I would have troubled myself about your letters?'

'No great pride, sir, to me *that*! For they gave you such an opinion of me, that you was resolved to ruin me. And what advantage have they brought *me*, who have been made a prisoner, and used as I have been–'

'Why, Pamela,' interrupted he, a little seriously, 'why this behaviour, for my goodness to you in the garden? This is not of a piece with your gentleness there. And you must not give me cause to think, that you are capable of taking advantage of my kindness to you.' 'Ah! sir,' said I, 'you know best your own heart and designs! But I fear I was too open-hearted then; and that you still keep your resolution to ruin me, and have only changed the form of your proceedings.'

'I tell you once again,' replied he, a little sternly, 'that you cannot oblige me more, than by placing some confidence in my honour. But I shall possibly account for the *cause* of your foolish and perverse doubts, in these papers. You have been sincere to your *father* and *mother*, I question not, though you begin to make *me* suspect you. It is impossible you should be thus disobliging, after what last passed in the garden, if you were not prepossessed in some *other* man's favour. And let me tell you, that if I find it so, it shall be attended with such effects as will make your heart bleed in every vein.'

He was going away in wrath. 'One word, sir, one word,' said I, 'before you read my papers, since you *will* read them: pray make allowances for all the harsh reflections you will find in them, on your own conduct to me: and remember only, that they were not written for your sight; but were penned by a poor creature hardly used, and who was in constant apprehension of receiving from you the worst treatment you could inflict upon her.'

'If that be all,' said he, 'and there be nothing of *another* nature, you have no cause for uneasiness; for read I not in your former letters as many saucy reflections upon myself as there were lines? and yet have I ever upbraided you on that score? Though, perhaps, I wished you had been more sparing of your freedoms of that sort.'

'I am not afraid, sir,' said I, 'of being found guilty of a falsehood in what I have told you. I remember not all I wrote, yet I know I wrote my heart at the time; and that is not deceitful. And be pleased, sir, to bear in mind, that I always declared I thought myself right to endeavour to make my escape from my illegal restraint; and I hope you will not be angry, that I would have done so, if I could.'

'I will judge you, never fear,' said he, 'as favourably as you deserve; for you have too powerful a pleader within me here,' putting his hand to his bosom: and saying so, went down stairs.

About nine o'clock he sent for me into the parlour. I went a little fearfully; and he held the papers in his hand, and said, 'Now, Pamela, you come upon your trial.' 'I hope, sir,' said I, 'that I have a *just* judge.' 'Ay,' returned he, 'and you may hope for a *merciful* one too, or else I know not what will become of you.

'I expect,' continued he, 'that you will answer directly, and plainly, to every question I shall ask you. In the first place, here are several love-letters between you and Williams.' 'Love-letters! sir,' said I. 'Well, call them what you will, I do not, with all the allowances you desired me to make for you, entirely like them.' 'Do you find, sir, that I gave any the least encouragement to his proposals?' 'Encouragement enough, Pamela! for one in your situation! and to a first declaration of love! The discouragement is no other than is practised by all your artful sex, in order to incite ours to pursue you.' 'I know nothing, sir,' said I, 'of the practices of artful women! I have no art. All I aimed at was all lawful means to preserve my innocence: and to avoid those snares which were laid to bring me to disgrace.'[198]

'Well, so much for that,' replied he. 'But where (since you have kept so exact a journal of all that has passed) are the accounts *previous* to these here in my hand?' 'My father has them, sir,' said I. 'By whose means?' 'By Mr Williams's, sir.' 'Well answered,' said he. 'But cannot you contrive to get me a sight of them?' 'Contrive to get you a sight of them, sir!' said I, 'I wish I could have contrived to have kept from you those you have.' 'I *must* see them, Pamela,' returned he, 'or I shall never be easy. I must know how this correspondence, between you and Williams, began: and if I *can* see them, it shall be better for you, if they answer what these papers in my hand give me hope they will.'

'I will tell you, sir, very faithfully,' said I, 'what the beginning was; for I was bold enough to be the *beginner*.' 'That won't do,' said he; 'for though this point may appear a punctilio[199] to *you*, to *me* it is of high importance.' 'If you will permit me, sir,' said I, 'to go to my father, I will send the papers to you by any servant you shall send for them.' 'Will you so? But I dare say, if you will write for them, they will send them to you: and I desire you will.'

'As, sir, you have seen all my *former* letters, through John's baseness, and now *these*, through your faithful housekeeper's wickedness, I think you *might* see *all the rest*. But I hope you will not desire it, till I know how much my obeying you in this particular, will be of use to myself.'

'You must trust to my honour for that. But tell me, Pamela,' said the artful gentleman, 'since I have seen *these*, would you have voluntarily shewn me *those*, had they been in your possession?'

I was not aware of his inference, and said, 'Yes, truly, sir, I think I should, if you commanded it.' 'Well, then, Pamela,' replied he, 'as I am sure you have found means to continue your journal, I desire, till the *former part* to these in my hand can come, that you will shew me the *succeeding*.' 'O sir, sir,' said I, 'have you caught me so! But indeed you must excuse me.'

'Why,' said he, 'tell me truly, have you not continued your account till now?' I begged he would not ask me. 'But I insist upon your answering truly,' said he. 'Why, then, sir, I will not tell an untruth; *I have*.' 'That's my good girl,' said he. 'I love sincerity at my heart. And you will greatly oblige me, to shew me voluntarily what you have written. I long to see the particulars of your plot, and your disappointment where these papers leave off. As I have furnished you with a subject, I think I have a title to see how you manage it. Besides, there is such a pretty air of romance, as you tell your story, in *your* plots, and *my* plots, that I shall be better directed how to wind up the catastrophe of the pretty novel.'

'If I were your equal, sir,' returned I, 'I should say – It is cruel to make a jest of the misfortunes you have studiously involved me in.'

'My equal, Pamela! You must have thought yourself my equal, at least, by the liberties you have taken with my character, in your letters.' 'I would not, sir,' pertly replied I, 'have taken those liberties, if you had not given me the cause: and the *cause*, sir, you know, is before the effect.'

'You chop logick[200] very prettily, Pamela,' said he. 'What the deuce do we men go to school for? If our wits were naturally equal to those of women, much time and pains might be spared in our education. Since nature teaches your sex, what in a long course of labour and study, ours can hardly attain to. But,' continued he, 'I believe, I must assume to myself, half the merit of *your* wit; for the innocent exercises you have had for it from me, have certainly sharpened your invention.'

'Could I, sir,' replied I, 'have been without those *innocent* exercises, as you are pleased to call them, I should have been glad to have been as dull as a beetle.'[201] 'But, then, Pamela, I should not have loved you so well.' 'But, then, sir, I should have been safe, easy, and happy.' 'Ay, may be so, and may be not; and the wife of some clouterly²⁰² plough-boy.'

'Sir, I should then have been content and innocent; and that's better than being a princess, and not so.' 'And may-be not,' said he; 'for with that pretty face, some of us keen fox-hunters would have found you out; and, in spite of your romantic notions, (which then too, perhaps, would not have had so strong a place in your mind) might have been more happy with the plough-man's wife, than I have been with my mother's Pamela.' 'I hope, sir,' said I, 'you would have been very much mistaken. My father and mother took care to instil into my mind lessons of virtue from my *very cradle*. My dear good lady, your mother, *found* them there, or she would not have honoured me as she did with her countenance. O, had the dear lady but have lived!' And I wiped my eyes.²⁰³

'Well, but,' resumed he, with quickness, as if he would fly from that subject, 'as to these writings of yours, that follow your fine plot, I *must* see them.' 'Indeed, sir, you *must not*, if I can help it.' 'Nothing,' said he, 'pleases me better, than to find that, in all your devices, you have had regard to truth; and have, in all your little pieces of deceit, told very few *wilful* falsehoods. Now, I expect you will continue this laudable regard to it in your answers to my questions. Let me know then, where you found supplies of pen, ink, and paper, when Mrs Jewkes was so vigilant, and gave you but two sheets at a time? Tell me truth.'

'I will, sir. Little did I think I should have such occasion for them as I have had; but, when I went away from your house, good Mr Longman, at my request, furnished me with a little store of each.' 'Yes, yes,' said he, 'it must be *good* Mr Longman! All *your* confederates, every one of them, are good; but such of my servants as have done their duty, and obeyed my orders, and myself too, are painted out by you, in your papers, as black as devils.'

'Sir,' said I, 'I hope you won't be angry; but do you think that I have painted some of your servants in worse colours than the parts they acted require?'

'I will not lose my question,' said he. 'Tell me, where did you hide your paper, pens, and ink?'

'Some, sir, in one place, some in another; that I might have some left, if others should be found.' 'That's a good girl! I love you for your sweet veracity. Now tell me, where it is you hide your other written papers, your saucy journal?' 'I must beg your excuse, sir.' 'But, indeed,' said he, 'you will not have it; for I *will* know, and I *will* see them!' 'This is very hard, sir,' said I; 'but I must say, you shall not, if I can help it.'

He then sat down, and took both my hands, and said, 'Well said, my pretty Pamela, *if you can help it*! But I will not let you help it. Tell me, are they in your pocket?' 'No, sir,' said I, my heart up at my mouth. 'I know you won't tell a downright *fib* for the world,' said he; 'but for *equivocation*! no jesuit[204] ever went beyond you. Answer me then, are they in *neither* of your pockets?'[205] 'No, sir,' said I. 'Are they not,' said he, 'about your stays?' 'No, sir,' replied I; 'but pray no more questions; for, excuse me, sir, but ask me ever so often, I will not tell you.'

'O,' said he, 'I have a way for your *will-not's*. I can do as they do abroad, when the criminals won't confess; torture them till they do.' 'But pray, sir,' said I, 'is this fair, just, or honest? I am no criminal.'

'O my girl!' said he, 'many an *innocent* person has been put to the torture. But let me know where they are, and you shall escape the *question*,[206] as it is called abroad.'

'Sir,' said I, 'the torture is not used in England, and I hope you won't bring it up.' 'Admirably said!' replied the naughty gentleman. 'But I can tell you of as great a punishment: if a criminal won't plead with us here in England, we *press* him to death, or till he does plead. And so now, Pamela, this is a punishment shall certainly be yours, if you won't tell without.'

Tears stood in my eyes, and I said, 'This, sir, is very cruel! very barbarous!' 'No matter,' returned he; 'it is but like a Lucifer, you know. And after I have done so many things by you, which *you* think heinous, what I shall further do on this occasion, ought not to surprize you.'

'But, sir,' said I, (dreadfully afraid he had some notion they were about me) 'if you *will* be thus unreasonably obeyed, let me go up to them, and read them over again, to see what I have written, that follows the letters you have.'

'I will see them all,' said he, 'down to this very day, if you have written so far! Or at least till within this week. But say, Pamela, tell me truth; *are* they *above*?' I was more affrighted. He saw my confusion. 'Tell me truth,' said he. 'Why, sir,' answered I, 'I have sometimes hid them under the dry mould in the garden; sometimes in one place, sometimes in another; and those you have in your hand, were several days under a rose-bush in the garden.' 'Artful girl,' said he; 'what's this to my question? Are they not *about* you?' 'If,' said I, 'I must pluck them from behind the tapestry, won't you see in which apartment?' 'Still more and more artful!' said he. 'Is this an answer to my question? I have searched every place above, and in your closet, for them, and can't find them; I *will* therefore know where they are. Now,' said he, 'it is my opinion they are about you; and I never undressed a girl in my life; but I will now begin to strip my pretty Pamela, and hope I shall not go far before I find them.' And he began to unpin my handkerchief.

I wept, and resisting said, 'I will not be used in this manner. Pray, sir, consider! Pray, sir, consider!' 'And, pray,' said he, 'do *you* consider. For I *will* see these papers. But, perhaps,' said the wicked wretch, (was ever any one so vile!) 'they are tied about your knees with your garters'; and stooped. I fell on my knees, excessively affrighted; but yet speechless for a few moments. He seemed alarmed at my being ready to faint. 'Will you, on your honour,' said he, 'if I let you go up, bring them down to me, uncurtailed, and not offer to make away a single paper?' 'I will, sir.' 'On your honour?' 'Yes, sir.'

And so he raised me, and let me go up stairs, I crying for vexation all the way.

I went to my closet, and there sitting down, and recollecting every thing, I could not bear the thoughts of giving up my papers; nor of undressing myself, as was necessary to be done, to untack them, so I writ thus:

'*SIR*,
'To expostulate with such an arbitrary gentleman, I am afraid will signify nothing. And most hardly do you use the power you so illegally have obtained over me. I can hardly bear the usage I receive from you, and my apprehensions of what I may have still to suffer. Let me beseech you, sir, not to insist upon the performance of the promise you extorted from me. Yet, if you do, allow me till to-morrow morning, that I may just run my papers over, and see what I put into your hands against myself; and if it must be so, I will then give them to you, without the least addition or diminution.'

In less than half an hour he sent up Mrs Jewkes for what I had promised; and I gave her the above note to carry to him. He read it, and sent me word, that I must keep my promise strictly, and he would give me till morning; but that I must bring to him what he expected, without his asking for them again.

So I took off my under-coat, and with great trouble of mind unscrewed the papers. There is a vast quantity of writing. I will just slightly mention the subjects; because I may not, perhaps, get them again for you to see.

They begin with an account of my getting out of the window; and throwing my petticoat and handkerchief into the pond. Of my disappointment in finding the lock of the back-door changed. Of my trying to climb over the door; and the bricks giving way, of my falling down, some of them tumbling upon me, and miserably bruising me; for so, my dear father and mother, it fell out. Then I relate, that finding I could not get off, and dreading the hard usage I expected to receive, I was so wicked as to think of throwing myself into the water; and my sad reflections upon this matter. How Mrs Jewkes used me on this occasion, when she found me. How my master had like to have been drowned in hunting; and my concern for his danger, notwithstanding his usage of me. I then mention Mrs Jewkes's wicked reports raised to frighten me, that I was to be married to an ugly Swiss; who was to sell me on the wedding-day to my master. Her vile way of talking to me like a London prostitute. My apprehensions on seeing preparations made for my master's coming. Her bad usage of me on a suspicion that I was trying to get away again. My master's dreadful arrival; and his hard, very hard treatment of me; and Mrs Jewkes's insulting me. His jealousy of Mr Williams; and of the vile Mrs Jewkes's instigating him to ruin me. And down to this place I made one parcel, hoping that would content him. But for fear it should not, I put into another parcel the papers that contain the following particulars.

A copy of his proposals to me, of a great parcel of gold, and fine clothes and rings, and an estate of I can't tell how much a year; and fifty pounds a year for the life of both you, my dear parents, on condition I would be his kept mistress; with an insinuation, that, perhaps, he would marry me at a year's end. All sadly vile; with threatenings, if I did not comply, that he would ruin me, without allowing me any thing. A copy of my answer, refusing all with just abhorrence; but begging, in the conclusion, his mercy, in the most moving manner I could think of. An account of his angry behaviour, and Mrs Jewkes's wicked advice hereupon. His trying to get me to his chamber; and my refusal to go. A deal of stuff and chit-chat between me and the odious Mrs Jewkes; in which she was very wicked and very insulting. Two notes I wrote, as if to be carried to church, to pray for his reclaiming, and my safety; which Mrs Jewkes seized, and officiously shewed him. A confession of mine, that notwithstanding his bad usage, I could not hate him. My concern for Mr Williams. A horrid contrivance of my master to ruin me; being in my room disguised in clothes of the maid, who lay with me and Mrs Jewkes. How narrowly I escaped, by falling into fits. Mrs Jewkes's detestable part in this sad affair. How he seemed moved at my danger, and forebore his abominable designs. How ill I was for a day or two after; and how kind he seemed. Of his making me forgive Mrs Jewkes. How, after this, and great kindness pretended, he made rude offers to me in the garden; which I escaped. How I resented them.

Then I had written, how kindly he behaved himself to me; and praised me, and gave me great hopes of his being good at last. Of the too tender impression this made upon me; and how I began to be afraid of my own consideration for him, though he had used me so ill. How sadly jealous he was of Mr Williams, and how I, as I justly could, cleared myself as to his doubts on that score. How, when he had raised me to the highest hope of his goodness, he went off more coldly. My free reflections upon this trying occasion.

This brought matters down from Thursday the 20th day of my imprisonment, to Wednesday the 41st. And here I resolved to end; for only what passed on Thursday, Friday, and Saturday, remain to give an account of; and Thursday he set out to a ball at Stamford; and Friday was an odd story about a gypsy; and this is Saturday, his return from a ball at Stamford. But I shall have little heart to take pen in hand for the future, if he is so resolved to see all I write.

These two parcels of papers I have got ready for him against tomorrow morning. I have indeed always used him very freely in my writings; but he must thank himself for that: since I have only writ the truth; and I wish he had deserved a better character at my hands, as well for his own sake, as mine.

SUNDAY *Morning*

Remembering he had sent me word, that I must bring him my papers, without obliging him to ask for them again, I thought it was better to do that which I should be forced to do, in such a manner as might shew I would not disoblige on purpose: and therefore on his sending Mrs Jewkes to tell me, that he should not go to church this morning, and was gone into the garden, I went with my two parcels, though stomaching the matter very heavily. Yet, on my entering the garden, as he walked in one walk, I took another; that I might not seem too forward neither.

He soon spied me, and said, 'Do you expect, Pamela, when I complied with your request yesterday, to be entreated to perform conditions with me? Why take you that walk, if you think of your promise, and of my goodness to you?' I say *goodness*! thought I. 'I might not know,' returned I (as I crossed the walk to attend him) 'but I should interrupt, you, sir, in your meditations this good day.'

'Was that the case,' said he, 'truly, and from your heart?' 'I don't doubt, sir,' answered I, 'but you have very good thoughts sometimes; though not towards me!' 'I wish,' said he, 'I could avoid thinking so well of you, as I do. But where are the papers? I dare say, you had them about you yesterday, for you say in those I have, that you will bury your writings in the garden, for fear you should be *searched*, if you do not escape. This,' added he, 'gave me a noble pretence to search you; and I have been vexing myself all night, that I did not strip you garment by garment, till I had found them. And I hope that you come now rather resolving to trifle with me, than to give them up with a grace; for I assure you, I had rather find them myself.'

I did not like this way of talk; and thinking it best, to cut it short, pulling the first parcel out of my pocket, 'Here, sir,' said I, 'since I cannot be excused, is the parcel, that goes on with my fruitless attempt to escape, and the terrible consequences it had like to have had. And it goes down to the wicked articles you sent me. You know all that has happened since.'

He was going to speak; but I said, to drive him from thinking of any more, than that parcel, 'And I must beg of you, sir, to read them with favour, in such places as I may have treated you with freedom; and allow for the occasions: but if you will be pleased to return them, without breaking the seal, it will be very generous: and I will take it for a great favour, and a good omen.'

He took the parcel, and broke the seal instantly. 'So much for your *omen*!' replied he. 'I am sorry for it,' said I, very seriously; and was walking away. 'Whither now?' said he. 'I was going in, sir, that you might read them (since you *will* read them) without interruption.' He put them into his pocket, and said, 'You have *more* than these. I am sure you have. Tell me truth.' 'I have, sir, I own. But *you* know as well as *I* all that they contain.' 'But I don't know,' said he, 'the light you represent things in. Give them to me, therefore, if you have not a mind that I should search for them myself.' 'Why then, unkind sir, if it must be so, here they are.'

And so I gave him, out of my pocket, the second parcel, sealed up, as the former, with this superscription; *From the wicked articles, down through vile attempts, to* Thursday *the 42nd day of my imprisonment*. 'This is last Thursday, is it?' 'Yes, sir; but now that you seem determined to see every thing I write, I will find some other way to employ my time.'

'I would have you,' said he, 'continue writing by all means; and I assure you, in the mind I am in, I will not ask you for any papers after these; except something very extraordinary happens. And if you send for those from your father, and let me read them, I may very probably give them all back again to you. I desire therefore that you will.'

This hope a little encourages me to continue my scribbling; but, for fear of the worst, I will, when they come to any bulk, contrive some way to hide them, that I may protest I have them not about me, which, before, I could not say of a truth.

He led me then to the side of the pond; and sitting down on the slope, made me sit by him. 'Come,' said he, 'this being the scene of part of your project, and where you so artfully threw in some of your clothes, I will just look upon that part of your relation here.' 'Sir,' said I, 'let me then walk about at a little distance; for I cannot bear the thought of it.' 'Don't go far,' said he.

When he came, as I suppose, to the place where I mentioned the bricks falling upon me, he got up, and walked to the door, and looked upon the broken part of the wall; for it had not been mended; and reading on to himself, came towards me; and took my hand, and put it under his arm.

'Why this,' said he, 'my girl, is a very moving tale. It was a very desperate attempt, and had you got out, you might have been in great danger; for you had a very bad and lonely way; and I had taken such measures, that let you have been where you would, I should have had you.'

'All I ventured, and all I suffered, was nothing, sir, to what I apprehended. You will be so good from hence to judge –' 'Romantic girl!' interrupted he, 'I know what you'd say,' and read on.

He was very serious at my reflections, on what God enabled me to escape. And when he came to my reasonings, about throwing myself into the water, he said, 'Walk gently before'; and seemed so moved, that he turned away his face from me; and I blessed this good sign, and began not so much to repent his seeing this mournful part of my story.

He put the papers in his pocket, when he had read my reflections, and my thanks for escaping from *myself*; and said, taking me about the waist, 'O my dear girl! you have touched me sensibly with your mournful tale, and your reflections upon it. I should truly have been very miserable had that happened which might have happened. I see you have been used too roughly; and it is a mercy you stood proof in that dangerous moment.'

Then he most kindly folded me in his arms. 'Let us, say I, my Pamela, walk from this accursed piece of water; for I shall never look upon it again with pleasure. I thought,' added he, 'of terrifying you to my will, since I could not move you by love; and Mrs Jewkes too well obeyed me, when the effect had like to have been so fatal to my girl.'

'O sir,' said I, 'I have reason to bless my dear parents, and my good lady, for giving me a religious education; since but for that, I should, upon more occasions than one, have attempted a desperate act: and I the less wonder how poor creatures, who have not the fear of God before their eyes, and give way to despondency, cast themselves into perdition.'

'Give me a kiss, my dear girl,' said he, 'and tell me you forgive me, for plunging you into so much danger and distress. If my mind hold, and I can see these former papers of yours, and that these in my pocket give me no cause to alter my opinion, I will endeavour to defy the world, and the world's censures, and, if it be in the power of my whole life, make my Pamela amends for all the hardships she has undergone by my means.'

I could hardly suppress my joyful emotions on this occasion. But fears will ever mingle with one's hopes, where a great and unexpected, yet uncertain good opens to one's view. And this shammarriage, then coming into my mind, 'O sir,' said I, 'what do you bid me look up to? Your poor servant can never wish to create envy to herself, and discredit to you! Therefore, sir, permit me to return to my parents, and that is all I have to ask.'

He flew into a violent passion. 'And is it *thus*,' said he, 'in my fond conceding moments, that I am to be answered? Precise, perverse, unseasonable Pamela! be gone from my sight, and know as well how to behave in a hopeful prospect, as in a distressed state; and then, and not till then, shalt thou attract the shadow of my notice.'

I was startled, and would have spoken: but he stamped with his foot, and said, 'Begone, I tell you. I cannot bear this romantic, this stupid folly.'

'One word,' said I; 'but one word, I beseech you, sir.'

He turned from me in great wrath, and took down another alley, and I went in with a very heavy heart. I fear I was indeed foolishly unseasonable: but if it was a piece of art of his side, as I apprehended, to introduce the sham-wedding, (and to be sure he is very full of his devices) I think I was not *so much* to blame.

I went up to my closet; and wrote thus far. He walked about till dinner was ready; and is now set down to it. Mrs Jewkes tells me he is very thoughtful, and out of humour; and asked, what I had done to him?

Now again, I dread to see him! When will my fears be over?

Three o'Clock

He continues exceedingly wroth. He has ordered his travelling chariot to be got ready with all speed. What is to come next, I wonder!

Sure I did not say *so much*! But see the lordliness of a high condition! A person of low degree must not put in a word, when the great take it into their heads to be angry! What a fine time a young creature of unequal condition would have, if she were even to marry such an one! My good lady, his dear mother, spoiled him at first. Nobody must speak to him, or contradict him, as I have heard, when he was a child; and so he has not been used to be controuled, and cannot bear the least thing that crosses his violent will. This is one of the blessings attending men of high condition! Much good may do them with their pride of birth, and pride of fortune! All that it serves for, as far as I can see, is to multiply their disquiets, and every body's else, that has to do with them.

So, so! where will this end! Mrs Jewkes has been with me from him, and she says, I must quit the house this moment! 'Well,' said I, 'but whither am I to be carried next?' 'Why, home,' said she, 'to your father and mother.' 'And, can it be?' said I: 'no, no, I doubt I am not to be so happy as that! To be sure, some bad design is on foot again! To be sure it is! Sure, sure, Mrs Jewkes,' said I, 'he has not found out some other house-keeper *worse than you*!'

She was very angry, you may well think; and went from me muttering.

She came up again. 'Are you ready?' said she. 'Bless me!' said I, 'you are very hasty: I have heard of this not a quarter of an hour ago. But I shall be soon ready; for I have but little to take with me, and no kind friends in this house to take leave of, to delay me.' Yet, like a fool, I could not help crying. 'Pray,' said I, 'just step down, and ask, if I may not have my papers?'

I don't know what to think, nor how to judge; but I shall never believe I am with you, till I am on my knees before you, begging both your blessings. Yet I am sorry he is so *angry* with me! I thought I did not say *so much*.

There is, I see, the chariot drawn out, the horses too, the grim *Colbrand* going to get on horse-back. What will be the end of all this?

I am quite ready now; and only wait for an answer about my papers. And so I will put in my bosom the few I have left. But did I say *so much*?

THE END OF VOLUME I

VOLUME II

THE JOURNAL CONTINUED

SUNDAY *Night,*[207] *near Nine o'Clock*

Well, my dear parents, here I am (would you believe it?) at an inn in a poor little village, almost such a one as yours; I shall learn the name of it by-and-by. And Robin assures me he has orders to carry me to you. O that he may say truth, and not deceive me again! But having nothing else to do (and I am sure I shall not sleep a wink to-night, were I to go to-bed) I will write my time away, and take up my story where I left off, at three o'clock this day.

Mrs Jewkes came up to me, with this answer about my papers, 'My master says he will not read them yet, lest he should be moved by any thing in them to alter his resolution. But, if he shall think it worth while to read them, he will send them to you afterwards to your father's. But,' said she, 'here is the money that I borrowed of you: for all is over with you now, I find.'

She saw me weep; and said, 'Do you repent?' 'Of what?' said I. 'Nay, I can't tell,' replied she; 'but to be sure he has had a specimen of your satirical flings,[208] or he would not be so angry. Oh!' continued she, and held up her hand, 'thou hast a spirit! But I hope it will now be brought down.' 'I hope so too,' said I. 'I am quite ready, Mrs Jewkes.'

She lifted up the sash,[209] and said, 'I'll call Robin to take your portmanteau: bag and baggage![210] I'm glad you're going.' 'I have no words,' replied I, 'to throw away upon *you*, Mrs Jewkes; but,' making her a very low curt'sy, 'I most heartily thank you for all your *virtuous* civilities to me. And so adieu! for I'll have no portmanteau, I assure you, nor any thing besides what I have on, except these few things that I brought with me in my handkerchief.' For I had all this time worn the clothes I had bought, though my master several times would have had it otherwise. Nevertheless, I had put up paper, ink, and pens.

So down I went; and as I passed by the parlour, she stepped in, and said, 'Sir, you have nothing to say to the girl, before she goes?' I heard him reply, though I did not see him, 'Who bid *you* say *the girl*, Mrs Jewkes, in that manner? She has offended only me!'

'I beg your honour's pardon,' said the wretch; 'but if I were your honour, she should not, for all the trouble she has cost you, go away scot-free.' 'No more of this! as I *told you before*,' said he: 'what! when I have such proof, that her virtue is all her pride, shall I rob her of that? No,' added he, 'let her go, perverse and foolish as she is; but she *deserves* to go away virtuous, and she *shall*.'

I was so overjoyed at this unexpected goodness, that I opened the door before I knew what I did, and I said, falling on my knees at the door, with my hands folded and lifted up, 'May God bless your honour! May God Almighty bless your honour, for this instance of your goodness! I will pray for you as long as I live, and so shall my father and mother!'

He turned from me, and went into his closet, and shut the door. He needed not; for I would not have gone nearer to him!

Surely I did not say *so much*, that he should be so *very* angry.

I think I was loth to leave the house. Can you believe it? What could be the matter with me, I wonder! I felt something *so* strange, and my heart was *so* heavy! I wonder what ailed me! But this instance of his goodness was so *unexpected*! I believe that was all! Yet I have a very strange heart still. Surely, surely, I cannot be like the murmuring Israelites of old, who hungered after the onions and garlick of Egypt, where they had suffered such a heavy bondage?[211] I'll take thee, O contradictory, ungovernable heart, to severe task for these thy strange emotions, when I get to my father's; and if I find any thing in thee that should not be, depend upon it, thou shalt be humbled, if strict abstinence, prayer, and mortification, will do it!

But yet, after all, this *last* goodness of his has touched me too sensibly: I almost wish I had not heard what he said; and yet, methinks I am glad I did; for I should rejoice to think the best of him, for *his own* sake.

Well, and so I went out to the chariot, the same that brought me down. 'So, Mr Robert,' said I, 'here I am again! a fine sporting-piece[212] for the great, a mere tennis-ball of fortune! You have your orders, no doubt.' 'Yes, madam,' said he. 'Don't call me madam,' said I, 'nor stand with your hat off to such a one as I.' 'Had not my master,' replied he, '*ordered* me not to be wanting in respects to you, I would have shewn you all I could.' 'That's very kind, Mr Robert,' said I, with my heart full.

Mr Colbrand (mounted on horseback, with pistols before him) came up to me, as soon as I got in, with *his* hat off too. 'What, Monsieur!' said I, 'are *you* to go with me?' 'Part of the way,' he said, to see me safe. 'I *hope* that's kind, too, in you, Mr Colbrand,' said I.

I had nobody to wave my handkerchief to now, nor to take leave of; and so I resigned myself to my contemplations, with this strange wayward heart of mine, that I never found so awkward before. And away drove the chariot! And when I had got out of the elm-walk, and into the great road, I could hardly think but I was in a dream all the time. A few hours before, said I to myself, so high in my master's favour, with twenty kind things said to me, and a generous concern for the misfortunes he had brought upon me; and now only for a rash half-word turned out of doors at an hour's warning; and all his kindness changed to hatred! And I now, from three o'clock to five, several miles off! But if I am going to my dear parents, thought I, all will be well again, I hope.

What strange creatures are men! *Gentlemen*, I should rather say. For you, my good mother, although poverty has been your lot, have had better fortune; and you and my father have always been blest in each other! Yet this pleases me too: he was so good, he would not let Mrs Jewkes speak ill of me, and scorned to take her unwomanly advice. O what a black heart has this poor wretch! So I need not rail against *men* so much; for my master, bad as I have thought him, is not half so bad as this woman! To be sure she must be an atheist! Do you think she is not?

We could not reach further than this little poor place, and sad alehouse, rather than inn;²¹³ for it soon began to be dark, and Robin did not make so much haste as he might have done. He is forced to make hard shift²¹⁴ for his horses.

Mr Colbrand, and Robert too, are very civil. I see he has got my portmanteau lashed behind the chariot. I did not desire it; but I shall not come quite destitute.

A thorough riddance of me, I see! Bag and baggage! as Mrs Jewkes says. Well, my story, surely, would furnish out a surprising kind of novel, if it were to be well told.

Ten o'Clock

Mr Robert came up to me just now, and begged me to eat something. I thanked him; but said I could not eat. I bid him ask Mr Colbrand to walk up; and he came; but neither of them would sit, nor put their hats on. What mockery is this to such a poor soul as I! I asked them, if they were at liberty to tell me the truth of what they were to do with me? They both said, Robin was ordered to carry me to my father's; and Mr Colbrand was to leave me within ten miles, and then strike off for the other house, and wait till my master arrived there. They spoke so seriously, that I could not but believe them.

But when Robin was gone down, the other said he had a letter to give me next day at noon, when we baited, as we were to do, at Mrs Jewkes's relations. 'May I not,' said I, 'beg the favour to see it to-night?' He seemed so loth to deny me, that I have hopes I shall prevail on him by-and-by.

Well, my dear father and mother, I have got the letter, on great promises of secrecy, and of making no advantage of the contents. I have opened it, without breaking the seal. This is a copy of it:

'When these lines are delivered to you, you will be far on your way to your father and mother, with whom you have so long desired to be: and, I hope, I shall forbear thinking of you with the least shadow of that fondness which my foolish heart had entertained for you. I bear you, however, no ill-will; but the end of my detaining you being over, I would not that you should stay with me an hour more than needed, after your ungenerous behaviour to me, at a time when I was inclined to pass over all other considerations, and make an honourable address to you.

'I will acknowledge another truth – That had I not parted with you as I did, but permitted you to stay till I had read your journal, (freely, as I doubt not you have treated me in it) and till I had heard your bewitching pleas in your own behalf, I feared I could not trust myself with my own resolution. And this was the reason, I frankly own, that I determined not to see you, nor hear you speak; for well I know my weakness in your favour.

'But since my fond folly was likely to cost me so dear, I am resolved to get the better of it. And yet, I cannot but say, that I could wish you would not think of marrying in haste; and particularly, that you would not have that cursed Williams. But what is all this to me now? Only I am weak enough to wish that, as I had already looked upon you as *mine*, and you have so soon got rid of your first husband, you will not refuse, to my *memory*, the regard that every decent woman observes on losing a husband; that is to say, that you will pay a twelve-month's compliment, though but in *mere* compliment, to my ashes.

'Your papers shall be faithfully returned. I have paid so dear for my curiosity, that you would look upon yourself amply revenged, if you knew what they have cost me.

'I thought of writing only a few lines; but I have run into length. I will now try to recollect my scattered thoughts, and resume my reason; and shall find trouble enough to supply the chasms you have made in my family: since, let me tell you, though I can forgive *you*, I never can my *sister*, nor my domesticks; for my vengeance must be wreaked somewhere.

'I doubt not your prudence in forbearing to expose me any more than is necessary for your own justification; and for the sake of *that*, I will suffer myself to be accused by you, and will also accuse myself, if it be needful. For I am, and will ever be,

Your affectionate Well-wisher.'

This letter, when I expected some new plot, has greatly affected me. For here plainly does he confess his great value for me; and accounts for his rigorous behaviour to me. And so all this wicked gypsey-story is, as it seems, a forgery, and has quite ruined me! For, O my dear parents, forgive me! but I found, to my grief, before, that my heart was too partial in his favour; but *now*, to find him capable of so much openness, so much affection, nay, and of so much *honour* too, I am quite over-come. This was a good fortune, however, I had no reason to expect. But to be sure, I must own to you, that I shall never be able to think of any body in the world but him! Presumption! you will say; and so it is: but love, I imagine, is not a voluntary thing – *Love*, did I say! But come, I hope not: at least it is not, I hope, gone so far, as to make me *very* uneasy: for I know not *how* it came, nor *when* it began; but it has crept, crept, like a thief, upon me; and before I knew what was the matter, it looked *like* love.

I wish, since it is too late, and that my lot is so absolutely, so irrevocably determined, that I had not had this letter, nor heard him take my part to that vile woman; for then I should have blessed myself for having escaped so happily his designing arts; but *now*, my poor mind is all topsy-turvied, as I may say,[215] and I have made an escape from my prison, only to be more a prisoner.

But, I hope, since thus it is, that all will be for the best; and I shall, with your prudent advice, and pious prayers, be able to overcome this weakness. But, to be sure, my dear sir, I will keep a longer time than a twelve-month, as a *true widow*, for a compliment, and *more* than a compliment, to your ashes! O the dear request! how kind, how affectionate! O that I had been the greatest duchess in the land! Then might I have been enabled to shew my gratitude to him; and not, as now, labour under the weight of obligation, that presses me to death;[216] and which, had I been a duchess, I never could have returned, but by a whole life of faithful love, and chearful duty and obedience!

Forgive, I beseech you, my dear father, forgive your poor daughter! How am I grieved to find this trial so severe upon me. O my unguarded youth, and tender years, will ye not in some measure excuse me? I never before knew, I could have no notion of what it was to be so affected! But prayer, and resignation to the Divine Will, and the benefits of your good lessons and examples, I hope, will enable me to get over this heavy trial.

Yet, O my treacherous, treacherous heart! How couldst thou serve me thus! And give no notice to me of the mischiefs thou wert about to bring upon me! How couldst thou thus inconsiderately give thyself up to the proud invader, without ever consulting thy poor mistress in the least! But thy punishment will be the *first* and the *greatest*: and well, perfidious traitor! deservest thou to smart, for giving up so weakly, thy *whole self*, before a summons came, and to one too, who had used me so hardly; and when likewise thou hadst so well maintained thy post against the most violent and avowed, and therefore, as I thought, only dangerous attacks!

After all, I must either not shew you this confession of my weakness, or tear it out of my writing. [*Memorandum*, to consider of this, when I get home.]

MONDAY *Morning, Eleven o'Clock*

We are just come in here, to the inn kept by Mrs Jewkes's relations. The first compliment I had, was, in a very impudent manner – How I liked the 'squire? I could not help saying, 'Bold, forward woman! is it for *you*, who keep an inn, to treat passengers with so much freedom?' She was but in jest, she said, and asked pardon: and she came and begged excuse again, very submissively, after Robin and Mr Colbrand had talked to her a little.

The latter here, in great form, gave me, before Robin, the letter, which I had returned him for that purpose. And I retired, as if to read it; and so I did; for I think I can't read it too often; though, for my peace of mind's sake, I might better try to forget it. I am sorry, methinks, I cannot bring you back a sound heart; but indeed it is an honest one, as to any body but me; for, wicked thing that it is, it has deceived nobody else.

More and more surprising things still!

Just as I had sat down, to try to eat a morsel before I set out to pursue my journey, came in Mr Colbrand, in a great hurry. 'O madam! madam!' said he, 'here is the groom from my master, all in a foam, man and horse!' How my heart fluttered! What now! thought I; what is to come next! He went out, and presently returned with a letter for me, and another, inclosed for himself. I shut the door; and (never, sure, was the like known!) found that to me to contain as follows:

'I find it in vain, my Pamela, to struggle against my affection for you. After you were gone, I ventured to look into your journal. Mrs Jewkes's bad usage of you, after your dreadful temptations and bruises, affected me greatly: but when in one place I read the unexpected declaration of your generous concern for me, on hearing how narrowly I escaped drowning (though my death would have been your *freedom*, and my treatment of you had made it your *interest* to wish it); and in another, your most agreeable confession, that notwithstanding all my hard usage of you, you could not *hate* me; and that expressed in so sweet, so innocent a manner, that I flatter myself you may be brought to *love* me, I began to regret parting with you; but, God is my witness! from no dishonourable motives, but the very contrary: and the more, when I reflected upon your behaviour at leaving my house: for, still that melodious voice praying for me at your departure, and thanking me for my rebuke to Mrs Jewkes, hangs upon my ears, and delights my memory. And though I went to-bed, I could not rest; but about two I arose, and ordered Thomas to get himself and one of the swiftest horses ready to overtake you with a letter, which is this, that I instantly sat down to write to you.

'Now, my dear Pamela, let me beg of you, on the receipt of this, to order Robin to bring you back to my house. I would have set out myself, for the pleasure of bearing you company back in the chariot, but am really indisposed; I believe, with vexation, that I should part thus with the delight of my soul, as I now find you are, and must be, in spite of the pride of my heart.

'You cannot imagine the obligation your return will lay me under to your goodness: and yet, if you will not so far favour me, you are to be under no restraint, as you will see by my letter unsealed, inclosed to Colbrand. But spare me, my dearest girl, the confusion of following you to your father's; which I must do, if you go on; for I find I cannot live without you.

'If you are the generous Pamela I imagine you to be, (for hitherto you have been all unmerited goodness to me) let me see, by your compliance, the further excellency of your disposition. Let me see you can forgive the repeated attempts of a man who loves you more than he loves himself. Let me see by it, that you are not prepossessed in any *other* person's favour: and one instance more of your consideration for me, I would beg you to give me, and then I will be all gratitude: and that is, that you would dispatch Colbrand with a letter to your father, desiring him to send to you, at my house, the letters you found means, by Williams's conveyance, to transmit to him. You may assure the good man from me, that all must and shall end happily. And when I have all my proud, and, perhaps, *punctilious* doubts answered, I shall have nothing to do, but to make my promise good, and you and myself equally happy: for I must be

Yours, and only yours.'

MONDAY *Morning, near Three o'Clock*

What, my dear parents, will you say to this letter? How my exulting heart throbbed, and even upbraided me for so lately reproaching it for giving way to the love of so dear a man! But take care thou art not too credulous neither, O fond believer! said I to myself; things that we wish, are apt to gain a too ready credit with us. This sham-marriage is not yet cleared up: Mrs Jewkes, the vile Mrs Jewkes! may yet instigate and influence the mind of this master: his pride of heart, and pride of condition, may again take place; and a man that could, in so *little* a space of time, change his professed love into avowed hatred, and so disgracefully banish me his house in consequence of that hatred, must be too unsteady to be depended upon; and though he sends for me now in such affectionate terms, he may again relapse, if *now* he mean honourably, and then may more effectually deceive, and ruin me. Therefore will I not acquit thee yet, O credulous, fluttering, throbbing mischief! that art so ready to believe what thou wishest: and I charge thee to keep better guard than thou hast lately done, and tempt me not to follow too implicitly thy flattering impulses.

Thus foolishly dialogued I with my heart; and yet, all the time, this heart was Pamela.

The letter to Monsieur Colbrand is as follows:

'I am sure, my honest Colbrand will excuse the trouble I give him. I have, for good reasons, besought Mrs Andrews, in a letter, which incloses this to you, wherever Tom shall overtake her, as a favour, to discontinue her journey to her father's, and instantly to set out on her return to Brandon Hall. I hope she will have the goodness to oblige me: but if she chuses to prosecute her journey, Robin is to pursue his first directions, and set her down at her father's door. If she *will* oblige me in her return, perhaps, she will give you a letter to her father, for some papers to be delivered to you for her: and if she do, you will carry it to Mr Andrews; and if he give you the papers, you will deliver them into her own hands *here*: but if she give you not such a letter, you will attend her on her return to the Hall, if she pleases to favour me so far; and that with all the expedition, that her health will permit. I am, &c.

'On second thoughts, let Tom go forward with Mrs Andrew's

letter, if she pleases to give one, and do you attend her in her
return hither.'

Now this is a generous manner of treating me. Surely I am not
of an ungenerous mind myself; for I love to be generously treated!
I wished at the time that I could have taken your directions in this
case.[217] I think I will trust in his generosity: yet is it not too great a
trust; especially as I have been treated? Then the gypsey's information came into my mind. Who, Pamela, thought I, if thou returnest,
will pity thee, should he take advantage of this confidence? The
world forms its judgment of our actions rather from events, than
from reason in undecided cases. And yet, if he meant not honourably now, he might have ordered Colbrand and Robin to carry me
back, whether I would or not. And will it not look as if I were
prepossessed, as he calls it, if I chuse to proceed to my father's?
If he intends *honour* to me, the least I can shew on my part, is, that
I have *gratitude*, and that my *heart is free*; so that I can return love
and duty for it. Hard would it be for a man of his rank and fortune,
if he were to undervalue himself, in preferring his poor servant to
ladies of rank and fortune, and could not be sure, that she could
love him above all the men in the world. He leaves me, as I have
observed above, generously at my liberty, when he could compel
me. And begs of me to spare him the confusion of following me to
my father's; which he must do, he says, if I proceed. Does not this
generosity, and open declaration, deserve in return some confidence?

He is not now, in my eye, the dreaded master, but the condescending one. And how amiable does he appear to me, to what he
did! Then he is indisposed: his illness is owing to his vexation for
parting with me. If he should die! (which God forbid.) And could
I think that I was the occasion – I will not tell you how this sad
thought affected me.

Recovering myself, Away with these fears, thought I, and with
all my apprehensions! I will return. I will obey him. The humble
Pamela will not lose this opportunity of laying an obligation on
her great master. Who knows, but he may owe his life to my return? And if so, that preserved life will enable one to bear the
lowering reflections that a sense of my unworthiness might otherwise, at times, fill me with, if he should be good to me.[218] I *will*

return. And if he should treat me ill hereafter, double will be his ungenerous guilt – I can then but die!

Having so resolved, I thought it right, to take to myself all the merit I could in obliging him, in hopes to engage the more securely his gratitude: and so I wrote the letter to you which he desired me to write, begging of you to return me, by the bearer, those papers and letters which I had sent you by Mr Williams's conveyance: for that they imported me much, for clearing up a point in my conduct, yet my master was desirous, to have cleared up, in order to make me happier than ever I could have hoped to be. But you will have that letter, before you can have *this*; for I would not send you this without the papers that precede it; and those are in my master's hands.

Having written this letter, and given it to Thomas, for him to carry to you, I sent for Monsieur Colbrand and Robin; and gave to the former *his* letter; and when he had read it, I said, 'You see how things stand. I am resolved to return to our master; and as he is not so well as were to be wished, the more haste you make, the better: don't mind my fatigue; consider only yourselves, and the horses.' Robin, who guessed the matter, by his conversation with Thomas, (as I suppose) said, 'God bless you, madam, and reward you, as your obligingness to my good master deserves; and may we all live to see you triumph over Mrs Jewkes!'

I wondered to hear him say so; for I was always careful of exposing my master, or even that wicked woman, before the common servants. But yet I question whether Robin would have said this, as he was not quite so good as he should be when he brought me down, if he had not guessed, by Thomas's message, and my resolving to return, that I might stand well with his master. So selfish are the hearts of poor mortals, that they are ready to change as favour goes!

They were not long getting ready. I wrote on till they were; and on my knees, prayed to God, that I might have no cause to repent my compliance.

Robin drove on at a very great rate; and when we came to the little town, where we put up on Sunday night, he gave his horses a bait; and said, he would push for his master's that night, as it would be moon-light, if I should not be too much fatigued; because there was no place between that and the village adjacent to Brandon

Hall fit to put up at for the night. I said, I wished not to lie on the road; and if it could be performed, I should bear it well enough. And so we pursued our journey.

But it was about one o'clock when we reached my master's gate. Every body was gone to rest. But one of the helpers got the keys from Mrs Jewkes, and opened the gates. The horses were so tired, that they could hardly crawl into the stables. And I, with the over-fatigue, when I went to get out of the chariot, fell down, and thought I had lost the use of my limbs.

Mrs Jewkes huddled on her clothes, and came down. She lifted up her hands and eyes, as if she wondered at my return: and I thought shewed more care of the horses than of me. Two of the maids came soon after; and I, supporting myself on the arms of each, made shift to get up stairs.

It seems my master was very ill, and had been upon the bed most part of the day. Abraham (who succeeded John) sat up with him. And he stepping out to us, told us, that my master was got into a fine sleep, and heard not the chariot come in. I was glad of that; for although his chamber lies towards the garden, on the other side of the house, I thought the coachman and the other servants (being awake themselves) talked loud enough to disturb the soundest sleeper, in the remotest part of the house; and Robin drove in the horses, farther over the rattling pavement, than he needed to have done.[219]

Mrs Jewkes said, he had a feverish complaint, and had been blooded. She prudently forbade Abraham, when my master awaked, to tell him I was come, for fear of surprising him, and augmenting his fever; or, indeed, to say anything of me, till she herself broke it to him in the morning, as she should see how he was.

Mrs Jewkes obliged me to drink almost half a pint of burnt wine,[220] made very rich and cordial, with spices; and then gave me a part of her bed; and I fell into a sound sleep, which I had little hoped for.

TUESDAY *Morning*

Mrs Jewkes, as soon as she got up, went to know how my master did, and he had had a good night; and having drank plentifully of sack-whey,[221] his fever was considerably abated. She told him, he must not be surprised, and she would tell him news. He asked, 'What?' And she said, Pamela was come back. He raised himself up, 'Can it be?' said he: 'What, already!' She told him, I came last night. Colbrand coming to the door to enquire of my master's health, he ordered him to come in, and was highly pleased with the account he gave him of my readiness to come back, and of my willingness to reach home that night. And he said, 'These tender fair-ones, I think, bear fatigue better than we men. But she is very good, to give me such an instance of her readiness to oblige me. Pray, Mrs Jewkes, take great care of her health. Let her not rise all day.' She told him, I had been up two hours. 'Ask her,' said he, 'if she will be so good as to make me a visit. If she will not, I will rise, and attend her.' 'Indeed, sir,' said she, 'you must lie still. To be sure she will think it her duty to wait on your honour.' 'But don't urge her too much,' said he, 'if she be unwilling.'

She came to me, and telling me this, I said, I would most willingly wait upon him. Indeed I longed to see my master, and was much grieved he was so ill. So I went with her. 'Will she come?' said he, as I entered the room. 'Yes, sir,' said she; 'and she said, at the first word, "Most willingly".' 'Sweet excellence!' he was pleased to say.

As soon as he saw me, he said, 'O my Pamela! you have made me quite well. I am concerned to return my acknowledgements to you in so unfit a place and manner; but will you give me your hand?' I did, and he kissed it with great eagerness. I expressed myself sorry to see him so ill. 'I can't be ill,' said he, 'while you are with me. I am well already'; and again kissing my hand, 'You shall not,' said he, 'repent of this goodness. I am sorry you have had so much fatigue. Life is no life without you! If you had refused to return (and yet I had hardly hopes you would oblige me) I should have had a very severe fit of it, I believe; for I was taken very oddly, and knew not what to make of myself: but now I shall be well instantly. You need not, Mrs Jewkes,' added he, 'send for Dr Harpur from Stamford; for this lovely creature is my doctor, as her absence was my disease.'

Mrs Jewkes looked so particularly odd, that I cannot describe how she looked. In short, no other features but her own could express such looks. Half surprized and half-displeased, and such a squint with her eyes! Yet instantly, as it were, the displeasure went off, as if she had bid it hide itself, and then a sort of vexed, forced, broad smile took place, as if (as I thought afterwards) she would have been glad to take to herself some merit, from being present at the favour shewn me, though by the first part of her countenance, I dare say she wished me an hundred miles off, and that I had never come back.[222]

My master desired me to sit down by his bedside; and I turning my head, as if looking for a chair, the officious woman reached one; and, at his repeated command, I sat down. He then asked me, if I had obliged him in the request he had made me, that I would send to my father for my former packet. I told him I had, and hoped it would be brought. It was doubly kind and good, he was pleased to say.

As rest, I said, was necessary for him, I desired leave to withdraw; and added, that I would pray for his honour's speedy recovery. 'Dear, good girl,' he called me; and bowed his head; and I retired with a look and behaviour, from which, I doubt (as I have since recollected) he might read a good deal of my heart. Forgive me, my dear parents. But if it was so, I could not help it.

He arose in the afternoon, and sent for me into his chamber. He seemed much amended in his health, as well as, I bless God for it, in his heart. How kind a dispensation is sickness sometimes! He was quite easy, and pleased with me. Mrs Jewkes was there, and he said to her, 'After this instance of my good Pamela's obligingness in her chearful return, I am sure, Mrs Jewkes, we ought to leave her entirely at her liberty; and, pray, if she chuses to take an airing in the chariot, let her be obliged, without asking her any questions.'

He took my hand, and said, 'One thing I will tell you, Pamela, because I know you will be glad to hear it, and yet will not care to ask about it: I had, before you went, taken Williams's bond for the money he owes me. How the poor man had behaved, I can't tell; but he could get no bail; and if I have no new reason given me, I shall hardly exact the payment of it. He has now been some time at liberty. But, methinks, I could wish, you would not see him at present.'

'Sir,' said I, 'I will not do any thing to disoblige you wilfully; and I am glad Mr Williams is at liberty; and the more, because I was the occasion of his misfortunes.' I durst say no more, though I wanted to plead for the poor gentleman. 'I am sorry, sir,' added I, 'that Lady Davers, who loves you so well, should have incurred your displeasure. I hope it was not on my account.'

He took out of his waistcoat-pocket his letter-case, and said, 'Here, Pamela; read *that* when you go to your chamber. You will find it to be a letter from Lady Davers; and let me have your thoughts upon it.'

He complained of heaviness,[223] and said he would lie down, and indulge for that day; and if he were better in the morning, would take an airing in the chariot. So I withdrew, and went to my closet, and read the letter he was pleased to put into my hands; which is as follows:

'Give me leave to tell you, brother, that I have had some people with me, who, with a good design, have made me acquainted with a certain proceeding of your's that *gives* me great uneasiness. I will, without apology, write to you my full mind on the occasion. Could I have thought that a brother of mine would so meanly run away with my mother's waiting-maid, and keep her a prisoner from all her friends? And yet I might have supposed, when you would not let the wench come to me on my mother's death, that you meant no good. You must either mean to marry her, or to make a kept creature of her; if the latter, are there not wretches enough to be had, without ruining a poor wench, whom my mother loved, and who really was a very good girl? As to marriage, I dare say you don't think of it. Your pride, surely, will set you above that. If it do not, you will be utterly inexcusable. It has been hinted to me, nevertheless, by *others*, that you have meanness enough in your pride, to think of such a thing; so bewitched are you, it seems, by this girl. This, though I think it must be a groundless surmise, excessively alarms me. Consider, brother, that ours is no upstart family. It is as ancient as the best in the kingdom: and, for several hundreds of years, it has never been known, that the heirs of it have disgraced themselves by unequal matches: and you know you have been sought to by some of the first families in the nation, for your alliance. If you were descended from a family of yesterday, from one who is but a remove or two from the dirt you seem so fond of, that would be another thing. Let me tell you, that I, and all mine, will renounce you for ever, if you can descend so meanly. A handsome man, as you are in your person, so happy in the gifts of your mind; and possessed of such a noble and clear estate; and very rich in money besides, left you by the behest of fathers and mothers, with such ancient blood in your veins, untainted. I cannot bear to think of your thus debasing yourself: and yet it would be very wicked in you to ruin the wench. Let me, therefore, beg of you, to restore her to her parents. Give her an hundred pounds or so, and make her happy with some honest fellow of her own degree; and that will equally become your honour, and your usual generosity of spirit.

'You must impute to my true sisterly love, and to my regard for your honour, the freedom of this expostulation; and then no other excuse will be wanting for it, from

> *Your affectionate sister,*
> B. DAVERS.'

What a letter is this, my dear father and mother! One may see by it how poor people are despised by the rich and the great! And yet we were all on a foot originally. Surely these proud people never think what a short stage life is; and that, with all their vanity, a time is coming, when they shall be on a level with us. The philosopher, who looked upon the skull of a king, and that of a poor man, saw no difference between them.[224] Besides, do they not know, that the richest of princes, and the poorest of beggars, are to have one great and just Judge, at the last day; who will not distinguish between them, according to their circumstances when in life? But, on the contrary, according to the neglected opportunities afforded to both? And how much greater then must be the condemnation of the one, than of the other? Poor souls! how do I pity their pride! O keep me, Heaven! from *their* high condition, if my mind shall ever be tainted with *their* vice! or polluted with so cruel and inconsiderate a contempt of the humble estate which they behold with so much scorn.

But, besides, how do these great people know, supposing they could trace back their ancestry, for one, two, three, or even five hundred years, that then the original stems of these poor families, though they have not kept such elaborate records of their good-for-nothingness, (as it often proves) were not as deeply rooted as theirs? And how can they be assured, that one or two hundred years hence, some of those now despised upstart families may not revel in their estates, while their descendants may be reduced to the other's dung-hills? And perhaps such is the vanity, as well as changeableness of human affairs, in *their* turns, aided by the heralds office, set up for pride of family, and despite the others!

On this occasion I recal the following lines, which I have read; where the poet argues in a much better manner:

> Wise Providence
> Does various parts for various minds dispense;
> The *meanest slaves*, or those who *hedge* and *ditch*,
> Are useful, by their toil, to feed the *rich*.
> The *rich*, in due return, impart their store;
> To comfort and reward the lab'ring poor.
> Nor let the *rich* the *lowest slave* disdain;
> He's *equally* a *link* of nature's *chain*;
> Labours to the *same end*, joins in *one view*;
> And *both alike* the *Will Divine* pursue:
> And, at the last, are levelled, *king* and *slave*,
> Without distinction, in the silent grave.[225]

WEDNESDAY *Morning*

My master sent me a message just now, that he was so much better, that he would take a turn after breakfast, in the chariot, and would have me give him my company. I hope, I shall know how to comport myself with humility, under all these favours.

Mrs Jewkes is become one of the most obliging creatures in the world; and, after her example, every one shews me high respect. But now, if this should all end in the sham-marriage! What would become of your poor girl, should returning health revive in him his wicked views! But I shall see what light this new honour will afford me! So I'll get ready. But I won't, I think, change my garb. Should I do it, it would look as if I would be nearer on a level with him: I will therefore go as I am, except he orders otherwise. Yet Mrs Jewkes says, I ought to dress as fine as I can. As my master is up, and at breakfast, I will venture down to ask him, how he will have me appear.

Well, he is kinder and kinder, and, thank God, purely recovered! How charmingly he looks, to what he did yesterday!

He arose as I entered the room, and, taking my hand, would make me sit down by him. 'My charming girl,' said he, 'seemed going to speak: what would she say?' 'Sir,' said I, (a little dashed[226] at his distinguishing favour) 'is it not too great an honour for me to attend you in the chariot?' 'No, my dear Pamela,' said he; 'your company will give me greater pleasure, than mine can give you honour; so say no more on that head.'

'But, sir,' said I, 'as to my appearance'; and I looked on my dress. 'I find no fault with your appearance, as you call it: and you look so pretty, that if you shall not catch cold, in that round-eared cap, you shall go just as you are.' 'Then, sir, you'll be pleased to go a by-way, that it mayn't be seen you do so much honour.' 'O my good girl,' interrupted he, 'I doubt you are more afraid of your own reputation, than of mine! But I intend by degrees to take off the world's wonder, and to teach them to expect what is to follow, as a due to my Pamela.'

O my dear father and mother! Did I not do well now to come back! And, now, could I get rid of my fears of this sham-marriage (for all this is not yet inconsistent with that frightful scheme) I should be too happy.

I withdrew (blushing, pleased, transported,) to fetch my gloves; and now do I wait his kind commands.

Dear, dear good sir! for God's sake, let me have no reverses, no more trials! for such, I verily think, I could not now bear!

O my dear father, I fear you will be apprehensive for the head, or at least for the humility, of your girl, when you shall read what I have to relate to you of what passed in this charming airing.

He handed me into the chariot before all the servants, as if I had been a lady! And I had the pleasure to hear one of the servants say to another, 'They are a charming pair! 'Tis pity they should be parted!'

He ordered dinner to be ready by two; and Abraham, who succeeds John, went behind the chariot. He bid Robin drive gently, and told me he wanted to talk to me about his sister Davers, and other matters. Indeed, at first setting out, he kissed me a little too often, that he did; and I was afraid of Robin's looking back, through the fore glass,[227] and of people seeing us as they passed; but he was exceedingly kind to me, in his words, as well. At last, he said, 'You have, I doubt not, read over and over, my sister's letter. You see she intimates in it, that some people had been with her; and who should they be but Mrs Jervis, and Mr Longman, and Jonathan! The knowledge of this, their bold officiousness, has laid me under the necessity of dismissing them from my service. I see,' said he, 'you are going to speak in their favour; but your time is not come to do that, if ever I shall permit it.

'As to Lady Davers, who threatens to renounce me, I have been beforehand with her; for I have renounced her. I have been a kind brother to her. When I entered upon my estate, I gave up pretensions to a considerable value, contrary to her own and to her lord's expectations, by way of present to her. She was surely beside herself when she wrote me such a letter; for well she knew that I would not bear it. But you must know, Pamela, that she is much incensed, that I will not give ear to a proposal of hers, of a daughter of a certain noble lord, who indeed wants not merit; and who probably might have attracted my regards, had I not had a dislike to marriage, and a girl in my view; with whom I hoped to live upon my own terms. Don't tell me, Pamela, by your blushes, that you know who the girl is. Be satisfied with this assurance' (for I was going to speak) 'that I have at present views quite different from those, which this girl had once reason to be apprehensive of. And yet, to be sincere, I must own, that the certainty there will be, that I shall incur the censures of the world, if I act up to my present intentions, still, at times, gives me thoughts not altogether favourable to those intentions. For it will be said by every one, that Mr B. a man not destitute of pride, a man of family, and ample fortunes, has been drawn in by the eye, to marry his mother's waiting-maid. Not considering, and not knowing, perhaps, that to her mind, to her virtue, as well as to the beauties of her person, she owes her well-deserved conquest: and that (as I firmly trust will be the case) there is not a lady in the kingdom who will better support the condition to which she will be raised, if I should marry her. And,' generously added he, putting his arm round me, 'I pity my dear girl too, for her part in this censure; for here will she have to combat the pride and slights of the neighbouring gentry all around us. Lady Davers, you see, will never be reconciled to you. The other ladies will not visit you; and you will, with a merit superior to them all, be treated as if unworthy their notice. Should I now marry my Pamela, how will my girl relish all this? Will not these be cutting things to my fair one, to whom the condition you will then be raised to, will have given some pride? And *some pride* I would have it give you: you have *now*, my Pamela, a dignity that seems natural to your person. As to myself, sensible as I am *beforehand*, of what the world will say, I shall have nothing to do, when *it is done*, but to brazen out the matter, of my former pleasantry on this subject, with my companions; stand their rude jests for once or twice, and my fortune will create me always respect enough. But, I say, what will my poor girl do, as to *her* part? For the ladies will shun your acquaintance. What says my girl to this?'

You may well guess, my dear father and mother, how transporting to me these generous and condescending expressions were! 'O sir,' said I, 'how inexpressibly kind and good is all this! Your poor servant has a much greater difficulty than this to overcome.'

'What is that?' said he, a little impatiently: 'I will not forgive your doubts now.' 'No, sir,' said I, 'I cannot doubt; but it is, how I shall *support*, how I shall *deserve*, YOUR goodness to me!' 'Dear girl!' said he, and pressed me to his bosom, 'I was afraid you would again have given me reason to think you had doubts of my honour. And this, at a time when I was pouring out my whole soul to you with a true and affectionate ardour, I could not so easily have forgiven: and yet I have been so much obliged by your chearful return to a house you had reason to detest, that I should have been very sorry to have had cause given me to be angry with you, whatever you had said.'

'But, good sir,' said I, 'my greatest concern will be for the rude jests you will have yourself to encounter with, for thus stooping beneath yourself. For as to *me*, considering my low birth, and little merit, even the slights and reflections of the ladies will be an honour to me: and I shall have the pride to place more than half their ill-will to their envying my happiness. And if I can, by my chearful duty, and grateful behaviour, render myself worthy of the continuance of your affection, I shall think myself but too happy, let the world say what it will.'

'You are very good, my dearest girl,' said he. 'But how will you bestow your *time*, when you will have no visits to receive or pay? No parties of pleasure to join in? No card-tables to employ your winter evenings, and even, as the taste is, half the day, summer and winter?'

'My mother, I know, in order to amuse herself, instructed you how to take part in those diversions, as well as in others: and I assure my girl, that I shall not desire you to live without such amusements as *my wife* might expect, had you been a woman of the first quality.'

'How, sir, shall I bear your goodness! But do you think, in such a family as yours, a person whom you shall honour with the rank of mistress of it, will not find useful employments for her time, without looking abroad for any others?

'In the first place, sir, if you will give me leave, I will myself look into all such parts of the family management, as may befit the mistress of it to inspect: and this I shall hope to do in such a manner, as not to incur the ill-will of any *honest* servant.

'Then, sir, I will ease you of as much of your family accounts, as I possibly can: you know, sir, my late good lady made me her treasurer, her almoner, and everything; and I will apply myself to learn what I may be defective in, to enable me to be a little useful to you, sir, in this particular.

'Then, sir, if I must needs be visiting or visited, and the ladies will not honour me so much, or even if they *would* now-and-then, I will visit, if your goodness will allow me so to do, the unhappy poor in the neighbourhood around you; and administer to their wants and necessities, in such small matters as may not be hurtful to your estate, but comforting to them; and entail upon you their blessings, and their prayers for your health and welfare.

'Then I will assist your housekeeper, as I used to do, in the making jellies, comfits,[228] sweetmeats, marmalades, cordials; and to pot, and candy, and preserve, for the uses of the family; and to make myself all the fine linen of it, for yourself and me.

'Then, sir, if you will indulge me with your company, I will take an airing in your chariot now-and-then: and when you return from your diversions, I shall have the pleasure of receiving you with chearful duty; as I shall have counted the moments of your absence. And I have no doubt of so behaving, as to engage you frequently to fill up some part of my time (the sweetest by far that will be) in your instructive conversation.'

'Proceed, my dear girl,' said he, 'I love to hear you talk.'[229]

'The breakfasting-time, sir, the preparation for dinner, and sometimes to entertain your chosen friends, and the company you shall bring home with you, *gentlemen*, if not *ladies*, and the supperings, will fill up a great part of the day, in a very necessary manner.

'Possibly, sir, a good-humoured lady will now-and-then drop in; and if so, I hope to behave myself in such a manner, as not to *add* to the disgrace you will have brought upon yourself: for indeed, I will be very circumspect, and try to be as discreet as I can; and as humble too, as shall be consistent with your honour.'

Generously pleased with my prattle, he again bid me talk on.[230]

'Cards, 'tis true, I can play at, in all the games that our sex usually delight in: but they are a diversion that I am not fond of; nor shall I ever desire to play, unless to induce such ladies, as you may wish to see, not to shun your house, for want of an amusement they are accustomed to.

'Music, which my good lady also had me instructed in, will fill up some intervals, if I should have any.

'Then, sir, you know, I love reading and scribbling; and though most of the latter will be employed in the family accounts, yet reading, at proper times, and in proper books, will be a pleasure to me, which I shall be unwilling to give up for the best company in the world, when I cannot have yours. Besides, sir, will not books help to polish my mind, and make me worthier of your company and conversation? And when I am at a loss to understand any thing I read, what a delightful instructor shall I have, if you will permit me to have recourse to you? And till you have time or inclination to instruct me, I can put down in a pocket-book the words and things I shall not know the meaning of.

'But one thing, sir, I ought not to forget, because it is the chief: my duty to God, and my prayers for you and for myself, will always employ some good portion of my time: for *myself* particularly, that I may be enabled to discharge my duty to you, and be found grateful for all the blessings I shall receive at the hands of Providence, by means of your generosity and condescension.

'With all this, sir, can you think I shall be at a loss to pass my time? But, as I know that every slight to me, if I come to be so happy, will be, in part, a slight to you, I will beg of you, sir, not to let me go very fine in dress; but appear only so, as that I may not be a disgrace to you, after the honour you shall have done me, in giving me a title to be called by your worthy name: for, sir, I humbly apprehend, that nothing so much excites the envy of my own sex, as seeing a person set above them in appearance. And if this plainness in apparel be known to be in compliance to my own choice and wishes, it will be a credit, sir, to your condescension, and save me many mortifications. If I am not gorgeous in my dress, this I promise you, sir, I will be always neat, and fit to be seen by you; and if by *you*, by *any body* you shall bring home with you. And I have heard my lady say, that gentlemen of taste are more pleased with intrinsic neatness, than with outward ornament.'

Here I stopped; for I had prattled a great deal; and he said, clasping me to him, 'Why stops my Pamela? Why does she not proceed? I could dwell upon your words all the day long. You shall be the directress of your own pleasures, and of your own time, so sweetly do you chuse to employ it: and then shall I find some of my own bad actions atoned for by your exemplary goodness, and God will bless *me* for *your* sake.'

I could not speak for joy; and he was pleased to proceed, 'What delight do you give me, my beloved Pamela, in this sweet foretaste of my happiness! I will now defy the saucy, busy censures of the world; and bid them know *your* excellence, and *my* happiness, before they, with unhallowed lips, presume to judge of *my* actions, and *your* merit! And let me tell you, my dearest girl, that I can add to your agreeable enumeration my hopes of a still more pleasing amusement for you, though it is what your bashfulness would not permit you to hint at; and which I will now no further touch upon (lest it should seem, to your nicety, to detract from the present purity of my good intentions) than to say – I hope you will have, superadded to all these, such an employment, as will give me a view of perpetuating my happy prospects, and my family at the same time; of which I am almost the only one, in a direct line.'

If I did blush, it was impossible so much as to *look* displeased, such was the charming manner with which he insinuated this distant hope.

Imagine, my dear parents, how my heart was affected with all these things!

He was pleased to add another charming sentiment, which shewed me the noble sincerity of his kind professions. 'I do own to you, my Pamela,' said he, 'that I love you with a purer flame than ever I knew in my whole life! A flame, to which I was a stranger, and which commenced for you in the garden; though you, unkindly, by your unseasonable doubts, nipped the opening bud, while it was too tender to bear the cold blasts of slight or negligence. And this I declare to you, that I have known, in this sweet hour's conversation, a higher and sincerer joy than it is possible I could have known, had I succeeded in my views upon you.'

'O sir!' said I, 'expect not words from your poor servant, equal to these generous professions. Both the means, and the will, are given to you, to lay me under an everlasting obligation. How happy shall I be, if, though I cannot be worthy of all this goodness and condescension, I can prove myself not entirely unworthy of it! But I can only answer for a grateful heart; and if ever I give you cause wilfully (and you will generously allow for *involuntary* imperfections) to be displeased with me, may I be an outcast from your house and favour, as much as if the law had divorced me from you!'

'Gratitude, my beloved girl,' said the generous man, 'is, *must be*, a part of your nature, or you could not, on this occasion, express yourself in a style so raised. But you were going to say something else. Speak on, my Pamela! say all that is in your heart to say. Speak on, my Pamela.'[231]

'I am so desirous, sir, to stand well in your opinion, that I was going to try to clear myself in relation to my behaviour in the garden, which you were pleased to think so unseasonable. Had you *then* been pleased to hear what I had to say, you would, I flatter myself, have forgiven me, and owned, that I had some cause to fear, and to wish to be with my father and mother; and this I the rather say to you now, that you should not think me ever capable of returning insolence for goodness; or appearing foolishly ungrateful to you, when you was so kind to me.'

'Indeed, Pamela,' said he, 'you gave me great uneasiness; for I love you too well not to be jealous of the least appearance of your indifference to me, or preference of any other person, not excepting your parents themselves. This made me resolve not to hear you; for I had not got over my reluctance to marriage; and a little weight, you know, turns the scale, when it hangs in an equal balance. But yet, you see, that though I could part with you, while my anger held, yet the regard I had then newly professed for your virtue, made me resolve not to offer to violate it; and you have seen likewise, that the painful struggle I underwent when I began to reflect, and to read your moving journal, between my desire to recall you, and my doubt whether you would return, (though yet I resolved not to force you to it) had like to have cost me a severe illness: but your kind and chearful return has dispelled all my fears, and given me hope (advantages of fortune out of the question) that you have not an indifference to me; and you see how your presence has chased away my illness.'

'I bless God for your recovery, sir,' said I; 'but since you are so good as to encourage me, and will not despise my weakness, I will acknowledge, that I suffered more than I could have imagined, in being forbidden your presence in so much anger; and I was still the more affected, when you answered the wicked Mrs Jewkes so generously in my favour, at my leaving your house: for this, sir, awakened all my reverence for you; and you saw I could not forbear, not knowing what I did, to break in upon you, and acknowledge your goodness on my knees.'

''Tis true, my dear Pamela,' said he, 'we have sufficiently tortured each other: but we shall soon, I hope, be able to sit down together, secured in each other's good opinion, and take pleasure in reflecting upon all our past difficulties. Meantime, let me hear what my dear girl would have said in her justification, (could I have trusted myself with her) as to her fears, and the reason of her wishing herself from me, at a time that I had begun to shew my fondness for her in a manner that I thought would have been agreeable to her and virtue.'

I pulled out of my pocket the gypsey letter; but, before I gave it to him, 'I have this letter, sir,' said I, 'to shew you, as what, I believe, you will allow, must have given me the greatest disturbance: but first, as I know not who is the writer, and it seems to be in a disguised hand, I would beg it as a favour, that if you guess whose it is, which I cannot, it may not turn to the person's prejudice.'

He took it and read it. And it being signed *Somebody*, he said, 'Yes, this is indeed from *Somebody*; and, disguised as the hand is, I know the writer: don't you see by the setness of some of these letters, and a little secretary²³² cut here and there, especially in that *c*, and that *r*, that it is the hand of a person bred in the law-way? Why, Pamela, 'tis old Longman's hand: an officious –' and there he stopt. 'But I have done with him,' resumed he, angrily.

'O sir,' said I, 'it would be too presuming in me to offer (so much overwhelmed as I am with your goodness) to defend any body you are angry with; yet, so far as any one has incurred your displeasure for my sake, and for no other want of duty or respect, I could wish – But I dare not say more.'

'But,' said he, 'as to the letter, and the information it contains: let me know, Pamela, when you received this.' 'On the Friday, sir, that you were gone to the wedding at Stamford.' 'How could it be conveyed to you,' said he, 'unknown to Mrs Jewkes, when I gave her such a strict charge to attend you, and you had promised me, that you would not throw yourself in the way of such intelligence? For, when I went to Stamford, I knew (from a private intimation given me) that there would be an attempt made to see you, or give you a letter, by somebody, if not to get you away; but I was not certain whether from Lady Davers, Mrs Jervis, Mr Longman, or John Arnold, or your father; and as I was then but struggling with myself, whether to give way to my honourable inclinations, or to free you, and let you go to your father, that I might avoid my own danger; (for I had absolutely resolved never again to wound your ears with any proposals of a contrary nature.) Hence it was, that I desired you to permit Mrs Jewkes to be on her guard till I returned, by which time I thought I should have decided this disputed point within myself between my pride and my inclinations.'

'This, sir,' said I, 'accounts well to me for your conduct in that case, and for what you said to me and to Mrs Jewkes on that occasion; and I see more and more how much I may depend upon your honour and goodness. But I will tell you all the truth.'

And then I recounted to him the whole affair of the gypsey, and how the letter was put among the loose grass, &c. And he said, 'The man who thinks a thousand dragons sufficient to watch a woman, when her inclination takes a contrary bent to his wishes, will find all too little; since she will engage the stones in the street, and the grass in the field, to act for her, and help on her correspondence, if she has no other way.' 'You are not angry, sir, I hope.' 'I am not,' said he. 'But I cannot help observing, that if the mind be not engaged, there is hardly any confinement sufficient to restrain the person. You have told me, Pamela, a very pretty story; and as you never, even in your severest trials, gave me reason to question your veracity, I make no doubt of the truth of what you have now mentioned: and I will, in my turn, give you a proof of my sincerity, that shall carry conviction with it.

'You must know then, my Pamela, that I had actually formed such a project, as is mentioned in this letter; so well informed was this officious *Somebody*; and the time was fixed, for the very person described in this letter, to be here. I had intended that he should have read some part of the ceremony (as little as was possible, to deceive you) in my chamber; and so I hoped to have you mine upon terms that *then* would have been much more agreeable to me than matrimony. Nor did I intend that you should soon be undeceived: so that we might have lived for years, perhaps, very agreeably together; while it would have been in my power to confirm or abrogate the marriage, as I pleased.'

'O sir,' said I, 'I am out of breath with the thoughts of my danger. But what good angel prevented the execution of this deep-laid design?'

'Why, *your* good angel, Pamela: for when I began to consider that it would have made *you* miserable, and *me* not happy; that if I should have a child by you, it would be out of my power to legitimate it, if I should wish it to inherit my estate; and that, being the last of my family, most of what I possess must descend to a new line, and to disagreeable and unworthy persons: when I further considered your unsullied virtue, and reflected upon the trials you had undergone, and the troubles I had involved you in, I was resolved, though I doubted not succeeding in this last plot, to overcome myself; and to part with you, rather than betray you under so black a veil. Besides, I remembered how much I had exclaimed against, and censured an action of this kind, that had been attributed to one of the first men of the law, and of the kingdom, as he afterwards became. And when I reflected, that if I were to proceed in this scheme, I should do no more than tread in a path that another had marked out for me; and, as I was assured, with no great satisfaction to himself, when he came to reflect; my pride was a little piqued; for, if I went at any time out of the way, I loved to be thought an original. All these considerations, put together, induced me to reject this project, and I sent word to the person, that I had better considered of the matter, and would not have him come, till he heard farther from me: and, in the interim, I suppose, some of your confederates, Pamela, (for we have been a couple of plotters, though your virtue and merit have procured *you* more faithful friends than my money and promises have made me) one way or other got knowledge of it, and gave you this notice. But perhaps it would have come too late, had not your white angel got the better of my black one. Upon the whole, I must needs own, that, from these appearances, you were but too well justified in your fears; and I have only one thing to blame you for; which is, that you, who have such a command of your pen, did not clear up this matter by a few lines to me: the rather, as you had reason then to have a better opinion of me than you had at any time before; and, as I see, you could so easily have done it. This would have saved us both much fatigue; you of person, me of mind; since, had I known what seeming good grounds you had for pouring cold water on a young flame, that was just then rising to an honourable expansion, I should not have ascribed your doubts, and desire of leaving me, as I thought I had reason to do, either to perverse nicety; or, which most alarmed me, to a prepossession in some other person's favour.'

'I wish, sir,' said I, 'I had taken that liberty. I am sure I should have saved myself, had such been the happy effect of my writing, as much fatigue of *mind* as of *person*: and I could not better manifest the truth of this, than by the chearfulness with which I obeyed you, on your recalling me to your presence.'

'Ay, that, my dear Pamela,' said he, 'was the kind, the inexpressibly kind compliance, that has rivetted my affections to you, and induced me to open to you, in this free and unreserved manner, my whole heart.'

'Indeed, sir,' said I, 'I had the less merit in my return (you are too generous to think hardly of me for the confession) because I was driven by an irresistible impulse to it, and could not help it if I would.'

'This,' said he (and honoured me by kissing my hand) 'is engaging indeed. And may I hope, that my Pamela's gentle inclination for her persecutor was the strongest motive to her return?'

I was silent. I felt myself blush. I looked down. I was afraid I had said too much; not for my heart, but for my interest in *his* heart. Men complain, I have heard, of women's reserves; yet slight them, if they are not reserved. But this *now* wholly good gentleman did not do so by me. On the contrary, he encouraged my frankness. 'Why blushes my girl?' said he. 'Why looks she down? Fear not to trust the tenderest secrets of your heart with me, if favourable to me. I do assure you, that I so much value a fervent and unquestionable love in the person I would wish for my wife, that even in the days of courtship, I would not have the least shadow of reserve, where there is no room for doubt, have place on her lips, when she inclines to favour me by a declaration of reciprocal love. And can you return me sincerely the honest compliment I now will make you? In the *choice* I have made, it is impossible I should have any view to my *interest*. Love, *true* love, is my *only* motive. And were I not what I am, as to fortune, could you give me the *preference* to any other person you know in the world, notwithstanding what has passed between us?'

'Why,' said I, 'should your so much obliged Pamela decline an answer to this kind question? Cruel as I have thought you, and truly shocking and detestable as your attempts ever were to me, you, sir, are the only man living, my father excepted, who ever was more than indifferent to me. Yet allow me to add, that not having the presumption to raise my eyes to you, I knew not myself the state of my own heart, till your kindness to me melted away, as I may say, the chilling frost that prudence and love of virtue had cast about the buds of – What shall I say? Excuse, sir –'233

'My dearest Pamela,' clasping me to his bosom, 'I do excuse, and will spare your sweet confusion. I am fully satisfied. Nor am I now so solicitous as I was, about the papers that you have kindly written for to your father: and yet I still wish to see them, for the sake of the sweet manner in which you relate what has passed; and to have before me the whole series of your sufferings, in order to recompence you for them.'

In this manner, my dear father and mother, did your happy daughter find herself blessed by her generous master! An ample recompence for all her sufferings, did she think this sweet conversation only. A hundred tender things he expressed besides, which, though they never can escape my memory, yet would be too tedious to write down. What a happy change is this! And who knows but my kind, my generous master, may put in my power, when he shall see me not quite unworthy of it, to be a means, without injuring him, to dispense, to many persons, the happy influences of the condition, to which I shall be, by his kind favour, exalted? Doubly blessed shall I be, in particular, if I can return the hundredth part of the obligations I owe to such honest good parents, to whose pious instructions and examples, under God, I owe all my present happiness, and future prospects.

I must sit down to ponder all these things, and to admire and bless the goodness of that Providence, which has, through so many intricate mazes, made me tread the paths of innocence, and so amply rewarded me, for what it has itself enabled me to do!

I will now continue my pleasing relation.

As the chariot was returning home from this sweet airing, he said, 'From all that has passed between us, in this more than agreeable excursion, my Pamela will see, and will believe, that the trials of her virtue are all over from me: but perhaps there will be some few yet to come of her patience and humility. For I have, at the earnest importunity of Lady Darnford, and her daughters, promised them a sight of my girl: I intend therefore to have that whole family, and Mrs Jones, and Mrs Peters's family, to dine with me in a few days. And although I believe you would hardly choose to grace my table, till you can do it in your own right, I should be glad you would not refuse coming down to us, if I should desire it; for I would preface our *nuptials*,' said the dear gentleman! [What a sweet word was that!] 'with their opinion of your merits (and to see you, will be enough for that purpose) and so, by degrees, prepare my neighbours to expect what is to follow. They already have your character from me, and are disposed to admire you.'

'I am afraid, sir,' said I, 'that weighed down as I am with the sense of my obligations to your goodness, on one hand, and of my own unworthiness on the other, I shall behave very aukwardly on such an occasion: but your will in every thing I *can* obey you in, shall me mine.'

'I am obliged to you, my Pamela,' said he; 'and pray be then dressed just as you are; for since they know your condition, and I have told them the story of your present dress, and how you came by it, one of the young ladies begs it as a favour, that they may see you in it: and the rather as I have boasted, that you owe nothing to dress, but make a much better figure with your own native stock of loveliness, than the greatest ladies they have seen, arrayed in the most splendid attire, and adorned with jewels.'

'Your goodness, sir,' said I, 'makes you behold your poor servant in a light greatly beyond her merit! But it must not be expected, that others, ladies especially, will look upon me with *your* favourable eyes: but as to dress, as well now, as at all times, it will be a pleasure to me to shew every one, that, with respect to my happiness in this life, I am entirely the work of your bounty.'

'Admirable Pamela! Excellent girl!' said he. 'I might have *addressed* a hundred fine ladies; but never could have had reason to *admire* one as I do you.'

I hope, my dear father, you will think, that I repeat these generous expressions rather to set forth my master's goodness to me, than that I have the vanity to think I deserve one of them. It shall be always my endeavour, I do assure you, to be more and more humble, as I am either complimented or obliged; for were I even to *deserve* the compliments that shall happen to be made me for any talents that may be imputed to me, to whom am I indebted for these talents but to God? Be His all the glory, therefore. And to whom but to you, my father, and to you, my mother, and to my dear departed lady, do I owe the cultivation of those talents? What a poor patched-up merit, therefore, is all the merit I have to boast of! And shall I be vain of it? And it is with very great pleasure, that I look forward on the high benefits my master seems determined to confer upon his poor servant, because I think I shall not be puffed up with my high condition; since thus I argue with myself: it is always the sign of a dependent condition to be forced to lie under obligations one cannot repay; as it is of a rich mind, when it can confer favours, without expecting or *needing* a return. It is, on one side, the state of the human creature, compared, on the other, to that of the Great Creator; and so, with due deference, may my master's beneficence be said to be God-like.

The chariot brought us home at near the hour of two; and, as my master is pure well, and chearful, I hope he does not repent of his generous treatment of me. He handed me out of the chariot, and to the parlour, with the same goodness, that he shewed, when he put me into it, before several of the servants. Mrs Jewkes came to enquire how he did. 'Quite well, Mrs Jewkes,' said he, 'quite well; I thank God, and this good girl, for it!' 'I am glad of it,' said she; 'but I hope you are not the worse for *my* care, and for my doctoring!' He told her he was not, and thanked her both for her care and skill.

Then he said, 'Mrs Jewkes, you and I have used this good girl very hardly.' 'I was afraid, sir,' said she, 'I should be the subject of her complaints.' 'I assure you,' replied he, 'she has not opened her lips about you. We have had quite a different subject to talk of. I hope she will forgive us both: you especially she must; because you have done nothing but by my orders. But I only mean, that the necessary consequence of those orders has been very grievous to my Pamela: and now comes our part to make her amends, if we can.'

'Sir,' said she, 'I always said to madam, that you was very good, and very forgiving.' 'No,' said he, 'I have been very wicked, and she, I hope, will be very forgiving. But all this preamble is to tell you, Mrs Jewkes, that now I desire you will study to oblige her, as much as you were forced, in obedience to me, to disoblige her before. And you will remember, that in every thing she is to be her own mistress.'

'Yes,' said she, 'and mine too, I suppose, sir?' 'Ay,' said the generous man, 'I believe it will be so in a little time.' 'Then,' said she, 'I know how it will go with me!' And put her handkerchief to her eyes. 'Pamela,' said my master, 'comfort Mrs Jewkes.'

This was very generous, already to seem to put her in my power; and I took her hand, and said, 'I shall never take upon me, Mrs Jewkes, to make a bad use of any opportunities that may be put into my hands, by my generous master; nor shall I ever wish to do you disservice: for I shall consider, that what you have done, was in obedience to a will, which it will become me also, for the future, to submit to.'

'See there, Mrs Jewkes,' said my master, 'we are both in generous hands; and, indeed, if Pamela did not pardon you, I should think she but half forgave me, because you acted by my instructions.' 'Well,' said she, 'God bless you both together, since it must be so; and I will double my diligence to oblige my lady, as I find she will soon be.'

Do you, my dear father and mother, join in prayer with me, that

God would remove from me all the delightful prospects before me, if, when I come to be what I am encouraged to look up to, my new condition should so far corrupt my mind, as to make me proud, and vain, and forget to acknowledge, with thankful humility, the blessed Providence, which has so visibly conducted me through the dangerous paths I have trodden to this happy moment.

My master was pleased to say, that he thought I might as well dine with him, since he was alone. But I begged he would excuse me, for fear, as I said, such excess of goodness and condescension, all at once, should turn my head; and that he would by slower degrees bring on my happiness, lest I should not know how to bear it.

'Persons who doubt themselves,' replied he, 'seldom do amiss. And if there was any fear of what you say, you could not have had it in your thoughts: for none but the presumptuous, the conceited, and the thoughtless, fall into great errors. But nevertheless,' added he, 'I have such an opinion of your prudence, that I shall generally think what you do, or wish to do right.'

'Sir,' said I, 'your kind expressions shall but task me with the care of endeavouring to deserve your good opinion.' And being then about to go upstairs, and nobody near, 'Permit me, sir,' said I, with some confusion, 'thus on my knees, to thank you, as I often wanted to do in the chariot, for all your goodness to me.' And I had the boldness to touch his hand with my lips.

I wonder since, how I could be so bold. But how could I help it? My heart was like a too full river, which overflows its banks. My gratitude, at the moment, got the better of my fear, and carried my shamefacedness away before it, as the river does every thing that opposes it.

He clasped me in his arms, and kissing me, said, 'You are a dear obliging girl: and here, on my knees, as you on yours, I vow to you everlasting truth and fidelity; and may God but bless us both with half the pleasures that seem to lie before us, and we shall have no reason to envy the felicity of the greatest princes!' 'O sir,' said I, 'how shall I support so much goodness!' I could say no more, at the time, but by my tears; for I wept with joy: yet my heart was full of grateful meaning, and wanted to relieve itself by words.

He raised me, and as I bent towards the door, led me to the stairs foot; and saluting me there again, left me to go up to my closet, where I threw myself on my knees, and blessed that gracious God, who had thus changed my distress to happiness, and so abundantly rewarded me for all the sufferings I had passed through. And oh! how light, how very light, do all those sufferings *now* appear, which *then* my repining mind made so grievous to me! Hence, in every state of life, and in all the changes and chances of it, for the future, will I trust in Providence, who knows what is best for its creatures, and frequently makes the very evils we most dread, the cause of our happiness, and of our deliverance from greater. My experiences, young as I am, as to this great point of reliance on Heaven, are strong, though my judgment in general may be weak; but you'll excuse these reflections, because they are your daughter's; and, so far as they are not amiss, are owing to the examples set me by you both; and to my late good lady's instructions.

I have written a vast deal in a little time: and shall conclude this delightful Wednesday, with saying, that in the afternoon my master was so well, that he rode out on horseback, and came home about nine at night; and then stepped up to me, and seeing me with pen and ink before me in my closet, was pleased to say, 'I come only to tell you I am very well, my Pamela; and since I have a letter or two to write, I will leave you to proceed in your's, as I suppose that was your employment'; for I had put by my papers at his coming up. He saluted me, bid me good-night, and went down; and I finished up to this place before I went to-bed. Mrs Jewkes told me, if it were agreeable to me, she would lie in another room; but I said, 'No, Mrs Jewkes; pray let me have your company.' And she made me a fine curt'sy, and thanked me. How times are altered!

THURSDAY

This morning my master came up to me, and talked to me on various subjects for a good while together in the most kind manner. Among other things he asked me, If I chose to order any new clothes against my marriage. (O how my heart flutters when he mentions this subject so freely!) I said, I left everything to his good pleasure, only repeating my request, for the reasons I gave yesterday, that I might not be too fine.

He said, 'I think, my dear, the ceremony shall be very privately performed: I hope you are not afraid of a sham-marriage; and pray get the service by heart, that you may see nothing is omitted.'

I glowed between bashfulness and delight. O how I felt my cheeks burn!

I answered, I feared nothing, I apprehended nothing, but my own unworthiness. 'I think,' said he, 'the ceremony shall be performed within these fourteen days, at this house.' O how I trembled! but not with grief, you may believe! 'What says my girl? Have you to object against any day of the next fourteen, because my affairs require me to go to my other house, and I think not to stir from this, till I am happy with you?'

'I have no will but your's,' said I (all glowing like the fire, as I could feel): 'but, sir, did you say in the *house*?' 'Ay,' said he; 'for I care not how privately it be done; and it must be very public, if we go to church.' 'It is a *holy rite*, sir,' said I, 'and would be better, methinks, solemnized in a *holy place*.'

'I see' (said he, most kindly) 'my lovely maid's confusion; and your trembling tenderness shews I ought to oblige you all I may. Therefore I will order my own little chapel, which has not been used for two generations for any thing but a lumber-room, because our family seldom resided here long together, to be got ready for the ceremony, if you dislike your own chamber or mine.'

'Sir,' said I, 'that will be better than a chamber; and I hope it will never be lumbered again, but kept to the use, for which, as I *presume*, it has been consecrated.' 'O yes,' said he, 'it has been consecrated, and that several ages ago, in my great-great-grandfather's time, who built that and the good old house together.

'But now, my dear girl, if I do not too much add to your sweet confusion, shall it be in the *first* seven days, or the *second* of the next fortnight?' I looked down, quite out of countenance. 'Tell me,' said he.

'In the second seven days, if you please sir,' said I. 'As *you* please,' returned he, most kindly; 'but I should thank you, Pamela, if you would choose the first.' 'I'd *rather*, sir, if you please,' replied I, 'it should be in the second.' 'Well,' said he, 'be it so; but don't defer it till the last day of the fourteen.'

'Pray, sir,' said I, 'since you embolden me to talk on this important subject, may I not send my father and mother word of my happiness?' 'You may,' replied he; 'but charge them to keep it secret, till you or I direct the contrary. I told you,' added he, 'that I would see no more of your papers; I meant I would not without your consent: but if you will shew me what you have written, since the last I saw, (and now I have no other motive for my curiosity, but the pleasure I take in reading what you write) I shall acknowledge it as a favour.'

'If, sir,' returned I, 'you will be pleased to let me write over again one sheet, I will; and yet, relying on your word, I have not written with the least precaution.' 'For that very reason,' said he, 'I am the more desirous to see what you write: but what is the subject of the sheet you mean to transcribe? And yet before-hand, I tell you, I cannot consent that you should with-hold it from me.'

'What I am loth you should see, sir,' returned I, 'are very severe reflections on the letter I received by the gypsey, when I apprehended your design of the sham-marriage; though there are other things; but those reflections are the worst.' 'They can't be worse, my dear sauce-box,' replied he, 'than what I have seen already; and I will allow of your treating me freely on that occasion, because, from the contents of that letter, I must have a very black appearance with you at that time.' 'Well, sir,' said I, 'I think I will obey you, and send you my papers before night.' 'But don't alter a word in them,' said he. 'I won't, sir,' replied I, 'since you command me not.'

While we were talking, Mrs Jewkes came up, and told my master, that Thomas was returned. 'Let him,' said he, 'bring up the papers.' For he hoped, and so did I, that you had sent them by him. But it was a great disappointment when he came up, and said, 'Sir, Mr Andrews did not care to deliver them; and would have it, that his daughter was forced to write that letter to him: and in apprehensions for his daughter, on her turning back, when on her way to them, (as I told him she did,' said Thomas) 'he took on sadly.'

I began to be afraid now, that all would be bad for me again.

'Well, Tom,' said he, 'don't mince the matter. Tell me what Mr and Mrs Andrews said.' 'Why, sir, they both, after they had withdrawn, to consult together upon their daughter's letter, came out, weeping so bitterly, that grieved my very heart; and they said, Now all was over with their poor daughter; and either she had written that letter by compulsion, or –' and there Thomas stopt.

'*Or* what?' said my master, 'speak out.' 'Or had yielded to your honour, so they said, and was, or would be ruined!'

My master seemed vexed, as I feared. And I said, 'Pray, sir, be so good to excuse the fears of my honest parents! They cannot know your goodness to me.'

'And so,' said my master, (without answering to what I said) 'they refused to deliver the papers?' 'Yes, and please your honour,' said Thomas, 'though I told them, that their daughter, of her own accord, on a letter I had brought her, very chearfully wrote what I carried. But Mr Andrews said, "Why, wife, there are in these papers twenty things nobody should see but ourselves, and especially not the 'squire. O the poor girl! She has had *many*, very many stratagems to struggle with! And now, at last, has met with one that has been too hard for her!" And then, and please your honour, the good old couple sat themselves down, and hand-in-hand, leaning upon each other's shoulder, did nothing but lament. I was piteously grieved; but all I could say could not comfort them; nor would they give me the papers, though I told them I should deliver them into their daughter's own hands. And so, and please your honour, I was forced to come away without them.'

My good master saw me all bathed in tears at this description of your distress and fears for me, and he said, 'I am not angry with your father. He is a good man; and I would have you write out of hand, and it shall be sent by the post to Mr Atkins, who lives within two miles of your father, and I'll inclose it in a cover of mine, in which I will desire Mr Atkins, the moment it comes to his hand, to convey it safely to your father. But say nothing in what you write of sending hither the papers, since they are so scrupulous about them. I want not now to see them on any other score than that of mere curiosity; and that will be answered at any other time.' And so saying, he was pleased to dry my eyes with my own handkerchief, before Thomas; and turning to him, said, 'The worthy couple don't know my honourable intentions by their dear daughter; who, Tom, will in a little time, be your mistress; though I shall keep the matter private for some days, and would not have it spoken of by my servants out of the house.'

Thomas said, 'God bless your honour! You know best.' And I said, 'O sir, you are all goodness! How kind is this, to forgive the disappointment, instead of being angry, as I feared you would be!'

Thomas then withdrew. And my master said, 'I need not remind you, Pamela, of writing immediately, to make the good couple easy. I will leave you to yourself for that purpose; only send me down such of your papers, as you are willing I should see, with which I shall entertain myself for an hour or two. But one thing,' added he, 'I forgot to tell you: the neighbouring gentry I mentioned, will be here to-morrow to dine with me.' 'And *must* I, sir,' said I, 'be shewn to them?' 'O yes,' replied he. 'The chief reason of their coming is to see you. And don't be concerned: you will see nobody equal to yourself.'

I opened my papers as soon as my master had left me, and laid out those which contain the following particulars:

They begin on the Thursday morning on which he set out for Stamford, and give an account of the morning visit he made me before I arose: of his strict instructions to Mrs Jewkes, but in a good-natured way, to be watchful over me, because of some private intimations he had received, that an access would be attempted to be made to me, by somebody: of the letter cunningly contrived to be put into my hands by a gypsey, informing me of a design of a sham-marriage to be set on foot against me: of my heavy reflections upon it, in which I call him a *truly diabolical man*, and am otherwise very severe upon him: of his return on Saturday, and of the terror he put me in by an offer he made to search me for the papers which followed those he had got by Mrs Jewkes's means; and to prevent which I was forced to give them up: of his behaviour to me after he had read them, and great kindness to me, because of the dangers I had escaped, and the troubles I had undergone: and how I, unseasonably, in the midst of his goodness, (having the intelligence of the sham-marriage, from the gypsey, in my thoughts) expressed my desire of being permitted to go home to you: of his being enraged on this occasion, and turning me that very Sunday out of his house, and sending me on my way to you: of the grief I had at parting with him, and of my free acknowledgment to you, that I found I loved him too well, and could not help it: of his sending after me to beg my return; but yet generously leaving me at my liberty, when he might have forced me back: of my resolution to oblige him: of my concern to find him very ill on my return: of his kind reception of me: the copy of Lady Davers's angry letter to him, upbraiding him with his behaviour to me, and desiring him to set me free, and to give me a sum of money in marriage with some one of my own degree, threatening to renounce him as a brother, if he should degrade himself by marrying me himself; and then follow my serious reflections on this letter, &c. (all which, I hope, with the others, you will shortly see). And this carried matters down to Tuesday night last.

And here I thought it best to stop; for the rest of my narrative being a relation of our charming chariot conference, on Wednesday morning, and of his great goodness to me ever since, I was a little ashamed to let him see all that I had written on those tender and most agreeable subjects; though his generous favours deserve all the acknowledgments I can possibly make.

When I had looked these out, I carried them down into the parlour to him, and said, putting them into his hands, 'Your allowances, good sir, as heretofore; and if I have been too open and free in my reflections or declarations, let my apprehensions on one side, and my sincerity on the other, be my excuse.' 'You are very obliging, my good girl,' said he. 'You have nothing now to apprehend either from my thoughts or actions.'

I then went up, and wrote the letter to you, briefly acquainting you with my present happy prospects, and expressing the gratitude which I owe to the most generous of men; requesting (notwithstanding his kind dispensing with the sight of them) the papers you have; and assuring you, that I should soon have the pleasure of sending to you, not only those, but all that succeeded them to this time, as I know you delight to amuse yourself in your leisure hours with my scribble.

I carried down this letter, before I sealed it, to my master. 'Will you please, sir,' said I, 'to take the trouble of reading what I have written to my father and mother?' He was pleased to thank me, and putting his arm round me[234] while he read it, seemed much pleased with the contents; and giving it me again, 'You are very happy, my beloved girl,' said he, 'in your expressions: and the affectionate things you say of me, are inexpressibly obliging; and with this kiss do I confirm for truth all that you have promised for my intentions in this letter.'

O my dear father and mother! What a happy creature is your girl! God continue my present prospects! A change now would kill me quite.

He went out in his chariot in the afternoon; and returning in the evening, sent to desire me to take a little walk with him in the garden: and down I went that very moment.

He came to meet me. 'So,' said he, 'how does my girl now? Who do you think I have seen since I have been out?' 'I don't know, sir,' answered I. 'There is a turning in the road,' said he, 'about five miles off, which goes round a meadow, that has a pleasant footway, on the banks of a little brook, and a double row of limes on each side, where the gentry in the neighbourhood sometimes walk and converse; and sometimes angle. (I'll shew it you in our next airing.) I stepped out of my chariot to walk across this meadow, and bid Robin meet me with it on the further part of it. And who should I 'spy there walking, with a book in his hand, but *your* humble servant, Williams? Don't blush, Pamela. His back was towards me. I thought I would speak to the man; and before he saw me, "How do you do, old acquaintance?" said I.

'We were of one college for a twelvemonth, you have heard. The man gave such a start at hearing my voice, and seeing me so near him, that I thought he would have leapt into the brook.'

'Poor man!' said I. 'Ay,' said he, 'but not too much of your *poor man*, in that soft accent, neither, Pamela. "What are you reading, Mr Williams?" said I. "Sir," answered he, "it is, it is," stammering with surprize, "it is the French Telemachus.[235] I am about perfecting myself in the French tongue." (Better so, thought I, than perfecting my Pamela in it.) "Don't you think, that yonder cloud may give us a small shower?" (It did a little begin to wet). He believed not, was his answer.

'"If," said I, "you are for the village, I'll give you a cast,[236] for I shall call at Sir Simon Darnford's, in my way home." "It would be too great an honour," the man too modestly said. "Let us walk to the further opening there," replied I, "and we shall meet my chariot."

'So, Pamela,' continued my master, 'we fell into conversation, as we walked. He said, he was very sorry he had incurred my displeasure; and the more, as he had been told by Mrs Jones, who had it from Sir Simon's family, that I had more honourable views than at first were apprehended. "We men of fortune, Mr Williams," said I, "take a little more liberty with the world than we ought to do; wantoning, very probably, as you contemplative folks would say, in the sun-beams of a dangerous affluence; and cannot think of confining ourselves to the common paths, though the safest and most eligible. And you may believe, I could not very well like to be supplanted in a view that lay next my heart; and that by an old acquaintance, whose good, before this affair, I was studious to promote."

"'I would only say, sir," answered he, "that my *first* motive was entirely such as became my function: and I am very sure, that however inexcusable I might seem in the *progress* of the matter, you would have been sorry to have had it said, that you had cast your thoughts on a person, that nobody could have wished for but yourself."

"'I see, Mr Williams," replied I, "that you are a gallant as well as religious man: but what I took most amiss was, that, if you thought me doing a wrong thing, you did not expostulate with me upon it, as your function might have allowed you to do; but immediately determined to circumvent me, and to secure to yourself, and that from my own house, a young creature, who held, as you must think, a first place in my heart; and by whom you knew not but I might do honourably at last, as I actually intend to do. But the matter is happily at an end, and my resentments too."

"'I am sorry, sir," said he, "that I should take any step to disoblige you; but I rejoice in your honourable intentions; and give me leave to say, that if you make young Mrs Andrews your lady, she will do credit to your choice with every body that sees and knows her."

'In this manner,' continued my master, 'did Mr Williams and I confabulate,²³⁷ and I set him down at his lodgings in the village. But he kept your secret, Pamela, and would not own, that you gave any encouragement to his addresses.'

'Indeed, sir,' replied I, 'he could not say that I did; and I hope you believe me.' 'I do,' said he: 'but 'tis still my opinion, that if I had not detected him as I did, the correspondence between you would have ended in the manner I have supposed.'

'When you consider, sir,' replied I, 'that my utmost presumption could not make me hope for the honour you are now so good as to design me; that I was very hardly used; and had no prospect before me but dishonour; you will allow, that I should have seemed very little in earnest in my professions of honesty, if I had not endeavoured to get away: but yet I resolved not to think of marriage; for I never saw the man I could love, till your goodness, I am not ashamed to say, emboldened me to look up to you.'

'I should, my dear Pamela,' returned he, 'make a very ill compliment to my vanity, if I did not believe you.'

I was glad to hear this account of the interview between Mr Williams and himself: I hope the good man will, in time, be reinstated in his favour.

He was so good as to tell me, he had given orders for the chapel to be cleared. With what inward joy, yet with fear and trembling, do I look forward!

FRIDAY

About twelve o'clock came Sir Simon, Lady Darnford, their two daughters, Mrs Jones,[238] a sister-in-law of her's, and Mr Peters, and his spouse, and niece. Mrs Jewkes, who is more and more obliging, was much concerned I was not dressed in some of my best clothes, and made me many compliments.

My master, conducting them into the garden, led them into the largest alcove, and stepped himself to me. 'Come, my Pamela,' said he, 'the ladies are impatient to see you.' I was in some confusion. 'The young ladies,' said he, 'are dressed out in their best attire; but they make not such an appearance as my charming girl in this humble garb. They are all in the great alcove.' 'Shan't I follow you thither, sir?' said I. 'I can't bear you should do me so much honour as to accompany me.' 'I'll go before you,' replied he, 'and do you bid Mrs Jewkes bring a bottle or two of Canary, and some cake.' So he left me, and went to attend his guests.

This alcove fronts the longest gravel-walk in the garden, so that they saw me all the way I came, for a good way: there was no by-path, as I wished there were, and would have chosen it if there had, could I have done it without appearing affected.[239] My master, with pleasure, told me, afterwards, all they said of me.

Will you forgive your vain daughter, if she tells you all he was pleased to tell me? *Vain* you will think me, and I cannot but say I am proud to be so distinguished by him. Then these agreeable circumstances are so *new* to me! When I am more used to these honours, I hope all my pride will be lost in my gratitude to God, and to him. I know, moreover, that my now happy tale rejoices your worthy hearts; and you will not think I can be too particular on these occasions. So, my dear father and mother, you must have some pride to answer for, as well as your daughter.

He said, 'spying me first, 'Look there, ladies, comes my pretty rustic!' They all, I saw, (which dashed me) stood at the opened windows of the alcove, and in the door-way, looking full at me. Was that pretty in them?

My master told me, that Mrs Jones said, 'She is a charming creature! I see that at this distance.' And Sir Simon, it seems, who has been a sad rake in his younger days, swore he never saw so easy an air, so fine a shape, and so graceful a motion. Lady Darnford said, I was a sweet girl. And Mrs Peters said very handsome things. Even Mr Peters said, I should be the pride of the county. The young ladies, he was pleased to add, blushed, and envied me! But that could not be so! To his partial favour for me, I owed this compliment.

When I came near, he saw me in a little confusion, and was so kind as to meet me, 'Give me your hand,' said he, 'my good girl; you walk too fast' (for indeed I wanted to be out of their gazing). I did so, with a curt'sy, and he led me up the steps of the alcove, and in a most gracious manner presented me to the ladies. They all saluted me, and said, They hoped to be better acquainted with me: and Lady Darnford was pleased to say I should be the flower of the neighbourhood. Sir Simon said, 'Good neighbour, by your leave'; and, saluting me, added, 'Now will I say, that I have kissed the loveliest maiden in England.'

But for all this, methought I owed him a grudge for a tell-tale, though all is likely to turn out so happily.

Mr Peters very gravely followed his example, and said, like a bishop, 'God bless you, fair excellence!' 'Pray, dear madam, sit down by me,' said Mrs Jones. And they all sat down.

I hesitated, as if looking for a place near the door. 'Sit down, my good girl,' said my master: 'these ladies, my neighbours, will indulge you for *my* sake, at present; and when they are acquainted with you, for *your own*.'

'Sir,' said I, but hesitatingly, 'I shall be proud to deserve their indulgence.'

They all so gazed at me, that I could not look up; for I think it is one of the distinctions of persons of condition, and the well-bred, to put bashful ones out of countenance. 'Well, Sir Simon,' said my master, 'what say you now to my pretty rustic!' He swore a great oath, that he should better know what to say to me, if he was as young as himself. Lady Darnford said, 'You will never leave,[240] Sir Simon.'

'You have walked too fast, my Pamela,' said my master. 'Recover yourself. You may the sooner, for I have told all my kind neighbours here, a good deal of your story, and your excellence.' 'Yes,' said Lady Darnford, 'my dear neighbour, as I *will* call you; we that are here present have heard your uncommon story.' 'Then, madam,' replied I, 'you have heard what must make your kind allowance for me very necessary.' 'No,' said Mrs Peters, 'we have heard what will always make you valued as an honour to our sex, and as a pattern for all the young ladies in the county.' I could only curt'sy to this high compliment.

Mrs Jewkes came in with the Canary, brought by Nan, to the alcove, and some cake on a salver; and I said, 'Mrs Jewkes, let me be your assistant; I will serve the ladies with the cake.' So I took the salver, and went round to the company with it, ending with my master. Mrs Jones said, she was not used to be served with such a grace; and they all praised me. Sir Simon particularly said, when I served him, that I should have a better office; and seeming to expect that I should make some answer,[241] 'I hope my good master's favour,' said I, 'will never make me forget, that it is my duty to wait upon his friends.' 'Master! Sweet-one,' said Sir Simon, 'I hope you won't always call Mr B. master, for fear our ladies should make the word a fashionable one to their husbands through the county.'

The elder Miss Darnford stood up when I served her, and addressed me thus: 'I beg your pardon, my dear madam, but I had heard how sweetly this garb became you, and was told the history of it; and I begged it as a favour, that you might oblige us with your appearance in it.' 'I am much obliged to you, madam,' said I, 'that your kind prescription was so agreeable to my choice.' '*Was* it your choice?' said she. 'I am glad of that: and yet the moment I beheld you, I excused myself, to myself; for I saw that your person *gave*, and could not *take* ornament from any dress.' I blushed, and curtsied;[242] but was unable to return an answer.

Lady Darnford told my master, that she hoped they should have my company at table. He said, very kindly, 'It is her time now, and I will leave it to her choice.' 'If the good ladies, then, will forgive me, sir,' said I, 'I had rather be excused.' They all said I must not. I begged I might. 'Your reason for it, my Pamela?' said my master: 'since the ladies request it, I wish you would dine with us.' 'Sir,' replied I, 'your goodness will make me, every day, more and more deserving of the honour the ladies do me; but at present I have too great a sense of my unworthiness to be easy under such a distinction.'

My master generously said, 'Well then, ladies, we will not urge this matter further: we must not make my good girl uneasy with herself.'

'And must we excuse you, my *amiable friend*?' most sweetly said Miss Darnford. 'Accept me as such,' said she. 'Allow me to love you as my sister.'

How encouraging to your girl, my dear parents, was the condescension of so fine a young lady. My master seemed delighted with the honour done me, by every one.

Lady Darnford was pleased to say, 'We will not oppress you, my sweet neighbour: but if we excuse you at dinner, we must insist upon your company at tea, and at the card-table; for' (turning to my master) 'we intend to pass the whole day with you, sir, as we told you.' 'What say you to Lady Darnford's kind expectation, my Pamela?' said my master. 'Sir,' replied I, 'whatever is your pleasure, and the ladies, I shall think it my duty to comply with.' They said, I was very obliging. But Sir Simon, rapping out an oath, said, That *they* might dine together, if they would; but *he* would dine with me, and with nobody else.

The young ladies each offered herself to take a turn about the garden with me. And we three, and Mrs Jones's sister-in-law, and Mr Peters's niece, walked together.

They were very affable, kind, and obliging; and we soon entered into a good deal of familiarity; and Miss Darnford every moment rose higher in my opinion. Her sister was a little more on the reserve; and I afterwards heard, that, about a year before, she would fain have had my master make his addresses to her; but though Sir Simon is reckoned rich, she was not thought a sufficient fortune for him. And, now, to have him look down so low as me, must be a sort of mortification to a poor young lady! And I pitied her. Indeed I did! I wish all young persons of my sex could be as happy as I am likely to be.

My master told me afterwards, that I left the other ladies, and Sir Simon and Mr Peters, so full of *admiration*, was his word, both of my person and behaviour; that they could hardly talk of any other subject. The dear gentleman, God bless him! told me this with a pleasure that doubly delighted me.

We walked in, and dinner not being ready, the young ladies desired me to give them one tune upon the harpsichord. They knew, Miss Darnford was pleased to say, that I could oblige them to advantage, both with my finger and my voice.

They would not be denied, and I obeyed.

The ladies were so kind as to approve my performance: and Miss Darnford complimented me highly upon it; and said, she wished Mr B. could be prevailed upon to give a ball on an approaching happy occasion. But I can't say *I* do; though I did not say so; for these occasions, I think, are too solemn for *principals* of our sex to take part in, especially if they have the same thoughts of the solemnity that I have: for, though I have before me a prospect of happiness that may be envied by women of high rank; yet I have something very awful upon my mind, when I think of the matter, and shall more and more, as it draws nearer.

About Four o'Clock

My master just now came up to me, and said, 'If you should see Mr Williams below, do you think, Pamela, you should not be surprized?' 'No, sir,' said I, 'I hope not. Why should I?' 'Expect,' said he, 'a stranger, then, when you come down to us in the parlour; for the ladies are preparing for the card-table, and they insist upon your company.' 'O sir,' said I, 'you seem disposed to try all my courage.' 'Does it want courage, Pamela, to see Mr Williams?' 'No, sir, were not so many of your neighbours present, some of whom refused me protection, when I thought myself in danger. They, perhaps, will be affected, and will affect me, on recollecting what passed on that occasion; Sir Simon Darnford particularly, will perhaps take notice of the application made to his lady; Mr Peters –' 'Well,' interrupted he, 'I would have you guard your heart against surprizes, though you should see a man you have very little expectation to see, and whom you perhaps dearly love.'

This speech equally surprizes and concerns me. What will become of me, if he should be jealous? He looked very gravely when he said this. If any turn should now happen! My heart aches. But I will assume as chearful an air as I possibly can, that nothing will be imputed to me. Yet I wish Mr Williams had not come now, that there is so much company: otherwise I should have been glad to see the poor gentleman; for indeed I think him a good man, and he has suffered for my sake.

I am now sent for down to cards. I'll go; but wish for the continuance of their good opinion of me: for I shall be very aukward. My master, by his serious question, and caution to guard my heart against surprizes, has quite alarmed me. I hope he loves me! But whether he does or not, I am in for it now, over head and ears, I doubt, and can't help loving him; 'tis a folly to deny it.

Now, my dear mother, must I write to *you*. Well might my master speak so mysteriously as he did, about guarding my heart against surprizes. I never was so surprized in my life; and never could see a man I love so dearly! O my mother, it was my dear, dear father (and not Mr Williams) that was below, ready to receive and to bless your daughter; and both my master and my father enjoined me to write how the whole matter was, and what my thoughts were on this joyful occasion.

I will take the matter from the beginning, that Providence directed his feet to this house, as I have had it from Mrs Jewkes, from my master, my father, the ladies, and from my own heart and behaviour, as far as I know of both.

It seems then, that my father and you were so uneasy to know the truth of the story which Thomas had told you, that, fearing I was betrayed, and absolutely ruined, he set out the day after Thomas was there; and on Friday morning got to the neighbouring town; and there he heard, that the gentry in the neighbourhood were at my master's, at a great entertainment. He put on fresh linen (which he had brought in his pocket) at an alehouse there, and got shaved; and then set out for my master's house, with a heavy heart, dreading for me, and in much fear of being himself brow-beaten. He had, it seems, asked at the alehouse, what family the 'squire had down here, in hopes to hear something of me; and they said, 'A housekeeper, two maids, and, at present, two coachmen, and two grooms, a footman, and a helper.' Was there no more of the family down? he asked. They told him, but said it must not come from them, that there was a young creature there, who had been his mother's waiting-maid; but was supposed to be his mistress. This, he said, grieved his heart, and confirmed his fears.

About three o'clock in the afternoon, he reached the iron gate; and ringing there, Sir Simon's coachman, who was nearest at hand, went to him. And my father asked for the housekeeper; though from what I had written, he could not in his heart abide her. Mrs Jewkes sent for him in, little thinking who he was, and asked him, in the little hall, what was his business with her? 'Only, madam,' said he, 'whether I cannot speak one word with the 'squire?' 'No, friend,' said she, 'he is engaged with several gentlemen and ladies.' 'I have business with his honour,' said my father, 'of greater consequence to me than either life or death.' And tears stood in his eyes.

At these words she went into the great parlour, where my master was talking very pleasantly with the ladies; and said, 'Sir, here is a good tight²⁴³ old man, who wants to see you on business of life and death, he says, and is very earnest.' 'Ay,' said he, 'Who can he be? Shew him into the little hall. I'll go to him presently.' At my master's going out, Sir Simon, in his free manner, said, 'No more nor less, my good friend, I dare say, than a bastard child. If it is, bring it in to us.' 'I will,' said my master.

Mrs Jewkes tells me my master was much surprised, when he saw my father; and she much more, when my father said, 'Good God! give me patience! but, sir, as great as you are, I must ask for my child!' and burst out into tears. [O my dear mother! what trouble have I given you both!] My master said, taking him by the hand, 'Don't be uneasy, Goodman Andrews, your daughter is in the way to be happy!'

This alarmed my father, and he said, 'What! then, is she dying?' And trembled so, he could hardly stand. My master made him sit down, and sat down by him, and said, 'No, God be praised! she is very well; and pray be comforted: she has written a letter to assure you, that she has reason to be well satisfied and happy.'

'Ah! sir,' said he, 'you told me once she was in London, waiting on a bishop's lady, when all the time she was a close prisoner here.'

'Well, that's all over now, Goodman Andrews,' said my master: 'times are altered; for now the sweet girl has taken me prisoner; and, in a few days, I shall put on the most agreeable fetters that ever man wore.'

'O sir,' said he, 'you are too pleasant for my griefs. My heart is almost broken. But may I not see my poor child?' 'You shall presently,' replied my master, 'for she is coming down to us; and I hope you will believe *her*, though you seem to doubt *me*.'

'I will ask you, sir,' said he, 'but one question till then, that I may know how to look upon her when I see her? Is she honest? Is she virtuous?' 'As the new-born babe, Mr Andrews,' said my master; 'and in twelve days time, I hope, will be my wife!'

'O flatter me not, good your honour,' said my father, with folded hands: 'it cannot be! I fear you have deluded her with strange hopes; and would make me believe impossibilities!' 'Mrs Jewkes,' said my master, 'do you tell my Pamela's father all you know concerning me, and your mistress that is to be. Meantime, set out what you have, and make him drink a glass of what he likes best. If this be wine,' added he, 'fill me a bumper.'[244]

She did so; and he took my father by the hand, and said, 'Believe me, good man, and be easy; for I can't bear to see you tortured in this cruel suspense: your daughter is the beloved of my soul. I am glad you are come: you will find us all in the same story. And here's your dame's health; and God bless you both, for being the happy means of procuring for me so great a blessing!' And so he drank this most obliging toast.

'What do I hear! it cannot surely be!' said my father. 'And your honour cannot, I hope, mock a poor old man! This ugly story, sir, of the bishop runs in my head! But you say I shall see my child! And I shall see her honest! If not, poor as I am, I would not own her!'

My master bid Mrs Jewkes not let me know yet, that my father was come; and went to the company, and said, 'I have been agreeably surprized. Here is honest Mr Andrews come, full of grief, to see his daughter; for he fears she is seduced; and tells me, worthy man, that, poor as he is, he will not own her, if she be not virtuous.'

'O,' said they all, with one voice almost, 'Dear sir! shall we not see the good old man you have so much praised for his plain good sense and honest heart; and for his love to his daughter, as well as his daughter for her duty to him?' 'I intend,' said my master, 'to surprize her. She shall not know her father is come till she sees him.' 'Dear, dear Mr B.' said Miss Darnford (and they all joined in the same request) 'let us be present at their first interview!' But was not this very cruel, my dear mother? For well might they think I should not support myself under such an agreeable surprize.

He said, kindly, 'I have but one fear; that the dear girl may be too much affected.' 'O,' said Lady Darnford, 'we'll all help to keep up her spirits.' 'I'll go up,' said he, 'and prepare her a little.'

Accordingly, he came up, and amused me, as I have told you, about Mr Williams.

My master went from me to my father, and asked if he had eaten any thing. 'No,' said Mrs Jewkes; 'the good man's heart's so full he cannot eat, nor take comfort, till he has seen his daughter.' 'That shall soon be,' said my master. 'I will have you come in with me; for she is going to sit down with my guests to quadrille,[245] and I will hasten her down.' 'O sir,' said my father, 'don't, don't let me; I am not fit to appear before your guests; let me see my daughter by myself, I beseech you.' 'All my guests know your honest character, Goodman Andrews,' said my master; 'and long to see you for Pamela's sake.'

He then took my father by the hand, and led him in, against his will, to the company. 'My good neighbours,' said my master, 'I present to you one of the honestest men in England; my Pamela's father.' Mr Peters went to him, and took him by the hand, and said, 'We are all glad to see you, sir; you are the happiest man in the world in a daughter, whom we never saw before to-day; but cannot enough admire her.'

'This gentleman, Mr Andrews,' said my master, 'is the minister of the parish; but is not young enough to be Mr Williams.' This airy expression, my poor father said, made him, for a moment, fear that all was a jest. Sir Simon also took him by the hand, and said, 'Ay, you have a sweet daughter, honestly; we are all in love with her.' And the ladies came, and said very fine things: Lady Darnford particularly, That he might think himself the happiest man in England, in such a daughter. 'If, and please you, madam,' said he, 'she be but virtuous, 'tis all in all: the rest is but accident. But, I doubt, his honour has been too much upon the jest with me.' 'No,'

said Mrs Peters, 'we are all witnesses, that he intends very honourably by her.' 'It is some comfort,' said he, and wiped his eyes, 'that
such good ladies say so! But I wish I could see her.'

They would have had him sit down by them, but he chose to sit
in the corner of the room, behind the door; so that he could not be
seen as one came in; because the door opened against him, as I
may say. The ladies all sat down. My master sent for me. And down
I came.

Miss Darnford, in order to engage me from looking at my father,
as I put to the door after me, welcomed me down. I saw not, therefore, my father presently: and his heart was so full that he could
not speak to me: but he got up and sat down three or four times
successively, in silence, and was quite unable to come to me. The
ladies all had their eyes upon him; but I would not look that way,
supposing Mr Williams was there: and they made me sit down
between Lady Darnford and Mrs Jones; and asked me what we
should play at. I referred myself to their choice, and wondered to
see them smile, and look now upon me, and then to that part of
the room; but still, as Mr Williams had not been presented to me,
I looked not that way, though my face was to the door, and the
table before me.

'Did you send your letter to the post-house, my good girl,' said
my master, 'for your father?' 'To be sure, sir,' answered I; 'I did
not forget that. Mr Thomas carried it.' 'What,' said he, 'I wonder,
will the good old couple say to it?' 'O sir,' replied I, 'the news of
your great goodness will be a cordial to their worthy hearts!'

At that, my father, not able to contain himself, nor yet to stir
from the place, gushed out into a flood of tears, and cried out, 'O
my child!'

I knew the voice, and lifting my eyes, and seeing my father, gave
a spring, overturned the table, without regard to the company, and
threw myself at his feet. 'O my father! my father!' said I, 'can it
be! Is it you? Yes, it is! it is! O bless your happy –' daughter! I
would have said, and down I sunk.

My master was concerned. 'I feared,' said he, 'that the surprize
would be too much for her spirits.' All the ladies ran to me, and
made me drink a glass of water; and recovering, I found myself in
the arms of my dearest father. 'O tell me,' said I, 'every thing! How

long have you been here? When did you come? How does my
mother?' And half a dozen questions more I asked, before he could
answer one.

They permitted me to retire, with my father; and then I poured
forth all my vows and thanksgivings to God for this additional
blessing; and confirmed all my master's goodness to me, to his joyful amazement. And after I had resolved all his doubts, and answered
all his questions, we kneeled together, blessing God, and each
other, and you also, my dear mother, for several ecstatic minutes;
and my master coming in soon after, my dear father said, 'O sir,
what a change is this! May God reward and bless you, in this world
and the next!'

'How does my sweet girl?' said my kind master. 'I have been in
pain for you! I am sorry I did not apprise you beforehand —'

'O sir,' said I, 'it was *you*! and all you do must be right. But this
was a blessing so unexpected!'

'Well,' said he, 'you have given painful delight to all the company. They will be glad to see you, when you can return. Mr
Andrews, do you make this house your own; and the longer you
stay, the more welcome you will be. After you have a little composed yourself, my dear girl, come to us again. I am glad to see
you so well already.' And he left us.

'See you, my dear father,' said I, 'what goodness there is in this
once naughty master! O pray for him, and pray, that I may deserve
it!'

'How long is it since this happy change has been wrought, my
dear child?' 'O,' said I, 'several happy days! I have written down
every thing; and you will see, from the depth of despair, what God
has done for your daughter!'

'Blessed be his name!' said he. 'But can it be, that such a great
gentleman will make a lady of the child of such a poor man as I?
O the Divine Goodness! How will your mother be able to support
these happy tidings? I will set out to-morrow, to acquaint her with
them: for I am but half happy, till the dear good woman shares my
joy! To be sure, my dear child, we ought to go into some far
country to hide ourselves, that we may not disgrace you by our
poverty!'

'Now, my dear father,' said I, 'you are unkind for the first time.
Your poverty has been my glory; your honesty and integrity have

been my riches. Do I not owe all I am, and am likely to be, to your and my dear mother's good lessons and example? And shall I be ashamed of my parentage? See you not already that this great and rich gentleman respects you for your goodness? And what is greatness to goodness?'

In this manner, my dear mother, did we pass the happy moments, till Miss Darnford came in, and enquiring kindly after my health, took my father's hand and mine, and, with the most engaging sweetness, led us both into the great parlour to the company; who all arose to congratulate us. My master took my father's hand, in the kindest manner, and obliged him to sit down by him, and pledge him in a glass of wine. Sir Simon, after his facetious manner, put his hands on my shoulders. 'Let me see, let me see,' said he, 'where do your wings grow? for I never saw any body fly like you. 'Why,' said he, 'you have broken Mrs Jones's shins with the table. Shew her, madam, the hurt she has done you.'

They were so kind as to excuse me at cards; and my master made me sit between the two dearest men in the world to me, each holding one of my hands! my father, every now and then, with tears, lifting up his eyes, and saying, 'Could I ever have hoped this!'

I asked him, if he had been so good as to bring the papers with him. He said he had, and looked at me, as if he asked, Must I give them to you now? I said, 'Be pleased to let me have them.' He gave them to me; and I stood up, and curt'sying, put them into my master's hands. 'Thank you, Pamela,' said he. 'Your father shall take all your papers with him, that he may see how faulty I have been, as well as be enabled to account for this happy alteration. But I must have them all returned me. I shall keep them for the writer's sake.'

My master was very urgent with them to stay supper; and, at last, they complied, on condition that I would grace the table, as they were pleased to call it. I begged to be excused. My master said, 'Don't be excused, Pamela, since the ladies desire it. And besides, we won't part with your father; and so you may as well stay with us.'

I was in hopes my father and I might sup by ourselves, or only with Mrs Jewkes.

When supper was brought in, Lady Darnford took me by the hand, and said to my master, 'Sir, by your leave'; and would have placed me at the upper-end of the table. 'Pray, pray, madam,' said I, 'excuse me; I cannot sit there, indeed I cannot.' 'Pamela,' said my master, to the great delight of my good father, as I could see by his looks, 'oblige Lady Darnford, since she desires it. It is but a little before your time.'

'Dear, good sir,' said I, 'pray don't command it! Let me sit by my father.' 'Here's ado indeed,' said Sir Simon; 'sit down at the upper-end, as you should do! and your father shall sit by you there.'

This put my father upon difficulties. And my master said, 'Come, I'll place you all': and so put Lady Darnford at the upper-end, Mrs Jones at her right hand, and Mrs Peters on the left, placing me between the two young ladies; but very genteelly put Miss Darnford below her younger sister; saying, 'Come, madam, I'll put you here, because you shall hedge in this pretty cuckow.'

This seemed to please both sisters; for had the younger been put there, it might have piqued her, as matters had been formerly, to be placed below me; whereas Miss Darnford, giving place to her younger sister, made it less particular she should to me.

My master kindly said, 'Come, Mr Andrews, you and I will sit together.' And took his place at the bottom of the table, and set my father on his right hand; and Sir Simon would sit on his left. 'For, parson,' said Sir Simon to Mr Peters, 'I think the petticoats[246] should sit together; do you, therefore, sit down by that lady' (his sister). They had heard, that I had been used, by my late lady's goodness, to carve at her table, when she had any of her select friends to dine with her; and they would put me upon that office; and were pleased with my performance; all kindly desirous to keep your poor girl in countenance. And Miss Darnford took occasion to praise my voice and my performance on the harpsichord. 'Foolish Polly,' said Sir Simon, 'who, that hears her speak, knows not that she has a voice? And who, that sees her fingers, believes not, that they were made to touch any key?' He laughed out, and, 'O parson!' added he, ''tis well you are by, or I would have provoked a blush from the ladies.' 'I hope not, Sir Simon,' said Mrs Jones; 'a man of your politeness would not say any thing that would make ladies blush.' 'No, not for the world,' replied he; 'but if I had, it would have been, as the poet says,

They blush, because they understand.'[247]

When the company went away, Lady Darnford, Mrs Jones, and Mrs Peters, severally, in a very pressing manner, invited my master to return their visit, and not to fail to bring me with him. And they said to me, 'We hope, when the happy knot is tied, you will induce Mr B. to reside more among us.' 'We were always glad,' said Lady Darnford, 'when Mr B. was here; but now shall have double reason.' What grateful things were these to the ears of my good father!

When the company was gone, my master made us both sit down by him; and said, 'I have been telling this sweet girl, that, in four-teen days (and two of them are gone) she must fix on one to make me happy; and have left it to her, to chuse either one of the first or last seven.' My father held up his hands and eyes. 'God bless your honour,' said he, 'is all I can say!' 'Now, Pamela,' said my master, taking my hand, 'don't let a little wrong-timed bashfulness take place; because I should be glad to return to my Bedfordshire house, as soon as possible; and I would not go thither, till I carry my servants there a mistress, who should assist me to repair the mischiefs she has made in my family.'

I could not look up for joyful confusion. And my father said, 'My dear child, I need not, I am sure, prompt your obedience in whatever will most oblige so good a gentleman.' 'What says my Pamela?' said my master: 'she does not use to be at a loss for expression.' 'Sir,' said I, 'were I too sudden, it would look as if I doubted whether you would hold in your mind, and was not willing to give you time for reflection. But otherwise, I have no doubt to say, that I ought to resign myself implicitly to your will.'

'I want not time for reflection,' replied he. 'I once would have been glad to have called you mine upon other terms: but now I wish not for you but upon your own; and the sooner the ceremony is performed, the better. What say you, Mr Andrews?' 'Sir,' said my father, 'there is so much goodness on your side, and, blessed be God! so much prudence on my daughter's, that I must be quite silent. But when it is done, I and my poor wife shall have nothing to do, but to pray for you both, and to look back, with wonder and joy, on the ways of Providence.'

'This,' said my master, 'is Friday night; and suppose, my girl, it be next Monday – Tuesday – Wednesday – Thursday morning? Say, my Pamela.'

'Will you, sir,' replied I, 'excuse me till to-morrow for an answer?' 'I will,' said he. And touched the bell, for Mrs Jewkes. And when she came in, 'Where,' said my master, 'does Mr Andrews sleep to-night? You'll take care of the good man. He will bring a blessing upon every house, in which he sets his foot.'

My father wept for joy; and I could not refrain keeping him company. My master saluting me, bid us good-night, and retired; and I waited upon my father to his chamber, and was full of prattle, of my master's goodness, and my future prospects.

SATURDAY

I arose early in the morning; but found my father was up before me, and was gone to walk in the garden. I went to him; enquiring after his rest. 'O my dearest child,' said he, 'I have had a blessed night. I ruminated on all the wonderful things that have passed till I fell asleep: and then I dreamt of nothing but of Jacob's ladder,[248] and angels descending to bless me, and my beloved daughter!'

We both joined to bless God and each other: and as we walked on in the garden, with what delight, with what thankfulness, did we go over every scene of it, that had before been so dreadful to me! The fish-pond, the back-door, and every place.

About seven o'clock my master joined us, in his gown and slippers; and looking a little heavy, I said, 'Sir, I fear you had not good rest last night.' 'That is your fault, Pamela,' said he: 'after I went from you, I could not forbear looking into your papers, and they held me till after three.' 'I wish, sir,' said I, 'you had had better entertainment.' 'The worst part of it,' answered he, 'was what I had brought upon myself; and you have not spared me. But I forgive you. You had too much reason for it. Yet I find, plainly enough, that if you had got away, you would soon have been Williams's wife. Indeed I can't see how it could have been otherwise.' 'I do assure you, sir,' said I, 'I had no notion of being his wife, or any body's.' 'I believe so,' said he; 'but it must have come on as of course; and I see your father was for it.' 'Sir,' said my father, 'it was impossible for me to think of the joyful prospect before me. I thought my child's virtue would be secured by her marriage with an honest man; and that Mr Williams, as a good clergy-man, would be a greater match for her than we could hope for: but when I found my daughter was averse to it, I resolved not to urge her; but leave all to her own prudence.'

'I see,' said my master, 'that all was sincere, honest, and open; and I am quite satisfied. But, Pamela, I am sorry to find, in some parts of your journal, that Mrs Jewkes carried her orders too far. I the rather take notice of it, because you have not complained to me of her behaviour, as she might have expected for some parts of it: she had the insolence to strike my girl! I find.' 'Sir,' said I, 'I was a little provoking, I believe; but as we forgave each other, I was the less entitled to complain.'

'Well,' said he, 'you are very good; but if you should not know how to forget her insolence, I will so far indulge your resentment, as to order that she shall hereafter have nothing to do where you are.' 'Sir,' said I, 'your kindness makes all past evils as nothing to me; and when I reflect, that I owe my happiness to my grievances, it would be wrong if I could not, for the sake of the event, forgive the means.' 'That,' said he, and kissed me, 'is sweetly considered! and it shall be my part to make you amends for what you have suffered.'

My father's heart was full; and he said, with his hands folded and lifted up, 'Pray, sir, let me go, let me go, to my wife, and tell her all these blessed things, while my heart holds! for it is ready to burst with joy!' 'Good man!' said my master, 'I love to hear that honest heart of your's speaking at your lips. I enjoin you, Pamela, to continue your narrative, as you have opportunity; and though your father be here, write to your mother, that your story may be perfect, and that we, your friends, may read and admire you more and more.' 'Ay, pray do, my child,' said my father.

And this, my dear mother, is the reason that I write on, when I thought it needless so to do, because my father could tell you all that passed while he was here.

My master would make us both breakfast with him; and he said, (Abraham at his command withdrawing) 'I would have you, Pamela, begin to dress as you used to do; for now, at least, you may call your *two other bundles* your own; and for whatever you may want against the approaching occasion, (private as I design it, for particular reasons respecting Lady Davers) I'll send to Lincoln for it, by a special messenger.' My good lady's bounty, and his own, I said, had set me much above my degree, and I had very good things of all sorts; and I did not desire any other, because I would not excite the censure of the ladies. At present, he was pleased to say, if I was satisfied, he would be so; and would defer dress and appearance till he publicly owned his nuptials.

'I hope, Mr Andrews,' said he to my father, 'you will not leave us till you see the happy solemnity over, and then you will be *sure* I mean honourably; and besides, Pamela will be thereby induced to give me an early day.' 'O sir,' said he, 'I bless God, I have no reason to doubt your honourable meaning; and I hope you will excuse me, if I set out on Monday morning, very early, to my wife, for I am impatient to make her as happy as I am myself.'

'Why, Pamela,' said my master, 'may not the ceremony be performed on Tuesday, and then your father, perhaps, will stay? I should have been glad to have had it to-morrow,' added he; 'but I have sent Colbrand for a licence, that you may not have the shadow of a scruple remaining; and he cannot be back here to-morrow night, or Monday morning.'

This was most agreeable news. My father urging me to second his desire to return to you, my mother, I said, 'Sir, I know my father will want to be at home: and as you were pleased to give me a fortnight from last Thursday, I should be glad you would indulge me still to some day in the second seven.'

'Well,' said he, 'I will not be too urgent; but the sooner you fix, the more obliging I shall think you. Mr Andrews, we must leave something to these Jephtha's daughters,[249] in these cases. I suppose, the little bashful folly, which, in the happiest circumstances, may give a kind of regret to a thoughtful mind, on quitting the maiden state, is a reason with Pamela; and so she shall name her day.'

As we sat at breakfast, my master was pleased to order the coach, and said he would give me and my father an airing. 'And do you, Pamela,' said he, 'go up and dress yourself, as heretofore.'

My father, dear man! looking upon himself, now on this side, now on that, because of his mean appearance, begged to be excused. But my master would have it so.

I went up soon after; and, in obedience to my master's commands, took possession, in a happy moment, I hope, of my *two bundles*, as my good master was pleased to call them, (alluding to my former division of those good things my lady and himself had bestowed upon me) and so put on fine linen, silk shoes, and fine white cotton stockings, a handsome quilted petticoat, a rich green Mantua silk gown and coat; a French necklace, and a laced cambric handkerchief, and clean gloves; and taking my fan in my hand, I, like a proud hussey, looked in the glass, and was ready to think myself a gentlewoman; but I forgot not to return due thanks, for being able to put on this dress with so light a heart.

Mrs Jewkes would help to dress me, and complimented me highly, saying, among other things, That now I looked like her lady indeed! And, as she said, the little chapel was ready, and Divine Service would be read in it to-morrow, she wished the happy knot might then be tied. 'Have you not seen the chapel, madam,' said she, 'since it has been cleared out?' 'No,' said I; 'but are we to have service in it to-morrow, do you say? I am glad of that; for I have been a sad heathen lately, sore against my will! But who is to officiate?' 'Somebody,' replied she, 'Mr Peters will send.' 'You tell me very good news,' said I, 'Mrs Jewkes. I hope it will never be a lumber-room again.' 'Ay,' said she, 'I can tell you more good news; for the two Miss Darnfords, and Mrs Jones, are to be here at the opening of it; and will stay and dine with you.' 'My master,' said I, 'has not told me that.' 'You must alter your style, madam,' replied she. 'It must not be *master* now, sure!' 'O,' returned I, 'that is a language I shall never forget. He shall always be my master; and I shall think myself more and more his servant.'

My father did not know I went up to dress myself; and, when first he saw me afterwards, he stood in admiration,[250] and said, 'O my dear child, how well will you become your happy condition! Why, you look like a lady already!' 'I hope, my dear father,' said I, and boldly kissed him, 'I shall always be *your* dutiful daughter, whatever my condition be.'

My master sent me word he was ready; and when he saw me, said, 'Dress as you will, Pamela, you are a charming girl'; and handed me to the coach, and would make my father and me sit both on the fore side; and sat backwards over-against me; and bid the coachman drive to the meadow; that is, where he once met Mr Williams.

The conversation was most agreeable to me, and to my father, as we went; and he more and more exceeded in goodness and generosity. And what do you think? Why, while I was gone up to dress, he presented my father with twenty guineas; desiring him to buy himself and my mother such apparel as they should think proper; and lay it all out. But I knew not this till after we came home; my father having had no opportunity of telling me of it.

He was pleased to inform me of the chapel being got in tolerable order; and said it looked very well; and against he came down next, it should be all new white-washed, and painted, and lined;[251] and a new pulpit-cloth, cushion, desk, &c. and that it should always be kept in order for the future. He told me, the two Miss Darnfords, and Mrs Jones, would dine with him on Sunday. 'And with their servants and mine,' said he, 'we shall make a tolerable congregation. And,' added he, 'have I not well contrived, to shew you, that the chapel is really a house of God, and has been consecrated before we solemnize our nuptials in it?' 'O sir,' replied I, 'your goodness to me is inexpressible!' 'Mr Peters,' said he, 'offered to come and officiate in it; but would not stay to dine with me, because he is to have company at his own house; and so I intend that Divine Service shall be performed in it, by one to whom I shall make a yearly allowance, as my chaplain! You look serious, Pamela,' added he: 'I know you think of your friend Williams.' 'Indeed, sir,' said I, 'if you won't be angry, I did. Poor man! I am sorry I have been the cause of his disobliging you.'

When we came to the meadow, where the gentry have sometimes their walk, the coach stopped, and my master alighted, and led me to the brook-side; and it was a very pretty summer walk. He asked my father, if he chose to walk out, or go on in the coach to the further end? He, poor man, chose to go on in the coach, For fear, he said, any gentry should be walking there; and he told me, that he spent every moment of his time in the coach in thanking God for his mercies to us, and in begging for a blessing upon my master and me.

I was quite astonished, when we came into the shady walk, to see Mr Williams there. 'See there,' said my master, 'there's poor Williams, taking his solitary walk again, with his book.' And it seems it was so contrived; for Mr Peters had been, as I since find, desired to tell him to be in that walk at such an hour in the morning.

'So, old acquaintance,' said my master, 'again have I met you in this place? What book are you now reading?' He said, It was

Boileau's Lutrin.[252] 'You see,' said my master, 'I have brought with me my little fugitive, that would have been: while you are per-fecting yourself in French, I am trying to learn honest English; and hope soon to be master of it.'

'Mine, sir,' said he, 'is a very beautiful piece of French: but your English has no equal.'

'You are very polite, Mr Williams,' said my master. 'But, Pamela, why so strange, where you have once been so well acquainted? I do assure you both, that I mean not, by this inter-view, to abash Mr Williams, or to reproach you.'

Then I said, 'Mr Williams, I am very glad to see you; and (though the generous favour of my master has happily changed the scene, since you and I last saw each other) to have this opportunity to acknowledge, with gratitude, your good intentions, not so much to serve me, as *me*, but as a person, who then had great reason to believe herself in distress.'

'You, Pamela,' said my master, 'may make what acknowledg-ments you please to Mr Williams's good intentions; and I would have you speak as you think; but I do not apprehend myself to be quite so much obliged to those intentions.'

'Sir,' said Mr Williams, 'I beg leave to say, that knowing your good sense, and worthy education, I had great hopes, that when you came to reflect, you would not be displeased with me, for endea-vouring to serve and to save an innocence, of which there are not many examples.'

'Recrimination, Mr Williams,' replied my master, 'is not my intent.[253] Pamela knew not that she should see you here; and now you are both present, I would ask you, sir, if, now you know my honourable designs towards this good girl, you can really be *almost*, I will not say *quite*, as well pleased with the friendship of my wife, as you could have been with the favour of Mrs Andrews?'

'Sir,' replied he, 'I will answer you truly. I think I could have preferred with her any condition of life, however low, had I con-sidered only *myself*. But, sir, I had not the least encouragement from her; and had far greater reason to believe, that if she could have hoped for your goodness, her heart would have been too much pre-engaged, to think of any body else. And give me leave further to say, sir, that though I tell you sincerely my thoughts, were I only to consider *myself*; yet when I consider *her good*, I should be highly ungenerous, were it put to my *choice*, if I could not wish her in a condition so greatly superior, and so very answerable to her merit.'

'Pamela,' said my master, '*you* are obliged to Mr Williams, and ought to thank him: he has distinguished well. But as for *me*, who had like to have lost you by his means, I am glad the matter was not left to his *choice*. Mr Williams,' said he, 'I give you Pamela's hand, in token of her friendship and esteem for you; and I give you mine, with an assurance that I will not be your enemy.'

Mr Williams kissed my hand; and my master said, 'Sir, you will go home and dine with me, and I will shew you my little chapel; and let me wish you, Pamela, to number Mr Williams in the list of your chosen friends.'

Mr Williams had tears of pleasure in his eyes. I was silent: but Mr Williams said, 'Sir, I shall be taught by your generosity, to think that I have been inexcusably wrong, in every step I took, that could give you offence; and my future life shall shew my respectful gratitude.'

We walked on till we came to the coach, where was my father. 'Pamela,' said my master, 'tell Mr Williams who that good man is.' 'O Mr Williams!' said I, 'it is my father'; and my master was pleased to say, 'One of the honestest men in England. Pamela owes every thing that she is to be, as well as her being, to him; for, I think, she would not have brought me to this, but for the good lessons, and religious education, she had received from him.'

Mr Williams, taking my father's hand, as he sat in the coach, before he entered it himself, said, 'You contemplate, good Mr Andrews, with inexpressible pleasure, no doubt, the fruits of your pious care; and now are in a way, with your beloved daughter, to reap the happy effects of it.' 'I am overcome,' said my dear father, 'with his honour's goodness. But I can only say, I bless *God*, and bless *him*.'

Mr Williams and I being nearer the coach than my master, and he offering to draw back, to give way to him, he kindly said, 'Pray, Mr Williams, oblige Pamela with your hand; and then step in yourself.' He bowed, and took my hand, and stept in, my master making him sit forwards next me.

'Mr Andrews,' said my master, as he stept in himself, 'I told you yesterday, that the Divine you saw, was *not* Mr Williams; I now tell you, this gentleman *is*: and though I have been telling him, I think not *myself* obliged to his intentions; yet I will own, that Pamela and *you* are; and I would have you love him.'

'Sir,' said Mr Williams, 'you have a way of over-coming, that hardly all my reading affords an instance of the like; and it is the more noble, as it is on this side, as I presume, the happy ceremony; which, great as your fortune is, will lay you under an obligation to so much virtue and beauty, when the lady becomes yours; for you will then have a treasure that princes might envy you for.'

'Mr Williams,' replied my generous master, (God bless him!) 'it is impossible that you and I should live at variance, when our sentiments agree so well together, on subjects the most material.'

Then taking my hand, 'Collect yourself, and look up, my good girl,' said he; 'and don't injure Mr Williams and me so much, as to think we are capping compliments, as we used to do verses,[254] at school. I dare answer for him, as well as for myself, that we say not a syllable we don't think.'

'O sir,' said I, 'how unequal am I to all this goodness! Every moment that passes, adds to the weight of the obligations you oppress me with.'

'Think not too much of that,' said he, most generously. 'Mr Williams's compliments to you, have great advantage of mine: for, though equally sincere, I have a great deal to say, and to do, to compensate your sufferings; and, at last, must sit down dissatisfied, because those will never be balanced by all I can do for you.'

He saw my father quite unable to support these affecting instances of his goodness; and he let go my hand, and took his; and said, seeing his tears, 'I wonder not, my dear Pamela's father, that your honest heart thus shews itself at your eyes, to see all your daughter's trials at an end. I will not pretend to say, that I had formerly either power or will to act thus. But I have reaped so much pleasure from my present way of thinking, that my own *interest* will keep me steady. Indeed I knew not, till within these few days, what it was to be happy.'

'How happily, sir,' said Mr Williams, tears of joy in his eyes, 'have you been touched by the Divine Grace, before you were hurried into the commission of sins, that the deepest penitence could hardly have atoned for! God has enabled you to stop short of the evil; and you have nothing to do, but to rejoice in the good, which now will be doubly so, because you can receive it without the least inward reproach.'

'You say well,' replied my master: 'and I hope from the good example of my dear girl here, and from *your* friendship, Mr Williams, in time, to be half as good as my tutoress. And that,' said he, 'I believe, you will own, will make me, without disparagement to any man, the best fox-hunter in England.'

Mr Williams was going to speak: and he said, 'You put on so grave a look, Mr Williams, that, I believe, what I have said, with you *practical* good folks, is liable to exception: but I see we were become quite grave; and we must not be too serious neither.'

What a happy creature, my dear mother, is your Pamela! I shall never enough acknowledge the value he is pleased to express for my unworthiness, and in particular, that he has prevented[255] my wishes, and, unasked, sought the occasion of being reconciled to a good man, who, for my sake, had incurred his displeasure; and whose name he could not, a few days before, permit to pass through my lips: but see the wonderful ways of Providence! The sight of the very things that I most dreaded he should see or know, that is to say, the contents of my papers, has, I hope, satisfied all his scruples, and been a means to secure my happiness. Let me lay down my pen, and meditate.

In the agreeable manner I have mentioned, did we pass the time in our second happy airing. But Mrs Jewkes seemed ready to sink into the ground, when she saw Mr Williams brought in the coach with us, and treated so kindly.

We dined together in a most pleasant, easy, and frank manner; and I found I needed not, from my master's generosity, to be under any restraint, as to my conduct to this good clergyman; for as often as he fancied I was reserved, he urged me to shew civilities and care of Mr Williams.

After dinner, we went and looked into the chapel, which is a very pretty one, and very decent.

My heart, my dear mother, when I first set my foot in it, throbbed a good deal, with awful joy, at the thoughts of the solemnity, which I hope will, in a few days, be performed in it. And when I came up towards the little pretty altar-piece, while they were looking at a communion-picture, and saying it was prettily done, I gently stepped into a corner, out of sight, and poured out my soul to God in thankfulness, that, after having been so long absent from Divine Service, the first time that I entered into a house dedicated to his honour, should be with such blessed prospects before me; and begging of God to continue me humble, and to make me not unworthy of his mercies; and that he would be pleased to bless the *next* author of my happiness, my good master.

My master, just as I joined the company, said to Mr Williams, 'You will not, I hope, sir, refuse to give us your instructions here to-morrow. Mr Peters was so kind to offer to officiate; but I knew it would be inconvenient for him; and besides, I was willing to make this request to you as a token of a thorough reconciliation on my part.'

'Sir,' said he, 'most willingly, and most gratefully, will I obey you: though if you expect a discourse, I am wholly unprepared for the *occasion.*' 'I would not have it,' replied my master, 'pointed to any particular occasion; but if you have one upon the text, " *There is more joy in heaven over one sinner that repenteth, than over ninety-nine just persons that need no repentance*"; [256] and if it draws not upon me the eyes of my own servants, and those of the ladies we shall have here, I shall be content. I mention this text, as it is an usual one with the gentlemen of your cloth; but any one you have at hand will do.'

'I have one upon that very text, sir,' replied Mr Williams; 'but I think, that a thanksgiving one, which I made on a great mercy to myself, if I may be permitted to make my own acknowledgments of your favour the subject of a discourse, will be suitable to my grateful sentiments. It is on the text, " *Now lettest thou thy servant depart in peace; for mine eyes have seen thy salvation.*"'[257]

'That text,' said I, 'will be a very suitable one for me.'

'Not so, Pamela,' said my master; 'because I don't let you *depart.*'

'But, sir,' said I, 'I have seen *God's salvation*! I am sure, if ever any body had reason, I have, to say, with the blessed Virgin, " *My soul doth magnify the Lord*; for *he hath regarded the low estate of his hand-maiden, and exalted one of low degree.*"'[258]

'Were there time for it,' said my father, 'the book of Ruth [259] would afford a fine subject for the honour done my child.'

'I know that story, Mr Andrews,' said my master; 'but Mr

Williams will confirm what I say, that my good girl here will confer as much honour as she will receive.'

'Sir,' said I, 'you are inexpressibly generous; but I shall never think so.' 'That, my Pamela,' said he, 'is another thing: it will be best for *me* to think you *will*; and it will be kind in *you* to think you *shall not*. And the result will be to the advantage of both, in our behaviour to each other.'

When we came out of the little chapel, Mr Williams said he would go home, and look over his discourses for a suitable one.

'I have one thing to say, before you go, Mr Williams,' said my master. 'It is this: when my jealousy, on account of this good girl, put me upon a very vindictive conduct to you, you know I took a bond for the money I had caused you to be troubled for: I really am ashamed of that proceeding. I intended not, at the time I lent it to you, nor even when I took the bond, ever to receive it again. Here it is cancelled' (taking it out of his pocket, and giving it to him). 'How poorly does the present atone for the cruelty I used you with! But what will not jealousy make a man guilty of! I think,' proceeded he, 'all the charges attending the trouble you had, were defrayed by my attorney: I ordered that they should.'

'They were, sir,' said he; 'and ten thousand thanks to you for this goodness!'

My father was a little uneasy about his habit, because of his being to appear at chapel next day, before Miss Darnfords, and the servants; not on his own account, he said, but for my master's and mine: and then he told me of my master's present of twenty guineas for clothes, for you both; which made my heart truly joyful. But is it not almost a *hard* thing, my dear mother, to lie under the weight of such deep obligations on one side, and such a sense of one's own unworthiness on the other! What a God-like power is that of doing good! I envy the rich and the great for nothing else!

My master coming to us just as the twenty guineas were mentioned, I said, 'Oh! sir, will your bounty know no limits! My father has told me what you have given him.' 'A trifle, Pamela,' said he; 'a little earnest only of my kindness. Say no more of it. But did I not hear the good man expressing some sort of concern for somewhat? Hide nothing from me, Pamela.' 'Only, sir,' replied I, 'he knew not how to absent himself from Divine Service, and yet from his poor garb –'

'Fie, Mr Andrews,' interrupted he, 'I thought you were above regarding outward appearance. But, Pamela, your father is not much thinner than I am, nor much shorter; he and I will walk up together to my wardrobe; though it is not so well stored here, as in Bedfordshire.'

He accordingly led him, not without some painful reluctance on my father's part, up stairs, and looked over several suits; and, at last, fixing his eye upon a fine drab,[260] which he thought looked the plainest, he would help him to try the coat and waistcoat on himself. Indeed they fit him surprisingly well: and being plain, and lined with the same colour, (being made for travelling in a coach) my father had the less objection to them.

My master gave him the whole suit, and directed, in the kindest and most generous manner, that he should have linen, and hat, and shoes, and stockings, of his own, looked out for him; and even gave him, instead of the shoe-strings he used to wear, a pair of silver buckles out of his own shoes. So, my good mother, you must expect to see my dear father a great beau. 'Wig,' said my master, 'you want not Mr Andrews; for your own venerable white locks become you better than the most costly peruke ever became the best-dressed man in England.'[261]

But my poor father could not refrain tears when he came to me, and told me all this. 'I know not how,' said he, 'to comport myself under these great favours. O my child, it is all owing to the Divine Goodness, and your virtue!'

SUNDAY

This blessed day all the family seemed to take delight to equip themselves for the celebration of the Sabbath, in the little chapel; and Mrs Jones, and Mr Williams, came in her chariot, and the two Miss Darnfords, in their own; each attended by a footman. And we breakfasted together, in a most agreeable manner. My father appeared quite spruce and neat, and was greatly caressed by the three ladies.

As we were at breakfast, my master told Mr Williams, we must let the Psalms alone, he doubted, for want of a clerk; but Mr Williams said, No, nothing should be wanting that he could supply. My father said, If it might be permitted, he would, as well as he was able, perform that office; for it was what he had always taken delight in. And as I knew he had learnt psalmody formerly, in his youth, and had constantly practised it in private, at home, on Sunday evenings, (as well as endeavoured to teach it in the little school he so unsuccessfully set up, at the beginning of his misfortunes, before he took to hard labour) I was in no pain for his undertaking it in this little congregation. They seemed much pleased with his offer. Mrs Jewkes, and all the servants, but the cook, attended: and I never saw Divine Service performed with more solemnity, nor assisted at with greater devotion and decency; my master, Mrs Jones, and the two young ladies, setting an amiable example.

My father performed his part with great applause, making the responses as if he had been a practised parish clerk. He gave out the xxiiird psalm,* which consisting of but three staves,[262] we had it all; and he read the line, and began the tune, with a heart so entirely affected with the duty, as enabled him to go through it distinctly, calmly, and fervently at the same time. Mrs Jones

> * The Lord is only my support,
>   And he that doth me feed:
> How can I then lack any thing,
>   Whereof I stand in need?
> In pastures green he feedeth me,
>   Where I do safely lie;
> And after leads me to the streams,
>   Which run most pleasantly.
>
> And when I find myself near lost,
>   Then doth he me home take;
> Conducting me in his right paths,
>   E'en for his own name's sake.
> And though I were e'en at death's door,
>   Yet would I fear no ill;
> For both thy rod and shepherd's crook
>   Afford me comfort still.
>
> Thou hast my table richly spread
>   In presence of my foe:
> Thou hast my head with balm refreshed;
>   My cup doth overflow:
> And finally, while breath doth last,
>   Thy Grace shall me defend;
> And in the house of God will I
>   My life for ever spend.

whispered me, That good men were fit for all companies, and present to every laudable occasion: and Miss Darnford said, 'God bless the dear good man!'

You must think how I rejoiced in my heart.

I know, my dear mother, you can say most of the shorter psalms by heart; so I need not transcribe this, especially as your chief treasure is a Bible: and a treasure indeed it is. I know nobody makes more or better use of it.

Mr Williams gave us an excellent discourse on liberality and generosity, and the blessing attending the right use of riches, from the xith chapter of *Proverbs*, ver. 24, 25. '*There is that scattereth, and yet increaseth; and there is that withholdeth more than is meet; but it tendeth to poverty. The liberal soul shall be made fat; and he that watereth, shall be watered also himself.*' And he treated the subject in so handsome a manner, (keeping to generals) that the delicacy of my master, who at first was afraid of some personal compliments, was not offended; and he called it an elegant and sensible discourse.

My father was in the clerk's place, just under the desk; and Mrs Jones, by her footman, desired him to favour us with another psalm, when the sermon was ended. He thinking, as he said afterwards, that the former was rather of the longest, chose the shortest in the book, which, you know, is the cxviith.*

My master thanked Mr Williams for his discourse, and so did the ladies: as also did I, most heartily: and my master was pleased to take my father by the hand, as did also Mr Williams, and thanked him for his part in the sacred service. The ladies likewise made him their compliments; and the servants all looked upon him with countenances of respect and pleasure.

At dinner, do what I could, I was obliged to take the upper end of the table; and my master said, 'Pamela, you are so dextrous,

---

* O all ye nations of the world,
  Praise ye the Lord always:
And, all ye people ev'rywhere,
  Set forth his noble praise.

For great his kindness is to us;
  His truth doth not decay:
Wherefore praise ye the Lord our God;
  Praise ye the Lord alway.

that I think you may help the ladies; and I will help my two good friends, (should I not?)' meaning my father and Mr Williams.

I should have told you though, that I dressed myself in a flowered pattern, that was my lady's, and looked as good as new, and which had been given me soon after her death by my master; and the ladies, who had not seen me out of my homespun before, made me abundance of compliments, when they saw me first.

Talking of the psalms, just after dinner, my master greatly abashed me: for he said to my father, 'Mr Andrews, I think, in the afternoon, as we shall have only prayers, we may have one longer psalm; and what think you of the cxxxviith?' 'O good sir!' said I, 'pray, pray, not a word more!' 'Say what you will, Pamela,' said he, 'you shall sing it to us, according to your own version, before these ladies leave us.' My father smiled, but was half concerned for me; and said, 'Will it bear, and please your honour?' 'O ay,' said he, 'never fear it; so long as Mrs Jewkes is not in hearing.'

This excited all the ladies curiosity; and Mrs Jones said, she should be loth to desire any thing that would give me concern; but should be glad I would give leave for it. 'Indeed, madam,' said I, 'I must beg you won't insist upon it: I cannot, cannot comply.' 'You shall see it, indeed, ladies,' said my master; 'and pray, Pamela, not always as you please, neither.' 'Then, sir,' said I, 'not in my hearing, I hope.' 'Sure, Pamela,' returned he, 'you would not write what is not fit to be heard!' 'But, sir,' said I, 'there are particular cases, times, and occasions, that may make a thing tolerable at one time, that would not be so at another.' 'O,' said he, 'let me judge of that, as well as you, Pamela. These ladies know a good deal of your story; and, let me tell you, what they know of it is more to your credit than mine; so that if I have no dislike to revive the occasion, you may very well comply. But I will put you out of your pain, Pamela: Here it is!' And took it out of his pocket.

I stood up, and said, 'I hope, sir, you will allow me to leave the room a minute, if you *will* read it.' 'Indeed, I will not,' answered he. Mrs Jones said, 'Pray, Mr B. let us not hear it, if Mrs Andrews be so unwilling.' 'Well, Pamela,' said my master, 'I will put it to your choice, whether I shall read it now, or you will sing it by-and-by.' 'That's very hard, sir,' said I. 'It must be one, I assure you,' said he. 'Why then, sir,' replied I, 'you must do as you please; for I cannot sing it.'

'Then,' said he, 'I find I must read it; though very little to my reputation, as you, ladies, will think. But, first, let me briefly tell you the occasion.

'It was this: Pamela, in the time of her confinement, as she thought it, one Sunday was importuned by Mrs Jewkes, whom she considered as her gaoler, and whom she thought employed in a design against her honour, to sing a psalm. But her spirits not permitting, she declined it. However, on Mrs Jewkes's leaving her, recollecting that the cxxxviith psalm was applicable to her supposed case, Mrs Jewkes having often on other days urged her to sing a song, she turned it as in the paper in my hand. But pray, Mr Williams, do you read one verse of the common translation,[263] and I will read one of Pamela's version.'

Mr Williams, pulling out his little pocket common-prayer book, read the first two stanzas.

I

When we did sit in Babylon,
The rivers round about:
Then in remembrance of Sion,[264]
The tears for grief burst out.

II

We hanged our harps and instruments
The willow-trees upon:
For in that place, men, for that use,
Had planted many a one.

My master then read:

I

When sad I sat in Brandon-hall,
All watched[265] round about,
And thought of ev'ry absent friend,
The tears for grief burst out.

II

My joys and hopes all overthrown,
My heart-strings almost broke;
Unfit my mind for melody,
Much more to bear a joke.

The ladies seemed pleased, and Mr Williams proceeded:

III

Then they, to whom we pris'ners were,
 Said to us tauntingly;
'Now let us hear your Hebrew songs,
 And pleasant melody.'

My master then read:

III

Then she, to whom I pris'ner was,
 Said to me tauntingly;
'Now chear your heart, and sing a song,
 And tune your mind to joy.'

Mr Williams proceeded:

IV

'Alas!' said we, 'who can once frame
 His heavy heart to sing
The praises of our living God,
 Thus under a strange king?'

'This,' said my master, 'is Pamela's version.'

IV

'Alas!' said I, 'how can I frame
 My heavy heart to sing,
Or tune my mind, while thus inthralled
 By such a wicked thing!'

They were so good as to praise the simplicity of this stanza. My
father said, They would make his daughter proud. 'No,' said my
master, very generously, 'Pamela cannot be proud. For no one is
proud to hear themselves praised, but those who are not used to it.
But proceed, Mr Williams.' He read;

V

But yet, if I Jerusalem
 Out of heart let slide;
Then let my fingers quite forget
 The warbling harp to guide.

'Well, now,' said my master, 'for Pamela's version.'

V

But yet, if from my innocence
   I, ev'n in thought, should slide;
Then let my fingers quite forget
   The harpsichord to guide.

Mr Williams proceeded.

VI

And let my tongue within my mouth
   Be tied for ever fast,
If I rejoice, before I see
   Thy full deliv'rance past.

My master read,

VI

And let my tongue within my mouth
   Be locked for ever fast,
If I rejoice, before I see
   My full deliv'rance past.

'Now, good sir,' said I, 'oblige me. Don't read any further: pray
don't!' 'O, pray, madam,' said Mr Williams, 'let me beg to have the
rest read; for I long to know whom you make the sons of Edom,[266]
and how you turn the psalmist's execrations against the insulting
Babylonians.'

'Well, Mr Williams,' replied I, '*you* should not have said so.' 'O,'
said my master, 'that is one of the best things of all. Poor Jewkes
stands for Edom's sons; and we must not lose this, because I think
it one of my Pamela's excellencies, that, though thus oppressed, she
prays for no harm upon the oppressor. Read, Mr Williams, the next
stanza.' He read;

VII

Therefore, O Lord, remember now,
   The cursed noise and cry,
That Edom's sons against us made,
   When they rased our city.

VIII

Remember, Lord, their cruel words,
   When, with a mighty sound,
They cried, 'down, yea, down with it,
   Unto the very ground.'

351

'Here seems,' said my master, 'in what I am going to read, a little bit of a curse, indeed; but I think it makes no ill figure in the comparison.'

VII

And thou, Almighty, recompence
 The evils I endure,
From those who seek my sad disgrace,
 So causeless! to procure.

'And now,' said he, 'for Edom's sons! Though a little severe in the imputation.'

VIII

Remember, Lord, this Mrs Jewkes,
 When with a mighty sound,
She cries, 'down with her chastity,
 Down to the very ground!'

'Now,' said my master, 'read the psalmist's heavy curses': and Mr Williams read;

IX

Ev'n so shalt thou, O Babylon!
 At length to dust be brought:
And happy shall that man be called,
 That our revenge hath wrought.

X

Yea, blessed shall that man be called,
 That takes thy little ones,
And dasheth them in pieces small
 Against the very stones.

'Thus,' (said he, very kindly) 'has my Pamela turned these lines.'

IX

Ev'n so shalt thou, O wicked one,
 At length to shame be brought:
And happy, shall all those be called,
 That my deliv'rance wrought.

X

Yea, blessed shall the man be called,
 That shames thee of thy evil,

And saves me from thy vile attempts,
And thee, too, from the D——l:

'You see, my good friends,' said my master, 'that my Pamela has not an implacable spirit. But I fancy' (smiling) 'that this blessed man was, at that time, if the truth were known, hoped to be you, Mr Williams.' 'Whoever it was intended for *then*,' replied Mr Williams, 'it can be nobody *now*, sir, but your self.'

I could hardly hold up my head for the praises the kind ladies were pleased to heap upon me. I am sure, by this, they are very partial in my favour; and all because my master is so good to me, and loves to hear me praised.

We all, as before, and the cook-maid too, attended the prayers of the church in the afternoon; and my father concluded with the following stanzas of the cxlvth psalm; suitably praising God for all his mercies; but did not observe altogether the method in which they stand; which was the less necessary, he thought, as he gave out the lines.

The Lord is just in all his ways:
  His works are holy all:
And he is near all those that do
  In truth upon him call.

He the desires of all of them
  That fear him, will fulfil;
And he will hear them when they cry,
  And save them all he will.

The eyes of all do wait on thee;
  Thou dost them all relieve:
And thou to each sufficient food,
  In season due, dost give.

Thou openest thy plenteous hand,
  And bounteously dost fill
All things whatever that do live,
  With gifts of thy good will.

My thankful mouth shall gladly speak
  The praises of the Lord:
All flesh, to praise his holy name,
  For ever shall accord.

We walked in the garden till tea was ready; and as we went by the back-door, my master said to me, '*Of all the flowers in the garden, the sun-flower is the fairest!*' 'O, sir,' said I, 'let that be now forgot!' Mr Williams heard him say so, and seemed a little out of countenance: whereupon my master said, 'I mean not to make you serious, Mr Williams. There are other scenes before me, which, in my Pamela's dangers, give *me* more cause of concern, than any thing you ever did, ought to give *you*.' 'Sir,' said he, 'you are very generous.'

My master and Mr Williams afterwards walked together, for a quarter of an hour, and talked about general things, and some scholastic subjects, and joined us, very well pleased with each other's conversation.

Mrs Jones said, putting herself on one side of me, as my master was on the other, 'But, pray, sir, when is the happy time to be? We want it over, that we may have you with us as long afterwards as you can.' 'I,' said my master, 'would have it to-morrow, or next day, at farthest, if Pamela consent: for I have sent for a licence, and the messenger will be here to-night, or early in the morning, I hope. But, my good girl, let me desire you not to take beyond Thursday.' 'Surely, madam,' said Mrs Jones to me, 'the ceremony will not be delayed by you.' 'Now *you*, Mrs Jones,' said my master, 'are on my side, I will leave you with her, to settle it: and I hope, she will not let little bashful niceties be important with her.' And then he joined the two Miss Darnford's.

Mrs Jones told me, I was to blame, she would take upon her to say, if I delayed it a moment longer than was necessary; because she understood Lady Davers was very uneasy in the apprehension that it would be so; and if any thing should happen, it would be a sad thing! 'Madam,' replied I, 'when my master was pleased to mention it to me at first, he said it should be in fourteen days; and afterwards, asked me, if I would have it in the first or the second seven. I answered (for how could I do otherwise?) In the second: he desired it might not be the last day of the second seven. Now, madam, as he was then pleased to speak his mind, I would not for any thing seem too forward.'

'Well, but,' said she, 'as he now urges you in so unexceptionable a manner for a shorter day, I think, if I was in your place, I would agree to it.' I answered, that if I found him very earnest, I should think I ought to oblige him.

We joined the two Miss Darnford's, and they both begged to be at the wedding, and to have a ball; and besought me to second their requests. 'Indeed, ladies,' said I, 'I cannot promise that.' 'Why so?' they asked. 'One may, with pleasure,' answered I, 'celebrate the *anniversary* of one's nuptials; but the *day itself* – Indeed, ladies, I think it is too solemn an affair, for the parties of our sex to be very gay upon it! And I am sure, in your own cases, you would be of my mind.' 'If it be such a solemn business,' said Miss Darnford, 'the more need one has to be as light-hearted and merry as one can.'

'I told you,' said my master, 'what sort of an answer you would have from Pamela.' The younger Miss said, She never heard of such grave folks in her life, on such an occasion! 'Why, sir,' said she, 'I hope you will sing psalms, and that your bride will fast and pray all day. Such sackcloth and ashes [267] doings, for a wedding, did I never hear of!' She spoke a little spitefully, I thought; and I returned no answer. I shall have enough to do, I suppose, in a-while, if I am to answer every one that will envy me!

We went in to tea, and all the ladies could prevail upon my master for, was a dance before he left this country; but Miss Darnford said, It should then be at their house; for, truly, if she might not be at the wedding, she would be affronted, and come no more hither, till we had been there.

When they were gone, my master would have had my father stay till the ceremony was over; but he begged he might set out as soon as it was light in the morning; for, he said, My mother would be doubly uneasy at his stay; and he burned with impatience, to let her know all the happy things that had befallen her daughter. When my master found him so desirous to go, he called Mr Thomas, and ordered him to get horses ready betimes in the morning, and a portmanteau, and to attend my father a day's journey to his own home. How good was this!

He said a great many kind things at supper-time, and gave my father all the papers he had of mine; but desired, when he and my mother had read them, that he might have them again. 'So affection-ate a father and daughter,' added he, 'may, perhaps, be glad to be by yourselves, for an hour or two. Remember me to your good wife,

Mr Andrews; and tell her, that I hope it will not be long, before I see you together on a visit to your daughter. And so I wish you a good night, and a good journey, if you set out before I see you.' And then, taking my father's hand, he retired, leaving my dear father almost speechless, from the sense of his favours and goodness.

You may believe, my dear mother, how loth I was to part with my father; and he was also unwilling to part with me; but he was so impatient to see you, and tell you the happy tidings, with which his heart overflowed, that I could hardly wish to detain him.

Mrs Jewkes brought two bottles of canary, and two of cinnamon-water,[268] and some cake; and they were put in the portmanteau, with my father's newly presented clothes; for he said, He would not, for any thing, be seen in them in his neighbourhood, till I was known, by every body, to be married; nor would he lay out any part of the twenty guineas till then, neither, for fear of reflections. 'All this, as you please, my dear father.' said I, 'and I hope now we shall often have the pleasure of hearing from one another, without needing any art or contrivances.'

He said, he would go to-bed betimes, that he might be up as soon as it was light; and so he took leave of me, and said, He would not love me, if I arose in the morning to see him go; since that would make us but more loth to part, and grieve us both all day.

Mr Thomas brought him a pair of boots, and told him, he would call him up at day dawn; every thing being put up over night; and so I received his blessing, and his prayers, and his promises of procuring the same from you, my dear mother, and went up to my closet with a heavy heart, and yet a half-pleased one, if I may so say; since that, as he must go, he was going to the best of wives, and with the best of tidings. But I begged he would not work so hard as he had done; for I was sure my master would not have given him twenty guineas for clothes, if he had not designed to do something else for him; and that he should be the less concerned at receiving benefits from my master, because he, who employed so many persons in his large possessions, could make him serviceable, to a degree equivalent to the benefit conferred; yet not hurt any body else.

He promised me fair; and pray, my dear mother, see he performs. I hope my master will not see this: for I will not send it you, at present, till I can send you the best of news; and the rather, as my father can acquaint you with the greatest part of what I have written *since* the papers he carries you. So good-night! my dear mother: and God send my father a safe journey, and a happy meeting to you both!

MONDAY

Mr Colbrand being returned, my master came up to me in my closet, and brought me the licence. How my heart fluttered at the sight of it! 'Now, Pamela,' said he, 'tell me, if you can oblige me with the day. Your word is all that is wanting!' I was so bold as to kiss the hand that held it; and though unable to look up, said, 'I know not how to express my gratitude, sir, for all your goodness to me! I would not for any consideration, that you should believe me capable of receiving negligently an honour, that all the humble duty of a long life, were it to be lent me, will not be sufficient to enable me to deserve. I ought to resign myself, in every thing I may or can, implicitly to your will. But — ' 'But what?' said he, with a kind impatience! 'Why, sir,' said I, 'when from last Thursday you mentioned fourteen days, I had reason to think that term your choice; and my heart is so wholly yours, that I am afraid of nothing, but that I may seem to be forwarder than you wish.' 'Impossible, my dear creature!' said he, and folded me in his arms; 'impossible! If this be all, this very day shall make you mine: I will send away immediately,' said the dear gentleman. – And was going.

I said, 'No, pray sir, pray sir, hear me! Indeed it cannot be to-day!' 'Cannot!' said he. 'No, indeed, sir!' And I was ready to sink to see his generous impatience! 'Why flattered you then my fond heart,' replied he, 'with the hope that it might!' 'Sir,' said I, 'I will tell you what I had thought, if you'll vouchsafe me your attention.' 'Do then,' said he.

'I have, sir,' proceeded I, 'a great desire, that whenever the day is, it may be on a Thursday: [269] on a Thursday my father and mother were married, and they are a very happy pair: on a Thursday your poor Pamela was born: on a Thursday my dear good Lady took me from my parents into her protection: on a Thursday, sir, you caused me to be carried away to this place, to which I now, by God's goodness, and your favour, owe all my present prospects;

and on a Thursday it was, you named to me that fourteen days from that, you would confirm my happiness. Now, sir, if you please to indulge my superstitious folly, you will greatly oblige me: I was sorry, sir, for this reason, when you bid me not defer till the last day of the fourteen, that Thursday in next week was that last day.'

'This, Pamela, is indeed superstitious; and I think you should begin now to make another day in the week a happy one: as for example; on a Monday, may you say, my father and mother concluded to be married on the Thursday following. On a Monday, so many years ago, my mother was preparing all her matters to be brought to-bed on the Thursday following. On a Monday, several weeks ago, it was that you had but two days more to stay, till you were carried away on Thursday. On a Monday, I myself,' said he, 'well remember, it was that I wrote you the letter, that prevailed on you so kindly to return to me; and on the same day, you *did* return to my house here; which I hope, my girl, will be as propitious an æra[270] as any you have named: and now, lastly, will you say, which will crown the work; and, on a Monday, I was married. Come, come, my dear,' added he, 'Thursday has reigned long enough, let us now set Monday in its place, or at least on an equality with it, since you see it has a very good title, and as we now stand in the week before us, claims priority: and then, I hope, we shall make Tuesday, Wednesday, Friday, Saturday, and Sunday, as happy days, as Monday and Thursday; and so, by God's blessing, move round, as the days move, in a delightful circle, till we are at a loss what day to prefer to the rest.'

How charmingly was this said! And how sweetly kind!

'Indeed, sir,' said I, 'you rally my folly very agreeably; but don't let a little matter stand in the way, when you are so generously obliging in greater! Indeed I like Thursday best, if I may chuse.'

'Well then,' said he, 'if you can say, you have a better reason than this, I will oblige you; else I'll send away for the parson this moment!'

And so, I protest, he was going! 'Stay, stay, sir,' said I: 'we have a great deal to say first; I have a deal of silly prate to trouble you with!' 'Well, speak then, in a minute,' replied he, 'the most material: for all we have to say may be talked of while the parson is coming!' 'O but indeed, and indeed,' said I, 'it cannot be to-day.'

'Well then, shall it be to-morrow?' 'Why, sir, if it must not be on a Thursday, you have given so many pleasant distinctions for a Monday, that let it then be next Monday!' 'What! a week still!' said he. 'Sir,' answered I, 'if you please; for *that* will be, as you enjoined, within the second seven days.' 'My dear girl,' said he, ' 'twill be seven months till next Monday. Let it,' said he, 'if not to-morrow, be on Wednesday; I protest I will stay no longer.'

'Then, sir,' returned I, 'please to defer it, however, for *one* day more, and it will be my beloved Thursday.' 'If I consent to defer it till then, may I hope, my Pamela,' said he, 'that next Thursday shall *certainly* be the happy day?' '*Yes, sir,*' said I. And I believe I looked very foolishly.

And yet, why should I, with such a fine gentleman! And whom I so dearly love! And so much to my honour too? But there is something greatly awful upon my mind, in the solemn circumstance, and a change of condition never to be recalled, though all the prospects are so desirable. And I can but wonder at the thoughtless precipitancy with which most young folks run into this important change of life.

Thus, my dear parents, have I been brought to fix so near a day as next Thursday; and this is Monday. O dear! I am almost out of breath to think of it. This, though, was a great cut-off; a whole week out of ten days. I hope I am not too forward, I'm sure, if it obliges my dear master, I am justified.

After this, he rode out, and did not return till night. How, by degrees, things steal upon one! I thought even this small absence tedious, and the more, as we expected him home to dinner. I wish I may not, by my over-fondness, make him indifferent to me: but yet, my dear father and mother, you two, let the world run as it would, were always fond of each other.

When he returned, he said, he had had a pleasant ride, and was led out to a greater distance than he intended. At supper he told me, that he had a great mind Mr Williams should marry us; because, he said, it would shew a thorough reconciliation on his part: 'But,' said he, most generously, 'I am apprehensive, from what passed between you, that the poor man will take it hardly, and as an insult, of which I am not capable. What says my girl? Do you think he would?' 'As to what he *may* think,' replied I, 'I cannot answer;

but as to any *reason* for such thoughts, I can. And indeed, sir, you have shewn so much generosity to him, in every respect, it is impossible he should mistake your motive.'

He then spoke with some resentment of Lady Davers's behaviour; and I asked, If any thing new had occurred? 'Yes,' said he, 'I have a letter from her impertinent lord, written professedly at her instigation; which amounts to little less than a piece of insolent bravery, on supposing I intended to marry you. I was so provoked,' added he, 'that after I had read it, I tore it into a hundred pieces, and scattered them in the air, and bid the man who brought it, let his master know what I had done with his letter; and so would not permit him to speak to me, as he would fain have done. I think the fellow talked something of his Lady coming hither; but she shall not set her foot within my doors; and I suppose this treatment will hinder her.'

I was much concerned at this: and he said, 'Had I a hundred sisters, Pamela, their opposition should have no weight with me; and I did not intend you should know it; but you, who have suffered so much from the pride of the brother, must expect a little difficulty from that of the sister. In short, we are too nearly allied in mind, as well as blood, I find. But this is not *her* business. And if she would have made it so, she should have done it with more *decency*. Little reason had *she* to boast of her birth, who knows not what belongs to good manners.'

'I am very sorry, sir,' said I, 'to be the unhappy occasion of a misunderstanding between so good a brother, and so worthy a sister.' 'Don't say so, Pamela, because this is an unavoidable consequence of the happy prospect before us. Only bear it well yourself, because she is my sister, and leave it to me to make her sensible of her own rashness.'

'If, sir,' said I, 'the most humble deportment to good Lady Davers, will have any weight with her ladyship, assure yourself of all my endeavours to mollify her.' 'You must not imagine, Pamela,' returned he, 'that when you are my wife, I will suffer you to do any thing unworthy of that character. I know the duty of a husband, and will protect your gentleness as much as if you were a princess by descent.'

'You are inexpressibly good, sir,' said I; 'but I am far from thinking a gentle disposition indicates a meanness of spirit. This is a trial I ought to expect; and well may I bear it, who shall have so many benefits to set against it.'

'Well,' said he, 'all the matter shall be this: we will talk of our marriage as if it were to be celebrated next week. I find I have spies upon me: and lest Lady Davers, were she to know the day, should make me an unwelcome visit before it comes, which might give us trouble, I have already ordered my servants to have no conference with any body out of the house for ten or twelve days to come. Mrs Jewkes tells me, every one names next Thursday sevennight for our nuptials. And I will get Mr Peters, who wants to see my little chapel, to assist Mr Williams, under the notion of breakfasting with me next Thursday morning (since you won't have it sooner) and there will nobody else be wanting; and I will beg of Mr Peters to keep it private, even from his own family, for a few days. Has my girl any objection?'

'O sir,' answered I, 'you are so generous in all your ways, I *can* have no objections to any thing you propose: but I hope Lady Davers and you will not proceed to irreconcileable lengths; and when her ladyship comes to see you, and to tarry with you two or three weeks, as she used to do, I will keep close up, and not enter into her presence.'

'Well, Pamela, we will talk of that afterwards. You must do then as I shall think fit: and I shall be able to judge what you and I ought to do. But what still aggravates the matter is, that she should instigate the titled ape her husband to write to me, after she had so ill succeeded herself. I wish I had kept this letter, that I might have shewn you how a man who generally *acts* like a fool, can take upon him to *write* like a Lord. But I suppose it is of my sister's penning, and he, poor man! is the humble copier.'

TUESDAY

My master has just now been making me play upon the harpsichord, and sing to it; and was pleased to commend me for both. But he does so for every thing I do; so partial does his goodness make him to me.

One o'Clock

We are just returned from an airing in the chariot; and I have been delighted with his conversation upon English authors, poets particularly. He entertained me also with a description of some of the curiosities he had seen in Italy and France, when he made what the polite world call the Grand Tour. He said he wanted to be at his other seat; for he knew not well how to employ himself here, having not purposed to stay half the time. 'When I get there, Pamela,' said he, 'and we are settled, you will hardly be troubled with so much of my company, as I give you now; for I have a great many things to adjust: and I must go to London; for I have accounts that have run on longer than ordinary with my banker there. And I don't know,' added he, 'but the ensuing winter, I may give you a little taste of the diversions of the town for a month or so.' I said, That I never would encourage a wish after any entertainments that were not of his own choice.

'I make no doubt,' said he, 'but I shall be very happy; and hope you will be so too. I have no very enormous vices to gratify; though I pretend not to the greatest purity neither, my girl.' I was half sorry to hear him say this; because he said it with an air of more levity than altogether suited the subjects preceding; and as if he was preparing me to expect, that he would not be from proper motives, respecting his own future happiness, a quite good man. It hurt me for his own dear sake; and I had a kind of impulse upon me to say, 'If, sir, you can account for your actions to your own mind, I shall always think you right. But our greatest happiness here, is of very short duration: this life at the longest, forgive my seriousness, is a poor transitory one; and I hope we shall be so happy as to be enabled to look forward to another, where our pleasures will be everlasting.'

'You say well, Pamela; and I shall, by degrees, be more habituated to this way of thinking, as I more and more converse with you. But you must not be over serious with me, all at once; yet I charge you, never forbear to mingle your sweet divinity in your conversation, whenever it can be brought in *à propos*,[271] and with such a chearfulness of temper, as shall not throw a cloud over our innocent enjoyments.'

I was abashed at this, and silent, fearing I had offended. What I said was, indeed, very bold, the early days considered: but he kindly said, 'If you attend rightly to what I said, I need not repeat, that I mean not to discourage you from suggesting to me, on every proper occasion, the pious impulses of your own amiable mind. You, my Pamela, are not good by chance; but on principle.' 'Sir,' said I, 'you will be always indulgent, I make no doubt, so long as I mean well.'

He made me dine with him, and would eat nothing but what I helped him to. Indeed my heart is, every hour, more and more enlarged with his goodness and condescension. But still, what ails me, I wonder! a strange sort of weight hangs upon my mind, which makes me often sigh involuntarily, and damps, at times, the pleasures of my delightful prospects. I hope this is not ominous. I hope it is owing only to the weakness of an over thoughtful mind, on an occasion the most solemn and important of one's life, next to the last scene, which shuts up all.

I could be very serious! But I will commit all my ways to that Providence, which hitherto has so wonderfully conducted me, through real evils, to this hopeful situation.

I only fear, and surely, I have great reason, that I shall be too unworthy to hold the affections of so fine a man. But my continual prayer shall be for humility, as what, next to the Divine Grace, will be my surest guard, in the state of life to which I am going to be exalted. And don't cease your prayers for me, my dear parents; for, perhaps, this new condition may be subject to still worse hazards than those I have escaped; as would be the case, were conceitedness, vanity, and pride, to take hold of my heart! and if, for my sins, I were to be left to my own conduct, a frail bark in a tempestuous ocean, without ballast, or other pilot than my own inconsiderate will. But my master said, on another occasion, that those who doubted most, always erred least; and I hope, I shall always doubt my own worthiness!

I will not trouble you with twenty sweet agreeable things that passed in conversation with my excellent benefactor; nor with an account of the civilities of Monsieur Colbrand, Mrs Jewkes, and all the servants, who seem to be highly pleased with me, and with my conduct to them: and as my master, hitherto, finds no fault, that I go too low, nor they that I carry it too high, I hope I shall continue to have every body's good-will. But yet, will I not seek to gain that of any one by meannesses or debasements: but aim at an uniform and regular conduct, willing to conceal *involuntary* errors, as I would have my own forgiven; and not too industrious to discover *real* ones, that may be of no bad consequence, and unlikely to be repeated: yet not to hide such as might encourage bad hearts, or unclean hands, in cases where my master shall receive damage, or where the morals of the transgressors shall appear wilfully and habitually corrupt. In short, I will endeavour, as much as I can, that good servants shall in me find a kind encourager; indifferent ones be made better, by exciting in them a laudable emulation; and bad ones, if not quite irreclaimable, reformed by kindness, expostulation, and if those are ineffectual, by menaces; but most *by a good example*.

All this, if God pleases.

WEDNESDAY

Now, my dear parents, I have but this *one* day, between me and the most solemn rite that can be performed. My heart cannot yet shake off this heavy weight. Sure I am ungrateful to the Divine Goodness, and the favour of the best of benefactors! Yet I hope I am not! For, at times, my mind is all joy, at the prospect of what good tomorrow's happy solemnity may possibly, by the leave of my generous master, put it into my power to do.

WEDNESDAY *Evening*

My dear master is all tenderness. He sees my weakness, and generously pities and comforts me. I begged to be excused supper; but he led me down himself from my closet; and placed me by him, bidding Abraham not wait. I could not eat, and yet I tried, for fear he should be angry. He kindly forbore to hint any thing of the awful, yet delightful to-morrow! and put, now-and-then, a little bit on my plate, and guided it to my lips. I was concerned to receive his goodness with so ill a grace; and told him I was really ashamed of myself. 'You are, indeed, my dear girl,' said he, 'too thoughtful: but I am not a very dreadful enemy, I hope.' 'All, all, sir,' said I, 'is owing to the sense I have of my own unworthiness.'

He rung for the things to be taken away; and then sat down by me, and put his kind arms about me, and said the most generous things that ever dropped from the honey-flowing mouth of love: all I have not time to repeat: some I will; and, O indulge your foolish daughter, who troubles you with her nonsense; because what she has to say, is so affecting to her; and because, if she went to-bed, she could not sleep.

'This sweet anxiety in my Pamela,' said he, 'on the near approach of the solemnity which shall make us one, when nothing of dishonour is apprehended, shews me most abundantly, what a wretch I was to attempt such purity with a worse intention! No wonder, that one so virtuous, should find herself deserted of life itself on a violence so dreadful to her, and seek a refuge in the shades of death. But now, my dearest Pamela, that you have seen a purity on my side, nearly equal to your now; why all this affecting, yet sweet confusion? You have a generous friend, my dear girl in me; a protector now, not a violater of your innocence: why then, this strange perplexity, this sweet confusion?'

'O sir,' said I, and hid my face on his arm, 'expect not reason from the foolish Pamela. You should have indulged me in my closet. I am ready to beat myself for this ungrateful return to your goodness. But goodness, added to goodness every moment, and the sense of my own unworthiness, quite overcome my spirits!'

'Now,' said the generous man, 'will I, though reluctantly, make a proposal to my sweet girl. If I have been too pressing for the day: if another day will be more obliging: if you have apprehensiveness that you will not *then* have; although I have for these three days past, thought every tedious hour a day, if you earnestly desire it, I will postpone it. Say, my dear girl, *freely* say; but accept not my proposal without great reason; which yet I will not ask for.'

'Sir,' said I, 'this is a most generous instance of your kind consideration for me. But I fear – yes, I fear, it will be too much the same thing, some days hence, when the happy, yet, fool that I am! Awful time, shall be equally near.'

'Kind, lovely girl,' said he, 'now do I see you are to be trusted with power, from the generous use you make of it! Not one light word, or free look, from me, shall wound your nicest thoughts; but try however, to subdue this unseasonable timidity. I persuade myself, you will, if you can.'

'Indeed, sir! I will; for I am quite ashamed of myself, with such charming views before me! The honours you do me! the kindness you shew me! quite overwhelm me; and raise in me *such* a sense of my unworthiness – *That*, sir, is the thing; for I do assure you that my heart has not the least misgiving thought of your generous goodness; and I should abhor it, if it were capable of the least affectation.'

'Sweet good girl,' he called me, and folded me to his bosom: 'but now tell me,' said he, 'what I can do to make this dear flutterer' (*my* heart he meant) 'entirely easy?'

'Leave me, dear good sir, leave me a little to myself, and I will take my heart more severely to task, than your goodness will let *you* do: and I will present it to you, a worthier offering than at present its wayward follies will let it seem to be. But one thing is, I have no kind friend of my own sex, to communicate my foolish thoughts to, and to be strengthened by her advice: and then left to myself. What a weak silly creature am I!'

He kindly withdrew, to give me time to recollect myself, and in about half an hour returned. And then, that he might not begin at once upon the subject, and yet might speak something very agreeable to me, he said, 'Your father and mother have had a great deal of talk, by this time, about you, Pamela.' 'Your goodness, sir,' returned I, 'has made them quite happy. But I can't help being concerned about Lady Davers.'

'I am vexed,' said he, 'I did not hear her servant out; because it runs in my head, he talked somewhat about her coming hither. She will meet with but an indifferent reception from me, unless she comes resolved to behave better than she writes.'

'Pray, sir,' said I, 'be pleased to bear with my good lady, for two reasons: first, because she is your sister, and, to be sure, may very well think, what all the world will, that you have greatly undervalued yourself in making me happy. And next, because, if her ladyship finds you out of temper with her, it will incense her still more against me.'

'We have more proud ladies than my sister Davers,' said he, 'in our other neighbourhood, who perhaps have still less reason than she to be punctilious about their descent, and yet will govern themselves by her example, and say, "Why, his own sister will not visit him!" If therefore I can subdue her spirit, which is more than her husband ever could, or indeed any body else, it is a great point gained: and, if she gives me reason, I'll try for it.'

'Well, but my dear girl,' continued he, 'may I not say one word about to-morrow?' 'I hope I shall be less a fool, sir,' replied I: 'I have talked as harshly to my heart, as Lady Davers can do, and the naughty thing suggests to me a better behaviour.'

Saluting me, 'I took notice, Pamela,' said he, 'of what you observed, that you have none of your own sex with you: I think it is a little hard upon you. I should have liked to have had Miss Darnford with you; but then her sister must have been asked; and in that case, I might as well make a public wedding; which, you know, would have required clothes, and other preparation. Besides,' added he, 'a proposal was once made me of that second sister, who has five or six[272] thousand pounds more than the other, left her by a godmother, and she can't help being a little piqued on her being disappointed: though,' continued he, 'it was a proposal they could not expect should succeed; for there is nothing attracting either in her person or mind: and her fortune, as that must have been the *only* inducement, would not do by any means.'

'I am thinking, sir,' said I, 'that were you to have married a lady of birth and fortune answerable to your own, all the eve to the day would be taken up in reading, signing and sealing of settlements, paying down the portion, and such like. But now the poor Pamela brings you nothing at all! And the very clothes she wears, so very low is she, are entirely the effects of your bounty, and that of my good lady, your mother! So much oppressed by your favours, it is the less wonder that I cannot look up with the confidence that otherwise I might have had on this awful occasion.'

'Where the power is wanting, there is,' replied he, 'as much generosity in the will, as in the action. To all that know your story and your merit, it will appear, that I cannot recompence you for what I have made you suffer. You have had too many exercises for your virtue; and have nobly overcome; and who shall grudge you the reward of the dear bought victory? This affair is entirely the act of my own will. I glory in being able to distinguish so much excellence; and my fortune is the more valuable to me, as it enables me, in the world's eye, to do credit to your virtue, and to make you happy.'

'Good, dear sir, what can I say! How poor is it to have nothing but words to return for such generous deeds! And to say, I *wish* – What is a wish, but the acknowledged want of power, and a demonstration of one's poverty in every thing but *will*.'

'And that, my dear girl, is every thing! 'Tis all I want! 'Tis all that heaven itself requires of us! But no more upon these topics; and yet all that you have said, arises from the natural impulses of a generous and grateful heart. But I want not to be employed in settlements. I have possessions ample enough for us both; and you deserve to share them with me; and you *shall*, with as little reserve, as if you had brought me what the world reckons an equivalent: for in my own opinion, you bring me what is infinitely more valuable, an experienced truth, a well-tried virtue, and an understanding and genteel behaviour that will do credit to the station you will be placed in: to say nothing of this sweet person, that itself might captivate a monarch; and of your natural meekness and sweetness of disposition, in which you have no equal.'

Thus kind, soothing, and affectionate, was the dear gentleman to the unworthy, doubting, yet assured Pamela; and thus patiently did he indulge, and generously pardon, my weakness.

He offered to go himself to Mrs Jones in the morning, and reveal his intentions to her, and desire her secrecy and presence; but I said, that would disoblige the Miss Darnfords. 'No, sir,' said I, 'I will entirely cast myself on your generous kindness; for why should I seem to fear my kind protector, and the guide and director of my future steps?'

'You cannot,' said he, 'forgive Mrs Jewkes (for *she* must know it) and suffer *her* to be with you?' 'Yes, sir, I can: she is very civil to me now: and her former wickedness I will forgive, because you, sir, seem desirous that I should.'

'Well,' said he, 'I will call her in, if you please.' I humbly bowed my assent. And he rung for her; and when she came in, he said, 'Mrs Jewkes, I am going to entrust you with a secret.' 'Sir,' answered she, 'I will be sure to keep it as such.' 'We intend to-morrow,' pursued he, 'for our wedding-day. I have particular reasons, respecting myself and Lady Davers, to have our marriage kept from the knowledge of all my other servants for some time.' 'Very well, sir,' said Mrs Jewkes, curtseying low to my master, and still lower, poor soul! to me. (How can I hurt such a one, wicked as she has been, were it in my power?)[273] 'I will take care that no living soul shall know it for me.' And looked highly delighted with the confidence placed in her. 'Mr Peters and Mr Williams,' continued my master, 'are to be here to breakfast with me, as if only to see my little chapel. As soon as the ceremony is over, we will take an airing in the chariot, as we have done at other times; and so it will not be wondered that we are dressed. And Mr Peters and Mr Williams have promised secrecy, and will go home. I believe, however, on second thoughts, you cannot well avoid letting one of the maids into the secret; but that I leave to you.'

'Sir,' replied she, 'we all concluded it would be in a few days; and I doubt it cannot be long a secret.' 'I don't desire it should,' replied he; 'but you know we are not provided for a public wedding, and I shall declare it when we go to Bedfordshire, which will not be long. But the men, who lie in the offices, need not know it; for, by some means or other, my sister Davers is acquainted with all that passes.'

'Do you know, sir,' said she, 'that her ladyship intends to be down here with you in a few days? Her servant told me so, who brought you the letter that you were displeased at.'

'I hope,' said he, 'we shall be set out for the other house first; and so shall be pleased she loses her labour.' 'Sir,' continued she, 'her ladyship proposes to be here time enough to hinder your nuptials; which she supposes, as we did, will be the latter end of next week.' 'Let her come,' said he; 'but yet I desire not to see her.'

Mrs Jewkes then took courage. 'I beg your honour's pardon,' said she, curtseying, 'for addressing myself to my lady that is soon to be.' Then turning to me, 'Give me leave, madam,' said she, 'to wish you all manner of happiness: but I am afraid I have too well obeyed his honour to be forgiven by you.' 'Indeed, Mrs Jewkes,' returned I, 'you will be more your own enemy than I will be. I will look forward: and shall not offer to set my good master against any one whom he pleases to approve. And as to his old servants, I shall always value them, and never presume to dictate to his choice, or influence it by my own caprices.'

'Mrs Jewkes,' said my master, 'you find you have no cause for apprehension. My Pamela is very placable; and as we have both been sinners together, we must be both included in one act of grace.'

'Such an example of condescension as I have before me, Mrs Jewkes,' said I, 'may make you very easy; for I must be highly unworthy, if I did not forego all resentment, at the command of so great and so kind a benefactor.'

'You are very good to me, madam,' said she; 'and you may depend upon it, I will endeavour to atone for all my past behaviour to you by my future duty and respect to you, as well as to my master.'

'That's well said on both sides,' said he; 'but, Mrs Jewkes, to assure you, that my good girl here has no malice in her heart, she chuses you to attend her in the morning, and you must keep up her spirits.' 'I shall,' replied she, 'be very proud of the honour.' And withdrew, curtseying, and repeating her promises of care and secrecy.

My beloved master parted from me with great tenderness; and I came up, and sat down to write to you, my dear parents, all these most agreeable particulars. It is now past twelve o'clock, and Mrs Jewkes being come up, I will go to-bed; but not one wink, I fear, shall I get this night. I could beat myself for my folly. Sure there is nothing ominous in this strange perverseness! But is it not usual for all thoughtful young women to have the same anxieties so near so great a change of condition, though they carry it off more discreetly than I?

THURSDAY, *Six o'Clock in the Morning*

I might as well have not gone to-bed last night, for what sleep I had. Mrs Jewkes often was talking to me, and said several things that would have been well enough from any body else of our sex; but the poor woman has so little purity of heart, that it is all *say* from her, and goes no further than the ear.

I fancy my master has not slept much neither; for I heard him up, and walking about his chamber, ever since break of day. To be sure, he must have some concern, as well as I; for here he is going to marry a poor foolish unworthy girl, brought up by the bounty of his worthy family! And this foolish girl must be, to all intents and purposes, after twelve o'clock this day, as much his wife as if he were to marry a duchess. And here he must stand the shock of common reflection. 'The great Mr B. has done finely! he has married his poor servant *wench*!' will some say. The ridicule and rude jests of his equals, and companions too, he must stand: and the disdain of his relations, and indignation of Lady Davers, his lofty sister! O how shall I compensate him for the disgraces which he will bring upon himself for my sake! I can only do the best I can; and pray to God to reward him, and resolve to love him with a pure heart, and serve him with a sincere obedience. I hope he will continue to love me for *this*; for, alas! I have nothing else to offer. But, as I can hardly expect so great a blessing, if I can be secure from his contempt, I shall not be unhappy; and must bear his indifference, if his rich friends should inspire him with it, and proceed with doing my duty with chearfulness.

Half an Hour past Eight o'Clock

My dear master, my kind friend, my generous benefactor, my worthy protector, and, oh! all the good words in one, my affectionate husband that is soon to be, (Be curbed in, my proud heart, know thyself, and be conscious of thy own unworthiness!) has just left me with the kindest, tenderest expressions, that ever were uttered to a happy maiden. He approached me with a sort of reined-in rapture. 'My Pamela!' said he, 'may I just ask after your employment? Why such anxiety in this lovely face?' and he tapped my cheek. 'Don't let me chide my dear girl *this day*. The two clergymen will be here to breakfast with us at nine; and yet you seem not to have thought of dressing! Why this absence of mind? Why this sweet irresolution?'

'Indeed, sir,' said I, 'I will correct myself this instant!'

He saw the common-prayer-book lying in the window. 'I hope,' said he, 'my lovely girl has been conning[274] the lesson she is by-and-by to repeat. Have you not, Pamela?' and clasped his arms about me, and kissed me. 'Indeed, sir,' said I, 'I have been reading over the solemn service!' 'And what thinks my fairest' (for so he called me) 'of it?' 'O sir,' said I, ''tis a very solemn, a very awful service; and, joined with the nearness of the great, though joyfully hoped-for solemnity, makes one tremble to reflect upon it!' 'No wonder,' said he, 'it should affect my sweet Pamela: I have been looking into it this morning, and cannot but say, as you do, that I think it a solemn office. But this I tell my dear love,' continued he, and again clasped me to him, 'there is not a tittle in it that I cannot joyfully subscribe to.' I kissed his hand; 'O my generous protector,' said I, 'how gracious it is to strengthen thus the mind of your Pamela, which apprehends nothing so much as her own unworthiness!' 'You must judge of yourself, my love,' said he, 'in some measure, as I judge of you. If I think you worthy, you have only to preserve those graces which have made you so in my eye, and banish all doubt of yourself, as my whole future conduct shall shew you, that you shall have no reason for any of me.'

'Forbid me not, sir, to doubt *myself*. It will become me to be diffident, in order to be secure. But *your* goodness I cannot doubt, after such instances of it. Love but your Pamela, *as she will endeavour to deserve your favour*, I hardly dare to say your *love*: and what a punishment does that imply, if I should not preserve that duty, and that gratitude, which have made me appear so worthy in your eyes, though it cannot in my own!'

'Call it favour, call it love, what you please, my dear girl, call it: but I shall know no other language to you, but what love, true and ardent love, inspires. For, let me tell my Pamela, that, after having been long tossed about by the boisterous winds of culpable passion, I am not now so much the admirer of your beauty, all charming as you are, as of your virtue. My love therefore must increase, even should this perishable beauty fail, as the station of life you are now entering upon, will afford you augmented opportunities to display your virtue!' The charming man! how nobly, how encouragingly kind was all this!

'But why loses my dear girl her time? I was willing to say something to assure your doubting mind. As I have acted heretofore, I could not say less than I have said. Adieu, my lovely girl, be chearful!'

He kissed me again, and then retired, as respectfully as if your happy daughter were his equal, or even of such high fortunes as to do him honour by her hand. And I set about dressing myself immediately in a rich white satin night-gown, that had been my lady's; and, never being long about it, I was ready in an instant; and not being called down, took up my pen, and wrote thus far.

I have got such a knack of writing, that, when I am by myself, I cannot sit without a pen in my hand. But I am now called to breakfast. I suppose the gentlemen are come. Courage, Pamela! Fie upon it! My heart begins to flutter again! Foolish heart, lie still! Never sure was any maiden's heart under so little command as mine!

THURSDAY, *near Three o'Clock*

I thought I should have found no time nor heart to write again this day. But here are three gentlemen come unexpectedly, with a determination to stay to dinner; though my beloved master did all he could in civility to dismiss them. Having, therefore, nothing to do but write till I go to dinner myself with Mrs Jewkes, I will begin with my happy story where I left off.

But first let me observe, that the dear man forbade me to use the word *master*, either in speech or writing. But I insisted, that I could not dispense with it for the present. In obedience to him, I said, it might wear off by degrees; but I must continue the style, at least, till he thought fit to declare the honour done me.[275]

When I went down to breakfast, I found Mr Peters and Mr Williams both there. My master met me at the door, and led me in with great tenderness. He had kindly spoken to them, as he told me afterwards, to mention no more of the matter to me than needs must. I paid my respects to them, I believe, a little aukwardly, and was almost out of breath; but said, I had come down a little too fast.

When Abraham came in to wait, my master said (that the servants should not mistrust), ' 'Tis well, gentlemen, you came as you did: for my good girl and I were going to take an airing till dinner-time. I hope you'll stay and dine with me.' 'Sir,' said Mr Peters, 'we will not hinder your airing. I came, having a little time upon my hands, to see your chapel; but must be at home at dinner; and Mr Williams will dine with me.' 'Well then,' said my master, 'we will pursue our intention, and ride out for an hour or two, as soon as I have shewn Mr Peters my little chapel. Will you, Pamela, after breakfast, walk with us to it?' '*If – if,*' said I, and had like to have stammered (foolish creature that I was!) '*if* you please, sir.'

I could eat nothing, though I attempted it; and my hand shook so, I spilled some of my chocolate, and so put it down again. They were all very good, and looked another way. My master said, when Abraham left the room, 'I have a quite plain ring here, Mr Peters. And I hope the ceremony will dignify the ring: and that I shall give my Pamela reason to think it the most valuable one that can be presented her.' Mr Peters kindly answered, he was sure I should set a higher value on it, than on the richest diamond one in the world.

I had bid Mrs Jewkes not to dress herself, lest she should give cause of mistrust.

When breakfast was over, my master said before Abraham, 'Well, gentlemen, we will step into the chapel; and you must give me your advice as to the alterations I design. Pamela, you'll give us your opinion, won't you?' 'Sir,' said I, 'I will attend you instantly.'

They went out, and I sat down in the chair again, and fanned myself. 'I am sick at heart,' said I, 'I think, Mrs Jewkes.' She would have given me her smelling-bottle; but I said, 'Keep it in your hand. Perhaps I shall want it; but I hope not.'

She gave me very good words; and I stood up, but my knees beat so against each other, I was forced to sit down again. But, at last, I held by her arm; and passing by Abraham, I said, 'Do you know what alterations there are to be in the chapel, that we must all give our opinions of them?'

Nan, she told me, was let into the secret; and she had ordered her to stay at the chapel-door, to see that nobody came in. My master came to me, at entering the chapel, and took my hand, and led me up to the altar. 'Be chearful, my dear girl,' whispered he. 'I am, I will, sir,' said I; but I hardly knew what I said; and so you may believe, when I said to Mrs Jewkes, 'Don't leave me; pray, Mrs Jewkes, don't leave me': as if I had all confidence in her, and none where it is most due. So she kept close to me. God forgive me! but I never was so absent in my life, as at first. Even till Mr Williams had gone on in the service so far as to the awful words *requiring us, as we should answer at the dreadful day of judgment*; and then the solemn words, and my master whispering, 'Mind this, my dear,' made me start. Said he, still whispering, 'Know *you* any impediment?' I blushed, and said softly, 'None, sir, but my great unworthiness.'

Then followed the sweet words, '*Wilt thou have this woman to thy wedded wife*', &c. and I began to take courage a little, when my dearest master answered audibly to this question, '*I will*.' But I could only make a curt'sy, when they asked *me*; though, I am sure, my *heart* was readier than my *speech*, and answered to every article of *obey*, *serve*, *love*, and *honour*.

Mr Peters gave me away; and I said after Mr Williams, as well as

I could (as my dear master did with a much better grace) the words of betrothment; and the ceremony of the ring passing next, I received the dear favour, at his worthy hands, with a most grateful heart; and he was pleased to say afterwards, in the chariot, That when he had done saying, '*With this ring I thee wed,*' &c. I made a curt'sy, and said, 'Thank you, sir.' Perhaps I did, for I am sure it was a most grateful part of the service; and my heart was overwhelmed with his goodness; and the tender grace wherewith he performed his whole part. I was very glad that what followed was the prayer, and kneeling; for I trembled so, I could hardly stand; but it was as much with joy as fear.

The joining of our hands afterwards, the declaration of our being married, to the few witnesses present; (one of which was Nan, whose curiosity would not let her stand at the door) the blessing, the psalm, and the subsequent prayers, and the concluding exhortation, were such welcome as well as beautiful parts of this sacred office, that my heart began to be delighted with them, and my spirits to be a little freer.

And thus, my dearest, dear parents, is your happy, happy, thrice happy Pamela, at last married! And to whom? Why, to her beloved, gracious master! the lord of her wishes! And thus the dear, once naughty assailer of her innocence, by a blessed turn of Providence, is become the kind, the generous protector and rewarder of it. God be ever more blessed and praised! and make me not wholly unworthy of such an honour! And bless and reward the dear, dear man, who has thus exalted his unworthy servant, and given her a place, which the greatest ladies would think themselves happy in!

My master saluted me most ardently, and said, 'God gives you, my dear love, reason for as much joy on this occasion, as I now have.' And he presented me to Mr Peters, who saluted me; and said, 'You may excuse *me*, dear madam; I gave you away: you are my daughter.' And Mr Williams modestly withdrawing a little way, 'Mr Williams,' said my master, 'pray accept my thanks, and wish your *sister* joy.' He then saluted me; and said, 'I do, madam, from my heart: and I will add, that to see so much innocence and virtue so eminently rewarded, is one of the greatest pleasures I have ever known.'

Mrs Jewkes, by surprize, snatched my hand, and kissed it at the chapel-door; had she kissed my cheek, I should not have been displeased. I had got a new recruit of spirits just then; and taking her hand, 'I thank you, Mrs Jewkes,' said I, 'for accompanying me. I have behaved sadly.' 'No, madam,' said she, 'pretty well, pretty well.'

Mr Peters walked out with me; and Mr Williams and my master followed us, talking together.

Mr Peters, when he came into the parlour, said, 'I once more, madam, must wish you joy on this happy occasion. May every day add to your felicity; and may you very long rejoice in one another! You are the loveliest couple I ever saw joined in matrimony.'

My master came in with Mr Williams. 'So, my dear life,' said he, 'how do you do? A little more composed, I hope! Well, you see this is not so dreadful an affair as you apprehended.'

'Sir,' said Mr Peters, very kindly, ' 'tis a very solemn circumstance, and I love to see it so reverently and awfully entered into. It is an excellent sign; for the most *thoughtful beginnings* promise the most happy proceedings.'

My master took a fine diamond ring from his finger, and presented it to Mr Peters. And to Mr Williams he said, 'My old acquaintance, I have reserved for you, against a variety of solicitations, the living I always designed for you; and I beg you'll prepare to take possession of it; and as the doing it may be attended with some expence, pray accept of *this* towards it,' giving him a bank-note of 100*l*. [276]

And thus did this generous man bless us all, and me in particular; for whose sake he was as bounteous as if he had married a woman of the noblest fortune.

The two gentlemen took their leaves; and none of the servants suspected any thing, as Mrs Jewkes believes. And then, being alone with my beloved master, I threw myself at his feet, and blessed God, and blessed *him* for his goodness. He overwhelmed me with kindness; he called me his lovely bride, and twenty sweet and endearing names, which swell my grateful heart beyond the power even of repetition.

He afterwards led me to the chariot; and we had a delightful airing round the neighbouring villages; in which he said an hundred charming things, in hopes to dissipate those still perverse anxieties that dwell upon my mind, and, do what I can, spread too thoughtful an air, as he tells me, over my countenance.

We came home again by half an hour after one; and he was pleasing himself with thinking not to be an hour out of my company this happy day, that (as he was so good as to say) he might inspire me with a familiarity that should improve my confidence in him; when he was told that a footman of Sir Charles Hargrave had been there, to let him know that his master, and two other gentlemen, were on the road to take a dinner with him, in their way to Nottingham.

He was vexed at this. He should have been glad of their companies at any other time, he told me, but that it was a cruel intrusion now. He wished they had been told he would not be at home at dinner, 'And besides,' said he, 'they are abominable drinkers. I shall hardly be able to get them away to-night; for they have nothing to do but to travel round the country, and beat up the quarters[277] of their friends all the way; and 'tis all one to them, whether they stay a night, or a month, at a place. But,' added he, 'I'll find some way, if I can, to dismiss them after dinner. Confound them,' said he, in a violent pet,[278] 'that they should come this day, of all the days in the year!'

We had hardly got in, before they came; three mad rakes, they seemed to be, as I looked through the window, setting up a hunting-note, as soon as they came to the gate, that made the court-yard echo again, and smacking their whips in concert.

I retired to my closet, and had recourse to my pen and ink, for my amusement, and to divert my anxiety of mind.

If one's heart is so sad, and one's apprehension so great, where one greatly loves, and is highly obliged; what must be the case of those poor young creatures, who are compelled, by their tyrannical parents, to marry the man they almost hate, and, perhaps, to the losing of the man they most love? That is a sad thing indeed! And what have not such cruel parents to answer for? And what do not such innocent victims suffer?

My master came up to me, and said, 'Well, I just come to ask my sweet bride' [O the charming, charming word!] 'how she does? I see you are writing, my dear,' said he. 'These confounded rakes are half mad, I think, and will make me so! However,' continued he, 'I have ordered my chariot to be got ready, pretending to be under an engagement at some miles distance, and will set them out of the house, if possible; and then ride round, and come back, as soon as I can get rid of them. I find,' said he, 'Lady Davers is full of our affairs. She has thought fit to speak of me to Sir Charles Hargrave, with great freedom; and they all three have been at me without mercy; and were so earnest to see you, that I was obliged to be half serious with them.' He saluted me, and retired, saying, 'I shall quarrel with them, if I cannot get them away; for I have lost two or three precious hours with the delight of my heart.'

Mrs Jewkes asked me to walk down to dinner in the little parlour. I went, and she was so complaisant as to offer to wait upon me at table. But I insisted on her sitting down with me. 'Whatever my new station may require of me, Mrs Jewkes,' said I, 'I hope I shall always conduct myself in such a manner, that pride shall have no part in my character.'

'You are very good, madam,' said she; 'but I will always know my duty to my master's lady.'

My master came in again, and said, 'Well, thank my stars! these rakes are going now; but, as I must set out with them, it shall be in my chariot; for if I took horse, I should have difficulty to part with them. They intend to gather company as they go, and resolve to make a mad tour of it for some days together.'

Abraham coming in to tell him, the gentlemen were going, he left me, and set out with them.

I took a turn in the garden with Mrs Jewkes, after they were gone: and having walked a-while, I said, I should be glad of her company down the elm-walk, to meet the chariot.

What a different aspect every thing in and about this house bears now, to my thinking, to what it once had! The garden, the pond, the alcove, the elm-walk. But my prison is become my palace; and no wonder every thing about it wears another face!

We sat down upon the broad stile, leading towards the road. How different, poor woman! thought I, as we sat, is thy behaviour to me now, to what it was the last time I sat here!

At last my best beloved returned, and alighted there. Mrs Jewkes retired at his approach. 'What, my Pamela,' (and saluted me) 'brings you hither? I hope, to meet me!' 'Yes, sir,' said I. 'That's kind,' said he; 'but why that averted eye? that downcast countenance, as if you were afraid of me?' 'You must not think so, sir,' replied I. 'Revive my heart then,'said he, 'with a more chearful aspect; and let that over-anxious solicitude, which appears in the most charming face in the world, be chased from it. Have you, my dear girl, any fears that I can dissipate; any doubts that I can obviate; any hopes that I can encourage; any request that I can gratify? Speak, my Pamela; and, if I have power, *but* speak, and to purchase one smile, it shall be done!'

'I cannot, sir,' said I, 'have any *fears*, any *doubts*, but that I shall never be able to deserve your goodness. I have no *hopes*, but that my future conduct may be agreeable to you, and my determined duty well accepted. Nor have I any *request* to make, but that you will forgive all my imperfections.'

'I know your grateful heart,' said he; 'but remember, my dear, what the lawyers tell us – That marriage is the highest consideration which the law knows. And this solemnity, my sweet bride, having made you mine, and me your's, let us talk of nothing henceforth but equality; although, if the riches of your mind, and your un-blemished virtue, be set against *my* fortune, (which is but an accidental good, as I may call it, and *all* I have to boast of) I shall not think I can possibly deserve you, till, after your sweet example, my future life shall become nearly as blameless as your's.'

'O sir,' said I, 'what pleasure do you give me, in making me hope, that, instead of being in danger of being insnared by the high condition to which your goodness has exalted me, that I shall be confirmed by you in my duty; and that we may have a prospect of promoting each other's happiness, till time shall be no more! But, sir, I will not, as you once cautioned me, be too serious. I will resolve, with these sweet encouragements, to be, in every thing, what you would have me be!' He kissed me very tenderly: and by this time coming to the house, we entered it together.

Ten o'Clock at Night

As we sat at supper, he was generously kind to me, as well in his actions as expressions. He took notice, in the most delicate manner, of my endeavour to conquer my follies. 'I told my dear girl once before,' said he, 'that I was more the admirer of her virtue, than even of her beauty. My behaviour to you, my pain for your concern, causeless as it is, must convince you that I am. Loveliest of women, behold in me lover, husband, protector, all in one; and let your affiance in me answer those tender characters.'

After supper, of which, with all his sweet persuasions, I could hardly taste, he made me drink two glasses of champaign, and afterwards a glass of sack; which he kindly forced upon me by naming your healths: and, as the time of retiring drew on, he said, 'My dearest girl, I fear you have had too much of my company for so many hours together; and would better recollect yourself, if your retired for half an hour to your closet.'

I wished for this liberty; but knew not how to propose it. 'You are all goodness, sir,' said I; and boldly taking his hand, pressed it to my lips, with both mine. And he, saluting me very fervently, conducted his trembling Pamela to her chamber-door, and withdrew.

I went to my closet; and the first thing I did, on my knees, again thanked God for the blessing of the day; and besought the Divine assistance in the conduct of my future life.

FRIDAY *Evening*

How does this excellent man indulge me in every thing! Every hour he makes me happier, than in the former, by his generous condescension.

No light, frothy [279] jests drop from his lips; no alarming railleries; no offensive expressions, nor insulting airs, reproach or wound the ears of your thrice happy daughter. In short, he says every thing that may encourage me to look up with pleasure to the generous author of my happiness.

At breakfast, he strengthened my heart, by talking of *you*, my dear parents; a subject he knew I *could* talk of: and gave me assurances, that he would make you both happy. He said, he would have me send you a letter, to acquaint you with my nuptials; and, as he could make business that way, Thomas should carry it to-morrow. 'Nor will I,' said he, 'my dear Pamela, desire to see your writings, because I told you I would not; for now I will, in every thing, religiously keep my word with my bride; and you may send all your papers to them from those they have, down to this happy moment; only let me beg they will return them when they have read them, as also those I have not seen; which, however, I desire not to see till then; but then shall take it for a favour to see.'

'It will be my pleasure, as well as my duty, sir,' said I, 'to obey you in every thing. And I will write up to the conclusion of this day, that they may see how happy you have made me.'

I know, my dear parents, that you will both join with me to bless God for his mercies and goodness to you, as well as to me: for he was pleased to ask me particularly after your circumstances, and said, he had taken notice that I had hinted, in some of my first letters, that you owed money; and he gave me fifty guineas, and bid me send them to you in my pacquet, to pay your debts as far as *they* would go (were his words) with his request that you should quit your present business, and give yourself, and my mother, a creditable appearance. He would find a better place of abode for you, he said, than that you had, when he returned to Bedfordshire. How shall I bear all these instances of his goodness?

To me he gave no less than one hundred guineas more; and said, 'I would have you, my dear, give Mrs Jewkes, when you go away from hence, what you think fit out of these, as from yourself.' I desired his direction as to the sum. 'Give her then,' said he, 'twenty guineas. Give Colbrand ten. The two coachmen five each; to the two maids at this house, five each; give Abraham five; give Thomas five; and give the gardeners, grooms, and helpers, twenty guineas among them. And when,' added he, 'I return with you to the other house, I will make you presents both of money and ornaments, that may be worthy of my love, and of your present station; for now, my Pamela, you are not to regard, as you once proposed, what other ladies will say, but to appear as my wife ought to do. I will shew the world, that I have as much regard for you as I could have had for a woman of the first quality and fortune, had I married such a one.'

He saw I was at a loss for words. 'I see, my dearest bride! my Pamela! your grateful confusion'; and kissing me, as I was recovering my speech, 'Thus will I stop your mouth; you shall not so much as thank me; for when I have done ten times more than I have hitherto told you I will do, I shall but imperfectly express my love to you, and my concern for what I have made you suffer.'

He then, thinking I seemed somewhat thoughtful, proposed a little turn in the chariot till dinner-time: and this was another sweet relief to me; for he diverted me with twenty agreeable relations of what observations he had made in his travels; and gave me the characters of the ladies and gentlemen in his other neighbourhood; telling me whose acquaintance he would have me most cultivate. And when I mentioned Lady Davers with apprehension, he said, 'I love my sister, notwithstanding her violent spirit; and I know she loves me. I can allow a little for her pride, because I know what my own so lately was; and because she knows not my Pamela, and her excellencies, as I do. But you must not, my dear, forget what belongs to your character as my wife, nor meanly stoop to her; though I know you will chuse by complaisance to try to move her to a proper behaviour. But it shall be my part to see that you do not submit too much.

'However,' continued he, 'as I would not publicly declare my marriage here, I hope she will not come near us till we are in Bedfordshire; and then, when she knows we are married, she will keep away, if she is not willing to be reconciled. But we will have no more of this subject, nor talk of any thing,' added he, 'that shall give you concern.'

And then he changed the talk to more pleasing subjects.

After dinner, he told me he had already written to his draper in town to provide him new liveries: and to his late mother's mercer, to send him down patterns of the most fashionable silks for my choice. I told him, I was unable express my gratitude for his favours and generosity; and as he knew best what befitted his own rank and condition, I would wholly refer myself to his good pleasure: but, by all his repeated bounties to me, I could not but look forward with awe upon the condition to which he had exalted me; and now I feared I should hardly be able to act up to it in such a manner as should justify the choice he had made. But that I hoped I should have not only his generous allowance for my imperfections, which I assured him should not be wilful ones, but his kind instructions; and that as often as he observed any part of my conduct to be such as he could not entirely approve, he would let me know it; and I would think his reproofs of beginning faults the kindest and most affectionate things in the world; because they would keep me from committing greater; and be a means to continue to me the blessing of his good opinion.

He answered me in the kindest manner; and assured me, that

nothing should ever lie upon his mind, that he took amiss, without giving me an opportunity either of convincing *him*, or being convinced *myself*.

He then asked me, when I should be willing to go to the Bedfordshire house? I said, whenever he pleased. 'We will come down hither again before the winter,' said he, 'if you please, in order to cultivate the acquaintance you have begun with Mr Peters, Mrs Jones, and Sir Simon's family; and if it please God to spare us to one another, in the winter I will give you, as I promised, for two or three months, my company in London. And I think,' added he, 'if you have no objection, we will set out about Tuesday next week for the other house.' 'I *can* have no objection, sir,' said I, 'to any thing you propose; but how will you avoid Miss Darnford's solicitation for an evening to dance?' 'We can make Monday evening to do for that,' answered he, 'if they won't excuse us. But, if you please, I will invite Mrs Jones, Mr Peters and his family, and Sir Simon and his, to my little chapel on Sunday morning, and to stay to dinner with me; and then I will declare my marriage to them, because my dear life shall not leave this country with the least reason for any body to doubt that she is my wife.' I most gratefully bowed as I sat. 'And then,' said he, 'they will perhaps excuse us till we return into this country again, as to the ball. Is there any thing,' added he, 'that you have still to wish? If there be, speak your whole heart, my dear.'

'Hitherto, sir,' replied I, 'you have prevented my wishes: and yet, since you so kindly command me to speak all my heart, I must own that I have one or two favours to beg; and if they *can* be granted, I shall be the happiest creature in the world.'

'Say, my love, what they are. My *wife* (methinks I am grown fond of a name I once despised) may speak all her mind; and I will promise, that, so far as I chearfully can comply, I will.'

'Then you will permit me, ever kind, ever generous, and ever dear sir,' said I, 'to become an humble petitioner, and that upon my knees, for the reinstating such of your servants as have incurred your displeasure by their kindness to me.'

He raised me. 'My Pamela,' said he, 'has too often been in this suppliant posture. Rise, my love, and let me know whom in particular you would reinstate'; kindly holding me in his arms, and pressing me to his bosom.

'Mrs Jervis, sir,' said I, 'in the first place. She is a good woman; and the misfortunes she has had in the world must make your displeasure most heavy to her.'

'Who next?' 'Mr Longman, sir,' said I; 'and I am sure, kind as they have been to me, yet would I not ask it, if I could not vouch for their integrity, and if I did not think it was the interest of their dear master to restore them.'

'Have you any other person to intercede for, my Pamela?' 'Your good old butler, sir, who has been in your family before the happy day of your birth. Forgive me, sir, he is also a good man.'

'I have only to say,' answered he, 'that had not these three joined together in an appeal to Lady Davers, which has given her the insolent handle she has taken to intermeddle in my affairs, I could easily have overlooked all the rest of their conduct; though they have taken great liberties with my character; for I would have every body admire and respect my Pamela. But at your request I will forgive all three. I will myself write to Mr Longman, to let him know what he owes to your mediation. Yet perhaps the estate he has acquired in my family, may have set him above the wish of returning to it. Do you, my dear, write to Mrs Jervis to go and take possession of her former charge; for now she will be more immediately your servant; and I know you love her so well, that you'll go thither with the more pleasure to find her there. But don't think,' added he, 'that all this compliance is to be for nothing.' 'Ah, sir,' said I, 'tell me but what I *can* do, poor as I am in power, but rich in will; and I will not hesitate one moment.' 'Why then,' said he, 'of your own accord, reward me for my chearful compliance with one sweet kiss.' 'How generous is this!' said I, and instantly clasped my arms about his neck, and was not ashamed to kiss him once, and twice, and three times, once for every forgiven person.

'Now, my dearest Pamela,' said he, 'what other thing have you to ask? Mr Williams is already taken care of; and, I hope, will be happy. Have you nothing to say for John Arnold?'

'You have seen, dear sir, the poor fellow's penitence in my letters.' 'I *have*,' replied he; 'but that is his penitence for having served me, against you; and, I think, when he would have betrayed me afterwards, he deserves nothing from either of us.'

'Let this, however, dear sir,' said I, 'be a day of jubilee. The less he deserves, poor fellow! the more will be your goodness. Permit me one word only: That as he was divided in his inclinations between his duty to you, and good wishes to me, and knew not how to distinguish between the one and the other, when he finds us so happily united, he will have no more puzzles in his duty; for he has not failed in any other part of it; but, I hope, will serve you faithfully for the future.'

'Well, then, suppose, my dear, I put Mrs Jewkes into some inn, and give her John for a husband? What think you of this? Your gypsey's prophecy will then be made out: she will have a husband younger than herself.'

'I can freely forgive poor Mrs Jewkes, sir, and wish her happy: but permit me to ask, would not this look like a very heavy punishment to poor John? And as if you could not forgive *him*, when you are so generous to every body else?'

'O my Pamela,' said he, smiling, 'this, from a forgiving spirit, is very severe upon poor Jewkes: but I shall never have any more such trying services, to put him or the rest upon; and if *you* can forgive him, I think *I* may; and so John shall be at your disposal. And now let me know, what my Pamela has further to wish?'

'Not one single wish more, my dearest sir, has your grateful Pamela. My heart is overwhelmed with your goodness!'

I wept for joy. And he took me in his kind arms, and with my own handkerchief dried my cheeks, and kissed me. 'You have left me nothing to pray for,' continued I, 'but that God will bless you with long life, health, and honour, and continue to me the blessing of your love; and I shall then be the happiest creature in the world.'

'You cannot, my dearest creature,' said he, clasping me to his bosom, 'be so happy in me, as I am in you. How heartily do I now despise all my former licentious pursuits! What true joy flows from virtuous love! Joy which the narrow soul of the libertine cannot take in. I myself, whilst a libertine, knew nothing of it.

'But,' said he, 'I expected that my Pamela had something to ask for herself: but since all her wishes are answered in the delight her generous heart takes in promoting the happiness of others, it shall be my study to make all care for herself unnecessary.'

How blessed, my dear parents, is your daughter in a *husband*! How my heart rejoices at the word!

I afterwards retired to my closet, and write you thus far. And having completed what I purpose for this pacquet, and put up the obliging present, what have I more to say, but that I hope soon to see you both, and receive your blessings on this happy occasion. And yet, *have* I nothing more to say? Yes; I have. It is to beg the continuance of your united prayers, that I may preserve an humble and thankful heart: that I may always look up with gratitude to the gracious First Cause of all this good: and that I may so behave to every creature, high and low, as not to be a discredit to my generous benefactor! And now I hasten to subscribe by my new name. But think not, my dear father, my dear mother, that pride leads me to glory in the change of it: your humbler name will be ever dear to me: but yet, for *such* an husband – What shall I say? since words are too faint to express my gratitude for being entitled, at the same time that I can call myself your ever-dutiful daughter, to style myself

The happy, thrice happy,
PAMELA B.

SATURDAY *Morning, the Third of my happy Nuptials*

I must still write on, till I come to be settled in the station to which I am so generously exalted, that you may participate with me the happiness that arises from my new condition, and rejoice with me on the favours that are hourly heaped upon me by the best of husbands. When I had got my pacquet for you finished, I then set about writing, as Mr B. had kindly directed me, to Mrs Jervis; and had no difficulty, till I came to sign my name; and so I brought it down with me, when I was called to supper, unsubscribed.

My good master, (for I delight, and always shall, to call him by that name) had been writing to Mr Longman. 'See here, my dear,' said he pleasantly, 'what I have written to your *Somebody*.' I read as follows: and afterwards, by his leave, took a copy of it for you.

'Mr LONGMAN,
'I have the pleasure to acquaint you, that last Thursday I was married to my beloved Pamela Andrews. I have had reason to be disobliged with you, and Mrs Jervis, and Jonathan, not for your kindness to her, but for the application you all jointly made to Lady Davers, on a concern with which that lady could not possibly have any thing to do; and which has occasioned a misunderstanding between her

and me. But as it was one of my bride's first requests, that I would overlook what had passed, and reinstate you all three in your former charges, I chearfully, and without the least hesitation, complied with it.

'I shall set out next Tuesday or Wednesday for Bedfordshire, and hope to find you and Jonathan there in the full exercise of those trusts, which both of you have always discharged with unquestionable integrity, and to the satisfaction of

Yours, &c.

'My wife writes herself to Mrs Jervis.'

Most cordially I thanked him; and then shewed him my letter to Mrs Jervis. This is a copy of it.

'*My dear Mrs* JERVIS,
'I have joyful tidings to communicate to you. For yesterday I was married to the best of men, *yours* and *my* beloved master. I have only now to tell you, that my generous benefactor denies me nothing, and even anticipates my wishes. You may be sure I could not forget my dear Mrs Jervis; and I made it my request, and had it granted as soon as asked, that you might return to the charge, which you executed with so much advantage to our master's interest, and with so much pleasure to all under your direction. All the power I have lent me, shall be exerted to make every thing easy and agreeable to you; and as I shall soon have the honour of attending my dear Mr B. to Bedfordshire, it will be a very considerable addition to my joy, to be received there by my dear Mrs Jervis, with that pleasure which I promise myself from her affection. For I am, and ever will be, with equal affection and gratitude,

Your true Friend,
PAMELA.'

Mr B. read this letter. 'Why don't you put your name to it?' said he. 'Your goodness, sir,' answered I, 'has given me a right to a very honourable one: but as this is the first occasion of the kind, except in a letter I have written to my father and mother, I think I ought to shew it you unsubscribed, that I may not seem – '

'Sweet creature!' said he, interrupting me with a kiss, 'this is an effect of your amiable humility! But it becomes me to tell you, that

I am every moment more and more pleased with the right you have to my name.' He then took a pen himself, and wrote, after the word Pamela, his worthy name; and I under-wrote thus: 'Rejoice with me, my dear Mrs Jervis, that I am entitled thus to write myself.'

These letters, and the pacquet to you, were sent away by Thomas early this morning.

My dearest master is just rode out; and intends to call upon Mrs Jones, Mr Peters, and Sir Simon Darnford, to invite them and their families to chapel and to dinner to-morrow. He chose to do this in person, because the time is so short, that they will, perhaps, excuse themselves to a message.

I forgot to mention, that Mr Williams was here yesterday, to ask leave to go to see his new living, and to provide for taking possession of it. He seemed greatly pleased with my master's generous behaviour to me, as well as with his kind reception of him. He owned, with gratitude, that he thought himself one of the happiest of men.

Great and good God! as thou hast enlarged my opportunities, enlarge also my will, and make me delight in dispensing to others a portion of that happiness which I have myself so plentifully received at the hands of thy gracious Providence! Then shall I not be useless in my generation![280] Then shall I not stand a *single* mark of thy goodness to a poor creature, who in herself is of little account in the scale of beings, a mere cypher[281] on the wrong side of a figure; but shall be placed on the right side; and though nothing worth in myself, shall give signification by my *place*, and multiply the blessings I owe to thy goodness, which has distinguished me by so fair a lot!

This, as I conceive, is the indispensable duty of a high condition; and what must be the condemnation of poor creatures, at the great day of account, when they shall be asked what uses they have made of the opportunities put into their hands; and are able only to say – We lived but to *ourselves*: we circumscribed all the power thou gavest us, into one *narrow*, *selfish* compass: we heaped up treasures for those who came after us, though we knew not whether they would not make a still worse use of them than we ourselves had done.

But sure, such persons can have no notion of the exalted pleasure that flows from the reflection of having had it put into one's power to administer comfort and relief to those who stand in need of it. A pleasure which of itself infinitely rewards the beneficent mind, were there to be no after account at all!

How often have I experienced this in my good lady's time; though but the dispenser of *her* bounty to the poor and sick, when she made me her almoner! How have I been affected with the blessings which the miserable have heaped upon her for her goodness, and upon me for being but the humble conveyer of her charity to them! And how delighted have I been, when the moving report I have made of a particular distress, has augmented my good lady's stipend in relief of it!

And now, my dear parents, that it is, by the Divine Goodness, and the favour of this dear man, become my part to supply to the deserving poor the loss they have sustained in the death of my honoured lady, let me beg of you to join your *incessant* prayers with mine, that I may not set up my rest in my *mean self*; that I may not so behave as if I thought nothing further was to be done with the opportunities put into my hands: in a word, that my prosperity may not become a snare to me, and make me incur a terrible woe by the abuse or neglect of those opportunities.

SATURDAY, *Seven in the Evening*

My beloved master returned home to dinner, though much pressed by Mrs Jones, to dine with her, as he was also by Sir Simon, to dine with him. But Mr Peters being unable, at so short a notice, to provide a preacher for his church to-morrow morning, (Mr Williams being gone, as I said, to his new living) and believing he could for the afternoon, he promised to give us his company to dinner, and to read the evening service in our own chapel: and this made my master invite the Darnford family, and Mrs Jones, as well as Mr Peters and his family, to dine with him. They all promised to come.

Miss Darnford, however, told him, pleasantly, she would not come, unless he would promise to let *her* be at his wedding; by which, I find, Mr Peters has kept the secret, as my master desired he would.

My dear Mr B. was pleased to give me an airing after dinner in the chariot, and renewed his generous assurances to me. Indeed, if possible, he is kinder to me than ever. I will give you a new instance of his goodness.

I begged leave to send a guinea to a poor person in the town, that I heard, by Mrs Jewkes, lay very ill, and was very destitute.

He bid me send two.

'I will never, sir,' said I, 'do any thing of this kind, without making you first acquainted with it, and having your approbation.'

He generously answered, 'I shall then, perhaps, have you do less good than you would otherwise do, from a doubt of me; though I hope, your discretion, and my own temper, which is not avaricious, will make such doubt causeless.

'Now, my dear,' continued he, 'I'll tell you how we will direct ourselves in this point, to avoid even the shadow of uneasiness on one side, or doubt on the other.'

'As to your father and mother, in the first place, they shall be quite out of the question; for I have already determined in my mind about them; and it is thus: they shall go down, if they and you think well of it, to my little Kentish estate; an offer which once, my dear,' smiling, 'you rejected: then to my pain, but now I think it happy for both that you did. There is a pretty little farm, untenanted, upon that estate, and tolerably stocked, and I will further stock it for them; since such an industrious pair will not know how to live without some employment: and it shall be theirs for both their lives; with the house upon it, a pretty good one, and in tolerable repair. And I will allow them fifty pounds a year besides, that they may keep up the stock, and be kind to any other of your relations, without being beholden to you or me, for small matters; and for greater, when needful, you shall always have it in your power to accommodate them; for I shall never question your prudence. And we will, so long as God spares our lives, go down once a year to see them, and they shall come up as often as they please, it cannot be too often, to see us; for I mean not this, my dear, to send them from me. Before I proceed further, does my Pamela approve of what I have said?'

'I have not words, sir,' said I, (my eyes, I am sure, glistening with grateful joy) 'to express sufficiently my gratitude. Teach me, dear sir,' and I pressed his hand to my lips, 'teach me some other language, if there be any, that abounds with more grateful terms, that I may not thus be choaked with meanings, for which I can find no utterance.'

'My charmer!' says he, 'your heart speaks at your eyes in a language that words *indeed* cannot utter. You most abound, when you seem most to want! But let me desire you to mention this to *them*, for their approbation. But if it be your choice, and theirs, to have them nearer to you, or even under the same roof, I will freely consent to it.'

'O no, sir,' said I, (and I fear I almost sinned in my grateful flight) 'I am sure they would not choose that; they could not, perhaps, serve God so well, if they were to live with you: for so constantly seeing the hand that blesses them, they would, it may be, (as must be also *my* care to avoid) be tempted to look no further in their gratitude, than to the dear dispenser of such innumerable benefits!'

'Excellent creature!' said he, clasping his arms about me; 'your kind acceptance of my proposal, repays the benefit with interest, and leaves me under obligation to you.

'But now, my dearest, I will tell you what we will do, with regard to the article of your own *private* charity. Far be it from me, to put under that name the subject we have been mentioning; since what I have proposed is no more than *duty*, to persons so worthy, and so nearly related to my Pamela, and now, through her, to *myself.*' O how the sweet man – But what shall I say? I will proceed with an account of his further generosity.

'And this,' said he, 'lies in very small compass; for I will allow you two hundred guineas a year, which Longman shall constantly pay you, at fifty guineas a quarter, for your own use, and of which I expect no account. The payment of the first fifty to be made on the day you enter into my other house, that you may have something to begin with. I myself would make you the quarterly payment with my own hands, instead of Longman: but that if I did, it would rather have the look of a *present* than a *due*: and no pecuniary matters shall be permitted to abase my love to my wife, or to be supposed to engage that affection, which I hope to be sure of from higher merits and motives.'[282]

I could not speak.

He proceeded, 'If what I have said be agreeable to my girl,

signify to me that it is, since you seem to want words, by such a sweet kiss as you gave me yesterday.'

I hesitated not a moment to comply with these obliging terms, and threw my arms about his neck, though in the chariot, and blessed him for his goodness to me. 'But indeed, sir,' said I, when I could speak, 'I cannot support myself under this generous treatment! I am quite oppressed with your goodness.'

'Don't be uneasy, my dear,' said the superlatively generous man, 'about these trifles: God has blessed me with a very good estate, and it is in a prosperous condition. I lay up money every year, and have, besides, large sums in government securities, as well as in private hands; so that you will find, what I have hitherto promised, is very short of that proportion of my substance, which, as my wife, you have a right to.'

This, you will say, was a most delightful airing! The chariot brought us home in the evening; and then our supper succeeded in the same agreeable manner.

SUNDAY, *the Fourth Day of my Happiness*

Not going to chapel this morning, the reason of which I told you, I bestowed the time, from the hour of Mr B.'s rising, to our breakfast, in prayer and thanksgiving, in my closet. And now I find myself quite easy, chearful and free in my spirits. And the more, as I see, on every occasion, such a sweet tranquillity, and even such an increased vivacity in his temper and behaviour, as cannot but fill me with hope, that he repents not of his goodness to me.

I attended him to breakfast, and drank my chocolate with great pleasure; and he seemed quite pleased with me, and said, 'Now does my Pamela begin to look upon me with an air of serenity. It shall be always my delight to give her occasion for an aspect that so sweetly becomes her features.'

'My heart, dear sir,' said I, 'is quite easy, and has lost all its foolish tumults, which combating with my gratitude, I am afraid, gave a disagreeable cast to my behaviour: but now it is all of *one* piece, and devoted to you, and grateful tranquillity. But, dear sir, have you nothing to find fault with me for? Is there not something that you would have me to be, in behaviour, in dress, in any thing, that I am not?'[283]

'You are every thing, my love,' he was pleased to say, 'that I wish you to be. Only continue to be what you are, and you will be sure of my affection to the end of my life.

'As to dress, now you have mentioned it, and as to personal elegance, I will observe to you, that I have too often seen, in married persons, that the lady grows careless in her dress; which, to me, looks as if she would take no pains to secure the affection she had gained; and shews a slight to her husband, that she did not shew to her lover: now, you must know, this has always given me great offence. Let me say then, that I shall expect of you always to be dressed by dinner-time, except something extraordinary happens to prevent it; and this, whether you are to go abroad, or to stay at home. Since this will continue to you that sweet ease in your dress and behaviour, of which you are so happy a mistress; and whomsoever I bring home with me to my table, you will be in readiness to receive them; and will not want to make those foolish apologies to unexpected visitors, that carry with them a reflection on the conduct of those who make them; and besides, will convince me, that you think yourself obliged to appear as graceful to your husband, as you would to persons less familiar to your sight.'

'This, sir,' said I, 'is a most obliging injunction. I will always take care to observe it.'

'You, my dear,' said he, 'may better do this than half your sex: because they too generally act in such a manner, as if they seemed to think it the privilege of birth and fortune, to turn day into night, and night into day, and seldom rise till 'tis time to sit down to dinner; and so all the good old rules are reversed: for they breakfast when they should dine; dine, when they should sup; and sup, when they should retire to rest; and, by the help of dear quadrille, sometimes go to rest when they should rise. In all things, but such as these, my dear, I expect you to be a fine lady. My mother was one of these old-fashioned ladies; and, at the same time, one of the worthiest in the kingdom: you will have the less difficulty, therefore, of following the example she set you.'

I besought him to give me more of his injunctions; and he proceeded to lay down such rules for the family order, as indeed my *lady* had been used to follow; but which both delighted and surprized me, coming from *him*. And these were his observations on the early and regular times of breakfasting, dining, and supping, which he prescribed:

'I shall, in the usual course,' said he, 'and generally, if not hindered by company, like to go to rest by eleven. I ordinarily now rise by six, in summer: you will, perhaps, chuse to lie half an hour after me.

'Then you will have some time you may call your own, till you invite me to breakfast with you: a little after nine.

'Then again will you have several hours at your disposal, till three o'clock, when I shall like to sit down at table.

'You will then have several useful hours more to employ yourself in, as you shall best like; and I would generally go to supper by nine.[284] When we are resolved to stick to these old-fashioned rules, as near as we can, we shall induce our visitors to expect them from us. I have always observed, that it is in every one's power to prescribe rules to himself. It is only standing a few ridiculous jests at first, and those from such, generally, as are not the most worthy of regard; and, after a while, they will say, "It signifies nothing to ask *him*: he will have his own way. There is no putting him out of his course. He is a regular piece of clock-work," will they perhaps sneeringly add. And why should I not be so? For man is as frail a piece of machinery, and, by irregularity, is as subject to be disordered as a clock.

'Then,' continued he, 'when my guests find themselves received, at my *own* hours, with an open countenance and chearful heart; when they see plenty and variety at my table, and meet a kind and hearty welcome, they will not grudge me my regularity. And who knows, my dear, but we may revive the good old-fashioned rules in our neighbourhood? At least, it will be doing our part towards it; and answering the good lesson I learned at school – *Every one mend one*.[285] And the worst that can happen will be, that when some of my brother rakes, such as those who broke in upon us, so unwelcomely, last Thursday, are got out of their way, if that can ever be, and begin to consider, whom they shall go to dine with in their rambles, they will only say, "His dinner-time is over"; and so they'll reserve me for another time, when they happen to suit it better; or, perhaps, they will take a supper and a bed with me instead of a dinner.'

'O dearest, dear sir,' said I, 'have you no more of your injunctions to favour me with? They delight and improve me at the same time!'

'I think of no more at present,' said he: 'for it would be needless to say, how much I value you for your natural sweetness of temper, and for that innocent vivacity which gives to your lovely countenance its principal grace; and which you must not permit any sudden accident to overcloud. When any thing unpleasing happens, let me expect that, in a quarter of an hour, at farthest, you will begin to mistrust yourself, and apply to your glass; and if you see a gloom arising or arisen, banish it instantly; resume your former chearfulness; and then, my lovely girl, whose heart must always be seen in her face, and who cannot be a hypocrite, will find this a means to smooth her temper also.'

He then took notice of the discomposure that he had seen in some ladies, on their being broken in upon by unexpected guests. 'I am sure,' said he, 'I never shall have reason to caution my Pamela on any subject that will make her husband look little, or herself unprepared to welcome his friends. But yet I will say, that I expect of my dearest love, that she will accustom herself to an uniform complaisance. That however ill or well provided we may be for the reception of unexpected guests, she shew no flutter or discomposure. That whoever she may have in her company at the time, she signify not, by the least reserved look, that the stranger is come at a time she wished he had not: and that she will be chearful, kind, obliging to all; and if to any one more than another, to such as have the least reason to expect it from her, or who are of the lowest rank at the table; for thus will she, at the very time that she chears the doubting mind, *assure* all the rest, and diffuse ease, pleasure, and joy, around my board.

'After what I have said, I need not warn my love, that she suffer not any sudden accident to ruffle her temper. I shall never forget the discomposure that Mrs Arthur gave herself on one of her footmen's happening to stumble, and let fall a fine China dish; and she was so sincere in it, that she suffered it to spread all round the table, and not one of the company, myself excepted, but either became her consoler, or fell into stories of the like misfortunes; and, for the rest of the evening, we were turned into blundering footmen, and careless servants.'

I thankfully promised to attend to his kind hints; and then I retired to dress, which I did in my best clothes; and, on enquiry, hearing he was in the garden, I went to attend him.

I found him reading in the little alcove. 'You are busy, sir?' said I.

He put up the paper he was reading, and said, 'I can have no business of equal value to your company. Sit down, my Pamela,' taking my hand, and placing me by him. 'You are a sweet, obliging girl! I see you have begun with observing one of my injunctions, as you call them. You are *early* dressed; and charmingly too! Now, my dear, be so kind as to find some fault with *me*, and tell me what you would wish me to do, to appear still more agreeable to you than I am.'

'O sir,' said I; and I could have kissed him, but for shame; 'I have not one single thing to wish for; no, not *one*. Do you think,' proceeded I, (for I knew not how to stop) 'that your Pamela has no conscience? Let me assure you, sir, that less, *much* less than one half of the favours you have so generously conferred upon me, would have exceeded my utmost wishes.'

'My angel,' said he, eagerly taking my hand between both his, and seemed about to say more agreeable things; but my overflowing gratitude *compelled* me, as I may say, to go on. 'Why don't you, dear sir! ask me *quite contrary* questions? Don't I see, with delight, that your lessons are strengthened by your own example? For here, sir, in the first place, you that have enjoined me to be dressed for the day before dinner, are most charmingly dressed yourself.

'Then, sir, when you command me, at your table, to chear the doubting mind, and to behave most kindly to those who have least reason to expect distinction, and are of the lowest rank; how sweetly, in every instance that could possibly occur, have you done this yourself, by your Pamela! And how have you (to use your own words) diffused ease, pleasure, and joy, around my heart!

'Then again, when you bid me not be disturbed by little accidents, or by strangers coming in upon me unexpectedly, what an example did you give me of your own observation of this excellent rule, when, on our wedding-day, you permitted not the intrusion of Sir Charles Hargrave, and the other two gentlemen, which prevented our dining together on that chosen day, so to disturb you, as to hinder your entertaining them pleasantly, and parting with them kindly! What charming instances are these of your practising what you teach!'

'These observations are very much to my advantage, my dear,' said he: 'but I fear these instances were too accidental to give me a title to your kind compliment: allow me therefore to say, that if I do not always make my practice so well confirm my doctrines, my Pamela must not expect that my imperfections will be a plea for her non-observance of my lessons, as you call them; for, I doubt, I shall never be half so perfect as you; and so I cannot permit you to recede in your goodness, although I may find myself unable to advance, as I ought, in my duty.'

'I hope, sir,' said I, 'by God's grace, I never shall.'

He was pleased to take notice of my dress; and, spanning my waist with his hands,[286] said, 'What a sweet shape is here! It would make one regret to lose it: and yet, my Pamela, I shall think nothing but that loss wanting, to complete my happiness.'

I put my bold hand before his mouth. He kissed my hand, and said, 'Tell me! Speak! Say! Would such a circumstance be unwelcome to my Pamela?' 'I will say, sir,' said I, and hid my blushing face on his shoulder, 'that your wishes, in every thing, shall be mine.' He pressed me to his kind heart, and changed the subject. I was not too free, I hope?

Thus we talked, till we heard the coaches; and then he said, 'Stay in the garden, my dear, and I'll bring the company to *you*.' He did so; and as soon as I beheld them, I hastened towards them to shorten the distance.

'How do you do, my dear?' said Miss Darnford. 'You look so easy, so chearful, that I know you will grant the request I have to make to you: you know what it is: to dance at your wedding. Indeed, I must not be refused; for I shall long to be there.' Mrs Jones was pleased to say, I looked like an angel. And Mrs Peters, that I improved upon them every time they saw me. Lady Darnford also made me a fine compliment, and said, I looked freer and easier every time she saw me. Dear ladies! thought I, I wish you would spare these compliments; for I shall have some jest, I doubt, passed upon me, by-and-by, that will make me suffer for them.

Mr Peters said, softly, 'God bless you, dear *daughter*! But not even my wife knows it.'

Sir Simon came to me last, and took my hand, and holding it with both his, 'Mr B. by your leave,' said he; and kissed my hand five or six times; making a very free jest, by way of compliment, in his way.

A *young* rake, my dear mother, is hardly tolerable; but an *old* rake, and an *old* beau, are two very unnatural things! And all this before daughters, women-grown! I whispered my Mr B. [what a proud word is that! *my* Mr B.!] a little after, 'I fear,' said I, 'I shall suffer from Sir Simon's free jests by-and-by, when you reveal the matter.' ' 'Tis his way, my dear,' said he; 'we must give him the hearing.'

Miss Nanny Darnford said to me, with a sort of half-grave, ironical air, 'Give me leave to hope, madam, that you will permit my sister, if not me, to be present at the ceremony: she is quite wild about it.' I curt'sied, and only said, 'You are all very good to me, ladies.'

My dear Mr B. [he says, I must speak to him, and write of him, as my husband and lover both in one] took me aside, and said, 'Shall I lead them to the alcove, and tell them there, or stay till we go in to dinner?' 'Be pleased, sir,' said I, 'to defer it till they are going away.' 'You have hitherto,' said he, 'concealed your ring from the servants. If you will not have me communicate the affair till then, you must pull it off, or the ladies and Sir Simon will see it.'

Before I could reply, Mrs Jewkes, attended by Nan, officiously[287] waddled to us with two bottles of Rhenish,[288] (what she herself dearly loves) and sugar on a salver; and, making an aukward apology, by Mr B.'s encouragement, poured out a glass, and to his surprize, (though not disagreeable to him, I saw) but much more to mine, offered it to me, with a low curt'sy, saying, 'Will you, madam, begin?' 'No,' said I; 'my master, to be sure': my face, as I felt, in a glow.

They all took the hint: 'I'll be hanged,' said Miss Darnford, 'if they have not stolen a wedding!' 'It must certainly be so!' said Mrs Peters. 'Ah! Mr Peters! Where were you, and Mr Williams, last Thursday morning?' 'Let me alone,' said Sir Simon, 'let me alone; if any thing has been stolen, I'll find it out; I'm a justice of peace, you know. Come, madam,' taking my hand, 'answer me by the oath you have taken: Are you married, or not?'

Mr B. smiled to see me so like a fool. 'Pray, Sir Simon,' said I. 'I thought,' replied he, 'you did not look so smiling upon us for nothing.' In the kindest manner my dear Mr B. took my other hand. 'Since your blushes, my dearest love, discover you, be not ashamed of your husband: I never can be of my wife.'

'Now,' said Miss Darnford, 'I am quite angry.' 'And I,' said Lady Darnford, 'am quite pleased; let me give you joy, dear Mrs B.' Every one joined in the wish, and saluted me; while Mrs Jewkes shook her sides, and seemed highly pleased to be a means of discovering it.

'Nobody,' said Mr B., 'wishes *me* joy.' 'Nobody need,' said Mrs Jones, very obligingly; 'since, with such a bride, you want no good wishes!' He saluted each of the ladies; and, when he came to me, he said before them all, 'Now, my lovely bride, my sweet Pamela, let me conclude with you. May my love and my life in this world end together!'

Every one applauded him for the honour he did to his own generous choice. But I was forced to stand many more jests afterwards. And Sir Simon said several times, as preludes to his freedoms, 'Come, come, madam, now you are become one of us, I shall be a little less scrupulous than I have been, I will assure you.'

When we went in to dinner, my dear Mr B. led me to the upper end of the table. I curtsied low to him, and to the elder ladies, and made no scruple to take the place he led me to; and performed the honours of it with pretty tolerable presence of mind.

Mr B. with difficulty got them to give up the ball; on promising to be down again before winter; and on accepting of an invitation to meet this whole company at Sir Simon Darnford's to-morrow evening; by way of taking leave of them, he designing to set out on Wednesday morning for Bedfordshire.

The company intended to have staid supper; but soon after we had dined, a man and horse came express from a gentleman of Mr B.'s acquaintance, whose name is Carlton, and who being taken dangerously ill, begged to see him as soon as possible. And so they all took leave of us.

Mr Carlton lives near sixteen[289] miles off. Mr B. has a mortgage upon a considerable part of his estate. There is a great friendship between them. At parting with me, he bid me not expect him this night, if he returned not by eleven. 'Poor Mr Carlton and I,' said he, 'have pretty large concerns together, and if he should be very ill, and would be comforted by my presence, charity will not let me refuse it.'

It is now eleven[290] o'clock at night, and I fear he will not return. I am afraid his friend is very ill. Methinks I should be sorry any grief should touch his generous heart; yet there is no living in this world without many occasions for concern, even in the most prosperous state. It is fit it should be so; or else, poor wretches as we are! we should look no further; but be like travellers on a journey homeward, who, meeting with good entertainment at some inn on the way, put up their rest there, and never think of pursuing their journey to their proper home. This, I remember, was often a reflection of my good old lady, to whom I owe it.

I made Mrs Jewkes sup with me. She was much pleased with my condescension, as she called it; and for my freedom with her, as we sat together. I could see by her manner, that she remembered with shame some parts of her past wickedness to me. She looked down, sat on the edge of her chair, her voice so gentle, and, 'Yes, madam,' and 'No, madam'; almost all she could say.[291] Poor wretch! I pitied her sometimes. May it be in my power to subdue her by kindness! That shall not be wanting, if I see it will do. Yet I am afraid that her change of behaviour is more owing to her respect for my present condition than to principle. Yet great is the force of a good example in superiors. Mine, I hope, will not be wanting.

How I long to be doing some good! All that is past yet, is my dear master's!

God return him safe to my wishes! Every hour seems ten since I saw him. If he would not think my love troublesome, I should be all love as well as duty; for I have a truly grateful spirit; and so I ought to have; for I have nothing but my love of him to value myself upon.

MONDAY *Morning, Seven o' Clock*[292]

I have just received a letter from my best friend. This is a copy of it; directed to me by my maiden name, because of the servant who brought it:

' *My dearest Love,*

Monday Morning, 3 o'Clock

'As I desired you not to expect me, if I returned not by eleven last night, I hope my absence did not discompose you.

'I sat up with my poor friend Carlton all night. He entreats me not to leave him. His hours seem to be numbered. A very few, it is believed, will shut up the solemn scene. He is, however, sensible. I have made his heart, and the hearts of his wife and children, easy in the assurances of my kindness to them. I left the poor man, for a few moments, praying for a release; and blessing me.

' I could have wished, so much has this melancholy scene affected me, that we had not engaged ourselves to Sir Simon and the good neighbourhood, for this night: but since the engagement must take place, let me beg of you, my dear, to take the chariot, and go to Sir Simon's; the sooner in the day, the more obliging it will be to all your admiring friends. I hope to join you there by your tea-time in the afternoon. It will be six miles difference to me, and I know the good company will excuse dress on the occasion.

'I count every hour of this little absence for a day: for I am, with the utmost sincerity, my dearest love,

For ever your's,
W.B.[293]

'If you could dine with Sir Simon and the ladies, it would be a freedom they would be delighted with; and the more, as they expect not such a favour.'

God preserve the health of my dearest Mr B. I hope it will not suffer by his fatigues; and God bless him for his goodness to his sick friend and the distressed family. The least intimation of his pleasure shall be a command to me. I have ordered the chariot to be got ready. I will go and dine with Lady Darnford. I am already dressed.

Mrs Jewkes is sent for down. The trampling of horses in the court-yard. Visitors are come. A chariot and six.[294] Coronets on the chariot. Who can they be? They have alighted, and come into the house.

Dreadful! Dreadful! What shall I do? Lady Davers! Lady Davers, her own self! And my kind protector a great, great many miles off!

Mrs Jewkes, out of breath, tells me this, and says, she is enquiring for my master and me. How I tremble! I can hardly hold my pen. She asked her, it seems, if I was *whored* yet? There's a word for a lady's mouth! Mrs Jewkes says, she knew not what to answer. 'She is not married, I hope!' said my lady. 'No,' replied Mrs Jewkes. 'I am glad of that!' said my lady. Mrs Jewkes apologized to me, as it was to be a secret at present, for denying that I was married.

I can write no more at present. Lord bless me! I am all in terrors! I will try to get away.

Let me tell you all, my dear mother, just as it passed. I have been dreadfully – But you shall hear all as it passed.

'I will run away, Mrs Jewkes,' said I. 'Let the chariot go to the further end of the elm-walk, and I will fly to it unperceived.' 'But she is enquiring for you, madam. I said you were within, but going out. She would see you presently, she said, as soon as she could have patience.' 'What did she call me, Mrs Jewkes?' '*The creature*, madam: "*I will see the creature*," said she, "*as soon as I can have patience.*"' 'Ay, but,' replied I, '*the creature* won't see her, if she can help it. Pray, Mrs Jewkes, favour my escape for this once; for I am sadly frighted.'

'I'll bid the chariot go down as you order,' said she, 'and wait till you come; and I'll step down, and shut the hall-door, that you may pass unobserved; for she sits cooling herself in the parlour over-against the stair-case.' 'That's a good Mrs Jewkes!' said I: 'but who has she with her?' 'Her woman,' answered she, 'and her nephew; but he came on horseback, and is gone into the stables; and they have three footmen.' 'And I wish,' said I, 'they were all three hundred miles off! What *shall* I do!'

Mrs Jewkes told me, I must go down, or my lady would come up. 'What does she call me now?' ' *Wench*, madam: "*Bid the wench come down to me.*" Her nephew and her woman are with her.'

'I can't go!' said I, 'and that's enough! You might contrive it, that I might get out, if you would.' 'Indeed, madam, I cannot: for I would have shut the door, and she bid me let it stand open; and there she sits over-against the stair-case.' 'Then,' said I, fanning myself, 'I'll get out of the window, I think; I am sadly frighted!' 'I wonder you so much disturb yourself, madam!' said Mrs Jewkes. 'You're on the right side of the hedge,[295] I'm sure; and were it my case, I would not be so discomposed for any body.' 'Ay,' said I, 'but who can help constitution? I dare say, *you* would no more be so discomposed, than I can help it.' 'Indeed, madam, if I were you, I would put on an air as mistress of the house, as you are, and go and salute her ladyship, and bid her welcome.' 'Fine talking!' replied I; 'and be cussed for my civility! How unlucky this is, that your good master is abroad!'

'She expects to see you, madam. What answer shall I give her?' 'Tell her I am sick in bed: tell her I am dying, and must not be disturbed: tell her I am gone out: tell her any thing!'

At that moment up came her woman. 'How do you do, Mrs Pamela?' said she; and stared; I suppose to see me dressed. 'My lady desires to speak with you.' Now, thought I, I must go. She won't beat me, I hope. Oh, that my dear protector were at home!

I followed her woman down; my gloves on, and my fan in my hand, that I might be ready to step into the chariot, when I could get away. I had hoped, that the occasion for all my tremblings had been over; but I trembled sadly; yet resolved to put on as easy an air as possible: and entering the parlour, and making a very low curt'sy, 'Your servant, my good lady,' said I. 'And *your* servant, again,' said she, '*my lady*; for I think you are dressed out like one.'

'A charming girl though!' said her rakish nephew, and swore a great oath: 'dear madam, forgive me, but I must kiss her.' And came up to me.

'Forbear, uncivil gentleman,' said I; 'I won't be used with freedom.'

'Jackey,' said my lady, 'sit down, and don't touch the creature: she's proud enough already. There's a great difference in her air, as well as in her dress, I assure you, since I saw her last.

'Well, child,' said she, sneeringly, 'how dost find thyself? Thou'rt mightily come on of late! I hear strange reports about thee! Thou'rt got into fool's paradise,[296] I doubt; but wilt find thyself terribly mistaken, in a little while, if thou thinkest my brother will disgrace his family for the sake of thy baby-face!'

'I see,' said I, sadly vexed, (her woman and nephew smiling by) 'your ladyship has no particular commands for me, and I beg leave to withdraw.'

'Worden,'[297] said she to her woman, 'shut the door; my young lady and I must not part so soon.

'Where's your well-mannered deceiver gone, child?' said she.

'When your ladyship is pleased to speak intelligibly,' replied I, 'I shall know how to answer.'

'Well, but my dear child,' said she in drollery, 'don't be too *pert* neither. Thou wilt not find thy master's sister half so ready as thy mannerly master is, to bear with thy freedoms. A little more of that modesty and humility, therefore, which my mother's waiting-wench used to shew, will become thee better than the airs thou givest thyself.'

'I would beg,' said I, 'one favour of your ladyship, that if you would have me keep my distance, you will not forget your own degree.'

'Why, suppose, *Miss Pert*, I *should* forget *my* degree, wouldst thou not *keep* thy distance?'

'If you, madam,' said I, 'lessen the distance yourself, you will descend nearer to the level you are pleased to consider me in, than I hope Lady Davers, for her own honour, will deign to do.'

'Do you hear? do you hear, Jackey? Did I not tell you, that I should know how to form a notion of her situation, either by her pertness, or her reverence! Ah, girl! girl!'

Her nephew, who swears like a fine gentleman at every word, rapped out an oath, and said, drolling,[298] 'I think, Mrs Pamela, if I may be so *bold* as to say so, you should know you are speaking to Lady Davers!' 'I hope, sir,' replied I (vexed at what my lady said, and at his sneering) 'that as there was no need of your information, you don't expect my thanks for it; and I am sorry you seem to think it wants an oath.'

He looked more foolish than I, if possible, not expecting such a reprimand. At last, 'Why, Mrs Pamela,' said he, 'you put me half out of countenance with your witty reproof.'

'Sir,' said I, 'you seem quite a fine gentleman. I hope, however, that you *can* be out of countenance.'

'How now, Pert-one,' said my lady, 'do you know to whom you talk?'

'I beg pardon, madam! But lest I should still further forget myself—'

And then I made a low curtsey, and was going. But she arose, and gave me a push, and pulled the chair, and setting the back against the door, sat down in it.

'Well,' said I, 'I can bear any thing at your ladyship's hands.'

Yet I was ready to cry. And I went and sat down, and fanned myself, at the other end of the room.

Her woman, who stood all the time, said softly, 'Mrs Pamela, you should not sit in my lady's presence.' My lady, though she did not hear *her*, said, 'You shall sit down, child, in the room where I am, when I give you leave.'

I stood up, and said, 'When your ladyship will hardly permit me to stand, I might be allowed to sit.'

'But I asked you,' said she, 'whither your master is gone?'

'To one Mr Carlton's, madam, about sixteen miles off, who is very ill.'

'And when does he come home?'

'This evening, madam.'

'And whither are you going?'

'To a gentleman's house in the town, madam.'

'And how were you to go?'

'In the chariot, madam.'

'Why, you must be a lady in time, to be sure! I believe you'd become a chariot mighty well, child! Were you ever out in it, with your master?'

'I beseech you, madam,' said I, very much nettled, 'to ask half a dozen such questions together; because one answer may do for all!'

'Why, Bold-face,' said she, 'you'll forget your distance, and bring me to your level before my time.'

I could no longer refrain tears, but said, 'Pray your ladyship, let me ask, What I have done to be thus severely treated? If you think I am deceived, as you were pleased to hint, ought I not rather to be entitled to your pity, than your anger?'

She came to me, and taking my hand, led me to her chair, and then sat down, still holding my hand.

'Poor wench!' said she, 'I did indeed pity you, while I thought you innocent; and when my brother brought you down hither, without your consent, I was concerned for you. I was still *more* concerned for you, and loved you, when I heard of your virtue and resistance, and your laudable efforts to get away from him. But when, as I fear, you have suffered yourself to be prevailed upon, and have lost your innocence, and added another to the number of the fools he has ruined' [*This shocked me a little*] 'I cannot help shewing you my displeasure.'

'Madam,' replied I, 'I must beg a less hasty judgment; I have *not* lost my innocence.'

'Take care, take care, Pamela: don't lose your veracity, as well as your virtue. Why are you here, when you are at full liberty to go whither you please? I will make one proposal to you, and if you are innocent, I am sure you'll accept of it. Will you go and live with me? I will instantly set out with you in my chariot, and not stay half an hour longer in this house, if you will go with me. Now, if you are innocent, and willing to keep so, deny me, if you can.'

'I am innocent, madam,' replied I, 'and willing to *keep* so; and yet I cannot consent to this.'

'Then, very flatly, thou liest, child,' said she; 'and I give thee up': rising, and walking about the room in great wrath. Her nephew and her woman said, 'Your ladyship is very good.'

' 'Tis a plain case; a very plain case,' said her nephew.

I would have moved the chair, to have gone out, but her nephew came and sat in it. This provoked me; for I thought I should be unworthy of the honour I was raised to, though I was afraid to own it, if I did not shew some spirit, and I said, 'What, sir, is *your* privilege in this house? And what is your pretence to detain me against my will?'

'Because,' said he, 'I like it.'

'Do you so, sir?' replied I: 'if that is the answer of a gentleman to me, a woman, it would not, I dare say, be your answer to a gentleman.'

'My lady! my lady!' said he, 'a challenge, a challenge, by Gad!'

'No, sir,' said I, 'I am of a sex that gives no challenges; and you think so too, or you would not have thought of the word.'

'Don't be surprised, nephew,' said my lady; 'the wench could not talk thus, if she had not been her master's bedfellow. Pamela, Pamela,' tapping my shoulder, two or three times, in anger, 'thou hast lost thy innocence, girl; and thou hast got some of thy master's assurance, and art fit to go any where.'

'Then, an please your ladyship,' said I, 'I am unworthy of your presence, and desire I may withdraw.'

'No,' replied she, 'I will know first, what reason you can give for not accepting my proposal, if you are innocent?'

'I *can* give,' said I, 'a very good one: but I beg to be excused.'

'I *will* hear it,' said she.

'Why then,' answered I, 'I should perhaps have less reason to like *this* gentleman, at your ladyship's house, than my abode where I am.'

'Well then,' said she, 'I'll put you to another trial. I'll set out this moment with you to your father and mother, and see you with them in safety. What do you say to that?'

'Ay, Mrs Pamela,' said her nephew, 'now what does your innocence say to that? 'Fore Gad, madam, you have puzzled her now.'

'Be pleased, madam,' said I, 'to relieve me from the questionings of this fine gentleman. Your kindness in these proposals makes me think you would not have me insulted.'

'Insulted, madam! Insulted!' returned he. 'Fine ladies will give themselves fine airs! May she not as well call me, insolent, madam? Who, Mrs Pamela, do you talk to?'

'Jackey, be quiet,' said my lady. 'You only give her a pretence to evade my questions. Answer me, Pamela.'

'I will, madam, and it is thus: I have no occasion to be obliged to your ladyship for this honour; for I am to set out on Wednesday on the way to my parents.'

'Now, again, thou liest, wench.'

'I am not of quality,' said I, curtseying, 'to answer such language.'

'Let me again caution thee, wench, not to provoke me by thy pertness to do something by thee, unworthy of myself.'

That, thought I, you have done already; but I ventured not to say so.

'But who is to carry you,' said she, 'to your father and mother?'

'Who my master pleases, madam.'

'Ay,' said she, 'I doubt not thou wilt do every thing he pleases, if thou hast not already. Why now, tell me, Pamela, from thy heart, Hast thou not been in bed with thy master? Hay, wench!' repeated she.

I was quite shocked. 'I have not,' said I, 'deserved such usage: I am sure your ladyship can expect no answer to such a question. My sex, and my youth, might have exempted me from such treatment, from a person of your ladyship's birth and quality; were it only for your own sake, madam.'

'Thou art a confident wench,' said she, 'I see!'

'Pray, madam, let me beg you to permit me to go. I am waited for in the town to dinner.'

'I can't spare you,' replied she; 'and whomsoever you are to go to, will excuse you, when they are told 'tis *I* that command you *not* to go; and *you* may excuse it too, young Lady *Would-be*,²⁹⁹ if you recollect, that 'tis the unexpected arrival of your late lady's daughter, and your master's sister, that requires your attendance on her.'

I pleaded, foolishly enough, as I might have expected she would ridicule me for it, pre-engagement.

'My stars!' said she, 'what will this world come to! Waiting-wenches plead pre-engagements in bar of³⁰⁰ their duty! O Pamela, Pamela! I am sorry thou givest thyself such airs, and triest to ape thy betters: I see thou art quite spoiled: of a modest, innocent girl, that thou wert, and humble too, thou now art fit for nothing in the world, but what, I fear, thou art.'

'Why, madam,' said her kinsman, 'what signifies all your lady-ship can say? The matter's over with her, no doubt; and she likes it; and she is in a fairy-dream, and 'tis pity to awaken her before her dream's out.'

'Bad as you take me to be, madam,' said I, 'I am not used to such language or reflections as this gentleman bestows upon me; and I won't bear it.'

'Won't *bear it*; wench! Well, but, Jackey, be silent'; and, shaking her head, 'Poor girl! what a sweet innocence is here destroyed! A thousand pities! I could weep over her! But she is quite lost, quite undone; and has assumed airs upon it, that all those creatures are distinguished by!'

I wept for vexation. 'Say what you please, madam: if I can help it, I will not answer another word.'

Mrs Jewkes came in, and asked, If her ladyship was ready for dinner? 'Let it be served,' said she. I would have gone out with Mrs Jewkes; but my lady, taking my hand, repeated, that she could not spare me. 'And, miss,' proceeded she, 'you may pull off your gloves, and lay your fan by; you shall not stir from my presence. If you behave better, you shall wait upon me at dinner, and then I shall have a little further talk with you.'

Mrs Jewkes stopping at the door, 'Madam,' said she to me, 'may I speak one word with you?'

'I can't tell, Mrs Jewkes,' returned I. 'My lady holds my hand, and you see I am a kind of prisoner.'

'Madam, dost thou call her, woman? And I suppose *thou* art called madam[301] too. But what thou hast to say, thou may'st speak before me.'

Mrs Jewkes went out, and seemed vexed for me. She says, my face looked like the very scarlet.

The cloth was laid in another parlour, and for *three* persons, and she led me in: 'Come, my little dear,' said she, with a sneer, 'I'll hand you in, and I would have you think as highly of the honour, as if it was done you by my brother.'

How dreadful, thought I, would be my lot, were I as wicked as this haughty lady thinks me!

'Jackey,' said my lady, 'come, let us go to dinner. Do you, Worden,' (to her woman) 'assist the girl in waiting on us. We will have no men-fellows. Come, my young lady, shall I help you off with your white gloves?'

'I have not, madam, deserved this at your ladyship's hands.'

Mrs Jewkes coming in with the first dish, she said, 'Do you expect any body else, Mrs Jewkes, that the cloth is laid for *three*?'

'I hoped your ladyship and madam,' replied Mrs Jewkes, 'would have been so well reconciled, that she would have sat down too.'

'What means the clownish[302] woman?' said my lady, in great disdain: 'could you think the creature should sit down with me?'

'She does, and please your ladyship, with my master.'

'I doubt it not, woman,' said she, 'and *lies* with him too, does she not? Answer me, Fat-face!'

How these women of quality are privileged! thought I.

'If she does, madam,' said she, 'there may be a *reason* for it, perhaps!' And went out.

'So!' said she, 'the wench has got thee over! Come, my little dear, pull off thy *gloves*, I say'; and off she pulled my left glove herself, and spied my ring. 'O my dear God!' said she, 'if the wench has not got a ring! Well! this *is* a pretty piece of foolery, indeed! Dost know, my friend, that thou art miserably tricked? And so, poor Innocent! thou hast made a fine exchange, hast thou not? Thy honesty for this bauble! And, I'll warrant, my little dear has topped her part, and paraded it like any real wife; and so mimicks still the condition! Why,' said she, and turned me round, 'thou art as mincing as any bride! No wonder thou art thus tricked out, and talkest of thy *pre-engagements*! Pr'ythee, child, walk before me to that glass: survey thyself, and come back to me, that I may see how finely thou canst act the theatrical part given thee.'

I was then resolved to try to be silent; although exceedingly vexed. I went to the window, and sat down in it, and she took her place at the table; and her saucy nephew, fleering at me most provokingly, sat down by her.

'Shall not the bride sit down by us, madam?' said he.

'Ay, well thought of,' answered my lady. 'Pray Mrs Bride, your pardon for sitting down in your place!' How poor was this for a great lady! I said nothing.

With a still poorer pun, 'Thou hast some modesty, however, child! For thou canst not *stand it*, so must *sit*, though in my presence!'

I kept my seat, and was still silent. It is a sad thing, thought I, to be thus barbarously treated, and hindered, besides, from going where I should be so welcome.

Her ladyship eat some soup, as did her kinsman; and then, as she was cutting up a chicken, said, with as little decency as goodness, 'If thou *longest*, my little dear, I will help thee to a pinion, or breast.'

'But, perhaps, child,' said her Jackey, 'thou likest the merry-thought:[303] shall I bring it thee?' And then laughed like an idiot, for all he is a lord's son, and may be a lord himself; being eldest son of Lord H. His mother was Lord Davers's sister; who, dying some years ago, he has received what education he has, from Lord Davers's direction. Poor wretch! for all his greatness! If I could then have gone up, I would have given you his picture. But for one of twenty-five, or twenty-six years of age, much about the age of my dear Mr B. he is a silly creature.

'Pamela,' said my lady, 'help me to a glass of wine. No, Worden, *you* shan't'; for she was offering to do it. 'I will have my Lady Bride confer that honour upon me; and then I shall see if she can *stand up*.' I was silent, and stirred not.

'Dost hear, *Chastity*?' said she: 'wilt thou help me to a glass of wine, when I bid thee? What! not stir! Then I'll come and help *thee* to one.'

Still I moved not; but, fanning myself, continued silent.

'When I have asked thee, Meek-one, *half a dozen questions to-gether*,' said she, 'I suppose thou wilt answer them *all at once*. Canst thou not find one word for me? Canst thou not find thy feet?'

I was so vexed, I bit out a piece of my fan, not knowing what I did; but still I said nothing, only fluttering it, and fanning myself.

'I believe,' said she, 'my next question will make up half a dozen; and then, Modest-one, I shall be entitled to an answer.'

Her nephew arose, and brought the bottle and glass. 'Come,' said he, 'Mrs Bride, be pleased to help her ladyship, and I will be your deputy.'

'Sir,' replied I, ' 'tis in a good hand; help my lady yourself.'

'Why, Creature,' said she, flying into a passion, 'dost thou think thyself above it? Insolence!' continued she, 'this moment, when I bid you, know your duty, and give me a glass of wine; or –'

I took a little spirit then. Thought I, I can but be beaten. 'If,' said I, 'to attend your ladyship at table, or even kneel at your feet, were required of me, as a token of respect to Lady Davers; and not as an insult to her brother, who has done me an honour that requires me to act a part not unworthy of his goodness to me, I would do it. But, as things are, I must say, I cannot.'

She seemed quite surprised, and looked now upon her kinsman, and then upon her woman.

'I'm astonished! quite astonished! Well then, I suppose you would have me conclude you to be my brother's wife; would you not?'

'Your ladyship,' said I, '*compels* me to say this.'

'But,' replied she, 'dost thou *thyself* think thou art so?'

'Silence,' said her kinsman, 'gives consent.[304] 'Tis plain enough she does. Shall I rise, madam, and pay my duty to my new aunt?'

'Tell me,' said my lady, 'what, in the name of impudence, possesses thee, to *dare* to look upon thyself as *my* sister?'

'Madam,' replied I, 'that is a question will better become your brother to answer, than me.'

She was rising in great wrath; but her woman said, 'Good your ladyship, you'll do yourself more harm than her; and if the poor girl has been deluded, as you have heard, with the sham-marriage, she will be more deserving of your ladyship's pity than anger.'

'True, Worden, very true,' said my lady; 'but there's no bearing the impudence of the creature.'

I would have gone out at the door; but her kinsman ran and set his back against it. I expected bad treatment from her pride, and violent temper; but this was worse than I could have thought of. And I said to him, 'Sir, when my master comes to know your rude behaviour, you will, perhaps, have cause to repent it.' I then went and sat down in the window again.

'Another challenge, by Gad!' said he; 'but I am glad she says her *master!* You see, madam, she herself does not believe she is married, and so has not been *so much* deluded as you think for.'

And coming to me with a barbarous air of insult, he said, kneeling on one knee before me, 'My new aunt, your *blessing*, or your *curse*, I care not which; but quickly give me one or other, that I may not lose my dinner!'

I gave him a most contemptuous look. 'Tinseled toy!' said I, (for he was laced[305] all over) 'twenty or thirty years hence, when you are *at age*, I shall know how to answer you better. Mean time, sport with your footmen, and not with me.'

I then removed to another window nearer the door, and he looked like the fool he is.

'Worden, Worden,' said my lady, 'this is not to be borne! Was ever the like heard! Is my kinsman and Lord Davers's to be thus used by such a wench?' And was coming to me. Indeed I began to be afraid; for I have but a poor heart, after all. But Mrs Jewkes, hearing high words, came in again, with the second course, and said, 'Pray your ladyship, don't discompose yourself. I am afraid this day's business will make matters wider than ever between your ladyship and your brother: for my master doats upon madam.'

'Woman,' said she, 'do thou be silent! Sure, I, that was born in this house, may have some privilege in it, without being talked to by the saucy servants in it!'

'I beg pardon, madam,' replied Mrs Jewkes; and turning to me, 'Madam,' said she, 'my master will take it very ill, if you make him wait for you.'

I again arose to go out; but my lady said, 'If it were only for *that* reason, she shan't go.'

She then went to the door. 'Woman,' said she, to Mrs Jewkes, shutting her out, 'come not in again till I call you'; and stepping to me, took my hand, saying, 'Find your legs, miss, if you please.'

I stood up. She tapped my cheek. 'How does that glowing face,' said she, 'shew thy rancorous heart, if thou daredst to speak out! But come this way.' And leading me to her chair, 'Stand there,' said she, 'and answer me a few questions, while I dine, and I'll dismiss thee, till I call thy impudent master to account; and then I'll have you face to face, and all this mystery of iniquity shall be unravelled; for, between you, I *will* come to the bottom of it.'

When she had sat down, I moved to the window on the other side the parlour, which looks into the private garden; and her woman said, 'Mrs Pamela, don't make my lady angry; stand by her ladyship, as she bids you.'

'Mrs Worden,' replied I, 'do you attend your *lady*'s commands, and lay not *yours* upon *me*.'

'Your pardon, sweet Mrs Pamela,' replied she: 'times are much altered with you, I assure you.'

'Lady Davers,' returned I, 'has a very good plea to be free in the house she was *born* in: but *you* may as well confine your freedom to the house in which you had your *breeding*.'

'Hey-day!' retorted she. 'This from you, Mrs Pamela! But since you provoke me, I'll tell you a piece of my mind.'

'Hush, hush! *good woman*,' said I, alluding to my lady's language to Mrs Jewkes; 'my lady wants not your assistance! Besides, I can't scold!'

The woman was ready to stutter with vexation; and her nephew laughed as if he would burst his sides; 'G—d— me, Worden,' said he, 'you had better let her alone to my lady here; for she will be too many for twenty such as you and I.'

And then he laughed again, and repeated, ' "I *can't scold*," quoth a! but, by Gad, miss, you can speak d—d spiteful words, I can tell you that! Poor Worden, poor Worden! 'Fore Gad, she's quite dumb-foundered!'

'Well, but, Pamela,' said my lady, 'come hither and tell me truly – Dost thou think thyself really married?'

'My good lady,' said I, and approached her chair, 'I'll answer *all* your commands, if you'll have patience with me: but I cannot bear to be used thus by this gentleman, and your ladyship's woman.'

'Child,' said she, 'thou art very impertinent to my kinsman; thou canst not be civil to *me*; and *my ladyship*'s woman is much thy betters. But that's not the thing! Dost thou think thou art really married?'

'I see, madam,' replied I, 'you are resolved not to be pleased with *any* answer I shall return: if I should say I am *not*, then your ladyship will call me hard names, and perhaps I should tell an untruth. If I should say, I *am*, your ladyship will ask me, how I have the impudence to be so; and will call it a sham-marriage.'

'I will,' said she, 'be answered more directly.'

'Why, madam, what does it signify what *I* think? Your ladyship will believe as you please.'

'But canst thou have the vanity, the pride, the folly,' said she, 'to think thyself actually married to *my* brother? He is no fool, child; and libertine enough of conscience; and thou art not the first in the list of his credulous harlots.'

'Well, well,' said I (in a violent flutter) 'I am easy and pleased with my lot, and pray, madam, let me continue to be so, as long as I can.'

'Pert wench! But I will have patience with thee, if possible. Dost thou not think I am concerned, that thou, a young creature, whom my mother loved so well, shouldst have cast thyself away, shouldst have suffered thyself to be deluded and undone, after such a noble stand that thou madest for so long a time?'

'I do not think myself deluded and undone, madam; and am as innocent and as virtuous as ever I was in my life.'

'Thou liest, child,' said she.

'So your ladyship told me *twice* before!'

She gave my hand a slap for this; and I made a low curtsey; and retiring, said, 'I humbly thank your ladyship!' But I could not refrain tears; and added, 'Your brother, madam, however, won't thank your ladyship for this usage of me, though *I* do.'

'Come a little nearer me, my dear,' said she, 'and thou shalt have a little more than *that* to tell him of, if thou thinkest thou hast not made mischief enough already between a sister and brother. But, child, if he were here, I would serve thee worse, and him too.'

'I wish he was,' said I.

'Dost thou threaten me, mischief-maker, and insolent as thou art?'

'Now, pray, madam,' said I, (but got a little further off) 'be pleased to reflect upon all that you have said to me, since I have had the *honour*, or rather *misfortune*, to come into your presence; whether you have said *one* thing befitting your ladyship's degree to me, even supposing I was the wench, and the creature, you take me to be?'

'Come hither, my pert dear,' replied she, 'come but within my reach for *one* moment, and I'll answer thee as thou deservest.'

To be sure she meant to box my ears. But I should be unworthy of my happy lot, if I could not shew some spirit.

When the cloth was taken away, I said, 'I suppose I may now depart your presence, madam?'

'I suppose *not*,' said she. 'Why, I'll lay thee a wager, child, thy stomach's too full to eat, and so thou may'st fast till thy mannerly [306] master comes home.'

'Pray your ladyship,' said her woman, 'let the *poor girl* sit down at table with Mrs Jewkes and *me*.'

'You are very kind, Mrs Worden,' replied I; 'but times, as you said, are much altered with me. I have been of late so much honoured by better company, that I can't stoop to your's.'

'Was ever such confidence!' said my lady.

'Poor Worden! poor Worden!' said her kinsman; 'why, she beats you quite out of the pit!'[307]

'Will your ladyship,' said I, 'be so good as to tell me how long I am to stay? For you will please to see by *that* letter, that I am obliged to attend my master's commands.' And so I gave her her brother's letter, written from Mr Carlton's, which I thought would make her use me better, as she might judge by it of the honour done me by him.

'Ay,' said she, 'this is my *worthy* brother's hand: it is directed to Mrs Andrews. That's to *you*, I suppose, child! Thy name will be always Andrews for him, I am sure!' And so she read on, making remarks as she went along, in this manner:

' "*My dearest love*," [DEAREST LOVE!' looking at me, from head to foot. 'What! this to thy baby-face! – DEAREST LOVE. – Out upon it! I shall never bear to hear those words again! Pray, Jackey, bid Lord Davers never call *me* dearest love.] "*as I desired you not to expect me, if I returned not by eleven last night, I hope*" [Lord be good unto me! Mind Jackey! – I HOPE] *"my absence did not discompose you."* [Who can bear this! A confession, Jackey! a plain confession!' 'And so it is, madam! As clear to me as the sun!' looking at me till he dashed me. And then laughing with *such* an impudent look. I hated him at the moment. 'Well, but *did it discompose his dearest love!*' said my lady. '*Wert* thou *discomposed*, dearest love? Vastly tender! A creature, in thy way of life, is more complaisantly treated than an honest wife: but mark the end of it!']

[She read to herself, till she came to the following words] ' *"I could have wished"* [Pr'ythee, Jackey, mind this, *"I could have wished"*] *"WE had not engaged* OURSELVES*"* [WE and OURSELVES - MY brother and THEE, reptile, put together! Give me patience!] *"to Sir Simon and the good neighbourhood for this night."* [And does Sir Simon, and the good neighbourhood, permit thy visits, child? They shall have none from me, I assure them.] *"But since the engagement must take place,"* [Mind, mind, Jackey] *"let me beg of you,"* [The wretch who could treat Lord Davers and me as he has done, to turn beggar to this creature! *"Let me beg of you"*] *"my dear,"* [My dear! I shall be sick before I get half through! Thou little witch! How hast thou brought this about? But I will read on.] *"to take the chariot,"* [And is the chariot ready? Thank Heaven, I am in time to save thee this presumption!] *"and go to Sir Simon's; the sooner in the day the more obliging"* [Say you so, brother? And can thy company, creature, *oblige Sir Simon* and the *good neighbourhood?*] *"to all your ad-"* [O Jackey, Jackey – sick – sick to death!] *"miring friends!"* ' [And away went the letter at my head. I would have stooped for it; but her Worden was too nimble for me, and put the letter again in to her lady's hands; who went on with her remarks.] ' *"I hope to join you there"* [Join *you* – Who? Pamela Andrews! A beggar's brat! Taken by my mother.' 'On charity, madam!' said I. 'I curtsey to the dear lady's memory for it. I can best bear this of all your ladyship's reflections. It is my glory!' 'Confidence! be silent. Dost thou glory in thy shame!' Thank God, thought I, I have a *truer* glory! And I was silent, proudly silent, my dear mother. ' *"I hope to join you there,"* proceeded she in reading] *"by your tea-time in the afternoon."* [So you are in very good time, child, an hour or two hence, to answer all your important *pre-engagements*. Now, Jackey, he would have been hanged before he would have wrote so complaisantly to a WIFE. No *admiring* friends would he have mentioned to a woman of birth and quality answerable to his own, after the first fortnight. Very evident to me how the case is. Is it not so to you, Jackey? To you, Worden?' 'Very true, madam,' said her woman. 'Clear as the sun,' said her nephew, sneering in my glowing face. 'Uncivil gentleman!' I muttered to myself: but still I was proud of my innocence; and I could the better be silent. My lady read on.] ' *"It will be six miles difference to me."* [Ah, wretched Pamela! Seest thou not that thy influence is already in the wane? Hadst thou kept thine innocence, and thy lover had been of thine own rank, sixty miles would have been no more than one to him. Thinkest thou that my brother's heart is to be held fast by that baby-face of thine? Poor wretch! How I pity thee!' I curtsied to her for her pity; but still in proud (because self-justified) silence. She read on.] ' *"And I know the good company will excuse dress on the occasion."* [Excuse dress! No doubt but they will. Any dress is good enough, I am sure, to appear in, to such company as *admire* thee, creature, for a companion, in thy ruined state! But, Jackey, Jackey! More fine things still!] *"I count every hour of this little absence for a day!"* [There's for you! Let me repeat it: *"I count every hour of this little absence for a day!"* Mind too the non-sense of the good man! One may see love is a new thing to him. Here is a very tedious time gone since he saw his dear; no less than, according to his amorous calculation, a dozen days and nights at least! And yet, TEDIOUS as it is, it is but a LITTLE ABSENCE. Well said, my good, accurate, and consistent brother. But wise men in love are always the greatest simpletons! But now comes the reason, *why* this LITTLE absence, which, at the same time, is so GREAT an ABSENCE, is so *tedious:*] *"For I am,"* [Ay, now for it!] *"with the* UTMOST *sincerity, my dearest love,"* [Out upon it! DEAREST LOVE, again!] *"For ever yours!"* [But, brother, thou liest! Thou know'st thou dost. And, so, my good Miss Andrews, or what shall I call you? Your *dearest love* will be *for ever yours*! And hast thou the vanity to believe this? But stay, here is a postscript. The poor man knew not when to have done to his *dearest love*. He's sadly in for't, truly! Why, *his dearest love*,' looking at me, 'you are mighty happy in such a lover!] *"If you could dine with Sir Simon and the ladies,"* [Cry your mercy, my *dearest love*, now comes the *pre-engagement*!] *"it would be a freedom"* [A freedom with a witness!] *"they would be delighted with."* [Wretched flatterers, and mean-spirited creatures,

if they are.] *"And the more, as they expect not such a favour."*
[*Favour!* Jackey! *Favour!* O thou poor painted doll! But I *will* have
patience, if possible! Thy company will indeed be a favour to those
who can be delighted with it.][308]

'Well, so much for this kind letter! Worden, you may go to
dinner with Fat-face!'

Her woman retired. 'But you see, miss,' proceeded my lady to
me, 'you cannot honour this *admiring* company with this *little-
expected*, and, but in complaisance to *his* folly, I dare say, *little-
desired freedom*. And indeed I cannot forbear *admiring* thee so much
myself, my *dearest love*, that I will not spare thee at all, this whole
evening.'

You see that I had shewn her my letter to very little purpose.
Indeed, I repented my giving it into her hands several times as she
read.

'Well then,' said I, 'I hope your ladyship will give me leave to
send my excuses to your good brother, and let him know that your
ladyship is come, and is so fond of me, that you will not let me
leave you.'

'Insolent creature!' said she; 'and wantest thou my *good*
brother, as thou callest him, to come and quarrel with his sister
on thy account? But thou shalt not stir from my presence; and
I would now ask thee, what it is thou meantest by shewing me this
letter?'

'To shew your ladyship,' replied I, 'how I was engaged for this
day and evening.'

'And for nothing else?' asked she.

'If your ladyship can collect from it any other circumstances, I
might hope not to be the *worse* treated for them.'

Her eyes sparkled with indignation. She took my hand, and said,
grasping it very hard, 'I know, confident creature, that you shewed
it me to insult me. You shewed it me, to let me see, that he could be
civiller to a beggar-born, than to me, or to my good Lord Davers.
You shewed it me, as if you would have me be as credulous a fool
as yourself, to believe you are married, when I know the whole
trick of it, and have reason to believe *you* know it. You shewed it
me, in short, to upbraid me with his stooping to such painted dirt,
to the disgrace of a family, ancient and unsullied beyond most in

the kingdom. And now will I give thee an hundred guineas for one bold word, that I may fell thee at my foot.'

This fearful menace, and her fiery eyes, and rageful countenance, made me lose all my courage.

I wept. 'Good your ladyship,' said I, 'pity me. Indeed I am honest; indeed I am virtuous; indeed I would not do a bad thing for the world.'

'Though I know,' said she, 'the whole trick of thy pretended marriage, and thy foolish ring, and all the rest of the wicked nonsense; yet I should not have patience with thee, if thou shouldst but offer to let me know thy vanity prompts thee to *believe* thou art married to *my* brother! So take care, Pamela; take care, beggar's brat; take care.'

'Spare, madam, I beseech you, my parents. They are honest: they are good: it is no crime to be poor. They were once in a very creditable way: they never were beggars. Misfortunes may attend the highest. I can bear the cruellest imputations on myself; but upon such honest, industrious parents, who have passed through the greatest trials, without being beholden to any thing but God's blessing, and their own hard labour; I cannot bear reflection.'

'What! art thou setting up for a family,[309] creature as thou art? God give me patience! I suppose my brother's folly, and his wickedness together, will, in a little while, occasion a search at the Herald's Office,[310] to set out thy wretched obscurity. Provoke me, Pamela; I desire thou wilt. One hundred guineas will I give thee, to say but thou *thinkest* thou art married to *my* brother.'

'Your ladyship, I hope, won't kill me. And since nothing I can say will please you; and your ladyship is resolved to be angry with me, let me beg of you to do whatever you design by me, and suffer me to depart your presence!'

She slapt my hand, and reached to box my ear; but Mrs Jewkes, and her woman, hearkening without, they both came in at that instant; and Mrs Jewkes said, pushing herself in between us, 'Your ladyship knows not what you do: indeed you don't. My master would never forgive me, if I suffered, in his house, one he so dearly loves, to be so used; and it must *not* be, though you are Lady Davers.'

Her woman too interposed, and told her, I was not worth her ladyship's anger. But my lady was like a person beside herself.

I offered to go out, but her kinsman again set his back against the door, and put his hand to his sword, and said, I should not go, till Lady Davers permitted it. He drew it half-way, and I was so terrified, that I cried out, 'O the sword! the sword!' And, not knowing what I did, ran to my lady, and clasped my arms about her, forgetting, just then, how much she was my enemy; and said, sinking on my knees, 'Defend me, good your ladyship! The sword! the sword!' Mrs Jewkes said, 'My lady will fall into fits.' But Lady Davers was herself so startled at the matter being carried so far, that she did not mind her words, and said, 'Jackey, don't draw your sword! You see, violent as her spirit is, she is but a coward.

'Come,' said she, 'be comforted: I will try to overcome my anger, and will pity you. So, wench, rise up, and don't be foolish.' Mrs Jewkes held her salts to my nose. I did not faint. And my lady said, 'Jewkes, if *you* wish to be forgiven, leave Pamela and me by ourselves; and, Jackey, do you withdraw; only you, Worden, stay.'

I sat down in the window, trembling like a coward, as her ladyship called me, and as I am.

'You should not sit in my lady's presence, Mrs Pamela,' again said her woman.

'Yes, let her sit, till she is a little recovered,' replied my lady. She sat down over-against me. 'To be sure, Pamela,' said she, 'you have been very provoking with your tongue, to be sure you have, as well to my nephew, (who is a man of quality too) as to me.' And, palliating her cruel usage, conscious she had carried the matter too far, she wanted to lay the fault upon me: 'Own,' said she, 'you have been very saucy, and beg my pardon, and beg Jackey's pardon; and I will try to pity you: for you would have been a sweet girl, after all, if you had but kept your innocence.'

' 'Tis injurious to me, madam,' said I, 'to imagine I have not!' 'Have you not been a-bed with my brother?' said she. 'Tell me that.'

'Your ladyship,' replied I, 'asks your questions in a strange way, and in strange words!'

'Oh! your delicacy is wounded, I suppose, by my plain question! This niceness will soon leave thee, wench: it will indeed. But answer me directly.'

'Then your ladyship's next question,' said I, 'will be – Am I married? And you won't bear my answer to that – and will beat me again.'

'I have not beat you yet; have I, Worden? So you want to make out a story, do you? But, indeed, I cannot bear thou shouldst so much as *think* thou art *my* sister. I know the whole trick of it; and so, 'tis my opinion, dost thou. It is only thy little cunning, to serve for a cloak to thy yielding. Pr'ythee, pr'ythee, wench, thou seest I know the world a little; know it almost as much at thirty-two, as thou dost at sixteen.'[311]

I arose from the window, and walking to the other end of the room, 'Beat me again, if you please,' said I; 'but I must tell your ladyship, I scorn your words, and am as much married as your ladyship!'

At that she ran to me, but her woman interposed again. 'Let the vain creature go from your presence, madam,' said she. 'She is not worthy to be in it. She will but vex your ladyship.'

'Stand away, Worden,' said my lady. 'That is an assertion that I would not take from my brother. I can't bear it. As much married as I? Is that to be borne?'

'But if the creature believes she is, madam,' said her woman, 'she is to be as much pitied for her credulity, as despised for her vanity.'

I was in hopes to have slipped out at the door; but she caught hold of my gown, and pulled me back. 'Pray, your ladyship,' said I, very much afraid of her, (for I have a strange notion of the fury of a woman of quality when provoked) 'don't kill me! I have done no harm.' She locked the door, and put the key in her pocket. And I, seeing Mrs Jewkes before the window, lifted up the sash, and said, 'Mrs Jewkes, I believe it would be best for the chariot to go to your master, and let him know, that Lady Davers is here; and I cannot leave her ladyship.'

She was resolved to be displeased, let me say what I would.

'No, no,' said she; 'he'll then think, that I make the creature my companion, and know not how to part with her.'

'I thought your ladyship,' replied I, 'could not have taken exceptions at this message.'

'Thou knowest nothing, wench,' said she, 'of what belongs to people of condition: how shouldst thou?'

Nor, thought I, do I desire it at this rate.

'What shall I say, madam, to your brother?'

'Nothing at all,' replied she; 'let him expect his *dearest love*, and be disappointed; it is but adding a few more *hours*, and every one will be *a day* in his amorous account.'

Mrs Jewkes coming nearer me, and my lady walking about the room, being then at the end, I whispered, 'Let Robert stay at the elms; I'll have a struggle for't by-and-by.'

'*As much married as I!*' repeated she. 'The insolence of the creature!' Talking to herself, to her woman, and now-and-then to me, as she walked; but seeing I could not please her, I thought I had better be silent.

And then it was, 'Am I not worthy of an answer?'

'If I speak,' replied I, 'your ladyship is angry with me, though it be ever so respectfully: would to Heaven I knew how to please your ladyship!'

'Confess the truth,' answered she, 'that thou art an undone creature; hast been in bed with thy master; and art sorry for it, and for the mischief thou hast caused between him and me; and then I will pity thee, and persuade him to pack thee off, with a hundred or two of guineas; and some honest farmer may patch up thy shame, for the sake of the money: or, if nobody will have thee, thou must vow penitence, and be as humble as I once thought thee.'

I was quite sick at heart, at all this passionate extravagance, and the more as I was afraid of incurring displeasure, by not being where I was expected: and seeing it was no hard matter to get out of the window, into the front-yard, the parlour floor being almost even with the yard, I resolved to attempt it; and to have a fair run for it. Accordingly, having seen my lady at the other end of the room, in her walks backward and forward, and having not pulled down the sash, which I put up when I spoke to Mrs Jewkes, I got upon the seat, and whipped out in a moment, and ran away as fast as I could; my lady at one window, and her woman at another, calling after me to return.

Two of her servants appeared at her crying out; and she bidding them stop me, I said, 'Touch me at your peril, fellows!' But their lady's commands would have prevailed, had not Mr Colbrand, who, it seems, had been ordered by Mrs Jewkes, when she saw how I was treated, to be within call, come up, and put on one of his deadly fierce looks, the only time, I thought, it ever became him, and said, He would *chine*[312] the man, (that was his word) who offered to touch his lady; and so he ran alongside of me; and I heard my lady say, 'The creature flies like a bird.' Indeed, Mr Colbrand, with his huge strides, could hardly keep pace with me. I never stopped till I got to the chariot. Robert had got down from his seat, seeing me running at a distance, and held the door in his hand, with the step ready down; and in I jumped, without touching the step, saying, 'Drive me, drive me, as fast as you can, out of my lady's reach!' He mounted his seat, and Colbrand said, 'Don't be frightened, madam; nobody shall hurt you.' He shut the door, and away Robert drove; but I was quite out of breath, and did not recover it, and my fright, all the way.

Mr Colbrand was so kind (but I did not know it till the chariot stopped at Sir Simon's) to step up behind it, lest, as he said, Lady Davers should send after me: and he told Mrs Jewkes, when he got home, that he never saw such a runner in his life.

This cruel lady detained me till about six o'clock. Miss Darnford, as soon as the chariot stopped, ran out to me. 'Welcome! ten times welcome, my dear!' said she: 'but you'll be beat, I can tell you; for Mr B. has been here these two hours, and is very angry with you.'

'That's hard indeed!' said I. 'Indeed I can't afford it!' hardly knowing what I said, having not recovered my fright. 'Let me sit down, any where: I have been hardly treated.'

I sat down, and was quite sick with the hurry of my spirits, and leaned upon her arm.

'Your lord and master,' said she, 'came in very moody; and when he had staid an hour, and you not come, he began to fret, and said, He did not expect so little complaisance from you. And he is now sat down, with great persuasions, to a game at loo.[313] Come, you must make your appearance, lady fair; for he's too sullen to attend you, I doubt.'

'You have no strangers, have you, madam?' asked I. 'Only two women relations from Stamford,' replied she, 'and an humble servant of one of them.' 'Only all the world, Miss Darnford!' replied I: 'what shall I do? I cannot bear his anger.'

Just as I had said so, in came Lady Darnford and Mrs Jones, to chide me, as they said, for not coming sooner. And before I could speak, came in Mr B. I ran to him. 'How do you, Pamela?' said he, and saluted me, with a little more formality than I could well bear. 'I expected, my dear, that you would have been here to dinner.'

'Dear sir,' said I, 'pray, pray, hear me; and then you'll pity me! Mrs Jewkes will tell you, that as soon as I had read your kind letter, I said I would obey you, and come to dinner with these good ladies; and prepared myself instantly to attend them.' 'Look you, stately one,' said Miss Darnford, 'did I not tell you, that something must have happened? O these tyrants! these men!'

'Why, what hindered you, my dear? Give yourself time; you seem out of breath.' 'Out of breath, sir! well I may: for, just as I was ready to come away, who should drive into the court-yard, but Lady Davers!' 'Lady Davers! Nay, then, my dear,' said he, and saluted me more tenderly, 'have you had a trial indeed, from one of the haughtiest women in England, though my sister! For she, too, my Pamela, was spoiled by my mother! But have you seen her?'

'Yes, sir, and more than *seen* her!' 'Why, *sure*,' said he, 'she has not had the insolence –' 'But tell me, sir,' interrupted I, 'that you forgive me; for indeed I could not come sooner: do you and these good ladies but excuse me; and I'll tell you all another time.'

'But say, my dear, was Lady Davers insolent to you? Did Lady Davers offer –' 'Lady Davers, sir,' interrupted I, 'is your sister, and I must not tell you all; but she has treated me a little severely.'

'Did you tell her,' said he, 'you were married?' 'Yes, sir, I did at last: but she will have it, 'tis a sham-marriage, and that I am a vile creature: and she was ready to beat me, when I said so; for she could not have patience, she said, that I should be deemed her sister.'

'How unlucky it was,' replied he, 'that I was not at home! Why did you not send to me here?' 'Send, sir! I was kept prisoner by force. They would not let me stir, or do you think I would have been hindered from obeying you? Nay, I told them, that I had a pre-engagement; but she ridiculed me, and said, "Waiting-wenches talk of pre-engagements!" and then I shewed her your kind letter! And she made a thousand remarks upon it, and made me wish I had kept it to myself. In short, whatever I could do or say, there was no pleasing her; and I was a *creature*, a *wench*, and all that was naught. But I must entreat you not to be angry with her on my account.'

'Well, but,' said he, 'I suppose she hardly asked you to dine with *her*; for she came before dinner, I presume, if it was soon after you had my letter?' 'Dine with my *lady*! No, indeed! Why, she would have made me wait at table upon her, with her woman, because she would not expose herself and me by her anger, before the men-servants; which, you know, sir, was very considerate in her lady-ship.'

'Well,' said he, 'but *did* you wait at table upon her?' 'Would you have had me, sir?' 'Only, Pamela,' replied he, 'I hope you knew what belonged to your character, as my wife.' 'I refused to wait at table on that consideration, sir,' said I, 'as my lady *must* intend an indignity by it. Else I could have waited on my knees upon your sister.'

He expressed his approbation of my conduct; and said, She was an insolent woman, and should dearly repent her usage of me. 'But, sir, she is to be excused,' said I, 'because she will not believe that I am indeed married: be not, therefore, very angry at her ladyship.'

Lady Darnford went in to the company, and told them the cause of my detention; for, it seems, my dear master *loved me too well* to keep to *himself* the disappointment my not being here to receive him, was to him; and they had all given the two Miss Boroughs's, and Mr Perry, the Stamford guests, such a character of me as made them impatient to see me.

'Whom, my dear,' said Mr B., 'had my sister with her, besides her woman?' 'Her nephew, sir.'

'That nephew is a coxcomb,' replied he: 'how did *he* behave to you?' 'Not extraordinarily well, sir.'

'By heaven!' resumed he, 'if I knew he behaved unhandsomely to my love, I will send him home to his uncle without his ears.' 'Indeed, sir,' returned I, 'I was even with him, for I thought I ought not to bear with him as with her ladyship.'

'But, sure, my dear, you might have got away, when you went to your own dinner?' 'Indeed, sir, her ladyship locked me in, and would not let me stir.' 'You have not dined then?' 'No, indeed, sir, nor had a stomach to dine.' 'But, then, how got you away at last?'

I told him briefly how, and the kind part that not only Mr Col-brand, but Mrs Jewkes likewise, took on the occasion.

He called me sweet creature, and said, I loved to speak well of every body. 'But come,' said he, 'we will now join the company, and try to forget all you have suffered, for two or three hours; and resume the subject as we go home.'

'But you forgive me, sir, and are not angry?'

'Forgive you, my dear! I hope you forgive me! I shall never make you amends for what you have suffered *from* me, and *for* me!' And with those words he led me in to the company.

He very kindly presented me to the two stranger ladies, and the gentleman; and Sir Simon, who was at cards, rose from table, and saluted me: 'Adad! madam,' said he, 'I'm glad to see you here. What, it seems, you have been a prisoner! 'Tis well you was, or Mr B. and I should have sat in judgment upon you, and condemned you to a fearful punishment for your first crime of *Læsæ Majestatis*.' [I had this explained to me afterwards, as a sort of treason against my liege lord and husband.] 'We husbands, in this neighbourhood,' proceeded he, 'are resolved to turn over a new leaf with our wives, and *your* lord and master shall shew us the way, I can tell you. But I see by your eyes, my sweet culprit,' added he, 'and by your heightened complexion, that you have had sour sauce to your sweet meat.'

'I think we are obliged to our lovely guest, at last,' said Miss Darnford; 'for she was forced to jump out at a window to come to us.' 'Indeed!' said Mrs Peters. And my master's back being turned, 'Lady Davers,' added she, 'when a maiden, was always passionate; but very good when her anger was over. She would make nothing of slapping her maids about, and begging their pardons afterwards, if they took it patiently; otherwise she used to say, The *creatures* were even with her.'

'All my fear is,' said I, 'that I took too impatiently, though so much provoked, her treatment of me: but I should have been unworthy of the rank I am raised to, had I not shewn some spirit. Some I did shew for her brother's sake, and have reason to think myself happy, that I escaped a good cuffing.'

Miss Boroughs, and her sister, and Mr Perry, seemed to look at me with pleasure; and Miss Darnford, addressing herself to me, was pleased to say, 'These, our friends, Mrs B. are strangely admiring you. Mr Perry says, you are the loveliest woman he ever saw; and says it to his own mistress's face, too, I assure you!' 'If he said otherwise,' answered Miss Boroughs, 'I should think he greatly flattered me.'

I curtseyed to her.

Miss Nanny Boroughs made me a still higher compliment; and I said, 'Lady Davers was very cruel to keep me from such company.'

'It is our loss, my dear neighbour,' said Miss Darnford. 'I'll allow it,' returned I, 'in degree; for you have all been deprived, several hours, of an humble admirer.'

Mr Perry attributed to me high things: and mentioning the word *shining* – 'O sir!' said I, (my master coming up just then, but not in his hearing) 'mine is but a borrowed shine, like that of the moon: here is the sun, to whose fervent generosity I owe all the faint lustre that your goodness is pleased to look upon with so much kind distinction.'

'Mr B.,' said Mr Perry, 'I will pronounce you the happiest man in England.'

'I know not your subject,' said the dear generous man; 'but if you believe me so, for a *single* instance of this dear girl's goodness, what must I think, who experience it on every occasion? I assure you, that my Pamela's *person*, lovely as you see it, is far short of her *mind*. It was indeed her person that first attracted me, and made me her *lover*: but they were the beauties of her mind, that made me her *husband*.'

'Well,' said Mr Perry, very politely, 'excellent as your lady is, I know not the man who could deserve her, but that one, who says such just and such fine things of her.'

I was abashed; and took Miss Darnford's hand, and whisperingly said to her, 'Save me, dear madam, by your sweet example, from my rising pride. Could I deserve half these kind things, what a happy creature should I be!'

The greatest part of the company having sat down at loo, my *master*, being pressed, (how can I forbear calling him my master?) consented to play a rubbers at whist;[314] though he said, he had rather be excused, having been up all night. I asked how his friend did. 'We will talk of poor Mr Carlton,' said he, 'another time.' This, and the solemnity he spoke it with, made me fear the poor gentleman was no more: as indeed it proved.

We cast in,[315] and Miss Boroughs and my master were together, and Mr Perry and I. I had all four honours[316] the first time, and we were up at one deal.[317] 'An honourable hand, Pamela,' said my master, '*should* go with an honourable heart; but you would not have been up, if a knave had not been one.' 'Whist, sir,' said Mr Perry, 'you know was a court game originally; and the knave, I suppose, signified always the prime-minister.'

This introduced a pretty conversation, though a brief one, in relation to the game at whist. Mr B. compared it to the English constitution. He considered, he said, the *ace* as the laws of the land; the supreme welfare of the people. 'We see,' said he, 'that the plain, honest-looking *ace*, is above and wins the king, the queen, and the wily knave. But, by my Pamela's hand, we may observe what an advantage accrues when all the court-cards get together, and are acted by one mind.'

Mr Perry having in the conversation, observed, that it is an allowed maxim in our laws, that the king can do no wrong, 'Indeed,' said Mr B., 'we make that compliment to our kings indiscriminately; and it is well to do so, because the royal character is sacred; and because it should remind a prince of what is expected from him: but if the force of example be considered, the compliment should be paid only to a sovereign who is a good man, as well as a good prince; since a good master generally, through all degrees of men, makes good servants.'

Supper was brought in sooner on my account, because I had had no dinner; and there passed very agreeable compliments on the occasion.

Mrs Jones brought up the discourse about Lady Davers again; and my master said, 'I fear, Pamela, you have been more hardly used than you'll own. I know my sister's temper too well, to believe she could be over-civil to you, especially as it happened so unluckily that I was from home. If,' added he, 'she had no pique to *you*, my dear, yet what has passed between *her* and *me*, has so exasperated her, that I know she would have quarrelled with my horse, if she thought I valued it, and nothing else was in her way.

'I know, my dear,' continued he, 'she came on purpose to quarrel. The treatment I gave to her lord's letter must have greatly incensed her. What sort of language had she for me, Pamela?' 'Only, sir, her *well-mannered brother*, and such like.'

Mrs Jones, and Mrs Peters, said, That as Lady Davers's violent temper, and her many good qualities, were equally known to the neighbours present; as Mr B. would expect to hear what her treatment of me had been, when he got home, when perhaps there would not be any mediators between my lady and him present; and as they presumed this would be the last trial I should meet with, they wished they might be favoured with the particulars; making a compliment to my manner. Lady Darnford pleaded the curiosity and attention of Mr Perry and the Miss Boroughs's, who having heard a part of the story, wished, as they had whispered her, to hear the rest; and Mr B. being as impatient to know if I had suffered any personal indignity, I, by his command, related all that had passed, as I have written to you, my dear parents; only palliating her violence, by owning sometimes the sauciness of my answers; and the provocation I gave her by once saying, that I was as much married as her ladyship; and by mentioning her great concern for my credulity and supposed forfeited innocence; insisting that my marriage was a sham-marriage; and my ring a mere grimace, in order to cloak my yielding.

He expressed high displeasure, however, at her slapping my hand; and at her intending farther violence, had it not been for the interposition of her woman and Mrs Jewkes; the latter of whom I praised for her behaviour on the occasion. This generosity, as it was called, got me many applauses, Mr B.'s in particular. And I was the less scrupulous in my relation, from the hint of Mrs Peters and Mrs Jones, that it was better to tell the worst, that his resentment might be weakened when he came face to face with Lady Davers; when all her violence might have come out, and no pacifiers, as now, present; for her ladyship wants not the respect of this neighbourhood, though every one blamed her for the way she always unhappily gave to her passionate temper. And what made me *still* the less earnest to disguise the truth, was, that he once said, when I was shy of telling him the worst, 'Be not afraid, my dear, to acquaint me with all you suffered from my sister's violence. I must love her, after all. I know she comes with a view to reconciliation; but it must be through a hearty quarrel: she can shew a great deal of sunshine; but it must be preceded by a storm.'

Mr Peters, on this occasion, with a kind view to mollify Mr B., said, 'I am pleased, sir, to see, that you can thus, like a brother, allow for your sister's failings; yet do justice to the merit of the most amiable of wives.'

To this Mr B. answered (which yet farther encouraged me in telling all that had passed), 'By all that's good, Mr Peters, I would present my sister with jewels to the value of a thousand pounds, if she would kindly take my Pamela by the hand, wish her joy, and call her sister! And yet I should be unworthy of the dear creature that smiles upon me there, if it was not principally for *her* sake, and for the pleasure it would give *her*, that I say this.'

I bowed to him as I sat; but could not speak: my eyes were filled with tears of gratitude: and all the company, with one voice, blessed him, and praised me. And upon my disclaiming a right to this extraordinary compliment, Mrs Jones was pleased to say, 'My dear Mrs B., you deserve more than I can express; for to all who know your story, you must appear to be a matchless person.'

Lady Darnford added, 'You are an ornament to our sex, my dear; and your virtue, though Mr B. is so kind and generous a husband, as we see him, has met with no more than its due reward. And God long bless you together!'

'You are,' said my dearest Mr B., 'very good to me, ladies. I have offended extremely, by trials glorious to my Pamela, but disgraceful to myself; and I shall not think I deserve her, till I can bring my manners to a conformity with hers.'

O my dear father and mother! What a happy creature am I! I owe it all to God's grace, and to your and my good lady's instructions. To these let me always look back with grateful acknowledgments, that I may not impute to myself my present happiness, and be proud.

On my dear Mr B.'s pitying me, when I related some of her ladyship's charges upon me, of having been deluded, of art, of design, and of being a lost creature: 'O sir,' said I, 'how much easier sat upon me these charges, heavy as they were, than they would have done, had they been just! Then would they have quite broken my heart. These reproaches, added to my own guilt, would have made me truly wretched!'

Lady Darnford, at whose right-hand I sat, snatched my hand in a kind of rapture; and called me an exemplar for all my sex. Mr Peters said very handsome things: so did Mr Perry; and Sir Simon, his eyes glistening, said to my master, 'Why, neighbour, neighbour, by my troth, this is excellent! There is certainly something in virtue, that we had not well considered. On my soul, there has been but one angel come down for these thousand years, and you have got her.'

My master was so good as to applaud me for my whole behaviour; and particularly for my refusing to wait upon her at table; and then enquiring after the particulars of my escape; I thus proceeded: 'I saw nothing was to be done; and I feared, sir, you would wonder at my stay, and be angry; and I watched my opportunity, till my lady, who was walking about the room, was at the further end; and the parlour being, as you know, sir, a ground-floor, I jumped out of the window, and ran for it.

'Her ladyship called after me; so did her woman; and I heard her say, I flew like a bird; and she called to two of her servants, in sight, to stop me; but I said, "Touch me at your peril, fellows": and Mr Colbrand, having been planted at hand by Mrs Jewkes, put on a fierce look, cocked his hat with one hand, and put the other on his sword, and said, he would chine the man who offered to touch me. And he ran along-side of me, and could hardly keep pace with me: And here, my dear sir,' concluded I, 'I am, at yours and the good company's service.'

They were highly pleased with my relation; and my master said, he was glad Mrs Jewkes and Colbrand behaved so well.

'My sister,' said he, 'was always passionate. My mother had enough to do with us both. For we neither of us wanted spirit. When I was a boy, I never came home from school or college for a few days, but though we longed to see each other before, yet, ere the first day was over, we quarrelled: for she, being seven years older than I, was always for domineering over me, and I could not bear it. I used, on her frequently quarrelling with the maids, and being always at a word and a blow with them, to call her Captain *Bab.* (Her name is Barbara.) In my Lord Davers's courtship of her, my mother has made up quarrels between them three times in a day; and I used to tell her, she would certainly beat her husband, marry whom she would, if he did not break her spirit. Yet has she,' continued he, 'very good qualities. She was a dutiful daughter; is a good wife, for a managing one; she is bountiful to her servants, firm in her friendships, charitable to the poor, and, I believe, never any sister better loved a brother, than she me: and yet, she always delighted to vex and teaze me; and as I would bear a resentment longer than she, she would be one moment the most provoking creature in the world, and the next would do any thing to be forgiven. Indeed I have made her, when she was the aggressor, follow me all over the house and garden to be upon good terms with me. But my marriage piques her the more, because she had found out a match for me, with a woman of quality, and had set her heart upon bringing it to effect. She had even proceeded far in it, without my knowledge; and cannot therefore bear the thoughts of my being now married, and to her mother's waiting-maid too, as she reminds my Pamela.

'This is the whole case,' said he; 'and allowing for the pride and violence of her spirit, and that she knows not the excellencies of my dear girl, she is a little to be allowed for: though never fear, my Pamela, but that I, who never had a struggle with her, wherein I did not get the better, will do you justice, and myself too.'

This account of Lady Davers pleased every body; and was far from being to her disadvantage in the main. I would do any thing in the world to have the honour to be in her good graces: yet I fear that will never be brought about.

When I had concluded my story, nothing would serve Miss Darnford, and Miss Boroughs, but we must have a dance; and Mr Peters urged it forward, proposing himself to take the violin, of which he is a master.

My dear Mr B., though in his riding-dress, danced with Miss Boroughs. He is noted for a fine dancer, and had every one's praises.

Sir Simon, for a man of his years, danced well. He took me out. In his free way he said, that I was fitter to dance with a younger man; and would have it, that as my master and I were the best dancers, we should dance once together *before* folks; as the odd gentleman expressed himself. Mr B. obliged him, and took me out. He afterwards danced with Miss Darnford; who far, very far surpassed me.[318]

We left the company, to their great regret, at about eleven. It was twelve before we got home.

Mrs Jewkes told us, that Lady Davers sat up till eleven; and often expressed her impatience for our return; threatening us both. I was very glad to hear she was retired to rest. She had expressed, it seems, a good deal of vexation, that I had escaped her; and was a little apprehensive of the report I should make of her treatment of me. She asked Mrs Jewkes, if she thought I was really married? And Mrs Jewkes answering her in the affirmative, she fell into a passion; and said, 'Begone, bold woman! I cannot bear thee: see not my face till I send for thee. Thou hast been very impudent to me once or twice to-day already, and art now worse than ever.'

She sent for her at supper-time: 'I have another question to ask thee, woman,' said she, 'and answer me, *Yes*, if thou darest.' (Was ever any thing so odd!) 'Why then,' said Mrs Jewkes, 'I will say, *No*, before your ladyship speaks.' Lady Davers called her *Insolence* and *Assurance*; and said, 'Begone, bold woman, as thou art! But yet come hither: dost thou know if that young harlot is to lie with my brother to-night?'

Mrs Jewkes said, she knew not what to answer, because she had threatened her, if she said, *Yes*. 'I *will* know the bottom of this iniquity,' proceeded my lady. 'I suppose they will not have so much impudence as to sleep in one room while I am in the house; but I dare say they have been bed-fellows.

'I will lie to-night,' said she, 'in the room I was born in; so get that bed ready.' That room being our bed-chamber, Mrs Jewkes, after some hesitation, replied, 'Madam, my master lies there, and I have not the key.' 'I believe, woman,' said she, 'thou tellest me a story.' 'Indeed, madam,' returned she, 'I do not.' And yet she did; but was afraid, she said, that her ladyship would beat her, if she went up, and found, by some of my clothes there, how it was.

'I will then,' resumed my lady, 'lie in the best room, as it is called; and Jackey shall lie in the little green-room. Hast thou got the keys of those, Fat-face?' 'I have, madam; and will order them to be made ready.'

'And where dost thou lay *thy* pursy sides?' asked she. 'Up two pairs of stairs, madam, next the garden.' 'And where lies the young harlotry?' 'Sometimes with me, madam.' 'And sometimes with thy virtuous master, I suppose? Hay, woman! what sayest thou?' 'I must not speak,' replied Mrs Jewkes. 'Well, thou *may'st* go; thou hast the air of a secret-keeper[319] of that sort: I dare say thou'lt set the good work forward most cordially.'

'Poor Mrs Jewkes!' said my master, and laughed heartily.

'Dear sir,' said I, 'pray, let me in the morning lock myself up in the closet, as soon as you rise; and not be called down on any account. And I will employ myself about my journal, while these things are in my head.' 'Don't be afraid, my dear,' said he: 'am not I with you?'

Mrs Jewkes told her master that she pitied me for what I had undergone in the day; and I said, 'Well, Mrs Jewkes, that's all over, and past; and here I am safe in the best protection. But,

I am much obliged to you; and I thank you, for your part on the occasion.'

'I did not more than my duty,' replied she. 'Lady Davers was very violent. I believe, sir, I saved my lady once. But I was most vexed at the behaviour of her ladyship's kinsman.'

'Her kinsman's behaviour! Mrs Jewkes,' said my master eagerly, 'let me know what his behaviour was.'

'Foolishly impertinent in his words, that was all,' said I; 'and as I spared him not, there is no room for your displeasure, sir.'

'How behaved her woman to my beloved, Mrs Jewkes?'

'She was now-and-then a little impertinent, as ladies' women will be,' answered Mrs Jewkes. 'But you know,' said I, 'that she interposed in my favour more than once:' 'Very true, madam,' returned Mrs Jewkes: 'and Mrs Worden praised you at table with me, for the sweetest creature she ever beheld; but indeed would have it that you had a spirit; and she was sorry you answered her lady as you did; for she had never borne so much contradiction before. But I told her,' added Mrs Jewkes, 'That if I had been in your place, madam, I should have taken much more upon me, and that you were all sweetness. And she said, I was got over, she saw.'

TUESDAY *Morning, the Sixth Day of my Happiness*

My master had given orders to Mrs Jewkes not to let him be disturbed till the usual breakfast-time, as he had sat up all night before; but it seems my lady, knowing his usual hour to be six, arose about that time, and being resolved to find out whether one chamber served us both, and if so, to have witness of our being together, raised also her kinsman and her woman, and at about half an hour after six rapped at our chamber-door.

My master, waking, asked, Who was there? 'Open the door,' said my lady; 'open it this minute!' I said, clinging about his neck, in great terror, 'Dear, dear sir, pray, pray, sir, don't open the door!' 'Fear nothing, Pamela,' said he. 'The woman is certainly mad.'

He then called out, 'Who are you? What do you want?' 'You know my voice well enough,' answered my lady: 'I *will* come in.' 'Pray, sir,' said I, 'don't let her ladyship in.' 'Don't be frighted, my dear,' said he: 'she thinks we are not married, and that we are afraid to be found together. I'll let her in; but she shall not come near my dearest.'

So slipping on some of his clothes, and putting on his gown and slippers, he opened the door. In rushed she. 'I'll be an eye-witness of your wickedness,' said she, 'I will! In vain shall you think to hide your vileness from me!'

'How dare you, madam, set a foot into my house, after the usage I have received from you?'

I had covered myself over head and ears, and trembled in every joint: perhaps discernibly trembled, and my lady cried out, 'Bear witness, Jackey, bear witness, Worden; the creature is *now* in his bed.' My master not seeing the young gentleman before, who was at the feet of the bed, said, 'How now, sir! What's your business in this apartment? Begone this moment.' And he went away directly.

'Worden,' repeated my lady, 'You see the creature is in his bed.' 'I do, madam,' answered she.

My master came to me, and uncovering my head, (for I had hid my face under the pillow) said, 'Ay, look, Worden, and bear witness: here is my Pamela! My dear angel,' speaking to me, 'my lovely creature, fear not: look up, and see how frantically this woman of quality behaves.'

At that instant I turned my face, and saw my furious lady: who, unable to bear this, was coming to me. 'Wicked, abandoned wretch! vile brother! to brave me thus! I'll tear the creature out of bed before your face, and, when I leave this house, will expose you both as you deserve.'

He took her in his arms, as if she had been nothing; and carrying her out of the room, she cried out, 'Worden, Worden! help me, Worden! the wretch is going to fling me down stairs.' Her woman ran to him, and said, 'Good sir, for Heaven's sake, offer no violence to my lady! her ladyship has been ill all night.'

He set her down in her own chamber, and she could not speak for passion. 'Take care of your lady,' said he to Mrs Worden; 'and when she has rendered herself more worthy of my attention, I'll see her: 'till then, at her peril, let her not come near my apartment.'

He then returned to me; and with words sweetly soothing, pacified my fears: and gave me leave to retire to write in my closet, and to stay there till my lady was more calm; and retiring, permitted me, at my desire, to fasten the door after him.

At breakfast-time my master tapped at the chamber-door; and answering to my question, 'Who is there?' I opened it with pleasure. I had written on a good deal; but I put it by when I ran to the chamber-door. I would have locked it again, when he was in; but he said, 'Am not I here? Don't be afraid.' He asked, If I chose to come down to breakfast? 'O no, dear sir,' said I; 'be pleased to excuse me.' 'I cannot bear,' said he, 'that the mistress of my house should breakfast in her closet, as if she durst not come down, and I at home!' 'O sir,' replied I, 'pray pass that over for *my* sake, and don't let me by my presence enrage your sister.' 'Then, my dear,' said he, 'I will breakfast with *you* here.' 'I beseech you, dear sir,' answered I, 'to breakfast with your sister.' 'That,' replied he, 'will too much gratify her pride, and look like a slight to you.' 'Your goodness is too great for me to want such a proof of it. Pray oblige her ladyship: she is your guest. Surely, sir, you need not stand upon punctilio with your happy wife.'

'She is a strange woman,' said he: 'I pity her. She threw herself into a violent fit of the cholic.' 'I hope, sir,' said I, 'when you carried her ladyship out, you did not hurt her.' 'No,' replied he, 'I love her too well. I set her down in her own apartment; and she but now being a little easier, desires to see me, and that I will breakfast with her, or refuses to touch any thing. But, if my Pamela pleases, I will make your presence a condition.'

'O no, no, dear sir,' said I, 'pray don't. I will not scruple on my knees, to beg her ladyship's favour to me, now I am in your presence, if you permit me to do it. And, dear sir, if my deepest humility will gratify her, allow me to shew it.'

'You shall do nothing,' returned he, 'unbecoming the character of my wife, to please the proud woman. But I will, however, permit you to breakfast by yourself this once, as I have not seen her since I have used her in what she calls so barbarous a manner.' He saluted me, and withdrew, and I again locked the door after him.

Mrs Jewkes soon after tapped at the door. When I knew who it was, I opened it. 'It is a sad thing,' said she, 'that you should be so much afraid in your own house.' She brought me some chocolate and toast; and I asked her about my lady's behaviour. She said, her ladyship would not suffer any body to attend but her woman, because she would not be heard in what she had to say; but she believed, she said, her master was very angry with the young lord, as Mrs Jewkes called her kinsman; for, as she passed by the door, she heard him say, in a high tone, 'I hope, sir, *you* did not forget yourself'; or words to that effect.

About one o'clock, my master came up again; and he said, 'Will you come down to dinner, Pamela, when I send for you?' 'Whatever you command, sir, I must do: but my lady won't desire to see me.' 'No matter, whether she will or no; I will not suffer her to prescribe to *my* wife in *your own house*. I will, by my tenderness to you, mortify her pride; and it cannot be done so well as to her face.'

'Dearest sir, pray indulge me, and let me dine here by myself. Your tenderness to me will make my lady but more inveterate.' 'I have told her,' said he, 'that we are married. She is out of all patience about it, and yet pretends *not* to believe it. Then I told her she should have it her own way, and that, perhaps I am *not*. And what, I asked her, had she to do with it either way? She has scolded and prayed, blessed and cursed me, by turns, twenty times in these few hours. And I have sometimes soothed her, sometimes stormed at her. At last I left her, and took a turn in the garden for an hour, to compose myself, because you should not see how the foolish woman had ruffled me; and just now, to avoid her, I came into the house, seeing her coming to me in the garden.'

Just as he had said so, 'Oh! my lady! my lady!' cried I, for I heard her voice in the chamber, saying, 'Brother, brother, one word with you'; stopping in sight of the closet where I was. He stepped out, and she went to the window that looks towards the garden, and said, 'Mean fool that I am, to follow you up and down the house in this manner, though I am shunned and avoided by you! You a brother! You a barbarian! Is it possible we could be born of one mother?'

'Why, madam,' said he, 'do you charge me with a behaviour you compel me by your violence to shew you? Is it not surprising that you should take the liberty with me, that the mother you have named, never gave you an example for, to *any* of her relations? Was it not sufficient, that I was insolently taken to task by you in your letters, but I must be insulted in my own house? My retirements invaded? And the person, justly more dear to me than every other, must be singled out for an object of your passionate excesses?'

'Ay,' said she, 'that one person is the thing! But though I came up with a resolution to be temperate, and to expostulate with you

437

on your avoiding me so brutally, yet cannot I have patience to look upon the bed in which I was born, as the guilty scene of your wickedness with such a –'

'Hush!' said he, 'I charge you, call not the dear creature by any name unworthy of her. You know not, as I told you, her excellence; and I desire you will not repeat the freedoms you have taken below.'

She stamped with her foot, and said, 'God give me patience! So much contempt to a sister; and so much tenderness to a vile –'

He put his hand before her mouth. 'Be silent,' said he, 'once more, I charge you. You know not the merit of the dear creature you abuse so freely! I *ought not*, neither *will* I bear it.'

She sat down and fanned herself, and burst into tears, intermingled with such sobs of passion, as concerned me to hear; and I trembled as I sat.

He walked about the room in great emotion, and at last said, 'Let me ask you, Lady Davers, why am I to be thus insolently called to account by you? Am I not independent? Am I not of age? Am I not at liberty to please myself? Would to Heaven that instead of a woman, and my sister, any man breathing had dared, whatever were his relation, to give himself the airs you have done! Why did you not send on this errand your lord, who could write me such a letter as no gentleman should write, nor any gentleman tamely receive? *He* should have seen the difference.'

'We all know,' said she, 'that since your Italian duel, you have commenced a bravo;[320] and all your airs breathe as strongly of the manslayer, as of the libertine.'

'This,' said he, 'I will bear; for I have no reason to be ashamed of the cause of that duel, since it was to save an innocent friend, and because your reflection is levelled at myself only. But suffer not your tongue to take too great a liberty with my Pamela.'

In a violent burst of passion, 'If I bear this,' said she, 'I may bear any thing! O the little strumpet.'

He interrupted her then, and said wrathfully, 'Begone, rageful woman! Leave my house this instant! I renounce you, and all relation to you; and never more let me see your face, or call me brother.'

And he took her by the hand to lead her out.

She laid hold of the curtains of the window, and said, 'I will not go! You shall not force me from you thus ignominiously in the sight and hearing of the wench! Nor give *her* a triumph in your barbarous treatment of me.'

Not considering any thing, I ran out of the closet, and threw myself at my master's feet, as he held her hand, in order to lead her out. 'Dearest sir,' said I, 'let me beg that no act of unkindness pass between a brother and sister, so justly dear to each other. Dear, dear madam,' on my knees, clasping her, 'I beg your ladyship to receive me to your grace and favour, and you shall find me incapable of any triumph but in your ladyship's goodness to me.'

'Creature,' said she, 'art *thou* to beg for me! Is it to *thee* I am to owe the favour, that I am not cast headlong from a brother's presence! Begone to thy corner, wench! Begone, I say, lest I trample thee under my foot, and thy paramour kill me for it.'

'Rise, my Pamela,' said my master; 'rise, dear life of my life, and expose not your worthiness to the ungrateful scorn of so violent a spirit.'

And, saying this, he led me back to my closet; and there I sat and wept.

Her woman came up just as my master was returning to her lady; and very humbly said, 'Excuse my intrusion, good sir! I hope I may come to my lady?'

'Yes, Mrs Worden,' answered he, 'you come in, and pray take your lady down stairs with you, lest I should forget what belongs either to my sister or to myself.'

Seeing her ladyship so outrageous with her brother, I began to think what a happy escape I had had the day before; hardly as I had then thought myself treated by her.

Her woman begged her ladyship to walk down; and she said, 'Worden, seest thou that bed? That is the bed in which I was born; and yet that was the bed, thou sawest, as well as I, the wicked Pamela in, this morning, and this brother of mine just risen from her!'

'True,' said he; 'you both saw it; and it is my pride, that you could see it. It is my bridal-bed, and it is intolerable, that the happiness I knew before you came hither, should be interrupted by so violent a woman.'

'Swear to me but, thou bold wretch,' said she, 'swear to me that Pamela Andrews is really and truly thy lawful wife, without deceit, without double-meaning; and I know what I have to say.'

'I will humour you for once,' said he; and then swore a solemn oath, that I was.

'I cannot *yet* believe you,' said she, 'because in this particular, I had rather have called you *knave* than *fool*.'

'Provoke me not too much,' said he; 'for if I should as much forget myself as you have done, you would have no more of a brother in me, than I have of a sister in you.'

'Who married you?' said she; 'tell me that: was it not a broken attorney in a parson's habit? Tell me truly! Tell me in the wench's hearing. When she is undeceived, she will know how to behave herself.'

Thank God! thought I, it is not so.

'No,' said he, 'and I will tell you, that I bless God, for enabling me to abhor that project, before it was brought to bear; and Mr Williams married us.'

'Nay then,' said she. 'But answer me another question or two: Who gave her away?'

'Mr Peters,' said he.

'Where was the ceremony performed?'

'In my own little chapel, which was put in order on purpose.'

'Now,' said she, 'I begin to fear there is something in it: but who was present?'

'What a fool do I look like,' said he, 'to suffer myself to be thus interrogated by an insolent sister! But, if you must know, Mrs Jewkes was present.'

'O the procuress!' said she: 'but nobody else?'

'Yes,' said he, 'my whole heart and soul!'

'Wretch!' said she; 'and what would thy father and mother have said, had they lived to this day?'

'Their consents,' replied he, 'I should have thought it my duty to ask, but not your's, madam.'

'Suppose,' said she, 'I had married my father's groom! what would you have said to that?'

'I could not have behaved worse,' replied he, 'than you have done.'

'And would you not have thought,' said she, 'I had deserved the worst behaviour?'

'Does your pride, Lady Davers, let you see no difference in the case you put?'

'None at all,' said she. 'Where can the difference be between a beggar's son married by a lady, or a beggar's daughter made a gentleman's wife?'

'Then I'll tell you,' replied he; 'the difference is, a man ennobles the woman he takes, be she *who* she will; and adopts her into his own rank, be it *what* it will: but a woman, though ever so nobly born, debases herself by a mean marriage, and descends from her *own* rank, to that of him she stoops to marry. When the royal family of Stuart allied itself into the low family of Hyde, (comparatively low, I mean) did any body scruple to call the lady Royal Highness, and Duchess of York?[321] And did any body think her daughters, the late Queen Mary and Queen Anne, less royal for the inequality between the father and mother? When the broken-fortuned peer goes into the city to marry a rich tradesman's daughter, be he duke or earl, does not his consort immediately become ennobled by his choice? And who scruples to call her duchess or countess?

'And let me ask you, madam, has not your marriage with Lord Davers, though the family you sprung from is as ancient, and (title excepted) as honourable as that you are ingrafted into, made you a lady and a peeress of Great-Britain, who otherwise would have been stiled but a spinster?

'Now, Lady Davers, do you not see a difference between *my* marrying my mother's deserving waiting-maid, with such graces of mind and person as would adorn any rank; and *your* marrying a sordid groom, whose constant train of education, conversation, and opportunities, could possibly give him no other merit, than that which must proceed from the vilest, lowest taste, in his sordid dignifier?'

'What palliations, wretch!' said she, 'dost thou seek to find for thy meanness!'

'Again, let me observe to you, Lady Davers, that when a duke lifts a private person into his own rank, he is still her *head*, by virtue of being her husband: but, when a lady descends to marry a groom, is not that groom her *head*? Does not that difference strike you? and what lady of quality ought to respect another, who has set a groom *above* her? If she did, would she not thereby put that groom upon a par with herself? Call this palliation, or what you will; but if you see not the difference, you are a very unfit judge for *yourself*, much more unfit to be censurer of *me*.'

'I would have you,' said she, 'publish your fine reasons to the world. If any young gentleman should be influenced by them, to cast himself away on the servant-wenches in his family, you will have his folly to keep yours in countenance.'

'If any young gentleman,' replied my master, 'stays till he finds such a woman as my Pamela, enriched with the beauties of person and mind, so well accomplished, and so fitted to adorn the degree to which she is raised, he will be as easily acquitted as I shall be to all the world that sees her, except there be many more Lady Davers's than I apprehend there can be.'

'And so,' returned she, 'you say, you are actually and really married, honestly, or rather foolishly, married to this *wench*?'

'I am indeed,' said he, 'if you presume to call her so! And why should I not, if I please? Who is there that has a right to censure me? Whom have I hurt by it? Have I not an estate, free and independent? Am I likely to be beholden to you or to any of my relations? And why, when I have a sufficiency in my own power, should I scruple to make a woman happy, who has, besides beauty, virtue, and prudence, more generosity than any lady I ever conversed with? Yes, Lady Davers, she has all these *naturally*: they are *born* with her; and a few years education, with her genius, has done more for her, than a whole long life has done for others.'

'No more, no more, I beseech you,' said she; 'thou surfeitest me, honest man! with thy weak folly. Thou art worse than an idolater; thou hast made a graven image, and thou fallest down and worshippest the works of thine own hands; and, Jeroboam like, thou wouldst have every body bow down before thy calf!' [322]

'Whenever your passion, Lady Davers, suffers you to descend to witticism, it is about to subside. But, let me tell you, though I myself worship this sweet creature, I want nobody else to do it; and should be glad you had not intruded upon me, to interrupt me in the course of our mutual happiness.'

'Well said, well said, my kind, my well-mannered brother! I

shall, after this, very little interrupt your happiness, I assure you. I thought you a gentleman once, and prided myself in my brother, but I will say now, in the words of the burial-service, *Ashes to ashes and dirt to dirt!*'

'Ay,' said he, 'Lady Davers, and there we must all end at last; you with your pride, and I with my plentiful fortune, must so end; and then where will be your distinction? Let me tell you, that except you and I both mend our lives, though you may have in some things less to answer for than I, this amiable creature, whom your vanity and folly teaches you so much to despise, will be infinitely more exalted above us, by that Power who is no regarder of persons, than the proudest monarch in the world can imagine himself above the meanest creature in it.'

'Egregious preacher!' said she: 'my brother already turned *puritan*! I congratulate this change! Well,' (and came towards me and I trembled to see her coming; but her brother followed to observe her, and I stood up at her approach, and she said) 'Give me thy hand, Mrs Pamela, Mrs Andrews, Mrs – What shall I call thee! Thou hast done wonders in a little time! thou hast not only made a rake a husband; but thou hast made a rake a preacher! But take care,' added she, after all, in ironical anger, and tapped me on the neck, 'take care, that thy vanity begins not where his ends; and that thou callest not thyself *my* sister.'

'She may, I hope, Lady Davers, when she can make as great a convert of you from pride, as she has of me from libertinism.'

Mrs Jewkes just then came up, and said, dinner was ready to be served.

'Come, my Pamela,' said my master: 'you desired to be excused from breakfasting with us; but I hope you will give my Lady Davers and me your company to dinner.'

'How dare you insult me thus?' said my lady.

'How dare you, madam,' replied he, 'insult me in my own house, especially after I have told you I am married? How can you think of staying here one moment, and yet refuse my wife the honours that belong to her, as my wife?'

'Merciful God,' said she, 'give me patience!' and held her hand to her forehead.

'Pray, sir, dear sir,' said I, 'excuse me; don't vex my lady.'

'Be silent, my dear love,' said he. 'You see already what you have gained by your condescension. You have thrown yourself at her feet; and, insolent as she is, she has threatened to trample upon you. She will ask you presently, if she is to owe her excuse to your interposition; and yet nothing else can make me forgive her.'

Poor lady! she could not bear this, and in a frantic way ran to her afflicted woman; and, taking her by the hand, 'Lead me down, lead me down, Worden!' said she. 'Let us instantly quit this house, this now hated house. Order the fellows to get ready, and I will never see it, nor its owner, more.' Away she flung; and her servants were ordered to make ready for her departure.

My dear Mr B. was troubled, as I saw. 'Pray, dear sir,' said I, 'follow my lady down, and pacify her.'Tis her love to you.'

'Poor woman!' said he; 'I am concerned for her! But I insist upon your coming down, since things are gone so far. Her pride will otherwise get new strength, and we shall be all to begin again.'

'Dearest sir,' said I, 'excuse me going down this once!'

'Indeed, my dear, I will not,' replied he. 'What! shall it be said, that my sister shall fright my wife from the table, and I present? No, I have borne too much already! and so have you. I charge you, come down, when I send for you.'

He departed, saying these words, and I dared not dispute: for I saw, he was determined. And there is as much majesty as goodness in him; as I have often had reason to observe, though never more than on the present occasion.

Her ladyship instantly put on her hood and gloves, and her woman tied up a handkerchief full of things; for her principal matters were not unpacked, and her coachman got her chariot ready, and her footmen their horses, and she appeared resolved to go. But her kinsman having taken a turn somewhere with Mr Colbrand, she sat down fretting on a seat in the fore yard,[323] her woman standing by her, expecting him, and refusing to come in: she at last said to one of the footmen, 'Do you, James, stay to attend my nephew: we will take the road we came.'

Mrs Jewkes went to her, and said, 'Your ladyship will be pleased to walk in to dinner; 'tis just coming upon table.' 'No,' said she, 'I have enough of this house; I have indeed! But make my compliments to your master, and tell him, that I wish him happier than he has made me.'

He had sent for me down, and I obeyed. The cloth was laid in the parlour I had jumped out of; and there I found my master, walking backwards and forwards in thoughtful vexation.

Mrs Jewkes came in, and asked, if he pleased to have dinner served; for my lady would not come in, but desired her compliments, and wished him happier than he had made her.

Seeing at the window, when he went to that side of the room, every thing prepared for her departure, he stepped to her, and said, 'Lady Davers, if I thought you would not scorn me for my tameness, I would ask you to walk in, and at least let your kinsman' (who then appeared) 'and your servants dine before they set out.'

She wept, and turned her face from him to hide her tears. He took her hand, and said, 'Let me prevail upon my sister to walk in.'

'No!' said she, 'don't ask me! I wish I could hate you, as much as you hate me!'

'You do,' said he, 'and a great deal more; or you would not vex me as you do. Pray walk in.'

'Don't ask me,' said she.

'Dear madam,' said Mr H. 'your ladyship won't go till you have dined, I hope.'

'Yes, Jackey, I will,' said she: 'I can't stay; I'm an *intruder* here, it seems!'

'Think,' said her brother, 'of the occasion you gave for that word. Your violent passions are the only *intruders*! Lay them aside, and never sister was dearer to a brother than you to me.'

'Don't say such another word,' said she, 'I beseech you; for I am too easy to forgive you any thing for one kind word.'

'You shall have one hundred,' said he, 'nay, ten thousand, if they will do, my dear Lady Davers. And,' saluting her, 'pray give me your hand. John,' said he, 'put up the horses. Come, Mr H. lead in your aunt: she won't permit me to have that honour.'

This quite overcame her; and giving her brother her hand, 'Yes, I will,' said she; 'and you shall lead me any whither: but don't think, I can forgive you, neither.'

He led her into the parlour, where I was. 'But,' said she, 'why do you lead me to this wench?' 'She is my wife, Lady Davers: and if you will not love her for my sake, do not, however, forget common civilities to her, for your own.'

'Pray, madam,' said her kinsman, 'since your brother is pleased to own his marriage, we must not forget common civilities, as Mr B. says. And, sir,' added he, 'permit me to wish you joy.'

'Thank you, Mr H.,' said he. 'And *may* I,' said he, looking hesitatingly at Mr B. and then my master presented me to him, and he very complaisantly[324] saluted me, and said, 'I vow to Gad, madam,' scraping and bowing to me, 'I did not know this yesterday; and, if I was guilty of a fault, I beg your pardon.'

'Thou'rt a good-natured foolish fellow,' said my lady; 'thou mightest have saved this nonsensical parade, till thou hadst my leave for it.'

'Why, if they are actually married, there's no help for it, and we must not make mischief between man and wife.'

'But, brother,' said she, 'do you think I'll sit at table with the creature?'

'No contemptuous names, I beseech you, Lady Davers! I tell you, she is really my wife; and what must I be to suffer her to be ill used? If you will permit her to love you, she will always love and honour you.'

'Indeed, indeed, I will, madam,' said I. My hands held up.

'I cannot, I will not, sit down at table with her,' said she: 'Pamela, I hope thou dost not think I will?'

'Indeed, madam,' said I, 'if your good brother will permit it, I will withdraw, and dine by myself, rather than give uneasiness to the sister of my honoured benefactor.'

'Let her then leave the room,' replied she, 'if you expect me to stay.'

'Indeed, you are out of the way, madam,' said her kinsman; 'that is not right, as things stand.'

'No, madam, that must not be,' said my master: 'but, if it will please you, we will have two tables; you and your nephew shall sit at one, and my Pamela and I will sit at the other: but in that case, imagine, my dear Lady Davers, what a figure you will make!'

She seemed irresolute; and her brother placed her in the second place at the table. The first course being brought in, my master, fearing she would say some disrespectful things of me, bid the menservants withdraw, and send in Mrs Jewkes. 'Worden,' said he, 'do you attend your lady; Jewkes shall wait upon us.'

'Where,' said she to me, (the servants, however, being gone) 'wouldst *thou* presume to sit? Wouldst have me give *place* to thee *too*, wench?'

'Come, come,' said my master, 'I'll put that out of dispute.' And so he sat himself down at the upper end of the table, and placed me on his left hand. 'Excuse me, my dear,' said he, 'this *once* excuse me!'

'Oh! your hated complaisance,' said she, 'to such a–'

'Hush, Lady Davers! Hush!' said he: 'I will not bear to hear her spoken slightingly of! 'Tis enough, that, to oblige your violent and indecent caprice, you make me compromise with you thus.'

'Mr H.,' added he, 'take your place next your *gentle* aunt.'

'Worden,' said she, 'do you sit down by Pamela there, since it must be so; we'll be hail-fellow[325] all!'

'With all my heart,' replied my master. 'I have so much honour for the sex, that I would not have the meanest person of it, who had intrinsic merit, stand, while I sit.'

'Well say'st thou *that*, wretch,' replied her ladyship, 'who hast raised one of the meanest of it to an equality with thyself! But were these *always* thy notions?'

'They were not, Lady Davers: like other proud fools of family, I did not always know, that there was merit in individuals of low degree, which many of a higher could not boast of.'

Mrs Jewkes came in.

'Shall I help you, Lady Davers, to some of that carp?' said her brother.

'Help your beloved!' said she.

'That's kind!' replied he. 'Here, my love, let me help you.'

'Mighty well!' returned she. But sat on one side, turning from me, as it were.

'Dear aunt, dear Lady Davers,' whispered, but not very softly, her kinsman, 'let's see you kiss and be friends. Since things are as they are, what signifies standing out!'

'Hold thy fool's tongue,' said she: 'is thy tone so soon turned since yesterday?'

'Since yesterday!' said Mr B. 'I hope nothing affronting was offered yesterday to my *wife in her own house*.' She hit him a smart slap on the shoulder: 'Take that, impudent brother,' said she: 'I'll *wife* you, and in *her own* house!'

She seemed half afraid; but he, in good humour, 'I thank you, sister, I thank you. But I have not had a blow from you before a great while.'

' 'Fore Gad, sir,' said her kinsman, ' 'tis very kind of you to take it so well. Her ladyship is as good a woman as ever lived; but I have had many a cuff from her *myself*.'

'I won't put it up neither,' said my master, 'except you'll assure me, you had seen her serve her lord so.'

I pressed my foot to his, and said softly, 'Don't, dear sir!'

'What,' said she, 'is the creature begging me off from insult? If good manners will not keep him from affronting me, I will not owe his forbearance to *thee*, wench.'

'Well does Lady Davers use the word *insult*!' said my master. 'But, come, let me see you eat, and I'll forgive you'; and he put the knife in one of her hands, and the fork in the other. 'As I hope to live,' said he, 'I am quite ashamed of your childishness.'

She cut a little bit, but laid it down in her plate again: 'I cannot eat,' said she; 'I cannot swallow. It will certainly choak me, if I attempt it.' He arose from table himself, and filled a glass of wine. Mean time, his seat between us being vacant, she turned to me: 'Confidence!' said she, 'how darest thou to sit next *me*? Why dost thou not rise, and take the glass from thy property?' [326]

'Sit still, my dear,' said he; 'I'll help you both.' But I arose; for I was afraid of a good cuff; and said, 'Pray, sir, let me help my lady!' 'So you shall,' replied he, 'when she is in a humour to receive it as she ought. Lady Davers,' said he, offering her a glass of wine, 'pray accept of this from my hands.' 'Is this to insult me?' said she. 'No, really,' returned he; 'but to induce you to eat.'

She took the glass, and said, 'God forgive you, wicked wretch, for your usage of me this day! This is a little as it used to be! I once had your love; and now it is changed; and for whom? that vexes me!' She wept, and set down the glass without drinking.

'You don't do well,' said he. 'You neither treat me like your brother, nor like a man. I love you as well as ever. But, for a woman of sense, you act quite a childish part. Come,' added he, and held the glass to her, 'let the brother whom you once loved, prevail on you.' She then drank it. He took her hand. 'How passion,' said he, 'deforms the noblest minds! You must not quite forfeit that agreeableness that used to distinguish my sister. Let me persuade you to recollect yourself, and be again my sister!' For Lady Davers is indeed a fine woman, and has a presence as majestic for a lady, as her dear brother has for a gentleman.

He then led me to my seat, and sat down between us again; and when the second course was served, 'Lest you may be wanted without, Mrs Jewkes,' said he, 'let the men come in and wait.' I touched his toe again; but he minded it not; and I saw he was right; for her ladyship, by this time, had seemed to recollect herself, and behaved with some little freedom; but she could not forbear a sigh and a sob now-and-then.

She called for a glass of the same wine she had drank before. 'Shall I help you again, Lady Davers?' said her brother. At the same time, rising, and going to the side-board, filled her a glass. 'I love,' said she, 'to be soothed by my brother! Your health, sir!'

'My dear, now I'm up,' said my master to me, 'I will fill for you! I must serve both sisters alike!' She looked at the men-servants, as if they were a check upon her, and said to my master, 'How now, sir! Not that you know of.' He whispered her, 'Don't shew any contempt before my servants to one I have so deservedly made their mistress. Consider, 'tis done.' 'Ay,' said she, 'that's the thing that kills me.'

He gave me a glass. 'Your ladyship's health,' said I, and stood up. 'That won't do,' said she, leaning towards me, softly; and was going to call me *wench*, or *creature*, or some such name. And my master, seeing Abraham look towards her, her eyes being red and swelled, said, 'Indeed, Lady Davers, I would not vex myself about it, if I were you.' 'About what?' said she. 'About your lord's not coming down, as he had promised,' replied he. He sat down, and she tapped him on the shoulder: 'Ah! Wicked-one,' said she, 'nor will *that* do neither!' 'Why, to be sure,' added he, 'it would vex a woman of your merit, to be slighted, if it *were* so; but you know not what may have happened.'

She shook her head, and said, 'That's like your art! This makes one amazed you should be so *caught*!' 'Who! my *lord* caught?' said he: 'no, no! he'll have more wit than to be caught! But I never heard you were jealous before.' 'Nor,' said she, 'have you any reason to think so now.' 'Honest friends,' to the footmen, 'you need not wait,' said she; 'my woman will help us to what we want.' 'Yes, let them,' replied my master. 'Abraham, fill me a glass of wine. Come,' said he, 'Lord Davers to you, madam: I hope he'll take care he is not found out!' 'You are very provoking, brother,' said she. 'I wish you were half as good a man as Lord Davers: but don't carry your jest too far.' 'Well,' said he, ' 'tis a tender point, I own. I have done!'

By these kind managements the dinner passed over better than I expected. And when the servants were withdrawn, my master said, still keeping his place between us, 'I have a question to ask you, Lady Davers; and that is, if you will bear me company to Bedfordshire? I was intending to set out thither to-morrow. But I will attend your pleasure, if you will go with me.'

'Is thy wife, as thou callest her, to go along with thee, friend?' said she. 'To be sure she is, my dear Quaker sister,'327 answered he; and took her hand, and smiled. 'And wouldst have me parade it with *her* on the road? Hay! And make one to grace her retinue? Hay! Tell me, how thou wouldst chalk it out,328 if I would do as thou wouldst have me, honest friend!'

'Why, I'll tell you how I would have it. Here shall you and my Pamela —' 'Leave out *my*, I desire you, if you would have me sit patiently.' 'No,' said he, 'I cannot do that. Here shall you, and my Pamela, go together in your chariot, if you please; and your nephew and I will sometimes ride, and sometimes, by turns, go into my chariot, to your woman.'

'Shouldst thou like this, creature?' said she to me. 'If your ladyship think it not too great an honour, madam,' said I. 'Yes,' replied she, 'but my ladyship does think it would be too great an honour. But, how then, sir?' 'Why, then, when we came home, we would get Lord Davers to come to us, and stay a month or two.' 'And what if he were to come?' 'Why I would have you, as I know you have a good fancy,329 give Pamela your judgment on some patterns I expect from London, for clothes.' 'Provoking wretch!' said she; 'now I wish I may keep my hands to myself.' 'I don't say it to provoke you,' said he; 'nor ought it to do so. But when I tell you, I am married, is it not a consequence, that we must have new clothes?'

'Hast thou any more of these obliging things to say to me?' said she. 'I will make you a present,' returned he, 'worth your acceptance, if you will grace us with your company at church, when we make our appearance.' 'Take that,' said she, 'if I die for't! Wretch that thou art!' lifting up her hand, but he caught hold of it. Her kinsman said, 'Dear Lady Davers, I wonder at you! Why, all these are things of course.'

I begged leave to withdraw; and, as I went out, my master said, 'There's a person! There's a shape! There's a sweetness! O Lady Davers, were you a man, you would doat on her, as I do.' 'Yes,' said the naughty lady, 'so I should for my harlot, but not for a wife.' I turned, upon this, and said, 'Indeed, your ladyship is cruel, and well may men take liberties, when women of distinction say such things!' I wept, and added, 'Your ladyship's disgust, were not your brother the most generous of men, would make me very unhappy.'

'No fear, wench; no fear,' said she: 'thou wilt hold him as long as any body can, I see that! Poor Sally Godfrey never had half the interest in him.'

'Stay, my Pamela,' said he, in a passion. 'Stay, I tell you. You have now heard two vile charges against me! I love you with an affection so sincere, that I ought to say something before this accuser, that you may not think your virtue linked to too black a villain.'

Her nephew seemed uneasy, and blamed her. I came back, but trembled as I stood. He seated me; and, taking my hand, said, 'I have been accused, my dear, as a dueller,[330] and now as a profligate, in *another* sense; and there *was* a time, I should not have received these imputations with so much concern as I now do, when I would wish, by a conformity of my manners to your virtue, to shew to every one the force your example has upon me. But this briefly is the case of the first.

'I had a friend, who was designed to have been basely assassinnated by bravoes, hired by a man of title in Italy, who, like many other persons of title, had no honour; and at Padua, I had the fortune to disarm one of these bravoes in my friend's defence, and made him confess his *employer*; and *him*, I own, I challenged. At Sienna we met, and he died in a month after, of a fever; but, I hope, not occasioned by the slight wounds he had received from me; although I was obliged to leave Italy upon it, sooner than I intended, because of the resentment of his numerous relations, who looked upon me as the cause of his death.

'This is one of the good-natured hints, that might shock your goodness, on reflecting that you are yoked with a murderer. The other –' 'Nay, brother,' said she, 'say no more. 'Tis your own fault, if you go further.' 'She shall know it all,' said he. 'I defy the utmost stretch of your malice.

'When I was at college, I was well received by a widow lady, who had several daughters, and but small fortunes to give them. The old lady set one of them (a deserving good girl she was) to draw me into marriage with her; and contrived many opportunities to bring us, and leave us together. I was not then of age; and the young lady, who was not half so artful as her mother, yielded to my importunities, before the mother's plot could be ripened, and, by that means, utterly frustrated it. This, my Pamela, is the Sally Godfrey that Lady Davers, with the worst intentions, has informed you of. And for this, and whatever other liberties I may have taken, (for I have not lived a blameless life) I desire Heaven will forgive me, only, till I revive its vengeance by the like offences in injury to my Pamela.

'And now, my dear, you may withdraw; for this worthy sister of mine has said all the bad she knows of me; and what, at a proper opportunity, when I could have convinced you, that they were not my *boast*, but my *concern*, I should have acquainted you with myself; for I am not fond of being thought better than I am: though I hope, from the hour I devoted myself to so much virtue, to that of my death, my conduct shall be irreproachable.'

She was greatly moved at this, and the noble manner in which he owned his penitence; and gushed out into tears, and said, 'No, don't yet go, Pamela, I beseech you. My passion has carried me too far'; and coming to me, she took my hand, and said, 'You must stay to hear me beg his pardon'; and offered to take his hand also; but, to my concern, he burst from her; and went out of the parlour into the garden, in a rage so violent, that it made me tremble.

She sat down, and leaned her head against my bosom, and made my neck wet with her tears, holding me by my hands; and I wept for company. Her kinsman walked up and down the parlour, in a fret; and going out afterwards, he came in, and said, 'Mr B. has ordered his chariot to be got ready, and won't be spoken to by any body.' 'Where is he?' said she. 'Walking in the garden till it is ready,' replied he.

'Well,' said she, 'I have indeed gone too far. I was bewitched! And now,' said she, 'will he not forgive me for a twelvemonth: for I tell you, Pamela, if ever you offend, he will not easily forgive.'

I was delighted, though sad for the occasion, at her ladyship's goodness to me. 'Will you venture,' said she, 'to accompany me to him? Dare you follow a lion into his retreat?' 'I'll attend your ladyship,' said I, 'wherever you command.' 'Well, wench,' said she, 'Pamela, I mean, thou art very good in the main! I should have loved thee as well as my mother did – if – But 'tis all over now. Indeed, you should not have married my brother. But come, I must love him. Let us find him out. And yet will he use me worse than he would use a dog. I should not,' added she, 'have so much exasperated him: for whenever I have, I have always had the worst of it. He knows I love him.'

In this manner she talked to me, leaning on my arm, and walked into the garden.

I saw he was still in tumults, as it were, and he took another walk to avoid us. She called after him, and said, 'Brother, brother, let me speak to you! One word with you!' And as we made haste towards him, and came near to him, 'I desire,' said he, 'that you will not farther oppress me with your violence. I have borne too much with you. And I will vow for a twelvemonth, from this day –' 'Hush,' said she, 'don't vow, I beg you; for too well will you keep your vow, I know, if you do. You see,' said she, 'I stoop to ask Pamela to be my advocate. Sure that will pacify you!'

'Indeed,' said he, 'I desire to see neither of you on this occasion; and let me be left to myself.' He was going away: but she said, 'One word, sir, I desire. If you will forgive *me*, I will forgive *you*!' 'For what,' said the dear man, haughtily, 'will you forgive *me*?' 'Why,' said she, (for she saw him too angry to mention his marriage, as a subject that *required* her pardon) 'I will forgive you for all your ill usage of me this day.'

'I will be serious with you, Lady Davers,' said he: 'I wish you well; but let us, from this time, study so much each other's quiet, as never to come near each other more.' '*Never!*' said she. 'And can you desire this, barbarous brother, can you?' 'I can, I do,' replied he; 'and what have I to do, but to hide from you, not a brother, but a murderer, and a profligate, unworthy of your relation? And let me be consigned to penitence for my past wickedness: a penitence, however, that shall not be broken in upon by so violent an accuser.'

'Pamela,' said he, and made me tremble, 'how dare you approach me, without leave, when you see me thus disturbed! Never, for the future, come near me, when I am in tumults, unless I send for you.'

'Dear sir!' said I – 'Leave me,' interrupted he. 'I will set out for Bedfordshire this moment.' 'What! sir, without me? What have I done?' 'You have too meanly,' said he, 'for my wife, stooped to this furious woman; and, till I can recollect, must say, I am not pleased with you: but Colbrand, and two other of my servants, shall attend you; and Mrs Jewkes shall wait upon you part of the way. And I hope you will find me in a better disposition to receive you there, than I am at parting with you here.'

Had I not hoped, that this was partly put on to intimidate my lady, I believe I could not have borne it.

'I was afraid,' said she, 'he would be angry at you, as well as at me; for well do I know his unreasonable violence, when he is provoked. But one word, sir,' said she: 'forgive Pamela, if you won't forgive me; for she has committed no fault. Her good-nature to me is her only one. I requested her to accompany me. I will be gone myself, directly, as I would have done before, had you not prevented me.'

'I prevented you,' said he, 'through love; but you have stung me for it, through hatred. But as for my Pamela, I know, that I cannot be angry with her beyond the present moment. But I desire her never to see me on such occasions, till I can see her in the temper I ought to be in, when such sweetness approaches me. 'Tis, therefore, I say, my dearest, leave me now.'

'But, sir,' said I, 'must I leave you, and let you go to Bedfordshire without me? O dear sir, how can I?' 'You may go to-morrow, both of you,' said my lady, 'as you had designed, and I will depart this afternoon; and since I am not to be forgiven, I will try to forget I have a brother.'

'May I, sir,' said I, 'beg that all your anger may fall on myself, on condition of your being reconciled to Lady Davers?' 'Presuming Pamela!' replied he, and made me start, 'are you then so well able to sustain a displeasure, which, of all things, I expected, from your affection, and your tenderness, you would have wished to avoid? Now,' said he, and took my hand, and, as it were, tossed it from him, 'be gone from my presence, and reflect upon what you have said!'

I was so affrighted, that I sunk down at his feet, and clasped his knees, as he was turning from me, and said, 'Forgive me, sir! you see I am *not* so hardy! I cannot bear your displeasure!' And was ready to faint.

His sister said, 'Only forgive Pamela; 'tis all I ask! You will break *her* spirit. You will carry your passion as much too far as I have done mine.'

'I need not say,' said he, 'how well I love her: but she must not intrude upon me in these my ungovernable moments! I had intended, as soon as I could have suppressed, by reason, the tumults, which you, Lady Davers, had caused by your violence, to have come in, and taken such a leave of you both, as became an husband and a brother: but she has, unbidden, broken in upon me, and must take the consequence of a passion, which, when raised, is as uncontroulable as your own.'

'Did I not,' said Lady Davers, 'love you, as sister never loved a brother, I should not have given you all this trouble.' 'And did I not,' said he, 'love you better than you are resolved to deserve, I should be indifferent to all you say. But this last instance, of poor Sally Godfrey, after the duelling-hint, (which you would not have mentioned, had you not known it to be a subject that I never can hear of without concern) carries with it such an appearance of spite and meanness, as makes me desirous to forget that I have a sister.'

'Well,' said she, 'I am convinced it was wrong. I am ashamed of it myself. It was poor, it was mean, it was unworthy of your sister: and it is from this conviction that I stoop to follow you, to beg your pardon, and even to procure one for my advocate, who, I thought, by your own professions in her favour, had some interest with you; which now I shall begin to think made purposely to insult me.'

'I care not what you think! After the meanness you have been guilty of, I can only look upon you with pity. For, indeed, you are sunk very low with me.'

'It is plain, I am,' said she. 'But I'll be gone. And so, brother, let me call you so this *once*! God bless you! And, Pamela,' said her ladyship, 'God bless you!' And saluted me, and wept.

I dared say no more; and my lady turning from him, he said, 'Your sex is the Devil! how strangely can you discompose, calm, and turn, as you please, us poor weathercocks of men! Your kind blessing of my Pamela, I cannot stand! Salute but each other again.' And he then took both our hands, and joined them; and my lady kissing me again, with tears on both sides, he put his kind arms about each of our waists, and kissed first her ladyship, then me, with ardour, saying, 'Now, God bless you both, the two dearest creatures in the world to me!'

'Well,' said she, 'you will quite forget my fault about Miss –' He stopped her, before she could speak the name, and said, 'For ever forget it! But, Pamela, let me hope that you will never again make my anger so light a thing to you, as you did just now.'

'She did not,' said my lady, 'make light of your anger; but the heavier she thought it, the higher compliment she made me, in saying, she would bear it all, rather than not see you and me reconciled.'

'It was a slight,' said he, '(by implication at least) that my niceness[331] could not bear from her. For, looked it not like her presuming on such an interest in my affections, that, offend as she would, she could make it up with me whenever she pleased? Which, I assure her, will not, in cases of wilful disobligation, be always in her power.'

'I can tell you, Pamela,' said my lady, 'that you have a gentleman to deal with in my brother; and you may expect such treatment from him, as that character, and his known good sense, will demand of him: but *if* you offend, the Lord have mercy upon you! You see how it is by me! And yet, I never knew him forgive so soon.'

'I am sure,' said I, 'I will take as much care as I can; for I have been excessively frighted; and had offended by intending to oblige.'

Thus happily did this storm blow over; and my lady was quite subdued and pacified.

When we came out of the garden, on seeing his chariot quite ready, he said, 'Well, Lady Davers, I had most assuredly set out for Bedfordshire, if things had not taken this happy turn. But, instead of it, if you please, you and I will take an airing. We will attend you, my dear, at supper.'

Mr B. asked Mr H. to escort his aunt on horseback. 'I will,' answered he; 'and am glad, at my soul, to see you all so good friends.'

My dear master (I think, after this instance of his displeasure with me, I must not forbear calling him so) handed Lady Davers into his chariot: her kinsman, and his servant, rode after them; and I went up to my closet, to ruminate on all that had passed. And, foolish thing that I am, this poor Miss Sally Godfrey runs in my head! How soon the name and quality of a wife gives one privileges, in one's own account! Yet, methinks, I want to know more about her; for, is it not strange, that I, who lived years in the family, should have heard nothing of this? But I was so constantly with my good lady, that it was the less likely I should; and she, I dare say, never knew it, or she would have told me.

But I dare not ask him about this poor Miss Godfrey. Yet I wonder what became of her? Whether she be living? And whether any thing came of it? Perhaps I shall hear full soon enough. But I hope all bad consequences from it are over.

As to the other unhappy case, I know it was talked of, that in his travels, before I was taken into the family, he was in one or two broils; and, from a youth, he was always remarkable for courage, and is reckoned a great master of his sword. God grant he may never be put to use it! And that he may always be preserved in honour and safety!

About seven o'clock, my master sent word, that he would not have me expect him to supper: for that he, and Lady Davers, and Mr H., were prevailed upon to stay with Mrs Jones; and that Lady Darnford, and Mr Peters's family, had promised to sup with them there. I was glad they did not send for me; and the rather, as I hoped those good families, being my friends, would confirm my lady in my favour.

At about half an hour after ten o'clock, having tired myself with writing, I came down, and went into the housekeeper's parlour, where were Mrs Jewkes and Mrs Worden, whom, notwithstanding they would have excused themselves, I made sit down by me. Mrs Worden asked me pardon, in a good deal of confusion, for the part she acted the day before; saying, That things had been very differently represented to her; and she little thought I was married, and that she was behaving so rudely to the mistress of the house.

I said, I very freely forgave her; and hoped my new condition would not make me forget how to behave properly to every one; but that I must endeavour to act not unworthy of it, for the honour of the gentleman who had so generously raised me to it.

Mrs Jewkes said, That my situation gave me great opportunities of shewing the excellency of my nature, in forgiving offences so readily, as she, for her own part, must always, she said, acknowledge, with confusion of face.

'People, Mrs Jewkes,' replied I, 'don't know how they shall act, when their wills are in the power of their superiors. I always thought it became me to distinguish between acts of malice, and of implicit obedience, to the will of principals; though no commands of another should make us do an evidently wrong thing. The great,' continued I, 'though at the time they may be angry they are not obeyed, will have no ill opinion of a person for withstanding them in their unlawful commands.'

Mrs Jewkes seeming a little concerned, I said, I spoke chiefly from my own experience: as they both knew my story, I might say, that I had not wanted either for menaces or temptations; and had I complied with the one, or been intimidated by the other, I should not have been what I was.

'Ah! madam,' replied Mrs Jewkes, 'I never knew any body like you: and I think your temper sweeter since the happy day than before; and that, if possible, you take less upon you.'

'A good reason, Mrs Jewkes, may be assigned for that: I thought myself in danger: I looked upon every one as my enemy; and it was impossible, that I should not be fretful, uneasy, jealous. But when my dearest Mr B. had taken from me the ground of my uneasiness, and made me quite happy, I should have been very blameable, if I had not shewn a satisfied and easy mind, and an endeavour to engage every one's respect and love at the same time: and the rather, as it is but justifying, in some sort, my dear master, in the honour he has done me; for were I, by a contrary conduct, to augment the number of my enemies, I should encrease that of his censurers, for stooping so low.'

This way of talking pleased them both; and they made me many compliments upon it.

We were thus engaged, when my best friend, and Lady Davers, and her nephew, came home: they made me quite happy, by the good humour in which they returned. My dear Mr B. came to me, and saluting me, said, 'I will hope, my love, that you will not think hardly of our absence, when you are told that it has not been to your disadvantage; for we have talked of nobody but you.'

My lady came up to me, and said, 'Ay, child, you have been all our subject. I don't know how it is; but you have made two or three good families in this neighbourhood, as much your admirers, as your friend here.'

'Lady Davers,' said he, 'has been hearing your praises, Pamela, from half a score mouths, with more pleasure than her pride will easily let her own to you.'

'I cannot express the joy I should have,' said I, 'if Lady Davers would look upon me with an eye of favour.'

'Well, child,' replied she, 'proud hearts do not come down all at once; though my brother, here, has this day taken mine a good many pegs lower than ever it was before: but I will say, I wish you joy.' And saluted me.

'I am now, my dear lady,' said I, 'quite happy. Your favour was all that was wanting to make me so. To the last hour of my life I will shew your ladyship, that I have the most grateful and respectful sense of your goodness.'

'But, child,' said she, 'I shall not give you my company when you make your appearance. Let your own merit make all your Bedfordshire neighbours your friends, as it has done here, by your Lincolnshire ones; and you will have no need of my countenance, nor any body's else.'

'Now,' said her nephew, ' 'tis my turn: I wish you joy with all my soul, madam; and by what I have seen, and by what I have heard, 'fore Gad, I think you have met with no more than you deserve; and so all the company says, where we have been. And pray forgive all my nonsense to you.'

'I shall always, sir, I hope, respect as I ought, so near a relation of my good Lord and Lady Davers; and I thank you for your kind compliment.'

'Gad, Worden,' said he to her, who attended her lady for her commands, 'I believe you've some forgiveness too to ask; for we were all to blame, to make Mrs B. here fly the pit, as she did! Little did we think we made her quit her own house.'

'Thou always,' replied my lady, 'say'st either too much or too little.'

My lady sat down with me half an hour; and told me, that her brother had given her a fine airing. He had quite charmed her, she said, with his kind treatment of her; and, in his discourse, had much confirmed her in the good opinion she had begun to entertain of my discreet and obliging behaviour. 'But,' continued she, 'when he

would make me visit, without intending to stay, my old neighbours, (for Mrs Jones being nearest, we visited her first; and she
scraped all the rest of the company together) they were all so full of
your praises, that I was quite borne down; and, truly, I was Saul
among the prophets!'[332]

You may believe how much I was delighted with this; and I
spared not my acknowledgements.

When her ladyship retired to her chamber, she said, 'Good-night
to you, heartily, and to your good man. I now kiss you out of *more*
than form.'

Join with me, my dear parents, in my joy for this happy turn;
the contrary of which I so much dreaded, and was the only difficulty
I had to labour with! This poor Miss Sally Godfrey, I wonder what
is become of her, poor soul! I wish he would, of his own head,[333]
mention her again. Not that I am *very* uneasy, neither. You will
say, I must be a little particular, if I were.

My dear Mr B. gave me an account, when we went up, of the
pains he had taken with his sister; and of all the kind things the
company they had been in had said in my behalf. He told me, that
when my health, as Mrs B. was toasted, and came to her, she drank
it, in these words, 'Come, brother, here's your Pamela to you. But
I shall not know how to stand this affair, when a certain lady and
her daughters come to visit me.' [One of those young ladies, my
dear parents, was the person she was so desirous of seeing the wife
of her brother.] 'Lady Betty, I know,' said she, 'will rally me
smartly upon it; and, you know, brother, she wants not wit.' 'I
hope Lady Betty,' replied he, 'whenever she marries, will meet
with a better husband than I should have made her; for, in my
conscience, I think, I should hardly have made a tolerable one to
any woman but my Pamela.'

He told me, that they rallied him on the stateliness of his temper;
and said, they agreed with him in opinion, that he would make an
exceeding good husband where he was; but that he did so, must be
owing more to my meekness, than to his complaisance: 'For,' said
Miss Darnford, 'I could see, well enough, when your ladyship'
(speaking to Lady Davers) 'detained her, though he had but hinted
to her, it seems, his desire of finding her at our house, he was so
much out of humour, at her supposed non-complaisance, that mine
and my sister's pity for her was more engaged than our envy.'

'Ay,' said my lady, 'he is a lordly creature; and cannot bear disappointment, nor ever could.'

'Well, Lady Davers,' replied he, 'you, of all persons, should not find fault with me; for I bore a great deal from you, before I was at all angry.'

'Yes,' replied she; 'but when I had gone a little too far, as, I own, I did; you made me severely pay for it. You know you did, Sauce-box. And he treated the poor thing too,' added she, 'whom I took with me for my advocate, so low had he brought me, in such a manner as made my heart ake for her: but part was *art*, I know, to make me think the better of her.'

'Indeed, madam,' said he, 'there was very little of that; for, at that time, I cared not either for your good or bad opinion of her or of me. And, I own, I was displeased to be broken in upon, after your provocations, by either of you; and Pamela must learn that lesson – Never to come near me, when I am in those humours; which shall be as seldom as possible; for, after a while, if let alone, I come to myself, and am sorry for a violence of temper so like my dear sister's here; and, for this reason, think it is no matter how few witnesses there are of its intemperance; especially since such witnesses, whether they deserve it or not, (as you see in my Pamela's case) must be sufferers by it, if, unsent for, they come in my way.'

He repeated the same lesson to me when alone; and, enforcing it, owned, that he was angry with me in earnest, just then; although more with himself, afterwards, for being so: 'But when, Pamela,' said he, 'you wanted to take all my displeasure upon yourself, I thought it was *braving* me with your *merit*, and depending on my weakness, as if I must *soon* lay aside my anger, if it were transferred to you. I cannot bear, my dear, the thought, that you should wish, on any occasion whatever, to have me angry with you, or not to look upon my displeasure, as the heaviest misfortune that could befal you.'

'But, sir,' said I, 'you know, that what I did was to try to reconcile my lady; and, as she herself observed, it was paying her a high regard.' 'It was so,' replied he; 'but never think of making a compliment to *her*, or to *any* body living, at my expence. Besides, she had behaved so intolerably, that I began to think you had stooped too much, and more than I ought to permit my wife to do;

and acts of meanness are what I cannot endure in any body, but especially in those I love; and as she had been guilty of a very signal one, I had much rather have renounced her, at that time, than been reconciled to her.'

'Sir,' said I, 'I hope I shall always behave so, as not to be thought *wilfully* disobliging for the future. I am sure, I shall want only to *know* your will to conform to it. But this instance shews me, that I may *much* offend, without designing it.'

'My dear Pamela,' replied he, 'must not be too serious: I hope I shall not be a very tyrannical husband: yet do I not pretend to be perfect, or to be always governed by reason in my first transports; and I expect, from your affection, that you will bear with me, when you find me in the wrong. I have not an ungrateful spirit; and can, when cool, enter as impartially into myself, as most men; and then I am always kind and acknowledging, in proportion as I have been out of the way.

'But, to convince you, my dear,' continued he, 'of your well-meant fault, (I mean, with regard to the consideration I wished you to have to the impetuosity of my temper; for I acknowledge there was no fault in your intention) I will remind you, that you met, when you came to me, while I was so much disordered, a reception you did not expect, and a harsh word or two that you did not deserve. Now, had you not broken in upon me, while my anger lasted, but staid till I had come to you, or sent to request your company, you would have seen none of this, but have met with that affectionate behaviour, which, I doubt not, you will ever merit. In *this temper* shall you always have a proper influence over me: but you must not suppose, whenever I am out of humour, that in opposing yourself to my passion, you oppose a proper check to it; but when you are so good as to bend like the slender reed, to the hurricane, rather than, like the sturdy oak, to *resist* it,[334] you will always stand firm in my kind opinion; while a contrary conduct would uproot you, with all your excellencies, from my soul.'

'Sir,' said I, (but tears were in my eyes, and I turned my head away to conceal them) 'I will endeavour, as I said before, to conform myself, in all things, to your will.'

'And I, my dear, will endeavour to make my will as conformable to reason as I can. And let me tell you, that the belief that you would, was one of the inducements I had to marry at all. For nobody was more averse to the state than myself; and now we are upon this subject, I will give you the reasons of my aversion to it.

'We people of fortune, or such as are born to large expectations, of both sexes, are generally educated wrong. You have occasionally touched upon this subject, Pamela, several times in your journal, and so justly, that I will say the less upon it now. We are usually headstrong in our wills, and being unaccustomed to controul from our parents, know not how to bear it.

'Humoured by our nurses, through the faults of our parents, we practise first upon them; and shew the *gratitude* of our dispositions, in an insolence that ought at first to have been checked and restrained.

'Next, we are to be favoured and indulged at school; and we take care to reward our *masters* for their required indulgences, with further *grateful* instances of our unruly dispositions.

'After our wise parents have bribed our way through the usual forms, with very little improvement in our learning, we are brought home; and then our parents take their *deserved* turn. We torture their hearts by our undutiful behaviour; which, however ungrateful in us, is but the natural consequence of their culpable indulgence, from infancy upwards.

'After we have, perhaps, half broken *their* hearts, a *wife* is looked for: birth, and fortune, are the first motives, affection the last (if it be at all consulted): and two people thus educated, thus trained up, in a course of unnatural ingratitude, and who have been headstrong torments to every one who had a share in their education, as well as to those to whom they owe their being, are brought together; and what can be expected, but that they should join most heartily in matrimony to plague one another? It is indeed just it should be so, because they by this means revenge the cause of all those who have been aggrieved and insulted by them, upon each other.

'Neither of them having ever been subject to controul, or even to a contradiction, the man cannot bear it from one, whose new relation to him, and whose vow of obedience, he thinks, should oblige her to yield her will entirely to his.

'The lady (well-read in nothing, perhaps, but Romances) thinks it very ungallant now, for the *first* time, to be controuled, and that by a man, from whom she expected nothing but tenderness.

'So great is the difference, between what they both expect *from*, and what they both find *in*, each other, that no wonder misunderstandings happen: that these ripen into quarrels; that acts of unkindness pass, which, even had the first motive to their union been *affection*, as usually it is not, would have effaced all manner of tender impressions on both sides.

'Appeals to parents or guardians often ensue: if, by mediation of friends, a reconciliation takes place, it hardly ever holds; for the fault is in the minds of *both*, and neither of them will think so: whence the wound (not permitted to be probed) is but skinned over, and rankles at the bottom, and at last breaks out with more violence than before. Separate beds are often the consequence; perhaps elopements, guilty ones sometimes; if not, an unconquerable indifference, possibly aversion. And whenever, for appearance-sake, they are obliged to be together, every one sees, that the yawning husband, and the vapourish[335] wife, are truly insupportable to each other; but, separate, have freer spirits, and can be tolerable company.

'Now, my Pamela, I would have you think, and I hope you will have reason for it, that had I married the first lady in the land, I would not have treated her better than I will you; for my wife *is* my wife; and I was the longer in resolving on the state, because I knew its requisites, and doubted my conduct in it.

'I believe I am more nice than many men; but it is because I have been a close observer of the behaviour of wedded folks, and hardly have ever seen it to be such as I could like in my own case. I shall, possibly, give you more particular instances of this, when we have been *longer* acquainted.

'Had I married with no other views than most men have, on entering into the state, my wife might have been a fine lady, brought up pretty much in my own manner, and accustomed to have her will in every thing.

'Some men come into a compromise; and, after a few struggles, sit down tolerably contented. But, had I married a princess, I could not have done so. Indeed, I must have preferred her to all her sex, before I had consented to go to church with her; for even in this *best* case, differences are too apt to arise in matrimony, that will sometimes make a man's home uneasy to him; and there are fewer instances, I believe, of men's loving better after matrimony, than of women's; into the reasons of which it is not my present purpose to enquire.

464

'Then I must have been morally sure, that she preferred me to all men; and, to convince me of this, she must have lessened, not aggravated, my failings; she must have borne with my imperfections; she must have watched and studied my temper; and if ever she had any points to carry, any desire of overcoming, it must have been by sweetness and complaisance; and yet not such a slavish one, as should make her condescension seem to be rather the effect of her insensibility, than of her judgment and affection.

'She should not have given cause for any part of my conduct to her, to wear the least appearance of compulsion or force. The words *command*, on my side, and *obedience* on hers, I would have blotted out of my vocabulary. For this reason I should have thought it my duty to have desired nothing of her that was not reasonable, or just; and that then she should, on hers, have shewn no reluctance, uneasiness, or doubt, to oblige me, even at half a word.

'I would not have excused her to let me twice enjoin the same thing, while I took such care to make her compliance with me reasonable, and such as should not destroy her own free agency, in points that ought to have been allowed her: yet, if I was not always right, I should have expected that she should bear with me, if she saw me determined; and that she should expostulate with me on the right side of compliance; for that would shew me, (supposing *small points* in dispute, from which the greatest quarrels, among *friends*, generally arise) that she differed from me, not for *contradiction's sake*, but desired to convince me for *my own*; and that I should, another time, take fitter resolutions.

'This would have been so obliging a conduct, that I should, in justice, have doubled my esteem for one, who, to honour me, could give up her own judgment; and I should see she could have no other view in her expostulations, after her compliance had passed, than to rectify my notions for the future; and it would have been impossible then, but I must have paid the greater deference to her opinion and advice in matters of greater moment.

'In all companies, she must have shewn, that she had, whether I altogether deserved it or not, an high regard and opinion of me; and this the rather, as such a regard would be not only a reputation, but a security, to herself; since, if ever we rakes attempt a married woman, our first encouragement, next to that of our own vanity, arises from her indifferent opinion, or from her slight, or contempt, of her husband.

'I should have expected, therefore, that she would draw a kind veil over my faults; that such as she could not hide, she should endeavour to extenuate; that she would place my better actions in an advantageous light, and shew that I had *her* good opinion, at least, whatever liberties the *world* took with my character.

'She must have valued my friends for my sake; been chearful and easy, whomsoever I had brought home with me; and whatever faults she had observed in me, have never blamed me before company; at least, with such an air as should have shewn she had a better opinion of her own judgment, than of mine.

'Now, my Pamela, this is but a faint sketch of the conduct I must have expected from my wife, let her quality have been what it would; or I must have lived with her on bad terms. Judge, then, if, to me, a woman of the modish taste could have been tolerable.

'The perverseness and contradiction, I have too often seen, even among people of sense, as well as condition, in the married state, had prejudiced me against it; and, as I knew I could not bear contradiction, surely I was in the right to decline entering into that state with a woman, who, by her education, was so likely to give it: and you see, my dear, that I have not gone among this class of people for a wife; nor know I, indeed, where, in any class, I could have found one so suitable to my mind as you. For here is my misfortune; I could not have been contented to have been but *moderately happy* in a wife.

'Judge you, from all this, if I could very well bear, that you should think yourself so well secured of my affection, that you could take the faults of others upon yourself; and, by a supposed supererogatory[336] merit, think your interposition sufficient to atone for them. I know my own imperfections: they are many and great: yet will not allow that they shall excuse those of my wife, or make her think I ought to bear faults in her, that she *can* rectify, because she sees greater in me.

'Upon the whole, I expect that you will bear with me, and consult my temper, *till*, and only *till*, you see I am capable of returning insult for condescension; and till you think I shall be so mean as to be the gentler, for negligent or pertinacious treatment. One thing more I will add, that I should scorn myself, if there was one privilege of a wife, that a princess, as such, might expect to be indulged in, that I would not allow to my Pamela. For you are the wife of my affection; I never wished for one before you, nor ever do I hope to have another.'

I thanked him for these kind hints, and generous assurances; and told him, that they had made so much impression on my mind, that these, and his most agreeable injunctions before given me, and such as he should hereafter be pleased to give me, should be the indispensable rules for my future conduct.

And, indeed, I am glad that I have fallen upon this method of making a journal of all that passes in these first stages of my happiness; because it will sink the impression still deeper; and I shall have recourse to my papers for my better regulation, as often as I shall mistrust my memory.

Let me see: What are the rules I am to observe from this awful lecture? Why, these:

1. I must not, when he is in great wrath with any body, break in upon him without his leave. – *I will be sure to remember this.*

2. I must think his displeasure the heaviest thing that can befal me. – *That I certainly shall.*

3. And so, that I must not wish to incur it, to save any body else from it. – *Let me suffer for it, if I do.*

4. I must never make a compliment to any body at his expence.

5. I must not be guilty of any acts of wilful meanness! – *There is a great deal meant in this; and I will endeavour to observe it. The occasion on which he mentions this, explains it;* That I must say nothing, though in anger, that is spiteful, malicious, disrespectful, or undutiful.

6. I must bear with him, even when I find him in the wrong. – *This may be a little hard, as the case may be circumstanced.*

I wonder whether poor Miss Sally Godfrey be living or dead.

7. I must be as flexible as the reed in the fable; lest, by resisting the tempest, like the oak, I be torn up by the roots. – *I will do the best I can. There is no great likelihood, I hope, that I should be very perverse; yet, surely, the tempest will not lay me quite level with the ground, if I mean not perverseness.*

8. The education of young people of condition, he says, is generally wrong. – Memorandum, *That if any part of children's*

education fall to my lot, I never indulge or humour them in things that they ought to be restrained in.

9. That I accustom them to bear disappointments and controul.

10. That I suffer them not to be too much indulged in their infancy.

11. Nor at school.

12. Nor spoil them when they come home.

13. For that children generally extend their perverseness from the nurse to the schoolmaster; from the schoolmaster to the parents.

14. And, in their next step, as a proper punishment for all, make themselves unhappy.

15. Undutiful and perverse children, he observes, generally make bad husbands and wives – *And, most probably, bad masters and mistresses.*

16. Not being subject to be controuled early, he observes, they cannot, when married, bear with each other.

17. That the fault lying deep, and in the minds of each, neither will mend it.

18. Whence follow misunderstandings, quarrels, appeals, ineffectual reconciliations, separations, elopements – or, at best, indifference; perhaps, aversion. – Memorandum, *A good image of unhappy wedlock, in the words,* YAWNING HUSBAND, *and* VAPOUR-ISH WIFE, *when together: but separate, both in high spirits, and quite alive.*

19. Few married persons, he says, behave as he likes. – *Let me ponder this with awe, for my improvement.*

20. Some men can compromise with their wives for quietness-sake; but he cannot. – *Indeed, I believe that's true; nor do I desire he should.*

21. Love before marriage, he thinks, is absolutely necessary. – *Generally speaking, I believe it is.*

22. He says, there are fewer instances of mens loving better after marriage, than of womens. – *But why so? I wish he had given his reasons for this! I fancy they would not have been to the credit of his own sex.*

23. He insists upon it, that a woman should give her husband reason to think she prefers him before all men. – *No doubt, this should be so.*

24. If she would overcome, he says, it must be by sweetness and complaisance. – *A hard lesson, I doubt, where one's judgment is not convinced. We all dearly love to be thought in the right, in any debated point. I am afraid this doctrine, if enforced, would tend to make an honest wife a hypocrite!*[337]

25. Yet she must not shew such a slavish complaisance, as should rather seem the effect of her insensibility, than of her judgment or affection. – *Pretty tolerable.*

26. The words COMMAND and OBEY, he says, shall be blotted out of his vocabulary. – *Very good! Most chearfully do I subscribe to this!*

27. A man should desire nothing of his wife, but what is reasonable and just. – *To be sure, that is right. Yet who, all this time, is to be the judge?*

28. She must not shew reluctance, uneasiness, or doubt, in obliging him; and that too at half a word; and must not be bidden twice to do one thing. – *Very lordly! But may not there be some occasions, where this may be a little dispensed with? But he says afterwards, indeed,*

29. That this must be only while he took care to make her compliance reasonable, and consistent with her free agency, in points that ought to be allowed her. – *Come, this is pretty well, considering. Yet, again I ask – Who is to be the judge?*

30. If he be set upon a wrong thing, she must not dispute with him, but do it, and expostulate afterwards. – *I don't know what to say to this! It looks a little hard, methinks! This would bear a smart debate, I fancy, in a parliament of women.*[338] *But then he says,*

31. Supposing they are only small points that are in dispute. – *Well, this mends it a little: for small points, I think, should not be stood upon. May I not say, on either side?*

32. The greatest quarrels among friends (*and wives and husbands are, or should be, friends*) he says, arise from small matters. – *I believe this is very true; for I had like to have had anger, when I intended very well.*

33. A wife, he says, should not desire to convince her husband for CONTRADICTION sake, but for HIS OWN. – *As both will find their account in this, if one does, I believe it is very just.*

34. In all companies a wife must shew respect and love to her husband.

35. And this for the sake of her own reputation and security: because,

36. That rakes cannot have a greater encouragement to attempt a married woman's virtue, than her slight opinion of her husband. – *To be sure, this stands to reason, and is a good lesson.*

37. A wife, he says, should therefore draw a kind veil over her husband's faults.

38. Such as she could not conceal, she should extenuate.

39. She should place his virtues in an advantageous light.

40. And shew the world, that he had *her* good opinion.

41. She must value his friends for *his* sake.

42. She must be chearful and easy in her behaviour, to whomsoever he brings home with him.

43. Whatever fault she sees in him, she must never blame him before company.

44. At least, with such an air of superiority, as if she had a less opinion of his judgment than of her own.

45. He says, he cannot be contented to be only *moderately* happy in a wife.

46. A wife should take care, he says, how she ascribe supererogatory merit to herself; so as to take the faults of others upon her. – *Indeed, I think it is well if we can bear our own! This is of the same nature with the third: and touches upon me, on the present occasion, for this wholesome lecture.*

47. *His* imperfections, he says, must not be a plea for *hers*. – *To be sure, a woman cannot be too good; but 'tis to be hoped, men, who, to the honour of our sex, he seems to think, cannot be so good as we, will allow a little. But, indeed, he hints,*

48. That a husband, who expects all this, is to be incapable of returning insult for condescension; and ought not to abridge her of any privilege of her sex.

Well, my dear parents, I think this last crowns the rest, and makes them all very tolerable; since a generous man, and a man of sense, cannot be too much obliged. And, as I have the happiness to call such a one mine, I shall be very unworthy, if I do not make the obliging of him my whole study.

Yet, after all, you will see I have not the easiest task in the world before me. But, knowing my own heart, and that I shall not wilfully err, I have the less to fear.

Not one hint did he give, that I durst lay hold of, about poor Miss Sally Godfrey. I wish my lady had not spoken of it: for it has given me a curiosity that seems to me myself not to be quite right; especially so early in my marriage, and in a case so long ago past. Yet he intimated too, to his sister, that he had had other faults, (of this sort, I suppose): but I make no doubt, he has seen his error, and will be very good for the future. I wish it, and pray it may be so, for his own sake, even more than for mine.

WEDNESDAY, *the Seventh*

When I arose in the morning, passing by Lady Davers's chamber-door, and seeing it open, and hearing her talking to her woman, I stept in, and enquired after her night's rest.

She was in bed, and took kindly my visit, and asked me, when we set out for Bedfordshire? 'I can't tell, madam,' said I: 'it was designed as to-day, but I have heard no more of it.'

'Sit down,' said she, 'on the bed-side. I find, by the talk we had yesterday, and last night, that you have had but a poor time of it, Pamela,' (I must call you so yet, said she) 'since you were brought to this house, till within these few days. Mrs Jewkes, too, has given Worden such an account, as makes me pity you.'

'Indeed, madam,' said I, 'if your ladyship knew all, you *would* pity me; for never poor creature was so hardly used. But I ought to forget it all, and be thankful.'

'Why,' said she, 'as far as I can find, 'tis a mercy you are here now. I was greatly moved with some part of your story: and you have really made a noble stand, and deserve the praises of all our sex.'

'It was God's goodness that sustained me, madam,' replied I.

'Why,' said she, ''tis the more extraordinary, because, I believe, if the truth were known, you loved the wretch not a little. Speak your mind freely, child. You may say anything before Worden.'

'While my trials lasted, madam,' answered I, 'I had not a *thought* of *any thing*, but to preserve my innocence; I did not, I could not, think of love.'

'But tell me truly,' said she, 'did you not love him all the time?'
'I had always, madam,' answered I, 'a great reverence for my
master, and thought highly of all his good actions; and, though I
abhorred his attempts upon me, yet I could not hate him; and
always wished him well; but I did not know, it was love. Indeed,
I had not the presumption.'

'Sweet girl!' said she; 'that's prettily said: but when he found
he could not gain his ends, and began to repent of his treatment of
you, and to admire your virtue, and to profess honourable love to
you, what did you think?'

'Think! and please your ladyship, I did not know what to think:
I could neither hope nor believe so great an honour would fall to
my lot: and I feared more from his kindness, for some time, than
I had done from his unkindness. And, having had a private intimation of a sham-marriage intended, by means of a man who was to
personate a clergyman, my mind was kept in too much suspense,
to be greatly overjoyed at his declaration.'

'I think,' said her ladyship, 'he did make two or three attempts
upon you in Bedfordshire?' 'Yes, madam, he was very wicked, to
be sure.'

'And *here*, at this house, he owns, he proposed very high
articles to you.' 'Yes, madam; but I rejected them with great disdain; and was resolved to die rather than to be a kept creature.'

'He after that attempted you, I think: did he not?'

'O yes, madam! a most sad attempt he made; and I had like to
have been lost; for Mrs Jewkes was not so good as she should have
been.'

I then, at her request, acquainted her with that dreadful attempt,
and how I fell into fits; which saved me.

'Any attempts after this very base one?' asked she.

'He was not, answered I, so good as he should have been, once
in the garden afterwards: but my watchfulness –'

'But,' said she, 'did he not threaten you, at times, and put on
his stern airs, every now-and-then?' 'Threaten, madam!' replied I;
'yes, I had enough of that! I thought I should have died for fear,
several times.'

'How could you bear his threatenings?' said she: 'for he is a
most daring mortal! He has none of your puny hearts, but is as
bold as a lion; and, boy and man, he never feared any thing. I

myself,' added she, 'have a pretty good spirit; but when I have made him really angry, I have always been forced to make it up with him, as well as I could. For, child, he is not, as you have heard me say before, one that is easily reconciled. But, after he had professed honourable love to you, did he never attempt you again?'

'No, indeed, madam, he did not. But he was a good while struggling with himself, and with his pride, as he was pleased to call it, before he could stoop so low; and considered, and considered again: and once, upon my saying but two or three words, that displeased him, when he was very kind to me, he turned me out of doors, in a manner, at an hour's warning; for he sent me above a day's journey towards my father's; and then sent a man and horse, post-haste,[339] to fetch me back again; and has been exceedingly kind and gracious to me ever since; and, at last, made me happy.'

'That turning you away,' said she, 'one hour, and sending after you the next, is exactly like my brother. If you were to vex him by any fault he should think wilful, I should not wonder, if he banishes you from one house to the other; and set out to bring you back before you had reached it. Had he married the first woman in the kingdom, we should often have had such banishments and recals; but not the latter, till he had made her submit: yet has he some good qualities; for he is generous, nay, he is noble in his spirit; hates little mean actions; he delights in doing good. He is wise, prudent, sober, and magnanimous; and will not disguise his faults; but you must not expect to have him all to yourself, I doubt. No more, however, will I harp upon that string:[340] you see how he was exasperated at an hint or two of that sort; though something of it was art, I believe. Don't you think so?'

'Indeed, madam, I believe not. When we retired, he gave me a most noble lecture; and I find he was angry with me in earnest, and that it will not be an easy task to behave unexceptionably to him: for he has very nice and delicate notions; but yet, as your ladyship says, exceeding generous.'

'Well,' said she, 'I am glad thou hadst a little specimen of his anger; else I should have thought it art; and I do not love to be treated with low art, any more than he. But I understand, child,' continued she, 'that you keep a journal of all matters that pass; and that he has several times found means to get at it: should you care I should see it? It could not be to your disadvantage; for I find it had no small weight with *him* in your favour; and I should take great pleasure to read all his stratagems, attempts, contrivances, menaces, and offers to you, on one hand; and all your counter-plottings, which he much praises, your resolute resistance, and the noble efforts you have made to preserve your virtue; and the steps by which his pride was subdued, till you were made what you now are: for it must be a rare, an uncommon story. I shall have great pleasure in reading it; and it will, probably, reconcile me to the step he has taken. And that, let me tell you, is what I never thought to be; for I had gone a great way in bringing about a match with him and Lady Betty C.; and had laboured it so much, that Lord C. approved of it, and so did the Duke of —, her uncle; and Lady Betty herself was not averse: and now I shall be railed to death about it; and this made me so outrageous as I was to you. When I find, by your papers, that your virtue is but suitably rewarded, I shall have an excuse to make for myself, to Lady Betty, and her friends: he will be better justified for what he has done; and I shall love **you**.'

'There is nothing that I would not do,' replied I, 'to oblige your ladyship; but my father and mother (who would rather have seen me buried quick in the earth, than to have been seduced by the greatest of princes) have my papers in their hands at present; and your brother has bespoke them, when they have done reading them; but if he gives me leave, I will shew them to your ladyship with all my heart, not doubting your generous allowances, as I have had his – (though I have treated him very freely all the way, while he had wicked views) – and that your ladyship will consider them as the genuine sentiments of my heart, delivered from time to time to those whose indulgence I was sure of; and for whose sight, only, they were written.'

'Let me kiss you,' said she, 'for your chearful compliance. I make no doubt but my brother will consent I shall see them, because they must needs make for *your* honour; and I see he loves you better than he loves any one in the world.

'I have heard,' continued her ladyship, 'a mighty good character of your parents, as industrious, honest, sensible folks; and, as I doubt not my brother's generosity, I am glad they will make no ill figure, in the world's eye, with a little of his assistance.'

'There is not in the world, madam,' said I, 'an honester, a more affectionate, a more conscientious couple. They once lived creditably; they brought up a great family, of which I am the youngest, and the only one left. Their misfortunes were owing to their doing beyond their abilities for two unhappy brothers, who are both dead, and whose debts they stood bound for; and, by harsh creditors, (I call them so, because the debts were not of their own contracting) turned out of all; and my father having, without success, set up a little country school, (for he understood a little of accompts, and writes a pretty good hand) he was forced to take to hard labour; but all the time they were honest, contented; never repining; and loving to each other. All their fear was, that their poverty should subject me, their poor daughter, to temptation; and they were continually warning me on this subject. To God's grace, and their good lessons, and those I imbibed from my dear good lady, your ladyship's mother, it is that I owe the preservation of my innocence, and the happy station I am exalted to.'

She was pleased to salute me again, and said, 'There is such a sweet simplicity in thy story, as thou tellest it; such an honest artlessness in thy mind, and such an amiable humility in thy deportment, that I believe I shall be forced to love thee, whether I will or not. The sight of your papers, I dare say, will crown the work.

'Worden,' said my lady to her woman, 'you will take no notice of this conversation. I see you are much touched with it.' 'Indeed, madam, I am,' answered she: 'and it is a great pleasure to me to see so happy a reconciliation taking place, where there is so much merit.'

'I have discovered,' said I, 'so much prudence in Mrs Worden, that, as well for that, as for the confidence your ladyship places in her, I have made no scruple of speaking my mind freely before her; and, in the progress of my story, of blaming your dear brother, while he was blame-worthy, as well as of acknowledging his transcendent goodness to me since; which exceeds all I can ever deserve.' 'Perhaps not,' replied my lady; 'I hope you will be happy in each other. I will now rise, and tell him my thoughts, and ask him to let me have the reading of your papers; for I promise myself much pleasure in them; and shall not grudge a journey, and a visit to you, to the other house, to fetch them.'

'If, madam, I am blessed with your favour, and the continuance of your dear brother's goodness to me, I shall be too happy.'

I withdrew; and she let me hear her say to Mrs Worden, "Tis a charming creature, Worden! I know not which excels, her person or her mind. So young a creature too! Well may my brother love her!'

I am afraid, my dear father and mother, I shall now be proud indeed.

I had a good mind to have asked her ladyship about Miss Sally Godfrey; but I thought it was better left alone, since she did not mention it herself. I wonder, though, whether she be living or dead.

My lady was equally kind to me at breakfast; and asking my dear friend, he gave leave very readily that she should see all my papers, when you returned them to me. He was sure, he told her, when she came to read them, she would say, that I had well deserved the fortune I had met with; and would be of opinion, that all the kindness of his future life would hardly make me amends for my sufferings.

My lady resolving to set out on Thursday morning to return to her lord, my master ordered every thing to be made ready for our journey to Bedfordshire; and this evening our good neighbours will sup with us, by way of taking leave of Lady Davers and us.

WEDNESDAY *Night*

Nothing having passed at supper, but the most condescending goodness, on my lady's side, to me; and the highest civilities from our neighbours, and reciprocal good wishes all round; and a promise obtained from *my* Mr B. (There's a proud word!) that he would endeavour to pass a fortnight or three weeks in these parts, before the winter set in, I shall conclude this day, with observing, that I disposed of the money my master was so good to put into my hands, in the method he was pleased to direct. I gave Mrs Jewkes hers, in such a manner, as highly pleased her; and she wished me, with tears, all kinds of happiness; and prayed me to forgive her all her past wickedness, as she herself called it. I begged leave of my master to present Mrs Worden with five guineas for a pair of gloves,[341] which he said was well thought of.

I should have mentioned, that Miss Darnford and I agreed upon a correspondence, which will be no small pleasure to me; for she is an admirable young lady, whom I prefer to every one I have seen; and I shall, I make no doubt, improve by her letters; for she is said to have a talent in writing, and is both learned and well-read.

SATURDAY

On Thursday morning Lady Davers, as she had intended, set out for her own seat; and my best friend and I, attended by Mr Colbrand, Abraham, and Thomas, for this dear house. Her ladyship parted with her brother and me with great tenderness, and made me promise to send her my papers; with which I find she intends to entertain Lady Betty, and another lady or two, her select friends, as also her lord; in hopes to find, in the reading of them, as I have the pleasure to think, some excuse for her brother's choice.

My dearest master was all love and tenderness on the road, as he is in every place, and on every occasion. What a delightful change was this journey to that which, so contrary to all my wishes, and so much to my apprehensions, carried me hence to the Lincolnshire house! Do you think I did not bless God at every turn, and at every stage? Indeed I did.

We arrived not here till yesterday noon. Abraham rode before, to let them know we were coming. And I had the satisfaction to find every body there I wished to see.

When the chariot entered the court-yard, I was so strongly impressed with the favour and mercies of the Almighty, on remembering how I was sent away the last time I saw this house; the leave I took; the dangers I afterwards encountered; a poor cast-off servant girl; and now returning a joyful wife, and the mistress of the noble house I was turned out of; that I was hardly able to support the joy I felt in my mind on the occasion.

The dear man saw my emotion, and tenderly asked, why I seemed so affected? I told him, and lifted his hand to my lips, saying, 'O sir! the sense I have of God's mercies, and your goodness to me, on entering this dear, dear place, gives me joy beyond expression. I can hardly bear my own reflections!' 'Welcome, thrice welcome, pride of my life!' said he, 'to your own house'; kissing my hand.

All the common servants stood at the windows, as unseen as they could, to observe us. He took my hand, with the most condescending goodness; and, with great complaisance, led me into the parlour, and saluted me. 'Welcome once more, my dearest wife,' said he, 'a thousand times welcome, to the possession of a house that is not more mine than yours.'

I threw myself on my knees, 'Permit me, sir, thus to bless *God*, and to thank *you*, for all *his* mercies, and *your* goodness. May I so behave as not to be *utterly unworthy*; and then how *happy* shall I be!' 'God give me life and health,' said he, 'to reward my Pamela; and no man can be then so blessed as I!'

'Where is Mrs Jervis?' said he to Abraham, who passed by the door. She bolted in. 'Here, good sir,' said she; 'here, good madam, am I, waiting impatiently, till called for, to congratulate you both.' I ran to her, and clasped my arms about her neck, and kissed her. 'O my dear Mrs Jervis!' said I, 'my other mother! receive your happy, happy Pamela: and join with me to bless God, and bless our master –'

I was ready to sink in her arms, through excess of joy, to behold the dear good woman, who had been so often a mournful witness of my distress, as she was now of my triumph. 'Dearest madam,' said she, 'you do me too much honour. Let my whole life shew the joy I take in your deserved good fortune, and in my duty to you, for the early instance I received of your goodness in your kind letter.' 'O Mrs Jervis,' replied I, '*there*, next to the Almighty, all thanks are due, both from you and me: for our dear master granted me this blessing, as I may justly call it, the very first moment I begged it of him.' 'Your goodness, sir,' said she, 'I will for ever acknowledge; and I beg pardon for the wrong step I made, in applying to Lady Davers.' 'All is over now, Mrs Jervis,' said he. 'I will forget that you ever disobliged me. I always respected you, and shall now more and more value you, for the sake of that dear good creature, whom, with joy unfeigned, I call my wife.' 'God bless your honour, for ever!' said she; 'and many, *many* happy years may ye live together, the envy and wonder of all who know you!'

'But where,' said my master, 'is honest Longman? And where is Jonathan?' 'Come, Mrs Jervis,' said I, 'you shall introduce them, and all the good folks, to me presently. Let me now go up with you to behold the apartments, which I have seen *before* with such different emotions to what I shall now do.'

We went up; and in the chamber I took refuge in, when my master pursued me, in my lady's chamber, in her dressing-room, in Mrs Jervis's apartment (not forgetting her closet) in my own little bed-chamber, the green-room, and in each of the others, I blessed God for my past escapes, and present happiness. The good woman was quite affected with the zeal and pleasure with which I made my thankful acknowledgments to the Divine Goodness. 'O my excellent lady!' said she, 'you are still the same good, pious, humble soul I knew you. Your marriage has added to your graces, as I hope it will to your blessings.'

'Dear Mrs Jervis,' said I, 'you know not what I have gone through! You know not what God has done for me! You know not what a happy creature I am now! I have a thousand, thousand things to tell you. A whole week will be too little, every moment of it spent in relating to you what has befallen me, to make you acquainted with it all. We shall be sweetly happy together, I make no doubt. But I charge you, my dear Mrs Jervis, whatever you call me before strangers, that when we are by ourselves, you call me nothing but *your* Pamela. For what an ungrateful creature should I be, who have received so many mercies, if I assumed to myself insolent airs upon them! No, my dearest Mrs Jervis, it is my hope that I shall be more and more thankful, as I am more and more blessed; and more humble, as God, the author of all my happiness, shall more distinguish me.'

We went down again to the parlour, to our master. 'Call in again Mr Longman,' said he: 'the good man longs to see you, my dear.'

He came in: 'God bless you, my sweet lady!' said he; 'as now, Heaven be praised, I may call you! Did I not tell you, madam, that Providence would find you out?' 'O Mr Longman,' said I, 'God be praised for all his mercies! I am rejoiced to see you.' And I laid my hand on his, and said, 'Good Mr Longman, how do you? I must always value you; and you don't know how much of my present happiness I owe to the sheets of paper, and pens and ink, you furnished me with. I hope my dear Mr B. and you are quite reconciled.' 'O madam,' said he, 'how good you are! I cannot contain myself for joy!'

And then he dried his eyes – good man!

'Yes, I have been telling Mr Longman,' said my master, 'that I am obliged to him for his ready return to me; and that I will entirely forget his appeal to Lady Davers; and I hope he will find himself easy and happy to the extent of his wishes. My dear partner here, Mr Longman, I dare promise you, will do all *she* can to make you so.'

'Heaven bless you both together!' said he. ''Tis the pride of my heart to see this! I returned with double delight, when I heard the blessed news; and I am sure, sir,' said he, '(Mark old Longman's words), God will bless you for this every year more and more. You don't know how many hearts you have made happy by this generous deed.'

'I am sure,' said my dear master, 'I have made my *own* happy: and, Mr Longman, though I must think you S O M E B O D Y,[342] yet, as you are not a young man, I can allow you to wish my wife joy in the tenderest manner.'

'Adad! sir,' said he, 'I am sure you rejoice me with your favour: 'twas what I longed for, but dared not presume.'

'My dear,' said my master, 'receive the compliment of one of the honestest men in England, who always revered your virtues!' The good man saluted me; and said (dropping down on one knee), 'The great God of Heaven bless you both! I must quit your presence. Indeed I must.' And away he went.

'Your goodness, sir,' said I, 'knows no bounds: may my gratitude never find any!' 'I saw,' said my master, 'when the good man approached you, that he did it with so much awe and love mingled together, that I thought he longed to salute my angel; and I could not but indulge his honest heart.'

When honest old Jonathan came in to attend at dinner, so sleek,[343] and so neat, as he always is, with his silver hair, I said, 'Well, Mr Jonathan, how do you? I am glad to see you: you look as well as ever, thank God!' 'O madam,' replied he, 'better than ever, to behold such a blessed sight! God bless you, and my good master! And I hope, sir, you will excuse all my past failings.' 'Ay, that I will, Jonathan,' said his kind master; 'because you never had any, but what were owing to your regard for my beloved wife. And now I can tell you, you can never err, because you cannot respect her too much.' 'O sir,' said he, 'your honour is exceeding good. I'm sure I shall always pray for you both.'

After dinner, Mr Longman coming in, and talking of some affairs under his care, he said afterwards, 'All your honour's servants are now happy; for Robert, who left you, has a pretty little fortune fallen to him, or he never would have quitted your service. He was here but yesterday, to enquire when you and my lady returned hither; and hoped he might have leave to pay his duty to you both.' 'I shall be glad to see honest Robin,' said my master; 'for he is another of your favourites, Pamela. It was high time, I think, I should marry you, were it but to engage the respects of all my family to myself.'

'But I was going to say,' said Mr Longman, 'that all your honour's old servants are now happy, but one.' 'You mean John Arnold?' said my master. 'I do indeed,' replied he, 'if you will excuse me, sir.' 'O,' said I, 'I have had my prayer for poor John answered, as favourably as I could wish.' 'Why,' said Mr Longman, 'to be sure poor John has acted no very good part, take it all together; but he so much honoured *you*, sir, and so much respected *you*, madam, that he would have been glad to be obedient to both; and so was faithful to neither. But indeed the poor fellow's heart is almost broken, and he won't look out for any other place; and says, he must live in your honour's service, or he must die wretched very shortly.'

Mrs Jervis was there when this was spoken: 'Indeed,' said she, 'the poor man has been here every day since he heard the tidings that have rejoiced us all; and he says, he hopes yet to be forgiven.' 'Is he in the house now?' asked my master. 'He is, sir; and was here when your honour came in; and played at hide-and-seek to have one look at you both, when you alighted; and was ready to go out of his wits for joy, when he saw your honour hand my lady in.' 'Pamela,' said my master, 'you are to do with John as you please: you have full power.' 'Then, pray,' said I, 'let John come in.'

The poor fellow came in, with so much concern, that I have never seen a countenance that expressed so lively a consciousness of his faults, mingled with so much joy and shame. 'How do you, John?' said I. 'I hope you are very well!' He could hardly speak, and looked with awe upon my master, and with pleasure upon me. 'Well, John,' said my master, 'there is no room to say any thing to a man that has so much concern upon him already. I am told you *will* serve me, whether I will or not; but I turn you over altogether to my wife here: and she is to do by you as she pleases.' 'You see, John,' said I, 'your good master's indulgence. Well may *I* forgive, that have so generous an example. I was always persuaded of your honest intentions. You were only at a loss what to do between your duty to your master, and your good-will to me: you will now, from his goodness, have no more puzzles on that account.' 'I shall be but too happy,' said the poor man. 'God bless your honour! God bless you, madam! I have now the joy of my soul, in serving you both; and I will, to my power, make the best of servants.' 'Well, then, John, your wages will go on, as if you had not left your master: may I not say so, sir?' said I. 'Yes, surely, my dear,' replied he, 'and augment them too, if you find his duty to you deserves it.' 'A thousand million of thanks,' said the poor man: 'I desire no augmentation.'

He withdrew overjoyed; and Mrs Jervis and Mr Longman were highly pleased; for though they were incensed against him for his fault to me, when matters looked badly for me, yet they, and the rest of his fellow-servants, always loved John.

My master then, filling a glass of wine, said, 'Mr Longman, I will toast to you, the health of one of the happiest and honestest couple in England; my Pamela's father and mother.' Tears were in my eyes. I could not speak for joy.

'I think,' continued he, 'that our little Kentish purchase, Mr Longman, as it is at distance from my other estates, the management of which fully employ all your kind cares, will be in happy hands if Mr Andrews will take upon him the trouble of managing it. We will well stock for him the farm we call Hodges's, that is in the middle of the purchase; and his directing eye over the whole, will be an employment for him, and ease to you, and a benefit to me. What think you, Mr Longman?'

'Your honour cannot do a better thing; and I have had some inkling given me, that you may, if you please, augment that estate, by a purchase, of equal amount, contiguous[344] to it; and as you have so much money to spare, I can't see your honour can do better.' 'Well,' said my master, 'let me have the particulars another

time, and we will consider of it. But, my dear,' added he, 'you will
mention this to your father.

'I have too much money, Mr Longman,' continued he, 'lying
useless; though, upon the present agreeable occasion, I shall lay
out as much in liveries, and equipages,[345] as if I had married a
woman of a fortune, equal, if possible, to my Pamela's merit.
I reckon you have a good deal in hand?' 'Yes, sir,' said he, 'more
than I wish I had. But I have a mortgage in view, if you don't buy
that Kentish thing, that I believe will answer very well; and when
matters are riper, will mention it to your honour.'

'I took with me to Lincolnshire,' said my master, 'six hundred
and fifty guineas, and thought to have laid most of them out there.'
[Thank God, thought I, you did not! for he offered me five hundred
of them, you know.] 'But I have not laid out above two hundred
and fifty: I left there two hundred in my escritoire;[346] intending to
go thither again for a fortnight or three weeks, before winter; and
two hundred I have brought back. I have besides money, I know
not what, in three places here; the account of which is in my
library.

'You have made some little presents, Pamela, to my servants
there, on our nuptials; and these two hundred that I have brought
up, I will leave to your disposal, to do with some of them here, as
you did there.'

'I am ashamed, sir,' said I, 'to be so costly and so worthless!'
'Pray, my dear,' replied he, 'not a word more in that style.'

'Why, madam,' said Mr Longman, 'with money in stocks, and
one thing or other, his honour could buy half the gentlemen round
him. He wants not money, and lays up every year. And it would
have been pity, but he should have wedded just as he has done.'
'Very true, Mr Longman,' said my master: and pulling out his
purse, 'Tell out, my dear,' said he, 'two hundred guineas.' I did
so. 'Now,' said he, 'take them yourself, for the purposes I mentioned. But, Mr Longman, do you, before sun-set, bring my dear
girl fifty guineas, which is due to her this day, by my promise;
and every three months, pay her fifty more; which will be two
hundred guineas per annum: and this for her to lay out at her own
discretion, and without account, in such a way, as shall derive a
blessing upon us all: for she was my mother's almoner, and shall
be mine, and her own too.'

'I'll go for it this instant,' said Mr Longman.

When he was gone, I looked on my dear Mr B., and on Mrs Jervis; and he gave me a nod of assent; and I took twenty guineas, and said, 'Good Mrs Jervis, accept of this, which is no more than my generous master ordered me to present to Mrs Jewkes, for a pair of gloves, on my happy nuptials.'

'Mrs Jewkes, madam,' said she, 'was on the spot, at the happy time.' 'Yes,' said my master; 'but Pamela would have rejoiced to have had you there instead of her.' 'That I should, sir,' replied I, 'or instead of any body, except my own mother.'

She gratefully accepted them, and thanked us both: but I don't know what she should thank *me* for. I was not worth a fourth part of them myself.

'I would have you, my dear,' said he, 'in some handsome manner, as you know how, oblige Longman to accept of the like present.'

Mr Longman returned from his office, and brought me the fifty guineas, saying, 'I have entered this new article with great pleasure: *To my lady – Fifty guineas: to be paid the same sum quarterly.*' 'O sir,' said I, 'what will become of me to be so poor in myself, and so rich in your bounty? It is a shame to take all that your profuse goodness thus heaps upon me: but indeed it shall not be without account.' 'Make no words, my dear,' answered he: 'are you not my wife? And have I not endowed you with my worldly goods? Hitherto you have had a very inconsiderable part of them.'

'Mr Longman,' said I, 'and Mrs Jervis, you both see how I am even oppressed with obligations.' 'God bless the donor, and the receiver too!' said Mr Longman: 'I am sure they will bring back good interest; for, madam, you had ever a bountiful heart; and I have seen the pleasure you used to take to dispense my late lady's alms and donations.'

'You would have me, Mr Longman,' said I, 'who am otherwise honoured beyond my desert, make no scruple of accepting large sums: pray, do not you make any, to accept of a pair of gloves on account of my happy nuptials.'

He hesitated, and seemed at a loss; and Mr B. said, 'If Mr Longman refuse you, my dear, he will refuse your *first* favour.' I then put twenty guineas in his hand. He begged that he might return fifteen. 'Don't give me reason to imagine,' said I, 'that I have affronted you.' 'Well, if I must,' returned he, 'I know what I know.' 'What is that, Mr Longman?' said I. 'Why, madam,' replied he, 'I will not lay it out till my young master's birth-day, which I hope will be within this twelvemonth.'

Not expecting any thing like this from the good old man, I looked this way and that, and blushed, and held down my head. 'Charmingly said, Mr Longman!' said my master, and clasped his arms about me: 'O my dear life! God send it may be so! You have quite delighted me, Mr Longman!' 'Madam,' said the old gentleman, 'I beg your pardon; I hope no offence. But I would speak it ten times in a breath to have it so, take it how you please, as long as my master takes it so well.' 'Mrs Jervis,' said Mr B., 'I hope you join in Mr Longman's good wishes.' She did, she said, with her whole heart.

Mr Longman withdrawing soon after, my master said, 'Why blushes and looks down my dearest love? Surely the old man said nothing that ought to shock you.' 'I did not expect it, sir, from him,' said I: 'I was not aware but of some innocent pleasantry.' 'What he said,' replied he, 'was both innocent and pleasant: and I will not forgive you, if you do not say as he says. Come, speak before Mrs Jervis.' 'May everything happen, sir,' said I, 'that will give *you* joy!' He called me dearest love, and saluted me with great tenderness.

When the servants had dined, I desired to see the maidens, and all four came up together. 'You are welcome home, madam,' said Rachel; 'we rejoice all to see you here, and more to see you our lady.' 'My good old acquaintances,' said I, 'I joy to see you! How do you, Rachel? How do you, Jane? How do you, Hannah? How do you, Cicely?' And I took each of them by the hand, and could have kissed them. For, said I to myself, I kissed you all, last time I saw you, in sorrow; why should I not kiss you all with joy? But I forbore, because of their dear master's presence.

They seemed quite transported with me; and my master was pleased with the scene. 'See here, my lasses,' said he, 'your mistress! I need not bid you respect her; for you always loved her; and she will have it as much in her power, as inclination, to be kind to the deserving.' 'Indeed,' said I, 'I shall always be a kind friend to you; and your dear good master has ordered me to give each of you this, that you may rejoice with me on my happiness.' I then gave them five guineas each; and said, 'God bless you every one. I am over-joyed to see you.' They withdrew with the greatest gratitude and pleasure, praying for us both.

I turned to my dear Mr B. 'It is to you, sir,' said I, 'next to God, who put it into your generous heart, that all my happiness is owing. My heart overflows with joy and gratitude!' And I would have kissed his hand; but he clasped me in his arms, and said, 'You deserve it, my dear! You deserve it all!' Mrs Jervis came in. 'I have seen,' said she, 'a very affecting sight: you have made your maidens quite happy, madam, with your kindness and condescension. I saw them all four, as I came by the hall-door, just rising from their knees, praying for you both!' 'Good creatures!' said I; 'and did Jane pray too? May the effect of their prayers be returned upon themselves!'

My master sent for Jonathan, and I held up all the fingers of my two hands; and he giving a nod of approbation as the honest man came in, I said, 'Well, Mr Jonathan, I could not be satisfied without seeing you by yourself, and thanking you for all your past good-will to me. You will accept of *that* for a pair of gloves, on this happy occasion.' And I gave him ten guineas, and took his honest hand between both mine: 'God bless you,' said I, 'with your silver hairs, so like my dear father! I shall always value such a good old servant of the best of masters!' 'Such goodness! Such kind words!' said he. 'They are balm to my heart! Blessed be God, I have lived to this day!' He withdrew, his eyes swimming in tears.

Then in came Harry, and Isaac, and Benjamin, and the two grooms of this house, and Arthur the gardener; for my dear master had ordered them by Mrs Jervis thus to be introduced. 'Where is John?' said he. Poor John was ashamed, and did not come in till he heard himself called for. I asked each by his name, how he did; and gave each five guineas to rejoice, as I said, in my happiness. Harry, in the names of them all, blessed us, and congratulated themselves on the honour their master had done them in giving them a mistress, whom they always loved; and hardly could now more respect as their lady, than they did before for her virtue and sweetness of temper.

When I came to John, I said, 'I saw you before, John; but I again tell you, I am glad to see you.' He said, he was quite ashamed and confounded. 'You must look forward, John,' said I, 'and forget all that is passed. Your good master will, and so will I. For God has wonderfully brought about all these things, by the very means I thought most grievous.'

'Arthur,' said my master, 'I have brought you a mistress that is a great gardener. She will shew you a new way to plant beans: and never any body had such a hand at improving a sun-flower, as she!' I believe I looked a little silly. I felt my cheeks glow: but the best answer (the servants present) was silence.[347]

To the postilion and two helpers,[348] at my master's motion, I gave three guineas; calling each by his christian name (for my master has here, as well as in Lincolnshire, fine hunting-horses. Hunting is the chief sport he takes delight in). Nor was the poor scullion-boy,[349] Tommy, forgot. I called for him, and gave him two guineas; and, by way of taking more notice of him, some good advice, not to spend it idly; but to give it to his mother, to lay it out for him. Mr Colbrand, Abraham, and Thomas, had been remembered at the other house.

When they were all gone but Mrs Jervis, I said, 'And now, dearest sir, permit me, on my knees, thus, to bless you, and pray for you. May God crown you with length of days, and give you increase of honour; and may your happy, happy Pamela, by her grateful heart, appear always worthy in your eyes, though she cannot be so in her own, nor in those of any others!'

'Mrs Jervis,' said my master, tenderly raising me, 'you see the excellency of this sweet creature! And when I tell you, that the charms of her person, lovely as she is, bind me not so strongly to her as the graces of her mind, I know you will think that my happiness is built on a stable basis, and congratulate me upon it. 'Indeed I do, most sincerely, sir,' said she: 'this is a happy day to me!'

I stepped into the library, while he was thus pouring out his kindness for me to Mrs Jervis; and blessed God there, for the difference between my present situation, and what I had once known in it. Mrs Jervis, it seems, had whispered to him the thankful heart I had expressed above; and he stept to the library door; and, unobserved by me, saw me upon my knees, with my back towards him: but he softly put to the door again, as he had opened it a little way. And I said, on my joining him, not knowing he had seen me, 'You have some charming pictures in your library, sir.'

'I have, my dear life,' said he; 'but none equal to that which your piety affords me! May the God you delight to serve, bless more and more my angel!' 'You are all goodness, sir,' said I. 'I hope, replied he, 'after your example, I shall be more and more worthy of my present happiness!'

Do you think, my dear parents, there ever was so happy a creature as your Pamela? To be sure it would be very ungrateful to think with uneasiness, or any thing but compassion, of poor Miss Sally Godfrey.

He ordered Jonathan to let the evening be passed merrily, but wisely, as he said, with what every one liked, whether wine or October.[350]

He was pleased afterwards to lead me up-stairs, and gave me possession of my lady's dressing-room and cabinet, and her fine repeating-watch[351] and equipage; and, in short, of a complete set of jewels, that were hers; as also of the two pair of diamond ear-rings, the two diamond rings, and necklace, he mentioned in his naughty articles, which her ladyship had intended for presents to Miss Tomlins, a rich heiress, who was proposed for his wife, soon after he returned from his travels, had the treaty been concluded; and which was set aside, after all was agreed upon by the friends on both sides, by reason of his objections to the masculine airs of the lady; though she liked *him* very well. He presented me also with books, pictures, linen, laces, and every thing that was in my late lady's apartment; and bid me call that apartment mine. Give me, give me, good God, an increase of humility and gratitude!

SUNDAY *Night*

This day, as things could not be ready for our appearance at a better place, we staid at home; and my dear master employed himself a good deal in his library. And I have been taken up pretty much, as I ought to be, in my newly-presented closet.

Several of the neighbouring gentry sent their compliments to him this day on his return, but not a word about his marriage; particularly Mr Arthur, Miss Towers, Mr Brooks, and Mr Martin of the Grove.

MONDAY

I have had a good deal of employment in chusing patterns for my new clothes. Mr B. thought nothing too good; and was so kind as to pick out six of the richest, for me to chuse three suits out of, saying, We would furnish ourselves with more in town, when we went thither. One was white, flowered richly with silver. He was pleased to say, that, as I was a bride, I should make my appearance in that, the following Sunday. And so we shall have, in two or three days, from several places, nothing but mantua-makers and taylors at work. Bless me! what a chargeable creature am I to this most generous of men! But his fortune and station require a great deal of it; and his value for me will not let him do less, than if he had married a fortune equal to his own: and then, as he says, it would be a reflection upon him, if he did. And so I doubt it will be as it is: for, either way, the world will have something to say. He made me also chuse some very fine laces and linen: and has sent a message on purpose, to hasten all down. What can be done in town, as the millenery matters, and such like, are to be completed there, and sent by particular messengers, as done. All to be finished and brought hither by Saturday afternoon.

I send away John this morning, with some more of my papers, to you, and with the few he will give you, separate. You will be so good as to send me all those you have done with, that I may keep my word with Lady Davers. I am sure of the continuance of your prayers and blessings. Be pleased also to give me your answer about my dear Mr B.'s proposal of the Kentish farm. I beg you will buy two suits of clothes each, of the finest cloth for you, my dear father, and a creditable silk for my dear mother; and good linen, and every thing answerable: and that you will, as my best friend bid me say, let us see you here as soon as possible. He will have his chariot come for you, when you tell John the day. How I long to see you both, my dear good parents, and to share with you in person my felicities!

You will have, I am sure, the goodness to go to all your creditors, which are chiefly those of my poor unhappy brothers, and get an account of all you are bound for; and every one shall be paid to the utmost farthing, and interest besides; though some of them have been very cruel and unrelenting. But they are all entitled to justice, and shall be thankfully paid.

Now I think of it, John shall take what I have written down to this place; that you may have something to amuse you of your child's, instead of those you part with. I will continue writing till I am settled, and you are determined; and then I shall apply myself to the duties of the family, in order to become as useful to my dear master, as my small abilities will let me.

If you think a couple of guineas will be of use to Mrs Mumford, who I doubt has not much aforehand, pray give them to her, from me, (and I will return them to you) as for a pair of gloves on my marriage; and look among your acquaintance, and neighbours, and let me have a list of such honest, industrious poor, as may be true objects of charity, and have no other assistance; particularly such as are blind, lame, or sickly, with their several cases; and also such families and housekeepers as are reduced by misfortunes, as ours was, and where a great number of children may keep them from rising to a state of tolerable comfort: and I will chuse as well as I can; for I long to be making a beginning, with the kind quarterly benevolence my dear Mr B. has bestowed upon me for such good purposes.

I am resolved to keep account of all these matters: and Mr Longman has already furnished me with a vellum book of white paper; some sides of which I hope soon to fill, with the names of proper objects. And though my beloved master has given me all this without account, yet shall he see, (but nobody else) how I lay it out from quarter to quarter; and I will, if any be left, carry it on, like an accomptant, to the next quarter, and strike a balance four times a year, and a general balance at every year's end. And I have written in it, *Humble* RETURNS *for* DIVINE MERCIES. And locked it up in my newly-presented cabinet.

I intend to let Lady Davers see no further of my papers, than to her own angry letter to her brother; for I would not have her see my reflections upon it; and she will know, down to that place, all that is necessary for her curiosity, as to the stratagems used against me, and the honest part I have been enabled to act: and I hope, when she has read them all, she will be quite reconciled; for she will see it is all God Almighty's doings, as I may say; and that a man of Mr B.'s parts and knowledge was not to be drawn in by such a poor young unexperienced creature as I am.

I will detain John no longer. He will tell you to read the last part of the writing I send you first, and while he stays. And so, with my humble duty to you both, and my dear Mr B.'s kind remembrance, I rest,

Your ever dutiful,
and gratefully happy Daughter.

WEDNESDAY *Evening*

I will now, my honoured parents, proceed with my journal.

On Tuesday morning, my dear Mr B. riding out, returned, in company of Mr Martin of the Grove, Mr Arthur, and Mr Brooks, and a Mr Chambers; and, stepping up to me, said, He had rid out too far to return to breakfast; but had brought with him some of his old acquaintance, to dine with me. 'Are you sorry for it, Pamela?' I remembered his lessons, and answered, 'No, sure, sir; I can't be sorry for any thing you are pleased to do.' 'You know Mr Martin's character,' said he, 'and have severely censured him, as one of my brother rakes, and for his three lyings-in. I met them all,' continued he, 'at Mr Arthur's. His lady asked me, if I were *really* married? I said, "Yes, *really*." "And to whom?" said Mr Martin. "Why," replied I, without ceremony, "to my mother's waiting-maid." They could not tell what to say to me on this answer; and looked one upon another: and I saw I had spoiled a jest, from each. Mrs Arthur said, "You have, indeed, sir, a charming creature as ever I saw, and she has mighty good luck." "True," returned I, "and so have I. But I shall say the less of that, because a man never did any thing of this nature, but he was willing to make the best of it." "Nay," said Mr Arthur, "if you have sinned, it is with your eyes open! For you know the world as well as any man of your years in it."

'"Why, really, gentlemen," said I, "I should be glad to please all my friends; but, be that as it will, I do assure you, I am exceedingly pleased *myself*."

'"I have heard my wife," said Mr Brooks, "praise your spouse that is, so much for her beauty, that I greatly wanted to see her." "If," replied I, "you will all go and take a dinner with me, you shall see her in her proper place, gracing my table. Mrs Arthur, will you bear us company?" "No, indeed, sir," answered she. "What, I suppose, my *wife* will not be able to reconcile you to my *mother's waiting-maid*; is not that it? Tell truth, Mrs Arthur." "Nay," said she, "I sha'n't be backward to pay your wife a visit, in company of the neighbouring ladies; but my declining this sudden invitation, need not hinder you, gentlemen."

'"It should not," they said; and, each sending home, they, and Mr Chambers, a gentleman lately settled in the neighbourhood, came with me: and so, my dear,' concluded he, 'when you make your appearance, next Sunday, you are sure of a party in your favour; for all that see you must admire you.'

He went down to them; and when dinner was ready, he was pleased to take my hand, at my entrance into the dining-parlour. 'My dear love,' said he, 'I have brought some of my neighbours to dine with you.' 'You are very good, sir,' said I. He then presented to me each gentleman, Mr Chambers first; and each saluted me, and wished us both joy.

'I, for my part,' said Mr Brooks, 'wish you joy most heartily, madam. My wife told me a good deal of the beauties of your person; but I did not think we had such a flower in the county.'

I felt my face glow even more than it did at my entrance: yet was not so weak as to take a compliment for a strict truth. I curtsied in silence;[352] and Mr B. led me to my seat. The gentlemen seemed to try which should say the handsomest things of me. Yet were very free with one another (Mr Martin particularly) upon matrimony in general. The married men, willing, as it seemed, to draw me out, called upon me to defend the state I had so newly entered into.

I was sorry, I said, that so sacred an institution was supposed to want it. I dared to say, it did not with any married gentleman present. *They* had doubtless reason, and I questioned not their justice, to defend the state against the reflections of the finest gentlemen.

I had compliments from every gentleman on this occasion. Mr Martin affected to be dashed; but it was only affectation. He is not easily put out of countenance.

Mr Brooks whispered Mr B. that he might call me what he would; and so might the women of condition in the neighbourhood; but that for behaviour, good sense, and politeness, he thought he had never (even beauty out of the question) seen a more accomplished woman.

'My dear friend,' answered my delighted master, 'I told you before, that her fine person made me a lover; but it was her mind, that made me an husband.'

The first course coming in, Mr Arthur was pleased to observe, much to my advantage, on the ease and freedom with which I did the honours of the table; and said, he would bring his lady to be a witness, and a learner both, of my manner. Mr B. looking at me, as wishing me to speak, I said, I should be proud of Mrs Arthur's favour; and if I could be honoured with it, and with that of the ladies of the other gentlemen present, I should be enabled by their example to think myself better qualified for the place, to which the goodness of my dear Mr B. had exalted me; and which, at present, I was sensible, I filled with much insufficiency.

Mr B. seemed pleased at the approbation given to what I said, by every gentleman.

Mr Arthur drank to my health and happiness; and said, 'My wife told Mr B. madam, you had very good luck in such a husband; but I now see who has the best of it.' 'Come, come,' said Mr Brooks, 'let us make no compliments; the truth of the matter is, our good neighbour's generosity and judgment have met with so equal a match, in his lady's beauty and merit, that I know not which has the best luck. But may you be both long happy together, say I!' And he drank a glass of wine.

Mr B. addressed himself to me, on all occasions, in the kindest, tenderest, and most respectful manner. Insomuch that the free Mr Martin said, 'Did you ever think our good friend here, who used to ridicule matrimony so much, would have made so complaisant a husband? How long do you intend, sir, that this shall hold?' 'As long as my good girl deserves it,' said he, 'and that I am sure will be for ever. But,' continued the kind gentleman, 'you need not wonder I have changed my mind as to wedlock; for I never expected to meet with one whose behaviour, and sweetness of temper, were so likely to make me happy.'

After dinner, and having drank in one glass good healths to their ladies, I withdrew; and they sat and drank, as they boasted, two bottles of Burgundy each; and went away full of my praises, and vowing to bring their ladies to see me.

John having brought me your kind letter, my dear father, I told my master, after his friends were gone, how gratefully you received his generous intentions as to the Kentish farm, and promised your best endeavours to serve him in that estate; and that you hoped your industry and care would be so well employed in it, that you should be very little troublesome to him as to the liberal manner in which he had intended to add to a provision, that of itself exceeded all you wished.

He was very well pleased with your chearful acceptance of it.

I am glad your engagements to the world[353] lie in so small a compass: as soon as you have gotten an account of them exactly, you will be pleased to send it me, with the list you are so kind to promise to procure for me of the deserving poor.

I think, as my dear Mr B. is so generous, you should account nothing, that is plain, too good. Pray, don't be afraid of laying out upon yourselves. My dear Mr B. will not, when you come to us, permit you to return to your old abode; but will engage you to stay with us, till you set out for Kent. Be pleased, therefore, to dispose of yourselves accordingly.

I hope, my dear father, you have quite left off all slavish business. As Farmer Jones has, as I have heard you say, been kind to you, pray, when you take leave of him and his family, present them with three guineas worth of good books: such as a Family Bible, a Common Prayer, a Whole Duty of Man,[354] or any other you think will be acceptable; for they live a great way from church; and in winter the ways from their farm thither are almost unpassable.

John has brought me my papers safe. I will send them to Lady Davers, the first opportunity, down to the place I mentioned in my last.

My dear Mr B. just now tells me, that he will carry me in the morning a little airing, about ten miles off, in his chariot and four, to breakfast at a farm-house, noted for a fine dairy, and whither, now-and-then, the neighbouring gentry of both sexes resort for that purpose. And he will send Abraham on horseback, before us, to let the good folks know it. How can I forbear making you a partaker with me of all my pleasures, and the distinction given me by this best of husbands!

THURSDAY

Prepare, my dear parents, to hear something very particular. We set out at about half an hour after six, in the morning; and got to the truly neat house I mentioned in my former, by half an hour after eight.

We were prettily received and entertained here, by the good woman, and her daughter; and an elegancy ran through every thing, persons as well as furniture, yet all plain. And my master said to the good housewife, 'Do your young boarding-school ladies still at times continue their visits to you, Mrs Dobson?' 'Yes, sir,' said she; 'I expect three or four of them every minute.'

'There is, my dear,' said he, 'within three miles of this farm, a very good boarding-school for ladies. The governess of it keeps a chaise and pair, which is to be made a double chaise[355] at pleasure; and in summer-time, when the misses perform their tasks well, she favours them with an airing to this place, three or four at a time, to breakfast: and this serves both for a reward, and for exercise. The young ladies who have this favour, are not a little proud of it; and it brings them forward in their respective talks.'

'A very good method, sir,' said I. And just as we were talking, the chaise came in with four misses, all pretty much of a size, and a maid-servant to attend them. They were shewn another little neat apartment, that went through ours; and made their honours[356] very prettily as they passed by us. I went into the room to them, and asked them questions about their work, and their lessons; and what they had done to deserve such a fine airing and breakfasting. They all answered me very prettily. 'And pray, little ladies,' said I, 'what may I call your names?' One was called Miss Burdoff, one Miss Nugent, one Miss Booth, and the fourth Miss Goodwin. 'I don't know which,' said I, 'is the prettiest; but you are all best, my little dears; and you have a very good governess, to indulge you with such a fine airing, and such delicate cream, and bread and butter. I hope you think so.'

My master came in. He kissed each of them; but looked more wistfully on Miss Goodwin, than on any of the others; but I thought nothing just then: had she been called Miss Godfrey, I had hit upon it in a trice.

When we returned to our own room, he said, 'Which do you

think the prettiest of those children?' 'Really, sir,' replied I, 'it is hard to say: Miss Booth is a pretty brown [357] girl, and has a fine eye. Miss Burdoff has a great deal of sweetness in her countenance, but her features are not so regular. Miss Nugent has a fine complexion: and Miss Goodwin has a fine black eye, and is, besides, I think, the genteelest-shaped child. But they are all pretty.'

Their maid led them into the garden, to shew them the beehives; and Miss Goodwin made a particular fine curtsey to my master. And I said, 'I believe miss knows you, sir.' And taking her by the hand, 'Do you know this gentleman, my pretty dear?' 'Yes, madam,' said she; 'he is my own uncle.' I clasped her in my arms: 'O, why did you not tell me, sir,' said I, 'that you had a niece among these little ladies?' And I kissed her, and away she tript after the others.

'But pray, sir,' said I, 'how can this be? You have no sister nor brother, but Lady Davers. How can this be?'

He smiled; and then I said, 'O, my dearest sir, tell me now of a truth, does not this pretty miss stand in a nearer relation to you, than that of a niece? I *know* she does! I *know* she does!'

''Tis even so, my dear,' replied he; 'and you remember my sister's good-natured hint of Miss Sally Godfrey –' 'I do, sir,' answered I: 'but this young lady is Miss Goodwin, not Godfrey.' 'Her mother chose that name for her,' answered he, 'because she would not have her called by her own.' 'You must excuse me, sir,' said I; 'I must go and prattle with her.' 'I will send for her in again,' replied he. He did; and in she came, in a moment. I took her in my arms, and said, 'Will you love me, my charming dear? Will you let me be your aunt?' 'Yes, madam,' answered she; 'and I will love *you* dearly: but I must not love my uncle.' 'Why so?' asked Mr B. 'Because,' replied she, 'you would not speak to me at first! And because you would not let me call you uncle' (for it seems she was bid not, that I might not guess at her presently); 'and yet,' said the pretty dear, 'I had not seen you a great while – so I had not.'

'Well, Pamela,' said he, 'now can you allow me to love this little innocent?' '*Allow* you, sir!' replied I; 'you would be very barbarous, if you did not; and I should be more so, if I did not promote it all I could, and love the little innocent myself, for your sake, and for her own sake, and in compassion to her poor mother, though unknown to me.' Tears stood in my eyes.

'Why, my love,' said he, 'are your words so kind, and your countenance so sad?' I drew to the window, from the child, he following me; and said, 'Sad it is not, sir; but I have a strange grief and pleasure mingled at once in my breast, on this occasion: it is indeed a twofold grief, and a twofold pleasure.' 'As how, my dear?' 'Why, sir, I cannot help being grieved for the poor mother of this sweet babe, to think, if she be living, that she must call her chiefest delight her shame: if she be no more, that she must have had sad remorse on her mind, when she came to leave the world, and her little babe: and, in the second place, I grieve, that it must be thought a kindness to the dear little soul, not to let her know how near the dearest relation she has in the world is to her. Forgive me, sir; I say not this in the least to reproach you: indeed, I do not. And I have a twofold cause of joy. First, that I have had the grace to escape the misfortune of this poor lady; and next, that this discovery has given me an opportunity to shew the sincerity of my grateful affection for you, sir, in the love I will always bear to this dear child.'

I then stepped to her again, and kissed her; and said, 'Join with me, my pretty love, to beg your uncle to let you come and live with your new aunt: indeed, my precious, I will love you dearly.'

'Will you, sir?' said the little charmer, 'will you let me go and live with my aunt?'

'You are very good, my Pamela,' said he. 'I have not been once deceived in the hopes my fond heart had entertained of your prudence.' 'But will you, sir,' said I, 'will you grant me this favour? I shall most sincerely love the little charmer; and she shall be entitled to all I am capable of doing for her, both by example and affection. My dearest sir,' added I, 'oblige me in this thing! I think already my heart is set upon it! What a sweet employment and companion shall I have!'

'We will talk of this some other time,' replied he; 'but I must, in prudence, put some bounds to your amiable generosity. I had always intended to surprize you into this discovery; but my sister led the way to it, out of a poorness in her spite, that I could hardly forgive. You have obliged me beyond expression: yet I cannot say, that you have gone much beyond my expectation on this occasion. For I have such a high opinion of you, that I think nothing could have shaken it, but a contrary conduct to this you have shewn on so tender a circumstance.'

'Well, sir,' said the dear little miss, 'then you will not let me go home with my aunt, will you? She will be my pretty aunt; and I am sure she will love me.' 'When you break up next, my dear,' said he, 'if you are a good girl, you shall pay your new aunt a visit.' She made a low curtsey, 'Thank you, sir.' 'Yes, my dear,' said I, 'and I will get you some pretty picture books against the time. You love reading, I dare say?' 'Indeed I do.' 'I would have brought some now,' said I, 'had I known I should have seen my pretty love.' 'Thank you, madam,' returned she.

I asked him, how old she was? He said, 'Between six and seven.' 'Was she ever, sir, at your house?' 'My sister,' replied he, 'brought her thither once, as a little relation of her lord's.' 'I remember, sir,' said I, 'a little miss, once brought thither by Lady Davers; and Mrs Jervis and I took her to be a relation of Lord Davers.'

'My sister,' returned he, 'knew the whole secret from the beginning: and it made her a great merit with me, that she kept it from the knowledge of my father, who was then living, and of my mother, to her dying-day; although she descended so low, in her passion, as to hint the matter to you.'

The little misses took their leaves soon after. I know not how, but I am strangely taken with this dear child. I wish Mr B. would let me have her home. It would be a great pleasure to have such a fine opportunity, obliged as I am, to shew my love for him, in my fondness for this dear miss.

As we came home together in the chariot, he gave me the following particulars of this affair, additional to what he had before mentioned:

This lady, he said, was of a good family, and the flower of it. Her mother was a person of great art; and, in hopes to draw him in, as she knew that he was heir to a great estate, encouraged his private visits to her daughter; yet, as he was known to be unsettled and wild, and that her daughter was young and inexperienced, and far from being indifferent to him, she seemed not to consider that Miss Godfrey was in more danger from him, than he was from her; but depended too much upon her instructions to her.

At last, the young couple being found in a way, not very creditable to the lady; and he not talking of marriage; the mother thought of taking advantage of his youth, and of intimidating him. Accordingly, the next time he came, when the lovers were together, and not less familiar than before, an half-pay officer,[358] her relation, accompanied by one who had been her servant, broke in upon the lovers; and, reproaching him with dishonourable intentions, drew their swords upon him, threatening him with instant death, if he did not engage to marry the young lady on the spot; they having a clergyman in readiness below to join their hands.

He suspected, from some strong circumstances, that the young lady was in the plot, and enraged at the supposed imposition, drew; and was so much in earnest, that he run the servant into the arm; and pressing pretty forward upon the other, as he retreated, he rushed in upon him, near the top of the stairs, and pushed him down one pair. He was much hurt with the fall: Mr B. owned, however, that he might have paid for his rashness; but that the business of his antagonists was rather to frighten than to kill him. He then, in sight of the old lady, the minister, and the other daughters, quitted the house, vowing never more to enter it; and that he would never again visit the young lady.

After this, however, Miss Godfrey found means to engage him to give her a meeting at Woodstock, in which she undertook to clear up his suspicions of her conduct. But there, poor lady! she found herself betrayed (wicked man!) into the grossest fault a young woman can be guilty of, in order to convince him of her innocence in a less.

They afterwards often met at Godstow, at Woodstock, and every neighbouring place to Oxford, where he was then studying, as it proved, guilty lessons, instead of improving ones; till, at last, the effect of their frequent interviews grew too obvious to be concealed. In vain did they endeavour to prevail on him by marriage to save the young lady's credit. At last, they resolved to complain to his father and mother. But he making his sister, then unmarried, and at home, acquainted with the affair, she so managed as to prevail upon them to hush up the matter for the sake of their own reputation; and Miss Godfrey was sent to Marlborough, where, at his sister's expense, which he answered to her again, she was provided for, and privately lay-in. Miss B. (afterwards Lady Davers) took upon herself the care of the little-one, till it was put to the boarding-school, where it now is.

Mr B. has settled upon the child such a sum of money as the interest of it will handsomely provide for her; and the principal be a tolerable fortune, fit for a gentlewoman, when she comes to be of age.

'This, my dear,' said Mr B., when he had given me the above particulars, 'is the story of Miss Sally Godfrey; and I do assure you, I am far from taking a pride in this affair: but since it has happened, I will do all I can to make the child happy.'

'And may she be so!' said I. 'How much will it add to my felicity, if I can contribute to it! O that you would permit me to have her home.' He made me no answer in words; but tenderly grasped my hand, and looked pleased.

I asked him, if Miss Goodwin had any notion of who were her father and mother? 'No,' answered he. 'Her governess has been told by my sister, that she is the daughter of a gentleman and his lady, who are related, at a distance, to Lord Davers, and now live at Jamaica; and she calls me uncle, only because I am the brother to Lady Davers, whom she calls aunt, and who is very fond of her, as is also my lord, who knows the whole matter. At all their little school-recesses they have her at their house. I believe,' added he, 'the matter is very little known or suspected; for as her mother *is* of a good family, her friends endeavour to keep it secret, as much as I; and Lady Davers, till her wrath boiled over, the other day, has managed the matter very dexterously and kindly.'

I wanted him to say, whether her mother is living; and his words, 'her mother *is* of a good family,' left me no room to doubt it. And I said, 'But how, sir, can the poor mother be content to deny herself the enjoyment of so sweet a child?' 'Ay, Pamela,' replied he, 'now *you* come in; I see you want to know what's become of the poor mother. I was willing to see how the little suspense would operate upon you.' 'Dear sir,' said I. 'Nay,' replied he, ''tis very natural, my dear! I think you have had a great deal of patience, and are come at this question so fairly, that you deserve to be answered.

'You must know, then, there is some foundation for saying, that her mother is in Jamaica: there she does live, and very happily too. She suffered so much in childbed, that nobody expected her life; and this made such an impression upon her, that she dreaded nothing so much as the thoughts of falling into her former fault. To say the truth, I had intended to make her a visit, as soon as her month was up.[359] She apprehended that I would; and, in order to avoid me, privately engaged herself to go to Jamaica, with two young ladies, who were born there; and were returning to their friends, after they had been four years in England for their education; recommending to me, by a very moving letter, her child, requesting that it might not be called by her name, but Goodwin, the better to conceal the disgrace she had brought upon her family.

'She prevailed upon her friends to assign her five hundred pounds, in full of all her demands upon them; and went up to London, and embarked, with her companions, at Gravesend, and sailed to Jamaica. There she is since well and happily married; passing to her husband for a young widow, with one daughter, which her first husband's friends take care of, and provide for. And so, you see, Pamela, that in the whole story, on both sides, the truth is as much preserved as possible.'

'Poor lady!' said I; 'how much does her story affect me! I am glad she is so *happy* at last.' 'And, my dear,' said he, 'are you not glad she is so *far off* too?' 'As to that, sir,' said I, 'I cannot be sorry, especially as she could not have been made happy *here*. For, sir, have you not hinted –' I stopt. 'I have, my love. I know what you would say. The mind once tainted –' He stopt. Ah, dear sir, thought I, *once tainted*! I am afraid. But let me hope the best.

'How greatly, sir,' said I, 'is this unhappy lady to be admired! how much in earnest was she to be good, that she should leave her native country, leave all her relations, leave you, whom she so well loved, leave her dear baby, to try a new fortune, in a new world, among absolute strangers, hazarding seas and winds, to preserve herself from further guiltiness! Indeed, sir, I grieve for what her distresses must have been, on taking so noble a resolution; I am grieved to think of her remorse, through her childbed terrors: and great it must be to have so worthy an effect upon her afterwards. I honour her resolution, and must rank such a true penitent in the class of those who are most virtuous; and doubt not God Almighty's mercies to her; and that her present happiness is the result of his gracious Providence, blessing her penitence. But, sir, did you not *once* see the poor lady before she went abroad?'

'I did not believe her so much in earnest,' answered he; 'and I went down to Marlborough, and heard she was gone from thence to Calne.[360] I went to Calne, and heard she was gone to Reading, to a relation's there. Thither I went, and heard she was gone to Oxford. I followed; and there she was; but would not see me.

'She at last received a letter from me, in which I begged a meeting with her; for I found her departure with the ladies was resolved upon, and that she was with her friends, only to take leave of them, and receive her agreed-on portion: and she appointed the Saturday following, and that was Wednesday, to give me a meeting at the old place at Woodstock.

'Then,' added he, 'I thought I was sure of her, and doubted not I should spoil her intended voyage.' [Naughty, naughty man! thought I.] 'I set out on Thursday to Gloucester on a party of pleasure; and on Saturday I went to the place appointed, at Woodstock: but, when I came thither, I found a letter instead of the lady; and, when I opened it, it was to beg my pardon for deceiving me; expressing her concern for her past fault, her affection for me; and the apprehension she had, that she should be unable to keep her good resolves, if she met me: she let me know, that she had set out the Thursday before for her embarkation; being apprehensive that no other measure could save her; and had appointed this meeting on Saturday, at the place of our mutual guilt, that I might be suitably impressed upon the occasion, and pity and allow for her; and that she might be out of my reach. She recommended again, as upon the spot to which the poor little-one owed its being, my tenderness to it for her sake: and that was all she had to request of me, she said; but would not forget to pray for me in all her own dangers, and in every difficulty she was going to encounter with.'

I wept at this moving tale: 'And did not this make a deep impression upon you, sir?' said I: 'surely such an affecting lesson as this, on the very guilty spot too (I admire the poor lady's pious contrivance!) must have had a great effect upon you. One would have thought, sir, it was enough to reclaim you for ever. All your naughty purposes, I make no doubt, were quite changed at the time.'

'Why, my dear,' replied he, 'I was much affected, you may be sure, when I came to reflect: but at first I was so assured of being a successful tempter, that I could not bear she should so escape me; so much transcend me in heroical bravery: and I hastened away to Lord Davers, and got a bill of credit from him, upon his banker in

London, for five hundred pounds; and set out for that metropolis, having called at Oxford, and got what light I could, as to the place where there was a probability of hearing of her, there.

'When I arrived in town, which was not till Monday morning, I went to a place called Crosby-square,[361] where the friends of the two ladies lived. She had set out in the flying-coach;[362] got to the two ladies the same night; and, on Saturday, had set out with them for Gravesend, much about the time she led me to expect her at Woodstock.

'You may suppose, that I was much concerned at this information. However, I got my bill of credit converted into money; and set out on Monday afternoon, and reached Gravesend that night; and there I understood, that she and the two ladies had gone on board from the very inn I put up at, in the morning, and the ship waited only for the wind, which then was turning about in its favour.

'I got a boat directly, and went on board the ship, and asked for Mrs Godfrey. But judge you her surprize and confusion when she saw me. She had like to have fainted away. I offered any money to put off the sailing till next day, but it could not be complied with; and fain would I have got her on shore, and promised to attend her (if she would go) over land, to any part of England the ship would touch at. But she was immoveable.

'Every one concluded me her humble servant, and was affected at the tender interview; the young ladies, and their female attendants, especially. With great difficulty, upon my solemn assurances of honour, she trusted herself with me in one of the cabins; and there I endeavoured, all I could, to prevail upon her to quit her purpose: but all in vain: she said, I had made her quite unhappy by this interview! She had difficulties enough upon her mind before: but now I had embittered all her voyage, and given her the deepest distress.

'I could prevail upon her but for one favour, and that she granted with the utmost reluctance; which was, to accept of the five hundred pounds, as a present from me; and she promised, at my earnest desire, to draw upon me for a greater sum, as upon a person who had her effects in my hands, when she arrived, if she should find it convenient for her. This, I say, was all the favour I could procure; for she would not promise so much as to correspond with me, and was so determined on going, that, I believe, if I would have married her, (which yet I had not in my head to do) she would not have been diverted from her purpose.'

'But how, sir,' said I, 'did you part?' 'I would have sailed with her,' answered he, 'and been landed at the first port they should touch at, either in England or Ireland: but she was too full of apprehensions to admit it; and the rough fellow of a master would not stay a moment, the wind being quite fair. He was very urgent with me to go ashore, or to go the voyage: I could have thrown him overboard in my mind; for being impetuous in my temper, *spoiled, you know, my dear, by my mother*, and not used to controul, I thought it very strange, that wind or tide, or any thing else, should be preferred to me and my money: finding myself obliged to submit, I wished the ladies and the other passengers a good voyage; I gave five guineas among the ship's crew, to be good to the ladies. The unhappy lady recommended, once more, to me, the dear *guest*, as she called the child, the ladies being present; and thanked me for all the instances of regard I had shewn her in this attendance, which, she said, would leave too strong impression on her mind for her peace. At parting, she threw her arms about my neck, and we took such a leave as affected every one present.

'With a truly heavy heart, I went into my boat; and stood up in it, looking at her, as long as I could see her, and she at me, with her handkerchief at her eyes; and then I gazed at the ship, *till* and *after* I had landed, as long as I could discern the least appearance of it; for she was under sail, in a manner, when I left her.

'I returned, highly disturbed, to my inn. I went to bed; but rested not; set out for London the next morning; and the same afternoon for the country. And so much, my dear, for poor Sally Godfrey.

'She sends, I understand, by all opportunities, with the knowledge of her husband, to enquire how her child, by her first husband, does; and has the satisfaction to know she is happily provided for. About half a year ago her husband sent a little *Negro* boy, of about ten years old, as a present, to wait upon her. But he was taken ill of the small-pox, and died in a month after he was landed.'

'Sure, sir,' said I, 'you must have been long affected with a case so melancholy in its circumstances.'

'I will own, that the whole of the affair hung upon me for some time: but I was full of spirits and inconsideration. New objects of pleasure danced before my eyes, and kept reflection from me. I pursued them, even to satiety; and, at last, thought it was a kind of virtue to resolve to confine myself to one woman; and hoped, for a long time together, as my Pamela advanced to maturity, one day to prevail with her to be Sally Godfrey the second.'

'O sir! what a sad, sad account this is! I bless God for this disappointment: for your own sake, dear sir, as well as mine, I bless God for it.'

'And so do I, my dear,' replied he. 'And you will the less doubt my sincerity, when I tell you, that I have the more pleasure in my reformation, for having seen my error so early; and that with such a stock of youth and health on my side, in all appearance, I can truly abhor my past liberties, and pity poor Sally Godfrey, from the same motives that I admire my Pamela's virtue; and resolve to make myself as worthy of them as possible. And, to be more serious still, let me add, that I hope your prayers, my dear, for my pardon and perseverance, and your example, will not want their efficacy.'

These agreeable reflections, on this melancholy, but instructive story, brought us in view of his own house; where we alighted, and took a walk in the garden till dinner-time. And now we are so busy about making ready for our appearance, that I shall hardly have time to write till all that be over.

MONDAY *Morning*

Yesterday we set out, attended by John, Abraham, Benjamin, and Isaac, in new liveries, in the best chariot, which has been new-fitted, and lined and harnessed; so that it looked like a quite new one. But I had no arms to quarter [363] with those of my dear husband. Upon my taking notice of my obscurity on this occasion, he smilingly said, that he had a good mind to have the olive-branch,[364] which would allude to his hopes, quartered for mine. I was dressed in the suit I mentioned, of white flowered with silver, and a rich head-dress, and the jewels I mentioned before: Mr B. had on a fine laced silk waistcoat, of blue Paduasoy[365]; his coat was a pearl-coloured fine cloth, with silver buttons and button-holes, and lined with white silk. He looked charmingly indeed.

I said, I was too fine, and would fain have had the jewels omitted;

but he would not allow it. 'Are you not my wife?' said he. 'I had rather people should have any thing to say, than that I do not put you, as such, upon a foot with any woman I might have married.' The neighbouring gentry, it seems, had expected us; and there was a great congregation; for (against my wish) we were a little of the latest; so that, as we walked up the church, to his seat, we had abundance of gazers and whisperers: but my dear Mr B. behaved with an air so chearful, and was so complaisant to me, that he did credit to his choice; and as it became me to think of nothing but the duties of the sacred day, and of thankfulness to God, for his mercies to me, my intentness to them so much engaged my heart, that I was much less concerned, than I should otherwise have been, at the gazings and whisperings of the ladies and gentlemen, as well as of the rest of the congregation; whose eyes were all turned to our seat.

When the sermon was ended, we staid till the church was near empty; but we found great numbers of people at the church-doors and in the porch: I had the pleasure of hearing many commendations, as well of my behaviour as my person and dress, and not one mark of disrespect. Mr Martin, who is a single man, was there, as well as Mr Chambers, Mr Arthur, and Mr Brooks, with their families. And the four gentlemen came up to us, before we went into the chariot, and, in a very kind and respectful manner, complimented us both. Mrs Arthur and Mrs Brooks were so kind as to wish me joy; and Mrs Brooks said, 'You sent Mr Brooks home, madam, t'other day, quite charmed with that easy and sweet manner, which you have convinced a thousand persons, this day, is so natural to you.' I courtsied gratefully to her; and said, she did me honour.

My dear Mr B. handed me into the chariot, but was prevented from stepping into it himself by the officiousness of Sir Thomas Atkyns, a ceremonious young baronet, who very unseasonably, as I thought, engaged him with fine speeches, though Mr B. made several motions to come into the chariot to me. Mean time, I was abashed to hear the praises of the country-people, and to see how they crouded about the chariot. Several poor people begged my charity. Beckoning John with my fan, I gave him all the silver I had, which happened to be between twenty and thirty shillings, and bid him divide it among them in the further part of the church-yard; and to tell them to come next morning to Mr B.'s, and I would give them more, if they would not importune me now. This drew away from me their clamorous solicitations.

While Sir Thomas Atkyns was thus unseasonably engaging Mr B., and telling him a story, at which he himself heartily laughed, Mr Martin came up to me on the other side of the chariot, and leaned on the door. 'By all that's good,' said he, 'you have charmed the whole congregation. Not a soul but is full of your praises. My neighbour knew, better than any body could tell him, how to chuse for himself. Why,' said he, 'the Dean himself looked more upon you, than upon his book.'

'It is generous in you, sir,' said I, 'to encourage a diffident heart.' 'I vow,' said he, 'I say no more than truth: I would marry to-morrow, if I were sure of meeting with a woman of but half your merit. You are,' continued he, 'and 'tis not my way to praise too much, an ornament to your sex, an honour to your husband, and a credit to religion. Every body is saying so,' added he; 'for you have, by your piety, edified the whole church.'

The Dean made me a compliment as he passed. And, at last, Mr B. forced himself from Sir Thomas; who aukwardly apologized to me for detaining him so long.

Mr Martin told Mr B., that if he would come to church every Sunday, with his bride, he would never be absent from it. I told Mr B. that I was obliged to Mr Martin, for his countenance on his being detained from me.

Mr B., in a very obliging manner, returned Mr Martin's compliment; who then went to his own chariot. When we drove away, the people kindly blessed us, and called us a charming pair.

As I have no other pride, I hope, in repeating these things, than in the countenance the general approbation gives to my dear master for his stooping so low, you will excuse me for it, I know.

In the afternoon, we went again to church, and a little early, at my request; but it was quite full, and, soon after, even crouded; so much does novelty attract the eyes of mankind. Mr Martin came in, after us, and made up to our seat; and said, 'If you please, my dear friend, I will take my seat with you this afternoon.' Mr B. let him in. I was sorry for it; but was resolved that my duty should not give place to bashfulness, or to any other consideration; and when divine service began, I withdrew to the further end of the pew, and left the gentlemen in the front.

The Dean preached again, which he was not used to do, out of compliment to us; and an excellent sermon he made on the relative duties of Christianity. Mr Martin addressed himself twice or thrice to me, during the sermon; but he found my attention so wholly ingrossed by the preacher, that he each time soon re-seated himself; yet I took care, according to the lesson formerly given me, to observe to him a chearful and obliging behaviour, as one of Mr B.'s friends. My master invited him to supper; and he said, 'I am so taken with your lady, that, if you encourage me, I shall be always with you.' 'The oftener the more obliging,' replied Mr B.; 'and who knows but my example may reform another rake?' '*Who* knows?' said Mr Martin; 'I know: for I am more than half reformed already.'

At the chariot-door, Mrs Arthur, Mrs Brooks, and Mrs Chambers, were brought to me, by their respective husbands; and presently they were joined by the lively Miss Towers, who bantered me before, as I once told you. Mrs Arthur said, that all the ladies, my neighbours, would collect themselves together, and make me a visit. 'This,' said I, 'will be an honour, madam, that I can never enough acknowledge.'

'I had a slight cold,' said Miss Towers, 'that kept me at home in the morning; but I heard you so much talked of, that I resolved not to stay away in the afternoon: and I join in the joy every one wishes you.' She turned to my master, and said, 'I always thought you a sly thief: where have you stolen this lady? How barbarous is it to bring her out upon us at once, to eclipse us all!' 'A lady,' replied Mr B., 'who can express herself with so much generosity as Miss Towers does, on this occasion, shews a greatness of mind that cannot be eclipsed.'

'I own,' said she, softly, 'I was one of your censurers; but I never liked you so well in my life, as now that I see how capable your bride is of doing credit to her condition.' And coming to me, 'My dear neighbour,' said she, 'excuse me for a certain flippancy that I was once guilty of. Will it make an atonement, to say, that I see you now with Mr B.'s eyes?'

'How shall I suitably return my acknowledgements?' said I.

'Nothing, madam, can be wanting to complete my happiness, but the example and instruction of so many worthy ladies, as adorn this neighbourhood. Give me, in particular, madam, your countenance; that will enable me to sustain the honours to which the most generous of men has raised me.'

'If I was in another place,' said she, 'I would kiss you for that answer. Happy, happy Mr B.,' turning to my master; 'what reputation have you given to your judgment! I won't be long before I see you,' added she, 'I assure you, if I come by myself.' 'It shall be your own fault, Miss Towers,' said Mrs Brooks, 'if you do.'

They passed on to their coaches. I gave my hand to my dear master. 'Accept of it, dear sir,' whispered I; 'my heart is with it. How happy have you made me!' The Dean, passing us, whispered Mr B., that he congratulated him on his happiness. 'Every mouth,' said he, 'is full of it.' Mr B. said, he should think himself honoured by a visit from him. 'My wife and daughters,' said he, 'are at my brother's at Bedford: when they return, we will attend your bride together'; bowing to me. I curtsied, and said, that would be doing me honour; and then I thanked him for his fine discourse; as he did me for my attention, which he called exemplary.

My dear master then handed me into the chariot; and we were carried home, *both* happy, thank God!

Mr Martin came in the evening, with another gentleman, his friend, one Mr Dormer; and he entertained us with the favourable opinion, he said, every one had of me, and of the choice my good Mr B. had made.

This morning the poor came, to the number of twenty-five; and I sent them away with glad hearts.

TUESDAY

My generous master has given me, this morning, a most considerate, but yet, from the nature of it, melancholy instance of his great regard for me, which I never could have wished, hoped for, or even thought of.

He took a walk with me, after breakfast, into the garden, and a little shower falling, he led me for shelter into the summer-house, in the private garden, where he formerly gave me apprehensions; and, sitting down by me, he said, 'I have now finished all that lies on my mind, my dear, and am easy: for have you not wondered, that I have so much employed myself in my library? been so much at home, and yet not in your company?' 'I have never, sir,' replied I, 'been so impertinent. And, besides, I know that the method you take of looking into your own affairs, engages so much of your time, that I ought to be very careful how I intrude.'

'You are very considerate, my dear: but I'll tell you what has been my last work: I took it into consideration, that, at present, my family is almost extinct; and that the chief part of my *maternal* estate, in case I die without issue, will go to another family. And that I ought not to leave my Pamela at the mercy of those to whom my *paternal* estate, on the like contingency, will devolve. I have, therefore, as human life is uncertain, made such a disposition of my affairs, as will render you absolutely independent; as will secure to you the means of doing a great deal of good, and living as my relict ought to do; and, at the same time, put it out of any body's power to molest your father and mother, in the provision I design them for the remainder of their days: and I have finished all, this very morning, except to naming trustees for you; and if you have any persons in whom you would more particularly confide on this occasion, I would have you name them.'

I was so touched with this mournful instance of his excessive goodness to me, and the thoughts necessarily flowing from what he had said, that I was unable to speak; and, at last, relieving my mind by a violent fit of weeping, could only say, clasping my arms around him, 'How shall I support this! So very cruel, yet so kind!'

'Let not *that*, my dearest life,' said he, 'give you pain, that gives *me* pleasure. I am not the nearer my end, for having made this disposition; but I think, the putting off these material articles, when life is so precarious, is one of the most inexcusable things a prudent man can be guilty of. My poor friend, Mr Carlton, who so lately died in my arms, convinced me of this truth, that temporal concerns should not be left to the last debilitating hour, when the important moments ought to be filled up with other and greater considerations: he, poor man! had to struggle with, at once, a disordered state of worldly affairs; a weakness of body, and concerns of still as much more moment, as the soul is to the body. I had the happiness to relieve his anxiety as to the first: but the difficulties he had to contend with, and the sense he had of his incapacity to contend with them; the horror, the confusion he was sometimes in, as life was drawing to its utmost verge; so many things left undone, and to others to do for him; that altogether made so great an impression upon my mind, that I was the more impatient to come to this house, where were most of my writings, in order to make the disposition I have now perfected: and, since it is grievous to my dear girl, I will myself think of proper trustees for her. I have only, therefore, to re-assure you, my dear, that, in this instance, I have contrived to make you quite easy, free, and independent.'

I could not speak. He proceeded, 'As, my dear creature, I am determined henceforth to avoid every subject that may discompose you, I will mention now one request, the only one I have to make to you. It is this; that if it please God, for my sins, to separate me from my Pamela, you will only resolve not to marry *one* person; for I would not be such a Herod,[366] as to restrain you from a change of condition with any other, however reluctantly I may think of any other person's succeeding me in your esteem.'

I thought my heart would have burst: but was unable to answer one word. 'To conclude at once,' proceeded he, 'a subject that is so grievous to you, I will tell you, that this person is Mr Williams. And now I will acquaint you with my motive for this request; which is wholly owing to my niceness for you, and to no dislike I have to him, or apprehension of any likelihood, that it will be so: but, methinks, it would reflect a little upon my Pamela, if she were to take such a step, as if she had married one man for his *estate*, when, but for *that*, she would rather have had *another*. Forgive me, my Pamela,' added he; 'but I cannot bear even the most distant apprehension, that I had not the preference with you to any man living: as I have shewn you, that I have preferred you to all your sex, of whatever degree.'

I was still silent. Might I have had the world, I could not speak. He took me in his arms. 'I have now,' said he, 'spoken all my mind, and expect no answer; and I see you too much moved to give me one. Only say, you forgive me. And I hope I have not one dis-agreeable thing to say to my angel, for the rest of my life.'

Grief still choaked up the passage of my words. 'The shower,' said he, 'is over'; and he led me out. Recovering myself a little, I would have spoken on the melancholy subject; but he said, 'I will not hear my dear creature say any thing in answer to my request: to hearken to your assurance of complying with it, would look as if I wanted it. I shall never more think on the subject.' He then changed the discourse.

'Don't you with pleasure, my dear,' said he, 'take in the delightful fragrance, that this sweet shower has given to these banks of flowers? Your company is so enlivening to me, that I could almost fancy, that what we owe to the *shower* is owing to your presence. All nature, methinks, blooms around me, when I have my Pamela by my side. I will give you a few lines, that I made myself on such an occasion as this I am speaking of, the presence of a sweet companion, and the fresh verdure, that, after a shower succeeding a long drought, shewed itself throughout all vegetable nature.' And then, in a sweet and easy accent, with his arms about me as we walked, he sung me the following verses; of which he afterwards favoured me with a copy:

I

All nature blooms when you appear;
The fields their richest liv'ries wear;
Oaks, elms, and pines, blest with your view,
Shoot out fresh greens, and bud anew;
   The varying seasons you supply;
   And when you're gone, they fade and die.

II

Sweet Philomel,[367] in mournful strains,
To you appeals, to you complains.
The tow'ring lark, on rising wing,
Your praise, delighted, seems to sing;
   Presaging, as aloft he flies,
   Your future progress through the skies.

III

The purple violet, damask rose,
Each, to delight your senses, blows.
The lilies ope', as you appear;
And all the beauties of the year
   Diffuse their odours at your feet,
   Who give to ev'ry flow'r its sweet.

IV

For flow'rs and women are allied;
Both Nature's glory, and her pride!
Of ev'ry fragrant sweet possest,
They bloom but for the fair-one's breast;
    And to the swelling bosom borne,
    Each other mutually adorn.[368]

Thus sweetly did he palliate the grief, which the generosity of his actions, mixed with the seriousness of the occasion, and the strange request he had vouchsafed to make me, had occasioned. And all he would permit me to say, was, that I was not displeased with him! 'Displeased with you, dearest sir!' said I: 'let me thus testify my obligations, and the force all your commands shall have upon me.' And I clasped my arms about his neck, and kissed him.

But yet my mind was pained at times, and has been to this hour. God grant that I may never see the dreadful moment, that shall shut up the precious life of this most generous of husbands! And – but I cannot bear to suppose – I cannot say more on a subject so deeply affecting.

Oh! what a poor thing is human life in its best enjoyments! Subjected to *imaginary* evils, when it has no *real* ones to disturb it; and that can be made as effectually unhappy by our apprehensions of even remote contingencies as if we were struggling with the pangs of a present distress! This, duly reflected upon, methinks, should convince every one, that this world is not a place for the immortal mind to be confined to; and that there must be an hereafter, in which the *whole* soul shall be satisfied.

But I shall get out of my depth: my shallow mind cannot comprehend, as it ought, these weighty subjects: let me, therefore, only pray, that after having made a grateful use of God's mercies here, I may, with my dear benefactor, rejoice in that happy state, where is no mixture, no unsatisfiedness; and where all is joy, and peace, and love, for evermore.

I said, when we sat at supper, 'The charming taste you gave me, sir, of your genius, makes me sure you have more favours of this kind, to delight me with, if you please: may I beg to be indulged on this agreeable subject?' 'Hitherto,' said he, 'my life has been too much a life of gaiety and action, to be busied so innocently. Some little essays I have now-and-then made; but very few have I finished. Indeed I had not patience, nor attention enough, to hold me long to any one subject. Now-and-then, perhaps, I shall occasionally shew you what I have essayed: but I never could please myself in this way.

'You, my dear love, are a pretty *rhimester*; I will not flatter you by calling you a poetess: yet I admire that beautiful simplicity which in all you do, all you write, all you speak, makes so distinguishing a part of your character. Did I not see on your toilette yesterday a few lines begun in praise of humility?'

'You did not tell me before, that you saw them, sir. Supposing myself reproached by the daughter of an earl with my low birth, I was placing my whole merit in humility. I have written but that one stanza as I may call it, which I find you saw.' 'Finish it, my dear,' said he, 'and let me see it.'

I obeyed him. He was so good as to praise me for the simple verses. These are they:

> Some boast their riches; some their birth;
>   Their beauty some; some their degree;
> Yet all must turn to common earth:
>   Should not this teach HUMILITY?
>
> 'Say, cottage-born, what mean'st thou, girl?
>   Wouldst thou pretend to vie with me?'
> 'O no! – Your sire's a noble earl:
>   My only pride's HUMILITY.
>
> 'But while you boast of what you are,
>   And scorn so much the low degree;
> You'd be as rich, as great, as fair,
>   Could you but boast HUMILITY.
>
> 'If wealth, and birth, and beauty, give
>   But pride and insolence to thee,
> O keep them all; and, while I live,
>   Make all *my* pride HUMILITY.'[369]

FRIDAY

We were yesterday favoured with the company of almost all the neighbouring gentry, and their ladies, who, by appointment with one another, met to make us a congratulatory visit. The ladies were extremely obliging, free, and even affectionate to me; the gentlemen exceedingly polite. All was performed (for they were prevailed upon to pass the evening) with decency and order, and much to every one's satisfaction; which was principally owing to the care and skill of good Mrs Jervis, who is an excellent manager.

For my part, I was dressed out only to be admired, as it seems. And, if I had not known, that I did not make *myself*, as you, my dear father, once hinted to me; and if I had had the vanity to think as well of myself, as the good company was pleased to do, I might possibly have been proud. But I know, as my lady Davers said, though in anger, yet in truth, that I am but a *poor bit of painted dirt*. What I value myself upon, is, that God has raised me to a condition to be useful to better persons than myself. This is my pride: and I hope this will be *all* my pride. For, what was I of myself? All the good I can do, is but a poor third-hand good! for my dearest master himself is but the second-hand. G o d, the All-gracious, the All-good, the All-bountiful, the All-mighty, the All-merciful G o d, is the first: to H I M, therefore, be all the glory!

As I expect the happiness, the unspeakable happiness, my ever-dear, and ever-honoured father and mother, of enjoying the company of you both, under this roof, so soon, (and pray let it be as soon as you can) I will not enter into the particulars of the last agreeable evening. I shall have a thousand things, as well as that, to talk to you upon. I fear you will be tired with my prattle, when I see you!

I am to return these visits singly; and there were eight ladies here, of different families. I shall find enough to do! I doubt my time will not be so well filled up, as I once promised my best friend it should. But he is pleased, cheerful, kind, affectionate! What a happy creature am I! May I be always thankful to G o d, and grateful to *him*!

When all these tumultuous visitings are over, I shall have my mind, I hope, subside into a family calm, that I may make myself a little useful to the household of my Mr B.; or else I shall be an unprofitable servant indeed!

Lady Davers sent this morning a billet with her compliments to us both; and her lord's good wishes and congratulations. She desired I would send my papers by the messenger; letting me know, that she will herself bring them to me again, with thanks, as soon as she has read them; and she and her lord will come and be *my* guests (that was her particularly kind word) for a fortnight.

Methinks I want your list of the honest and worthy poor; for the money lies by me, and brings me no interest. You see I am become a mere usurer; indeed I want to make use upon use of it: and yet, when I have done all, I cannot do so much as I ought.

I tell my dear Mr B. that I long for another dairy-house visit. If he will not, at *present*, indulge me, I shall, when the sweet girl is a little *older*, teaze him like any over-indulged wife, to permit me the pleasure of forming her tender mind, as well as I am able. I am providing many pretty presents for her against I see her next.

Just now I have the blessed news, that you will set out, for this happy house, on Tuesday morning. The chariot shall be with you without fail. God give us a happy meeting![370] How I long for it! Forgive your impatient daughter, who sends this to amuse you on your journey; and is, and will be,

Ever most dutifully yours.

THE END OF VOLUME II

NOTES

ENTRIES which indicate revisions in the 1801 edition of *Pamela* (cited as 1801) are based on my own collation of that text with the editions of 1740, 1742 and 1761; only major additions, alterations, and a few of the numerous deletions could, however, be considered here. Other notes are indebted to several sources, including C. Willett and Phillis Cunnington, *Handbook of English Costume in the Eighteenth Century* (Faber, 1957), cited as Cunnington; T. C. Duncan Eaves and Ben D. Kimpel, 'Richardson's Revisions of *Pamela*' (*Studies in Bibliography*, 20, 1967, 61–88); *Johnson's England*, ed. A. S. Turberville (Clarendon Press, 1933); Samuel Johnson, *A Dictionary of the English Language* (1755); M. P. Tilley, *A Dictionary of the Proverbs in England in the Sixteenth and Seventeenth Centuries* (University of Michigan Press, 1950): and the *Oxford English Dictionary* (OED). I have also drawn on Eaves and Kimpel's edition of *Pamela* (Houghton Mifflin, 1971); and on Jocelyn Harris's edition of *Sir Charles Grandison* (Oxford University Press, 1972).

1. Title page (p. 27) *In Her Exalted Condition:* referring to Richardson's continuation of *Pamela*, Volumes III and IV of the 1801 edition.

2. (p. 29) *Anne Richardson:* she had hoped that her sister, Martha Bridgen, would correct the manuscript of the revised *Pamela*, but Martha died in 1785 without having done so. Anne then planned to undertake the task herself, but it cannot be determined if she ever worked on the manuscript; nor is it known why she finally arranged for its publication in 1801 (see Eaves and Kimpel, 'Richardson's Revisions', pp. 73–8).

3. (p. 31) Richardson's preface, included in the first edition, was reprinted, with various revisions, in each of the subsequent editions. In a letter to Aaron Hill of 1741 he described it as 'assuming and very impudent', able to make its lofty claims because Richardson had 'the umbrage of the editor's character to screen [himself] behind' (*Selected Letters*, ed. Carroll, p. 42). The version of 1801 follows the octavo text, but omits a postscript explaining why the introductory letters on the novel have been deleted and asserting that the work is based on a real life story.

4. (p. 33) The Contents had previously appeared only in the octavo edition. A brief preface explaining their purpose is omitted in 1801, and they are reduced to little more than half of their original length.

In general, descriptions of characters' motives and emotions are replaced by summaries of action; thus in Letter I, 'She is all grateful Confusion upon it, and thinks him the best of Gentlemen' (octavo) is altered to the terse 'Sends them money'. The present edition follows the octavo in placing the Contents together; in 1801 they were printed at the beginning of each volume.

VOLUME I

5. (p. 43) *cast accompts:* reckon accounts.

6. (p. 43) *mourning:* costumes appropriate for mourning.

7. (p. 44) *pill-boxes:* shallow boxes, often made of cardboard, used for carrying pills or other small objects.

8. (p. 49) *shifts, and six fine handkerchiefs:* shifts were women's undergarments, like chemises; handkerchiefs were neckwear, folded diagonally, draped around the neck and knotted in front in a breast knot.

9. (p. 50) *cambric aprons, and four Holland ones:* the aprons made of cambric, a fine French linen, would be worn as decorative additions to Pamela's dress; the Holland aprons, made of a linen fabric from the province of Holland in the Netherlands, would be used as working aprons.

10. (p. 50) *closet:* 'a small room of privacy and retirement' (Johnson).

11. (p. 50) *Flanders laced head-clothes:* head-dress, edged with lace from Flanders. The costliness of this material indicates Pamela's special status; her clothing is more elegant than that of a typical servant.

12. (p. 50) *silk shoes:* silk was commonly used as a material for shoe uppers.

13. (p. 51) *ribands and top-knots:* ribbons and bunches of ribbon loops, usually brightly coloured, worn on the hair or in a lace cap.

14. (p. 51) *stockings . . . stays:* stockings reached above the knee, supported by garters; stays were corsets, laced behind and stiffened with whalebone.

15. (p. 52) *As you say . . . was not so:* an insertion in 1801 that confirms Pamela's analysis of the situation, vindicating her judgement and countering charges by Richardson's critics that she was at fault in her dealings with Mr B.

16. (p. 54) *flowering him a waistcoat:* embroidering with a floral design. The waistcoat was a long garment for men, reaching to just above the knee, and often heavily embroidered.

17. (p. 57) *russet:* dress made of coarse, homespun woollen cloth of a brownish colour; worn by working women.

18. (p. 58) *toilet:* dressing-table.

19. (p. 58) *loft:* an upper chamber, or a chamber in general.

20. (p. 60) *silly:* simple.

21. (p. 60) *gypsey:* 'a name of slight reproach to a woman' (Johnson); cunning, deceitful, fickle.

22. (p. 63) *Angels and saints . . . defend me:* Pamela has probably been reading *Hamlet*, and here misquotes Hamlet's 'Angels and ministers of grace defend us' (I. iv. 39).

23. (p. 63) *Lucretia:* the wife of the Roman Tarquinius Collatinus. Her 'ravisher' was Tarquinius Sextus; after the rape she stabbed herself, as Pamela threatens to do. For a servant-girl she is indeed 'well read', as Mr B. mockingly observes.

24. (p. 64) *upon the floor:* in the fifth and subsequent editions Pamela falls face down, probably in response to a complaint in the anonymous *Pamela Censured* (1741) that her supine position 'must naturally excite Passions of Desire' in the reader. In 1801, however, Richardson restored her to her original position, perhaps aware that 'Passions of Desire' could also be aroused by a view of Pamela from behind.

25. (p. 64) *smelling-bottle:* a small bottle containing smelling-salts or perfume; listed in OED only from 1771.

26. (p. 64) *cut my laces:* cutting the laces of tight-fitting corsets was a common and effective method of restoring women from faints.

27. (p. 64) *chariot:* a light, four-wheeled carriage, with only back seats.

28. (p. 72) *coach:* a large carriage, 'distinguished from a chariot by having seats facing each other' (Johnson).

29. (p. 73) *If he can stoop . . . his own pride:* inserted in 1801 to make Pamela's moral purity more explicit; the author of *Pamela Censured* had objected that she seemed less afraid of being Mr B.'s mistress than of becoming a cast-off mistress. Mrs Jervis's tearful admiration that follows is also an insertion in 1801.

30. (p. 75) *Mrs Pamela:* Mrs, when followed by the Christian name, was a more respectful term of address for young women than Miss.

31. (p. 75) *foolatum:* a humorously archaic term for 'fool'.

32. (p. 75) *Mrs Jervis is very desirous . . . for her care:* in previous editions it was Pamela, not Mrs Jervis, who wanted the embroidery to be completed. The anonymous *Lettre sur Pamela* (1742) ridicules her pleasure in working on the waistcoat at a time when she should be leaving Mr B.'s household with all possible speed.

33. (p. 76) *night-gown, silken petticoats:* a night-gown was an informal gown, worn both indoors and out; petticoats were not under-garments but a prominent feature of women's clothing, worn under-neath an open overskirt.

34. (p. 76) *laced:* embroidered with lace.

35. (p. 76) *linsey-woolsey:* cheap textile material, woven from a mixture of wool and linen.

36. (p. 76) *sad-coloured:* sober, plain in colour.

37. (p. 76) *robings and facings:* robings were trimmings in the form of bands or stripes on a woman's robe; facings were trimmings of any kind, used to cover one kind of material with another.

38. (p. 76) *camblet quilted coat:* a petticoat padded with camlet, a mixed fabric of silk and camel, or goat's, hair. Quilted petticoats 'began to be worn after 1710 (rare before) and reached their height of popu-larity in the 1740's' (Cunnington, p. 138).

39. (p. 76) *under-coats . . . swan-skin:* under-coats were worn to give added thickness to petticoats, and also for warmth, as Pamela observes; swan-skin was a closely woven flannel material.

40. (p. 76) *Scots cloth:* a cheap textile fabric.

41. (p. 77) *round-eared caps:* originally called coifs, they curved round the face to the ears. They became popular in the 1740s; this is the earliest example in OED.

42. (p. 77) *hose . . . with white clocks:* stockings with patterns, either knitted in or embroidered.

43. (p. 77) *perquisite:* casual emolument; 'perk'.

44. (p. 77) *I am forced . . . Mrs Jervis:* a telling alteration in 1801, demonstrating Pamela's self-possession. In previous editions she had broken off the letter on hearing footsteps, assuming that the intruder must be Mr B.; here she waits until she can identify the person as Mrs Jervis, relying on the evidence of her senses, rather than her imagination.

45. (p. 79) *one-horse-chaise:* a light carriage seating one to three persons, normally drawn, as here, by one horse.

46. (p. 79) *wife and daughter:* in previous editions Pamela, less con-scious of propriety, does not mention Farmer Nichols's wife and daughters; the chaise was merely a 'cart', and Pamela hoped that no one would see her on her journey.

47. (p. 80) *wafers:* discs used for sealing letters.

48. (p. 81) *dickens:* slang for devil.

49. (p. 81) *out of the way:* angry.

50. (p. 81) *trow?:* do you think?

51. (p. 82) *Mrs Arthur . . . Mrs Brooks, Miss Towers:* changed from

'Lady' in previous editions, in response to Lady Bradshaigh's comment on the 'many mistakes ... with regard to the *Titles* of several characters'; Richardson admitted his 'Ignorance of Proprietys of those kinds' (Eaves and Kimpel, 'Richardson's Revisions', p. 81).

52. (p. 83) *two reigns ago:* during the reign of William III. In a preface to the first edition of *Pamela II*, Richardson dated the events of the novel 1717–30: the reigns of George I and George II.

53. (p. 83) *passionate:* 'easily moved to anger' (Johnson).

54. (p. 83) *quality:* people of good social position.

55. (p. 83) *the poet ... nobility:* misquoting 'Virtue alone is true Nobility'; the poet is George Stepney, 'The Eighth Satire of Juvenal translated' (1693), l. 37.

56. (p. 84) *out of the abundance of the heart the mouth speaketh:* Matthew, xii. 34; Jesus is admonishing the Pharisees, after asking them 'how can ye, being evil, speak good things?'

57. (p. 85) *some call her lady:* as Richardson himself had done in previous editions; Pamela's reference to 'we simple bodies' is a way of justifying the error.

58. (p. 87) *tricked myself up:* dressed up.

59. (p. 88) *green knot:* top-knot; see n. 13.

60. (p. 88) *tucker:* 'a slip of fine Linnen or Muslin that used to run in a small kind of ruffle round the uppermost Verge of the Womens Stays, and by that means covered a great part of the Shoulders and Bosom' (*Guardian*, no. 100).

61. (p. 89) *tight:* neat in appearance, shapely.

62. (p. 95) *slip-shoed:* in slippers.

63. (p. 95) *morning gown:* 'a loose gown worn before one is fully dressed' (Johnson); it resembled the modern dressing-gown.

64. (p. 95) *coat:* petticoat; see n. 33.

65. (p. 96) *wrapper:* a loose robe or gown.

66. (p. 99) *O the difference between the minds of thy creatures:* proverbial; cf. 'O, the difference of man and man' (*King Lear*, IV. ii. 26).

67. (p. 99) *But the Divine Grace is not confined to space:* proverbial; cf. 'In space comes grace'.

68. (p. 100) *birth-day suit:* a suit fit to wear at court on a royal birthday.

69. (p. 100) *stood on end with lace:* was completely covered with lace; the lace was gold in editions prior to 1761, then silver, but here Mr B.'s taste is less extravagant.

70. (p. 102) *with a witness:* proverbial for 'without a doubt' (Tilley, W591).

71. (p. 102) *But do you think . . . a poor girl:* one of several insertions in 1801 that exculpate Mr B.'s shortcomings; Pamela points out here that while he has been foolish in his dealings with her, such behaviour is unusual for him. In the previous paragraph one of Mr B.'s bawdy jokes, his desire to have Pamela 'as *quick another way,* as thou art in thy Repartees!' is omitted in 1801 for the same reason.

72. (p. 106) *Ads-bobbers:* God's mockers. This and other words used by Longman which were already archaic in Richardson's time indicate the steward's rusticity.

73. (p. 106) *well-a-day:* alas.

74. (p. 107) *elbow-chair:* 'a chair with arms to support the elbows' (Johnson).

75. (p. 107) *Ads-heartlikins:* God's little heart.

76. (p. 107) *wainscot:* wooden panelling, which was becoming fashionable in the first half of the eighteenth century.

77. (p. 108) *cot:* cottage.

78. (p. 108) *plain-work:* plain needlework or sewing.

79. (p. 108) *grasshopper in the fable:* Richardson printed his version of Sir Roger L'Estrange's translation of *Aesop's Fables* in November 1739, the same month in which he began writing *Pamela.* The grasshopper fable is number 164 in his edition, which he advertised in a note to this passage in the fifth edition of *Pamela.*

80. (p. 109) *I have read of a good bishop:* Pamela has probably been reading John Foxe's *Book of Martyrs* (1563), in which Thomas Bilney (who was not, however, a bishop) places his hand in a candle in preparation for his death by burning. Pamela (or Richardson) seems to have conflated this story with that of Bishop Bonner, who put not his own but Thomas Tomkins's hand in a candle, to discourage him from maintaining his Protestant views.

81. (p. 109) *blood-pudding:* black pudding; a sausage made of blood and suet.

82. (p. 109) *beechen trencher:* platter made of beech wood.

83. (p. 109) *city mouse and the country mouse: Aesop's Fables,* Richardson's edition, no. 11. The country mouse, feasting at the house of her city sister, declares after their meal has been disrupted by some noisy servants, 'I had much rather be nibbling of Crusts, without Fear or Hazard in my own Hole, than be Mistress of all the Delicates in the World, and subject to such terrifying Alarms and Dangers'.

84. (p. 109) *betimes:* early in the morning.

85. (p. 110) *sash-door:* door with a window in the upper part.

86. (p. 110) *calimanco:* glossy woollen material from Flanders.

87. (p. 110) *burn:* burnish; Pamela will polish the silver braid on her shoes, and sell it along with some old silver buckles.

88. (p. 112) *hips and haws ... pig-nuts:* fruits of rose and hawthorn, and earth-nuts, a type of tuber.

89. (p. 113) *fetch:* trick.

90. (p. 121) *Verses on my going away:* Richardson revised this poem thoroughly for the 1801 edition; seven stanzas were deleted, four altered, three new ones added and only three left unchanged. The change of tone from pathos to dignified stoicism exemplifies Richardson's changing attitude to his heroine.

91. (p. 123) *beset:* the most didactic part of Richardson's editorial commentary is deleted at this point in 1801, making the disruption in the stream of letters less obtrusive.

92. (p. 129) *vilely tricked:* Richardson uses italics in this letter to indicate changes made by Pamela to the words dictated by Mr B.; see below, p. 155.

93. (p. 133) *diet-bread:* special bread for invalids, made from finely ground floor; not normally eaten by servants, it is another sign of Pamela's special status.

94. (p. 133) *Canary wine:* light sweet wine from the Canary Islands.

95. (p. 133) *Jehu-like:* proverbial, alluding to II Kings, ix. 20: 'The driving is like the driving of Jehu ... for he driveth furiously.'

96. (p. 133) *bait:* feed.

97. (p. 135) *cordial:* 'any medicine that increases strength' (Johnson).

98. (p. 136) *The regard:* in previous editions the more amorous but less discreet Mr B. expressed 'passion' here for Pamela, and signed himself not 'Your true Friend' but 'Your passionate Admirer'.

99. (p. 137) *wife:* the following passage, describing Pamela's overnight stay at Farmer Monkton's, is completely recast in 1801, and contains several pages of new material. Anne Richardson states in a letter to her sister Martha of 1784 that 'the conversation at the farmer's ... was *not* an improvement, as the stile is different from the rest of the two first vols.', but Eaves and Kimpel admire the 'sharp characterization, realistic presentation of manners, and accurate reporting of conversation' displayed here ('Richardson's Revisions', pp. 81, 84). Pamela's vigorous arguments and witty asides throughout this passage are somewhat incongruous with her dejection on entering the farmer's house, but they are in keeping with Richardson's bolder depiction of his heroine; her fleeting desire to have both Robert's and Mr B.'s necks broken (p. 143) is a typically aggressive touch in 1801.

100. (p. 138) *Farmer Monkton:* Farmer Norton in previous editions; Richardson probably changed the name because he had also used it for Mrs Judith Norton, nurse of the heroine of *Clarissa* and a sympathetic character.

101. (p. 141) *nerst:* rustic dialect for next to, near.

102. (p. 141) *otherguess:* different kind of.

103. (p. 145) *prepossessed:* already won over, prejudiced.

104. (p. 145) *baffled:* eluded, defeated.

105. (p. 145) *'Ifackins:* in faith.

106. (p. 147) *She calls me madam . . . to be insolent:* the first of several insertions in 1801 in which Pamela exercises her powers of analysis in descriptions of Mrs Jewkes.

107. (p. 147) *gambol . . . may-game:* merrymaking; laughing-stock.

108. (p. 152) *pursy:* short-winded, puffy or fat.

109. (p. 154) *an affair with Lady Davers:* the 'affair' is Mr B.'s attempt to gain his sister Lady Davers's approval of his interest in Pamela; the sentence is inserted in 1801 to explain Mr B.'s delay in making a proposal of marriage to Pamela.

110. (p. 157) *hoods, and a velvet scarf:* hoods could either be attached to cloaks or, as here, were separate; they were large enough to cover caps worn underneath and completely covered the head. A scarf was a large wrap enveloping the body.

111. (p. 159) *turfted:* covered with turf.

112. (p. 159) *Argus:* Argus Panoptes, the all-seeing, was less fortunate than Mrs Jewkes, however; set by Juno to guard Io from the attentions of Zeus, he was killed by Hermes and his one hundred eyes were placed by Juno on the peacock's tail.

113. (p. 161) *hussey:* abbreviation for 'housewife', a case for needles and thread.

114. (p. 162) *din their ears:* repeat *ad nauseam*.

115. (p. 163) *stand shill-I, shall-I:* remain irresolute or undecided.

116. (p. 163) *Jezebel:* the infamous wife of Ahab, King of Israel (I Kings, xvi. 31 ff.); hence a wicked, abandoned woman.

117. (p. 163) *Marry come up:* interjection expressing indignant surprise or contempt.

118. (p. 164) *mal-pertness:* impudence.

119. (p. 164) *settle-bench:* a long wooden bench, usually with arms and a high back that extended to the ground, with a locker or box under the bench.

120. (p. 166) *post-house:* post-office.

121. (p. 166) *can:* cup.

122. (p. 168) *horse-beans:* beans used as food for horses and cattle, or made into bean-meal and used for coarse bread.

123. (p. 168) *five ells:* 18¾ feet; an ell is 45 inches.

124. (p. 171) *True friend . . . alarming danger:* Pamela's analysis of Mr B.'s letter is inserted in 1801. It is one of several passages in which she demonstrates her ability to see through a specious argument, while displaying her own high moral standards.

125. (p. 171) *struck:* taken root.

126. (p. 171) *a most wicked jest:* in previous editions we learn that the joke is 'about Planting, &c.'; the more refined Pamela of 1801 does not make this explicit.

127. (p. 172) *for he bears an irreproachable character:* inserted in 1801; see n. 128.

128. (p. 173) *I besought Mr Peters . . . in the case:* this and the previous insertion exculpate Mr Peters's failings, answering several critics who objected to Richardson's treatment of the clergy in *Pamela*.

129. (p. 175) *Ruin . . . horse-lip:* one of Pamela's sharp descriptions of Mrs Jewkes inserted in 1801.

130. (p. 176) *Prayers and tears . . . when she cries:* Pamela's argument with Mrs Jewkes here and her penetrating asides are extensively revised in 1801.

131. (p. 176) *cunning as a serpent:* alluding to Matthew, x. 16, where Jesus warns his disciples to be 'wise as serpents, and harmless as doves'.

132. (p. 179) *Brandon-hall:* 'B—n' in previous editions. Brandon must be Mr B.'s surname, since Richardson contracts the names of people but not of places. The name resembles that of Richardson's 'good man', Grandison (whose residence, similarly, is called Grandison Hall), and the similarity contributes to Richardson's rehabilitation of his much criticized hero. Mr B. was badly in need of an authentic name; he was variously known as Booby in Fielding's *Shamela*, Belmour in *The Life of Pamela*, Belvile and Beaulove in two dramatic adaptations of 1741, Belton in the first French translation of *Pamela* (a name furnished, according to the preface, by Richardson himself), and as Bonfil in Goldoni's *Pamela Nubile* (1741).

133. (p. 181) *ingenious:* intellectually able, talented.

134. (p. 182) *She wondered at that . . . I said nothing:* inserted in 1801; see n. 106.

135. (p. 186) *was before-hand in:* had previously made.

136. (p. 186) *Nought can restrain consent of twain:* the saying, which

originated in Harington's version of Ariosto's *Orlando Furioso* (Book XXVIII, *Moral*), is a translation of Ovid's '*Non caret effectu, quod volvere duo*'.

137. (p. 188) *Mrs Jewkes said . . . memory ever since:* an insertion in which Pamela's fear of the bull is given both a logical and a psychological explanation: Mrs Jewkes informs her that it has injured others, as well as the cook-maid, and Pamela's mother, we learn, habitually compared bulls to 'wicked men'. This justifies the half-heartedness of her first attempt to escape, and answers criticisms that she had no real desire to escape at all.

138. (p. 188) *My reverence . . . disgrace the character:* inserted in 1801 to indicate Pamela's respect for the clergy; see n. 128. *Character* is public role or position.

139. (p. 189) *my snuff-box, my seal-ring:* snuff became fashionable around 1700, after which gentlemen normally carried an ornate snuff-box; a seal-ring was a ring bearing a seal.

140. (p. 190) *in a sweet pickle:* proverbial for an awkward predicament; Tilley, P276. 'Sweet' is used ironically here, since pickle juice is salt or acidic.

141. (p. 191) *my heart up at my mouth:* proverbial for fear (Tilley, H331).

142. (p. 191) *saucer eyes:* eyes as large and round as saucers; generally applied to spectres and ghosts.

143. (p. 192) *As I continue writing . . . and my fears:* an insertion, responding to complaints that Pamela spent too much time writing and not enough acting; she herself is now aware of this.

144. (p. 192) *there can be no prudence without apprehension:* proverbial; cf. 'Fear (suspicion) is one part of prudence' (Tilley, F135).

145. (p. 193) *grabbling:* scrambling.

146. (p. 194) *watchments:* task of watching. The word was rarely used, as Pamela's disdainful 'as you call them' suggests; this is the only example in OED.

147. (p. 196) *Gainsborough:* in Lincolnshire.

148. (p. 198) *in course:* in their proper order.

149. (p. 201) *the fool's plaything:* Pamela is the plaything and Williams the fool; cf. the proverbial 'What is a fool without a bauble?' (Tilley, F511).

150. (p. 201) *instantly into gaol:* eighteenth-century law gave a creditor the power of putting his debtor in prison and keeping him there until the debt was repaid; this could amount to a life sentence (see Turberville, I, 325).

151. (p. 201) *gewgaw:* 'a showy trifle; a toy; a bauble; a splendid plaything' (Johnson).

152. (p. 201) *speaking picture:* the phrase, used in Sidney's *Defence of Poetry* in an analogy between poetry and art, derives from Horace's *Ars Poetica* and Plutarch's *Moralia.*

153. (p. 204) *What cruel reproaches ... broken-hearted:* the second-longest insertion in 1801, this is one of several in which Pamela writes a critical commentary on letters by other characters; see n. 124.

154. (p. 206) *blubber:* swollen, protruding.

155. (p. 206) *bag:* a silken pouch, used to contain the back hair of a wig or of natural hair; it was tied by a running string, concealed by a stiff black bow.

156. (p. 206) *wen:* tumour, or large wart.

157. (p. 206) *knot:* a bunch of decorative ribbons, attached to the hilt of a sword; bright colours were often used.

158. (p. 207) *Stamford:* in Lincolnshire.

159. (p. 208) *I have read of a great captain:* I have not identified the captain whom Pamela wishes to emulate.

160. (p. 209) *hear her fast:* fast asleep; Pamela will hear her snoring.

161. (p. 210) *hied:* hurried.

162. (p. 210) *broke:* bruised.

163. (p. 211) *into my head:* Pamela's lengthy meditation on suicide which follows is probably influenced by that of her namesake in Sidney's *Arcadia*, which Richardson printed, at least in part, for the 1724–5 edition, and to which he alludes in *Pamela II.*

164. (p. 212) *the dreadful stake, and the highway interment:* Pamela refers to the practice of burying suicides by the highway with a stake through the body. By 1788, however, Horace Walpole could refer to the 'absurd stake and highway of our ancestors' (quoted in A. Alvarez, *The Savage God*, 1971, p. 147).

165. (p. 213) *unjust imprisonment:* Joseph, son of Jacob and Rachel, was imprisoned by Pharaoh on a false accusation by his master's wife, but found favour through his skill in interpreting Pharaoh's dreams (Genesis, xxxix–xli).

166. (p. 215) *some angel:* Peter, imprisoned by Herod, was delivered by an angel who caused his chains to fall off and the prison doors to open (Acts, xii. 7–10).

167. (p. 215) *hap:* fate.

168. (p. 216) *billet:* a thick stick used as a weapon.

169. (p. 217) *family plaster:* a domestic remedy for wounds.

170. (p. 218) *a wife in every nation:* in *Pamela II* Mr B. himself expresses approval of polygamy to the countess with whom Pamela suspects him of having an affair. Lovelace also favours polygamy

in *Clarissa*, and in 1752 Richardson began a series of teasing letters to Lady Bradshaigh advocating polygamy as a solution for Sir Charles Grandison's dual attachment to Harriet and Clementina.

171. (p. 220) *Seeing myself . . . sight of pursuers:* an insertion supplying two further reasons for Pamela's failure to escape: lack of shelter in the surrounding countryside, and her fear of the warrant that Mr B. has taken out for her arrest.

172. (p. 220) *handle:* a fact or circumstance that may be taken advantage of for some purpose.

173. (p. 224) *pucker:* a state of agitation or excitement; this is the earliest example in OED.

174. (p. 224) *the wolf:* Aesop's *Fables*, no. 29. Pamela's version, however, is somewhat different from that in Richardson's edition, where a dog, not a wolf, accuses a sheep, with a kite, a wolf and a vulture as witnesses. In his 'Reflection' drawn from the fable, Richardson states that 'no Innocence can be safe, where Power and Malice are in Confederacy against it'.

175. (p. 226) *stand in your own light:* proverbial (Tilley, L276).

176. (p. 227) *Samson:* Samson, blinded and imprisoned by the Philistines, was taken from prison to make sport for them (Judges, xvi. 25–7).

177. (p. 228) *noisome:* ill-smelling.

178. (p. 229) *solitaire:* a precious stone, usually a diamond, set by itself.

179. (p. 229) *When I come . . . chastity inviolate:* inserted in 1801; Pamela's professed indifference to her outward appearance here counters objections that she was excessively interested in her attire.

180. (p. 230) *at all adventures:* at any risk; whatever the consequence.

181. (p. 230) *Give me leave . . . on such terms:* this spirited retort in 1801 replaces a more servile response in previous editions.

182. (p. 230) *greatest monarch:* the commander is Manius Curius Dentatus, a Roman consul (d. 270 BC), who gained a decisive victory over the Samnites in 290 BC and was celebrated for his simplicity and frugality.

183. (p. 234) *fleers:* mocking looks or speeches.

184. (p. 236) *chariot-and-six:* chariot drawn by six horses.

185. (p. 237) *betimes:* at once.

186. (p. 237) *rated at:* scolded angrily.

187. (p. 238) *bating:* except for.

188. (p. 240) *in my hand:* in previous editions Pamela had been more ostentatiously naked; as well as holding her underclothes she specified that she was 'all undressed'.

189. (p. 242) *I abhor violence:* inserted in 1801 as part of Richardson's endeavour to rehabilitate Mr B. before his marriage.

190. (p. 242) *grimace:* pretence, sham.

191. (p. 242) *in my bosom:* Eaves and Kimpel note that this is the only one of Mr B.'s four 'mammary explorations' retained in 1801 ('Richardson's Revisions', p. 81).

192. (p.247) *which having a passage . . . without stopping:* inserted in 1801 to justify Pamela's venturing into the alcove with Mr B.

193. (p. 250) *affiance:* 'trust in the divine promises and protection' (Johnson).

194. (p. 257) *saluted:* kissed.

195. (p. 258) *full dressed, and very richly:* inserted in 1801 to indicate Mr B.'s concern for propriety.

196. (p. 260) *cramp:* handwriting which is difficult to make out, or understand.

197. (p. 262) *broken:* failed in business; bankrupt.

198. (p. 267) *I know nothing . . . disgrace:* an insertion, stressing Pamela's ingenuousness.

199. (p. 267) *punctilio:* 'a small nicety of behaviour; a nice point of exactness' (Johnson).

200. (p. 268) *chop logick:* exchange logical arguments.

201. (p. 268) *dull as a beetle:* proverbial (Tilley, B220).

202. (p. 269) *clouterly:* clumsy, awkward; from 'clouter': one who mends, or patches.

203. (p. 269) *My father and mother . . . eyes:* inserted in 1801 to show that Pamela's exemplary virtue had been with her from birth.

204. (p. 270) *equivocation! no jesuit:* the Jesuits, a Catholic religious order founded in 1530 by St Ignatius Loyola, were proverbially associated with equivocation; in 1601 Anthony Shirly complained of their doctrine of 'equivocating, which you may term in plain English lying and cogging' (quoted in G. B. Harrison, *A Last Elizabethan Journal*, 1933, p. 218).

205. (p. 270) *pockets:* worn beneath the dress, they were joined by tape tied around the waist.

206. (p. 270) *question:* 'examination by torture' (Johnson). Pressing to death, or *la peine forte et dure*, was, as Mr B. points out in his reply, still used as a torture for criminals who refused to speak in court. Cases are recorded in the *London Magazine* for 21 August 1735 and in the *Universal Spectator*, no. 674, for October 1741.

VOLUME II

207. (p. 279) *Sunday Night:* 'Monday' in previous editions; an error, since Pamela is writing on Sunday evening, shortly after dusk.

208. (p. 279) *flings:* gibes, scoffs.

209. (p. 279) *sash:* window.

210. (p. 279) *bag and baggage:* proverbial for 'a thorough riddance', as Pamela notes on p. 281 below.

211. (p. 280) *bondage:* the Israelites, living on manna, displeased God through their longing for fish, cucumbers, melons, leeks, onions and garlic (Numbers, xi. 5).

212. (p. 280) *sporting-piece:* plaything.

213. (p. 281) *alehouse, rather than inn:* an alehouse, unlike an inn, would not normally receive overnight guests.

214. (p. 281) *make hard shift:* do the best he can.

215. (p. 284) *topsy-turvied, as I may say:* thrown into utter confusion. 'As I may say' is an insertion in 1801, Pamela now being aware that the use of 'topsy-turvy' as a verb is unusual.

216. (p. 284) *presses me to death:* Mr B. refers to pressing as a form of capital punishment above, p. 270.

217. (p. 288) *in this case:* deleted in 1801 is a sentence that gives a different reason for Pamela's return: 'I doubt he has got too great Hold in my Heart, for me to be easy presently, if I should refuse.'

218. (p. 288) *He is not now . . . good to me:* an insertion, emphasizing that Mr B.'s illness is the primary reason for Pamela's return; she is thus impelled by a moral obligation, not by an emotional compulsion.

219. (p. 290) *I thought the coachman . . . have done:* an insertion that also underlines Pamela's changed emotions in 1801; her concern that the noisy servants and the sound of the carriage might disturb Mr B.'s sleep indicates her sympathy and kindness, rather than an ungovernable passion.

220. (p. 290) *burnt wine:* heated wine; 'the precise early sense is doubtful' (OED).

221. (p. 290) *sack-whey:* a medicinal drink, consisting of sack, a white wine from Spain or the Canaries, mixed with whey.

222. (p. 292) *Mrs Jewkes looked . . . come back:* an insertion, containing another of Pamela's sharp observations of Mrs Jewkes.

223. (p. 293) *heaviness:* drowsiness.

224. (p. 294) *between them:* the philosopher is Diogenes, who told Alexander the Great that he could find no difference between the bones of Alexander's father and those of his slaves.

225. (p. 295) *the silent grave:* I have not identified these lines, which might be by one of Richardson's circle.

226. (p. 296) *dashed:* abashed.

227. (p. 296) *fore glass:* glass between horseman and passenger in a chariot; the only example in OED.

228. (p. 299) *comfits:* 'a dry sweetmeat; any kind of fruit or root preserved with sugar, and dried' (Johnson).

229. (p. 299) *Proceed, my dear . . . talk:* Richardson made several alterations in 1801 to prevent Pamela from monopolizing the genteel conversations in which she participates after her engagement and marriage. In this insertion Mr B. asks her to continue her monologue, providing a pretext for her garrulousness.

230. (p. 300) *Generously pleased . . . talk on:* another insertion; see n. 229.

231. (p. 302) *Gratitude, my beloved . . . my Pamela:* an insertion; see n. 229.

232. (p. 303) *secretary:* a style of handwriting used chiefly in legal documents; its archaic quality makes Mr B. suspect that the hand is Longman's.

233. (p. 307) *Yet allow me . . . Excuse, sir:* inserted in 1801 to show that Pamela loves Mr B. for himself, not for his fortune as hostile critics had suggested.

234. (p. 317) *putting his arm round me:* in previous editions Mr B. sits Pamela on his knee.

235. (p. 318) *Telemachus: Les Aventures de Télémaque* (1699), a long, didactic allegorical prose epic by François de Salignac de la Mothe-Fénelon (1651–1715).

236. (p. 318) *cast:* a casual lift, ride.

237. (p. 319) *confabulate:* converse, chat.

238. (p. 320) *Mrs Jones:* Lady Jones in previous editions; see n. 51.

239. (p. 320) *there was no by-path . . . appearing affected:* an insertion, justifying Pamela's dramatic entrance; the subjunctive 'were' here is characteristic of Pamela's improved grammar in 1801.

240. (p. 322) *leave:* desist.

241. (p. 322) *seeming to expect . . . some answer:* an insertion, giving Pamela a reason to contradict Sir Simon. A second contradictory reply is deleted in 1801.

242. (p. 322) *I blushed, and curtsied . . . an answer:* an insertion, indicating Pamela's increased modesty on social occasions in 1801; see n. 229.

243. (p. 326) *tight:* see n. 61.

244. (p. 327) *bumper:* a brimful glass.

245. (p. 328) *quadrille:* a fashionable card game for four people.

246. (p. 332) *petticoats:* often used as a term for women, the word here includes Mr Peters because of the skirt of his gown.

247. (p. 332) *understand:* Swift, 'Cadenus and Vanessa' (1713), l. 171.

248. (p. 334) *Jacob's ladder:* Jacob dreamed of a ladder reaching from earth to heaven, with angels ascending and descending (Genesis, xxviii. 12).

249. (p. 336) *Jephtha's daughters:* proverbial for virgins. Jephtha unwittingly offered his daughter to God as a burnt offering; before her death, however, she bewailed her virginity for two months (Judges, xi. 30–40).

250. (p. 337) *admiration:* in previous editions Mr Andrews was at first unable to recognize Pamela in her finery, and suspected that another lady was to be Mr B.'s wife.

251. (p. 338) *lined:* with wooden panelling.

252. (p. 339) *Boileau's Lutrin: Le Lutrin* (1674–83), a mock epic by Nicolas Boileau-Despréaux (1636–1711).

253. (p. 339) *Recrimination . . . my intent:* an insertion, increasing Mr B.'s magnanimity; in previous editions he reproached Mr Williams for his devious behaviour.

254. (p. 341) *verses:* to cap compliments is to follow one compliment with a better; to cap verses is to reply to a verse previously quoted with another that begins with the final or initial letter of the first, or that rhymes or otherwise corresponds with it.

255. (p. 342) *prevented:* anticipated.

256. (p. 343) *repentance:* quoted from the parable of the lost sheep (Luke, xv. 7).

257. (p. 343) *salvation:* spoken by Simon, who has just seen the infant Jesus (Luke, ii. 29–30).

258. (p. 343) *degree:* from the Magnificat (Luke i. 46, 52); the 'hand-maiden' is the speaker, the Virgin Mary.

259. (p. 343) *Ruth:* Ruth the Moabitess lost her first husband and worked in the fields to support herself and her mother-in-law; her virtue was rewarded through her marriage to Boaz, 'a mighty man of wealth', and she became an ancestress of King David.

260. (p. 345) *drab:* thick woollen cloth of a yellowish colour.

261. (p. 345) *England:* natural hair would be more appropriate than a wig for a man of Mr Andrews's social standing; he is not, despite Pamela's hyperbole, a 'great beau'. The best wigs, as Mr B. notes, were very expensive, costing as much as forty guineas, or the rough equivalent of five hundred pounds today.

262. (p. 346) *staves:* stanzas.

263. (p. 349) *common translation:* the metrical arrangement by Thomas Sternhold, John Hopkins and others; first published in 1562, it was printed, with various modifications, more than a thousand times between then and the end of the eighteenth century. It was, however, rivalled in the eighteenth century by Nahum Tate and Nicholas Brady's *New Version of the Psalms*, first published in 1596.

264. (p. 349) *Sion:* Zion, or Jerusalem.

265. (p. 349) *watched:* Richardson had altered 'watched' to 'guarded' in the octavo edition when Pamela first reads her poem (p. 179), but in both the octavo and 1801 he failed to make the alteration when Mr B. reads her poem aloud.

266. (p. 351) *sons of Edom:* descendants of Esau, at war much of the time with the Israelites; they aided the Babylonians in sacking Jerusalem.

267. (p. 355) *sackcloth and ashes:* worn for mourning or repentance.

268. (p. 356) *cinnamon-water:* an aromatic beverage, prepared from cinnamon.

269. (p. 357) *Thursday:* a private reference; Thursday was one of the second Mrs Richardson's two lucky days. Eaves and Kimpel note that in Pamela's insistence on being married on a Thursday, Richardson 'was permitting himself a little fun with his wife's superstition' (*Samuel Richardson: A Biography*, 1971, p. 485).

270. (p. 358) *æra:* epoch.

271. (p. 362) *à propos:* opportunely, pertinently.

272. (p. 367) *five or six:* she had only two or three thousand more in previous editions, but the B. of 1801 is worth a greater fortune.

273. (p. 369) *Very well, sir ... power:* an insertion, contributing to Pamela's study of Mrs Jewkes.

274. (p. 371) *conning:* learning by heart.

275. (p. 373) *But first let me ... done me:* an insertion, justifying Pamela's continued use of the word 'master', rather than 'husband'.

276. (p. 376) *100l.:* the one hundred pounds had been fifty pounds in previous editions; another example of Mr B.'s increased largesse.

277. (p. 377) *beat up the quarters:* visit unceremoniously.

278. (p. 377) *pet:* temper.

279. (p. 380) *frothy:* empty, trifling.

280. (p. 388) *useless in my generation:* Pamela wishes to be a model of good conduct to her contemporaries and, with a play on 'generation', does not wish to be barren.

281. (p. 388) *cypher:* 'an arithmetical mark, which, standing for nothing in itself, increases the value of the other figures' (Johnson).

282. (p. 391) *I myself would make . . . motives:* an insertion, explaining why Mr B. will not pay Pamela her quarterly allowance in person. Richardson's interest in the financial provisions made by a man for his wife was advanced for his time.

283. (p. 392) *But, dear sir . . . am not:* in this insertion Pamela asks Mr B. for his rules of conduct; in previous editions he had delivered them without her prompting, and their tone was more dictatorial.

284. (p. 394) *supper by nine:* in previous editions Mr B. dined at two and had supper at eight; the later times here reflect changing fashion in the 1750s. He is still keeping country hours ('old-fashioned rules'), however; dinner in a fashionable household would not begin until four or five, while supper could take place even after midnight (see Turberville, I, 346).

285. (p. 394) *Every one mend one:* proverbial; 'If every man mend one all shall be mended' (Tilley, M196).

286. (p. 397) *with his hands:* an anonymous correspondent, several of whose criticisms of *Pamela* were printed in the introduction to the second edition, complained that 'the Passage where the Gentleman is said to span the Waist of *Pamela* with his Hands, is enough to ruin a Nation of Women by Tight-lacing'; the passage, however, was never altered.

287. (p. 398) *officiously:* used here with the older meaning of 'dutifully'.

288. (p. 398) *Rhenish:* Rhine wine. Several details in this paragraph are insertions, including 'waddled', 'what she herself dearly loves', and Mr B.'s surprise and encouragement as Mrs Jewkes pours the wine for Pamela.

289. (p. 399) *near sixteen:* eighteen in previous editions.

290. (p. 400) *eleven:* ten in previous editions.

291. (p. 400) *She looked down . . . say:* an insertion; see n. 106.

292. (p. 400) *Seven o'Clock:* this is altered from 'Eleven' in previous editions, while Mr B.'s letter is now written not at one but at three in the morning. The delivery time is thus reduced from ten to four hours, suggesting that Mr B. has more efficient messengers in 1801. They also, however, have two miles less to travel; see n. 289.

293. (p. 401) *W.B.:* William Brandon; in *Pamela II* Pamela names her firstborn son William after his father.

294. (p. 401) *chariot and six:* a chariot drawn by six horses. The coronets are small crowns, indicating nobility.

295. (p. 402) *right side of the hedge:* proverbial; 'on the safer (better) side of the hedge' (Tilley, S428).

296. (p. 403) *fool's paradise:* proverbial (Tilley, F523).

297. (p. 403) *Worden:* addressed, with greater familiarity, by her Christian name Beck in previous editions.

298. (p. 404) *drolling:* making fun of.

299. (p. 408) *Lady Would-be:* this fictitious surname was first used to indicate aspiration in Sir Politick Would-be, the schemer in Jonson's *Volpone* (1606).

300. (p. 408) *in bar of:* as a reason for not doing.

301. (p. 409) *madam:* in the sense of bawd; hence Pamela's scarlet face.

302. (p. 409) *clownish:* ill-bred, ill-mannered.

303. (p. 410) *merry-thought:* the wishbone of a chicken; Jackey laughs because whoever gets the longer piece will be married before the other. In previous editions the joke was more bawdy; Jackey there inquired if Pamela wanted the 'rump'.

304. (p. 411) *Silence . . . gives consent:* proverbial (Tilley, S446).

305. (p. 412) *laced:* covered in lace.

306. (p. 415) *mannerly:* well-mannered.

307. (p. 415) *beats you quite out of the pit:* the metaphor is taken from the then popular sport of cock-fighting; the pit is the cockpit, resembling a small amphitheatre, in which cock-fights were held.

308. (p. 418) *My dearest love . . . with it:* Lady Davers's commentary on Mr B.'s letter to Pamela is considerably expanded in 1801.

309. (p. 419) *setting up for a family:* pretending to come from a good family.

310. (p. 419) *Herald's Office:* founded in 1483 to settle questions of precedence and trace pedigrees.

311. (p. 421) *sixteen:* Pamela was 'little more than fifteen years of age' on p. 52; about a year elapses, however, between then and her wedding. See Dorothy Parker, 'The Time Scheme of *Pamela* and the Character of B.', *Texas Studies in Language and Literature*, 11 (1969), 695–704.

312. (p. 422) *chine:* break the back of; latest example in OED.

313. (p. 423) *loo:* card game in which the loser is required to pay a certain sum, or 'loo', to the pool.

314. (p. 427) *whist:* whist, an early form of bridge, became immensely popular in the early 1740s; Horace Walpole described it as a 'universal opium' in 1742 (Turberville, I, 358).

315. (p. 427) *cast in:* chose partners at cards; only example in OED.

316. (p. 427) *honours:* the four highest trumps: ace, king, queen and knave.

317. (p. 427) *up at one deal:* ahead after one round.

318. (p. 432) *who far, very far surpassed me:* an insertion, displaying Pamela's modesty.

319. (p. 433) *secret-keeper:* procuress; bawd.

320. (p. 438) *bravo:* 'a man who murders for hire' (Johnson).

321. (p. 441) *York:* in 1660 the Duke of York, later James II, married Anne, daughter of Edward Hyde, a commoner.

322. (p. 442) *calf:* Jeroboam, who in fact made two golden calves, offended God in doing so and was cursed (I Kings, xii–xiv).

323. (p. 444) *fore yard:* courtyard in front of a building.

324. (p. 446) *complaisantly:* courteously, agreeably.

325. (p. 447) *hail-fellow:* on intimate terms; from the proverbial 'hail fellow well met' (Tilley, H15).

326. (p. 448) *thy property:* Lady Davers stresses that Mr B. now belongs to Pamela as a husband, not to herself as a brother.

327. (p. 450) *Quaker sister:* Mr B. calls Lady Davers a Quaker because of the exaggerated formality of her 'thy', 'thee' and 'thou' in the previous sentence, and her use of the word 'friend' instead of 'brother'.

328. (p. 450) *chalk it out:* plan or arrange it.

329. (p. 450) *a good fancy:* good taste.

330. (p. 451) *dueller:* Richardson's own aversion to duelling is expressed in his 'Six Original Letters Upon Duelling', *Candid Review*, March 1765, pp. 227–31; and in the Concluding Note to *Sir Charles Grandison.*

331. (p. 456) *niceness:* 'superfluous delicacy or exactness' (Johnson).

332. (p. 460) *Saul among the prophets:* before Saul was made King of Israel he surprisingly prophesied among a company of Philistine prophets, instead of doing battle with them; 'Therefore it became a proverb, *Is* Saul also among the prophets?' (I Samuel, x. 12). In his contribution to *The Rambler*, no. 97, Richardson refers to the same story, noting that 'even a Saul was once found prophesying among the prophets whom he had set out to destroy'.

333. (p. 460) *of his own head:* spontaneously, of his own accord.

334. (p. 462) *resist it:* in Richardson's *Aesop's Fables*, no. 163, 'An Oak and a Willow', the willow bends and withstands the storm undamaged, while the oak resists it and is destroyed.

335. (p. 464) *vapourish:* inclined to depression or low spirits.

336. (p. 466) *supererogatory:* supererogation, in Roman Catholic theology, is the performance of good works beyond what God commands or requires, constituting a state of merit which the Church may dispense to others to make up for their deficiencies. Mr B. is

thus accusing Pamela of attempting to atone for Lady Davers's fault.

337. (p. 469) *A hard lesson . . . hypocrite:* this and the next response to Mr B.'s rules of conduct were inserted in 1801, while Pamela's responses to nos. 26–29 were expanded; as elsewhere the commentary thus becomes more astringent than in previous editions; see n. 99.

338. (p. 469) *a parliament of women:* alluding to the courts of love presided over by women in the Middle Ages. To characterize his own female correspondents, with whom he exchanged numerous lengthy letters on topics such as the duties of wives to husbands, Richardson borrowed the term 'little senate' from Pope's Prologue to Addison's *Cato*, l. 23.

339. (p. 473) *post-haste:* 'haste like that of a courier' (Johnson); hence, with all possible haste.

340. (p. 473) *harp upon that string:* proverbial (Tilley, S936).

341. (p. 476) *a pair of gloves:* a gratuity given ostensibly for a pair of gloves; Mrs Worden is given the same amount here as the coachmen, maids, Abraham and Thomas received on p. 381.

342. (p. 480) *Somebody:* alluding to Longman's signature on the anonymous letter, p. 262.

343. (p. 480) *sleek:* smooth-haired.

344. (p. 482) *contiguous:* adjacent.

345. (p. 483) *equipages:* 'the Provision of all things necessary for a Voyage or Journey; as Attire, Furniture, Horses, Attendance, &c.' (Nathan Bailey, *An Universal Etymological Dictionary*, 8th ed., 1737).

346. (p. 483) *escritoire:* a writing-desk constructed to contain stationery and documents.

347. (p. 487) *but the best answer . . . was silence:* a sign of Pamela's increased sense of decorum in 1801; in previous editions she makes a surprisingly *risqué* comment about 'Improvements in every kind of Thing'.

348. (p. 487) *postilion and two helpers:* a postilion is 'one who guides the first pair of a set of six horses in a coach' (Johnson); helpers are groom's assistants in a stable.

349. (p. 487) *scullion-boy:* 'the lowest domestic servant that washes the dishes and the kettles in a kitchen' (Johnson).

350. (p. 488) *October:* strong ale brewed in October.

351. (p. 488) *repeating-watch:* 'a watch that strikes the hours at will by compression of a spring' (Johnson).

352. (p. 492) *I curtsied in silence:* Pamela's silence in 1801 replaces a

witty reply in previous editions, which led to an indecorous debate about marriage.

353. (p. 494) *engagements to the world:* debts.

354. (p. 494) *Whole Duty of Man:* a highly popular devotional work, first published in 1658; probably by Richard Allestree (1618–91), chaplain to the King and provost of Eton.

355. (p. 495) *double chaise:* carriage with four, as opposed to two, horses ('chaise and pair').

356. (p. 495) *made their honours:* curtsied.

357. (p. 496) *brown:* with brown hair and/or brown complexion.

358. (p. 499) *half-pay officer:* an officer receiving half-pay when not in actual service, or after retirement at a prescribed time.

359. (p. 501) *her month was up:* a month after childbirth.

360. (p. 502) *Calne:* in Wiltshire.

361. (p. 503) *Crosby-square:* a square of good houses, off Bishopgate.

362. (p. 503) *flying-coach:* a swift stagecoach.

363. (p. 505) *arms to quarter:* alluding to the practice of adding another's coat of arms to one's hereditary arms.

364. (p. 505) *olive-branch:* representing children; 'thy children like olive plants round about thy table' (Psalms, cxxviii. 3).

365. (p. 505) *Paduasoy:* a strong, corded silk fabric.

366. (p. 511) *such a Herod:* alluding to the story of Herod's jealousy and eventual murder of his wife, Mariamne, as told by Flavius Josephus and translated into English by l'Estrange. Anna Howe refers to the same story in *Clarissa*, complaining that Lovelace loves Clarissa with 'such a love as Herod loved his Mariamne' (1748, IV, 340).

367. (p. 512) *Philomel:* the nightingale.

368. (p. 513) *adorn:* this poem, which was in the first edition of *Pamela*, is probably by Richardson himself.

369. (p. 514) *You, my dear love … Humility:* an insertion in 1801, intended to show that Pamela has poetic ability, as well as moral virtue. The verses may be by one of Richardson's circle.

370. (p. 516) *meeting:* the meeting, which is indeed a happy one, is summarized by Richardson in a headnote to the Contents of Volume III; the old couple were 'received by Mr B. with great kindness, and by their beloved daughter with transports of dutiful joy'.

READ MORE IN PENGUIN

READ MORE IN PENGUIN

A CHOICE OF CLASSICS

Oliver Goldsmith	**The Vicar of Wakefield**
Gray/Churchill/Cowper	**Selected Poems**
William Hazlitt	**Selected Writings**
George Herbert	**The Complete English Poems**
Thomas Hobbes	**Leviathan**
Samuel Johnson	**Gabriel's Ladder**
	History of Rasselas, Prince of Abissinia
	Selected Writings
Samuel Johnson/ James Boswell	**A Journey to the Western Islands of Scotland and The Journal of a Tour of the Hebrides**
Matthew Lewis	**The Monk**
John Locke	**An Essay Concerning Human Understanding**
Andrew Marvell	**Complete Poems**
Thomas Middleton	**Five Plays**
John Milton	**Complete Poems**
	Paradise Lost
Samuel Richardson	**Clarissa**
	Pamela
Earl of Rochester	**Complete Works**
Richard Brinsley Sheridan	**The School for Scandal and Other Plays**
Sir Philip Sidney	**Arcadia**
Christopher Smart	**Selected Poems**
Adam Smith	**The Wealth of Nations (Books I–III)**
Tobias Smollett	**Humphrey Clinker**
	Roderick Random
Edmund Spenser	**The Faerie Queene**
Laurence Sterne	**The Life and Opinions of Tristram Shandy**
	A Sentimental Journey Through France and Italy
Jonathan Swift	**Complete Poems**
	Gulliver's Travels
Thomas Traherne	**Selected Poems and Prose**
Henry Vaughan	**Complete Poems**